MW00831099

Parable of the Talents

BOOKS BY OCTAVIA E. BUTLER

Parable of the Talents

OCTAVIA E. BUTLER

Seven Stories Press
NEW YORK • OAKLAND

Seven Stories Press
140 Watts Street
New York, NY 10013
www.sevenstories.com

Library of Congress Cataloging-in-Publication Data

Names: Butler, Octavia E., author.
Title: Parable of the talents : a novel / Octavia E. Butler ; introduction by
   Toshi Reagon.
Description: Seven Stories Press edition. | New York : Seven Stories Press,
   [2016]
Identifiers: LCCN 2016033092 | ISBN 9781609807207 (hardcover)
Subjects: LCSH: Young women--Fiction. | Twenty-first century--Fiction. |
   Political fiction. | BISAC: FICTION / Science Fiction / General. | FICTION
   / Literary. | GSAFD: Science fiction.
Classification: LCC PS3552.U827 P38 2016 | DDC 813/.54--dc23
LC record available at https://lccn.loc.gov/2016033092

Printed in the USA.

9 8

All That You Touch You Change

by Toshi Reagon

Octavia E. Butler's Parable novels—*Parable of the Sower* and *Parable of the Talents*—have become bibles for grassroots revolutionaries. They've become temples and gathering stones. Many folks have Earthseed or God Is Change as their religion on social media sites. The post-Parable generations of Black Sci-fi, Afrofuturistic Comic Book Nerd Kids, students, professors, and artists have taken possession of the mainstream idea of who gets to imagine and create a future on Earth and in the stars. Octavia Butler's never-ending yet full of endings universe laid a foundation and held up that soulful spot upon which revolutionaries can stand.

It was very hard for me to read *Parable of the Sower*. My mother, Bernice Johnson Reagon, introduced Octavia Butler's work to me in the late '80s. I read *Dawn* first. Then *Kindred*. Then *Wild Seed*. And on and on until, one year around Christmas, I saw a new book on the shelves at the bookstore—*Parable of the Sower*. I bought two. One for me, and one for Mom. I wrapped Mom's book and put it under the tree. When we opened our gifts, we had each given the other *Parable of the Sower* and purchased another copy for ourselves.

Mom read hers right away. I read two pages and closed mine, thinking, *Nope. Not now.* I was not yet ready to face it.

In 1997 Mom and I taught a semester at Princeton University for Toni Morrison's Atelier. We taught songs from the African American song tradition. Because we had to teach a text alongside the music, Mom suggested *Parable of the Sower*.

This was when I first read the book. This was when we learned we could sing this book, leading us on our journey to create Octavia E. Butler's *Parable of the Sower: The Opera*.

Octavia Butler gets us back home again in *Parable of the Sower*.

After reading it I couldn't imagine the need for anything else. A book that was so hard for me to read past the first page. It was a story that swallowed me up and told me it was true even though it was placed in the fiction section of the bookstore. True even though it took place in the future, a future thirty years away from the time I first read it. It moved my feet across a highway where feet are not supposed to travel. It took me along. It landed me home.

But I did need the something else that is *Parable of the Talents*.

Parable of the Talents is the part we don't want to face. That denial trigger hits and hits and we act like we don't know what to do, or how to do. All of sudden our skill and mastery duck deep inside us and we whisper, *No. Not again.* We are unable to count on or stand on our strength and knowledge.

Parable of the Talents says, "Stay here and watch the future look back at you."

In looking at what narrative to tell for the opera, my mind kept traveling to this Parable. Here in the teen years of the twenty-first century, not so far away from the year 2024, when *Parable of the Sower* starts, we are, right now, at the beginning of *Parable of the Talents*. We are at the opening of that unimaginable, horrible era of human destruction—of each other, of the world—stated so clearly on the pages of both of these books that long after her death Octavia Butler is being praised as a predictor of our current events.

Octavia Butler the time traveler, the wall bender, the space explorer and community maker, the race builder. Sometimes she can be too literal for me, like the town oracle you go to sit in front of when you're extra desperate. The town oracle who never lies, whose eyes won't twinkle and let you see something else or let you think that maybe you heard wrong.

No, you heard right.

Parable of the Talents is delicious plain human speak. It is what you are actually working with. It is another map for anyone looking for where they are. It is unfolded in your lap and you can see yourself on it. You see the roads you have traveled and the ones you have yet to travel. You see the space where there was no road and you climbed over, under, and through wilderness. You see your good company and your alone places. You see your deserts and your too-much-rain places. You see the years roll on no matter what. You see your wondering how far have you gone.

As you look, you trace scars on your own body where someone cut you, or you tripped running, or the earth burned or shuddered open and things fell on top of you while you covered others. You learn the geography on the map, practice memorizing routes. You forget where you buried things in the past and that's okay—if you have an imagination.

If you believe in something beyond yourself.

If you know that you are a part of a changing universal narrative and that there is home on the journey, and rest for the weary.

If you are available to stand inside the ever-turning possibilities of breathing.

But if you are not, you might find yourself in a oneness of fear and hatred, only wanting and serving one thing. You might think you own the elements themselves and all other living creatures must bend to serve your narrow-minded vision of domination. You might look at the map and, as slave masters did centuries ago, think it is a plaything for your pleasure only. You will never learn.

Embrace diversity
Unite—
Or be robbed,
ruled,
killed
By those who see you as prey.
Embrace diversity
Or be destroyed.

—EARTHSEED: THE BOOKS OF THE LIVING

TO MY AUNTS
IRMA HARRIS AND
HAZEL RUTH WALKER,
AND IN MEMORY OF MY MOTHER
OCTAVIA MARGARET BUTLER

Prologue

○ ○ ○

from EARTHSEED: THE BOOKS OF THE LIVING
by Lauren Oya Olamina

Here we are—
Energy,
Mass,
Life,
Shaping life,
Mind,
Shaping Mind,
God,
Shaping God.
Consider—
We are born
Not with purpose,
But with potential.

They'll make a God of her.

I think that would please her, if she could know about it. In spite of all her protests and denials, she's always needed devoted, obedient followers—disciples—who would listen to her and believe everything she told them. And she needed large events to manipulate. All gods seem to need these things.

Her legal name was Lauren Oya Olamina Bankole. To those who loved her or hated her, she was simply "Olamina."

She was my biological mother.

She is dead.

I have wanted to love her and to believe that what happened between her and me wasn't her fault. I've wanted that. But instead, I've hated

11

her, feared her, needed her. I've never trusted her, though, never understood how she could be the way she was—so focused, and yet so misguided, there for all the world, but never there for me. I still don't understand. And now that she's dead, I'm not even sure I ever will. But I must try because I need to understand myself, and she is part of me. I wish that she weren't, but she is. In order for me to understand who I am, I must begin to understand who she was. That is my reason for writing and assembling this book.

It has always been my way to sort through my feelings by writing. She and I had that in common. And along with the need to write, she also developed a need to draw. If she had been born in a saner time, she might have become a writer as I have or an artist.

I've gathered a few of her drawings, although she gave most of these away during her lifetime. And I have copies of all that was saved of her writings. Even some of her early, paper notebooks have been copied to disk or crystal and saved. She had a habit, during her youth, of hiding caches of food, money and weaponry in out-of-the-way places or with trusted people, and being able to go straight back to these years later. These saved her life several times, and also they saved her words, her journals and notes and my father's writings. She managed to badger him into writing a little. He wrote well, although he didn't like doing it. I'm glad she badgered him. I'm glad to have known him at least through his writing. I wonder why I'm not glad to have known her through hers.

"God is Change," my mother believed. That was what she said in the first of her verses in *Earthseed: The First Book of the Living*.

All that you touch
You Change.

All that you Change
Changes you.

The only lasting truth
Is Change.

God
Is Change.

The words are harmless, I suppose, and metaphorically true. At least she began with some species of truth. And now she's touched me one last time with her memories, her life, and her damned Earthseed.

2032

○ ○ ○

From EARTHSEED: THE BOOKS OF THE LIVING

We give our dead
To the orchards
And the groves.
We give our dead
To life.

1

○ ○ ○

From EARTHSEED: THE BOOKS OF THE LIVING

Darkness
Gives shape to the light
As light
Shapes the darkness.
Death
Gives shape to life
As life
Shapes death.
The universe
And God
Share this wholeness,
Each
Defining the other.
God
Gives shape to the universe
As the universe
Shapes
God.

From *MEMORIES OF OTHER WORLDS*
by Taylor Franklin Bankole

I have read that the period of upheaval that journalists have begun to refer to as "the Apocalypse" or more commonly, more bitterly, "the Pox" lasted from 2015 through 2030—a decade and a half of chaos. This is untrue. The Pox has been a much longer torment. It began well before 2015, perhaps even before the turn of the millennium. It has not ended.

I have also read that the Pox was caused by accidentally coinciding climatic, economic, and sociological crises. It would be more honest to say that the Pox was caused by our own refusal to deal with obvious problems in those areas. We caused the problems: then we sat and watched as they grew into crises. I have heard people deny this, but I was born in 1970. I have seen enough to know that it is true. I have watched education become more a privilege of the rich than the basic necessity that it must be if civilized society is to survive. I have watched as convenience, profit, and inertia excused greater and more dangerous environmental degradation. I have watched poverty, hunger, and disease become inevitable for more and more people.

Overall, the Pox has had the effect of an installment-plan World War III. In fact, there were several small, bloody shooting wars going on around the world during the Pox. These were stupid affairs—wastes of life and treasure. They were fought, ostensibly, to defend against vicious foreign enemies. All too often, they were actually fought because inadequate leaders did not know what else to do. Such leaders knew that they could depend on fear, suspicion, hatred, need, and greed to arouse patriotic support for war.

Amid all this, somehow, the United States of America suffered a major nonmilitary defeat. It lost no important war, yet it did not survive the Pox. Perhaps it simply lost sight of what it once intended to be, then blundered aimlessly until it exhausted itself.

What is left of it now, what it has become, I do not know.

Taylor Franklin Bankole was my father. From his writings, he seems to have been a thoughtful, somewhat formal man who wound up with my strange, stubborn mother even though she was almost young enough to be his granddaughter.

My mother seems to have loved him, seems to have been happy with him. He and my mother met during the Pox when they were both home-less wanderers. But he was a 57-year-old doctor—a family practice phy-sician—and she was an 18-year-old girl. The Pox gave them terrible memories in common. Both had seen their neighborhoods destroyed—his in San Diego and hers in Robledo, a suburb of Los Angeles. That seems to have been enough for them. In 2027, they met, liked each other, and got married. I think, reading between the lines of some of my father's writing, that he wanted to take care of this strange young girl that he had found. He wanted to keep her safe from the chaos of the time, safe from the gangs, drugs, slavery, and disease. And of course he was flat-tered that she wanted him. He was human, and no doubt tired of being alone. His first wife had been dead for about two years when they met.

He couldn't keep my mother safe, of course. No one could have done that. She had chosen her path long before they met. His mistake was in seeing her as a young girl. She was already a missile, armed and tar-geted.

From *THE JOURNALS OF LAUREN OYA OLAMINA*
SUNDAY, SEPTEMBER 26, 2032

Today is Arrival Day, the fifth anniversary of our establishing a com-munity called Acorn here in the mountains of Humboldt County.

In perverse celebration of this, I've just had one of my recurring nightmares. They've become rare in the past few years—old enemies with familiar nasty habits. I know them. They have such soft, easy beginnings. . . . This one was, at first, a visit to the past, a trip home, a chance to spend time with beloved ghosts.

My old home has come back from the ashes. This doesn't surprise me, somehow, although I saw it burn years ago. I walked through the rubble that was left of it. Yet here it is restored and filled with people—all the people I knew as I was growing up. They sit in our front rooms in rows of old metal folding chairs, wooden kitchen and dining room chairs, and plastic stacking chairs, a silent congregation of the scattered and the dead.

Church service is already going on, and, of course, my father is preaching. He looks as he always has in his church robes: tall, broad, stern, straight—a great black wall of a man with a voice you not only hear, but feel on your skin and in your bones. There's no corner of the meeting rooms that my father cannot reach with that voice. We've never had a sound system—never needed one. I hear and feel that voice again.

Yet how many years has it been since my father vanished? Or rather, how many years since he was killed? He must have been killed. He wasn't the kind of man who would abandon his family, his community, and his church. Back when he vanished, dying by violence was even easier than it is today. Living, on the other hand, was almost impossible.

He left home one day to go to his office at the college. He taught his classes by computer, and only had to go to the college once a week, but even once a week was too much exposure to danger. He stayed overnight at the college as usual. Early mornings were the safest times for working people to travel. He started for home the next morning, and was never seen again.

We searched. We even paid for a police search. Nothing did any good.

This happened many months before our house burned, before our community was destroyed. I was 17. Now I'm 23 and I'm several hundred miles from that dead place.

Yet all of a sudden, in my dream, things have come right again. I'm at home, and my father is preaching. My stepmother is sitting behind him and a little to one side at her piano. The congregation of our neighbors sits before him in the large, not-quite-open area formed by our living room, dining room, and family room. This is a broad L-shaped space into which even more than the usual 30 or 40 people have crammed themselves for Sunday service. These people are too quiet to be a Baptist congregation—or at least, they're too quiet to be the Baptist congregation I grew up in. They're here, but somehow not here. They're shadow people. Ghosts.

Only my own family feels real to me. They're as dead as most of the others, and yet they're alive! My brothers are here and they look the way they did when I was about 14. Keith, the oldest of them, the worst, and the first to die, is only 11. This means Marcus, my favorite brother and always the best-looking person in the family, is 10. Ben and Greg, almost as alike as twins, are eight and seven. We're all sitting in the front row, over near my stepmother so she can keep an eye on us. I'm sitting between Keith and Marcus to keep them from killing each other during the service.

When neither of my parents is looking, Keith reaches across me and punches Marcus hard on the thigh. Marcus, younger, smaller, but always stubborn, always tough, punches back. I grab each boy's fist and squeeze. I'm bigger and stronger than both of them, and I've always had strong hands. The boys squirm in pain and try to pull away. After a moment, I let them go. Lesson learned. They let each other alone for at least a minute or two.

In my dream, their pain doesn't hurt me the way it always did when we were growing up. Back then, since I was the oldest, I was held responsible for their behavior. I had to control them even though I couldn't escape their pain. My father and stepmother cut me as little slack as possible when it came to my hyperempathy syndrome. They refused to let me be handicapped. I was the oldest kid, and that was that. I had my responsibilities.

Nevertheless, I used to feel every damned bruise, cut, and burn that my brothers managed to collect. Each time I saw them hurt, I shared their pain as though I had been injured myself. Even pains they pretended to feel, I did feel. Hyperempathy syndrome is a delusional disorder, after all. There's no telepathy, no magic, no deep spiritual awareness. There's just the neurochemically-induced delusion that I feel the pain and pleasure that I see others experiencing. Pleasure is rare, pain is plentiful, and, delusional or not, it hurts like hell.

So why do I miss it now?

What a crazy thing to miss. Not feeling it should be like having a toothache vanish away. I should be surprised and happy. Instead, I'm afraid. A part of me is gone. Not being able to feel my brothers' pain is like not being able to hear them when they shout, and I'm afraid.

The dream begins to become a nightmare.

Without warning, my brother Keith vanishes. He's just gone. He was the first to go—to die—years ago. Now he's vanished again. In his place beside me, there is a tall, beautiful woman, black-brown-skinned and slender with long, crow-black hair, gleaming. She's wearing a soft, silky green dress that flows and twists around her body, wrapping her in some intricate pattern of folds and gathers from neck to feet. She is a stranger.

She is my mother.

She is the woman in the one picture my father gave me of my biological mother. Keith stole it from my bedroom when he was nine and I was twelve. He wrapped it in an old piece of a plastic tablecloth and buried it in our garden between a row of squashes and a mixed row of corn and beans. Later, he claimed it wasn't his fault that the picture was ruined by water and by being walked on. He only hid it as a joke. How was he supposed to know anything would happen to it? That was Keith. I beat the hell out of him. I hurt myself too, of course, but it was worth it. That was one beating he never told our parents about.

But the picture was still ruined. All I had left was the memory of it.

And here was that memory, sitting next to me.

My mother is tall, taller than I am, taller than most people. She's not pretty. She's beautiful. I don't look like her. I look like my father, which he used to say was a pity. I don't mind. But she is a stunning woman.

I stare at her, but she does not turn to look at me. That, at least, is true to life. She never saw me. As I was born, she died. Before that, for two years, she took the popular "smart drug" of her time. It was a new prescription medicine called Paracetco, and it was doing wonders for people who had Alzheimer's disease. It stopped the deterioration of their intellectual function and enabled them to make excellent use of whatever memory and thinking ability they had left. It also boosted the performance of ordinary, healthy young people. They read faster, retained more, made more rapid, accurate connections, calculations, and conclusions. As a result, Paracetco became as popular as coffee among students, and, if they meant to compete in any of the highly paid professions, it was as necessary as a knowledge of computers.

My mother's drug taking may have helped to kill her. I don't know for sure. My father didn't know either. But I do know that her drug left its unmistakable mark on me—my hyperempathy syndrome. Thanks to the addictive nature of Paracetco—a few thousand people died trying to break the habit—there were once tens of millions of us.

Hyperempaths, we're called, or hyperempathists, or sharers. Those are some of the polite names. And in spite of our vulnerability and our high mortality rate, there are still quite a few of us.

I reach out to my mother. No matter what she's done, I want to know her. But she won't look at me. She won't even turn her head. And somehow, I can't quite reach her, can't touch her. I try to get up from my chair, but I can't move. My body won't obey me. I can only sit and listen as my father preaches.

Now I begin to know what he is saying. He has been an indistinct background rumble until now, but now I hear him reading from the twenty-fifth chapter of Matthew, quoting the words of Christ:

"For the kingdom of Heaven is as a man traveling into a far country who called his own servants, and delivered unto them his goods. And unto one he gave five talents, to another two, and to another one; to every man according to his several ability; and straightway took his journey."

My father loved parables—stories that taught, stories that presented ideas and morals in ways that made pictures in people's minds. He used the ones he found in the Bible, the ones he plucked from history, or from folk tales, and, of course he used those he saw in his life and the lives of people he knew. He wove stories into his Sunday sermons, his Bible classes, and his computer-delivered history lectures. Because he believed stories were so important as teaching tools, I learned to pay more attention to them than I might have otherwise. I could quote the parable that he was reading now, the parable of the talents. I could quote several Biblical parables from memory. Maybe that's why I can hear and understand so much now. There is preaching between the bits of the parable, but I can't quite understand it. I hear its rhythms rising and falling, repeating and varying, shouting and whispering. I hear them as I've always heard them, but I can't catch the words—except for the words of the parable.

"Then he that had received the five talents went and traded with the same and made them another five talents. And likewise he that had received two, he also gained another two. But he that had received one went out and digged in the earth, and hid his lord's money."

My father was a great believer in education, hard work, and personal responsibility. "Those are our talents," he would say as my brothers' eyes glazed over and even I tried not to sigh. "God has given them to us, and he'll judge us according to how we use them."

The parable continues. To each of the two servants who had traded well and made profit for their lord, the lord said, "Well done, thou good and faithful servant; thou hast been faithful over a few things, I will make thee ruler over many things: enter thou into the joy of thy lord."

But to the servant who had done nothing with his silver talent except bury it in the ground to keep it safe, the lord said harsher words. "Thou wicked and slothful servant. . . ." he began. And he ordered his men to, "take therefore the talent from him and give it unto him which hath ten talents. For unto everyone that hath shall be given, and he shall have in abundance: but from him that hath not shall be taken away even that which he hath."

When my father has said these words, my mother vanishes. I haven't even been able to see her whole face, and now she's gone.

OCTAVIA E. BUTLER

I don't understand this. It scares me. I can see now that other people are vanishing too. Most have already gone. Beloved ghosts. . . .

My father is gone. My stepmother calls out to him in Spanish the way she did sometimes when she was excited, "No! How can we live now? They'll break in. They'll kill us all! We must build the wall higher!"

And she's gone. My brothers are gone. I'm alone—as I was alone that night five years ago. The house is ashes and rubble around me. It doesn't burn or crumble or even fade to ashes, but somehow, in an instant, it is a ruin, open to the night sky. I see stars, a quarter moon, and a streak of light, moving, rising into the sky like some life force escaping. By the light of all three of these, I see shadows, large, moving, threatening. I fear these shadows, but I see no way to escape them. The wall is still there, surrounding our neighborhood, looming over me much higher than it ever truly did. So much higher. . . . It was supposed to keep danger out. It failed years ago. Now it fails again. Danger is walled in with me. I want to run, to escape, to hide, but now my own hands, my feet begin to fade away. I hear thunder. I see the streak of light rise higher in the sky, grow brighter.

Then I scream. I fall. Too much of my body is gone, vanished away. I can't stay upright, can't catch myself as I fall and fall and fall. . . .

I awoke here in my cabin at Acorn, tangled in my blankets, half on and half off my bed. Had I screamed aloud? I didn't know. I never seem to have these nightmares when Bankole is with me, so he can't tell me how much noise I make. It's just as well. His practice already costs him enough sleep, and this night must be worse than most for him.

It's three in the morning now, but last night, just after dark, some group, some gang, perhaps, attacked the Dovetree place just north of us. There were, yesterday at this time, 22 people living at Dovetree— the old man, his wife, and his two youngest daughters; his five married sons, their wives and their kids. All of these people are gone except for the two youngest wives and the three little children they were able to grab as they ran. Two of the kids are hurt, and one of the women has had a heart attack, of all things. Bankole has treated her before. He says she was born with a heart defect that should have been taken care of when she was a baby. But she's only twenty, and around the time she was born, her family, like most people, had little or no money. They worked hard themselves and put the strongest of their kids to work at ages eight or ten. Their daughter's heart problem was always either going to kill her or let her live. It wasn't going to be fixed.

Now it had nearly killed her. Bankole was sleeping—or more likely staying awake—in the clinic room of the school tonight, keeping an eye on her and the two injured kids. Thanks to my hyperempathy syndrome, he can't have his clinic here at the house. I pick up enough of other people's pain as things are, and he worries about it. He keeps wanting to give me some stuff that prevents my sharing by keeping me sleepy, slow, and stupid. No, thanks!

So I awoke alone, soaked with sweat, and unable to get back to sleep. It's been years since I've had such a strong reaction to a dream. As I recall, the last time was five years ago right after we settled here, and it was this same damned dream. I suppose it's come back to me because of the attack on Dovetree.

That attack shouldn't have happened. Things have been quieting down over the past few years. There's still crime, of course—robberies, break-ins, abductions for ransom or for the slave trade. Worse, the poor still get arrested and indentured for indebtedness, vagrancy, loitering, and other "crimes." But this thing of raging into a community and killing and burning all that you don't steal seems to have gone out of fashion. I haven't heard of anything like this Dovetree raid for at least three years.

Granted, the Dovetrees did supply the area with home-distilled whiskey and homegrown marijuana, but they've been doing that since long before we arrived. In fact, they were the best-armed farm family in the area because their business was not only illegal, but lucrative. People have tried to rob them before, but only the quick, quiet burglartypes have had any success. Until now.

I questioned Aubrey, the healthy Dovetree wife, while Bankole was working on her son. He had already told her that the little boy would be all right, and I felt that we had to find out what she knew, no matter how upset she was. Hell, the Dovetree houses are only an hour's walk from here down the old logging road. Whoever hit Dovetree, we could be next on their list.

Aubrey told me the attackers wore strange clothing. She and I talked in the main room of the school, a single, smoky oil lamp between us on one of the tables. We sat facing one another across the table, Aubrey glancing every now and then at the clinic room, where Bankole had cleaned and eased her child's scrapes, burns, and bruises. She said the attackers were men, but they wore belted black tunics—black dresses, she called them—which hung to their thighs. Under these, they wore ordinary pants—either jeans or the kind of camouflage pants that she had seen soldiers wear.

"They were like soldiers," she said. "They sneaked in, so quiet. We never saw them until they started shooting at us. Then, bang! All at once. They hit all our houses. It was like an explosion—maybe twenty or thirty or more guns going off all at just the same time."

And that wasn't the way gangs operated. Gangsters would have fired raggedly, not in unison. Then they would have tried to make individual names for themselves, tried to grab the best-looking women or steal the best stuff before their friends could get it.

"They didn't steal or burn anything until they had beaten us, shot us," Aubrey said. "Then they took our fuel and went straight to our fields and burned our crops. After that, they raided the houses and barns. They all wore big white crosses on their chests—crosses like in church. But they killed us. They even shot the kids. Everybody they found, they killed them. I hid with my baby or they would have shot him and me." Again, she stared toward the clinic room.

That killing of children . . . that was a hell of a thing. Most thugs—except for the worst psychotics—would keep the kids alive for rape and then for sale. And as for the crosses, well, gangsters might wear crosses on chains around their necks, but that wasn't the sort of thing most of their victims would get close enough to notice. And gangsters were unlikely to run around in matching tunics all sporting white crosses on their chests. This was something new.

Or something old.

I didn't think of what it might be until after I had let Aubrey go back to the clinic to bed down next to her child. Bankole had given him something to help him sleep. He did the same for her, so I won't be able to ask her anything more until she wakes up later this morning. I couldn't help wondering, though, whether these people, with their crosses, had some connection with my current least favorite presidential candidate, Texas Senator Andrew Steele Jarret. It sounds like the sort of thing his people might do—a revival of something nasty out of the past. Did the Ku Klux Klan wear crosses—as well as burn them? The Nazis wore the swastika, which is a kind of cross, but I don't think they wore it on their chests. There were crosses all over the place during the Inquisition and before that during the Crusades. So now we have another group that uses crosses and slaughters people. Jarret's people could be behind it. Jarret insists on being a throwback to some earlier, "simpler" time. *Now* does not suit him. Religious tolerance does not suit him. The current state of the country does not suit him. He wants to take us all back to some magical time when everyone believed in the same God, worshipped him in the same way, and understood that their safety in the universe depended on completing the same religious rituals and stomping anyone who was different. There was never such a time in this country. But these days, when more than half the people in the country can't read at all, history is just one more vast unknown to them.

Jarret supporters have been known, now and then, to form mobs and burn people at the stake for being witches. Witches! In 2032! A witch, in their view, tends to be a Moslem, a Jew, a Hindu, a Buddhist, or, in some parts of the country, a Mormon, a Jehovah's Witness, or even a Catholic. A witch may also be an atheist, a "cultist," or a well-to-do eccentric. Well-to-do eccentrics often have no protectors or much that's worth stealing. And "cultist" is a great catchall term for anyone who fits into no other large category, and yet doesn't quite match Jarret's version of Christianity. Jarret's people have been known to beat or drive out Unitarians, for goodness' sake. Jarret condemns the burnings, but does so in such mild language that his people are free to hear what they want to hear. As for the beatings, the tarring and feathering, and the destruction of "heathen houses of devil-worship," he has a simple answer: "Join us! Our doors are open to every nationality, every race! Leave your sinful past behind, and become one of us. Help us to make America great again." He's had notable success with this carrot-and-stick approach. *Join us and thrive, or whatever happens to you as a result of your own sinful stubbornness is your problem.* His opponent Vice President Edward Jay Smith calls him a demagogue, a rabble-rouser, and a hypocrite. Smith is right, of course, but Smith is such a tired, gray shadow of a man. Jarret, on the other hand, is a big, handsome, black-haired man with deep, clear blue eyes that seduce people and hold them. He has a voice that's a whole-body experience, the way my father's was. In fact, I'm sorry to say, Jarret was once a Baptist minister like my father. But he left the Baptists behind years ago to begin his own "Christian America" denomination. He no longer preaches regular CA sermons at CA churches or on the nets, but he's still recognized as head of the church.

It seems inevitable that people who can't read are going to lean more toward judging candidates on the way they look and sound than on what they claim they stand for. Even people who can read and are educated are apt to pay more attention to good looks and seductive lies than they should. And no doubt the new picture ballots on the nets will give Jarret an even greater advantage.

Jarret's people see alcohol and drugs as Satan's tools. Some of his more fanatical followers might very well be the tunic-and-cross gang who destroyed Dovetree.

And we are Earthseed. We're "that cult," "those strange people in the hills," "those crazy fools who pray to some kind of god of change." We are also, according to some rumors I've heard, "those devil-worshiping hill heathens who take in children. *And what do you suppose they do with them?*" Never mind that the trade in abducted or orphaned children or children sold by desperate parents goes on all over the country, and everyone knows it. No matter. The hint that some cult is taking in children for "questionable purposes" is enough to make some people irrational.

That's the kind of rumor that could hurt us even with people who aren't Jarret supporters. I've only heard it a couple of times, but it's still scary.

At this point, I just hope that the people who hit Dovetree were some new gang, disciplined and frightening, but only after profit. I hope. . . .

But I don't believe it. I do suspect that Jarret's people had something to do with this. And I think I'd better say so today at Gathering. With Dovetree fresh in everyone's mind, people will be ready to cooperate, have more drills and scatter more caches of money, food, weapons, records, and valuables. We can fight a gang. We've done that before when we were much less prepared than we are now. But we can't fight Jarret. In particular, we can't fight *President* Jarret. President Jarret, if the country is mad enough to elect him, could destroy us without even knowing we exist.

We are now 59 people—64 with the Dovetree women and children, if they stay. With numbers like that, we barely do exist. All the more reason, I suppose, for my dream.

My "talent," going back to the parable of the talents, is Earthseed. And although I haven't buried it in the ground, I have buried it here in these coastal mountains, where it can grow at about the same speed as our redwood trees. But what else could I have done? If I had somehow been as good at rabble-rousing as Jarret is, then Earthseed might be a big enough movement by now to be a real target. And would that be better?

OCTAVIA E. BUTLER

I'm jumping to all kinds of unwarranted conclusions. At least I hope they're unwarranted. Between my horror at what's happened down at Dovetree and my hopes and fears for my own people, I'm upset and at loose ends and, perhaps, just imagining things.

2

○ ○ ○

From EARTHSEED: THE BOOKS OF THE LIVING

Chaos
Is God's most dangerous face—
Amorphous, roiling, hungry.
Shape Chaos—
Shape God.
Act.

Alter the speed
Or the direction of Change.
Vary the scope of Change.
Recombine the seeds of Change.
Transmute the impact of Change.
Seize Change.
Use it.
Adapt and grow.

The original 13 settlers of Acorn, and thus the original 13 members of Earthseed, were my mother, of course, and Harry Balter and Zahra Moss, who were also refugees from my mother's home neighborhood in Robledo. There was Travis, Natividad, and Dominic Douglas, a young family who became my mother's first highway converts. She met them as both groups walked through Santa Barbara, California. She liked their looks, recognized their dangerous vulnerability—Dominic was only a few months old at the time—and convinced them to walk with Harry, Zahra, and her in their long trek north where they all hoped to find better lives.

Next came Allison Gilchrist and her sister Jillian—Allie and Jill.

But Jill was killed later along the highway. At around the same time, my mother spotted my father and he spotted her. Neither of them was shy and both seemed willing to act on what they felt. My father joined the growing group. Justin Rohr became Justin Gilchrist when the group found him crying alongside the body of his dead mother. He was about three at the time, and he and Allie wound up coming together in another small family. Last came the two families of ex-slaves that joined together to become one growing family of sharers. These were Grayson Mora and his daughter Doe and Emery Solis and her daughter Tori.

That was it: four children, four men, and five women.

They should have died. That they survived at all in the unforgiving world of the Pox might qualify as a miracle—although, of course, Earthseed does not encourage belief in miracles.

No doubt the group's isolated location—well away from towns and paved roads—helped keep it safe from much of the violence of the time. The land it settled on belonged to my father. There was on that land when the group arrived one dependable well, a half-ruined garden, a number of fruit and nut trees, and groves of oaks, pines, and redwoods. Once the members of the group had pooled their money and bought handcarts, seed, small livestock, hand tools, and other necessities, they were almost independent. They vanished into their hills and increased their numbers by birth, by adoption of orphans, and by conversion of needy adults. They scavenged what they could from abandoned farms and settlements, they traded at street markets and traded with their neighbors. One of the most valuable things they traded with one another was knowledge.

Every member of Earthseed learned to read and to write, and most knew at least two languages—usually Spanish and English, since those were the two most useful. Anyone who joined the group, child or adult, had to begin at once to learn these basics and to acquire a trade. Anyone who had a trade was always in the process of teaching it to someone else. My mother insisted on this, and it does seem sensible. Public schools had become rare in those days when ten-year-old children could be put to work. Education was no longer free, but it was still mandatory according to the law. The problem was, no one was enforcing such laws, just as no one was protecting child laborers.

My father had the most valuable skills in the group. By the time he married my mother, he had been practicing medicine for almost 30 years. He was a multiple rarity for their location: well educated, professional, and Black. Black people in particular were rare in the mountains. People wondered about him. Why was he there? He could have been making a better living in some small, established town. The area was littered with tiny towns that would be glad to have any doctor. Was he competent? Was he honest? Was he clean? Could he be trusted looking after wives and daughters? How could they be sure he was really a doctor at all? My father apparently wrote nothing at all about this, but my mother wrote about everything.

She says at one point: "Bankole heard the same whispers and rumors I did at the various street markets and in occasional meetings with neighbors, and he shrugged. He had us to keep healthy and our work-related injuries to treat. Other people had their first aid kits, their satellite phone nets, and, if they were lucky, their cars or trucks. These vehicles tended to be old and undependable, but some people had them. Whether or not they called Bankole was their business.

"Then, thanks to someone else's misfortune, things improved. Jean Holly's appendix flared up and all but ruptured, and the Holly family, our eastern neighbors, decided that they had better take a chance on Bankole.

"Once Bankole had saved the woman's life, he had a talk with the family. He told them exactly what he thought of them for waiting so long to call him, for almost letting a woman with five young children die. He spoke with that intense quiet courtesy of his that makes people squirm. The Hollys took it. He became their doctor.

"And the Hollys mentioned him to their friends the Sullivans, and the Sullivans mentioned him to their daughter who had married into the Gama family, and the Gamas told the Dovetrees because old Mrs. Dovetree—the matriarch—had been a Gama. That was when we began to get to know our nearest neighbors, the Dovetrees."

Speaking of knowing people, I wish more than ever that I could have known my father. He seems to have been an impressive man. And, perhaps, it would have been good for me to know this version of my mother, struggling, focused, but very young, very human. I might have liked these people.

From *THE JOURNALS OF LAUREN OYA OLAMINA*
MONDAY, SEPTEMBER 27, 2032

I'm not sure how to talk about today. It was intended to be a quiet day of salvaging and plant collecting after yesterday's uncomfortable Gathering and determined anniversary celebration. We have, it seems, a few people who think Jarret may be just what the country needs—apart from his religious nonsense. The thing is, you can't separate Jarret from the "religious nonsense." You take Jarret and you get beatings, burnings, tarrings and featherings. They're a package. And there may be even nastier things in that package. Jarret's supporters are more than a little seduced by Jarret's talk of making America great again. He seems to be unhappy with certain other countries. We could wind up in a war. Nothing like a war to rally people around flag, country, and great leader.

Nevertheless, some of our people—the Peralta and Faircloth families in particular—might be leaving us soon.

"I've got four kids left alive," Ramiro Peralta said yesterday at Gathering. "Maybe with a strong leader like Jarret running things, they'll have a chance to stay alive."

He's a good guy, Ramiro is, but he's desperate for solutions, for order and stability. I understand that. He used to have seven kids and a wife. He'd lost three of his kids and his wife to a fire set by an angry, frightened, ignorant mob who decided to cure a nasty cholera epidemic down in Los Angeles by burning down the area of the city where they thought the epidemic had begun. I kept that in mind as I answered

OCTAVIA E. BUTLER

him. "Think, Ramiro," I said. "Jarret doesn't have any answers! How will lynching people, burning their churches, and starting wars help your kids to live?"

Ramiro Peralta only turned away from me in anger. He and Alan Faircloth looked across the Gathering room—the school room—at one another. They're both afraid. They look at their children—Alan has four kids, too—and they're afraid and ashamed of their fear, ashamed of their powerlessness. And they're tired. There are millions of people like them—people who are frightened and just plain tired of all the chaos. They want someone to do something. Fix things. Now!

Anyway, we had a stormy Gathering and an uneasy anniversary celebration. Interesting that they fear Edward Jay Smith's supposed incompetence more than they fear Jarret's obvious tyranny.

So this morning, I was ready for a day of walking, thinking, and plant collecting with friends. We still travel in groups of three or four when we leave Acorn because the mountains, on the roads and off them, can be dangerous. But for nearly five months now, we've had no trouble while salvaging. I suppose, though, that that can be dangerous in itself. Sad. Raids and gangs are dangerous because they kill outright. Peace is dangerous because it encourages complacency and careless-ness—which also kills sooner or later.

In spite of the Dovetree raid, we were, to be honest, more compla-cent than usual because we were heading for a place that we knew. It was a burned, abandoned farmhouse far from Dovetree where we'd spotted some useful plants. In particular, there was aloe vera for use in easing burns and insect bites, and there were big mounds of agave. The agave was a handsome, variegated species—blue-green leaves edged in yellow-white. It must have been growing and propagating untended for years in what was once the front yard of the farmhouse. It was one of the large, vicious varieties of agave, each individual plant an upturned rosette of stiff, fibrous, fleshy leaves, some of them over a meter long in the big parent plants. Each leaf was tipped with a long, hard, dagger-sharp spike, and for good measure, each leaf was edged in jagged thorns that were tough enough to saw through human flesh. We intended to use them to do just that.

On our first visit, we had taken some of the smallest plants, the youngest offsets. Now we meant to dig up as many of the rest as we could bundle into our handcart. The cart was already more than half full of things we had salvaged from the rotting storage shed of a collapsed cabin a couple of miles from where the agave grew. We had found dusty pots, pans, buckets, old books and magazines, rusted hand tools, nails, log chains, and wire. All had been damaged by water and time, but most could be cleaned and repaired or cannibalized for parts or at least copied. We learn from all the work we do. We've become very competent makers and repairers of small tools. We've survived as well as we have because we keep learning. Our customers have come to know that if they buy from us, they'll get their money's worth.

Salvaging from abandoned gardens and fields is useful, too. We collect any herb, fruit, vegetable, or nut-producing plant, any plant at all that we know or suppose to be useful. We have, always, a special need for spiny, self-sufficient desert plants that will tolerate our climate. They serve as part of our thorn fence.

Cactus by cactus, thornbush by thornbush, we've planted a living wall in the hills around Acorn. Our wall won't keep determined people out, of course. No wall will do that. Cars and trucks will get in if their owners are willing to absorb some damage to their vehicles, but cars and trucks that work are rare and precious in the mountains, and most fuels are expensive.

Even intruders on foot can get in if they're willing to work at it. But the fence will hamper and annoy them. It will make them angry, and perhaps noisy. It will, when it's working well, encourage people to approach us by the easiest routes, and those we guard 24 hours a day.

It's always best to keep an eye on visitors.

So we intended to harvest agave.

We headed for what was left of the farmhouse. It was built on a low rise overlooking fields and gardens. It was supposed to be our last stop before we went home. It came near to being our last stop, period.

There was an old gray housetruck parked near the ruin of the house. We didn't see the truck at first. It was hidden behind the larger of two chimneys that still stood like head- and footstones, commemorating the burned house. I mentioned to Jorge Cho the way the chimneys looked. Jorge was with us because in spite of his youth, he's good at spotting useful salvage that other people might dismiss as junk.

"What are head- and footstones?" he asked me. He meant it. He's 18 and an escapee from the Los Angeles area like I am, but his experience has been very different. While I was being cared for and educated by educated parents, he was on his own. He speaks Spanish and a little remembered Korean, but no English. He was seven when his mother died of flu and twelve when an earthquake killed his father. It collapsed the old brick building in which the family had been squatting. So at 12, Jorge alone was responsible for his younger sister and brother. He took care of them, somehow, and taught himself to read and write Spanish with occasional help from an old wino acquaintance. He worked at hard, dangerous, often illegal jobs; he salvaged; and when necessary, he stole. He and his sister and brother, three Korean kids in a poor neighborhood of Mexican and Central American refugees, managed to survive, but they had no time to learn nonessentials. Now we're teaching them to read, write, and speak English because that will enable them to communicate with more people. And we're teaching them history, farming, carpentry, and incidental things—like what head- and footstones are.

The other two members of the salvage team were Natividad Douglas and Michael Kardos. Jorge and I are sharers. Mike and Natividad aren't. It's too dangerous to send out a majority of sharers on any team. Sharers are too vulnerable. We suffer no matter who gets hurt. But two and two is a good team, and the four of us work well together. It's unusual for us all to be careless at the same time, but today, we managed it.

The fireplace and chimney that had concealed the truck from us had been the end wall of what was once a large living room. The fireplace was big enough to roast a whole cow. The whole affair was just big enough to conceal a medium-sized housetruck.

We saw the thing only an instant before it opened fire on us.

We were armed, as usual, with our automatic rifles and our sidearms, but against the armor and the firepower of even a modest housetruck, those were nothing.

We dropped to the ground under a spray of dirt and rock kicked up by bullets hitting the ground around us. We scrambled backward, down the rise on which the house was built. The crest of the rise was our only cover. All we could do was lie at the foot of its slope and try to keep all our body parts out of sight. We didn't dare stand or even sit up. There was nowhere for us to go. Bullets chewed the ground in front of us, then behind us, beyond the protection of the rise.

There were no trees nearby—not even a large bush between us and the truck. We were in the thinnest part of the remains of a desert garden. We had not reached our agaves yet—could not reach them now. They couldn't have shielded us anyway. The only thing some of us might have at least concealed ourselves behind was a young, far-from-bullet-proof young Washingtonia palm tree that we had passed on the way in. Its fronds were spread around it, low and green like a big bush, but it was at the north end of the house, and we were pinned down at the south end. The truck, too, was parked at the south end. The tree would be of no use to us. Nearest to us were a few aloe vera plants, a prickly pear, a small yucca, and a few weeds and tufts of grass.

None of these would do us any good. If the people in the truck had been making full use of their equipment, even the rise would not have done us any good. We would already be dead. I wondered how they had managed to miss us when we arrived. Were they just trying to scare us off? I didn't think so. The shooting had gone on for too long.

At last, it stopped.

We lay still, playing dead, listening for the whine of a truck engine, for footsteps, for voices, for any of the sounds that might tell us we were being hunted—or that our assailants had gone. There was only the low moan of the wind and the rustling of some of the plants. I lay, thinking about the pine trees that I had seen on the high ridge far behind the house. I could see them in my mind's eye, and somehow, it was all I could do to stop myself from raising my head to get a look at them, to see whether they were as far away as I thought they were. The weed-strewn fields of what had been the farm swept back and up into the hills. Above them were the pines that could shelter and conceal, but they were far beyond our reach. I sighed.

Then we heard the sound of a child, crying.

We all heard it—a few short sobs, then nothing. The child sounded very young—not a baby, but young, exhausted, helpless, hopeless.

The four of us looked at one another. We all care about kids. Michael has two and Natividad has three. Bankole and I have been trying to have one. Jorge, I'm glad to say, hasn't made anyone pregnant yet, but he's been a surrogate father to his younger sister and brother for six years. He knows as well as the rest of us do what dangers lie in wait for unprotected children.

I raised my head just enough to get a quick look at the truck and the area around it. A housetruck, armed, armored, and locked up tight shouldn't—couldn't—let the sound of a child's crying escape. And the sound had seemed normal, not amplified or modified by truck speakers.

Therefore, one of the truck's doors must be open. Wide open.

I couldn't see much through the weeds and grasses, and I didn't dare to raise my head above them. All I could make out were the sunlit shapes of the chimney, the truck beside it, the weeds in the fields behind both chimney and truck, the distant trees, and. . . .

Movement?

Movement far away in the weeds of the field, but coming closer.

Natividad pulled me down. "What is the matter with you?" she whispered in Spanish. For Jorge's sake, it was best to stay with Spanish while we were in trouble. "There are crazy people in that truck! Do you want to die?"

"Someone else is coming," I said. "More than one person, coming through the fields."

"I don't care! Stay down!"

Natividad is one of my best friends, but sometimes having her along is like having your mother with you.

"Maybe the crying is intended to lure us out," Michael said. "People have used children as lures before." He's a suspicious man, Michael is. He questions everything. He and his family have been with us for two years now, and I think it took him six months to accept us and to decide that we had no evil intentions toward his wife or his twin girls. This, even though we took them in and helped them when we found his wife alone, giving birth to the twins in a ruin of a shack where they had been squatting. The place was near a stream, so they had water, and they had a couple of scavenged pots. But they were armed only with an ancient, empty .22 target pistol and a knife. They were all but starving, eating pine nuts, wild plants, and an occasional small animal that Michael trapped or killed with a rock. In fact, he was away looking for food when his wife Noriko went into labor.

Michael agreed to join us because he was terrified that in spite of his odd jobs, begging, stealing, and scavenging, his wife and babies might starve. We never asked more of them than that they do their share of the work to keep the community going and that they respect Earthseed by not preaching other belief systems. But to Michael, this sounded like altruism, and Michael didn't believe in altruism. He kept expecting to catch us selling people into slavery or prostituting them. He didn't begin to relax until he realized that we were, in fact, practicing what we preached. Earthseed was and is the key to us. We had a way of life that he thought was sensible and a goal, a Destiny that he thought was crazy, but we weren't up to anything that would harm his family. And his family was the key to him. Once he accepted us, he and Noriko and the girls settled in and made Acorn very much their home. They're good people. Even Michael's suspiciousness can be a good thing. Most of the time, it helps us keep alert.

"I don't think the crying was intended to lure us out," I said. "But something is wrong here. That's obvious. The people in that truck should either make sure we're dead or they should leave."

"And we shouldn't hear them," Jorge said. "No matter how loud that kid yells, we shouldn't hear a thing."

Natividad spoke up. "Their guns shouldn't have missed us," she said. "In a truck like that, the guns should be run by a computer. Automatic targeting. The only way you can miss is if you insist on doing things yourself. You might forget to put your guns on the computer or you might leave the computer off if you just wanted to scare people. But if you're serious, you shouldn't *keep* missing." Her father had taught her more about guns than most of the rest of our community knew.

"I don't think they missed us on purpose," I said. "It didn't feel like that."

"I agree," Michael said. "So what's wrong over there?"

"Shit!" Jorge whispered. "What's wrong is the bastards are going to kill us if we move!"

The guns went off again. I pressed myself against the ground and lay there, frozen, eyes shut. The idiots in the truck meant to kill us whether we moved or not, and their chances for success were excellent.

Then I realized that this time, they weren't shooting at us.

Someone screamed. Over the steady clatter of one of the truck's guns, I heard someone scream in agony. I didn't move. When someone was in pain, the only way I could avoid sharing the suffering was not to look.

Jorge, who should have known better, raised his head and looked.

An instant later he doubled up, thrashing and twisting in someone else's agony. He didn't scream. Sharers who survive learn early to take the pain and keep quiet. We keep our vulnerability as secret as we can. Sometimes we manage not to move or give any sign at all. But Jorge hurt too much to keep his body still. He clutched himself, crossing his arms over his belly. At once, I felt a dull echo of his pain in my own middle. It is incomprehensible to me that some people think of sharing as an ability or a power—as something desirable.

"Fool," I said to Jorge, and held him until the pain passed from both of us. I concealed my own pain as best I could so that we wouldn't develop the kind of nasty feedback loop that I've learned we sharers are capable of. We don't die of the pains that we see and share. We wish we could sometimes, and there is danger in sharing too much pain or too many deaths. These are individual matters. Five years ago I shared three or four deaths fast, one after another. It hurt more than anything should be able to hurt. Then it knocked me out. When I came to, I was numb and sick and dazed long after there was any pain to share. With lesser pains, it's enough to turn away. In minutes, the pain is over for us. Deaths take much longer to get over.

The one good thing about sharing pain is that it makes us very slow to cause pain to other people. We hate pain more than most people do.

"I'm okay," Jorge said after a while. And then, "Those guys out there . . . I think they're dead. They must be dead."

"They're down anyway," Michael whispered as he looked where Jorge had looked. "I can see at least three of them in the field beyond the chimney and the truck." He squirmed backward so that he could relax and no longer see or be seen over the rise. Sometimes I try to imagine what it must be like to look at pain and feel nothing. My current recurring nightmare is the closest I've come to that kind of freedom, not that it felt like freedom. But to Michael, feeling nothing must be . . . well . . . normal.

Everything had gone quiet. The truck had not moved. It did nothing.

"They seem to need a moving target," I said.

"Maybe they're high on something," Natividad said. "Or maybe they're just crazy. Jorge, are you sure you're okay?"

"Yes. I just want to get the hell out of here."

I shook my head. "We're stuck here, at least until it gets dark."

OCTAVIA E. BUTLER

"If the truck has even the cheapest night-vision equipment, the dark won't help us," Michael said.

I thought about that, then nodded. "Yes, but it shot at us and missed. And it hasn't moved, even though two sets of people have found its hiding place. I'd say either the truck or the people in it are not in good working order. We'll stay here until dark, then we'll run. If we're lucky, no one will wander in behind us before then and give us trouble or draw the truck's attention back this way. But whatever happens, we'll wait."

"Three people are dead," Michael said. "We should be dead ourselves. Maybe before the night is over, we will be."

I sighed. "Shut up, Mike."

We waited through the cool autumn day. We were lucky that two days before, the weather had turned cool. We were also lucky that it wasn't raining. Perfect weather for getting pinned down by armed lunatics.

The truck never moved. No one else came along to trouble us or to draw fire. We ate the food we had brought along for lunch and drank what was left of our water. We decided that the truckers must think we were dead. Well, we were content to play dead until the sun had set. We waited.

Then we moved. In the dark, we began to crawl toward the northward edge of our cover. Moving this way, we hoped to put so much of the big chimney between ourselves and the truck that the people in the truck would not have time to see us and open fire before we got to better cover behind the second chimney. Once we reached the second chimney, we hoped to keep both chimneys between ourselves and the immobile truck as we escaped. That was fine as long as the truck remained immobile. If it moved, we were dead. Even if it didn't move, there would be a moment when we were easy targets, when we had to run across open ground.

"Oh god, oh god, oh god," Jorge whispered through clenched teeth as he stared at the stretch of open ground. If the truck managed to shoot anyone, and he saw it, he would collapse. So would I.

"Don't look around," I reminded him. "Even if you hear shots, look straight ahead, and run!"

But before we could start, the crying began again. There was no mistaking the sound. It was the open, uninhibited sobbing of a child, and this time, it didn't stop.

We ran. The sound of the crying might help to cover any sounds we made over the uneven ground—although we weren't noisy. We've learned not to be.

Jorge reached the smaller chimney first. I was next. Then Michael and Natividad arrived together. Michael is short and lean and looks as quick as he is. Natividad is stocky and strong and doesn't look quick at all, but she tends to surprise people.

We all made it. There were no shots fired. And in the time it took us to reach the smaller chimney, I found that I had changed my mind about things.

The crying had not stopped or even paused. When I looked around the small chimney toward the truck, I could see light—a broad swatch of dim, blue-gray light. I couldn't see people, but it was clear that we had guessed right. A side door of the truck was wide open.

We were all bunched together at the smaller chimney, the others peering toward the down slope north of us. That was where they still expected to go. There was starlight enough to light the way, and I could see Jorge, bent down, his hands on his thighs as though he were about to run a race.

The child was not sobbing now, but wailing—a thin, exhausted sound. Best to move before the crying stopped. Also best to move before the others understood what I meant to do—what I now knew I had to do. They would follow me and back me up as long as I moved fast and didn't give them time to think or argue.

"Let's go," Michael said.

I paid no attention. There was, I realized, a bad smell in the air, swelling and fading in the evening breeze. It seemed to be coming from the truck.

OCTAVIA E. BUTLER

"Come on," Michael urged.

"No," I said, and waited until all three of them had turned to look at me. Timing, now. "I want to see about that child," I said. "And I want that truck."

I moved then, just ahead of their restraining hands and words.

I ran. I ran around the carcass of the house, shifting for an instant from reality into my dream. I was running past the stark ruin of a house, its chimneys, its few remaining black bones just visible against the stars.

Just for an instant, I thought I saw shadowy dream forms. Shadows rising, moving. . . .

I shook off the feeling and stopped as I reached the larger chimney. I edged around it, willing the truckers not to shoot me, terrified that they would shoot me, moving fast in spite of the terror.

The blue-gray light was brighter now, and the smell had become a sickening stench of rottenness that I found all too familiar.

I crouched low, hoping to be out of sight of the truck's cameras, and I crossed in front of the truck—near enough to it to put out my hand and touch it. Then I had reached the far side of it where the light was, where the door must be open.

As I went, I almost fell over the crying child. It was a little girl of perhaps six or seven. She was filthy beyond my ability to describe filthiness. She sat in the dirt, crying, reaching up to wipe away tears and rearrange some of the mud on her face.

She looked up and saw me just as I managed to stop myself from falling over her. She stared at me, her mouth open, as I swung past her to level my rifle into the blue-gray light of the truck's interior.

I don't know what I expected to see: Drunken people sprawled about? An orgy? More filth? People aiming their weapons at me? Death?

There was death nearby. I knew that. The smell was unmistakable.

What I did see in the blue-gray light was another child, another little girl, asleep at one of the truck's monitors. She had put her head down against the edge of the control board, and was snoring a little. The blue-gray light came from the three screens that were on. All three showed only gray, grainy electronic "snow."

There were also three dead people in the truck.

That is, I thought they must be dead. It was clear that all had been wounded—shot, I thought—several times. In fact, they must have been shot some time ago—days ago, perhaps. The blood on their bodies had dried and darkened.

I don't share any feeling with the unconscious or the dead, I'm glad to say. No matter how they look or smell, they don't bother me that much. I've seen too many of them.

I climbed into the truck, leaving the crying child outside to the care of the others. I could already hear Natividad talking to her. Natividad loves kids, and they seem to trust her as soon as they meet her.

Jorge and Michael had come up behind me as I climbed into the truck. Both froze as they saw the sleeping child and the sprawled bodies. Then Michael moved past me to check the bodies. He, Natividad, Allie Gilchrist, and Zahra Balter have learned to assist Bankole. They have no official medical or nurse training, but Bankole has trained them—is training them—and they're careful and serious about their work.

Michael checked the bodies and discovered that only one, a slender, dark, middle-aged man, was dead. He had been shot in the chest and abdomen. The other two were a big, naked, middle-aged, blond woman shot in the legs and thighs and a clothed blond boy of about 15 shot in the legs and left shoulder. These people were covered with dried blood. Nevertheless, Michael found faint heartbeats in the woman and the boy.

"We've got to get them to Bankole," he said. "This is too much for me."

"Oh, shit," Jorge moaned, and he ran outside and threw up. I couldn't blame him. He had just noticed the maggots in the man's eyes, mouth, and wounds, and in the wounds of the other two. I looked away myself. All of us can deal with that kind of thing, but no one enjoys it. To tell the truth, I was more concerned about whether one or both of the wounded people would come to. I positioned myself

OCTAVIA E. BUTLER

so that I would not have to look at them. They were in no shape to attack us, of course, but they would drag me into their pain if they were conscious.

Keeping my back to Michael and his patients, I awoke the sleeping child. She wasn't quite as filthy as the little girl we'd found outside, but she did need a bath.

She squinted up at me, groggy, uncomprehending. Then she gave a little squeal and tried to dart past me, and out the door.

I caught her and held her while she struggled and screamed. I spoke to her, whispered to her, tried to reassure her, did all I could to bring her out of her hysteria. "It's all right, honey, it's all right. Don't cry. You'll be all right. We'll take care of you, don't worry. We'll take care of you. . . ." I rocked her and crooned to her as though to a much younger child.

The dead and wounded were no doubt her family. She and the other child had been alone here with them for . . . how long? They would need all the care we could give them. After much more screaming and struggling, she began to take refuge in my arms, holding on to me instead of trying to escape. From my arms, she stared, huge-eyed, at the others.

Jorge stood watch at the monitors once his stomach settled. Natividad had calmed the other little girl and found a clean cloth and some water. These she used to wash the child's face, hands, and arms. Michael had left the wounded woman and boy to examine the truck's controls. Of the four of us, he was the only one who knew how to drive.

"Any trouble?" I asked him.

He shook his head. "Not even any sign of boobytraps. I guess they would have worried about the kids springing them."

"Can you drive it?"

"No problem."

"Drive it, then. It's ours. Let's go home."

The truck was all right. There was plenty of power in its batteries, and Michael had no trouble finding and using its night-vision equipment. It carried infrared, ambient light, and radar devices. All of these were of good quality, and all worked. The little girls must not have understood how to use them—as they had not known how to drive. Or perhaps they had known how to operate everything, but had not known where to go with it. Who could little children go to for help, after all? If they had no adult relatives, even the police would either sell them illegally or indenture them legally. Indenturing indigents, young and old, is much in fashion now. The Thirteenth and Fourteenth Amendments—the ones abolishing slavery and guaranteeing citizenship rights—still exist, but they've been so weakened by custom, by Congress and the various state legislatures, and by recent Supreme Court decisions that they don't much matter. Indenturing indigents is supposed to keep them employed, teach them a trade, feed them, house them, and keep them out of trouble. In fact, it's just one more way of getting people to work for nothing or almost nothing. Little girls are valued because they can be used in so many ways, and they can be coerced into being quick, docile, disposable labor.

No doubt these two girls have been taught to be terrified of strangers. Then, with their parents and brother out of action, they had been left on their own to defend their family and their home. In their blind fear, they had, they must have, shot at us and shot and hit three men who gave no sign of being anything worse than wanderers, perhaps salvagers. Michael and Natividad did go out to check on these men before we left while Jorge and I loaded our handcart and its contents onto the truck.

The three men were dead. They had hard currency and holstered guns—which Michael and Natividad collected. We covered them with rocks and left them. But they had been even less of a danger to the housetruck than we were. If they had walked right up to the truck, a locked door would have kept them out. Their old nine-millimeter semiautomatics would have had no chance against the truck's armor. But the little girls hadn't realized that.

We got them home to Acorn, and they're getting baths, food, comfort, and rest. Bankole is working on their mother and brother. He was not happy to have new patients. Our clinic has never been so full, and he has all his students and some volunteers helping him. He says he doesn't know whether he'll be able to save this new mother and son. He has a few simple instruments and an intricate little diagnostic unit that he saved when he fled his home in San Diego five years ago. And he has a few medicines—drugs to ease pain, fight infection, and otherwise keep us healthy. If the boy lives, Bankole doesn't know whether he'll walk again.

Bankole will do his best for them. And Allie Gilchrist and May are taking care of the little girls. The girls have been lucky, at least, in having us find them. They'll be safe with us.

And now, at last, we have something we've needed for years. We have a truck.

WEDNESDAY, SEPTEMBER 29, 2032

With all the work that my Bankole has had to do to help the wounded woman and boy and the wounded Dovetrees, he didn't get around to shouting at me over the truck incident until last night. And, of course, he didn't shout. He tends not to. It's a pity. His disapproval might be easier to take if it were quick and loud. It was, as usual, quiet and intense.

"It's a shame that so many of your unnecessary risks pay off so well," he said to me as we lay in bed last night. "You're a fool, you know. It's as though you think you can't be killed. My god, girl, you're old enough to know better."

"I wanted the housetruck," I said. "And I realized we might be able to get it. And we might be able to help a child. We kept hearing one of them crying."

He turned his head to look at me for several seconds, his mouth set. "You've seen children led down the road in convict collars or chains," he said. "You've seen them displayed as enticements before houses of prostitution. Are you going to tell me you did this because you heard one crying?"

"I do what I can," I said. "When I can do more, I will. You know that."

He just looked at me. If I didn't love him, I might not like him much at times like these. I took his hand and kissed it, and held it. "I do what I can." I repeated, "And I wanted the housetruck."

"Enough to risk not only yourself, but your whole team—four people?"

"The risk in running away empty-handed was at least as great as the risk of going for the truck."

He made a sound of disgust and withdrew his hand. "So now you've got a battered old housetruck," he muttered.

I nodded. "So now we have it. We need it. You know we do. It's a beginning."

"It's not worth anyone's life!"

"It didn't cost any of our lives!" I sat up and looked down at him. I needed to have him see me as well as he could in the dim light from the window. I wanted to have him know that I meant what I was saying. "If I had to die," I said, "if I had to get shot by strangers, shouldn't it be while I was trying to help the community, and not just while I was trying to run away?"

He raised his hands and gave me an ironic round of applause. "I knew you would say something like that. Well, I never thought you were stupid. Obsessed, perhaps, but not stupid. That being the case, I have a proposition for you."

He sat up and I moved close to him and pulled the blankets up around us. I leaned against him and sat, waiting. Whatever he had to say, I felt that I'd gotten my point across. If he wanted to call my thinking obsessive, I didn't care.

"I've been looking at some of the towns in the area," he said. "Saylorville, Halstead, Coy—towns that are a few miles off the highway. None of them need a doctor now, but one probably will someday soon. How would you feel about living in one of those towns?"

I sat still, surprised. He meant it. Saylorville? Halstead? Coy? These are communities so small that I'm not sure they qualify as towns. Each has no more than a few families and businesses huddled together between the highway—U.S. 101—and the sea. We trade at their street markets, but they're closed societies, these towns. They tolerate "foreign" visitors, but they don't like us. They've been burned too many times by strangers passing through—people who turned out to be thieves or worse. They trust only their own and long-established neighboring farmers. Did Bankole think that they would welcome us? Except for a larger town called Prata, the nearest towns are almost all White. Prata is White and Latino with a sprinkling of Asians. We're you name it: Black, White, Latino, Asian, and any mixture at all—the kind of thing you'd expect to find in a city. The kids we've adopted and the ones who have been born to us think of all the mixing and matching as normal. Imagine that.

Bankole and I, both Black, have managed to mix things up age-wise. He's always being mistaken for my father. When he corrects people, they wink at him or frown or grin. Here in Acorn, if people don't understand us, at least they accept us.

"I'm content here," I said. "The land is yours. The community is ours. With our work, and with Earthseed to guide us, we're building something good here. It will grow and spread. We'll see that it does. But for now, nothing in any of those towns is ours."

"It can be," he said. "You don't realize how valuable a physician is to an isolated community."

"Oh, don't I? I know how valuable you are to us."

He turned his head toward me. "More valuable than a truck?"

"Idiot," I said. "You want to hear praise? Fine. Consider yourself praised. You know how many of our lives you've saved—including mine."

He seemed to think about that for a moment. "This is a healthy young group of people," he said. "Except for the Dovetree woman, even your most recent adoptees are healthy people who've been injured, not sick people. We have no old people." He grinned. "Except me. No chronic problems except for Katrina Dovetree's heart. Not even a problem pregnancy or a child with worms. Almost any town in the area needs a doctor more than Acorn does."

"They need any doctor. We need you. Besides, they have what they need."

"As I've said, they won't always."

"I don't care." I moved against him. "You belong here. Don't even think about going away."

"Thinking is all I can do about it right now. I'm thinking about a safe place for us, a safe place for you when I'm dead."

I winced.

"I'm an old man, girl. I don't kid myself about that."

"Bankole—"

"I have to think about it. I want you to think about it too. Do that for me. Just think about it."

3

○ ○ ○

From EARTHSEED: THE BOOKS OF THE LIVING

God is Change,
And in the end,
God prevails.
But meanwhile . . .
Kindness eases Change.
Love quiets fear.
And a sweet and powerful
Positive obsession
Blunts pain,
Diverts rage,
And engages each of us
In the greatest,
The most intense
Of our chosen struggles.

From *MEMORIES OF OTHER WORLDS*

I cannot know what the end will be of all of Olamina's dreaming, striving, and certainty. I cannot recall ever feeling as certain of anything as she seems to be of Earthseed, a belief system that she herself created—or, as she says, a network of truths that she has simply recognized. I was always a doubter when it came to religion. How irrational of me, then, to love a zealot. But then, both love and zealotry are irrational states of mind.

Olamina believes in a god that does not in the least love her. In fact, her god is a process or a combination of processes, not an entity. It is

55

not consciously aware of her—or of anything. It is not conscious at all. "God is Change," she says, and means it. Some of the faces of her god are biological evolution, chaos theory, relativity theory, the uncertainty principle, and, of course, the second law of thermodynamics. "God is Change, and, in the end, God prevails."

Yet Earthseed is not a fatalistic belief system. God can be directed, focused, speeded, slowed, shaped. All things change, but all things need not change in all ways. God is inexorable, yet malleable. Odd. Hardly religious at all. Even the Earthseed Destiny seems to have little to do with religion.

"We are Earthseed," Olamina says. "We are the children of God, as all fractions of the universe are the children of God. But more immediately we are the children of our particular Earth." And within those words lies the origin of the Destiny. That portion of humanity that is conscious, that knows it is Earthseed, and that accepts its Destiny is simply trying to leave the womb, the Earth, to be born as all young beings must do eventually.

Earthseed is Olamina's contribution to what she feels should be a species-wide effort to evade, or at least to lengthen, the specialize-growdie evolutionary cycle that humanity faces, that every species faces.

"We can be a long-term success and the parents, ourselves, of a vast array of new peoples, new species," she says, "or we can be just one more abortion. We can, we must, scatter the Earth's living essence—human, plant, and animal to extrasolar worlds: 'The Destiny of Earthseed is to take root among the stars.'"

Grand words.

She hopes and dreams and writes and believes, and perhaps the world will let her live for a while, tolerating her as a harmless eccentric. I hope that it will. I fear that it may not.

My father has, in this piece, defined Earthseed very well, and defined it in fewer words than I could have managed. When my mother was a child, protected and imprisoned by the walls of her neighborhood, she dreamed of the stars. Literally, at night she dreamed of them. And she dreamed of flying. I've seen her flying dreams mentioned in her earliest writings. Awake or asleep, she dreamed of these things. As far as I'm concerned, that's what she was doing when she created her Earthseed Destiny and her Earthseed verses: dreaming. We all need dreams—our fantasies—to sustain us through hard times. There's no harm in that as long as we don't begin to mistake our fantasies for reality as she did. It seems that she doubted herself from time to time, but she never doubted the dream, never doubted Earthseed. Like my father, I can't feel that secure about any religion. That's odd, considering the way I was raised, but it's true.

I've seen religious passion in other people, though—love for a compassionate God, fear of an angry God, fulsome praise and desperate pleading for a God that rewards and punishes. All that makes me wonder how a belief system like Earthseed—very demanding but offering so little comfort from such an utterly indifferent God—should inspire any loyalty at all.

In Earthseed, there is no promised afterlife. Earthseed's heaven is literal, physical—other worlds circling other stars. It promises its people immortality only through their children, their work, and their memories. For the human species, immortality is something to be won by sowing Earthseed on other worlds. Its promise is not of mansions to live in, milk and honey to drink, or eternal oblivion in some vast whole of nirvana. Its promise is of hard work and brand-new possibilities, problems, challenges, and changes. Apparently, that can be surprisingly seductive to some people. My mother was a surprisingly seductive person.

There is an Earthseed verse that goes like this:

> *God is Change.*
> *God is Infinite,*
> *Irresistible,*
> *Inexorable,*

Indifferent.
God is Trickster,
Teacher,
Chaos,
Clay—
God is Change.
Beware:
God exists to shape
And to be shaped.

This is a terrifying God, implacable, faceless, yet malleable and wildly dynamic. I suppose it will soon be wearing my mother's face. Her second name was "Oya." I wonder whatever possessed my Baptist minister grandfather to give her such a name. What did he see in her? "Oya" is the name of a Nigerian Orisha—goddess—of the Yoruba people. In fact, the original Oya was the goddess of the Niger River, a dynamic, dangerous entity. She was also goddess of the wind, fire, and death, more bringers of great change.

From *THE JOURNALS OF LAUREN OYA OLAMINA*
MONDAY, OCTOBER 4, 2032

Krista Noyer died today.

That was her name: Krista Koslow Noyer. She never regained consciousness. From the time we found her beaten, raped, and shot, lying naked in her family's housetruck, she's been in a deep coma. We've kept her and her wounded son in the clinic together. The five Dovetrees have moved in with Jeff King and his children, but it seemed best to keep Krista Noyer and her son at the clinic.

Zahra Balter and Allie Gilchrist helped to clean them up, then assisted Bankole when he removed five bullets from their bodies—two from the mother and three from the son. Zahra and Allie have been

OCTAVIA E. BUTLER

working with Bankole longer than Mike and Natividad have. They're not doctors, of course, but they know a lot. Bankole says he thinks they could function well as nurse practitioners now.

He, all four of his helpers, and others who gave volunteer nursing care did their best for the Noyers. After Krista Noyer's surgery, Zahra, Natividad, Allie, Noriko Kardos, Channa Ryan, and Teresa Lin took turns sitting with her, tending her needs. Bankole says he wanted women around her in case she came to. He thought the sight of male strangers would panic her.

I suspect that he was right. Poor woman.

At least her son was with her when she died. He lay on the bed next to hers, sometimes reaching out to touch her. They were only separated by one of our homemade privacy screens when personal things had to be done for one of them. There was no screen between them when Krista died.

The boy's name is Danton Noyer, Junior. He wants to be called Dan.

We burned the body of Danton Noyer, Senior, as soon as we got it back to Acorn. Now we'll have to burn his wife. We'll hold services for both of them when Dan is well enough to attend.

SUNDAY, OCTOBER 17, 2032

We had a double funeral today for Danton Noyer, Senior, and his wife Krista.

Under Bankole's care, Dan Noyer is recovering. His legs and shoulder are healing, and he can walk a little. Bankole says he can thank the maggots for that. Not only did the disgusting little things keep his wounds clean by eating the dead tissue, but they did no harm. This particular kind have no appetite for healthy, living tissue. They eat the stuff that would putrefy and cause gangrene, then, unless they're removed, they metamorphose and fly away.

The little girls, Kassia and Mercy, had, at first, to be kept inside so that they would not run away. They had nowhere to go, but they were so frightened and confused that they kept trying to escape. When they were allowed to visit their brother, they had to be kept from hurting him. They ran to him and would have piled onto his bed for reassurance and comfort if May and Allie had not stopped them. May seems best able to reach them. They seem to be adopting both women—and vice versa—but they seem to have a special liking for May.

She's something of a mystery, our May. I'm teaching her to write so that someday she'll be able to tell us her story. She looks as though she might be a Latina, but she doesn't understand Spanish. She does understand English, but doesn't speak it well enough to be understood most of the time. That's because sometime before she joined us, someone cut out her tongue.

We don't know who did it. I've heard that in some of the more religious towns, repression of women has become more and more extreme. A woman who expresses her opinions, "nags," disobeys her husband, or otherwise "tramples her womanhood" and "acts like a man," might have her head shaved, her forehead branded, her tongue cut out, or, worst case, she might be stoned to death or burned. I've only heard about these things. May is the first example of it that I've ever seen—if she is an example. I'm glad to say her terrible wound had healed by the time she came to us. We don't even know whether May is her real name. But she can say, "May," and she's let us know we're to call her that. It's always been clear that she loves kids and gets along well with them. Now, with the little Noyer girls, it seems that she has a family. She's been sharing a cabin with Allie Gilchrist and Allie's adopted son Justin for the better part of a year. Now I suppose we'll have to either expand Allie's cabin or begin work on a new one. In fact, we need to begin work on two or three new ones. The Scolari family will be getting the next one. They've been cooped up with the Figueroas long enough. Then the Dovetrees, then the Noyers and May.

Dan Noyer is staying with Harry and Zahra Balter and their kids now that he's well enough to get around on his own a little. It seemed best to get him out of the clinic as soon as possible once his mother died. May is already sharing her one room with the two little girls, so Bankole looked for space for Dan elsewhere. The Balters volunteered. Also, May's a sharer, and Dan still has bouts of pain. He doesn't complain, but May would notice. I do when I'm around him. There's no hyperempathy in the Balter family, so they can care for injured people without suffering themselves.

It's been a busy few weeks. We've done several salvage runs with the truck and gathered things we've never been able to gather in quantity before: lumber, stone, bricks, mortar, cement, plumbing fixtures, furniture, and pipe from distant abandoned ruins and from the Dovetree place. We'll need it all. We're 67 people now with the Noyer children. We're growing too fast.

And yet in another way, we're only creeping along. We're not only Acorn, we're Earthseed, and we're still only a single tiny hill community squeezed into too few cabins, and sharing an almost nineteenth-century existence. The truck will improve our comfort, but . . . it's not enough. I mean, it may be enough for Acorn, but it's not enough for Earthseed.

Not that I claim to know what would be enough. The thing that I want to build is so damned new and so *vast*! I not only don't know how to build it, but I'm not even sure what it will look like when I have built it. I'm just feeling my way, using whatever I can do, whatever I can learn to take one more step forward.

Here, for our infant Earthseed archives, is what I've learned so far about what happened to the Noyers. I've talked to Kassia and Mercy several times. And over the past three days, Dan has told me what he could remember. He seemed to need to talk, in spite of his pain, and with me around to complain to Bankole for him and see that he has his medicine when he needs it, he's had less pain. On his own, he seems willing to just lie there and hurt. Well, there's nothing wrong with being stoic when you have to be, but there's enough unavoidable suffering in the world. Why endure it when you don't have to?

The Noyers had driven up from Phoenix, Arizona, where food

and water are even more expensive than they are in the Los Angeles area. They sold their houses—they owned two—some vacant land, their furniture, Krista Noyer's jewelry, sold everything they could to get the money to buy and equip an armed and armored housetruck big enough to sleep seven people. The truck was intended to take the family to Alaska and serve as their home there until the parents could get work and rent or buy something better. Alaska is a more popular destination than ever these days. When I left southern California, Alaska was a popular dream—almost heaven. People struggled toward it, hoping for a still-civilized place of jobs, peace, room to raise their children in safety, and a return to the mythical golden-age world of the mid-twentieth century. They expected to find no gangs, no slavery, no free poor squatter settlements growing like cancers on the land, no chaos. There was to be plenty of land for everyone, a warming climate, cheap water, and many towns, new and old, privatized and free, eager for hardworking newcomers. As I said, heaven.

If what I've heard from travelers is true, the few who've managed to get there—to buy passage on ships or planes or walk or drive hundreds, even thousands, of miles, then somehow sneak across the closed border with Canada to the also-closed Canadian-Alaskan border—have found something far less welcoming. And last year, Alaska, weary of regulations and restrictions from far away Washington, D.C., and even more weary of the hoard of hopeful paupers flooding in, declared itself an independent country. It seceded from the United States. First time since the Civil War that a state's done that. I thought there might be another civil war over the matter, the way President Donner and Alaskan Governor—or rather, Alaskan *President*—Leontyev are snarling at one another. But Donner has more than enough down here to keep him busy, and neither Canada nor Russia, who have been sending us food and money, much liked the idea of a war right next door to them. The only real danger of civil war is from Andrew Steele Jarret if he wins the election next month.

OCTAVIA E. BUTLER

Anyway, in spite of the risks, people like the Noyers, hopeful and desperate, still head for Alaska.

There were seven people in the Noyer family just a few days before we found the truck. There was Krista and Danton, Senior; Kassia and Mercy, our seven- and eight-year-old orphans; Paula and Nina, who were 12 and 13; and Dan, the oldest child. Dan is 15, as I guessed when I first saw him. He's a big, baby-faced, blond kid. His father was small and dark-haired. He inherited his looks and his size from his big, blond mother, while the little girls are small and dark like Danton, Senior. The boy is already almost two meters tall—a young giant with an oldest child's enhanced sense of responsibility for his sisters. Yet he, like his father, had been unable to prevent Nina and Paula from being raped and abducted three days before we found the truck.

The Noyers had gotten into the habit of parking their truck in some isolated, sunny place like the south side of that burned-out farmhouse. There they could let the kids spend some time outside while they cleaned and aired the truck. They could unroll the truck's solar wings and spread them wide so that the sun could recharge their batteries. To save money, they used as much solar energy as possible. This meant driving at night and recharging during the day—which worked all right because people walked on the highways during the day. It's illegal to walk on highways in California, but everyone does it. By custom now, most pedestrians walk during the day, and most cars and trucks run at night. The vehicles don't stop for anything that won't wreck them. I've seen would-be hijackers run down. No one stops.

But during the day, they park to rest and refuel.

Danton and Krista Noyer kept their children near them, but didn't post a regular guard. They thought their isolation and general watchfulness would protect them. They were wrong. While they were busy with housekeeping, several men approached from their blind side— from the north—so that the chimney that had not quite hidden them had blocked their view. It was possible that these men had spotted the truck from one of the ridges, then circled around to attack them. Dan thought they had.

The intruders had rounded the wall and, an instant later, opened fire on the family. They caught all seven Noyers outside the truck. They shot Danton, Senior, Krista, and Dan. Mercy, who was nearest to the truck, jumped inside and hid behind a box of books and disks. The intruders grabbed the three other girls, but Nina, the oldest, created such a diversion with her determined kicking, biting, gouging, and struggling, breaking free, then being caught again, that Kassia, free for an instant, was able to slither away from her captor and scramble into the truck. Kassia did what Mercy had not. She slammed the truck door and locked it, locked all doors.

Once she had done that, she was safer than she knew. Intruders fired their guns into the truck's armor and tires. Both were marked, but not punctured, not much damaged at all. The intruders even built a fire against the side of the truck, but the fire went out without doing damage.

After what seemed hours, the men went away.

The two little girls say they turned on the truck's monitors and looked around. They couldn't find the intruders, but they were still afraid. They waited longer. But it was terrible to wait alone in the truck, not knowing what might be happening just beyond the range of the monitors—on the other side of the chimney wall, perhaps. And there was no one to take care of them, no one for them to turn to. At last, staying in the truck alone was too much for them. They opened the door nearest to the sprawled bodies of their parents and big brother.

The intruders were gone. They had taken the two older girls away with them. Outside, Kassia and Mercy found only Dan and their parents. Dan had come to, and was sitting on the ground, holding his mother's head on his lap, stroking her face, and crying.

Dan had played dead while the intruders were there. He had given no sign of life, even when one of the intruders kicked him. Stoic, indeed. He heard them trying to get into the truck. He heard them cursing, laughing, shouting, heard two of his sisters screaming as he had never heard anyone scream. He heard his own heart beating. He thought he was dying, bleeding to death in the dirt while his family was murdered.

Yet he did not die. He lost consciousness and regained it more than once. He lost track of time. The intruders were there, then they were gone. He could hear them, then he couldn't. His sisters were screaming, crying, moaning, then they were silent.

He moved. Then gasping and groaning with pain, he managed to sit up. His legs hurt so as he tried to stand that he screamed aloud and fell down again. His mind blurred by pain, blood loss, and horror, he looked around for his family. There, near his legs, wet with his blood and her own was his mother.

He dragged himself to her, then sat holding her head on his lap. How long he sat here, all but mindless, he did not know. Then his little sisters were shaking him, talking to him.

He stared at them. It took him a long time to realize that they were really there, alive, and that behind them, the truck was open again. Then he knew he had to get his parents inside it. He had to drive them back down to the highway and into a town where there was a hospital, or at least a doctor. He was afraid his father might be dead, but he couldn't be sure. He knew his mother was alive. He could hear her breathing. He had felt the pulse in her neck. He had to get help for her.

Somehow, he did get them both into the truck. This was a long, slow, terrible business. His legs hurt so. He felt so weak. He had grown fast, and been proud of being man-sized and man-strong. Now he felt as weak as a baby, and once he had dragged his parents into the truck, he was too exhausted to climb into one of the driver's seats and drive. He couldn't get help for his parents or look for his two lost sisters. He had to, but he couldn't. He collapsed and lay on the floor, unable to move. His consciousness faded. There was nothing.

It was a familiar sort of story—horrible and ordinary. Almost everyone in Acorn has a horrible, ordinary story to tell.

Today we gave the Noyer children oak seedlings to plant in earth that has been mixed with the ashes of their parents. We do this in memory of our own dead, present and absent. None of the ashes of my family are here, but five years ago when we decided to stay here, I planted trees in their memory. Others have done the same for their dead. Nina and Paula Noyer's ashes aren't here of course. Nina and Paula may not even be dead. But they will be remembered here along with their parents. Once Dan understood the ceremony, he asked for trees for Nina and Paula as well as for his parents.

He said, "Some nights I wake up still hearing them screaming, hearing those bastards laughing. Oh, god. . . . They must be dead. But maybe they're not. I don't know. Sometimes I wish I were dead. Oh god."

We've phoned our neighbors and friends in nearby towns about Nina and Paula Noyer. We've left their names, their descriptions (garnered from what Dan told me), and the offer of a reward in hard currency—Canadian money. I doubt that anything will come of it, but we have to try. It isn't as though we have an abundance of hard currency to spread around, but because we're so careful, we do have some. Because of the truck, we'll soon have more. To tell the truth, I'd try to buy the girls back even if there were no truck. It's one thing to know that there are children on the roads and in the towns being made to suffer for someone else's pleasure. It's another to know that the two sisters of children you know and like are being made to suffer. But there is the truck. All the more reason for us to do what we can for the Noyer children.

We brought Dan to the funeral services on a cot that we used as a stretcher. He can stand and walk. Bankole makes him do a little of that every day. But he's still not up to standing or sitting for long periods of time. We put him next to the slender young trees that Bankole planted five years ago in memory of his sister and her family, who had lived on this property before us. They were murdered before we arrived. Their bodies were burned with their home. All we found of them were their charred bones and a couple of rings. These are buried beneath the trees just at the spot where Dan lay for the funeral.

The little girls planted their seedlings under our guidance, but not with our help. The work was done by their hands. Perhaps the planting of tiny trees in earth mixed with ashes doesn't mean much now, but they'll grow up knowing that their parents' remains are here, that living trees grow from those remains, and that today this community began to be their home.

We moved Dan's cot so that he could use the garden trowel and watering can, and we let him plant his own seedlings. He, too, did what he had to do without help. The ritual was already important to him. It was something he could do for his sisters and his parents. It was *all* he could do for them.

When he had finished, he said the Lord's Prayer. It was the only formal prayer he knew. The Noyers were nominal Christians—a Catholic mother, an Episcopalian father, and kids who had never seen the inside of a church.

Dan talked his sisters into singing songs in Polish—songs their mother had taught them. They don't speak Polish, which is a pity. I'm always glad when we can learn another language. No one in their family spoke Polish except Krista, who had come with her parents from Poland to escape war and uncertainty in Europe. And look what the poor woman had stepped into.

The girls sang their songs. As young as they were, they had clear, sweet voices. They were a delight to hear. Their mother must have been a good teacher. When they had finished, and all the seedlings were watered in, a few members of the community stood up to quote from Earthseed verses, the Bible, The Book of Common Prayer, the Bhagavad-Gita, John Donne. The quotations took the place of the words that friends and family would have said to remember and give respect to the dead.

Then I said the words of the Earthseed verses that we've come to associate with funerals, and with remembering the dead.

"God is Change," I began.

Others repeated in soft voices, "God is Change. Shape God." Habits of repetition and response have grown up almost without prompting among us. Sad to say, we've had so many funerals in our brief existence as a community that this ritual in particular is very familiar. Only last week, we planted trees and spoke words for the Dovetrees. I said,

> *"We give our dead*
> *To the orchards*
> *And the groves.*
> *We give our dead*
> *To life."*

I paused, took a deep breath, and continued in slow, measured tones.

> *"Death*
> *Is a great Change—*
> *Is life's greatest Change.*
> *We honor our beloved dead.*
> *As we mix their essence with the earth,*
> *We remember them,*
> *And within us,*
> *They live."*

"We remember," the others whispered. "They live."

I stood silent for a moment, gazing out toward the tall persimmon, avocado, and citrus trees. Bankole's sister and brother-in-law had planted these trees, had brought them as young plants from southern California, half expecting them to die here in a cooler climate.

According to Bankole, many of them did die, but some survived as the climate changed, warmed. Old-timers among our neighbors complain about the loss of their fog, rain, and cool temperatures. We don't mind, those of us from southern California. To us it's as though we've come to a somewhat gentler version of the homes we were forced to leave. Here, there is still water, space, not too much debilitating heat, and some peace. Here, one can still have orchards and groves. Here, life can still come from death.

The little girls had gone back to sit with May. May hugged them, one small, dark-haired child in each arm, all three of them still, solemn, listening.

I began a new verse, almost a chant,

> *"Darkness*
> *Gives shape to the light*
> *As light*
> *Shapes the darkness.*
> *Death*
> *Gives shape to life*
> *As life*
> *Shapes death.*
> *God*
> *And the universe*
> *Share this wholeness*
> *Each*
> *Defining the other:*
> *God*
> *Gives shape to the universe*
> *As the universe*
> *Shapes God."*

And then, after a moment of silence, the last, the closing words:

> *"We have lived before*
> *We will live again*

We will be silk,
Stone,
Mind,
Star,
We will be scattered,
Gathered,
Molded,
Probed.
We will live,
And we will serve life.
We will shape God
And God will shape us
Again,
Always again
Forevermore."

Some people whispered that last word—echoed it. Zahra quoted in a voice almost too soft to be heard,

"God is Change,
And in the end
God prevails."

Her husband Harry put his arm around her, and I saw that her eyes were bright with unshed tears. She and Harry may be the most loyal, least religious people in the community, but there are times when people need religion more than they need anything else—even people like Zahra and Harry.

4

○ ○ ○

From EARTHSEED: THE BOOKS OF THE LIVING

To shape God
With wisdom and forethought,
To benefit your world,
Your people,
Your life,
Consider consequences,
Minimize harm
Ask questions,
Seek answers,
Learn,
Teach.

From *MEMORIES OF OTHER WORLDS*

Our coast redwood trees are dying.

Sequoia sempervirens is the botanical name for this tallest of all trees, but many are evergreen no longer. Little by little from the tops down, they are turning brown and dying.

I do not believe that they are dying as a result of the heat. As I recall, there were many redwoods growing around the Los Angeles area—Pasadena, Altadena, San Marino, places like that. I saw them there when I was young. My mother had relatives in Pasadena and she used to take me with her when she went to visit them. Redwoods growing that far south reached nothing like the height of their kind here in the north, but they did survive. Later, as the climate changed, I suppose they died as so many of the trees down south died—or they were chopped down and used to build shelters or to feed the cooking fires of the homeless.

And now our younger trees have begun to die. This part of Humboldt County along the coast and in the hills—the local people call these coastal hills "mountains"—was cooler when I was a boy. It was foggy and rainy—a soft, green climate, friendly to most growing things. I believe it was already changing nearly 30 years ago when I bought the land that became Acorn. In the not-too-distant future, I suppose it will be little different from the way coastal southern California was a few decades ago—hot, semiarid, more brown than green most of the time. Now we are in the middle of the change. We still get a few substantial fall and winter storms each year, and there are still morning fogs in the spring and early summer.

Nevertheless, young redwood trees—those only about a century old, not yet mature—are withering. A few miles to the north and south of us in the old national and state parks, the groves of ancient giants still stand. A few hundred acres of them here and there have been released by the government, sold to wealthy, usually foreign interests, and logged. And squatters have cut and burned a number of individual trees, as usual, to build shelters and feed cooking fires, but the majority of the protected ones, millennia old, resistant to disease, fire, and climate change, still stand. If people let them alone, they will go on, childless, anachronistic, but still alive, still reaching futilely skyward.

My father, perhaps because of his age, seems to have been a loving pessimist. He saw little good in our future. According to his writing, our greatness as a country, perhaps even the greatness of the human species, was in the past. His greatest desire seems to have been to protect my mother and later, to protect me—to somehow keep us safe.

My mother, on the other hand, was a somewhat reluctant optimist. Greatness for her, for Earthseed, for humanity always seemed to run

OCTAVIA E. BUTLER

just ahead of her. Only she saw it, but that was enough to entice her on, seducing her as she seduced others.

She worked hard at seducing people. She did it first by adopting vulnerable, needy people, then by finding ways to make those people want to be part of Earthseed. No matter how ridiculous Earthseed must have seemed, with its starry Destiny, it offered immediate rewards. Here was real community. Here was at least a semblance of security. Here was the comfort of ritual and routine and the emotional satisfaction of belonging to a "team" that stood together to meet challenge when challenge came. And for families, here was a place to raise children, to teach them basic skills that they might not learn elsewhere and to keep them as safe as possible from the harsh, ugly lessons of the world outside.

When I was in high school, I read the 1741 Jonathan Edwards sermon, "Sinners in the Hands of an Angry God." Its first few words sum up the kinds of lessons so many children were forced to learn in the world outside Acorn. Edwards said, "The God that holds you over the pit of hell, much as one holds a spider, or some loathsome insect over the fire, abhors you, and is dreadfully provoked; his wrath towards you burns like fire; he looks upon you as worthy of nothing else, but to be cast into the fire." You're worthless. God hates you. All you deserve is pain and death. What a believable theology that would have been for the children of the Pox. No wonder, some of them found comfort in my mother's God. If it didn't love them, at least it offered them some chance to live.

If my mother had created only Acorn, the refuge for the homeless and the orphaned. . . . If she had created Acorn, but not Earthseed, then I think she would have been a wholly admirable person.

From *THE JOURNALS OF LAUREN OYA OLAMINA*
SUNDAY, OCTOBER 24, 2032

Dan is much better. He's still limping, but he's healing fast. He sat through Gathering today for the first time. We held it indoors at the school because it's been raining—a good steady cold rain—for two days.

Dan sat through a welcoming and a discussion that his family's truck had helped to provoke. The welcoming was for Adela Ortiz's baby, Javier Verdugo Ortiz. Javier was the child of a brutal highway gang rape, and Adela, who came to us pregnant only seven months ago, had not known whether she wanted us to welcome him, had not even known whether or not she wanted to keep him. Then he was born and she said he looked like her long-dead younger brother, and she loved him at once, and couldn't think of giving him up and would we welcome him, please? Now we have.

Adela has no other family left, so several of us made little gifts for him. I made her a pouch that she can use to carry the baby on her back. Thanks to Natividad, who has carried each of her babies that way, backpacking babies has become the custom for new mothers here at Acorn.

Adela chose Michael and Noriko to stand with her. They took their places on either side of her as the baby slept in her arms, and we filed past, each of us looking at Javier and giving him gentle, welcoming touches on each tiny hand and the black-haired head. He has the full head of hair of a much older child. Adela says her brother was that way too. She had helped to take care of her brother when he was a baby, and now she feels very much that God has given him back to her. I know that when she talks about God, she doesn't mean what I mean. I'm not sure that matters. If she stays with us, obeys our rules, joins in our joys, sorrows, and celebrations, works alongside us, it doesn't matter. And in the future, when her son says "God," I think he will mean what I mean.

These are the words of welcoming:

> *"Javier Verdugo Ortiz*
> *We, your people*
> *Welcome you.*

OCTAVIA E. BUTLER

We are Earthseed.

You are Earthseed—
One of many
One unique,
One small seed,
One great promise.
Tenacious of life,
Shaper of God,
Water,
Fire,
Sculptor,
Clay,
You are Earthseed!
And your Destiny,
The Destiny of Earthseed,
Is to take root
Among the stars."

They're good words. Not good enough to welcome a child into the world and into the community. No words are good enough to do that, and yet, somehow, words are needed. Ceremony is needed. As I spoke the words, the people sang them softly. Travis Douglas and Gray Mora have set several Earthseed verses to music. Travis can write music. Gray can hear it inside himself and then sing it to Travis.

When the words, the music, and the touching were over, when the Kardoses had accepted Adela as their sister and Javier as their nephew and Adela had accepted them, when all three had given their sworn promise before the community, Javier woke up wanting to nurse and Adela had to go back to her seat with him. Beautiful timing.

So many members of our community have come to us alone or with only little children that it seems best for me to do what I can to create family bonds that take in more than the usual godparent-godchild relationship. All too often, back in my old neighborhood in Robledo, that was no relationship at all. Aside from giving occasional gifts, people did not take it seriously. I want it taken seriously here. I've made that clear to everyone. No one has to take on the responsibility of joining in this way to another family, but anyone who does take that responsibility has made a real commitment. The family relationship is not only with the new child, but with its parents as well. We are too young a community for me to say for sure how well this will work in the future, but people seem to accept it. We're used to depending on one another.

Once the welcoming was over, we moved on to the weekly discussion. Our Gatherings, aside from weddings, funerals, welcomings, or holiday celebrations, are discussions. They're problem-solving sessions, they're times of planning, healing, learning, creating, times of focusing, and reshaping ourselves. They can cover anything at all to do with Earthseed or Acorn, past, present, or future, and anyone can speak.

During the first Gathering of the month, I lead a looking-back-looking-forward discussion to keep us aware of what we've done and what we must do, taking in any necessary changes, and taking advantage of any opportunities. And I encourage people to think about how the things we do help us to sustain purposeful religious community.

This morning Travis Douglas wanted to talk about expanding our community business, a subject dear to my own heart. First he read his chosen Earthseed texts—verses that, like any good texts, could be used to start any number of different discussions.

> *"Civilization is to groups what intelligence is to individuals. Civilization provides ways of combining the information, experience, and creativity of the many to achieve ongo-ing group adaptability."*

And then,

OCTAVIA E. BUTLER

"Any Change may bear seeds of benefit.
Seek them out.
Any Change may bear seeds of harm.
Beware.
God is infinitely malleable.
God is Change."

"We have an opportunity that we have to take advantage of," Travis said. "We have the truck, and we have no real competition. I've gone over the truck, and in spite of the way it looks, it's in damned good shape. The solar wings just drink sunlight—really efficient. If we recharge the batteries during the day, we should save a bundle in fuel. For short trips there isn't even any need to use anything but the batteries. We have the best vehicle in the area. We can do minor professional hauling. We can buy goods from our neighbors and sell them in the cities and towns. People will be glad to sell us their stuff for a little less if we're the ones who do the work of getting it to market. And we can contract to grow crops for businesses in Eureka-Arcata, maybe down in Garberville."

Several of us have talked about this off and on, but today was our first Gathering on the subject since we got the truck. Travis, more than most of us, wanted to risk becoming more involved with our neighbors. We could contract with them to buy the specific handicrafts, tools, and crops that they produce well. We know by now who's good at what, who's dependable, and who's honest and sober at least most of the time.

Travis and I have already been asking around on our now more frequent trips to Eureka to see which merchants might be interested in contracting to buy specific produce from us.

Travis cleared his throat and spoke to the group again. "With the truck," he said, "only our first truck if we're successful, we've got the beginnings of a wholesale business. Then, instead of depending only on what we can produce and instead of only bartering with near neighbors, we can grow a business as well as a community and a movement. It's important that we become a self-sustaining economic entity or we're liable never to move out of the nineteenth century!"

Well put, but not all that well received. We say "God is Change," but the truth is, we fear change as much as anyone does. We talk about changes at Gathering to ease our fears, to desensitize ourselves and to consider consequences.

"We're doing all right," Allie Gilchrist said. "Why should we take on more risk? And why, when this guy Jarret is liable to win the election, should we draw attention to ourselves?" She had already lost her infant son and her sister. She had only her adopted son Justin, and she would do almost anything to protect him.

Michael surprised me. "We could do it, I suppose," he said, and I waited for the "but." There was bound to be one with Michael. He obliged. "But she's right about Jarret. If he gets elected, the last thing we'll need is higher visibility."

"Jarret is down in the polls," Jorge said. "His people are scaring everyone to death with their burning churches, burning people. He might not win."

"Who the hell do they poll these days?" Michael asked, shaking his head. And then, "We'd better keep an eye on Jarret anyway. Win or lose, he'll still have plenty of followers who are eager to create scapegoats."

Harry spoke up. "We aren't invisible now," he said. "People in the nearby towns know us, know what we are—or they think they do. I want my kids to have a chance at decent lives. Maybe this wholesaling idea will be the beginning of that chance."

Next to him, his wife Zahra nodded and said, "I'm for it too. We didn't settle here just to grub in the ground and live in log huts. We can do better."

"We might even improve things for ourselves with the neighbors," Travis said, "if more people in the area know us, know that we can be trusted, it might be a little harder for a rabble-rouser like Jarret or one of his local clones to make trouble for us."

OCTAVIA E. BUTLER

I doubted that that would prove true—at least not on a large scale. We would meet more people, make more friends, and some of these would be loyal. The rest . . . well, the best we could hope for from them would be that they ignore us if we get into trouble. That might be the kindest gesture they could manage—to turn their backs and not join the mob. Others, whether we thought of them as friends or not, would be all too willing to join the mob and to stomp us and rob us if stomping and robbing became a test of courage or a test of loyalty to country, religion, or race.

On the other hand, making more of the right kinds of friends couldn't hurt us. We've already made some that I trust—near neighbors, a couple of people in Prata, and a few more in Georgetown, the big squatter settlement outside Eureka. And the only way to make more good friends is to make more friends period.

Adela Ortiz spoke up in her quick, soft, little-girl voice. She's only 16. "What if people think we're cheating them?" she said. "People always think that. You know, like you're trying to be nice to them and they just think everybody's a liar and a thief but them."

I was sitting near her, so I answered. "People will think whatever they like," I said. "It's our job to show by our behavior that we're not thieves, and we're not fools. We've got a good reputation so far. People know we don't steal. They know better than to steal from us. And they know we're neighborly. In emergencies, we help out. Our school is open to their kids for a little hard currency, and their kids are safe while they're here." I shrugged. "We've made a good start."

"And you think this wholesaling business is the way for us to go?" Grayson Mora asked.

I looked over at him with surprise. He sometimes manages to get through a whole Gathering without saying anything. He isn't shy at all, but he's quiet. He and his wife were slaves before they met. Each had lost family members to the effects and neglects of slavery. Now between them they have two girls and two boys. They're ferocious in guarding their children, and suspicious of anything new that might affect those children.

"I do," I said. I paused, glanced up at Travis who stood at the big handsome oak podium that Allie had built. Then I continued. "I believe we can do it as long as the truck holds up. You're our expert there, Travis. You've said the truck is in good shape, but can we afford to maintain it? What new, expensive part will it be needing soon?"

"By the time it needs anything expensive, we should be making more money," he said. "As of now, even the tires are good, and that's unusual." He leaned over the podium, looking confident and serious. "We can do this," he said. "We should start small, study the possibilities, and figure out how we should grow. If we do this right, we should be able to buy another truck in a year or two. We're growing. We need to do this."

Beside me, Bankole sighed. "If we're not careful," he said, "our size and success will make us the castle on the hill—everyone's protector in this area. I don't think that's wise."

I do think it's wise, but I didn't say so. Bankole still can't see this place as anything more than a temporary stop on the way to a "real" home in a "real" town—that is, an already established town. I don't know how long it will take for him to see that what we're building here is as real and at least as important as anything he's likely to find in a town that's been around for a century or two.

I foresee a time when our settlement is not only "the castle on the hill," but when most or all of our neighbors have joined us. Even if they don't like every aspect of Earthseed, I hope they'll like enough of it to recognize that they're better off with us than without us. I want them as allies and as members, not just as "friends." And as we absorb them, I also intend to either absorb some of the storekeeper, restaurant, or hotel clients that we'll have—or I want us to open our own stores, restaurants and hotels. I definitely want to begin Gathering Houses that are also schools in Eureka, Arcata, and some of the larger nearby towns. I want us to grow into the cities and towns in this natural, self-supporting way.

I don't know whether we can do all this, but I think we have to try. I think this is what a real beginning for Earthseed looks like.

OCTAVIA E. BUTLER

I don't know how to do it. That scares me to death sometimes—always feeling driven to do something I don't know how to do. But I'm learning as I go along. And I've learned that I have to be careful how I talk about all this, even to Acorn. Bankole isn't the only one of us who doesn't see the possibility of doing anything he hasn't seen done by others. And . . . although Bankole would never say this, I suspect that somewhere inside himself, he believes that large, important things are done only by powerful people in high positions far away from here. Therefore, what we do is, by definition, small and unimportant. This is odd, because in other ways, Bankole has a healthy ego. He didn't let self-doubt or the doubts of his family or the laughter of his friends stop him from going to college, and then medical school, surviving by way of a combination of scholarships, jobs, and huge debts. He began as a quietly arrogant Black boy of no particular distinction, and he ended as a physician.

But in a way, I suppose that's normal. I mean, it had been done before. Bankole himself had been taken to a Black woman pediatrician when he was a child.

What I'm trying to do isn't quite normal. It's been done. New belief systems have been introduced. But there's no standard way of introducing them—no way that can be depended on to work. What I'm trying to do is, I'm afraid, a crazy, difficult, dangerous undertaking. Best to talk about it only a little bit at a time.

Noriko, Michael's wife, spoke up. "I'm afraid for us to get involved in this new business," she said, "but I think we have to do it. This is a good community, but how long can it last, how long can it grow before we begin to have trouble feeding ourselves?"

People nodded. Noriko has more courage than she gives herself credit for. She can be shaking with fear, but she still does what she thinks she should do.

"We can grow or we can wither," I agreed. "That's what Earthseed is about on a larger scale, after all."

"I wish it weren't," Emery Mora said. "I wish we could just hide here and stay out of everything else. I know we can't, but I wish. . . . It's been so good here." Before she escaped slavery, she'd had two young sons taken from her and sold. And she's a sharer. She and Gray and his daughter Doe and her daughter Tori and their sons Carlos and Antonio—all sharers. No other family is so afflicted. No other family has more reason to want to hide.

We talked on for a while, Travis listening as people protested, then either answering their protests or letting others answer them. Then he asked for a vote: Should we expand our business? The vote was "yes" with everyone over 15 voting. Only Allie Gilchrist, Alan Faircloth, Ramiro Peralta, and Ramiro's oldest daughter Pilar voted "no." Aubrey Dovetree, who couldn't vote because she was not yet a member, made it clear that she would have voted "no" if she could have.

"Remember what happened to us!" she said.

We all remembered. But we had no intention of trading in illegal goods. We're farther from the highway than Dovetree was, and we couldn't refuse this opportunity just because Dovetree had been hit.

We would expand our business, then. Travis would put together a team, and the team would talk to our neighbors—those without cars or trucks first—and talk to more merchants in the cities and towns. We need to know what's possible now. We know we can sell more at street markets because now with the truck we can go to more street markets. So even if we don't manage to get contracts at first, we'll be able to sell what we buy from our neighbors. We've begun.

When the Gathering was over, we shared a Gathering Day meal. We spread ourselves around the two large rooms of the school for food, indoor games, talk, and music. At the front of the room near the podium, Dolores Figueroa Castro was planning to read a story to a group of small children who would sit at her feet. Dolores is Lucio's niece, Marta's daughter. She's only 12, but she likes reading to the younger kids, and since she reads well and has a nice voice, the kids like to listen. For the adults and older kids, we were to have an original play, written by Emery Mora, of all people. She's too shy to act, but she loves to write and she loves to watch plays. Lucio Figueroa has discovered that he enjoys staging plays, shaping fictional worlds. Jorge and a few others are hams and love acting in plays. Travis and Gray provide any needed music. The rest of us enjoy watching. We all feed one another's hungers.

Dan Noyer came over to me as I helped myself to fried rabbit, baked potato, a mix of steamed vegetables with a spicy sauce, and a little goat cheese. There were also pine nut cookies, acorn bread, and sweet potato pie. On Gathering Day, the rule is, we eat only what we've raised and prepared. There was a time when that was something of a hardship. It reminded us that we were not growing or raising as much as we should. Now it's a pleasure. We're doing well.

"Can I sit with you?" Dan asked.

I said, "Sure," then had to fend off several other people who wanted me to eat with them. Dan's expression made me think it was time for him and me to have some version of the talk that I always seem to wind up having with newcomers. I thought of it as the "What the hell is this Earthseed stuff, and do I have to join?" talk.

Right on cue, Dan said, "The Balters say my sisters and I can stay here. They say we don't have to join your cult if we don't want to."

"You don't have to join Earthseed," I said. "You and your sisters are welcome to stay. If you decide to join us someday, we'll be glad to welcome you."

"What do we have to do—just to stay, I mean?"

I smiled. "Finish healing first. When you're well enough, work with us. Everyone works here, kids and adults. You'll help in the fields, help with the animals, help maintain the school and its grounds, help do some building. Building homes is a communal effort here. There are other jobs—building furniture, making tools, trading at street markets, scavenging. You'll be free to choose something you like. And you'll go to school. Have you gone to school before?"

"My folks taught us."

I nodded. These days, most educated poor or middle-class people taught their own children or did what people in my old neighborhood had done—formed unofficial schools in someone's home. Only very small towns still had anything like old-fashioned public schools. "You might find," I said, "that you know some things well enough to teach them to younger kids. One of the first duties of Earthseed is to learn and then to teach."

"And this? This Gathering?"

"Yes, you'll come to Gathering every week."

"Will I get a vote?"

"No vote, but you'll get a share of the profit from the sale of the crop, and from the other businesses if things work out. That's after you've been here for a year. You won't have a decision-making role unless you decide to join. If you do join, you'll get a larger share of the profit and a vote."

"It isn't really religious—your service, I mean. You guys don't believe in God or anything."

I turned to look at him. "Dan, of course we do."

He just stared at me in silent, obvious disbelief.

"We don't believe the way your parents did, perhaps, but we do believe."

"That God is Change?"

"Yes."

"I don't even know what that means."

"It means that Change is the one unavoidable, irresistible, ongoing reality of the universe. To us, that makes it the most powerful reality, and just another word for God."

"But . . . what can you do with a God like that? I mean . . . it isn't even a person. It doesn't love you or protect you. It doesn't know anything. What's the point?"

"The point is, it's the truth," I said. "It's a hard truth. Too hard for some people to take, but that doesn't make it any less true." I put my food down, got up, and went to one of our bookcases. There, I took down one of our several copies of *Earthseed: The First Book of the*

Living. I self-published this first volume two years ago. Bankole had looked over my text when it was finished, and said I should copyright and publish for my own protection. At the time, that seemed unnecessary—a ridiculous thing to do in a world gone mad. Later, I came to believe he was right—for the future and for a reason in the present that Bankole had not mentioned.

"Things will get back to normal someday," he had said to me. "You should do this in the same way that we go on paying their taxes."

Things won't get back to what he calls normal. We'll settle into some new norm someday—for a while. Whether that new norm will recognize our tax paying or my copyright, I don't know. But there's a more immediate advantage to be had here.

People are still impressed, even intimidated, by bound, official-looking books. Verses, handwritten or printed out on sheets of paper just don't grab them the way a book does. Even people who can't read are impressed by books. The idea seems to be, "If it's in a book, maybe it's true," or even, "If it's in a book, it must be true."

I went back to Dan, opened the book, and read to him,

> *"Do not worship God*
>
> *Inexorable God*
> *Neither needs nor wants*
> *Your worship.*
> *Instead,*
> *Acknowledge and attend God,*
> *Learn from God,*
> *With forethought and intelligence,*
> *Imagination and industry,*
> *Shape God.*
> *When you must,*
> *Yield to God.*
> *Adapt and endure.*

For you are Earthseed,
And God is Change."

I paused, then said, "That's what we believe, Dan. That's what we strive to do—part of what we strive to do, anyway."

Dan listened, frowning. "I'm still not sure what all that means."

"You'll learn more about it in school. We say education is the most direct pathway to God. For now, it's enough to say that verse just means that flattering or begging God isn't useful. Learn what God does. Learn to shape that to your needs. Learn to use it, or at least, learn to adapt to it so that you won't get squashed by it. That's useful."

"So you're saying praying doesn't work."

"Oh, no. Praying does work. Praying is a very effective way of talking to *yourself*, of talking yourself into things, of focusing your attention on whatever it is you want to do. It can give you a feeling of control and help you to stretch yourself beyond what you thought were your limits."

I paused, thinking of how well Dan had done just that when he tried to rescue his parents. "It doesn't always work the way we want it to," I said. "But it's always worth the effort."

"Even if when I pray, I ask God to help me?" he asked.

"Even so," I said. "You're the one your words reach and strengthen. You can think of it as praying to that part of God that's within you."

He thought about that for a while, then looked at me as though he had a big question, but hadn't yet decided how to ask it. He looked down at the book.

"How do you know you're right?" he asked at last. "I mean, that guy who wants to be President, that Jarret, he would call you all heathens or pagans or something."

Indeed, he would. "Yes," I said. "He does seem to enjoy calling people things like that. Once he's made everyone who isn't like him sound evil, then he can blame them for problems he knows they didn't cause. That's easier than trying to fix the problems."

"My dad says. . . ." The boy stopped and swallowed. "My dad said Jarret's an idiot."

"I agree with your dad."

"But how do you know you're right?" he insisted. "How do you know Earthseed is true? Who says it's true?"

"You do, Dan." I let him chew on that for a while, then went on. "You learn, you think, you question. You question us and you question yourself. Then, if you find Earthseed to be true, you join us. You help us teach others. You help others the way we've helped you and your sisters." Another pause. "Spend some time reading this book. The verses are short and they mean what they say, although that may not be all that they mean. Read them and think about them. Then you can begin asking questions."

"I've been reading," he said. "Not this book, but other things. Nothing to do but read while I could hardly move. The Balters gave me novels and things. And . . . I've been thinking that I shouldn't be here, living soft, eating good food, and reading books. I've been thinking that I ought to be out, looking for my sisters Nina and Paula. I'm the oldest, and they're lost. I'm the man of the family now. I should be looking for them."

That was the most alarming thing he had said so far. "Dan, we have no way of knowing—"

"Yeah. No one knows if they're alive or where they are or if they're still together. . . . I know. I keep thinking about all that. But they're my sisters. Dad and Mom always told me to look out for them." He shook his head. "Hell, I didn't even look out for Kassi and Mercy. If they hadn't saved themselves, I guess we'd all be dead." He shoved his dinner away in self-disgust. He had already eaten most of it. But because we were on a bench rather than at a table, there was little room for shoving things. His plate fell off onto the floor and broke.

He stared at it, tears in his eyes—tears that had nothing to do with broken china.

I reached for his hand.

He flinched away, then looked up from the plate and stared at me through his tears.

I took his hand again, and looked back at him. "We have friends in some of the nearby towns," I said. "We've already left word with them. We're offering a reward for the girls or for information that leads us to them. If we can, we'll snatch them. If we have to, we'll buy them." I sighed. "I can't promise anything, Dan, but we'll do what we can. And we need you to help us. Travel with us to street markets, stores, and shops in nearby communities. Help us to look for them."

He went on staring at me as though I might be lying, as though he could find the truth in my face, if only he stared hard enough at it. "Why? Why would you do that?"

I hesitated, then drew a deep breath and told him. "We've all lost people," I said. "Everyone here has lost members of their families to fire, to murder, to raids. . . . I had a father, a stepmother, and four younger brothers. All dead. All. When we can save life . . . we do. We couldn't stand it any other way."

And still, he stared at me. But now he was shaking. He made me think of a crystal thing, vibrating to sound, about to shatter. I pulled him to me, held him, this big child, taller than me. I felt his tears, wet on my shoulder, then felt his arms go around me, hugging back, still shaking, silent, desperate, hanging on.

OCTAVIA E. BUTLER

5

○ ○ ○

From EARTHSEED: THE BOOKS OF THE LIVING

Beware:
At war
Or at peace,
More people die
Of unenlightened self-interest
Than of any other disease.

The selections I've offered from my mother's journal make it clear that in spite of her near nineteenth-century existence she paid attention to the wider world. Politics and war mattered very much. Science and technology mattered. Fashions in crime and drug use and in racial, ethnic, religious, and class tolerance mattered. She did see these as fashions, by the way—as behaviors that went in and out of favor for reasons that ran the gamut from the practical to the emotional to the biological. Human competitiveness and territoriality were often at the root of particularly horrible fashions in oppression. We human beings seem always to have found it comforting to have someone to look down on—a bottom level of fellow creatures who are very vulnerable, but who can somehow be blamed and punished for all or any troubles. We need this lowest class as much as we need equals to team with and to compete against and superiors to look to for direction and help.

My mother was always noticing and mentioning things like that. Sometimes she managed to work her observations into Earthseed verses. In November of 2032 she had bigger reasons than usual to pay attention to the world outside.

From *THE JOURNALS OF LAUREN OYA OLAMINA*
SUNDAY, NOVEMBER 7, 2032

News.

Tucked away at Acorn as we are, we have to make a special effort to get news from outside—real news, I mean, not rumors, and not the "news bullets" that purport to tell us all what we need to know in flashy pictures and quick, witty, verbal one-two punches. Twenty-five or thirty words are supposed to be enough in a news bullet to explain either a war or an unusual set of Christmas lights. Bullets are cheap and full of big, dramatic pictures. Some bullets are true virtuals that allow people to experience—safely—hurricanes, epidemics, fires, and mass murder. Hell of a kick.

Well-made news disks, on the other hand, or good satellite news services cost more. Gray and Emery Mora and one or two others say news bullets are enough. They say detailed news doesn't matter. Since we can't change the stupid, greedy, vicious things that powerful people do, they think we should try to ignore them. No matter how many times we're forced to admit we can't really hide, some of us still find ways to try.

Well, we can't hide. So it's best to pay attention to what goes on. The more we know, the better able we'll be to survive. So we subscribe to a good phone news service and now and then we buy detailed world-news disks. The whole business makes me long for free broadcast radio like the kind we had when I was a kid, but that's almost nonexistent in this area. We listen to what little is left when we go into one of the larger towns. We can hear more now because the truck's radio picks up more than our little pocket radios can.

So here are some of the most significant news items of the past week. We listened to some of them on a new Worldisk today after Gathering.

Alaska is still claiming to be an independent nation, and it seems to have gotten into an even closer, more formal alliance with Canada and Russia—northerners sticking together, I suppose. Bankole shrugged

OCTAVIA E. BUTLER

when he heard that and shook his head. "Why not?" he said. "They've got all the money."

Thanks to climate change, they do have most of it. The climate is still changing, warming. It's supposed to settle at a new stable state someday. Until then, we'll go on getting a lot of violent, erratic weather around the world. Sea level is still rising and chewing away at low-lying coastal areas like the sand dunes that used to protect Humboldt Bay and Arcata Bay just north of us. Half the crops in the Midwest and South are still withering from the heat, drowning in floods, or being torn to pieces by winds, so food prices are still high. The warming has made tropical diseases like malaria and dengue normal parts of life in the warm, wet Gulf Coast and southern Atlantic coast states. But people are beginning to adapt. There's less cholera, for instance, and less hepatitis. There are fewer of all the diseases that result from bad sanitation, spoiled food, or malnutrition. People boil the water they drink in cities where there's a problem and in squatter settlements with their open sewers—ditches. There are more gardens, and old-fashioned skills in food preservation are being revived. People barter for goods and services where cash is rare. They use hand tools and draft animals where there is no money for fuel or no power equipment left. Life is getting better, but that won't stop a war if politicians and business people decide it's to their advantage to have one.

There are plenty of wars going on around the world now. Kenya and Tanzania are fighting. I haven't yet heard why. Bolivia and Peru are having another border dispute. Pakistan and Afghanistan have joined forces in a religious war against India. One part of Spain is fighting against another. Greece and Turkey are on the edge of war, and Egypt and Libya are slaughtering one another. China, like Spain, is tearing at itself. War is very popular these days.

I suppose we should be grateful that there hasn't been another "nuclear exchange." The one three years ago between Iran and Iraq scared the hell out of everyone. After it happened, there must have been peace all over the world for maybe three months. People who had hated one another for generations found ways to talk peace. But insult by insult, expediency by expediency, cease-fire violation by cease-fire violation, most of the peace talks broke down. It's always been much easier to make war than to make peace.

Back in this country, in Dallas, Texas, some fool of a rich boy went adventuring among the free poor of a big squatter settlement. He wound up wearing the latest in electronic convict control devices—also known as slave collars, dog collars, and choke chains. And with the collar to encourage him, he learned to make himself useful to a local pimp. I've heard that the new collars are damned sophisticated. The old ones—worn more often as belts—could only cause pain. They delivered shocks and sometimes damaged or killed people. The new collars don't kill, and they can be worn for months or years at a time and used often to deliver punishment. They're programmed to resist being removed or destroyed by delivering jolts of pain severe enough to cause unconsciousness. I've heard that some collars can also give cheap, delicious rewards of pleasure for good behavior by encouraging changes in brain chemistry—stimulating the wearer to produce endorphins. I don't know whether that's true, but if it is, the whole business sounds a little like being a sharer—except that instead of sharing what other people feel, the wearer feels whatever the person holding the control unit wants him to feel. This could initiate a whole new level of slavery. After a while, needing the pleasure, fearing the pain, and always being desperate to please the master could become a person's whole life. I've heard that some collared people kill themselves, not because they can't stand the pain, but because they can't stand the degree of slavishness to which they find themselves descending.

The Texas boy's father spent a lot of money. He hired private cops—the kind who'll do anything if you pay them enough—and they sliced through the squatter camp as though it were a ripe melon until they found the boy. And with that, bingo! Slavery was discovered in Texas in 2032. Innocent people—not criminals or indigents—were being held against their wills and used for immoral purposes! How about that! What I'd like to see is a state of the union where slavery isn't being practiced.

Here's another news item. On the planet Mars, living, multicellular organisms have been discovered . . . sort of. They're very small and very strange inside, although outside they look like tiny slugs . . . some of the time. They live at least four meters down in certain polar rock formations, and they're not exactly animals. They're a little like Terrestrial slime molds. And, like slime molds, they go through independent single-celled stages during which they eat their way through the rocks, multiplying by dividing, resembling little antifreeze-filled amoeba. When they've exhausted the food supply in their immediate neighborhoods, they unite into sluglike multicellular masses to travel to new sites where the minerals they ingest are available. They don't reproduce in their slug form as Terrestrial slime molds do. They seem to need the slug form only to produce enough of their corrosive antifreeze solution to enable them to migrate through rock to a fresh supply of food. They make soil in two ways. They eat minerals, pass these through their bodies, and shed a dust so fine and so slippery that, like graphite, it can work as a kind of lubricant. And they ooze through the rocks in their slug form, their corrosive slime dissolving trails, cracks, and making more dust.

These creatures are living Martians! So far, though, all the specimens captured and examined at Leal Station died soon after being taken from their cold, rocky home. For that reason and others, they are both a great discovery and a great sadness. They are the last discoveries that will be made by scientists working for the U.S. Government.

President Donner has sold the last of our Mars installations to a Euro-Japanese company, in fulfillment of one of his earliest campaign promises. The idea is that all nonmilitary space travel, manned and unmanned, should be privatized. "If it's worth doing at all," Donner said, "it should be done for profit, and not as a burden on the taxpayers." As though profit could be counted only as immediate financial gain. I was born in 2009, and for as long as I can remember, I've heard people complaining about the space program as a waste of money, and even as one of the reasons for the country's deterioration.

Ridiculous! There is so much to be learned from space itself and from the nearby worlds! And now we've found living extraterrestrials, and we're going to quit. I suppose that if the Martian "slime molds" can be used for something—mining, perhaps, or chemistry—then they'll he protected, cultivated, bred to be even more useful. But if they prove to be of no particular use, they'll be left to survive or not as best they can with whatever impediments the company sees fit to put in their paths. If they're unlucky enough to be bad for business in some way—say they develop a taste for some of the company's building materials—they'll be lucky to survive at all. I doubt that Terrestrial environmental laws will protect them. Those laws don't even really protect plant and animal species here on Earth. And who would enforce such laws on Mars?

And yet, somehow, I'm glad our installations have been sold and not just abandoned. Selling them was bad, but it was the lesser evil. Most people wouldn't have minded seeing them abandoned. They say we have no business wasting time or money in space when there are so many people suffering here on Earth, here in America. I wonder, though, where the money received in exchange for the installations has gone. I haven't noticed any new government education or jobs programs. There's been no government help for the homeless, the sick, the hungry. Squatter settlements are as big and as nasty as ever. As a country, we've given up our birthright for even less than bread and pottage. We've given it up for nothing—although I'm sure some people somewhere are richer now.

Consider, though: a brand-new form of life has been discovered on Mars, and it got less time on the news disk than the runaway Texas boy. We're becoming more and more isolated as a people. We're sliding into undirected negative change, and what's worse, we're getting used to it. All too often, we shape ourselves and our futures in such stupid ways.

More news. Scientists in Australia have managed to bring a human infant to term in an artificial womb. The child was conceived in a petri dish. Nine months later, it was taken, alive and healthy, from the last in a series of complex, computer-controlled containers. The child is the

OCTAVIA E. BUTLER

normal son of parents who could not have conceived or borne a child without a great deal of medical help.

Reporters are already calling the womb containers "eggs," and there's some foolish popular argument over whether a "hatched" person is as human as a "normally born" person. There are ministers and priests arguing that this tampering with human reproduction is wrong, of course. I doubt that they'll have much to worry about for a while. The whole process is still experimental and would be available only to the very rich if it were being marketed to anyone—which it isn't, yet. I wonder whether it will catch on at all in this world where so many poor women are willing to serve as surrogate mothers, carrying to term the child of wealthier people even when the wealthy people are able to have a child in the normal way. If you're rich, you can have a surrogate for not much more than the price of feeding and housing her for nine months. If she's smart and you're generous, you might also wind up agreeing to feed, house and help educate her children. And you might give her husband a job. Channa Ryan's mother did this kind of work. According to Channa, her mother bore 13 surrogate children, none of them genetically related to her. Her marriage didn't survive, but her two genetic daughters were given a chance to learn to read and write, cook, garden, and sew. That isn't enough to know in this world, of course, but it's more than most poor people learn.

It will be a long while—years, decades perhaps—before human surrogates are replaced by computerized eggs. Consider, though: eggs combined with cloning technology (another toy of the rich) would give men the ability to have a child without the genetic or the gestational help of a woman. Such men would still need a woman's ovum, stripped of its genetic contents, but that would be all. If the idea caught on, they might be willing to use the ovum of some animal species.

And, of course, women will be free to do without men completely, since women can provide their own ova. I wonder what this will mean for humanity in the future. Radical change or just one more option among the many?

I can see artificial wombs being useful when we travel into extrasolar space—useful for gestating our first animals once they're transported as frozen embryos and useful for gestating children if the nonreproductive work of women settlers is needed to keep the colony going. In that way, perhaps the eggs may be good for us—for Earthseed—in the long run. But what they'll do to human societies in the meantime, I wonder.

I've saved the worst news item for last. The election was on Tuesday, November 2. Jarret won. When Bankole heard the news, he said, "May God have mercy on our souls." I find that I'm more worried about our bodies. Before the election, I told myself that people had more sense than to elect a man whose supporters burn people alive as "witches," and torch the churches and homes of people they don't like.

We all voted—all of us who were old enough—and most of us voted for Vice President Edward Jay Smith. None of us wanted an empty man like Smith in the White House, but even a man without an idea in his head is better than a man who means to lash us all back to his particular God the way Jesus lashed the money changers out of the temple. He used that analogy more than once.

Here are some of the things that Jarret said back when he was shouting from his own Church of Christian America pulpit. I have copies of several of his sermons on disk.

"There was a time, Christian Americans, when our country ruled the world," he said. "America was God's country and we were God's people and God took care of his own. Now look at us. Who are we? What are we? What foul, seething, corrupt heathen concoction have we become?

"Are we Christian? Are we? Can our country be just a little bit Christian and a little bit Buddhist, maybe? How about a little bit Christian and a little bit Hindu? Or maybe a country can be a little bit Christian and a little bit Jewish? How about a little bit Christian and a little bit Moslem? Or perhaps we can be a little bit Christian and a little bit pagan cultist?"

And then he thundered, "We are God's people, or we are filth! We are God's people, or we are nothing! We are God's people! God's people!

"Oh my God, my God, why have we forsaken thee?

"Why have we allowed ourselves to be seduced and betrayed by these allies of Satan, these heathen purveyors of false and unchristian doctrines? These people. . . . These pagans are not only wrong. They're dangerous. They're as destructive as bullets, as contagious as plagues, as poisonous as snakes to the society they infest. They kill us, Christian American brothers and sisters. They kill us! They rouse the righteous anger of God against us for our misguided generosity to them. They are the natural destroyers of our country. They are lovers of Satan, seducers of our children, rapists of our women, drug sellers, usurers, thieves, and murderers!

"And in the face of all that, what are we to them? Shall we live with them? Shall we let them continue to drag our country down into hell? Think! What do we do to weeds, to viruses, to parasitic worms, to cancers? What must we do to protect ourselves and our children? What can we do to regain our stolen nation?"

Nasty. Very nasty. Jarret was the junior senator from Texas when he preached the sermon that contained those lines. He never answered the questions he asked. He left that to his listeners. And yet he says he's against the witch burnings.

His speeches during the campaign have been somewhat less inflammatory than his sermons. He's had to distance himself from the worst of his followers. But he still knows how to rouse his rabble, how to reach out to poor people, and sic them on other poor people. How much of this nonsense does he believe, I wonder, and how much does he say just because he knows the value of dividing in order to conquer and to rule?

Well, now he's conquered. In January of next year, he'll be sworn in, and he'll rule. Then, I suppose we'll see just how much of his own propaganda he believes.

Another, happier, more local event happened here at Acorn yesterday. Lucio Figueroa, Zahra Balter, and Jeff King came in with a huge load of books for our library. Some look almost new. Others are old and worn, but they've all been protected from the weather, from water, and from fire. There are textbooks, up to graduate level in several subjects, specialized dictionaries, a set of encyclopedias—2001 edition—books of history, how-to books, and dozens of novels. Jeff King ran across the books being all but given away at a street market in Arcata.

"Someone was clearing out a room so that relatives could move into it," he told me. "The owner of the books had died. He was considered the family eccentric, and no one else in the household shared his enthusiasm for reading big, bulky books made of paper. I didn't think you'd mind my buying them for the school."

"Mind?" I said. "Of course not!"

"Lucio said he wasn't sure we should spend the money, but Zahra said you were crazy for more books. I figured she'd know."

I grinned. "She knows. I thought everyone knew."

There were fifteen boxes of books. We took them into the school, and today we recovered as best we could from the stuff on the Worldisk by looking through the books and shelving them. We read bits of this and that to one another. People got excited and interested, and everyone carried away a book or two to read. After hearing the news, we all needed to read something that wasn't depressing.

I wound up with a couple of books on drawing. I haven't tried to draw anything since I was seven or eight. Now, all of a sudden, I find myself interested in learning to draw, learning to draw well—if I can. I want to learn something new and unrelated to any of our troubles.

SUNDAY, NOVEMBER 14, 2032

I'm pregnant!

No surrogates, no computerized eggs, no drugs. Bankole and I did it the good old-fashioned way—at last!

It's crazy that it should happen now, just when America has elected a wild man to lead it. Bankole and I began trying as soon as we could see that we were going to survive here at Acorn. Bankole's first wife couldn't have children. As a young woman back in the 1990s, she was in a serious car accident and wound up with a hysterectomy, among other things. Bankole claimed he never minded. He said the world was going to hell just as fast as it could, and it would be an act of cruelty to bring a child into it. They talked about adopting, but never did.

Now he's going to be a father, and in spite of all his talk, he's almost jumping up and down—that is, whenever he isn't being scared to death. He's talking about moving into an established town again. He hadn't said anything about that since right after we got the truck, but now the subject is back, and he's serious. He wants to protect me. I realize that. I suppose I should be glad he feels that way, but I wish he would show his protective feelings in another way.

"You're a kid yourself," he said to me. "You don't have the sense to be afraid."

I can't seem to get angry with him for saying things like that. He says them, then he thinks for a moment, and if he doesn't watch himself, he begins to grin like a boy. Then he remembers his fears and looks panicked. Poor man.

6

○ ○ ○

From EARTHSEED: THE BOOKS OF THE LIVING

God is Change
And hidden within Change
Is surprise, delight,
Confusion, pain,
Discovery, loss,
Opportunity, and growth.
As always,
God exists
To shape
And to be shaped.

It's a good thing, I suppose, that my mother's God was Change. Her life had a way of changing in abrupt, important ways. I don't suppose she was really any more prepared for sudden changes than anyone else, but her beliefs helped her cope with them, even take advantage of them when they came.

I enjoyed reading about the way she and my father reacted to my conception. Such mismatched people, yet such a normal reaction. She couldn't know that she was in for other major changes even before she could get used to being pregnant.

From *THE JOURNALS OF LAUREN OYA OLAMINA*
SUNDAY, DECEMBER 5, 2032

Spokesmen for Christian America have announced that the Church will be opening homeless shelters and children's homes—

orphanages—in several states, including California, Oregon, and Washington. This is just a beginning, they say. They hope in time to "extend a helping hand to the people of every state in the union, including Alaska." I heard this on a newsdisk that Mike Kardos bought at a Garberville street market yesterday. Time to begin to clean up the Christian America image, I suppose. I just hope the California shelters and orphanages will be put where they're most needed—down around San Diego, Los Angeles, and San Francisco. I don't want them up here. Christian America is made up of scary people, and I find it impossible to believe that they intend only to do good and to help others.

FRIDAY, DECEMBER 17, 2032

Today I found my brother Marcus.

This is impossible, I know, but I found him. He's sick, fearful, confused, and angry—hut he's alive!

I found him in Eureka, California, although five years ago, down in Robledo, he died.

I don't know what to say about this. I don't know how to deal with it. Writing about it helps. Somehow, writing always helps.

Before dawn this morning, five of us drove into Eureka. Bankole needed medical supplies and we had a couple of deliveries of winter vegetables and fruit to make to small, independent stores who have already begun to buy our produce. After that, we had a special errand.

Bankole hadn't wanted me to come. He worries about me more than ever now, and he's always after me to move to an established town. We could have a nice little house and he could be town doctor. We could live nice empty little antique lives, and I could forget I've spent the past five years struggling to establish Acorn as the beginning of Earthseed. Now that we've got the truck, traveling is a lot less dangerous than it used to be, but my Bankole is more worried than ever.

OCTAVIA E. BUTLER

And, to tell the truth, there are still things to worry about. We've all been looking over our shoulders since Dovetree. But we've got to live. We've got work to do.

"So Acorn is safe now?" I said to Bankole. "I'll be safe if I stay there?"

"Safer than you are traveling all over the county," he muttered, but he knew me well enough to let it go. At least he would be along to keep an eye on me.

Dan Noyer would also be along because our special errand concerned him. On our way home we were going to meet with a man who had contacted us through friends in Georgetown, claiming that he had one of Dan's younger sisters, and that he would sell her to us. The man was a pimp, of course—"a livestock man, specializing in lamb and chicken" as one of the euphemisms went. That is, a man who puts slave collars on little children and rents their bodies to other grown men. I hate the idea of having anything to do with a slug like that, but he was exactly the kind of walking filth who would have Nina and Paula Noyer.

I had asked Travis and Natividad Douglas to come along with us, to ride shotgun, and in Travis's case, to fix the truck if anything went wrong with it. I've trusted them both more than once with my life. I trust their judgment and their ability to fight. I felt a need to have people like that behind me when I was dealing with a slaver.

We made our deliveries to the two independent markets early, as we had promised—produce from our fields and from what was left of Dovetree's huge kitchen garden and small grove of fruit trees. The Dovetree truck and farm tractor had both been stolen during the raid that destroyed Dovetree. The houses and outbuildings had been torched along with the stills and fields. But a number of fruit trees and garden crops survived. Since the five surviving Dovetrees have decided to stay with us—to join us as members of Earthseed once their required probationary year has ended—we've felt free to take what we could from the property. The two Dovetree women have relatives elsewhere in the mountains, but they don't much like them, and they don't want to be squeezed into crowded houses with them. They do get along with us, and they know that while they're crowded now, they will have their own cabin by the time they're Welcomed as members.

Of course, they could go back and live on their own land. But two women and three children wouldn't survive on their own. They wouldn't survive alone even in a place as hidden and protected as Acorn. Trying to live right off the highway at Dovetree, they would be enslaved or killed in no time. Any house or farm that can be seen from the highway is bound to be tempting to the desperate and the opportunistic, and now the fanatical. Dovetree as it was survived because the family was large, well armed, and had a reputation for toughness. That worked until a small, determined army came along. The attackers really were Jarret loyalists, by the way. They came from the Eureka-Arcata area, from the new Christian America churches that have sprung up there. They have no government-sanctioned authority, but they believe God is on their side, and the cleansing work they do is God's work. Somehow, this kind of thing doesn't tend to make it to the news nets or disks. I've picked it up by talking to people. I know a few good sources of local news.

Bankole bought his supplies next. They're the most expensive things we buy, but they're also the most necessary. We are, as Bankole says, a healthy, young community, but the world around us isn't healthy. Thanks to malnutrition, climate change, poverty, and ignorance, a lot of old diseases are back, and some of them are contagious. There was an outbreak of whooping cough in the Bay Area last winter, and it came up the highway as far north as Ukiah down in Mendocino County. Why it stopped there, I don't know. And there was rabies last summer. Several people in squatter camps were bitten by rabid dogs or rats. They died of it, and a couple of teenagers were shot because they pretended to have rabies just to scare people. Whatever money it costs to keep us healthy, it's worth it.

When our business in Eureka was finished, we went to meet the slaver at the place he and I had agreed on, just south and east of Eureka in Georgetown. The squatter settlement called Georgetown extends

OCTAVIA E. BUTLER

well back from the highway in coastal hills. The place is a human-made desert, dusty when the weather is dry, muddy when it rains, almost treeless, plantless, filled with the poorest of the poor and their open sewers, their malnutrition, their drugs, crime, and disease. Bankole says it was once a beautiful area of farms, trees, and hills. That must have been a long time ago. The settlement is called Georgetown because the most permanent-looking thing in it is a cluster of shabby-looking redwood buildings. They're on a flattened hilltop and can be seen from just about everywhere in the settlement. There's a store, a café, a games hall, bar, a hotel, a fuel station, and a repair shop where tools, guns, and vehicles of all kinds might be restored to usefulness. The whole complex is called George's, and is run by a huge family surnamed George. At the café, George's has a lot of rentable cubbyhole mailboxes where packages and paper messages can be left, and there's a big bank of pay phones where, for a serious fee, you can access almost any network, service, group, or individual. This service in particular has made the place a combination message center, meeting place, and Old West saloon. It's natural to arrange to meet people there to transact business of all kinds. Elroy George and his sons, his sons-in-law, his brothers, and his brothers' sons see to it that people behave themselves. The Georges are a formidable tribe. They stick together, and people respect them. Their prices are high, but they're honest. You get what you pay for with the Georges. Sad to say, some of the things that get paid for in the café or elsewhere at the complex are slaves and drugs. The Georges aren't slavers, but they've been known to handle drugs. I wish that weren't so, but it is. I just hope they don't go the way of the Dovetrees. They're stronger and more entrenched, and better connected politically than the Dovetrees, but who knows? Now that Jarret has been elected, who knows?

Dolores Ramos George, the matriarch of the tribe, runs the store and the café, and she knows everyone. She's got a reputation for being a hard, mean woman, but as far as I'm concerned, she's just a realist. She speaks her mind. I like her. She's one of the people with whom I left word about the Noyer girls. When she heard the story, she just shook her head. "Not a chance," she said. "Why didn't they keep a watch? Some parents got no sense at all."

"I know," I said. "But I have to do what I can—for the sake of the other three kids."

"Yeah." She shrugged. "I'll tell people. It won't do no good."

But now it looked as though it had done some good. And in thanks, I had brought Dolores a basket of big navel oranges, a basket of lemons, and a basket of persimmons. If we found one or both of the Noyer girls as a result of her spreading the word, I would owe her a percentage of the reward—a kind of finder's fee. But it seemed wise to make sure she came out ahead, no matter what.

"Beautiful, beautiful fruit," she said, smiling as she looked at it and handled it. She was a stout, old-looking 53, but the smile took years off her. "Around here, if you don't guard a fruit tree and shoot a couple of people to prove you mean it, they'll tear off all the fruit, then cut down the tree for firewood. I won't let my boys kill people to save trees and plants, but I really miss oranges and grapes and things."

She called some of her young grandchildren to come and take the fruit into the house. I saw the way the kids were looking at everything, so I warned them not to eat the persimmons until they were soft to the touch. I cut one of the hard ones up and let each child have a taste of it so they would all know just how awful something so pretty could taste before it was ripe. Otherwise, they would have ruined several pieces of fruit as they tried to find a tasty, ripe persimmon. Just yesterday, I caught the Dovetree kids doing that back at Acorn. Dolores just watched and smiled. Anyone who was nice to her grandkids could be her friend for life—as long as they didn't cross the rest of her family.

"Come on," she said to me. "The shit pile that you want to talk with is stinkin' up the café. Is this the boy?" She looked up at Dan, seeming to notice him for the first time. "Your sister?" she asked him.

Dan nodded, solemn and silent.

"I hope she's the right girl," she said. Then she glanced at me, looked me up and down. She smiled again. "So you're finally starting a family. It's about time! I was 16 when I had my first."

I wasn't surprised. I'm only two months along, and not showing at all yet. But she would notice, somehow. No matter how distracted and grandmotherly she can seem when she wants to, she doesn't miss much.

We left Natividad in the housetruck, on watch. There are some very efficient thieves hanging around Georgetown. Trucks need guarding. Travis and Bankole went into the café with Dan and me, but Dan and the two men took a table together off to one side to back me up in case anything unexpected happened between the slaver and me. People didn't start trouble inside George's Café if they were sensible, but you never knew when you were dealing with fools.

Dolores directed us to a tall, lean, ugly man dressed completely in black, and working hard to look contemptuous of the world in general and George's Café in particular. He wore a kind of permanent sneer.

He sat alone as we had agreed, so I went over to him alone and introduced myself. I didn't like his dry, papery voice or his tan, almost yellow eyes. He used them to try to stare me clown. Even his smell repelled me. He wore some aftershave or cologne that gave him a heavy, nasty, sweet scent. Honest sweat would have been less offensive. He was bald, cleanshaved, beak-nosed, and so neutral-colored that he could have been a pale-skinned Black man, a Latino, or a dark-skinned White. He wore, aside from his black pants and shirt, an impressive pair of black leather boots—no expense spared—and a wide heavy leather belt decorated with what I first thought were jewels. It took me a moment to realize that this was a control belt—the kind of thing you use when you're moving around a lot and controlling several people through slave collars. I had never seen one before, but I'd heard descriptions of them.

Hateful bastard.

"Cougar," he said.

Crock of shit, I thought. But I said, "Olamina."

"The girl's outside with some friends of mine."

"Let's go see her."

We walked out of the café together, followed by my friends and his. Two guys sitting at the table off to his right got up when he did. It was all a ridiculous dance.

Outside, near the big, mutilated, dead stump of a redwood tree, several kids waited, guarded by two more men. The kids, to my surprise, looked like kids. They were not made up to look older or, for that matter, younger. The boys—one looked no older than 10—wore clean jeans and short-sleeved shirts. Three of the girls wore skirts and blouses, and three wore shorts, and T-shirts. All the jeans were a little too tight, and the skirts were a little too short, but none were really worse than things free kids of the same ages wore.

The slaves were clean and they looked alert and wary. None of them looked sick or beaten, but they all kept an eye on Cougar. They looked at him as he emerged from the café, then looked away so that they could watch him without seeming to. They weren't really good at this yet, so I couldn't help noticing. I looked around at Dan, who had followed us out with Bankole and Travis. Dan looked at the slave kids, stopped for a second as his gaze swept over the older girls, then shook his head.

"None of them are her," he said. "She's not here!"

"Hold on," Cougar said. He tapped his belt and four more kids came around the great trunk of the tree—two boys and two girls. These were a little older—mid-to-late teens. They were beautiful kids—the most beautiful I had ever seen. I found myself staring at one of them.

Somewhere behind me, Dan was whimpering, "No, no, she's still not here! Why did you say she was here? She's not!" He sounded much younger than his 15 years.

And I heard Bankole talking to him, trying to calm him, but I stood frozen, staring at one of the boys—a young man, really. The young man stared back at me then looked away. Perhaps he had not recognized me. On the other hand, perhaps he was warning me. I was late taking the warning.

"Like that one, do you?" Cougar purred.

Shit.

"He's one of my best. Young and strong. Take him instead of a girl."

I made myself look at the girls. One of them did look like the description we had given out of Dan's sisters: small, dark-haired, pretty, 12 and 13 years old. Nina had a scar just at the hairline where she had been burned when she was four and she and Paula and Dan had found some matches to play with. Some of her hair had caught fire. Paula had a mole—she called it a beauty mark—on the left side of her face near her nose. The girl that Cougar hoped we would buy did have a scar just at the hairline like Nina. She even resembled little Mercy Noyer quite a bit. Same heart-shaped face.

"Did she say she was Nina Noyer?" I asked Cougar.

He grinned. "Can't talk," he said. "Can't write either. Best kind of female. She must have said something bad to somebody, though, back when she could talk. Because before I bought her, somebody cut her tongue off."

I didn't let myself react, but there was no way I could avoid thinking of our May back at Acorn. We still don't know whose work this tongue cutting is, but we know that some Christian America types would be happy to silence all women. Jarret preached that woman was to be treasured, honored, and protected, but that for her own sake, she must be silent and obey the will of her husband, father, brother, or adult son since they understood the world as she did not. Was that it? The woman could be silent or she could be silenced? Or was it simpler than that—some pimp in the area just liked cutting out women's tongues? I didn't believe Cougar had done it. There was nothing about his body language that said he was lying or being evasive. That might just mean he was a very good liar, but I didn't think so. It seemed to me that he was telling the truth because he didn't care. He didn't give a damn who had cut the girl or why. I did. I couldn't help it. How much more of this kind of mutilation would we be seeing?

The beautiful young man moved his feet in a restless, noisy way, dragging my attention back to him. Not that I was in any danger of forgetting him. And he was the one I had to buy now.

"How much for him?" I asked. It was too late to pretend I wasn't interested. I had all I could do to just keep functioning—speaking sensible words in normal tones of voice, pretend that the impossible was not in the process of happening.

"Buying, are we?" asked Cougar, smirking.

I turned to face him. "I came here to buy," I said. In fact, I would chance making an enemy of the Georges and kill Cougar if I had to. I would not leave my brother in this man's hands. The thought that I had to leave any of these kids in his hands was sickening.

"I hope you can afford him," Cougar said. "Like I told you, he's one of my best."

I haven't had to do much haggling in my life, but something occurred to me as Cougar and I began. "He looks like one of your oldest," I said. My brother Marcus would be almost 20 now. How old did one of Cougar's child-slaves have to be before he was too old?

"He's 17!" Cougar lied.

I laughed and told a lie of my own. "Maybe five or six years ago he was 17. Good god, man, I'm not blind! He's great-looking, but he's no kid." It amazed me that I could lie and laugh and behave as though nothing unusual were happening when my long-dead brother stood alive and well just a few meters away.

To my further amazement, we haggled for over an hour. It seemed to me to be the right thing to do. Cougar was in no hurry, and I took my cue from him. He even seemed to be enjoying himself some of the time. Everyone else sat around on the ground, waiting, and looking bored or confused and angry. My people were the confused, angry ones. Dan in particular looked first disbelieving, then disgusted, then furious. But he followed the example of the two men. He kept quiet. He sat staring at the ground, his face expressionless. Travis watched me, then looked from me to Bankole, trying to figure out what was going on. But he wouldn't ask in front of Cougar. Bankole maintained a perfect poker face. Later, the three of them would have a lot to say to me. But not now.

And Cougar did want to get rid of Marcus. Maybe it was Marcus's age, maybe something else, but I couldn't miss that veiled eagerness of his. What he said just didn't jibe with his body language. I think being a sharer makes me extra sensitive to body language. Most of the time, this is a disadvantage. It forces me to feel things that I don't want to feel. Psychotics and competent actors can cause me a lot of trouble. This time, though, my sensitivity was a help.

I bought my brother. No shooting, no fighting, not even much cussing. In the end, Cougar smirked, took his hard currency, and released Marcus from the slave collar. He had offered me the collar and a control unit too—at added cost. Of course I didn't want it. Filthy things.

"Nice doin' business with you," Cougar said.

No. It hadn't been nice at all. "I still want the Noyer girls," I said.

He nodded. "I'll keep my eyes open. That young one over there is a real good fit to the description you gave."

I turned to Dan. "Is she . . . anything like your sisters?"

The girl and Dan stared at one another, and it hit me again that I was going to have to walk away and leave these children to their pimp. I avoided looking at the girl.

"Yeah, she looks a little like Nina," Dan mumbled. "But what good is that? She's not Nina. What good is anything?"

"Can you tell him anything more that would help him recognize either of your sisters if he sees them?" I asked.

"I don't want him to recognize them," Dan turned to stare at Cougar. "I don't want him to touch them. I'd kill him! I swear I would!"

Bankole took him to the truck, and Travis, in spite of his confusion, followed with Marcus. I went back into George's and took care of Dolores. She hadn't found Dan's sister, but she had done me a favor that I would never have imagined anyone could do. She had more than earned her fee.

As for Dan I couldn't really blame him for his attitude. But we couldn't afford a fight now. I was too close to my own edge. Leaving the rest of the kids, especially the little ones, was horrible. I had been willing to fight for Marcus if I had to, but I might have gotten him and others killed. I would have gotten someone killed. I don't know how to stop people like Cougar, but I don't think killing off their victims, their human property, is the best way.

Inside the truck, I hugged my brother. He was as unresponsive as a stick at first, but after a moment he held me away from him and stared at me for at least a full minute. He didn't say anything. He just shook his head. Then he hugged me. After a while, he put his hand to his throat. He felt all around his neck where the damned collar had been. Then he just kind of curled up on himself. He lay on his side in fetal position, and I sat beside him. He flinched when I touched him, so I just sat there.

And I told the others. "He's my brother," I said. "I . . . for five years, I believed . . . that he was dead." And then I couldn't say anything more. I just sat with him. I don't know what the others did apart from keeping watch and driving us home. If they talked, I didn't hear them. I didn't care what they did.

In all, Bankole told me, my brother had three active venereal infections. Also, his upper back and shoulders, his left arm, and the outside of his left leg were covered with an ugly network of old burn scars. No wonder Cougar had wanted to get rid of him. He probably thought he'd cheated me, palmed a defective off on me. Someone might once have done the same to him. Marcus was so good-looking that Cougar might have been persuaded to buy him in a rush without stripping him to look him over. But Marcus had suffered terrible burns sometime in the past, and Bankole said he had been shot, too.

When Bankole had finished examining him, he gave him something to help him sleep. That seemed best. Marcus had not objected to being examined. I assured him before I left them together that Bankole was a doctor and my husband as well. He didn't say anything. I asked him what he wanted to eat.

OCTAVIA E. BUTLER

He shrugged and whispered, "Nothing. I'm okay."

"He's far from okay," Bankole told me later. But because Marcus wasn't in serious physical pain, we could keep him with us. We gave him a space behind screens—room dividers—in our kitchen. It was warm there, and we had set up a bed, a dresser, a pitcher and basin, and a lamp. Like every other household in the community, we sometimes had to take people in—strangers who were visiting, new people joining us, or neighbors within the community who weren't getting along with others in their own households.

I worried that Marcus, in his present state of mind, might get up in the night and run away. How long must he have dreamed of running away from Cougar and his friends? Now, waking up in a strange place, and not quite remembering how he had gotten there. . . . Just to be sure, even after he had taken his sleeping pill, I went out and told our night watch—Beth Faircloth and Lucio Figueroa—to be careful. I told them Marcus might awake confused, and try to run away, and that they should be careful about shooting at a lone figure trying to get away from Acorn. Under normal circumstances, such a figure would be thought a thief, and might be shot. We'd had great trouble with thieves during our first year, and we learned that if we were to survive, we couldn't afford to have much sympathy for them.

But Marcus must not be shot.

"You told me Zahra Balter saw your stepmother and your brothers shot down back in Robledo," Bankole said to me as we lay in bed together. "Well, he's been beaten, shot, and burned. I can't imagine how he survived. Someone must have taken care of him, and it wouldn't have been your friend Cougar."

"No, it wouldn't have been Cougar," I agreed. "I want to know what happened. I hope he'll tell us. How was he with you when I left you two alone together?"

"Silent. Responsive and unembarrassed, but not speaking one unnecessary word."

"You're sure you can cure his infections?"

"They shouldn't be a problem. Let alone, any one of them would have killed him sooner or later. But with treatment, he should be all right—physically, anyway."

"He was 14 when I saw him last. He liked playing soccer and reading about the past and about foreign places. He was always taking things apart and sometimes getting them back together again, and he had a huge crush on Robin Balter, Harry's youngest sister. I don't know anything about him now. I don't know who he is."

"You'll have plenty of time to find out. I've told him he's going to be an uncle, by the way."

"Reaction?"

"None at all. At the moment, I don't think that even he knows who he is. He seems willing enough to be looked after, but I get the feeling he doesn't much care what happens to him. I think . . . I hope that that will change. You may be his best medicine."

"He was my favorite brother—and always the best-looking person in the family. He's still one of the best-looking people I've ever seen."

"Yes," Bankole said. "In spite of his scars, he's a good-looking boy. I wonder whether his looks have saved him or destroyed him. Or both."

It seems that things can never go well for long.

Dan Noyer has run away. He slipped past the watch and out of Acorn at least in part because of the instructions I gave to the night watch. Beth Faircloth says she saw someone—a man or boy, she thought.

"I thought the figure was too tall to be Marcus," she said when she phoned me. "But I wasn't sure—so I didn't shoot." The running figure had been dressed in dark clothing with something dark over the head and face.

Not until I had verified that Marcus was still there did I think of Dan. To tell the truth, I had forgotten about Dan. My mind had been filled with Marcus—getting him back, keeping him, wondering what had happened to him. I had paid no attention to Dan. Yet Dan had suffered a terrible disappointment. He was in real pain. I knew that, and I left him to the Balters, who, after all, have two energetic little kids of their own to deal with.

I got Zahra out of bed and asked her to check on Dan. He had been staying with them for four months now. Of course, he was gone. His note said, "I know you'll think I'm wrong, but I have to find them. I can't let them be with someone like that Cougar. They're my sisters!" And after his signature, a postscript: "Take care of Kassi and Mercy until I come back. I'll work for you and pay you. I'll bring Paula and Nina back and they'll work too."

He's only 15. He saw Cougar and his crew. He saw my brother. He saw Georgetown. And seeing all that, he learned nothing!

No, that's not true. He's learned—or finally realized—all the wrong things. I had assumed he knew what his sisters' fate might be if they were alive—that they might be prostitutes, might wind up in some rich man's harem or working as slave farm or factory laborers. Or, I suppose, they might wind up with some pervert who likes cutting out female tongues. They might even wind up as the property of someone who cares for them and looks after them even as he makes sexual use of them. That would be the best possibility. The worst, perhaps, is that they might survive for a while as "specialists"—prostitutes used to serve crazies and sadists. These don't live long, and that's a mercy. Theirs is a fate that could also befall a big, baby-faced, well-built boy like Dan. I wonder how much of this Dan understands. He is a good, brave, stupid boy, and I suspect he'll pay for it.

He might come back, of course. He might come to his senses and come home to help take care of Kassia and Mercy. Or we might find him through our outside contacts. I'll have to make sure that the word is out on him as well as on Nina and Paula. Problem is, finding him won't help if he's still intent on hunting for his sisters. We can't chain him here. Or rather, we won't. If he insists on dying, he will die, damn him. Damn!

7

○ ○ ○

From EARTHSEED: THE BOOKS OF THE LIVING

The child in each of us
Knows paradise.
Paradise is home.
Home as it was
Or home as it should have been.

Paradise is one's own place,
One's own people,
One's own world,
Knowing and known,
Perhaps even
Loving and loved.

Yet every child
Is cast from paradise —
Into growth and destruction,
Into solitude and new community,
Into vast, ongoing
Change.

From *WARRIOR* by Marcos Duran

When I was a kid, I never let anyone know how much the future scared me. In fact, I couldn't see any future. I was born into a world that was no bigger than the walled neighborhood enclave where my family lived. My father had lived there as a boy and inherited the house from his father.

My world was a cage. When one of my brothers dared to leave the cage, to run away from home, someone outside caught him and cut and burned all the flesh from his living body. Sometimes I catch myself wondering how long it took him to die.

I admit, my brother was no angel. He was mean and not very bright. He loved our mother, and he was her favorite, but I don't think he ever gave a damn about anyone else. Still, even though he was as tall as our father, he was only 14 when he was killed. To me, that makes the men who killed him worse than he ever was. How could they be human and do a thing like that to somebody? I used to imagine them—the killers—waiting for me whenever neighborhood adults with guns risked taking us out of the cage for a little while. The world outside was like my brother at his worst multiplied by about a thousand: stupid, mean, so out of control that it might do anything. It was like a dog with rabies, tearing itself to pieces, and wanting to do the same to me.

And then it did just that.

Oh, yes. It did.

I could return the compliment. I could have reached for the power to do that. But I would rather fix the problem. What happened to me shouldn't happen to anyone, yet such things have happened to thousands of people, perhaps millions. I've read history. Things weren't always this way. They don't have to go on being this way. What we have broken we can mend.

M y Uncle Marc was the handsomest man I've ever seen. I think I fell more than half in love with him before I even met him. There were also times when I was afraid for him. I don't know what to make of our family. My grandfather was, from what I've heard, a good and dedicated Baptist minister. He looked after his family and his community and insisted that both be armed and able to defend themselves in an armed and dangerous world, but beyond that, he had no ambitions. It never seemed to occur to him that he could or should fix the world. Yet he was the father of two would-be world-fixers. How did that happen?

Well, my mother was a sharer, a little adult at 15, and a survivor of the destruction of her whole neighborhood at 18. Perhaps that was why she, like Uncle Marc, needed to take charge, to bring her own brand of order to the chaos that she saw swallow so many of the people she loved. She saw chaos as natural and inevitable and as clay to be shaped and directed. As she says in one of her verses:

> Chaos
> Is God's most dangerous face—
> Amorphous, roiling, hungry.
> Shape Chaos—
> Shape God.
> Act.
>
> Alter the speed
> Or the direction of Change.
> Vary the scope of Change.
> Recombine the seeds of Change.
> Transmute the impact of Change.
> Seize Change,
> Use it.
> Adapt and grow.

And so she tried to adapt and to grow. Perhaps she feared being like her own mother, who looked for help in a "smart" drug and wound up damaging her child and killing herself. Chaos. Whatever my mother's reasoning, she decided that she knew what was wrong with her world, and she knew what would fix it: Earthseed. Earthseed with all its definitions, admonitions, requirements, *purpose*. Earthseed with its Destiny.

My Uncle Marc, on the other hand, hated the chaos. It wasn't one of the faces of his god. It was unnatural. It was demonic. He hated what it had done to him, and he needed to prove that he was not what it had forced him to become. No Christian minister could ever hate sin as much as Marc hated chaos. His gods were order, stability, safety, control. He was a man with a wound that would not heal until he could be certain that what had happened to him could not happen again to anyone, ever.

My father called my mother a zealot. I think that name applies even more to Uncle Marc. And yet, I think Uncle Marc was more of a realist. Uncle Marc wanted to make the Earth a better place. Uncle Marc knew that the stars could take care of themselves.

From *THE JOURNALS OF LAUREN OYA OLAMINA*
SATURDAY, DECEMBER 18, 2032

Dan hasn't come back. I had no reason to expect him to give up and come home so quickly, but I did hope. Jorge, Diamond Scott, and Gray Mora are going to trade at the Coy street market today. I've told them to leave word with the few people we know in Coy, and on the way back, to tell the Sullivan family. Their quickest way home takes them past the Sullivan place.

Marcus slept through the night, causing no trouble to himself or to us. Bankole happened to be in the kitchen when he awoke, and that was good. Bankole took him out to one of our composting toilets. I didn't see him until later when he had washed and dressed. Then he came hesitant and tentative, to my kitchen table.

"Hungry?" I asked. "Sit down."

He stared at me for several seconds, then said, "When I woke up, I thought all this was just a dream."

I put a piece of fruit-laden acorn bread in front of him. We had both been raised on the stuff because our old neighborhood happened to have several very fruitful California live oak trees within the walls. My father didn't believe in waste, so he found out how to use acorns

OCTAVIA E. BUTLER

as food. Native Americans did it. We could do it. He and my mother worked at learning to use not only acorns but cactuses, palm fruit, and other plants that might otherwise be seen as useless. For Marcus and me, all this was food from home.

Marcus took the acorn bread, bit into it, and chewed slowly. First he looked delighted, then tears began to stream down his face. I gave him a napkin and a glass of what had once been a favorite morning drink of his—a mug of hot, sweet apple juice with a lemon squeezed into it. The apples we pressed in southern California were of a different variety, but I don't think he noticed. He ate, wiped his eyes, looked around. He stared at Bankole as Bankole came in, then focused on the rest of his breakfast, all but huddling over it the way a hawk does when it's claiming and protecting its kill. There was no more talk for a while.

When we had all had enough to eat, Bankole looked at Marcus and said, "I've been married to your sister for five years. During all that time, we believed that you and the rest of her family were dead."

"I thought she was dead, too," Marcus said.

"Zahra Balter—she was Zahra Moss when you knew her—she said she saw all of you killed," I told him.

He frowned. "Moss? Balter?"

"We didn't know Zahra very well back home. She was married to Richard Moss. He was killed and she married Harry Balter."

"God," he said. "I never thought I'd hear those names again. I do remember Zahra—tiny, beautiful, and tough."

"She's still all three. She and Harry are here. They've got two kids."

"I want to see them!"

"Okay."

"Who else is here?"

"A lot of people who've been through hard times. No one else from home, though. This community is called Acorn."

"There was a little girl . . . Robin. Robin Balter?"

"Harry's little sister. She didn't make it."

"You thought I didn't."

"I . . . saw Robin's body, Marc. She didn't make it."

He sighed and stared at his hands resting in his lap. "I did die back in '27. I died. There's nothing left."

"There's family," I said. "There's me, Bankole, the niece or nephew who'll be born next year. You're free now. You can stay here and make a life for yourself in Acorn. I hope you will. But you're free to do what you want. No one here wears a collar."

"Have you ever worn one?" he asked.

"No. Some of us have been slaves, but I never was. And I believe you're the first of us who's worn a collar. I hope you'll talk or write about what happened to you since the old neighborhood was destroyed."

He seemed to think about that for a while. "No," he said. "No."

Too soon. "Okay," I said, "but . . . do you think any of the others could have survived? Cory or Ben or Greg? Is it possible . . . ?"

"No," he repeated. "No, they're dead. I got out. They didn't."

Sometime later, as we got up from the table, two men arrived by truck from the little coastal town of Halstead. Like Acorn, Halstead is well off the main highway. In fact, Halstead must be the most remote, isolated town in our area with the Pacific Ocean on three sides of it and low mountains behind it.

In spite of all that, Halstead has a major problem. Halstead used to have a beach and above the beach was a palisade where the town began. Along the palisade, some of the biggest, nicest houses sat, overlooking the ocean. On one side of the peninsula were the old houses, large, well-built wood frame structures. On the other side were newer houses built on land that was once a seaside golf course. All of these are . . . were lined up along the palisade. I don't know why people would build their homes on the edge of a cliff like that, but they did. Now, whenever we have heavy rains, when there's an earthquake, or when the level of the sea rises enough to saturate more land, great blocks of the palisades drop into the sea, and the houses sitting on them break apart and fall. Sometimes half a house falls into the sea. Sometimes it's several houses. Last night it was three of them. The people of Halstead were still fishing victims out of the sea. Worse, the community doctor had been delivering a baby in one of the lost houses. That's why the community was turning to Bankole for help. Bankole had been on good terms with their doctor. The people of Halstead trusted Bankole because their doctor had trusted him.

"What are you people thinking?" Bankole demanded of the weary, desperate Halstead men as he and I snatched up things he would need. He was adding to his medical bag. I was packing an overnight case for him. Marcus had looked from one of us to the other, then moved off to one side, out of the way.

"Why do you still have people living on the cliffs?" Bankole demanded. He sounded angry. Unnecessary pain and death still made him angry. "How many times does this kind of thing have to happen before you get the idea?" he asked. He shut his bag and grabbed the overnight case that I handed him. "Move the damned houses inland, for heaven's sake. Make it a long-term community effort."

"We're doing what we can," a big red-haired man said, moving toward the door. He pushed his hair out of his face with a dirty, abraded hand. "We've moved some. Others refuse to have their houses moved. They think they'll be okay. We can't force them."

Bankole shook his head, then kissed me. "This could take two or three days," he said. "Don't worry, and don't do anything foolish. Behave yourself!" And he went.

I sighed, and began to clear away the breakfast things.

"So he really is a doctor," Marcus said.

I paused and looked at him. "Yes, and he and I really are married," I said. "And I'm really pregnant. Did you think we were telling you lies?"

". . . no. I don't know." He paused. "You can't change everything in your life all at once. You just can't."

"You can," I said. "We both have. It hurts. It's terrible. But you can do it."

He reached for the plate I was about to take, and scavenged a few crumbs of Acorn bread from it. "It tastes like Mama's," he said, and he looked up at me. "I didn't believe it was you at first. Yesterday in that godforsaken shantytown, I saw you, and I thought I had finally lost my mind. I remember, I thought, 'Good. Now I'm crazy. Now nothing matters. Maybe I'll see Mama, too. Maybe I'm dead.' But I could still feel the weight of the collar around my neck, so I knew I wasn't dead. Just crazy."

"Then you knew me," I said. "And you looked away before Cougar could see that you knew me. I saw you."

He swallowed. Nodded. A long time later, he shut his eyes and leaned his face into his hand. "If you still want me to," he said, "I'll tell you what happened."

I managed not to sigh with relief. "Thank you."

"I mean, you've got to tell me things, too. Like how you wound up here. And how you wound up married to a man older than Dad."

"He's a year younger than Dad. And when we had both lost almost everything else and everyone else, we found each other. Laugh if you want to, but we were damned lucky."

"I'm not laughing. I found good people too, at first. Or rather, they found me."

I sat down opposite him, and waited. For a time, he stared at the wall, at nothing, at the past.

"Everything was burning on that last night," he said. His voice was low and even. "There was so much shooting. . . . Hoards of bald, painted people, mostly kids, had rammed their damned truck through our gate. They were everywhere. And they had their fun with Ben and Greg and Mama and me. In all the confusion, Lauren, we didn't even know you were gone until we had almost reached the gate. Then a blue-painted guy grabbed Ben—just snatched him and tried to run off with him. I was too small to do any good fighting him one-on-one, but I was fast. I ran after him and tackled him. I might not have been able to bring him down by myself, but Mama jumped on him too. We dragged him down, and when he fell, he hit his head on the concrete and he dropped Ben. Mama grabbed Ben and I grabbed Greg. Greg had hurt his foot—stepped on a rock and twisted it—while we were running.

"This time, we made it out through the wrecked gate. I didn't know where we were going. I was just following Mama, and we were both looking around for you." He paused. "What happened to you?"

"I saw someone get shot," I said, remembering, shuddering with the memory. "I shared the pain of the gunshot, got caught up in the death. Then when I could get up, I found a gun. I took it from the hand of someone who was dead. That was good because a moment later, one of the paints grabbed me, and I had to shoot him. I shared his death, and in the confusion of that, I lost track of you guys and of time. When I could, I ran out of the gate and spent the rest of the night a few blocks north of our neighborhood huddling in someone's half-burned garage. The next day I came back looking for you. That's when I found Harry and Zahra. We were all pretty beaten up. Zahra told me you guys were dead."

Marcus shook his head. "I wish we had been with you. Then we could have been just 'beaten up.' Everything went wrong for us. Just as we went through the gate another group of paints arrived."

He paused. "You know, I met some paints later. Most of them killed themselves off, with their drugs, or with their drug-induced love of fire. But there are still a few around. Anyway . . . I was collared with some a few months ago. They said their whole deal was to help the poor by killing off the rich and letting the poor take their stuff. If you lived in a place where the houses weren't falling down, and especially if you had a wall around your neighborhood or your house, that meant you were rich. The crazy thing was, a lot of the paint kids really were rich. One of the girls I met, her family had more money than our whole neighborhood put together. She had pretty much given up everything for the paints, but in the end her friends betrayed her. One day while she was spaced out on something, they sold her to be collared because she was still young and cute, and they needed money for drugs. But she still thought she'd done some good. We couldn't convince her. We figured the drugs had wiped out her mind."

"She had to believe in something," I said. "And after all, what did she have left?"

"I guess. Anyway, we were caught between these two groups of god-damn saviors of the poor." He sighed. "They were shooting—most of them firing into the air at first—and waving torches. . . . More fire. . . . We couldn't do anything but run back in through the gate.

"Everything was crazy. Ben and Greg were crying. People were running everywhere. All the houses were burning. Then someone shot me. I was knocked down, stunned. At first I didn't understand what had hit me. Then I felt this unbelievable pain. I must have dropped Greg. I tried to look around for him. That's when I understood that I was down on the sidewalk. I felt slammed down, stomped, plus stabbed through the right shoulder and arm by a hot poker. I never knew who shot me or why. We didn't have guns. I guess they just shot us for fun.

"Then I saw Mama get shot. The truth is, it all happened so fast—first me, Then her, bang, bang. I know that. But at the time. . . . I remember seeing it all, taking it all in as though I had plenty of time. And yet I was desperate to get out of there, and scared to death. Jesus God, there's no way I can make you know how bad it was.

"I saw Mama stagger and collapse. She made a horrible noise, and I saw blood pouring from her neck. I knew then that . . . she . . . that she was dying. I knew it.

"I tried to get up, tried to make myself go to her. But while I was struggling to stand, a green-painted woman ran up and shot her through the head.

"I slipped in my own blood and fell back. From the ground, I saw a red guy shoot Ben twice through the head, then step over him and shoot Greg. I saw him. I was yelling. The red guy had an automatic rifle—an old AK-47. He shot Ben while Ben was trying to get up. Ben's head . . . just . . . broke apart.

"But Greg was down on the sidewalk—moving, but down. When the guy shot him, the bullets must have ricocheted off the concrete.

They hit another paint in the legs. He screamed and fell down. That made all the paints nearby mad. It was like they thought we had shot their man—like his being wounded was our fault. They grabbed all four of us and dragged us over to the Balter house. It was burning, and they threw us into the fire.

"They did that. They threw us into the fire. I was the only one who was conscious. I was maybe the only one alive, but I couldn't stop them. Somehow, though, once they threw me in, I got up and ran out. I just ran, panicked out of my mind, blind with smoke and pain, not human anymore. I should have died.

"Later, I wished I had died. Later, all I wanted to do was die."

Marcus stopped and sat silent for several seconds.

"Someone must have helped you," I said when I thought the silence had gone on long enough. "You were only 14."

"I was only 14," he agreed. After another silence, he went on. "I think I must have fallen down in the Balter yard. I was on fire. I didn't think about rolling on the ground to put the fire out, but I must have done it. I was just scrambling around in panic and pain, and the fire did go out. Then all I could do was lie there. I must have passed out at some point. When I woke up—I have a clear memory of this—I was on a big wooden wagon on top of a lot of scorched clothes and some pots and pans and junk. I could see the sidewalk passing under me— broken concrete, weeds growing in the holes and cracks, and I could see the backs of a man and woman walking ahead, leaning forward, pulling the wagon with rope harnesses. Then I passed out again.

"A pair of scavengers picking over the bones of our neighborhood had found me groaning—although I don't remember groaning or being found—and they had loaded me onto their salvage wagon. They were a middle-aged couple named Duran, believe it or not. Maybe they were distant relatives or something. It's a pretty common name, though."

I nodded. Not unusual at all, but the only Duran I happened to know was my stepmother. Duran was her maiden name. Well, if these

Durans had saved my brother's life five years ago when he couldn't have lived without their help, I was more than willing to be related to them.

"They had had an 11-year old daughter kidnapped from them the year before they found me," Marcus said. "They never found her, never found out what happened to her, but I can guess. You could sell a pretty little girl for a lot then. Just like now. I've heard people say things are getting better. Maybe so, but I haven't noticed. Anyway, the Durans were handsome people. Their daughter could have been really pretty."

He sighed. "The kid's name was Caridad. They said I looked enough like her to be her brother. The woman said that. Inez was her name. She was the one who insisted on collecting what was left of me and taking it home to nurse back to health.

"I'm surprised I even looked human when she found me. My face wasn't too bad—blood and bruises from falling down a few times. But the rest of me was a hell of a mess.

"There was no way these people could afford a doctor—not even for themselves. So Inez herself worked on me. She worked so hard to save me—like a second mother. The man thought I would die. He thought it was stupid to waste time, effort, and valuable resources on me. But he loved her, so he let her have her way.

"These people were a lot poorer than we used to be, but they did what they could with what they had. For me that meant soap and water, aspirin and aloe vera. Why I didn't die of 20 infections, I don't know. I goddamn sure wanted to die. I'll tell you, I'd rather blow my own brains out than go through that again."

I shook my head. I had no medical training beyond first aid, and I doubt that I'd be much good administering that, but I'd lived with Bankole long enough to know how nasty burns could be. "No complications at all?" I demanded.

Marcus shook his head. "I don't know, really. Most of the time I was in so much pain I didn't know what was going on. How could I tell a complication from the general run of misery?"

OCTAVIA E. BUTLER

I shook my head, and wondered what Bankole would say when I told him. Soap and water and aspirin and aloe vera. Well, a little humility would be good for him. To Marcus, I said, "What Happened to the Durans?"

"Dead," he whispered. "At least I guess they're dead. So many died. I never found their bodies, though, and I tried. I did try."

Long silence.

"Marcus?" I reached over and put my hand on his.

He pulled away and put his hand to his face. I heard him sigh behind them. Then he began to talk again. "Four years after our neighborhood burned, the city of Robledo decided to clean itself up. The Durans and I were squatters. We shared a big, abandoned stucco house with five other families. That meant that we were part of the trash that the new mayor, the city council, and the business community wanted to sweep out. It seemed to them that all the trouble of the past fewyears was our fault—poor people's fault, I mean. Homeless people's fault. Squatters' fault. So they sent an army of cops to drive out everyone who couldn't prove they had a right to be where they were. You had to have rent receipts, a deed, utility receipts, something. At first, there was a hell of a business in fake paper. I wrote some of it myself—not for sale, but for the Durans and their friends. Most people couldn't read or write or at least not in English, so they needed help. I saw that some of them were paying hard currency for crap, so I started writing—rent receipts, mostly. In the end, it was all for nothing. Between them, the city and the county owned most of the rotting buildings in our area, and the cops knew we didn't belong there, no matter what papers we had. They drove us all out—poor squatters, drug dealers, junkies, crazies, gangs, whores, you name it."

"Where were you living?" I asked. "What part of town?"

"Valley Street," Marcus said. "Old factory buildings, parking structures, ancient houses and stores, all packed with people."

"And vacant lots full of weeds and trash where people dump inconvenient dead bodies," I continued for him.

"That's the area, yes. The Durans were poor. they worked all the time, but sometimes they didn't even get enough to eat—especially sharing with me. When I was well enough, I worked with them. We cleaned, repaired, and sold everything we could salvage. We took whatever jobs we could get—cleaning, assembling, constructing, repairing.

They never lasted long. There were a lot of people like us and not so many jobs, so wages were terrible. Just food and water sometimes, or some old clothes or shoes or something. They'd even pay you in American money if they thought they could get away with palming it off on you. Hard currency if they gave a damn about treating you right. Most didn't. Also, hard currency if they were a little bit afraid of you or of your friends.

"In spite of all our efforts, there was no way we could afford to rent even a shabby little apartment or house. We lived on Valley Street because we couldn't do any better. With all that, though, it probably wasn't as bad as you think. People looked after one another there, except for the worst junkies and thugs. Everyone knew who they were. I did reading and writing for people even before the fake-paper craze. They paid me what they could. And . . . I helped some of them hold church on Sundays. There was an old carport behind the house we lived in. It projected from a garage where three families lived, but as it happened, no one lived under the carport. We met for church there and I would preach and teach as best I could. They let me do it. They came to hear me even though I was a kid. I taught them songs and everything. They said I had a gift, a calling. The truth was, thanks to Dad, I knew more about the Bible than any of them, and more about real church."

He paused, looked at me. "I liked it, you know? I prayed with them, helped them any way I could. Their lives were so terrible. There wasn't much I could do, but I did what I could. It was important to them that I had recovered from burns and gunshots. A lot of them had seen me back when I looked like vomit. They thought if I could recover from that, God must have something in mind for me.

"The Durans were proud of me. They gave me their name. I was Marcos Duran. That's who I was during my four years with them. That's who I still am. I found a real home there.

"Then the cops came and drove us into the street. Behind them came demolition crews to push down the houses, blow up the buildings, and destroy everything we had been forced to leave behind. People were dragged or driven into the street without all kinds of things—spare clothing, money, pictures, personal papers. . . . Some people who couldn't speak English were even driven out without relatives who had managed to hide or who were too sick or disabled to run. The cops dragged some of these out and put them in trucks. They didn't find them all. I sent them to get seven that I knew of, and they brought them out.

"But everything was chaos. People kept trying to run back to get their things, and the cops kept stopping them—or trying to. Some of the cops were in armored personnel carriers. The ones on foot had full body armor, masks, shields, automatic rifles, gas, whips, clubs, you name it, but still, some people tried to stop them, or at least to hurt them. The people threw rocks, bottles, even precious cans of food.

"Then someone fired three shots, and one of the cops went down. I don't know whether he was wounded or he tripped, but there were the shots, and he fell. And that was that. Everything went to hell.

"The cops started shooting. People ran, screamed, shot back if they had guns. I got separated from the Durans. I started looking for them even before the shooting stopped. No one shot me this time, but I didn't find the Durans. I never found them. I tried for days. I looked at as many dead bodies as I could before they were collected. I did everything I could think of, but they were gone. After a while, I knew they must be dead, and I was alone again."

Marcus sat still, staring into space. "I loved them," he said, his voice soft and filled with pain. "And I loved being Marcos Duran—the little preacher. People trusted me, respected me. . . . It was a good life. Most of them were good people—just poor. They deserved so much better than they got." He shook his head.

"I didn't know what to do," he continued after a moment. "I hung around the Valley Street area for two more weeks, saw all the buildings go down and the rubble carried away. I stole food where I could, avoided the cops, and kept looking for the Durans. I'd said they were dead, and on some level, I believed they were, but I couldn't stop looking.

"But there was nothing. No one." He hesitated. "No, that's not quite right. Some people from my poor, half-assed church came back to see what was left. I met three families of them. They all asked me to stay with them. They had relatives squatting in other hovels, over-crowded like you wouldn't believe, but they figured they could take in one more. I had nothing, but they wanted me. I should have gone with them. I probably would have set up another church outside of town, gotten married, and raised a family—Dad all over again. I would have been okay. Poor, but okay. Poor doesn't matter as much if you can make a place for yourself and be respected. I know that now, but I didn't then.

"I was 18. I figured it was time for me to be a man, get out on my own. I figured there was nothing for me in southern California. It was a place where you could only be poor unless you were born rich or you were a really successful crook. I thought that meant I had to go north. There was always a river of people walking north on the freeway. I thought they must know something. I talked to people about Alaska, Canada, Washington, Oregon . . . I never intended to stay in California."

"Neither did I," I said.

"You walked up?"

"I did. So did Bankole, Harry, Zahra. . . . A lot of us did."

"Nobody bothered you?"

"A lot of people bothered us. Harry, Zahra and I survived because we stuck together and one of us always kept watch. We started out with my one gun. We gathered more people and more guns along the way. I lost count of the number of times we were nearly killed. One

OCTAVIA E. BUTLER

of us was killed. There may be an easy way to get here, but we didn't find it."

"Neither did I. But why did you come here? I mean, why didn't you keep going to Oregon or someplace?"

"Bankole owns this land," I said. "By the time we got near here, well, he and I wanted to stay together, but I also wanted . . . I wanted to keep the rest of the group together. I was building a community—a group of families and single people who were still human."

"You walk the roads for a while, and you wonder if anyone is still human."

"Yeah."

"The people you brought here—they built this place?"

I nodded. "There was nothing here when we got here but the ashes of a house, the bones of Bankole's relatives, some untended crops and trees, and a well. There were only 13 of us then. There are 66 of us now—67 with you."

"You just let people come here and stay? What if they rob you, cheat you, kill you? What if they're crazy?"

"Give me some credit, Marc."

His face changed in an odd way. "You. You personally." He paused. "I thought at first this was Bankole's place, that he'd taken you in."

"I told you, this is his land."

"But it's your place."

"It's our place. I've shaped it, but it doesn't belong to me. I've invited people to come here and build lives for themselves, to join us." I hesitated, wondering how much he still believed in religion as our father had taught it to us. When he was little, he always seemed to take Dad's religion as real, as obvious, as a given. But what did he believe now that he had suffered the destruction of two homes and the loss of two families, then endured prostitution and slavery? He still had not talked about that last part of his story. Had his religion given him hope, or had it withered and fallen away when his God did not rescue him? Back in Robledo, he had run a simple outdoor church, had been serious about it. But where was he now? I made myself continue. "And I've given them a belief system to help them deal with the world as it is and the world as it can be—as people like them can make it."

"You mean you're their preacher?" he asked.

I nodded. "We don't call it that, but yes."

He looked surprised, then gave a short bark of laughter. "Religion is in our genes," he said. "It must be. Either that or Dad did a hell of a job on us."

"We call our system Earthseed," I said. "My actual title is 'Shaper.'"

He stared at me for several seconds, saying nothing. He still looked surprised, and now confused. "Earthseed?" he said at last. "My god, I've heard of you guys. You're that cult!"

"So we've been called."

"There was a politician. He was running for the state senate, I think. He won. He was a Jarret supporter. He was making a speech in Arcata when I was up there, and he was listing devil-worshiping cults. He named Earthseed as one of them. I'd never heard of it, but I remember because he was going on about how the name actually referred to the devil, the seed deep in the earth and growing like a poisonous fungus to spread its evil to more and more people."

"Oh, Marc. . . ."

"I didn't make it up. He really said that."

I drew a deep breath. "We don't worship the devil. In fact, we don't worship anyone. And we are Earthseed. Human beings are Earthseed. We have no devils. But we're so small that I'm surprised your politician had ever heard of us. And I wish he hadn't. Such lies!"

He shrugged. "It was just politics. You know those guys will say anything. But why would you stop being a Christian? Why would you make up a new religion?"

"I didn't make it up. It was something I had been thinking about since I was 12. It was—is—a collection of truths. It isn't the whole truth. It isn't the only truth. It's just one collection of thoughts that are true. I could never say anything about it at home. I never wanted to hurt Dad. But his way didn't work for me. I wanted it to. I would have been a lot more comfortable if it had. But it didn't. Earthseed does."

"But you made Earthseed up. Or if you didn't make it up, you read it or heard about it somewhere."

I had heard this many times before. It seemed to be one of the things that every new potential member said. I even kept a simple teaching tool near at hand to deal with it. I got up and went to a bookshelf where a beautiful piece of rose quartz that Bankole had given me acted as a bookend for the few books I kept here in the house and not in the library section of the school.

"Look at this," I said, "and tell me something." I put the rock in his hands. "If I were to analyze this stone and find out exactly what it's made of, would that mean I made it up?"

"That's not a good comparison, Lauren. The rock exists. Earthseed didn't exist until you made it up."

"All the truths of Earthseed existed somewhere before I found them and put them together. They were in the patterns of history, in science, philosophy, religion, or literature. I didn't make any of them up."

"You just put them together."

"Yes."

"Then you did make Earthseed up the same way you would have made a novel up if you wrote one. You wouldn't have to find anything brand-new for your characters to do or be in a novel. I don't think you could if you wanted to."

"Except that by definition, a novel is fiction. Don't call Earthseed fiction. You don't know anything about it except the lies told by an opportunistic politician." I took down a copy of *The First Book of the Living* and handed it to him. "Come and talk to me after you've read this."

"You wrote this?"

"Yes."

"And you believe in it?"

"I believe it. I wouldn't teach people that things were true if I didn't believe them."

"Back in Robledo, I remember you were always writing. Keith used to sneak into your room and read your diary. Or at least he said he did."

I thought about that for a moment. "I don't think he ever read my journal," I said. "I mean, I know I was always chasing him out of my room. I chased you out, too, plenty of times. But I think if Keith had read my journal, he wouldn't have been able to resist using it against me. Besides, Keith never read anything unless he had to."

"Yeah." He paused, gazing down at the table. "It's weird to think I'm older now than he ever got to be. He still seems older and bigger when I think about him. He was such a goddamn asshole." He shook his head. "I think I really hated him, you know, the way he was always making trouble for everybody, beating the rest of us up—except you. He was afraid of you because you were so much bigger. And Mama . . . she loved him more than she loved all of us put together."

"It wasn't that bad, Marc."

He looked up at me, solemn-eyed. "It was, though. She wasn't your mother, so maybe you didn't feel it the way I did, but it was that bad and then some."

"I felt it. Toward the end when she and I needed each other most, I'm not sure she loved me at all. But she was so scared and so desperate. . . . Forgive her, Marc. She was in a hellish place with four children to look out for. If it made her less rational than she should have been . . . well, forgive her."

There was a long silence. He stared at the book, open at the first page:

> All that you toucttleh
> You Change.
>
> All that you Change
> Changes you.

OCTAVIA E. BUTLER

The only lasting truth
Is Change.

God
Is Change.

I couldn't tell whether he had read the words at first. He seemed to stare the way blind people do, unseeing, blank. Then he whispered, "Oh, god," and it sounded like a prayer. He shut the book and closed his eyes. "I'm not sure I want to read your book, Lauren," he said. He opened his eyes and looked at me. "You haven't asked how I wound up with Cougar."

"I want to know," I admitted.

"Simple. My first night walking the freeway, three guys jumped me—big guys. I didn't have much money and that pissed them off—you know, like I was supposed to be rich so that robbing me would be worth their while. If I wasn't rich, then I had cheated them, and they had a right to get me for it. Shit."

He was staring at the table again, and I imagined him as he must have been then, facing three big men. He had always been slight and much too attractive for his own good—a beautiful boy, and now, such a handsome young man. I had seen the girls and women of the community staring at him as we brought him from the truck to the house last night. If he stayed, they would be all over him.

He would be stronger now. He had a look of wiry strength about him. But even now, he wouldn't be strong enough to hold off three attackers. And he'd had no friends with him, watching his back on the freeway that night.

After a while, he spoke again, still staring at the table. "They didn't just beat the hell out of me and rape me and let me go," he said. "They kept me so they could do it over and over again. And when they got tired of me, they sold me to a pimp. Not Cougar. He came later. The first one called himself Zorro. All these guys seem to have stupid names. Anyway, Zorro was the first to put a collar around my neck. After that people didn't have to bother beating me up—unless they felt like it. Some people get turned on by beating the shit out of a guy who can't fight back. And. . . . You know the worst thing about a collar, Lauren? They can torture you with it every day. Every goddamn day. And you never have any marks to mess you up and drive down your price, and you never die of it! Or most people don't die of it. Some are lucky. They have heart attacks or strokes and they die. But the rest of us live no matter what. And if we try to find some other way to die, to kill ourselves, they can stop us. The guy with the control unit can play you the way Mama used to play her piano. You get so you'll do anything—anything!—just to get him to let you alone for a few minutes. You walk past a corpse on the road—some poor old guy who couldn't walk any farther or a woman someone had raped and killed. You walk past the corpse, and you wish like hell it was you."

He sighed and shook his head. "That's it, really. I had one more owner between Zorro and Cougar, but he was walking shit too. You can't own people and torture them for fun and profit without being shit. A pimp would sell his mother and his daughter if the price were right. And if I ever get the chance, I swear to god, Lauren, I'll stake all three of them out and I'll burn them—like Jarret's people do with their so-called witches." After a moment, he added, "I saw that done once—a burning. Sargent—my second owner—did it to a woman who tried to kill him in his sleep. She was a beautiful woman. Sargent and his friends wiped out her family to get her, but then he slept with her before she had learned the rules.

"These are the rules: Once you've got a collar on, you can't run. Get a certain distance from the control unit and the collar chokes you. I mean it gives you so much pain that you can't keep going. You pass out if you try. We called that getting choked. Touch the control unit and the collar chokes you. It won't work for you anyway. It's got a fingerprint lock. And if the fingers trying to use it are wrong or are dead, it chokes you and stays on choke until someone with the right

OCTAVIA E. BUTLER

living fingers turns it off. Or until you die. When someone threatens a pimp, sometimes he'll make his oldest, least popular whores fight for him, shield him. The truth is, while they're wearing the collars, all his whores will fight for him, no matter how much they hate him. They'll fight hard. They might not even care whether or not they get killed.

"And, of course, if you try to cut, burn, or otherwise damage the collar, it chokes you.

"The girl, she tried to take revenge for her family. She never knew why the other whore Sargent had with him that night stopped her. The other whore begged her not to do it. He tried to explain, but she wouldn't listen. Then Sargent woke up. The next day, he gathered all his whores together and he staked the girl out naked and made us all gather wood and stack it around her and on top of her with just her head showing. Then he made us watch while he . . . while he burned her."

It occurred to me that Marcus was the "other whore" who saved Sargent's life. Maybe he was. I would not ask. Perhaps on some level, the "other whore" was him even if it wasn't, really. A collar, my brother was saying, makes you turn traitor against your kind, against your freedom, against yourself. This was what had been done to him. And what had it made of him? Who and what was he now? No one could go through what he has gone through and not change somehow. No wonder the first of the Earthseed verses had reached him.

I took him to see Zahra and Harry, and they both hugged him, amazed. Zahra, in particular, who had seen him shot and thrown into the fire, kept staring at him and touching him. He stared back at them the way I've seen half-starved people stare at food that they couldn't beg, buy, or steal.

SUNDAY, DECEMBER 19, 2032

"Call me Marcos," my brother said to me as I showed him our school-library-Gathering Hall. He was about to attend his first Gathering, but I had brought him to the school early so that he could see more of what we had built. He seemed impressed with the building and with our collection of salvaged, purchased, and bartered books, but I had gotten the impression that there was something else on his mind. Now here it was.

"I've been Marcos Duran for more than five years now," he said. "I don't really know how to be Marcus Olamina anymore."

I didn't know what to make of that. After a while, I said, "Do you . . . ? Is it that you don't want people to think of me as your sister?"

He looked horrified. "No, Lauren. It's not like that." He paused, thought for a moment. "It's more like Marcus Olamina was my childhood name. I'm not that kid anymore. I'll never be him again."

I nodded. "Okay." And then, "Thanks to Bankole, just about everyone here calls me Olamina, so maybe it's just as well. Less confusing."

"Your husband calls you by your maiden name?"

"He doesn't like my first name, so he ignores it. That's fair. I didn't like his first name either. It's 'Taylor,' by the way, and I ignore it."

My brother shrugged. "Your business, I guess. Just call me Marcos."

I shrugged too. "All right," I said.

WEDNESDAY, DECEMBER 22 , 2032

Bankole is home. He says the doctor in Halstead is dead, and the people there—the mayor and town council—have asked him to move there and become their doctor full time.

He wants to. For my sake and the baby's as well as his own, he wants to more than anything. It's a chance that may not come his way again, he says. He's an old man, he says. He's got to think of the future, and I've got to think of the baby, he says. I've got to be realistic, for god's sake, and stop dreaming, he says.

I'm not conveying the full flavor of this. It's the same old stuff. He's said most of it before, and I'm damned tired of it. But it's worse now. It's scarier. Bankole means it more than he ever has before because he has an offer now—a real offer. And he means it because there is this

OCTAVIA E. BUTLER

small new life between us, growing inside me. I've had no morning sickness, none of the swellings and discomforts and moodiness that Zahra has when she's pregnant. And yet, I don't doubt for a moment that my daughter is within me. Bankole's checked, and he says she's a girl. In gentler moments, we bicker about her name—Beryl like his mother or, from my point of view, almost anything that isn't Beryl. Such an old-fashioned name.

But sometimes all of the ease and the joy and the love that I feel because of our child growing and developing within me seems lost on Bankole. All he seems to see is what he calls my immaturity, my irrational, unrealistic faith in Earthseed, my selfishness, my shortsightedness.

2033

○ ○ ○

From EARTHSEED: THE BOOKS OF THE LIVING

Partnership is giving, taking, learning, teaching, offering the greatest possible benefit while doing the least possible harm. Partnership is mutualistic symbiosis. Partnership is life.

Any entity, any process that cannot or should not be resisted or avoided must somehow be partnered. Partner one another. Partner diverse communities.

Partner life. Partner any world that is your home. Partner God. Only in partnership can we thrive, grow, Change. Only in partnership can we live.

8

○ ○ ○

From EARTHSEED: THE BOOKS OF THE LIVING

Purpose
Unifies us:
It focuses our dreams,
Guides our plans,
Strengthens our efforts.
Purpose
Defines us,
Shapes us,
And offers us
Greatness.

I'm not entirely sure why I've spent so much time looking at my mother's life before I was born. Perhaps it's because this seems the most human, normal time of her life. I wanted to know who she was when she was a young wife and soon-to-be mother, when she was a friend, a sister, and, incidentally, the local minister.

Should she have left Acorn and gone to live in Halstead as my father asked? Of course she should have! And if she had, would she, my father, and I have managed to have normal, comfortable lives through Jarret's upheavals? I believe we would have. My father called her immature, unrealistic, selfish, and shortsighted. Shortsighted, of all things! If there are sins in Earthseed, shortsightedness, lack of forethought, is the worst of them. And yet shortsighted is exactly what she was. She sacrificed us for an idea. And if she didn't know what she was doing, she should have known—she who paid so much attention to the news, to the times and the trends. As an adolescent, she saw her father's error when he could not see it—his dependence on walls and guns, religious faith, and a hope that the good old days would return. Yet what more than that did she have? If her good days were to be in the future on some extrasolar world, that only made them more pathetically unreal.

From *THE JOURNALS OF LAUREN OYA OLAMINA*
SUNDAY, JANUARY 16, 2033

People keep pet dogs in Halstead, as they do in most local cities and towns.

I know that, but I grew up down south, where poor people and dogs didn't run together. They ate one another. Dogs ran in packs, and they were one of the things we were glad our walls kept out. Some of the very rich used vicious dogs to guard their property. They were the only ones who could afford to buy meat, then feed it to a dog. The rest of us, if we got meat, were glad to eat it ourselves.

Even now, it startles me every time I see people and dogs together and peaceful. But the people of local towns and family farms, while not rich, have food enough to share with dogs—even dogs who do no work and only lie around all day with their mouths open and their long, sharp teeth showing. Children play with them. More than once in the past few days, I've had to quell my impulse to snatch a child away from those teeth and beat off the dog.

It's interesting to see that dogs don't like me any more than I like them. We keep out of one another's way. Bankole, on the other hand, likes dogs. He scratches their ears and talks to them. They like him. When he was a boy down south, he kept two or three big ones as pets. Hard to believe that people did that in San Diego or Los Angeles, even thirty or forty years ago.

To please Bankole, I went with him into cold, windy Halstead for a couple of days. I told him it would do no good, but he wanted me to go anyway. I've pleased him so little recently that I agreed to go. He's in love with the place. It's just what he wants: long established, yet

146   OCTAVIA E. BUTLER

modern, familiar, and isolated. There are comfortable big houses—three and four bedrooms. And, thanks to the wind turbines in the hills, along the ridges, there's plenty of electricity most of the time. And there's modern plumbing. We have a little of that now, but it's been a long struggle. Halstead, except for its crumbling coastline, is about as well protected as any town could be. Its population is about 250. That includes the nearest farm families.

Bankole and I have been promised the home of a family who is emigrating—going to homestead in Siberia. Two young-adult sons and the husband of the family have already gone to prepare a place for the women, the younger children, and the grandparents. For this family named Cannon, Bankole's protected, promised land of Halstead is just one more piece of the worn-out, unlivable "old country" that they want to leave behind. They're nice people, but they can't wait to get out of the United States. They say it just doesn't work anymore. The election of Jarret was, for them, the last straw.

And yet the Halstead trip was a good experience for me. I don't get to travel as much as I did before I got pregnant—no salvaging and not as much trading. Bankole nags me to stay home and "behave myself," and most of the time, I give in.

I had forgotten what living in a big modern house was like. Even the cold and the wind weren't that bad. I kind of liked them. The house rattled and creaked, but it was warmed both by electric heaters and by fires in the fireplaces, and it was set far enough back from the coastal bluffs to be in no danger for many years, if ever.

During the first day, I walked out to the bluffs and stood looking at the Pacific Ocean. We can see the ocean every time we travel up the highway to the Eureka-Arcata area and farther north. Up there, it has washed away long stretches of sand dunes and done real damage along the Humboldt and Arcata Bay coastlines. This is all the fault of the steadily rising level of the sea and of occasional, severe storms.

But still, the sea is beautiful. I stood there in the buffeting wind, staring out at the whitecaps and enjoying the sheer vastness of the water. I didn't hear Bankole come up behind me until he was almost beside me. That says something about how safe I felt. I'm more watchful at home in Acorn.

Bankole put his arm around me, and the wind whipped his beard. He smiled. "It is beautiful, isn't it?"

I nodded. "I wonder how people used to living here are going to like living on the vast Siberian plains, even if the plains are warmer than they once were."

He laughed. "When I was a boy, Siberia was a place where the Russians—the Soviets, we called them then—sent people they thought of as criminals and political troublemakers. If anyone then had said that Americans would be giving up their homes and their citizenship and going to make new lives in Siberia, the rest of us would have looked around for a straitjacket for him."

"I suspect it's a human characteristic not to know when you're well off," I said.

He glanced at me sidewise. "Oh, it is," he said. "I see it every day."

I laughed, wrapped an arm around him, and we went back to the Cannon house to a meal of broiled fish, boiled potatoes, Brussels sprouts, and baked apples. The Cannon house sits on a large lot, and, like Bankole and I, the Cannons raise much of their own food. What they can't raise, they buy from local farmers or fishermen. They're also part of a cooperative that evaporates salt for their own use and for sale. But unlike us, they use few wild foods or seasonings—no acorns, cactus fruit, mint, manzanita, not even pine nuts. Surely there will be new foods in Siberia. Would they learn to eat them or would they cling to whatever they could grow or buy of their bland familiar foods?

"Sometimes I can't stand the thought of leaving this house," Thea Cannon said as we sat eating. "But there'll be more opportunity for the children when we leave. What is there for them here?"

I'm not so pregnant that most people notice, and I do wear loose clothing now. But I did think that Thea Cannon, who has seven kids of her own, would have noticed. Maybe she's just too wrapped up in

OCTAVIA E. BUTLER

her own worries. She's a plump, pretty, tired-looking blond woman in her forties, and she always seems a little distracted—as though she has a lot on her mind.

That night, I lay awake beside Bankole, listening to the sounds of the sea and the wind. They're good sounds as long as you don't have to be outside. Back at Acorn, being on watch during rough weather is no joke.

"The mayor tells me the town is willing to hire you to replace one of their teachers," Bankole said, his mouth near my ear and his hand on my stomach where he likes to rest it. "They've got one teacher who's in her late fifties and one who's 79. The older one has been wanting to retire for years. When I told them that you had pretty much set up the school at Acorn and that you taught there, they almost cheered."

"Did you tell them that all I've got is a high school education, a lot of reading, and the courses I audited on my father's computer?"

"I told them. They don't care. If you can help their kids learn enough to pass the high school equivalency tests, they'll figure you've earned your pay. And by the way, they can't actually pay you much in hard currency, but they're willing to let you go on living in the house and raising food in the garden even after I'm dead."

I moved against him, but managed not to say anything. I hate to hear him always talking about dying.

"Aside from the older teacher," he continued, "no one around here has a teaching credential. The older people who do have college degrees *do not* want second or third careers teaching school. Just install some reading, writing, math, history, and science in these kids' heads, and everyone will be happy. You should be able to do it in your sleep after what you've had to put up with in Acorn."

"In my sleep," I said. "That sounds like one definition of life in hell."

He took his hand off my stomach.

"This place is wonderful," I said. "And I love you for trying to provide it for the baby and me. But there's nothing here but existence. I can't give up Acorn and Earthseed to come here and install a dab of education into kids who don't really need me."

"Your child will need you."

"I know."

He said nothing more. He turned over and lay with his back to me. After a while, I slept. I don't know whether he did.

Later, back at home, we didn't talk much. Bankole was angry and unforgiving. He has not yet said a firm "No" to the people of Halstead. That troubles me. I love him and I believed he loves me, but I can't help knowing that he could settle in Halstead without me. He's a self-sufficient man, and he truly believes he's right. He says I'm being childish and stubborn.

Marc agrees with him, by the way, not that either of us has asked Marc what he thinks. But he's still staying with us, and he can't help hearing at least some of our disagreement. He could have avoided mixing in, but I don't think that ever occurred to him.

"What's the matter with you?" he demanded of me this morning just before Gathering. "Why do you want to have a baby in this dump? Just think, you could live in a real house in a real town."

And I got so angry so fast that my only choices were either to be very quiet or to scream at him. He, of all people, should have known better than to say such a thing. We had reached out from our *dump* with money made at our dump. We had found him and freed him. But for us and our *dump*, he would still be a slave and a whore!

"Come to Gathering," I said in almost a whisper. And I walked out of the house away from him.

He followed me to Gathering, but he never apologized. I don't think he ever realized that he had said something vile.

After Gathering, Gray Mora came up to me and said, "I hear you're leaving."

I was surprised. I don't suppose I should have been. Bankole and I don't scream at one another and broadcast our troubles the way the Figueroas and the Faircloths do, but no doubt it's clear to everyone that there's something wrong between us. And then there was Marc.

He might tell people—just out of a need to be important. He does have a consuming need to be important, to reassert his manhood.

"I'm not leaving," I told Gray.

He frowned. "You sure? I heard you were moving to Halstead."

"I'm not leaving."

He drew in a long breath and let it out. "Good. This place would probably go to hell without you." And he turned and walked away. That was Gray. I thought back when he joined us that he might be trouble, or that he wouldn't stay. Instead, he turned out to be dependability itself—as long as you didn't want a lot of conversation or demonstrative friendliness. If you were loyal to Gray and his family, he was loyal to you.

Later, after dinner, Zahra Balter pulled me out of a set of dramatic readings that three of the older kids were giving of their own work or of published work that they liked. I was enjoying Gray's stepdaughter Tori Mora's reading of some comic poetry that she had written. The more laughter in Acorn, the better. And I was drawing Tori, tall and lean and angular, a handsome girl rather than a pretty one. I had discovered that drawing was so different from everything else I did that it relaxed me, and at the same time, it roused me to a new alertness—a new kind of alertness. I've begun to perceive color and texture, line and shape, light and shadow with new intensity. I go into these focused, trancelike states and draw really terrible stuff. My friends laugh at the drawings, but they tell me they're getting better, getting recognizable. Zahra told me a couple of weeks ago that a drawing I'd done of Harry looked almost human.

But this time Zahra hadn't come to talk about my drawing.

"So you're going to leave!" she hissed at me as soon as we were alone. She looked angry and bitter. Here and there around us, people found their own Gathering Day amusements. May was teaching Mercy Noyer how to weave a small basket from tree bark. A few adults and older kids had gotten a soccer game going in spite of the cold. Marc and Jorge were out there on opposite sides, having a great time running up and down the field, getting filthy, and collecting more than their share of bruises. Travis, who also loves soccer, has said, "I think those two would kill each other for a chance to score."

If only Marc would confine himself to scoring in soccer.

Of course, I wasn't as surprised at Zahra's question as I had been at Gray's. "Zee, I'm not leaving," I said.

Like Gray, she didn't believe me at first. "I heard you were. Your brother said. . . . Lauren, tell me the truth!"

"Bankole wants me to move to Halstead," I said. "You know that. I don't want to go. I think we've got something worthwhile going here, and it's ours."

"I heard they offered you a house by the ocean?"

"Within sight of the ocean, but not that close. You don't want to be too close to the ocean in Halstead."

"But a real house, I mean. A house like back in Robledo."

"Yes."

"And you turned them down?"

"Yes."

"You're crazy as hell."

That did startle me. "You mean you want me to go, Zee?"

"Don't be stupid. You're the closest thing I got to a sister. You know damned well I don't want you to go. But . . . you should go."

"I'm not."

"I would."

I stared at her.

"I'd go to a better place if I could. I got two kids. Where do they go from here? Where's your little baby going from here?"

"Where would they go from Halstead? Halstead is like Robledo with a better wall. Why do you think there are people there who are planning to emigrate to Russia or Alaska and others who are just trying to hang on to their little piece of the twentieth century until they die? None of them is trying to build anything to replace what we've lost or to boost us to something better."

"You mean like Earthseed? The Destiny?"

"Yes."

"It ain't enough."

"It's a beginning. It's a way of trying to build tomorrow instead of cycling back into some form of yesterday."

"Do you ever stop preaching?"

"Am I wrong?"

She shrugged. "You know I'm not religious the way you are. Besides, even if you go to Halstead, we'll still be here. And Earthseed will still be Earthseed."

Would it? Maybe. But Earthseed is a young movement. I couldn't walk away and leave it to a "maybe." I *wouldn't* walk away from it any more than I'd walk away from the baby I would soon be having. Someday, I want people to go from here and teach Earthseed. And I want what they teach to still be recognizable as Earthseed.

"I'm not going," I said. "And, Zee, I think you're a liar. I don't think you'd go either. You know that here at Acorn we're with you if you get into trouble. And you know we would take care of your kids if anything happened to you and Harry. Who else would do that?" She had been raised in some of the nastier streets of Los Angeles, and she knew about loyalty, about depending on her friends and having them depend on her.

She looked at me, then looked away. "It's good here," she said, staring out toward the hills to the west of us. "It's better than I thought it could be when we got here. But you know it's nothing like as good as we had back in Robledo. For your baby's sake, you ought to go."

"For my baby's sake, I'm staying."

And she met my eyes again. "You sure? Think about the future."

"I'm sure. And you know damned well I am thinking about the future."

She was silent for a moment. Then she sighed. "Good." Another silence. "You're right. I wouldn't want to go, and I wouldn't want you to go either. Maybe that's because I'm as big a fool as you are. I don't know. But . . . we do have something good here. Acorn and Earth-seed—they're both too good to let go of." She grinned. "How's Bankole dealing with things?"

"Not well."

"No. He tries to give you what any sane woman would want, and you don't want it. Poor guy."

She went away, smiling. I was heading back to the reading and my sketch pad when Jorge Cho came up to me, sweaty and filthy from the game. He was with his girlfriend Diamond Scott, tiny and black and every hair in place as usual. I saw the question on their faces before Jorge spoke.

"Is it true that you're leaving?"

THURSDAY, JANUARY 20 , 2033

Jarret was inaugurated today.

We listened to his speech—short and rousing. Plenty of "America, America, God shed his grace on thee," and "God bless America," and "One nation, indivisible, under God," and patriotism, law, order, sacred honor, flags everywhere, Bibles everywhere, people waving one of each. His sermon—because that's what it was—was from Isaiah, Chapter One. "Your country is desolate, your cities are burned with fire: your land, strangers devour it in your presence, and it is desolate as overthrown by strangers."

And then, "Come now, and let us reason together, saith the Lord: though your sins be as scarlet, they shall be as white as snow; though they be red like crimson, they will be as wool. If ye be willing and obedient, ye shall eat the good of the land. But if ye refuse and rebel, ye shall be devoured with the sword: for the mouth of the Lord hath spoken it."

Then, he spoke of peace, rebuilding and healing. "A strong Christian America," he said, "needs strong Christian American soldiers to reunite, rebuild, and defend it." In almost the same breath, he spoke of both "the generosity and the love that we must show to one another, to all of our fellow Christian Americans," and "the destruction we must visit upon traitors and sinners, those destroyers in our midst."

I'd call it a fire-and-brimstone speech, but what happens now?

SUNDAY, FEBRUARY 6 , 2033

Yesterday Marc told Bankole that he intended to hold services of his own on Gathering Day. He would, he said, speak just before our regular gathering. It seemed that he was remembering his time with the Durans in Robledo, remembering his carport church, and wanting to recapture that image of himself.

Bankole sent him to me. "Don't go out of your way to make trouble," Bankole told him. "Your sister has been good to you. Tell her what you intend to do."

"She can't stop me!" my brother said.

"Do what's right," Bankole told him. "You have a conscience. Don't go behind your sister's back."

So later in the day, Marc found me sitting with Channa Ryan, sorting and cataloging books. We're always behind in that, and it needs to be done. All of our kids work on projects as part of their education. Each kid does at least one group project and one individual project per year. Most kids find the two unrelated projects influencing one another in unexpected ways. This helps the kids begin to learn how the world works, how all sorts of things interact and influence one another. The kids begin to teach themselves and one another. They begin to learn how to learn. With their mentors' help, they each choose some aspect of history, science, math, art, or whatever and learns it well enough to teach it. Then they do just that. They teach it. To do a good job, they need to be able to find out what information we have available here and what they're going to have to go to the nets for. Since we aren't rich yet, the more we can offer them from our own library, the better.

Still, cataloging is tedious. I was almost glad when Marc came and interrupted my work. He and I went outside to talk.

"I want to get back to what I really care about," he said as we sat together on a handsome bench that Allie Gilchrist had made. Allie's discovered a real liking for building furniture, and she's worked as hard to learn to do it well as she has to learn to assist Bankole well.

"What?" I asked Marc, hoping that what he wanted was something that we could accommodate. No one wanted more than I did for him to find his own interests and get into work that he cared about.

"I want to start my church again," he said. "I want to preach. I'm not asking your permission. I'm just letting you know. With Jarret in office, you need someone like me anyway so that you'll be able to say you're not a Satanist cult."

I sighed. All of a sudden I could feel myself all but sagging with weariness and dread. But I only said, "If Jarret noticed us and wanted to call us a Satanic cult, your preaching wouldn't stop him. Would you be willing to speak *at* Gathering?"

That surprised him. "You mean while you're having your services?"

"Yes."

"I won't talk about Earthseed. I want to preach."

"Preach, then."

"What's the catch?"

"You should know. You've been to our services. You choose the topic. You say what you want. But afterward there will be questions and discussion."

"I'm not out to teach a class. I want to preach a sermon."

"That's not our way, Marc. If you speak, you have to face questions and discussion. You need to be ready for that. Besides, no matter what you call it, a good sermon is just a lesson that you're trying to teach."

"But . . . you won't try to get in the way of my preaching at the Gathering if I take questions afterward?"

"That's right."

"Then I'll do it."

"It's no joke, Marc."

"I know. It's no joke to me either."

"I mean we're as serious about the discussion as you are about the sermon. Some of our people might probe and dissect in ways you won't like."

"Okay, I can handle it."

No, I didn't think he could. But an unpleasant thing should be done quickly if it must be done at all. My brother had a sermon ready. He'd been working on it in his spare moments. Since I was scheduled to speak at the Gathering this morning, I was able to step aside for him, let him speak at once.

He didn't pull his punches. He confronted us, challenged us directly from the Bible—first from Isaiah again, "The grass withereth, the flower fadeth; but the word of our God will stand for ever." Then later from Malachi, "For I am the Lord. I change not." And then from Hebrews, "Jesus Christ the same yesterday, and today, and for ever. Be not carried about with divers and strange doctrines."

Marc doesn't have our father's impressive voice, and he knows it. He uses what he has skillfully, and, of course, it helps that he's so good-looking. But once he had preached his sermon on the change-lessness of God, Jorge Cho spoke up. Jorge was next to Diamond Scott as usual. He has told me he intends to marry Di, but Di has been looking at my brother in a way that Jorge doesn't like at all. There's a rivalry between Marc and Jorge anyway. They're both young and competitive.

"We believe that all things change," Jorge said, "Even though all things don't necessarily change in all ways. Why do you believe God doesn't change?"

My brother smiled. "But even you believe that your God doesn't change. Your God promotes change, but he stays the same."

That surprised me. Marc shouldn't have made such avoidable mistakes. He's had plenty of time to read, talk, and hear about Earthseed, but somehow, he's misunderstood.

Travis was the first to point out the error. "God *is* Change," he said. "God *promotes* nothing. Nothing at all."

And Zahra, of all people, said, "Our God isn't male. Change has no sex. Marc, you don't know enough about us yet even to criticize us."

Jorge began repeating his question before Zahra had finished. "Why do you think your God doesn't change? How can you prove it."

"I have faith that it's true," Marc said. "Belief must be based on faith as much as on proofs."

"But there must be some test," Jorge said. "You must have a way to know when your faith is sensible and when it makes no sense."

"The test is the Bible, of course. When the Bible tells us something—in this case, it tells us several times—we can believe it. We can have faith that it is true."

Antonio Cortez, Lucio's oldest nephew, jumped in. "Look," he said, "in the Bible, God does things. Things happen and he reacts. He makes things. He gets angry. He destroys things. . . ."

"But he, himself, doesn't change," my brother said.

"Oh, come on," Tori Mora shouted in open disgust. "To take action is to change. It's to go from action to inaction. And he goes from calmness to anger—he gets angry a lot. And—"

"And in Genesis," her stepsister Doe said, "he lets some of his favorite men have children with their sisters or daughters. Then in Leviticus and Deuteronomy, he says anyone who does that should be killed."

"Right," Jorge said. "I was just reading that last week. It is no good to say that something is true because the Bible says it is true and then forget that a few pages later, the Bible says—or shows—something completely different."

"Every time any god is accepted by a new group of people, that god changes," Harry Balter said.

"I think," Marta Figueroa Castro said in her gentlest voice, "that the verses you read, Marc, mean that God is always God, always there for us, always dependable that way. And, of course, it means that God and God's word will never die."

"Yes, so much of the Bible is metaphor," Diamond Scott said. She, too, spoke very gently. "I remember that my mother used to try to take it absolutely literally, but it just meant she had to ignore some things and twist others." Beside her, Jorge smiled.

The discussion went on for a while longer. Then other people began to take pity on Marc. They let him end the discussion. They had never been out to humiliate him. Well, maybe Jorge had, but even Jorge had been polite. Things would have gone better for Marc if he had done his homework, and things would have been more interesting and involving for his audience. He might even have won over a Faircloth or a Peralta. I had worried about that.

The truth is, I let him speak today because I wanted him to speak before he was truly ready. I wish I hadn't had to do that. I wish he had wanted to do something else—anything else—to get his self-respect back and begin to rebuild himself. I have tried to interest him in the several kinds of work we do here. He isn't lazy. He pulls his weight. But he doesn't like fieldwork or working with animals or trading or teaching or salvaging or carpentry. He tried repairing salvaged tools, but it bothered him that he had so much to learn even about simple things. He all but ruined a pair of heavy-duty shears that he was supposed to be sharpening. He tried to grind their almost square edges to thin, sharp blades, and Travis gave him the chewing out he deserved.

"If you don't know, *ask*," Travis had shouted. "Nobody expects you to know everything. Just ask! This shit is easy to do if you just take the trouble to learn a few basics. Work with me for a while. Don't try to go off on your own."

But my brother needed to "go off on his own," to have his own turf where he was the one who said yes or no, and where everyone respected him. He needed that more than he needed anything, and he meant to have it all at once.

But now, instead of feeling important and proud, he feels angry and embarrassed. I had to let him inflict those feelings on himself. I couldn't let him begin to divide Acorn. More important—much more important—I couldn't let him begin to divide Earthseed.

9

○ ○ ○

From EARTHSEED: THE BOOKS OF THE LIVING

To make peace with others,
Make peace with yourself:
Shape God
With generosity
And compassion.
Minimize harm.
Shield the weak.
Treasure the innocent.
Be true to the Destiny.
Forgive your enemies.
Forgive yourself.

My mother was quite open in her journal about the fact that she
didn't know what she was doing, and that this was a terrible frustration to her. She meant to make Earthseed a nationwide movement,
but she had no idea how to do this. She seemed to have vague plans
to someday send out Earthseed missionaries, to use Acorn as a kind
of school for such missionaries. Perhaps this is what she would have
done if she'd had the chance. It might even have worked. It's worked
for other cults. It might have gained her a larger following, more
recognition.

But she didn't want simple recognition. She wanted people to
believe. She had a truth that she wanted to teach and an outer-space
Destiny that she wanted taken seriously and someday fulfilled. And it's
obvious from her treatment of Uncle Marc that she was very territorial
about the whole thing. I don't know whether Uncle Marc ever realized
how she set him up to fail and to make a bad first impression with her

people. Such a simple, subtle thing. He imagined that she had done something much more obvious and complicated.

She didn't fight people unless she was pretty sure she was going to win. When she wasn't sure, she found ways to avoid fighting or go along with her opponents until they tripped themselves up or put themselves in a position for her to trip them up. Smart, I suppose—or treacherous, depending on your point of view.

She learned from everyone, used everyone and everything. I think if I had died at birth, she would have managed to learn something from my death that would be useful to Earthseed.

From *THE JOURNALS OF LAUREN OYA OLAMINA*
SATURDAY, FEBRUARY 19, 2033

I feel more strongly than I ever have that there will soon be war.

President Jarret is still stirring up bad feelings over Alaska, or as he describes it, "our truant forty-ninth state." He paints Alaska's President Leontyev and the Alaskan legislature as the real enemies—as "that gang of traitors and thieves who are trying to steal a vast, rich portion of these *United* States for themselves. These people want to treat all of Alaska as their own personal, private property. Can we let them get away with it? Can we let them cheat us, rob us, destroy our country, use our sacred constitution as waste paper? Can we forget that 'If a house be divided against itself, that house cannot stand?' Jesus Christ spoke those words 2000 years ago. President Abraham Lincoln paraphrased them in 1858. Was Lincoln wrong? Was—dare we ask it? Dare we imagine it? Was Christ wrong? Was our Lord, wrong?"

He's so good at asking nasty rhetorical questions—so good at encouraging young men—not young women, only men—to "Do your duty, to your country and to yourselves. Prove yourselves men worthy to be called good Christian American soldiers. Serve your country, now that it has such great need of you." They're to do all this by joining the armed services. I've never heard a president talk this way—although I have read about presidents and leaders of other nations who talked this way when they were preparing for war. Jarret said nothing about drafting people, but Bankole says that may be next. Bankole was down in Sacramento a couple of days ago, and he says a lot of people think it's "time we taught that bunch of traitors up in Alaska a lesson."

It shouldn't be so easy to nudge people toward what might be their own destruction.

"Who was doing the talking?" I asked him as he unpacked medical supplies. He keeps most of his supplies in our cabin until they're needed at the clinic. That way they're less likely to tempt children or thieves. "I mean, was it most of the people you talked to or just a few?"

"Mostly men," he said. "Some young and some old enough to know better. I think a lot of the younger ones would like a war. War is exciting. A boy can prove himself, become a man—if he lives. He'll be given a gun and trained to shoot people. He'll be a powerful part of a powerful team. Chances are, he won't think about the people who'll be shooting back at him, bombing him, or otherwise trying to kill him until he faces them."

I thought about the young single men of Acorn—Jorge Cho, Esteban Peralta, Antonio Figueroa, and even my brother Marc, and shook my head. "Did you ever want to go to war?" I asked.

"Never," Bankole answered. "I wanted to be a healer. I was damned idealistic about it. Believe me, that was a daunting enough challenge for a young Black boy in the late twentieth century—much harder than learning to kill. It never occurred to me back in the 1990s when I was in medical school that in spite of my ideals, I would have to learn to do both."

MONDAY, FEBRUARY 28 , 2033

Marc spoke at Gathering yesterday. This is the third time he's done it. Each time he learns more about Earthseed and tries harder to convince us that our beliefs are nonsense. He seems to have decided that the unity, the Christianity, and the hope that Jarret has brought to the country makes Jarret not the monster we all feared but a potential savior. The country, he tells us, must get back to God or it is finished.

"The Earthseed Destiny," he said yesterday, "is an airy nothing. The country is bleeding to death in poverty, slavery, chaos, and sin. This is the time for us to work for our salvation, not to divert our attention to fantasy explorations of extrasolar worlds."

Travis, trying to explain, said, "The Destiny is important for the lessons it forces us to learn while we're here on Earth, for the people it encourages us to become. It's important for the unity and purpose that it gives us here on Earth. And in the future, it offers us a kind of species adulthood and species immortality when we scatter to the stars."

My brother laughed. "If you're looking for immortality in outer space," he said, "you've been misled. You already have an immortal soul, and where that soul spends eternity is up to you. Remember the Tower of Babel! You can follow Earthseed, build your way to go to the stars, fall down into chaos, and wind up in hell! Or you can follow the will of God. And if you follow God's will, you can live forever, secure and happy, in God's true heaven."

Zahra Balter, loyal in spite of her personal beliefs, spoke up before I could. "Marc," she said, "if we have immortal souls, don't you think we'll take them with us even if we go to the stars?"

"Why do you find it so easy," Michael Kardos asked, "to believe we go to heaven after we die, but so hard to believe we can go into the heavens while we're alive? Following the Earthseed Destiny is difficult. Massively difficult. That's the challenge. But if we want to do it, someday we'll do it. It's not impossible."

I had spoken the same words to him shortly after he came to live at Acorn. He had said then with bitter contempt that the Destiny was meaningless. All he wanted to do, he said, was to earn enough money to house, feed, and clothe his family. Once he was able to do that, he said, then maybe he'd have time for science fiction.

Indeed.

OCTAVIA E. BUTLER

Marc has gone.

He left yesterday with the Peraltas. They're gone for good too. They were the ones Marc managed to reach. They've always felt that we should be more Christian and more patriotic. They say Andrew Jarret is our elected leader—Ramiro Peralta and his daughter Pilar helped elect him—and a minister of God, so he deserves our respect. Esteban Peralta is going to enlist in the army. He believes—the whole family believes—it's our patriotic duty, everyone's duty, to support Jarret in his "heroic" effort to revive and reunify the country. They don't believe Jarret's a fascist. They don't believe that the church burnings, witch burnings, and other abuses are Jarret's doing. "Some of his followers are young and excitable," Ramiro Peralta says. "Jarret will put their asses into uniform. Then they'll learn some discipline. Jarret hates all this chaos the way I hate it. That's why I voted for him. Now he'll start putting things right!"

It's true that there haven't been any burnings or beatings since Jarret was inaugurated—or none that I've heard of, and I've been paying attention to the news. I don't know what this means, but I don't believe it means everything's all right. I don't think the Peraltas believe it either. I think they're just scared, and getting out of any potential line of fire. If Jarret does crack down on people who don't fit into his religious notions, they don't want to be here at Acorn.

My brother, on the other hand, used to despise Jarret. Now he says Jarret is just what America needs. And I'm afraid that it's me he's begun to despise. He blames me for the failure of his Gathering Day sermons. He's gained no followers. The Peraltas like him and sort of agree with him. Pilar Peralta is more than half in love with him, but even they don't see him as a minister. They see him as a nice boy. In fact, that's the way most people here in Acorn see him. He thinks this is my fault. He believes, he insists, that I coached people to attack and humiliate him at all three Gatherings. And he says with a weary, irritating, *honest* smile, "I forgive you. I might have done the same thing to protect my turf if I had any turf to protect."

I think it was the smile that made me say more than I should have. "The truth is," I told him, "You were given a special privilege. If you were anyone else, you could have been expelled for preaching another belief system. I let you do it because you've been through so much hell, and I knew it was important to you. And because you're my brother." I would have called back the words if I could have. He would hear pity in them. He would hear condescension.

For a long moment, he stared at me. I watched him get angry—very angry. Then he seemed to push his anger away. He refused to react to it. He shrugged.

"Think of the Gatherings you've attended," I said to him. "Name even one that didn't involve questions, challenges, argument. It's our way. I did warn you. Anyone can be questioned on any subject they choose to teach or advocate. I told you that we were serious about it. We learn at least as much by discussion as by lecture, demonstration, or experience."

"Forget about it," he said. "It's done. I don't blame you. Really. I shouldn't have tried my hand here. I'll make a place for myself somewhere else."

Still no anger expressed. Yet he was furious. He wouldn't show it and he wouldn't talk about it, but it came off him like heat. Perhaps that's what a collar teaches—a horrible kind of self-control. Or perhaps not. My brother was always a self-contained person. He knew how to be unreachable.

I sighed and gave him as much money as I could afford, plus a rifle, a sidearm, and ammunition for both. He's not a very good shot with anything yet, but he knows the basics, and I couldn't let him go out and wind up in the hands of someone like Cougar again. The Peralta family had been with us for two years, so they had money and possessions as a result of their work with us. Marc did not. We drove him and the Peraltas into Eureka. There, they might find homes and jobs, or at

OCTAVIA E. BUTLER

least they might find temporary shelter until they could decide what to do.

"I thought you knew me," I said to my brother just before he left us. "I wouldn't do what you're accusing me of."

He shrugged. "It's okay. Don't keep worrying about it." He smiled. And he was gone.

I don't know how to feel about this. So many people have come here and stayed or wanted to stay even if, for some reason, they couldn't. I had to expel a thief a year ago, and he cried and begged to stay. We had caught him stealing drugs from Bankole's medical supplies, so he had to go, but he cried.

As they left us, even the Peraltas looked grim and frightened. They were Ramiro, the father; Pilar, 18; Esteban, 17; and Eva, who was only two and whose birth at a rest stop along the highway had cost her mother's life. They had no other relatives left alive, no friends outside of Acorn who would help them if they got into trouble. And Esteban would be leaving them soon to enlist. They had good reason to look worried.

Marc would be in the same situation once he left us. Worse, he would be all alone. Yet he smiled.

I don't know whether I'll ever see him again. I feel almost as though he's died . . . died again.

THURSDAY, MARCH 17 , 2033

Dan Noyer found his way back to us last night.

He came back. Amazing. I think he's been gone longer than he was with us. We tried to find him—for his little sisters' sakes as much as for his. But unless you have the money to hire a small army of private cops like that guy in Texas, finding people in today's chaos is almost impossible. My finding Marcus was an accident. Anyway, Dan came home on his own, poor boy.

It was a cold night. We had all gone to bed except for the first watch of the night.

The watchers were Gray Mora and Zahra Balter.

Zahra was the one who spotted the intruders. As she described it to me later, she saw two people running, staggering, sometimes seeming to hold one another up. If not for the staggering, Zahra might have fired a warning shot, at least. But before she revealed herself, she wanted to see who or what the runners were escaping from.

As she scanned the hills behind them, she tapped out our emergency signal on her phone.

There were five people chasing the staggering runners—or, with her night-vision glasses, she could see five. She kept looking for more.

One of the five shouted, then fell, and Zahra realized that that one must have blundered into the edge of our thorn fence. In the dark, some of our thorn bushes don't look that savage. They're pretty if you don't touch them. Some will even be covered with flowers soon. But they grab clothing and flesh, and they tear.

The injured one's four companions slowed, seemed to hesitate, then sped up again as the injured one limped after them.

Zahra put her rifle on automatic and fired a short burst across the path of the two front runners. They stopped short and dived into the thorn bushes and cactuses. One began to fire in Zahra's general direction. There were shouts of pain and loud curses. Then all five were shooting. Down in Acorn, we could hear the gunfire. Even without the phone, we would have known that it was coming from the area around Zahra's watch station.

Zahra and Harry are my oldest friends, and I'm Change-sister to them and Change-aunt to their kids Tabia and Russell. For that reason, I paid no attention to Bankole when he told me to stay in the house. I remember thinking that if this were another Dovetree-like raid, staying inside was only asking to burn.

But this didn't sound like what happened at Dovetree. It wasn't loud enough. There weren't enough attackers. This sounded like a small gang raid of a kind we hadn't had for years.

Bankole and I slipped out of the house together and headed for the truck. For most of the run, we were protected by the bulk first of our own cabin, then of the school. I suppose that's why Bankole didn't try as hard as he might have to make me stay behind. We couldn't be seen, let alone shot at. We keep the truck parked in its own space on the south side of the school. It's protected there in the center of the community, and during the day we can spread its solar wings and let it recharge its batteries.

Harry Balter reached the truck just as Bankole and I got there. He opened a side door, and all three of us scrambled in.

Harry and I have gotten comfortable with the truck's computers. In our earlier lives down south, we both used our parents' computers. We're unusual. Most adults at Acorn had never touched or even seen a computer before. Still others are afraid of them. For now, although we're passing on our knowledge, we're still among the few who take full advantage of what the truck can do with its weapons, maneuverability, and sensory systems.

We turned everything on, and Bankole drove us toward Zahra's current watch station. As we rode, we used the truck's infrared viewer to locate each of the intruders. Bankole is a good, steady driver, and he has confidence in the truck's armor. It didn't seem to bother him at all that people were shooting at us. In fact, it was a good thing the intruders were wasting ammunition on us. That gave Zahra some relief.

Then we had a look around, and we decided that one of the intruders was much too close to Zahra—and creeping closer. He could have been trying to get away, but he wasn't. None of them were. We made sure the targets we had identified were, in fact, targets, and not our own people. Once we were sure, we pointed them out to the truck and let it open up on them. Along with the truck's ability to "see" in the dark via infrared, ambient light, or radar, it also has very good "hearing," and an incorrectly designated sense of "smell." This last is based on spectroscopic analysis rather than on actual smelling, but it is a kind of chemical analysis over a distance. It could be used on anything that emitted or reflected electro-magnetic radiation—light—of some kind.

And the truck had plenty of memory. It could, and had, recorded all that it could of each of us—our voices, hand and foot prints, retinal prints, body sounds, and our general shapes in several positions to help it recognize us and not shoot us.

When the truck began shooting, I left the forward monitors to Harry. I didn't need to see anything that might make me useless, and the truck didn't need any more help from me. Once we were between Zahra and the attackers, I checked Zahra on an aft screen. She was alive and still at her station. Most of her body was concealed within the depression and behind the stone shelter that was intended to shield her. Some distance away, Gray Mora was still at his station and still alive. He wasn't involved in this, and his duty was to hold his position and guard the other most likely approach to Acorn. It had taken a while for us to learn not to be distracted by people who might rattle the front door while their friends slipped in through the back.

The intruder nearest to Zahra was dead. According to the truck, he was no longer changing the chemistry of the air in his immediate vicinity in a way that indicated breathing, and he wasn't moving. Once the truck was stopped, its ability to detect motion was as good as its hearing. Put the two together and we could detect breathing and heart-beat—or their absence. We've tried to trick it—fool it into mistaking one of us playing dead for an actual corpse—and we've never been able to. That's comforting.

"All right," Harry said, looking up from his screen. "How's Zee?"

"Alive," I told him. "Are all the shooters down?"

"Down and dead, all five of them." He drew a deep breath. "Bankole, let's go pick up Zahra."

"Has anyone given Gray an all-clear?" I asked.

"I have," Bankole answered. "You know, I've got the next watch. In another hour, I would have relieved Zahra."

"For the rest of the night," I said, "whoever's on duty should watch from the truck. Whoever these guys are, they might have friends."

Bankole nodded.

OCTAVIA E. BUTLER

He stopped us as close to Zahra's watch station as the truck could get. We all took one more look around, then Harry opened the door. Before we could call her, Zahra darted from cover and jumped into the truck. She was bleeding from the left side of her face and neck, and that took me by surprise. At once, I felt pain in my own face and neck, but managed not to react. Habit. Harry grabbed Zahra and yelled for Bankole.

"I'm okay," Zahra said. "I just got hit by broken rock when those guys were shooting. There was rock flying everywhere."

I went up to take Bankole's place, and he went back to check on her. I'm a pretty decent driver now, so I got us back to the houses. "I'll take what's left of Zahra's watch," I said. "Your watch, too, Bankole. I think you're going to be busy."

"Watch from the truck!" Bankole ordered as though I hadn't just made the same suggestion myself.

"Of course."

"Whatever happened to the two people those gunmen were chasing?" Zahra asked.

We all looked at her.

"They were staggering toward Acorn." she said. "They couldn't have gotten far. I didn't shoot them. They were already hurt."

This was the first we knew of the running pair. Zahra thought they were both wounded, and both men. Yet we hadn't spotted them. Of course, we hadn't looked back toward Acorn for more intruders. I hadn't even used the aft screens to do that. Stupid of me.

We looked around Acorn now, and found the usual signs of life— plenty of heat and some sound from the houses. The people were no doubt watching, but in the middle of the night, they wouldn't come rushing out until they got an all-clear from us. The older kids would be keeping an eye on the younger ones, and the adults would be watching us. No one was showing a light or moving around where they could be seen. The only loud sound was that of a baby crying from the Douglas house. Even that came to an abrupt stop.

If this had been a drill, it would have been a good drill.

But where were the two runners? Were they hiding? Had they found their way into the school or into one of the houses? Were they crouching behind one of the trees?

Were they armed?

"I don't think they had guns," Zahra said when I asked her.

Then I spotted them—or spotted something. I drove toward it, toward our own cabin, in fact—Bankole's and mine.

"The truck says they're still alive," I said. "They're not moving much, and Zee's right. They're not armed. But they're alive."

The runners were Dan Noyer and a young girl. The moment I saw her—tall like Dan, but slender, pretty, dark-haired with a sharp little chin like Mercy's—I knew she must be one of Dan's sisters. As it turned out, she was Nina Noyer.

Both brother and sister had been beaten bloody with both fists, and with something else. Bankole says they look as though they've been lashed with whips.

"I suppose," he said with great bitterness, "that people who don't have access to convict collars might have to exert themselves—resort to older methods of torture."

Brother and sister have rope burns at their wrists, ankles, and necks. Also, Bankole says, they've suffered a great deal of sexual abuse. The girl told him they were forced "to do it with strangers for money." Dan has endured even more beating than Nina has, and both have what Bankole calls, "the usual infections and tissue damage." Nina says she got pregnant, but one night during her captivity, she had a miscarriage. She hadn't known what was happening, but one of the other slaves told her. Well, I suppose it would be surprising if she hadn't gotten pregnant. For her sake, I'm glad she miscarried.

And Dan had somehow found her, rescued her, and brought her home in spite of pursuers chasing him right down into our valley. How had one 15-year-old done so very much?

OCTAVIA E. BUTLER

And in the end, what would it cost him? In the end, did that matter?

FRIDAY, MARCH 18, 2033

"This is no way to live," Bankole said to me when he came in from tending Dan and Nina this morning. He sat at the table and put his head down on his arms.

I had taken his watch, as I promised, to free him to do what he could for Dan and Nina. Allie and May were helping him, since they have all but joined the Noyer family by taking care of Kassia and Mercy for so long.

Bankole had spent most of his time with his two patients, and had once again found himself fighting for Dan's life. The boy stopped breathing twice, and Bankole revived him. But at last, the young body, once strong and healthy, just gave up. It had taken an incredible amount of abuse over the past few months.

"His heart just quit," Bankole said. "If I had more modern equipment, maybe. . . . Goddamnit, Olamina, can you see now why I need to get out of here and get you out of here?"

"He's really dead?" I whispered, not believing it—not wanting to believe it.

"He's dead. It's obscene! A young boy like that."

"What about his sister."

"She wasn't as badly beaten as he was. I believe she'll be all right."

Would she, after all that had happened? I doubted it. Bankole and I sat silent for a while, each of us thinking our own thoughts. What would it have meant to Dan that he had saved his sister, even though he had not been able to save himself? Did he ever imagine such a thing? Would it somehow have been all right? Enough?

"Where's the other sister—Paula?" I asked. "What happened to her?"

Bankole sighed. "Dead. Some trouble on the road up north around

Trinidad. Three men tried to steal her. They got caught. Her owners and the thieves shot it out, and she was in the middle. Nina says her owners just cursed her for getting in the way and getting killed. They left her body lying among the rocks by the sea. Nina said Paula loved the sea when the family saw it for the first time last year. She said she hoped the tide came in and carried her away.

I shook my head. Bankole got up and went to lie on the bed.

"But Dan did it," I said more to myself than to him. "He found his sister, and he brought her home. It was *impossible*, but he did it!"

"Shit," Bankole said, and turned his face to the wall.

Now the long day is over.

We've cleaned up the hillside battlefield and thrown ground pepper over parts of it so that any smell of blood that still clings to it wouldn't hold the attention of wild dogs.

We've collected the dead, searched their bodies, then after dark, surrounded them with scrap wood, soaked them in lamp oil, and burned them. We do a thorough job, and the smoke is less noticeable at night—less of a lure to scavengers and to the curious.

I hate doing this—burning the dead. Of course, whether they're our dead or someone else's, it has to be done, but I hate it.

We burned Dan separate from his attackers. I set his pyre alight myself. Allie chose the verse and spoke it. We'll have a full service for Dan when Nina is well enough to attend. For now, though, I think Allie made a good choice.

> *"As wind,*
> *As water,*
> *As fire,*
> *As life,*
> *God*
> *Is both creative and destructive,*
> *Demanding and yielding,*
> *Sculptor and clay.*

OCTAVIA E. BUTLER

God
Is Infinite Potential.
God
Is Change."

The other dead—the intruders—were four men and a woman, all in their twenties or early thirties. They were dirty and scratched up, but well-dressed, well-armed, well-heeled. They had plenty of Canadian money in their pockets. Were they slavers? Drug dealers? Thieves? Rich kids slumming? Even Nina wasn't sure. She and Dan had escaped from their original captors and had been on the highway, headed for Acorn when this new group spotted them and came after them.

The intruders weren't carrying identification or even a change of clothing. That means they had homes or a base of some kind nearby. We thought about that and decided to burn their clothing along with their bodies. It's of much better quality than our own—newer, more fashionable, and more expensive. If we wear it, it might be recognized at one of the street markets. And another thing. Two of the intruders were wearing black sweatshirts with white crosses embroidered on them—embroidered, not printed. These weren't the long tunics that Aubrey Dovetree mentioned, but they were interesting imitations. The intruders were thugs of some kind who had decided it was fashionable to look like Jarret's people.

The intruders' guns are, like our own, good-quality, well-cared-for automatic rifles with laser sites. One is German, one's American, and the three newest are Russian. They're all as illegal as hell and as common as oranges. We'll hide them in our survival caches scattered through the mountains. The only thing they had that we'll keep with us and use, as we need it, is some of their money. Most of that will go in the caches too. It's all worn and wrinkled and not identifiable. The fact that there's so much of it—more per person than any group of us would carry around—tells us that these people were either rich or involved in some profitable illegal activity, or both.

Well, now they're gone. People vanish in this world. Even rich people out for fun and greater profit vanish. It happens all the time.

OCTAVIA E. BUTLER

10

○ ○ ○

From EARTHSEED: THE BOOKS OF THE LIVING

We can,
Each of us,
Do the impossible
As long as we can convince ourselves
That it has been done before.

Life at Acorn involved a lot of hard physical work. It says a great deal about the world of the early 2030s that most of the people who stumbled onto the community chose to join Earthseed and stay. That being the case, it must have taken a lot to get the Peralta family to leave. There may have been more reasons than my mother gives for their leaving, but I haven't been able to find evidence of them. Perhaps the Peraltas actually did disagree with the religious and political feelings of the rest of Acorn. Perhaps also, they were afraid of the way the political situation in the country was going. They had reason to be.

On the other hand, I'm not at all surprised that Uncle Marc left. There really was no place for him at Acorn. He was "Olamina's little brother" or, as my mother said, a nice boy. He could have married and begun a family in one more little cabin. That would have been intolerable to him. He was a world saver, after all, like my mother. Or not like her, since Earth was the only world that interested him. Like the Peraltas, he was in religious and political disagreement with Acorn, and, like the Peraltas, he was probably wise to leave when he did.

I got the impression that my mother didn't pay much attention to being pregnant. It wasn't that she resented it. There's no indication that she did. She simply ignored it. I was due in July. Between running out

177

into the firefight with the thugs who chased Dan and Nina Noyer and actually giving birth to me, she worked hard to increase both Acorn's wholesaling and its retailing businesses. She was so successful at this that by the time I was born, the community was in the process of negotiating to buy another truck. They did eventually buy it. Most people had been nervous about having only the one truck. Travis and his helpers had kept the old housetruck running well, and hadn't had to spend much money on it since they made repairs themselves, but one major accident would put the whole community out of business—or at least, out of its new businesses.

With two trucks, the beginnings of a fleet, my mother was looking forward to what she saw as a pleasant, reasonably secure future. She began to think less about Acorn and more about Earthseed—about spreading Earthseed to whole groups of new people. She wrote more than once in her journal that she hoped to use missionaries to make conversions in nearby cities and towns and to build whole new Earthseed communities—clones of Acorn. I think she especially liked this last idea. She even imagined names for the Acorn clones like a girl thinking up names for imaginary children that she hopes to have someday. There was a Hazelnut, a Pine, a Manzanita, a Sunflower, an Almond. . . . "They should be small communities," she said. "No more than a few hundred people, never more than a thousand. A community whose population grew to more than a thousand should split and 'parent' a new community."

In small communities, she believed, people are more accountable to one another. Serious misbehavior is harder to get away with, harder even to begin when everyone who sees you knows who you are, where you live, who your family is, and whether you have any business doing what you're doing.

My mother was not a fanciful woman apart from her belief in Earthseed. That, I think, was why the people of Acorn trusted her so. She was practical, straightforward, fair, honest, and she liked people. She enjoyed working with them. She was a better-than-average community leader. But beneath it all was always Earthseed and a longing, an obses-

OCTAVIA E. BUTLER

sion, that was far stronger than anyone seemed to realize. People who are intelligent, ambitious, and at the same time, in the grip of odd obsessions can be dangerous. When they occur, they inevitably upset things.

In *The First Book of the Living*, my mother says,

> *Prodigy is, in its essence, adaptability and persistent,*
> *positive obsession. Without persistence, what remains*
> *is an enthusiasm of the moment. Without adaptability,*
> *what remains may be channeled into destructive fanati-*
> *cism. Without positive obsession, there is nothing at all.*

From *THE JOURNALS OF LAUREN OYA OLAMINA*
FRIDAY, JULY 22, 2033

On July 20, I turned 24. More important, on that day my daughter Larkin Beryl Ife Olamina Bankole was born.

We've named her all that, poor little one. "Larkin" is from the same root as "Lauren" and my father's name, "Laurence." All three names derive from "Laurel" and that from the ancient Greek habit of rewarding the victorious by crowning them with wreaths of laurel leaves. And there is a pleasant similarity between "Larkin" and "lark," the name of a songbird that neither Bankole nor I have ever seen or heard, but whose voice, we have read, is beautiful. I had planned to call our daughter Larkin even before she was born on my and my father's birthday. What a lovely connection. Three generations of beginning on July 20 is more than just a coincidence. It's almost a tradition.

"Beryl" was the name of Bankole's mother. Bankole and I had been bickering over it for months, and I had known that it would show up somewhere in our daughter's name. As long as it wasn't her first name, it was endurable. It has a good denotative meaning. A beryl is a very hard clear or cloudy mineral which, when properly shaped and polished has great potential for beauty. The emerald is a kind of beryl.

"Ife" is the Yoruba personal name we've chosen to go with our two Yoruba surnames—since my grandfather and Bankole's father had chosen to take Yoruba surnames back in the 1960s. "Ife" was Bankole's idea. I didn't remember it. We had pooled our memories of Yoruba names, and as soon as Bankole came up with "Ife," it seemed right to both of us. It means "love," Bankole says.

And, of course, she was "Olamina" and "Bankole." So many names for one little girl. When she's older, she'll no doubt choose a couple of them and drop the others.

She's whole and beautiful and healthy, and I love her more than I would have thought possible. I'm still sore and tired, but it doesn't matter. She weighs three and a half kilos, has a big appetite, and a good loud voice.

Bankole sits, now, holding her as she sleeps—holding her and looking down at her, rocking her in the beautiful, ornate wooden rocking chair that Gray Mora paid Allie Gilchrist to make for him. Gray likes to build big things—cabins, storehouses, buildings of any kind. He designs them, organizes the building, and works on them. As long as he's building something, he's a happy man. The school is his doing, and if he were any more proud of it, he'd be impossible. But he leaves the designing and building of small things, furniture in particular, to Allie Gilchrist. She taught herself her craft not only by reading salvaged books, but by taking apart salvaged furniture to see how it was made. Now, at street markets, she sells the chairs, tables, cabinets, chests, toys, tools, and decorative items that she makes, and she gets good prices for them. Her son Justin is only nine, but he's already pleased her very much by picking the work up from her, learning it and enjoying it. May and the Noyer girls are also beginning to learn the craft, although May is more interested in weaving grasses, roots, bark, and other fibers into mats, baskets, and bags.

Four years ago, after Bankole delivered Gray's first son, Gray paid Allie to build a fine rocking chair for "the doctor." Gray and Bankole hadn't gotten along very well at first—Gray's fault, and he knew it.

He pretended to be contemptuous of Bankole—"a pussy-whipped old man!"—when, in fact, Bankole's age, education, and personal dignity intimidated him. Until Gray's wife bad become pregnant with their first son, the two men barely spoke. Then Bankole took care of Emery during her pregnancy and during Joseph's difficult birth—he was breech. After that, the handsome, oaken chair, given in stolid silence, had served as Gray's peace offering. Now Bankole sits in it, rocking, looking into his daughter's sleeping face, touching it as though he can't quite believe it's real, and yet, as though it's more real, more important than anything else in his world.

He seems to have taken his cue from Adela Ortiz. He says Larkin looks just like his younger sister did when she was a baby. That's the sister whose bones we found when we arrived here. Her bones, her husband's, her children's. After their deaths, Bankole must have felt cut off from the future, from any immortality of the flesh, the genes. He had no other relatives. Now he has a daughter. I'm not sure he even realizes how much of the time over the past couple of days that he's been smiling.

SUNDAY, JULY 24 , 2033

Today we Welcomed Larkin into the community—into Acorn and into Earthseed.

So far, I've been the one to Welcome each new child or adult adoptee. I don't conduct every Sunday Gathering, but I have Welcomed every newcomer. By now, it's expected—something I'm *supposed* to do. This time, though, I asked Travis to perform the ceremony. And, of course, we asked Harry and Zahra to stand with us. Bankole and I are already Change-sister and -brother to them and Change-aunt and -uncle to their children. Now it goes the other way as well. We each stand ready to parent one another's children. The Balters are my oldest friends and I trust them, but I hope the pledges we've given one another will never have to be kept.

It makes us more truly a community, somehow, now that so many of us have had children here . . . now that I've had a child here.

Larkin Beryl Ife Olamina Bankole,
We, your people
Welcome you. . . .

SATURDAY, JULY 30, 2033

"I don't think you can truly understand how I feel," Bankole said to me last night as he sat down to eat the dinner I had kept warm for him. He had been on evening watch, sitting with binoculars at a mountain overlook where he could see whether some new gang of thugs was approaching to destroy his family. He's more serious than ever about maintaining our 24-hour watch, but for each of us, standing watch is still a tiresome duty. I didn't expect him to come home in a good mood, but he was still on enough of a new-daddy high not to be too bad-tempered.

"You just wait until Larkin starts waking him up more," Zahra has warned me.

No doubt she's right.

Bankole sat down at the table and sighed. "Before I met you," he said, "there were times when I felt as though I were already dead." He looked at me, then at Larkin's crib where she slept, full of milk and, so far, dry. "I think you've saved me," he said. "I wish you'd let me save you."

That again. The people of Halstead had found themselves another doctor, but they didn't like him. There was some doubt as to whether he really was a doctor. Bankole thought he might have some medical training, but that he was something less than or other than an M.D. He was only about 35, and these days, almost all young physicians—those under 50—were working in privatized or foreign-owned cities, towns, or huge farms. There, they could earn enough to give their families good lives and the company police would keep them safe from marauding thugs or desperate poor people. There had to be something wrong with a 35-year-old doctor who was still looking for a place to hang out his shingle.

Bankole said he thought a sick or injured person would be safer in the hands of Natividad or Michael than with Halstead's new "Doctor" Babcock. He had warned several of his Halstead friends, and they had let him know that he was still welcome. They didn't doubt his medical knowledge, and they preferred to have him. And he still wanted to save me by taking me to live among them.

"Acorn is a community of people who have saved one another in all kinds of ways," I told him. "Acorn is home."

He looked at me again, then set to work on his dinner. It was late, and I had already eaten. I had taken the baby and gone to eat with Zahra and Harry and their kids. But now, I sat with him, sipping hot mint tea with honey and enjoying the peace. The fire in our antique, salvaged woodstove had burned to almost nothing, but the stove's cast-iron body was still warm and the July night wasn't cold. We were using only three small oil lamps for light. No need to waste electricity. The lamplight was soft and flickering.

I stared into the shadows, enjoying the quiet, family togetherness, content and drowsy until Bankole spoke again.

"You know," he said, "it took me a long time to trust you. You seemed so young—so vulnerable and idealistic, yet so dangerous and knowing."

"What?" I demanded.

"Truth. You were quite a contradiction. You still are. I thought you would grow out of it. Instead, I've gotten used to it—almost."

We do know one another after six years. I can often hear not only what he says but what he does not say. "I love you too," I said, not quite smiling.

Nor did he allow himself to smile. He leaned forward, forearms on the table, and spoke with quiet intensity. "Talk to me, girl. Tell me exactly what you want to do in this place, with these people. Leave out the theology this time, and give me some step-by-step plans, some material results that you hope to achieve."

"But you know," I protested.

"I'm not sure that I do. I'm not sure that *you* do. Tell me."

I understood then that he was looking for reasons to reevaluate his position. He still believed that we should leave Acorn, that we could be safe only in a bigger, richer, longer-established town. "Convince me," he was saying.

I drew a long, ragged breath. "I want what's happening," I said. "I want us to go on growing, becoming stronger, richer, educating ourselves and our children, improving our community. Those are the things that we should be doing for now and for the near future. As we grow, I want to send our best, brightest kids to college and to professional schools so that they can help us and in the long run, help the country, the world, to prepare for the Destiny. At the same time, I want to send out believers who have missionary inclinations—send them in family groups to begin Earthseed Gathering Houses in non-Earthseed communities.

"They'll teach, they'll give medical attention, they'll shape new Earthseed communities within existing cities and towns and they'll focus the people around them on the Destiny. And I want to establish new Earthseed communities like Acorn—made up of people collected from the highways, from squatter settlements, from anywhere at all. Some people will want to stay where they are and join Earthseed the way they might join the Methodists or the Buddhists. Others will need to join a closer community, a geographical, emotional, intellectual unit." I stopped and drew a long breath. Somehow I had never dared to say this much about my plans to any one person. I had been working them out in my own mind, writing about them, talking about them in bits and pieces to the group at Gathering, but never assembling it all for them. Maybe that was a mistake. Problem was, we'd been focused for so long on immediate survival, on solving obvious problems, on business, on preparing for the near future. And I've worried about scaring people off with too many big plans. Worst of all, I've worried about seeming ridiculous. It *is* ridiculous for someone like me to aspire to do the things I aspire to do. I know it. I've always known it. It's never stopped me. "We are a beginning," I said, thinking as I spoke. "It's as though Earthseed is only an infant like Larkin—'one small seed.' Right now we would be so very easy to stamp out. That terrifies me. That's why we have to grow and spread—to make ourselves less vulnerable."

"But if you went to Halstead," he began, "if you moved there—"

"If I went to Halstead, the seed here might die." I paused, frowned, then said, "Babe, I'm no more likely to leave Acorn now than I am to leave Larkin."

That seemed to rock him back a little. I don't know why, after all that I've already said. He shook his head, sat staring at me for several seconds. "What about President Jarret?"

"What about him?"

"He's dangerous. His being President is going to make a difference, even to us. I'm sure of it."

"We're nothing to him, so small, so insignificant—"

"Remember Dovetree."

Dovetree was the last thing I wanted to remember. So was that state senate candidate that Marc mentioned. Both were real, and perhaps both meant danger to us, but what could I do about either of them? And how could I let the fear of them stop me? "This country is over 250 years old," I said. "It's had bad leaders before. It survived them. We'll have to watch what Jarret does, change when necessary, adapt, maybe keep a little quieter than we have for a while. But we've always had to adapt to changes. We always will. God is Change. If we have to start saying long live Jarret' and 'God bless Christian America,' then we'll say it. He's temporary."

"So are we. And living with him won't be that easy."

I leaned toward him. "We'll do what we have to do, no matter who's warming the chair in the Oval Office. What choice do we have? Even if we run and hide in Halstead, we'll still be subject to Jarret. And we'll have no good friends around us to help us, lie for us if necessary, take risks for us. In Halstead, we'll be strangers. We'll be easy to pick out and blame and hurt. If vigilante crazies or even cops of some kind come asking questions about us or accusing us of witchcraft or something, Halstead might decide we're more trouble than we're worth. If things get bad, I want my friends around me. Here at Acorn, if we can't save everything, we can at least work together to save one another. We've done that before."

"This is like nothing we've faced before." Bankole's shoulders slumped, and he sighed. "I don't know that this country has ever had a leader as bad as Jarret or as bad as Jarret might turn out to be. Keep that in mind. Now that you're a mother, you've got to let go of some of the Earthseed thinking and think of your child. I want you to look at Larkin and think of her every time you want to make some grand decision."

"I can't help doing that," I said. "This isn't about grand decisions. It's about her and her future." I drank the last of my tea. "You know," I said, "for a long time, it terrified me—honestly terrified me—to think that the Destiny itself was so big, so complex, so far from the life I was living or anything that I could ever bring about alone, so far from anything that even seemed possible. I remember my father saying that he thought even the pitiful little space program that we've just junked was stupid and wrong and a huge waste of money."

"He was right," Bankole said.

"He was not right!" I whispered, my feelings flaring. After a moment, I said, "We need the stars, Bankole. *We need purpose!* We need the image the Destiny gives us of ourselves as a growing, purposeful species. We need to become the adult species that the Destiny can help us become! If we're to be anything other than smooth dinosaurs who evolve, specialize, and die, we need the stars. That's why the Destiny of Earthseed is to take root among the stars. I know you don't want to

hear verses right now, but that one is . . . a major key to us, to human beings, I mean. When we have no difficult, long-term purpose to strive toward, we fight each other. We destroy ourselves. We have these chaotic, apocalyptic periods of murderous craziness." I stopped for a moment, then let myself say what I had never said to anyone. He had a right to hear it. "Early on, when I told people about the Destiny, and most of them laughed, I was afraid. I worried that I couldn't do this, couldn't reach people and help them see truth. Later, when the people of Acorn began to accept all the Earthseed teachings except the Destiny, I worried more. People seem to be willing to believe all kinds of stupid things—magic, the supernatural, witchcraft. . . . But I couldn't get them to believe in something real, something that they could make real with their own hands. Now . . . now most of the people here accept the Destiny. They believe me and follow me, and . . . damned if I don't worry even more."

"You never said so." Bankole reached out and took my hands between his.

"What could I say? That I believe in Earthseed, yet I doubt my own abilities? That I'm afraid all the time?" I sighed. "That's where faith comes in, I guess. It always comes sooner or later into every belief system. In this case, it's have faith and work your ass off. Have faith and work the asses off a hell of a lot of people. I realize all that, but I'm still afraid."

"Do you think anyone expects you to know everything?"

I smiled. "Of course they do. They don't believe I know it all, and they wouldn't like me much if I did, but somehow, they do expect it. Logic isn't involved in feelings like that."

"No, it isn't. I suspect that logic isn't involved in trying to found a new religion and then having doubts about it either."

"My doubts are personal," I said. "You know that. I doubt myself, not Earthseed. I worry that I might not be able to make Earthseed anything more than another little cult." I shook my head. "It could happen. Earthseed is true—is a collection of truths, but there's no law that says it has to succeed. We can always screw it up. *I* can always screw it up. There's so much to be done."

Bankole went on holding my hands, and I let myself go on talking, thinking aloud. "I wonder sometimes whether I'll make it. I might grow old and die without seeing Earthseed grow the way that it should, without leaving the Earth myself or seeing others leave, maybe without even focusing serious attention on the Destiny. There are so many little cults—like earthworms twisting and feeding, forming and splitting, and going nowhere."

"I'll die without seeing the results of most of your efforts," Bankole said.

I jumped, looked at him, then said, "What?"

"I think you heard me, girl."

I never know what to say when he starts talking that way. It scares me because, of course, it's true.

"Listen," he said. "Do you really think you can spend your life—your life, girl!—struggling and risking yourself, maybe risking our child for a . . . a cause whose fulfillment you . . . probably won't live to see? Should you do such a thing?" I could feel him holding himself back, trying so hard to discourage me without offending me.

He let my hands go, then moved his chair around closer to me. He put his arm around me. "It's a good dream, girl, but that's all it is. You know that as well as I do. You're an intelligent person. You know the difference between reality and fantasy."

I leaned against him. "It's more than a good dream, babe. It's right. It's true! And it's so big and so difficult, so long-term, and as far as money is concerned, it's potentially so profitless, that it'll take all the strong religious faith we human beings can muster to make it happen. It's not like anything humanity has ever done before. And if I can't have it, if I can't help to make it happen. . . ." To my amazement, I felt myself on the verge of tears. "If I can't give it the push it needs, if I can't live to see it succeed. . . ." I paused, swallowed. "If I can't live to see it succeed, then, maybe Larkin can!" I found the words all but impossible to say. It was not a new idea to me that I might not live to see the Destiny fulfilled. But it felt new. Now Larkin was part of it, and it felt new and real. It felt true. It made me frantic inside, my thoughts leaping around. I felt as though I didn't know what to do. All of a sudden, I wanted to go stand beside Larkin's crib and look at her, hold her. I didn't move. I leaned against Bankole, unsettled, trembling.

After a while, Bankole said, "Welcome to adulthood, girl."

I did cry then. I sat there with tears running down my face. I couldn't stop. I made no noise, but of course, Bankole saw, and he held me. At first I was horrified and disgusted with myself. I don't do that. I don't cry on people. I've never been that kind of person. I tried to pull away from Bankole, but he held me. He's a big man. I'm tall and strong myself, but he just folded his arms around me so that I couldn't get away from him without hurting him. After a moment, I decided I was where I wanted to be. If I had to cry on someone's shoulders, well, his were big and broad.

After a time, I stopped, all cried out, exhausted, ready to get up and go to bed. I wiped my face on a napkin, and looked at him. "I wonder if that was some kind of postpartum something-or-other?"

"It might have been," he said, smiling.

"It doesn't matter," I told him. "I meant everything I said."

He nodded. "I guess I know that."

"Then let's go to bed."

"Not yet. Listen to me, Olamina."

I sat still and listened.

"If we stay here, if I agree that you and Larkin and I are going to stay here, this place is not going to be just one more squatter's shanty."

"It was never that!"

He held up his hand. "My daughter will not grow up grubbing for a living through the ruins of other people's homes and trash heaps. This place will be a town—a twenty-first-century town. It will be a decent place to raise a child—a place with some hope of survival and success. Whatever other grand things we do or fail to do, we will do that much!"

"It's an Acorn," I said, stroking his face, his beard. "It will grow."

He almost smiled. Then he was solemn again. "If I accept this, I'm in it for good! If you change your mind after a few hard times. . . ."

"Do I tend to do that, babe? Am I like that?"

He stared hard at me, silent, weighing.

"I helped you build this house," I said, referring to the literal meaning of his name, *help me build a house.* "I helped you build this house. Now there's so much more work to do."

OCTAVIA E. BUTLER

11

○ ○ ○

From EARTHSEED: THE BOOKS OF THE LIVING

Choose your Leaders
        with wisdom and forethought.
To be led by a coward
        is to be controlled
        by all that the coward fears.
To be led by a fool
        is to be led
        by the opportunists
        who control the fool.
To be led by a thief
        is to offer up
        your most precious treasures
        to be stolen.
To be led by a liar
        is to ask
        to be told lies.
To be led by a tyrant
        is to sell yourself
        and those you love
        into slavery.

I'm not certain how to write about the next episode in my parents' lives
and in my life. I'm glad to have no memory of it. I was only two months
old when it happened.

It's all very strange, very bad, very confused. If only my mother had
agreed to go with my father to live peacefully, normally in Halstead, it
wouldn't have happened. Or at least, it wouldn't have happened to us.

They didn't shoot their way in. It seems that they don't intend to kill us. Yet. Since Dovetree, they have changed. Their leader has come to power. They have acquired . . . if not legitimacy, at least a shadow of sophistication. Roaring in, shooting everyone, and burning everything is perhaps too crude for them now. Or maybe it's just not as much fun.

I write, not knowing how long I will be able to write. I write because they have not yet robbed us of everything. Our freedom is gone, our two trucks, our land, our business, our homes are gone, stolen from us. But somehow, I still have paper, pens, and pencils. None of our captors values these things, so no one has yet taken them from me. I must keep them hidden or they will be taken. All possessions will be taken. They will strip us. They've made that all too clear. They will break us down, reshape us, teach us what it means to love their country and fear their God.

Our several secret caches of food, weapons, money, clothing, and records have not been found. At least, I don't believe they have been. No one has heard that they have.

We're shut up in two of the rooms of the school. Our books are still here on their shelves. The various projects of our students are still here. Our several phones and our five new teaching computers are gone. They have hard-currency value. Also, they were a means of communicating with the outside. We are not permitted to do that. That would inhibit our reeducation.

I must make a record of all this. I don't want to, but I must. And I must hide that record so that, someday, Earthseed will know what Earthseed has survived.

We will do that. We will survive. I don't yet know how. How is always a problem. But, in fact, we will survive.

Here is what happened.

Late Tuesday afternoon last week, I was sketching two of the Faircloth kids and talking with them about the project they wanted to work on for school. They had, in their required study of history, just discovered World War II, and they wanted to build models of the battleships, submarines, and airplanes of the time. They wanted to report on the big battles and find out more about the atomic bombs dropped on Hiroshima and Nagasaki. They were fascinated by all of the loud, explosive events of the War, but they had no idea what a huge subject they had chosen or, beyond the barest outline, why the War had been fought. I had decided to sketch them while the three of us talked about it and narrowed things down.

The Faircloth family had always been poor, had lived in a squatter settlement before they came to us. Alan Faircloth had small, badly creased, paper photos of the boys as babies, but nothing recent. He had pleased me more than I would have been willing to admit by asking me to draw the two of them. I had become vain about my drawing. It was finally somewhere near good. Even Harry, Zahra, and Allie had said so, and they were the ones who had the most fun with my earlier efforts.

The boys and I were outside behind the school, enjoying a warm, easy day. Larkin lay next to me, asleep in her crib in spite of the noise the boys made. She was already used to noise. The boys were 11 and 12, small for their age, always loud, and unlikely to be still for more than two or three minutes at a time. First they peeked at Larkin, then they lost interest and shouted first at each other, then at me about weapons and battles, dive-bombers and aircraft carriers, Hitler, Churchill, Tojo, London, Stalingrad, Tokyo, on and on. Interesting that a thing as terrible and as massive as a worldwide war could seem so wonderful and exciting to a pair of preadolescent boys whose grandparents weren't born in time for it—although they did have paternal grandparents who were born and raised in London.

I sketched the boys quickly while listening to their enthusiasm and making suggestions. I was just finishing the sketches when the maggots arrived.

A maggot, nicknamed for its ugly shape, is something less than a tank, and something more than a truck. It's a big, armed and armored, all-terrain, all-wheel-drive vehicle. Private cops and military people use them, and people with plenty of money drive them as private cars. Maggots can go almost anywhere, over, around, or through almost anything. The people of Halstead have one. They've used it now and then to collect Bankole. Several small local towns have one or two for their cops or for search and rescue in the hills. But the things are serious fuel eaters—expensive to run.

That Friday, seven maggots came crawling out of the hills and through our thorn fence toward us. There had been no warning from the watchers. Nothing at all. That was my first thought when I saw them coming: Where were Lucio Figueroa and Noriko Kardos? Why hadn't they warned us? Were they all right?

Seven maggots! That was three or four times as much firepower as we could muster if we brought out every one of our guns. Only our truck guns would have even a ghost of a chance of stopping a maggot, anyway.

Seven of the damned things!

"Go home!" I said to the two boys. "Tell your father and sisters to get the hell out. No drill. The real thing! Get out, fast and quiet! Run!"

Both boys ran.

I took my phone from my pocket and tapped out the emergency bug-out signal. We've had bug-out exercises. Bankole called them that, and the name spread. I thought of them as "melt into the mountains" exercises. Now we faced the real thing. It had to be real. No one came visiting in seven armed and armored maggots.

I grabbed my Larkin as fast as I could and ran for the hills. I tried to keep the school building between the two of us and the nearest maggots. They were crawling toward us in what could have been a military formation. They could run us down, shoot us, do whatever they chose to do. The only thing we might be able to do that they couldn't do was vanish into the mountains. But could we even do that? If we kept still, the maggots' sensory equipment would spot us. And if we ran, the rocks and trees and thorn bushes wouldn't give us much protection from the maggots' guns. But what could we do but run? As long as no one came out of the maggots, we had nothing to shoot at.

Where was Bankole? I didn't know. Well, we had rendezvous points. We would find each other. The idea was *not* to waste time running around looking for relatives. Except for babies and very young children, everyone knew from the drills that a command to get out meant exactly that. *"Get out now!"*

And we were to go in all directions. We were not to follow one another or group together and provide our enemies with big, easy targets. As much as possible, we were to put trees and geographical features between ourselves and the enemy.

But what were we to do when the enemy was everywhere?

Then, in the same instant, all seven of the maggots began firing. It took me a moment to realize that they were not firing bullets, that, perhaps, we were not about to be killed. They were firing gas canisters. I kept running, hoping that others were doing the same. No matter what the gas was, it was not intended to do us good.

I headed through the young oak grove that was our cemetery toward the fold of a hill that I hoped would both shelter me and give me an easier path up over the first hill.

Then just ahead of me, a canister landed. Before it hit the ground, it began to spew out gas.

And my legs wouldn't hold me. I was running. Then I felt myself begin to fall. It was all I could do to manage not to fall on my baby, instead to have her fall on me. I heard her begin to cry—a thin, un-Larkinlike whimpering. I don't believe I cried out. I know I never lost consciousness. It was a terrible gas. I still don't know the name of it. It took away most of my ability to move, but left me wide awake, able to hear and see, able to know that my people were being collected like driftwood, being carried or dragged away by uniformed men.

Someone came to me, bent, and took Larkin from me. I couldn't move my head to see what he did with her. I couldn't struggle or protest or plead. I couldn't even scream.

Someone came for me and took me by the feet and dragged me over the ground, down the hill to the school. I was wearing denims and a light cotton shirt, and I could feel my back scraping over rocks and weeds. I could feel pressure—bumping and thudding. It didn't hurt as it was happening, but I knew it would hurt. All the adults and older kids had been carried or dragged to the school. I could see several of them sprawled on the floor wherever their captors had dropped them. What I could not see were the babies and young children.

I could not see my Larkin.

At one point, I heard shooting outside. It came from the south side of the school, not far away. It sounded like the guns of our older truck. Perhaps one of us had reached the truck and tried to use it as Bankole, Harry, and I had back when Dan and Nina Noyer came home. That was hopeless. Our old housetruck wouldn't have been a match for even one maggot. Then I heard a huge explosion. After that there was silence.

What had happened? Were the children involved? Not knowing was an agonizing torment. Utter helplessness was even worse. I could breathe. I could twitch a hand or a foot. I could blink. Nothing more.

After a while, I could whimper a little.

Sometime later, a man wearing the uniform of the day—black pants and a belted, black tunic with a white cross on its front, came to do something to us, to each of us. I couldn't see what he was doing until he got to me, unbuttoned three buttons of my shirt, raised my head, and fastened the slave collar around my neck.

It was that simple. They took Acorn. Its name is Camp Christian now. We captives were not able to do more than twitch, blink, or moan for over an hour. That was plenty of time to collar almost all of us.

No one collared Gray Mora. He had been a slave earlier in his life. He had never worn a collar, but he had spent his childhood and young manhood as the property of people who treated him not quite as well as they treated their cattle. They had taken his wife from him and sold her to a wealthy man who had seen her and wanted her. She was, according to Gray, a short, slight, very pretty woman, and she brought a good price. Her new owner made casual sexual use of her and then somehow, by accident or not, killed her. When Gray heard about that, he took his daughter Doe and broke free. He never told us exactly how he got free. I've always assumed he killed one or more of his masters, stole their possessions, and took off. That's what I would have done.

But this time, there was no escape. And yet Gray would not be a slave again.

I found out later that he managed to get to the housetruck, lock himself in, and fire on some of the maggots. That scratched them more than a little. Then, as the maggots began to fire on him and blow the housetruck's armor to hell, he charged one of them. He rammed it. There was an explosion. There shouldn't have been. The housetruck was as safe as it could be. Making it explode had to take a conscious effort—unless it was the maggot that exploded. I don't know for sure. But knowing Gray, I suspect he did something to cause the explosion. I believe he chose to die.

He is dead.

I can't believe that any of this is true. I mean . . . there ought to be a different way to write about these things—a way that at least begins to express the insanity and the terrible, terrible pain of it all. Acorn has always been full of ugly stories. There wasn't an adult among us who didn't have one. But we'd come together, lived together, helped one another, survived, thrived, we'd done that! *We'd done all that!* We'd made a good, home for ourselves, were making an honest living. Now people with crosses have come and put slave collars on us.

And where is my baby? Where is Larkin?

They separated the women and older girls from the men and older boys while we were paralyzed. They left the men in the larger room of the school and dragged us women into one of the smaller ones. I didn't think about it at the time, but that was an odd thing to do because there were more women than men in the community. We were dumped onto the wooden floor, half atop one another, and left there. The windows were open, and I remember thinking it strange that no one bothered to board them up or even close them.

The only good thing was that as I was half lifted and half dragged, I saw Bankole. I don't believe he saw me. He was lying on his back, staring straight up, one scraped, bloody hand on his chest. I saw him blink. I did see that, so I knew he was alive. If only he had gotten away. He would have been more likely than anyone else to find some way to help the rest of us. Besides, what will our captors do to a man his age? Would they care that he was old? No. From the way he looked, it was clear that he had been dragged across the ground just as I was. They didn't care.

Would they care that my Larkin was only a baby?

And where was she? *Where was she?*

I was terrified every time someone came near me. All our captors were young men, and I'd seen two or three angry, bloody ones. I didn't know at the time that this was Gray's work. I didn't know anything. All I could think about was Larkin, Bankole, my people, and the damned slave collar around my neck.

As the sun went down, my body began to hurt—my back and my hands and arms burned where they had scraped along the ground as I was dragged. My head felt lumpy and sore. It also ached in a hard, throbbing way that might have had something to do with the gas.

It was dark when I began trying to move. For a long time, all I could do was flop around a little. Someone in the room groaned. Someone else began to cry. Someone gasped, choked, and began to cough. Someone said over and over again, "Ah shit!" and I recognized Allie Gilchrist's voice.

OCTAVIA E. BUTLER

"Allie?" I said. I slurred the word, sounded drunk to my own ears, but she heard me.

"Olamina?"

"Yeah."

"Look, did you see Justin before they dragged you in here?"

"No. Sorry. Did you see Larkin?"

"No. Sorry."

"They took my baby too," Adela Ortiz said in a hoarse whisper. "They took him and I don't know where he is." She began to cry.

I wanted to cry myself. I wanted to just to lie there and cry because I hurt so much in so many ways. I felt too weak and uncoordinated to do anything but cry. Instead, I sat up, bumped someone, apologized, sat stupidly for a while, then found the sense to say, "Who else is here? One by one, say your names."

"Noriko," a voice said just to my left. "They took Deborah and Melissa," she continued. "I had Melissa and Michael had Deborah. We were running. I thought we were going to make it. Then that damned gas. We fell down, and someone came and pulled both girls away from us. I couldn't see anything but hands and arms taking them."

"And my babies," Emery Mora said. "My babies. . . ." She was crying, almost incoherent, "My little boys. My sons. They took my sons again. *Again!*" She had had two young sons when she was a slave years ago, and they had been sold away from her. She had been a debt slave—a legally indentured person bound for her family's unpaid debts. The debts were accumulated because she worked for an agribusiness corporation that underpaid its workers in company script instead of money, then overcharged them for food and shelter so that they could stay in ever-increasing debt. It was against the law for the company to break up families by selling minor children away from their parents or husbands from their wives. It was against both local and federal law, so it shouldn't have happened. Just as what's happened to us now shouldn't have happened.

I thought about Emery's older daughter and stepdaughter. "What about Tori and Doe?" I said. "Are they here? Tori? Doe?"

At first, there was no answer, and I thought of Nina and Paula Noyer. I didn't want to think of them, but Doe and Tori Mora were 14 and 15—far from babyhood. If they weren't here, where were they?

Then a very small voice said, "I'm here. Get off me."

"I'm trying to get off you," a stronger voice said. "There's no room in here. I can hardly move."

Tori and Doe, alive, and as well as the rest of us were. I shut my eyes and took a long, deep, grateful breath. "Nina Noyer?" I asked.

She began to answer, then coughed several times. "I'm here," she said at last, "but my little sisters. . . . I don't know what happened to them."

"Mercy?" I called. "Kassi?"

No answer.

"May?"

No answer. She couldn't talk, but she would have made a noise to let us know she was there.

"She had Kassia and Mercy with her," Allie said. "She's strong and fast. Maybe she got them away. She loved them like she gave birth to them."

I sighed. "Aubrey Dovetree?" I asked.

"I'm here," she said. "But I can't find Zoë or the kids. . . . Zoë had all three of them with her."

And Zoë had a heart condition, I thought. She might be dead, even if no one meant to kill her. Not knowing what else to do, I went on with my role call. "Marta Figueroa?"

"Yes," she whispered. "Yes, I'm here, all alone. My brother. . . . My children. . . . Gone."

"Diamond Scott? Cristina Cho?

"I'm here," said two voices at once, one in English and the other in Spanish. Cristina's English was good now, but under stress, she still reverted to Spanish.

"Beatrice Scolari? Catherine Scolari?"

"We're here," Catherine Scolari's voice said. She sounded as though she had been crying. "Vincent is dead." she said. "He fell against a rock, hit his head. I heard them say he was dead." Vincent was her husband and Beatrice's brother. He had only one arm because of an accident that happened before he joined us. He was, perhaps, more likely than most of us to be off balance when the gas collapsed him. But still. . . .

"He might not be dead," I said.

"He is. We saw him. . . ." There were more sounds of crying. I didn't know what to say to them. All I could think was that maybe Larkin was dead too. And what about Bankole? I didn't want to think about death. I didn't really want to think at all.

"Channa Ryan?" I said.

"I'm here. Oh god, I wish I wasn't."

"Beth Faircloth? Jessica Faircloth?"

There was no sound at first, then in nearly inaudible whispers, "We're here. Both of us are here."

"Natividad?" I said. "Zahra?"

"I'm here," Natividad said in Spanish. Then, "If they've hurt my babies, I'll cut their throats. I'll kill all of them. I don't care what they do to me." She began to cry. She's strong, but her kids mean more than life to her. She had a husband and three kids. Now, they're all gone from her.

"All of our babies are gone," I said. "We have to find out where they're being kept and who's guarding them and . . . and what's going to happen to them." I shifted, trying to get more comfortable, but that was impossible. "My Larkin should be nursing now. Right now. We have to find out what we can."

"They've put slave collars on us," Marta Figueroa said in almost a moan. "They took our kids and our men, and they put slave collars on us! What the hell more do we need to know than that?"

"We have to know as much as we can," I answered. "They're not killing us. They could have wiped us out. They separated us from the men and from the young kids, but we're alive. We have to find a way to get our kids back. Whatever we can do to get our kids back, we have to do it!" I felt myself falling toward hysteria, toward weeping and screaming. I tensed my body. Milk was leaking from my breasts onto my shirt, soaking the front of it, and I ached so.

For a long time no one said anything. Then Teresa Lin, who had not spoken before, whispered, "That window is open. I can see the stars."

"Did they put a collar on you?" I heard myself ask. I sounded almost normal to my own ears. My voice was soft and low.

"What, this wide flat thing? They put one on me. I don't care. That window is open! I'm getting out of here!" And she began scrambling over people toward the window. Someone cried out in pain. Several voices cursed her.

"Everybody down," I said. "Down on your face!"

I could not see who obeyed me. I hoped all the sharers did. I wasn't sure what the collar would do to Teresa when she tried to get out the window. Maybe it was a fake. Maybe it wouldn't do anything. Maybe it would cut off her breath. Maybe it would collapse her, and cause her terrible pain.

She dived out of the window. She's a slim woman, quick and lithe like a boy. I looked up in time to see her arc out the window as though she expected to land on something soft or on water.

Then she began to scream and scream and scream. Allie Gilchrist got up, stepped to the window, and looked out at her. Then Allie tried to climb out to help her. The moment Allie touched the window, she screamed, then fell back into our prison room. Allie curled on her side against me, and grunted several times—hard, agonized grunts. I turned my face away, her pain twisting in my own middle. It helped that I hadn't been able to see Teresa once she fell below the level of the window, but I had already gotten a taste of her pain too.

Outside, Teresa went on screaming and screaming.

"No one's around," Allie said, still gasping. "She's just lying there on the ground, screaming and twisting. No one's even come out to see."

She lay there all night. We couldn't help her. Her voice deteriorated from full-throated screaming, the way any of us might scream in fear and pain, to hoarse terrible grunting. She didn't pass out—or rather, she did, but she kept coming to again and making her terrible noises.

Going near the door meant pain. Going to the window meant pain. Even if you didn't try to get out, just being there hurt, hurt bad. Diamond Scott volunteered to crawl around the floor, letting her own collar tell her what was forbidden. People complained when she crawled over them, but I asked them to put up with it and Di apologized and the complaints stopped. We were still human, still civilized. I wondered how long that would last.

"Someone's here!" Di said. She almost screamed the words. "Someone's dead here!"

Oh, no. Oh, no.

"Who is it?" I asked.

"I don't know. She's cool. Not cold yet, but . . . I'm sure she's dead!"

I followed Di's voice, and spotted her silhouette, a darker shape in the darkness. She was moving more than the others, scrambling away from the body that she was sure must be dead.

Who was it?

Then, as I crawled toward the body, trying to be careful, trying not to hurt anyone, I had a feeling, a memory. I was afraid I knew who it was.

The body was sitting upright in a corner, against the wall. It was small—child-sized. It was a black woman's body—a black woman's hair, nose, mouth, but so small. . . .

"Zahra?"

She had not answered when I called her before. She was a bold, outspoken little woman, and she would not have kept quiet in all this. She might have been the one to go out the window before poor Teresa . . . if she could have.

She was dead. Her body wasn't yet stiff, but it would be soon. It was cooling. It wasn't breathing. I took the small hands between mine and felt the ring that Harry had worked so hard to buy for her. He's old-fashioned, Harry is, even though he's my age. He wanted his wife to wear his ring so that no one would make a mistake. Back when Zahra was the most beautiful woman in our Robledo neighborhood, she was beyond his reach, married to another man. But when that man was dead and Harry saw his chance, he moved right in. They were so different—black and white, tiny and tall, street-raised and middle class. She was three or four years older than he was. None of it mattered. They had managed, somehow, to have a good marriage.

And now she was dead.

And where were her children? I had another sudden, horrible thought. I felt for wounds on her, found scratches and dried blood, but no penetrating wound, no terrible soft place on her head. She had been brought in with the rest of us. Chances were, she was alive when she was brought in. Wouldn't our captors have noticed if she were dead? We were all dumped into this room and locked in by way of our collars during the same few minutes.

After that, no one had come in.

Perhaps, then, it was the gas that had been used on us. Could she have died of that? She was the smallest adult in the community, smaller, even, than Nina, Doe, and Tori. Was it possible that she got too much of the gas for her small size, and that killed her?

And if so, what did that say about our children?

Somehow, time passed. I sat rigid beside the body of my friend, and couldn't think or speak. I cried. I cried in grief and terror and rage. People told me later that I made no sound at all, but within myself, I cried. Within myself, I screamed with Teresa, and I cried and cried and cried.

After a time, I lay down on the floor, still crying, yet still making no noise. I could hear people around me moaning, crying, cursing, talking but their words made no sense to me. They might as well have been in a foreign language. I couldn't think of anything except that I wanted to die. Everything that I had worked to build was gone, stolen or dead, and I wanted to be dead too. My baby was dead. She must be. If I could have killed myself, just then I would have. I would have been glad to do it. I awoke, and there was sunlight streaming through the window. I had slept. How could I have slept?

I awoke with my head on someone's lap. Natividad's lap. She had come to sit against the wall next to Zahra's body. She had lifted my head off the floor and put it on her lap. I sat up, blinking and looking around. Natividad herself was asleep, although my moving woke her. She looked at me, then at Zahra's body, then back at me, as though the world were just coming back into focus for her, and it distressed her more and more every second. Her eyes filled with tears. I hugged her for a long time, then kissed her on the cheek.

The room was filled with sleeping women and girls. I counted 19 of us including myself and . . . not including Zahra and Teresa. Everyone looked dirty and scratched and abraded, and they lay in every possible position, some sprawled alone on the floor, some in pairs or larger groups, heads pillowed on laps, shoulders, or legs.

My breasts ached and leaked and I felt sick. I needed to use the bathroom. I wanted my child, my husband, my home. Near me, Zahra was cold and stiff, her eyes closed, her face beautiful and peaceful, except for its gray color.

I got up, stepped over people as they began to wake up. I went to an empty corner that I knew needed repair. A small earthquake a few months ago had caused a slight separation between the wall and floor in that corner. It wasn't obvious, but ants came in there, and water spilled near there ran out. Gray had promised to fix it, but hadn't gotten around to it.

I moved people away from the area—told them what I was doing and why. They nodded and gave no trouble. I wasn't the only one with a full bladder. I squatted there and urinated. When I finished, others followed my example.

"Is Teresa still there?" I asked Diamond Scott, who was nearest to the window.

Di nodded. "She's unconscious—or maybe dead." Her own voice sounded dead.

"I'm so hungry," Doe Mora said.

"Forget hungry," Tori said. "If I could just have some water."

"Hush," I said to them. "Don't talk about it. It just makes you feel worse. Has anyone seen our captors this morning?"

"They're building a fence," Diamond Scott said. "You can stand back from the window and see them. In spite of the collars they've put on us, they're building a fence."

I looked and saw maggots being used to string wire behind several of our homes, up the slope. As I watched, they smashed through our cemetery, breaking down some of the young trees that we planted to honor our dead. The maggots were well named. They were like huge insect larvae, weaving some vast, suffocating cocoon.

Our captors were keeping our land, then. Until that moment, this had not occurred to me. They were not just out to steal or burn, enslave or kill. That was what thugs had always done before. That was what they did in my old neighborhood in Robledo, in Bankole's San Diego neighborhood, and elsewhere. A lot of elsewheres. But these were staying, building a fence. Why?

"Listen," I said.

Most of the room paid no attention to me. People had focused on their own misery or on the maggots.

"Listen!" I said, putting as much urgency as I could into my voice. "There are things we need to talk about."

Most of them turned to look at me. Nina Noyer and Emery Mora still stared out the window.

"Listen," I said once more, wanting to shout, but not daring to. "Sooner or later, our captors will come in here. When they do, we need to be ready for them—as ready as we can be." I stopped, drew a deep breath, and saw that now they were all looking at me, all paying attention.

"We need to pretend to go along with them as much as we can," I continued. "We need to obey them and watch them, learn what they are and what they want, and where they're weak!"

People looked at me either as though they thought I'd lost my mind or as though it was good and hopeful news that our captors might, perhaps, have weaknesses.

"Anything they tell us may be lies," I said. "Probably will be. So any of us who get the chance should spy and eavesdrop and share information with the rest. We can escape from them or kill them if we can learn about them and pool our knowledge. Learn about the collars, too. Any little thing might help. And most important, most essential, learn about the kids."

"They'll rape us," Adela said, all but whimpering. "You know they will." *She* knew they would—she who had already suffered so much rape. She and Nina and Allie and Emery. The rest of us had been lucky—so far. Now our luck has run out. Somehow, we'll have to cope with that.

"I don't know," I said. "They could already have raped us, and they haven't. But . . . I suspect you're right. When men have absolute power over women who are strangers, the men rape. And we're collared." I glanced toward the window that Teresa's panic had driven her through. "If someone decides to rape one of us, we won't be able to stop him." I paused again. "I think . . . if you can't talk a guy out of it or beg and cry and get his pity or bluff him into believing you have a disease, then you'll have to put up with it." I paused, feeling inadequate and stupid. I shouldn't be giving these women this kind of advice. I, who had never been raped, had no right to tell them anything. I told them anyway. *"Do put up with it!"* I said. "Don't throw your lives away. Don't end up like Teresa. Learn everything you can from these people, and bring what you learn back to the rest of us. Even the stupid, ugly things that they say and do might be important. Their lying promises might hide a truth. If we collect what we see and hear, if we stay united, work together, support one another, then the time will come when we can win our freedom or kill them or both!"

There was a long silence. They just stared at me. Then someone—Nina Noyer—began to cry. "I was supposed to be free," she said through her tears. "All this was supposed to be over. My brother died to bring me here."

And all of a sudden, I felt *such* shame. All I wanted to do was lie down on the floor in a tight knot around my uselessness and my aching breasts and scream and scream. And I couldn't. I couldn't let myself fail my people in one more miserable way.

And these were my people—*my people.* They had trusted me, and now they were captives. And I could do nothing—nothing but give them galling advice and try to give them hope. "God is Change," I heard myself saying. "Our captors are on top now, but if we do this right, we will beat them. It's that or just . . . die."

"I haven't been able to take my medicine," Beatrice Scolari said into the near silence. "Maybe I will die." She had, in the past year, developed high blood pressure, and Bankole had put her on medication. Nina was still crying, now gathered against Allie, who rocked her a little as though she were much younger. Allie herself was crying, but in complete silence. Beatrice Scolari stared at me as though I could produce her medicine.

"Your medicine is one of the first things we've got to ask for when they start talking to us," I told Beatrice. "The very first thing we need is help for Teresa—if it isn't too late." But they must have seen Teresa. They must have heard her screaming earlier. Maybe they just didn't care. They knew she couldn't get away. Maybe they wanted to use her to make sure we understood our position. "We ask about our kids and about your medicine, Beatrice," I continued. "Then. . . . Then maybe they'll let us . . . take care of Zahra."

We waited until afternoon, hungry, thirsty, scared, miserable, worried about our children, and wondering about our men. No one paid any attention to us. We saw the invaders going in and out of our homes, finishing their fence, eating our food, but we saw them only

OCTAVIA E. BUTLER

from a distance. Even Teresa, lying on the ground outside our window, was ignored.

The younger girls cried and quarreled and complained. The rest of us sat silent most of the time. We had all been through one kind of hell or another. We had all survived enough to know that crying, complaining, and quarreling did no good. We might forget that in time, but not yet.

Sometime around two or three o'clock, the door of our prison opened. A huge, bearded man filled the doorway, and we stared up at him. He wore the usual uniform—black tunic with white cross and black pants, and he was at least two meters tall. He stared down at us as though we smelled—which we did—and as though that were our fault.

"You and you," he said, pointing to me and to Allie. "Get out here and pick up this corpse."

By reflex, Allie got a stubborn look on her face, but we both stood up. "She's dead, too," I said, pointing to Zahra.

I never saw his hand move, but he must have done something. I screamed, convulsed, dropped to the floor from a jolt of agony that seemed to come from nowhere and everywhere. I was on fire. Then I wasn't. Searing agony. Then nothing.

The man waited until I was able to look up at him, until I did look up.

"You don't speak unless you're spoken to," he said. "You do what you're told when you're told to do it, and you keep your mouths shut!"

I didn't say anything. Somehow, I managed to nod. It occurred to me that I should do that.

Allie stepped toward me to help me up, her hands already out to help me. Then she doubled up in agony of her own. Echoes of her pain burned through me, and I froze, teeth clenched. I was desperate not to announce my extra vulnerability, my sharing. If I was held captive long enough, they would find out. I knew that. But not now. Not yet.

The man didn't seem to take any special notice of me. He watched us both and waited in seeming patience until Allie looked up, bewildered and angry.

"You do what you're told and only what you're told," he said. "You don't touch one another. Whatever filth you're used to, it's over. It's time for you to learn to behave like decent Christian women—if you've got the brains to learn."

So that was it, then. We were a dirty cult of free lovers, and they had come to straighten us out. Educate us.

I believe Allie and I were chosen because we were the biggest of the women. We were ordered to carry first Zahra, then Teresa, out to a patch of ground where we grew jojoba plants for their oil. There, we were given picks and shovels and ordered to dig graves—long, deep holes—among the jojobas. We had had no food and no water. All we got was a jolt of agony now and then when we slowed down more than our overseer was willing to permit. The ground was bad—rocky and hard. That was why we used it for jojoba plants. The plants are tough. They don't need much. Now, it seemed that we were the ones who didn't need much. I didn't think I could do it—dig the damned hole. It's been a long time since I've felt so bad in every possible way, so horrible, so scared. After a while, all I could think of was water, pain, and where was my baby? I lost track of everything else.

I was digging Zahra's grave, and I couldn't even think of that. I just wanted the digging to be over. She was my best friend, my Change-sister, and she lay uncovered, waiting beside the hole as I dug, and it didn't matter. I couldn't focus on it.

The other women were brought out of the school and made to watch us dig. I knew that because my attention was caught by the sudden movement of silent, approaching people. I looked up, saw the women shepherded toward us by three black-tunic-and-cross-wearing men. Sometime later, I realized that the men had also been marched out. They were kept separate, and it seemed that some of them were digging too.

I froze, staring at them, looking for Bankole . . . and for Harry.

The sudden pain tore a grunt from me. I fell to my knees in the hole I was digging.

"Work!" my slave driver said. "It's time you heathens learned to do a little work."

I had not seen whom the men were burying. I saw Travis, shirt off, swinging a pick into the hard ground. I saw Lucio Figueroa digging another hole and Ted Faircloth digging a third. So they had three dead to our two. Who were their dead? Which of our men had these bastards killed?

Where was Bankole?

I hadn't spotted him. I had had such a quick look. I managed to look again and again as I shoveled dirt out of the hole. In the cluster of men, I spotted Michael, then Jorge, then Jeff King. Then the pain hit again. I didn't fall this time. I held on to the shovel and leaned back against the side of the hole I was digging.

"Dig!" the son of a bitch above me said. "Just dig!"

What would he do if I passed out? Would he go on triggering the collar until I died like Teresa? Was he enjoying himself? He didn't smile as he hurt me. But he did keep hurting me, even though I had shown no signs of rebellion.

Submission was no protection. If any of us were to survive, we must escape these people as quickly as possible.

The big, bearded slaver and perhaps three dozen of his kind stood around us as we stood around the graves. We were made to parade past each grave and look down at the dead. That was how Harry learned that Zahra was dead and how Lucio Figueroa, who had only this year begun to take an interest in Teresa Lin, came to know of her death. That was how I learned that Vincent Scolari was dead, as his wife and sister believed. And Gray Mora was dead—bloody and broken and dead. And that was how I learned that my Bankole was dead.

There was chaos. Emery Mora and both her daughters began to scream when they saw Gray's mangled body. Natividad and Travis ran into each other's arms. Lucio Figueroa dropped to his knees beside Teresa's grave, and his sister Marta tried to comfort him. Both Scolari women tried to go down into the grave to touch Vincent, to kiss him, to say good-bye. We were all lashed electronically for talking, screaming, crying, cursing, and demanding answers.

And I was lashed into unconsciousness for trying to kill my bearded keeper with a pickax. It would have been worth any amount of pain if only I could have succeeded.

OCTAVIA E. BUTLER

12

○ ○ ○

From EARTHSEED: THE BOOKS OF THE LIVING

Beware:
Ignorance
Protects itself.
Ignorance
Promotes suspicion.
Suspicion
Engenders fear.
Fear quails,
Irrational and blind,
Or fear looms,
Defiant and closed.
Blind, closed,
Suspicious, afraid,
Ignorance
Protects itself,
And protected,
Ignorance grows.

I miss Acorn. Of course, I have no memory of being there, but it was where my parents were together and happy during their brief marriage. It was where I was conceived, born, and loved by them both. It could have been, should have been, where I grew up—since it was where my mother had insisted on staying. And even if, in spite of my father's intentions and my mother's dreams, the place had gone on looking more like a nineteenth-century farming village than a stepping-stone toward the Destiny, I wouldn't have minded. It couldn't have been as grim as where I did grow up.

From the coming of Jarret's Crusaders—that is what they called themselves—my life veers away from Acorn and from my mother. The only surprising thing is that we ever met again.

My mother was right about the gas. It was intended to be used to stop riots, to subdue masses of violent people. Unlike poison gases that kill or maim or gases that caused tears and choking, or nausea, this gas was supposed to be merciful. It was called merciful. It was a paralysis gas. Most of the time, it worked fast and caused no pain and had no nasty aftereffects. But occasionally, children and small adults died of it. For that reason, an antidote was developed to be administered to small people who were overcome. It was given to me, to the rest of the little children of Acorn. For some reason it wasn't given to Zahra Batter. She was obviously an adult, in spite of her small size. Maybe the Crusaders thought age was more important than size. There were no physicians among them. There were no health workers of any kind. These were God's people come to bring the true faith to the cultist heathens. I suppose if some of the heathens died of it, that wasn't really very important.

From *THE JOURNALS OF LAUREN OYA OLAMINA*
THURSDAY, NOVEMBER 24, 2033

Thanksgiving Day.

Should I be thankful still to be alive? I'm not sure.

Today is like Sunday—better than Sunday. We have been given extra food and extra rest, and once services were over this morning, we were let alone. I am thankful for that. For once, they aren't watching us. They don't want to spend their holiday guarding us or "teaching" us, as they put it. This means that today I can write. On most days, by the time they let us alone, it's too dark to write and we're exhausted. After our work outside, we're watched and made to memorize and recite sections of the Bible until we can't think or keep our eyes open. I'm thankful to be writing and I'm thankful not to hear my own voice chanting something like, "Unto woman he said, I will greatly multiply thy sorrow and thy conception; in sorrow thou shalt bring forth children; and thy desire shall be to thy husband, and he shall rule over thee."

We're not permitted to speak to one another in our "teachers'" presence, and yet not allowed to be quiet and rest.

Now I must find a way to write about the past few weeks, to tell what has happened to us—just to tell it as though it were sane and rational. I'll do that, if for no other reason than to give some order to my scattered thoughts. I do need to write about . . . about Bankole.

All of our young children are gone. All of them. From Larkin, the youngest, to the Faircloth boys, the oldest, they've vanished.

Now we are told that our children have been saved from our wickedness. They've been given "good Christian homes." We won't see them again unless we leave our "heathenism" behind and prove that we've become people who can be trusted near Christian children. Out of kindness and love, our captors—we are required to address them each as "Teacher"—have provided for our children. They have put our children's feet on the pathway to good, useful American citizenship here on Earth, and to a place in heaven when they die. Now we, the adults and older kids, must be taught to walk that same path. We must be reeducated. We must accept Jesus Christ as our Savior, Jarret's Crusaders as our teachers, Jarret as God's chosen restorer of America's greatness, and the Church of Christian America as our church. Only then will we be Christian patriots worthy to raise children.

We do not struggle against this. Our captors order us to kneel, to pray, to sing, to testify, and we do. I've made it clear to the others through my own behavior that we should obey. Why should anyone resist and risk torture or death? What would be the good of that? We'll lie to these murderers, these kidnappers, these thieves, these slavers. We'll tell them anything they want to hear, do all that they require us to do. Someday they'll get careless or their equipment will malfunction or we'll find or create some weakness, some blind spot. Then we'll kill them.

But even though we obey, the Crusaders must have their amusements. In their loving kindness, they use the collars to torment us. "This is nothing compared to the fires of hell," they tell us. "Learn your lessons or you'll suffer like this for all eternity!" How can they do what they do if they believe what they say?

They eat our food and feed us their leavings, either as bowls of obvious table scraps or boiled up in a watery soup with turnips or potatoes from our gardens. They live in our houses and sleep in our beds while we sleep on the floor of the school, men in one room, women in another, no communication between the two permitted.

None of us is decently married, it seems. We were not married by a minister of the Church of Christian America. Therefore, we have been living in sin—"fornicating like dogs!" I heard one Crusader say. That same Crusader dragged Diamond Scott off to his cabin last week and raped her. She says he told her it was all right. He was a man of God, and she should be honored. Afterward, she kept crying and throwing up. She says she'll kill herself if she's pregnant.

Only one of us has done that so far—committed suicide. Only one: Emery Mora. She took revenge for what happened to her husband and for the abduction of her two little boys. She seduced one of the Crusaders—one of those who had moved into her own cabin. She convinced him that she was willing and eager to sleep with him. Then sometime during the night, she cut his throat with a knife she had always kept under her mattress. Then she went to the Crusader sleeping in her daughters' room and cut his throat. After that, she lay down in her bed beside her first victim and cut her own wrists. The three of them were found dead the next morning. Like Gray, Emery had taken substantial revenge.

For her own sake and the sake of her daughters, I wish she had chosen to live. I knew she was depressed, and I tried to encourage her to endure. At night when we were locked up together, we all talked, exchanged news, and tried to encourage one another. But the truth is, if Emery had to die, she chose the best possible way to do it. She's let

OCTAVIA E. BUTLER

us know that we can kill our captors. Our collars would not stop us. If Emery had not been confined by her collar to that one cabin, she might have killed even more of them.

But *why* had her collar not stopped her from killing? According to what Marc told me about his captivity, collars protected holders of control units. Was this a matter of a different kind of collar? Perhaps. We couldn't know that. None of the information we had collected and shared in the night had to do with different kinds of collars. What we had learned was that all our collars were linked together somehow in a kind of collar network. All could be controlled by the units that our captors wore as belts, but the belts themselves were powered or coordinated or somehow controlled from a larger master unit that Diamond Scott believed was kept in one of the two maggots that are always here. Things Di's rapist had said while she was with him waiting to be raped again made her certain that this was true.

A master control unit protected by the guns, locks, and armor of a maggot was beyond our reach, for now. We had to learn more about it. It occurred to me, though, that the reason the belt unit of Emery's rapist had not saved its owner's life was simple: he had taken it off. What man wore his belt to bed? Both of the men Emery had killed had taken their belts off. Why not? Emery was a slender little woman. A man of ordinary size wouldn't doubt his ability to control her with or without the collar.

Once she had killed, Emery would have tried to use the belt units to free herself, either to escape, to try to free us, or to take further revenge. She would have tried. I'm sure of that. And she would have failed either because she had the wrong fingerprints or because she lacked some other necessary key. It was important to know that, but there was more: she had tried the units, no doubt caused herself pain, but she had failed to set off any alarms. Perhaps there were no alarms. That could be very important someday.

We were all lashed for what Emery did. The men were made to watch.

We were marched out of the school and lashed as we were made to kneel and pray, to scream out our sins, to beg for forgiveness, and quote Bible verses on command. I kept thinking they would make a mistake and kill some of us. This was an orgy of abuse and humiliation. It went on and on for hours with our "teachers" taking turns, trading off, screaming their hate at us, and calling it love. I had no voice at all left by the time it was over. I was sore all over. An actual beating couldn't have left me feeling any worse. And if anyone had been paying attention to me in particular, they would have seen that I was a sharer. I lost control. I couldn't have concealed anything.

I remember wishing I could die. I remember wondering if in the end they would force us all to go the way Emery did, each of us taking a few of them with us.

New people have been brought to live among us—men and women from squatter camps and from nearby towns. Most of them seem to be just plain poor people. Some were like the Dovetrees. They produced and sold drugs or homemade beer, wine, or whiskey. And our neighbors the Sullivan and the Gama families have been rounded up and brought here. Some of their children used to attend our school, but none were captured with us. I haven't seen any of them since our capture. Why have they been taken captive and brought here now? No one seems to know.

The new women were stuffed in with us or put into the empty third room of the school—the room that was once our clinic. The men were housed in the big room with our men.

I need to write about Bankole.

I meant to do that when I began. I need to but I don't want to. It just plain hurts too much.

The Crusaders are making us enlarge our prison and enlarge our cabins, which are now their homes. And we work in the fields as before. We're feeding livestock and cleaning their pens. We're turning compost, we're planting herbs, we're harvesting winter fruits, vegetables and herbs, clearing brush from the hills. We're expected to feed ourselves and our captors. They eat better than we do, of course. After all, we owe them more than we can ever pay, you see, because they're teaching us to forsake our sinful ways. They keep talking about teaching us the meaning of hard work. They tell us that we're no longer squatters, parasites, and thieves. I've earned myself more than one lashing by saying that my husband and I own this land, that we've always paid our taxes on it, and that we've never stolen from anyone.

They've burned our books and our papers.

They've burned all that they could find of our past. It's all ungodly trash, they say. They made us do most of the fetching and carrying, the stacking and piling of so much that we loved. They watched us, their hands on their belts. All the books on paper and on disk. All the collections that our younger kids had assembled of minerals, seeds, leaves, pictures . . . All the reports, models, sculptures and paintings that our older kids have done. All the music that Travis and Gray wrote. All the plays that Emery wrote. All the bits of my journal that they could find. All the legal papers, including marriage licenses, tax receipts, and Bankole's deed to the land. All these things, our teachers threw lamp oil on and burned, then raked and stirred and burned again.

In fact, they've only burned copies of the legal papers. I'm not sure that matters, but it's true. Since we got our first truck, we've kept the originals in a safe-deposit box in Eureka—Bankole's idea. And we keep other copies in our various caches, along with a few books, other records, and the usual weapons, food, money, and clothing. I had been scanning Bankole's writing and my journal notebooks and hiding disk copies of them in the caches too. I don't know why I did this. In the case of my journals, it's an indulgence that I've always been a little ashamed of—wasting money copying my own stuff. But I remember I felt much better when I began to do it. Now I only wish I had scanned Emery's plays and Travis's and Gray's music. At least, as far as I know, the caches are still safe.

I've hidden my writing paper, pens, and pencils away in our prison room. Allie and Natividad have helped me loosen a couple of floorboards near the window. With only sharp stones and a couple of old nails as tools, we made a small compartment by scraping a hollow in one of the big lumber girders that supports the floor joists. The joists themselves were too slender and too obvious if anyone noticed a loose board. We hoped no "teacher" would peer down into the darkness to see whether anything might be in the girder. Natividad put her wedding ring there too, and Allie put in some drawings that Justin had done. Noriko put in a smooth, oval green stone. She and Michael had found it back when they had gone out salvaging together—back when they could be together.

Interesting that we could scrape into the girder without pain from our collars. Allie thought it meant we might be able to escape by loosening more floorboards and crawling out under the school. But when we got Tori Mora, the slenderest of us, to try to go down, she began to writhe in pain the moment her feet reached the ground. She convulsed and we had to pull her out. So we know one more thing. It's a negative thing, but we needed to know it.

So much is gone. So much has been taken from us and destroyed. If we haven't found a way out, at least we've found a way to keep a few small things. I find myself thinking sometimes that I could bear all this better if I still had Larkin and Bankole, or if I could see Larkin and know that she was alive and all right. If I could only just see her. . . .

I don't know whether the actions of these so-called Crusaders have any semblance of legality. It's hard to believe they might—stealing the land and freedom of people who've followed the law, earned their own livings, and given no trouble. I can't believe that even Jarret has so mangled the constitution as to make such things legal. At least, not yet. So how could a vigilante group have the nerve to set up a "reeducation" camp and run it with illegally collared people? We've been here for over a month and no one has noticed. Even our friends and customers don't seem to have noticed. The Gamas and the Sullivans aren't rich or powerful, but they've been in these hills for a couple of generations. Hasn't anyone come asking questions about them?

Maybe they have. And who has answered the questions? Crusaders in their other identities as ordinary, law-abiding patriots? I don't think it's too much to assume they have such identities. What lies have they told? Any group wealthy enough to have seven maggots, to support at least several dozen men, and to have what seems to be an endless number of expensive collars must be able to spread any lies it chooses to spread. Perhaps our friends outside have been told believable lies. Or perhaps they've just been frightened into silence, given to know that they shouldn't ask too many questions lest they get into trouble themselves. Or maybe it's just that none of us has powerful enough friends. We were nobodies, and our anonymity, far from protecting us, had made us vulnerable.

We at Acorn were told that we were attacked and enslaved because we were a heathen cult. But the Gamas and the Sullivans aren't cultists. I've asked women from both families why they were attacked, but they don't know either.

The Gamas and the Sullivans owned their land just as we did, and unlike the Dovetrees, the Gamas and the Sullivans had never raised marijuana or sold alcoholic beverages. They worked their land and they took jobs in the towns whenever they could find them. They worked hard and behaved themselves. And in the end, what did it matter? All their hard work and ours, all Bankole's attention to dead-and-gone laws, and all my hopes for my Larkin and for Earthseed. . . . I don't know what's going to happen. We will get out of this! We'll do that somehow! But what then? From what I've been able to hear, some of our "teachers" come from important families in the Churches of Christian America in Eureka, Arcata, and the surrounding smaller towns. This land is mine now. Bankole, with his trust in law and order, made a will. I've read it. The copy we kept here has been destroyed, of course, but the original and other copies still exist. The land is mine, but how can I take it back? How can we ever rebuild what we had?

When we break free of our "teachers," we will kill at least some of them. I see no way to avoid this. If they have to, and if they can, they'll kill us to stop our escape. The way they rape us, the way they lash us, the way they let some of us die—all that tells me they don't value our lives. Do their families know what they're doing? Do the police know? Are some of these "teachers" cops themselves or relatives of cops?

A great many people must know that something is going on. Each shift of our "teachers" stays with us for at least a week, then goes away for a week. Where do they tell people they've been? The area must be full of people who know, at least, that something unusual is happening. That's why once we've freed ourselves, I don't see how we can stay here. Too many people here will hate us either because we've killed their men in our escape or because they won't be able to forgive us for the wrongs that they, their families, or their friends have done us.

Earthseed lives. Enough of us know it and believe it for it to live on in us. Earthseed lives and will live. But Jarret's Crusaders have strangled Acorn. Acorn is dead.

I keep saying that I need to write about Bankole, and I keep not doing it. I was a zombie for days after I saw his body thrown into the bare hole they made Lucio Figueroa dig. They said none of their prayers over him, and, of course they refused to allow us to have services for him.

I saw him alive on the day the Crusaders invaded. I know I did. What happened? He was a healthy man, and no fool. He would not have provoked armed men to kill him. We're not allowed to talk to our men, but I had to find out what happened. I kept trying until I found a moment to talk to Harry Balter. I wanted it to be Harry so I could tell him about Zahra.

We managed to meet in the field as we worked with only our own community members nearby. We were harvesting—often in the

OCTAVIA E. BUTLER

rain—salad greens, onions, potatoes, carrots, and squashes, all planted and tended by Acorn, of course. We should also have been harvesting acorns—should already have harvested them—but we weren't permitted to do that. Some of us were being made to cut down both the mature live oak and pine trees and the saplings that we had planted. These trees not only commemorated our dead and provided us with much protein, but also they helped hold the hillside near our cabins in place. Somehow, our "teachers" have gotten the idea that we worshipped trees, thus we must have no trees nearby except those that produce the fruit and nuts that our "teachers" like to eat. Funny how that worked out. The orange, lemon, grapefruit, persimmon, pear, walnut, and avocado trees were good. All others were wicked temptations.

This is what Harry told me, bit by bit, during the times we managed to be near one another in our work.

"They used the collars, you know?" he said. "On that first day, they waited until we were all conscious. Then they came in and one of them said, 'We don't want you to make any mistakes. We want you to understand how this is going to work.' Then they started with Jorge Cho, and he screamed and writhed like a worm on a hook. Then they got Alan Faircloth, then Michael, then Bankole.

"Bankole was awake, but not really alert. He was just sitting on the floor, holding his head between his hands, staring down. They had taken all the furniture out by then, and piled it in a heap out where the trucks were. So none of us fell on anything but the floor. When they used the collar on him, he didn't make a sound. He just toppled over onto his side and twitched, sort of convulsed. He never screamed, never said a word. But he went into worse convulsions than any of the others had. Then he was dead. That was all. Michael said the collar had triggered a massive heart attack."

Harry didn't say more for a long time—or maybe he did, and I just didn't hear it. I was crying in spite of myself. I could be quiet, but I couldn't stop the tears. Then I heard him whisper, as we passed one another again, "I'm sorry, Lauren. God, I'm sorry. He was a good guy."

Bankole had delivered both of Harry's children. Bankole had delivered everyone's children, including his own daughter. Without believing in Earthseed, or even in Acorn, he had stayed and worked hard to make it all work. He had done more than anyone to make it work. How stupid and pointless that he should die at the hands of men who didn't know him or care about him or even intend to kill him. They just didn't know how to use the powerful weapons they possessed. They gassed Zahra to death by mistake because they didn't take her size into consideration. They shocked Bankole into a heart attack by mistake because they didn't take his age into consideration. It must have been his age. He'd had no heart trouble before. He was a strong, healthy man who should have lived to see his daughter grow up and maybe later father a son or another daughter.

It was all I could do not to fold up among the rows of plants and just lie there and moan and cry. But I stayed upright, somehow managed not to attract our "teachers" attentions.

After a time, I told him about Zahra. "I really believe it was her size," I finished. "Maybe these people don't know much about their weapons. Or maybe they just don't care. Maybe both. None of them lifted a finger to help Teresa."

There was another long, long silence. We worked and Harry got himself under control. When he spoke again, his voice was steady. "Olamina, we've got to kill these bastards!"

He almost never called me Olamina. We'd known each other since we were both in diapers. He called me Lauren except during the more important Gathering Day ceremonies. He had called me Olamina for the first time when I welcomed his first child into the Acorn community, and into Earthseed. It was as though for him the name were a title.

"First we've got to get rid of these collars," I said. "Then we have to find out what happened to the kids. If . . . if they're alive, we have to find out where they are."

"Do you think they are alive?"

OCTAVIA E. BUTLER

"I don't know." I drew a deep breath. "I'd give almost anything to know where my Larkin is and whether she's all right." Another pause. "These people lie about almost everything. But there must be records somewhere. There must be *something*. We've got to try to find out. Gather information. Seek weakness. Watch, wait, and do what you have to to stay alive!"

A "teacher" was coming toward us. Either he had spotted us whispering as we worked or he was just checking. I let Harry move past me. Our few moments of talk were over.

13

○ ○ ○

From EARTHSEED: THE BOOKS OF THE LIVING

When vision fails
Direction is lost.

When direction is lost
Purpose may be forgotten.

When purpose is forgotten
Emotion rules alone.

When emotion rules alone,
Destruction . . . destruction.

From Acorn, I was taken to a reeducation camp that was housed
in an old maximum-security prison in Del Norte County, just north
of Humboldt County. Pelican Bay State Prison, the thing had been
called. It became Pelican Bay Christian Reeducation Camp. I have
no memory of it, I'm glad to say, but people who spent time there as
adults and older kids have told me that even though it was no longer
called a prison, it reeked of suffering. Because of its prison structure,
it lent itself more easily than did Acorn to isolating people, not only
from society but from one another. It also provided enough room for
a nursery that was completely separate from the heathen inmates who
might contaminate the children. I was cared for at the Pelican Bay
nursery for several months. I know this because I was fingerprinted,
footprinted, and geneprinted there, and my records were stored at the
Christian American Church of Crescent City. They were supposed to
be accessible only to camp authorities, who were to prevent me from

being adopted by my heathen biological parents, and to whoever did adopt me. Also, there I was given my name: Asha Vere. Asha Vere was the name of a character in a popular Dreamask program.

Dreamasks—also known as head cages, dream books, or simply, Masks—were new then, and were beginning to edge out some of the virtual reality stuff. Even the early ones were cheap—big ski-mask-like devices with goggles over the eyes. Wearing them made people look not-quite-human. But the masks made computer-stimulated and guided dreams available to the public, and people loved them. Dreamasks were related to old-fashioned lie detectors, to slave collars, and to a frighteningly efficient form of audiovisual subliminal suggestion. In spite of the way they looked, Dreamasks were lightweight, clothlike, and comfortable. Each one offered wearers a whole series of adventures in which they could identify with any of several characters. They could live their character's fictional life complete with realistic sensation. They could submerge themselves in other, simpler, happier lives. The poor could enjoy the illusion of wealth, the ugly could be beautiful, the sick could be healthy, the timid could be bold. . . .

Jarret's people worried that this new entertainment would be like a drug to the "morally weak." To avoid their censure, Dreamasks International made a number of religious programs—programs that particularly featured Christian American characters. Asha Vere was one of those characters.

Asha Vere was a tall, beautiful, Amazon-like, Black Christian American woman who ran around rescuing people from heathen cults, anti-Christian plots, and squatter-camp pimps. I suppose someone thought that naming me after such an upright character might stifle any hereditary inclination in me toward heathenism. So I was stuck with the name. And so, by the way, were a lot of other women. Strong female characters were out of fashion in the fiction of the time. President Jarret and his followers in Christian America believed that one of the things that had gone wrong with the country was the intrusion of women into "men's business." I've seen recordings of him saying this and large audiences of both men and women cheering and applauding wildly. In fact, I've discovered that Asha Vere was originally intended to be a man, Aaron Vere, but a Dreamask executive convinced his colleagues that it was time for a hit series staring a tough-tender, Christian American female. He was right. There was such a hunger for interesting female characters that, as silly as the Asha Vere stories were, people liked them. And surprising numbers of people named their girl children "Asha" or "Vere" or "Asha Vere."

My name, eventually, was Asha Vere Alexander, daughter of Madison Alexander and Kayce Guest Alexander. These were middle-class Black members of the Church of Christian America in Seattle. They adopted me during the Al-Can war when they moved from Seattle—which had been hit by several missiles—down to Crescent City, where Kayce's mother Layla Guest lived. Ironically, Layla Guest was a refugee from Los Angeles. But she was a much richer refugee than my mother had been. Crescent City, a big, booming town among the redwoods, was so near Pelican Bay that Layla volunteered at the Pelican Bay nursery. It was Layla who brought Kayce and me together. Kayce didn't really want me. I was a big, dark-skinned, solemn baby, and she didn't like my looks. "She was a grim, stone-faced little thing," I heard her say later to her friends. "And she was as plain as a stone. I was afraid for her—afraid that if I didn't take her, no one would."

Both Kayce and Layla believed it was the duty of good Christian Americans to give homes to the many orphaned children from squatter settlements and heathen cults. If one couldn't be an Asha Vere, rescuing all sorts of people, one could at least rescue one or two unfortunate children and raise them properly.

Five months after Layla introduced her daughter to me, the Alexanders adopted me. I didn't exactly become their daughter, but they meant to do their duty—to raise me properly and save me from whatever depraved existence I might have had with my biological parents.

They have begun to let us alone more on Sundays after services. I suppose they're tired of using up their own Sundays to lash us into memorizing chapters of the Bible. After five or six hours of services and a meal of boiled vegetables, we are told to rest in our quarters and thank God for his goodness to us.

We aren't permitted to do anything. To do anything other than Bible study would be, in their view, "work," and a violation of the Fourth Commandment. We're to sit still, not speak, not repair our clothing or our shoes—we're all in rags since all but two sets per person of our clothing have been confiscated. We're allowed to read the Bible, pray, and sleep. If we're caught doing anything more than that, we're lashed.

Of course, the moment we're left alone, we do as we like. We hold whispered conversations, we clean and repair our things as best we can, we share information. And I write. Only on Sundays can we do these things in daylight.

We're permitted no electric light and no oil lamps, so we have only the window for light. During the week, it's dark when we get up and dark when we're shut in to sleep. During the week, we are machines—or domestic animals.

The only conveniences we're permitted are a galvanized bucket which we must all use as a toilet and a 20-liter plastic bottle of water fitted with a cheap plastic siphon pump. We each have one plastic bowl from which we both eat and drink. It's odd about the bowls. They're bright shades of blue, red, yellow, orange, and green. They're the only colorful things in our prison room—bright, cheerful lies. They're what you see first when you walk in. Mary Sullivan calls them our dog dishes. We hate them, but we use them. What choice do we have? Our only "legal" individual possessions are our bowls, our clothing, our blankets—one each—and our Camp Christian–issued paper King James Bibles.

On Sundays when we're fortunate enough to be let alone early, I take out paper and pencil and use my Bible as a desk.

My writing is a way for me to remind myself that I am human, that God is Change, and that I will escape this place. As irrational as the feeling may be, my writing still comforts me.

Other people find other comforts. Mary Sullivan and Allie combine their blankets and make love to one another late at night. It comforts them. Their sleeping place is next to mine, and I hear them at it. They aren't the only ones who do it, but they're the only pair so far that stays together.

"Do we disgust you?" Mary Sullivan whispered to me one morning with characteristic bluntness. We had been awakened later than usual and we could just see each other in the half-light. I could see Mary sitting up beside a still-sleeping Allie.

I looked at her, surprised. She's a tall woman—almost my size—angular and bony, but with an interesting-looking, expressive face. She looked as though she had always had plenty of hard, physical work to do, but not always enough to eat. "Do you love my friend?" I asked her.

She blinked, drew back as though she was about to tell me to mind my own business or to go to hell. But after a moment, she said in her harsh voice, "Of course I do!"

I managed a smile, although I don't know whether she could see it, and I nodded. "Then be good to one another," I said. "And if there's trouble, you and your sisters stand with us, with Earthseed." We're the strongest single group among the prisoners. The Sullivans and the Gamas have tended to group themselves with us, anyway, although nothing had been said. Well, now I've said something, at least to Mary Sullivan.

After a moment, she nodded, unsmiling. She wasn't a woman who smiled often.

I worry that someone will break ranks and report Allie and Mary, but so far, no one has reported anyone for anything, although our "teachers" keep inviting us to report one another's sins. There has been trouble now and then. Squatter-camp women have gotten into fights over food or possessions, and the rest of us stopped things before they got too loud—before a "teacher" arrived and demanded to know what was going on and who was responsible.

And there is one young squatter-camp woman, Crystal Blair, who seems to be a natural bully. She hits or shoves people, takes their food or their small possessions. She amuses herself by telling lies to cause fights. ("Do you know what she said about you? I heard her! She said . . .") She snatches things from people, sometimes making no secret of what she's doing. She doesn't want the pitiful possessions. Sometimes she makes a show of breaking them. She wants the other women to know that she can do what she damned well pleases, and they can't stop her. She has power, and they don't.

We've taught her to let Earthseed women and our possessions alone. We stood together, and let her know we're willing to make her life even more of a misery to her than it already is. We discovered by accident that all we had to do was hold her down and tug on her collar. The collar punishes her, and it punishes me and the other sharers among us if we were stupid enough to watch her suffering, but it leaves no marks. If we use her clothing to tie and gag her, then with just an occasional tug on her collar we can give her a hellish night. After we put her through one such night, she let us alone. She tormented other women. Tormenting people was her particular comfort.

We worry about her. She's crazier than most of us, and she's trouble, but she hates our "teachers" more than we do. She won't go to them for help. In time, though, one of her victims might. We watch her. We try to keep her from going too far.

SUNDAY, DECEMBER 11, 2033

More new people have been brought here—ragged, scrawny people, all strangers. Every day this week, a maggot has arrived to unload

OCTAVIA E. BUTLER

new people in groups of three, four, or five. We've finished building a long, shedlike extension onto the school with lumber that the "teachers" trucked in. This extension is four bare rooms of shelf beds intended to house 30 people each. Each wall is covered with three layers of shelves and plus an access ladder or two. Each shelf is to be a long, narrow bed intended to sleep two people, usually either feet to feet or head to head. The new people are each given what we have: a blanket, a plastic bowl, a Bible, and a shelf where they must sleep and store their things. We still sleep on the floor in our rooms, but everything else is the same.

Like us, the new people are using buckets as toilets. Some of us are being made to dig a cesspit. I took some lashes for pointing out that it was being put in a bad place. It could contaminate the underground water that feeds our wells. That could make us all sick, including our "teachers."

But our "teachers" know everything. They don't need advice from a woman, and a heathen woman at that. It was entirely their own decision a few days later to relocate the cesspit downhill and far away from the wells.

Someone has put up a sign at the logging-road gate: "Camp Christian Reeducation Facility." The Crusaders have surrounded the place with a Lazor-wire fence, so there's no safe entry or exit except at the gate. Lazor wire is made up of strands of wire so thin that they're hard to see. They slice into the flesh of the wild animals who blunder into them.

I've asked some of the strangers what's happening outside. Do people know what a reeducation camp really is? Are there other camps? Is there resistance? What's Jarret doing? What's going on?

Most of the new people won't talk to me. They're weary, frightened, beaten people. Those who are willing to talk know only that they were either arrested or snatched from their lives as squatters, drifters, or petty crooks.

Several of the new people are sharers. "Bad seed if there ever was bad seed," our "teachers" say. "The heathen children of drug addicts." They treat known sharers as objects of suspicion, contempt, and ugly amusement. They're so easy to torment. No challenge at all.

We have not given ourselves away, yet, we sharers of Earthseed. We've worked hard at concealing ourselves, and, I admit, we've been lucky. None of us has been pushed beyond our limits at a time when our "teachers" might notice. All of us have had years of hiding in plain sight to help us. Even the Mora girls, only 14 and 15, have managed to hide what they are.

I kept up my search for someone who could tell me at least a little about the outside. In the end, I didn't find my informant. He found me. He was a young Black man, bone thin, scarred, careful, but not beaten down. His name was David Turner.

"Day," he said when we found ourselves digging side by side in the stupid, dangerous cesspit that was later abandoned. I think now that he only spoke to me because we weren't supposed to speak.

I looked a question at him as I threw a shovelful of dirt out of the hole.

"Name of David," he said. "Call me Day."

"Olamina," I said without thinking.

"Yeah?" he said.

"Yes."

"Different kind of name."

I sighed, glanced at him, liked the stubborn, unbeaten look of him, and said, "Lauren."

He gave me a quick grin. "People call you Laurie?"

"Not if they expect me to answer," I said.

I guess we were a little careless. Above, one of our "teachers" lashed me hard, and I convulsed and fell. I've noticed before that if a collared man and woman are talking together, it's the woman who tends to be lashed. Women are temptresses, you see. We drag innocent men into trouble. From the time of Adam and Eve women have dragged innocent men into trouble. Anyway, I was lashed hard, but only once. After that, I was more careful.

Being lashed hard several times is enough to induce temporary coordination problems and memory loss. Day told me later that he'd seen a man lashed until the man didn't know his own name. I believe him. I know that when I saw Bankole's dead body, and I turned on my bearded guard, I had never in my life been more intent on killing another person. I was dropped where I stood with a hard shock, then lashed several more times, and Allie tells me that the way I jerked and flopped around the ground, she thought I'd break my bones. I woke up very sore, covered in bruises, sprains, abrasions, and bloody rock cuts, but that wasn't the worst.

The worst was the way I felt afterward. I don't mean the physical pain. This place is a university of pain. I mean what I wrote before. I was a zombie for several days after the lashing. At first I couldn't even remember that Bankole was dead. Natividad and Allie had to tell me that all over again more than once. And I couldn't remember what had happened to Acorn, why we were all shut up in one room of our own school, where the men were, where the children were. . . .

I haven't written about this until now. When I understood it, it scared me to death. It scared me into mewling in a corner like a terror- ized three-year-old.

After surviving Robledo, I knew that strangers could appear and steal or destroy everything and everyone I loved. People and posses- sions could be snatched away. But somehow, it had not occurred to me that . . . that *bits of my own mind* could be snatched away too. I knew I could be killed. I've never had any illusions about that. I could be disabled. I knew that too. But I had not thought that another person, just by pushing a small button, then smiling and pushing it again and again. . . .

He did smile, my bearded teacher. That came back to me later. All of it came back to me. When it did. . . . Well, that's when I retreated to my corner, whimpering and moaning. The son of a bitch smiled and pressed his button over and over as though he were fucking me, and he grinned while he watched me groaning and thrashing.

My brother said a collar makes you envy the dead. As bad as that sounds, it didn't, couldn't, convey to me, how a collar makes you hate. It teaches you whole new magnitudes of utter hatred. I knew almost nothing about hate until this thing was put around my neck. Now, sometimes it's all I can do to stop myself from trying again to kill one of them and then dying the way Emery did.

I've been talking off and on to Day Turner. Whenever we can, when we pass one another or are put to work in the same general area, we've talked. I've encouraged Travis and Harry and the other men to talk to him. I think he'll tell us anything he can that will help us. This is a summary of what he's passed on to us so far:

Day had walked over the Sierras from his last dead-end, low-paying job in Reno, Nevada. He had drifted north and west, hoping to find at least a chance to work his way out of poverty. He had no family, but for protection, he walked with two friends. All had been well until he and his friends reached Eureka. There, they had heard that one of the churches offered overnight shelter and meals and temporary work to willing men. The church was, no surprise, the Church of Christian America.

The work was helping to repair and paint a couple of old houses that the church intended to use as part of their orphaned-children's home. There were no orphans on site—or none that Day saw, or I suppose we would all have badgered him to death about our own children. You would think that there were enough real orphans in this filthy world. How dare anything that calls itself a church create new orphans with its maggots and its collars?

Anyway, Day and his friends liked the idea of doing something for kids and earning a few dollars as well as a bed and a few meals. But they were unlucky. While they slept on their first night in the church's men's dormitory, a small group of the men there tried to rob the place. Day says he had nothing to do with robbery. He says he doesn't give a damn

OCTAVIA E. BUTLER

whether we believe him or not, but that he's never stolen, except to eat, and he'd never in his life steal from a church. He was raised by a very religious uncle and aunt, now dead, and thanks to their early training, there were some things he just wouldn't do. But the thieves were said to be Black, and Day and his friends were Black, so Day and his friends were presumed guilty.

I found myself believing him. That may be stupid of me, but I like him, and he doesn't strike me as a liar or a church robber.

He says the church's security people swarmed over the dormitories, and the men awoke and ran in all directions. They were all free poor men. When trouble erupted, and there was no real profit to be had, most of them never thought of doing anything other than getting away—especially when the shooting started.

Day didn't have a gun. One of his friends did, but the three of them got separated. Then they all got caught.

He and 18 or 20 other men were caught, and all the Black ones went to jail. Some were charged with violent crimes—armed robbery and assault. The rest were charged with vagrancy—which is a far more serious crime than it once was. The vagrants were found guilty and indentured to the Church of Christian America. Day's friends were charged with felonies as part of the first group because they were found together and one had a gun. Day was in the vagrant group. He had been indentured to work for 30 days for the church. He had already been shifted around and forced to work for more than two months. They lashed him when he complained that his sentence was up. At first they said he could go free if he could prove he had a job waiting for him outside. Of course since he was a stranger to the area, and since he had no free time to look for a job, it was impossible for him to get outside work. Local vagrants, on the other hand, were, one by one, rescued by relatives and friends, who promised to either give them jobs or feed and house them so that they would no longer be vagrant.

Day had done construction work, painting, groundskeeping, and janitorial work. He had been given a thorough physical examination, then been required to donate blood twice. He had been encouraged to offer to donate a kidney or a cornea, after which he could heal and go free. This terrified him. He refused, but he couldn't help knowing that his organs, and, in fact, his life could be taken from him at any time. Who would know? Who would care? He wondered why they had not already killed him already.

Then they moved him to Camp Christian for reeducation. He was told that there was hope for him—that he could, if he chose, learn to be a servant of God and God's true church and a loyal citizen of the greatest country in the world. He said he was already a Christian. They said, in effect, "Prove it." They said he would be accepted among them when they judged him truly penitent and educated in the truths of the Bible.

Then Day quoted them Exodus 21:16—"And he that stealeth a man and selleth him, or if he be found in his hand, he shall surely be put to death." Day was lashed for his choice of scripture, of course, and he was told that the people of Christian America well knew that the devil could quote scripture.

Most people don't know about the camps, Day says. He's learned from talking to other collared men that there are a few small camps like Camp Christian and at least two big ones—much bigger than Camp Christian. One of the big ones is up at an abandoned prison in Del Norte County and the other is down in Fresno County. People don't realize how free poor vagrants are being treated, but he's afraid that even if they did know, they wouldn't care. The likelihood is that people with legal residences would be glad to see a church taking charge of the thieving, drug-taking, drug-selling, disease-spreading, homeless free poor.

"Back when I was at home, my aunt and uncle would have felt like that," Day said. "We walk the highways and scrounge and scavenge and ask for work, and all of that reminds people that what's happened to us can happen to them. They don't like to think about stuff like that, so they get mad at us. They make the cops arrest us or run us out of town. They call us names and wish somebody would do something to make us disappear. And now, somebody is doing just that!"

He's right. There are plenty of people who would think the Church was doing something generous and necessary—teaching deadbeats to work and be good Christians. No one would see a problem until the camps were a lot bigger and the people in them weren't just drifters and squatters. As far as we of Earthseed are concerned, that's already happened, but who are we? Just weird cultists who practice strange rites, so no doubt there are nice, ordinary people who would be glad to see us taught to behave ourselves too.

How many people, I wonder, can be penned up and tormented—reeducated—before it begins to matter to the majority of Americans? How does this penning people up look to other countries? Do they know? Would they care? There are worse things happening here in the States and elsewhere, I know. There's war, for instance.

In fact, we are at war. The United States is at war with Alaska and Canada. People are calling it the Al-Can war. I know Jarret wanted a war, was working to get one started. But until Day told me, I hadn't realized it had begun. There have already been exchanges of missiles and a few vicious border battles. I told Allie about this later, and she thought about it for a moment.

"Who's winning?" she asked.

I shook my head. "Day didn't tell me. Hell, I didn't ask."

She shrugged. "Yeah. It doesn't much matter to us, does it?"

"I don't know," I said.

We are roughly 250 inmates, and, by my most recent count, 20 guards. Just think: if we could all move at the same time, 10 or 12 people per guard, we might be able to . . . to. . . .

We might be able to die like Teresa. Just one "teacher" could, with one finger, send us all sprawling and writhing on the ground. We might be able to die, every one of us, without doing much more than startling our guards.

SUNDAY, DECEMBER 18, 2033

Now I have been raped.

It happened twice. Once on Monday, and again yesterday. It is my Christmas gift from Christian America.

SUNDAY, DECEMBER 25, 2033

I need to write about what has been happening to me. I don't want to, but I need to.

To be a sharer is to feel the pleasure and the pain—the apparent pleasure and the apparent pain—of other people. There have been times when I've felt the *pleasure* of one of our "teachers" when he lashed someone. The first time it happened—or rather, the first time I understood what was happening, I threw up.

When someone cries out in pain, I'm careful not to look. If I happen to see someone double up, so far I've been able to lean against a wall or a tool or a friend or a tree. Somehow, though, it never occurred to me that I had to protect myself from the pleasures of our "teachers."

There are a few men here, though, a few "teachers," who lash us until they have orgasms. Our screams and convulsions and pleas and sobs are what these men need to feel sexually satisfied. I know of three who seem to need to lash someone to get sexual pleasure. Most often, they lash a woman, then rape her. Sometimes the lashing is enough for them. I don't want to know this as clearly as I do know it, but I can't help myself. These men feast on our pain—and they call us parasites.

Rape is done with a pretense of secrecy. After all, these men come to the camp and do a tour of duty. Then at least some of them must go home to their wives and kids. Except for Reverend Joel Locke and his three top assistants, who work here full time, the men who come here still live in the real world. They rape, but they pretend they don't. They say they're religious, but power has corrupted even the best of them. I don't like to admit it, but some of them are, in a strange way,

OCTAVIA E. BUTLER

decent, ordinary men. I mean that they believe in what they are doing. They're not all sadists or psychopaths. Some of them seem truly to feel that collecting minor criminals in places like Camp Christian is right and necessary for the good of the country. They disapprove of the rape and the unnecessary lashings, but they do believe that we inmates are, somehow, enemies of the country. Their superiors have told them that parasites and heathens like us brought down "America the mighty." America was the strongest country on Earth, but people like us went whoring after foreign religions and refused to do our duty as citizens. We women lost all modesty and offered ourselves in the streets, and the men who should have controlled us became our pimps.

That's the short version of how evil we are and why we deserve to be in collars. The other side of this picture is how our hardworking, long-suffering "teachers" are trying to "help" us.

One of the men who has been after Jorge's sister Cristina specialized in this strange, self-pitying attitude. He talked to her about his wheel-chair-bound wife, about his disrespectful children, about how poor they all are. She says she begged him to let her alone, and he threw her down and forced her. He said he was a loyal, hardworking Christian American, and he was entitled to some pleasure in his life. But when he had finished, he begged her to forgive him. Insanity.

My rape happened at the end of a very cold, rainy day. I had been given cooking duties. This meant I got to clean myself up, stay warm and dry, and, for once, get enough to eat. I was feeling both grateful for this and ashamed of my gratitude. I worked with Natividad and two of the Gama women, Catarina and Joan, and at the end of the day, we were all taken away to the cabins and raped.

Of the four of us, only I was a sharer. Of the four of us, only I endured not only my own pain and humiliation, but the wild, intense pleasure of my rapist. There are no words to explain the twisted, schizoid ugliness of this.

We can't bathe often enough. We get no hot water and little soap unless we get kitchen duty. If we ask to be allowed to bathe, it's called vanity. Yet we are viewed with disgust and contempt if we stink. We are said to "stink with sin."

So be it.

I have decided to stink like a corpse. I have decided that I would rather get a disease from being filthy than go on attracting the attentions of these men. I will be filthy. I will stink. I will pay no attention to my hair or my clothing.

I must do this, or I will kill myself.

OCTAVIA E. BUTLER

2035

○ ○ ○

From EARTHSEED: THE BOOKS OF THE LIVING

Self is.
Self is body and bodily
perception. Self is thought, memory,
belief. Self creates. Self destroys.
Self learns, discovers, becomes.
Self shapes. Self adapts. Self
invents its own reasons for being.
To shape God, shape Self.

14

○ ○ ○

From EARTHSEED: THE BOOKS OF THE LIVING

Take comfort.
Each move toward the Destiny,
Each achievement of the Destiny,
Must mean new beginnings,
New worlds,
A rebirth of Earthseed.
Alone,
Each of us is mortal.
Yet through Earthseed,
Through the Destiny,
We join.
We are purposeful
Immortal
Life!

Somehow, my mother endured more than a year of slavery at Camp Christian. How she did it, how she survived it, I can only guess from her writings of 2033 and 2035. Her record of 2034 has been lost. She did write during 2034. I have no doubt of that. She couldn't have gone for a year without writing. I've found occasional references to notes made then. No doubt by then, she was writing on whatever scraps of paper she could find.

She obviously liked to keep her writing when she could, but I suspect that somehow it helped her just to do it, whether she was able to keep it or not. The act of writing itself was a kind of therapy.

The most important loss is this: There was at least one major escape attempt. The people of Acorn took no part in it, but of course they suffered for it later along with the rest of Camp Christian. Its leader was the same David Turner that my mother had met and liked in 2033. I know this because I've spoken to people who were there, who survived the effort, and who remember the suffering.

My best informant was a plainspoken woman named Cody Smith, who in December of 2034 had been arrested for vagrancy in Garberville and transported to Camp Christian. She was one of the survivors of the rebellion, although as a result of it, she suffered nerve damage and eventual blindness. She was beaten and kicked as well as electronically lashed. Here's her story as she told it to me:

"Day Turner's people were convinced that they could overwhelm the guards by piling onto them three or more to one. They believed they could kill the guards before their collars disabled them. Lauren Olamina said no. She said the guards were never all together, were never all outside at the same time. She said one guard missed was one guard who could kill all of us with just one finger. Day liked her. I don't know why. She was big like a man and not pretty, but he liked her. He just didn't believe she was right. He thought she was scared. But he forgave her because she was a woman. That drove her crazy. The more she tried to talk him out of it, the more determined he was to do it. Then he asked her if she was going to give him away, and she got really quiet and so mad he actually took a step back from her. She could do that. She didn't get loud when she got mad, she got real quiet. She scared people.

"She asked him who the hell did he think she was, and he said he was starting to not be sure. There was some bad feeling after that. She stopped talking to him and began talking to her own people. It was hard to talk, dangerous to talk. It was against the rules. People had to whisper and mutter and talk without moving their lips and not look at the people they were talking to. They got lashed if they were caught. Messages got passed from one person to another. Sometimes they got changed or messed up and you couldn't tell what people were trying to tell you. Sometimes someone told the guards. New people brought in from the road would do that—tell what they had no business telling.

OCTAVIA E. BUTLER

They got a little extra food for it or a warm shirt or something. But if we caught them at it, they never did it again. We saw to that. There were always a few, though. They did it for a reward or because they were scared or because they had started to believe all those sermons and Bible classes and prayer meetings and the other stuff they made us sit through or stand through when we were almost too tired to live. I think a few of the women did it so the guards would treat them better in bed. Some guards liked to hurt you. So for us, talking was dangerous even if no guard saw you do it.

"Anyway, it didn't seem that anyone gave Day Turner away. Lauren Olamina just told her people that when it happened, they should lie face-down on the ground with their hands behind their necks. Some of them didn't want to. They thought Day was right. But she kept at them, pushing them, asking them about lashings they had seen—one guard lashing eight or nine people at the same time with just one finger. . . . She got herself lashed over and over, trying to talk to them—to the men in her group espe-cially. I think Day worked on them at night when men and women were Locked up separate. You know the kind of shit men say to one another when they want to stop other men from listening to a woman. From what I heard, Travis Douglas was the one who kept Olamina's men in line. He wasn't all that big, but he had a force to him. People trusted him, listened to him, liked him. And for some reason, Travis trusted Olamina. He didn't like what she was telling them to do, but he . . . like he believed in her, you know.

"When the break came, most of Olamina's people did what she had told them to do. That saved them from being shot or from being beaten as badly as the ones like me who didn't get on the ground fast enough. Day's people started grabbing guards, and the Acorn people dropped like stones. When the pain hit, they were already getting down on the ground, all but a guy named King—Jeff King—big, good-looking blond guy—and three women. Two were named Scolari—sisters or some-thing—and Channa Ryan. I knew Channa Ryan. She just couldn't stand it anymore. She was pregnant, but not showing much yet. She figured if she died taking one of the guards and a guard's baby with her, it would be a good deal. There was this one particular guy—ugly son of a bitch who washed himself maybe once a week. But he used to make her go to his cabin two or three times a week. He had his fun with her. She wanted to get him. She didn't, though.

"Day's people killed one guard. Just one, and it was a woman who got him—that evil bitch Crystal Blair. She died for it, but she got him. I don't know why she hated the guards so much. They didn't rape her, didn't pay that much attention to her. I guess it was just that they took her freedom. She was a big pain in the ass while she was alive, but people kind of respected her after she was dead. She ripped that guard's throat out with her teeth!

"Day's people hurt a couple of other guards, but it cost them 15 of their own. Fifteen dead just to start with. Some others were lashed to death or almost to death later. Some were kicked and stomped as well as lashed. I was because I was too close to Crystal Blair when she killed that one guard. Day got killed too, but not until later. Later, they hanged him. By then, he was so busted up, I doubt he knew what was going on. The rest of us got hurt, but not so bad. The ones who could walk had to go out the next day to work. If we had headaches or teeth kicked in or bad gashes or bruises from being kicked with boots, it didn't matter. The guards said if they couldn't beat the devil out of us, they'd work him out of us. The ones who couldn't walk disappeared. I don't know what happened to them—maybe killed, maybe taken away for medical treatment. We never saw them again. Everyone else worked for sixteen hours straight. They lashed you if you stopped to pee. You had to just do it on yourself and keep working. They did that for three days straight. Work sixteen hours—dig a hole. Fill it up. Chop trees. Make firewood. Dig another hole. Fill it up. Paint the cabins. Chop weeds. Dig a hole. Fill it up. Drag rocks from the hills. Break them to gravel. Dig a hole. Fill it up.

"A couple of people went crazy. One woman just fell down on the ground and started screaming and crying. She wouldn't stop. The other one, a big man with scars all over his face, he started running

OCTAVIA E. BUTLER

and screaming—going nowhere, running in circles. They disappeared too. Three days. We didn't get enough to eat. You never got enough to eat unless you got kitchen duty. Every night they preached hellfire and damnation at us and made us memorize Bible verses for at least an hour before they'd let us sleep. Then it was like we hadn't slept at all and they were getting us up to do it all again. It was hell. Plain hell. No devil could have made a better one."

Cody Smith. She was an old woman when I met her—illiterate, poor, and scarred. If her version of the break and its aftermath is true, it's no wonder my mother never wrote much about it after her captivity. I've never found anyone who heard her talk much about it.

But at least she got most of her own people through the rebellion. She lost only three, and two others—the Mora sisters—had given away their status as sharers. I wonder that all the sharers hadn't given themselves away. On the other hand, when everyone is screaming, I suppose sharers' screams don't draw special attention. I don't know how the Moras gave themselves away, but Cody Smith and other informants have told me they did. It may have been the reason that after the rebellion, they were raped more often than the other women were. They never gave any other sharer away.

That was my mother's 2034. I wouldn't have wished it on her. I wouldn't have wished it on anyone.

What was done to my mother and to many other interned people of her time was illegal in almost every way. It was never legal to collar noncriminals, never legal to confiscate their property or separate husband from wife or to force either to work without pay of some kind. The matter of separating children from parents, however, might have been managed almost legally.

Vagrancy laws were much expanded, and vagrant adults with children could lose custody of the children, unless they were able to establish homes for them within a specified period of time. In some counties, job-placement help was available from churches and local businesses, and the jobs had to provide at Least room and board for the family, even if there were no salary. Vagrant women often became unsalaried household help or poorly paid surrogate mothers. In other counties, there was no help at all for vagrants. They had to make a proper home for their children or their children would be rescued from their inadequate, unfit hands.

Not surprisingly, children were "rescued" this way much more often from vagrants who were considered heathens than from those who were seen as acceptable Christians. And "heathens" who were poor, but not true vagrants, not homeless, might find themselves reclassified as vagrants so that their children could be placed in good Christian America homes. The idea, of course, was to make good Christian Americans of them in spite of the wickedness, or at best, the errors of their parents.

It's hard to believe that kind of thing happened here, in the United States in the twenty-first century, but it did. It shouldn't have happened, in spite of all the chaos that had gone before. Things were healing. People like my mother were starting small businesses, living simply, becoming more prosperous. Crime was down in spite of the sad things that happened to the Noyer family and to Uncle Marc. Even my mother said that things were improving. Yet Andrew Steele Jarret was able to scare, divide, and bully people, first into electing him President, then into letting him fix the country for them. He didn't get to do everything he wanted to do. He was capable of much greater fascism. So were his most avid followers.

For people like my mother, Jarret's fanatical followers were the greater danger. During Jarret's first year in office, the worst of his followers ran amok. Filled with righteous superiority and popular among the many frightened, ordinary citizens who only wanted order and stability, the fanatics set up the camps. Meanwhile, Jarret himself was busy with the ridiculous, obscene Al-Can war. If Jarret's thugs weren't locking poor people into collars, Jarret himself was seducing them into the military and feeding them into what turned out to be a useless, stupid exercise in destruction. The already-weakened country all but collapsed. Too many Americans, whether or not they belonged to CA, had family

OCTAVIA E. BUTLER

and friends in both Canada and Alaska. People deserted or left the country to avoid the draft—there was one, at last—and the saying was, during the war, that healthy young men were America's biggest export.

There was much slaughter on both sides of the Canadian border and there were air and naval attacks on the coastal cities of Alaska. The war was like an exaggeration of the attempted breakout at Camp Christian. Much blood was shed, but little was accomplished. The war began in anger, bitterness, and envy at nations who appeared to be on their way up just as our country seemed to be on a downward slide.

Then the war just petered out. At first, there was much fighting, much destruction, much screaming and flag-waving. Then, gradually, over 2034, a terrible, bitter weariness seemed to creep over people. Poor families saw their sons drafted and killed, as they said, "for nothing!" It was harder than ever to buy decent food. Much of our grain over the past few years of climate change and chaos had been imported from Canada, after all. In the end, in late 2034, peace talks began. After that, except for a lot of hard feelings and occasional nasty incidents, the war was over. The border between Canada and America stayed where it had been, and Alaska remained an independent country. It was the first state to officially, completely, successfully secede from the union. People were saying that Jarret's home state of Texas would be next.

In less than a year, Jarret went from being our savior, almost the Second Coming in some people's minds, to being an incompetent son of a bitch who was wasting our substance on things that didn't matter. I don't mean that everyone changed their feelings toward him. Many people never did. My adopted parents never did, even though he cost them a beautiful, intelligent, loving daughter. I grew up hearing about that daughter endlessly. Her name was Kamaria, and she was perfect. I know this because my mother told me about her at least once during every day of my childhood. I could never look as good as Kamaria did or straighten my room as well or do as well with my studies or even clean a toilet as well—although I find it difficult to believe the perfect little bitch ever cleaned a toilet—or used one.

I didn't know I was still bitter enough to write a thing like that. I shouldn't be. It's foolish to hate someone you've never met, someone who's never harmed you. I believe now that I shifted my resentment safely onto Kamaria, who wasn't there, so that at least until my adolescence, I could love Kayce Alexander. She was, after all, the only mother I knew.

Kamaria Alexander died in a missile attack on Seattle when she was 11 years old, and my adopted parents never stopped blaming—and hating—the Canadians in their grief for her. But they never blamed Jarret—"that good man," "that fine man," "that man of God." Kayce talked that way. So did her friends when she finally moved back to them in Seattle where her neighborhood and her church were scarred, but still standing. Madison Alexander barely spoke at all. He murmured agreement with whatever Kayce said, and he felt me up a lot, but apart from that, he was quiet. My strongest memory of him, when I was four or five, was of his picking me up, putting me in his lap, and feeling me. I didn't know why I didn't like this. I just learned early to stay out of his way as much as I could.

From *THE JOURNALS OF LAUREN OYA OLAMINA*
SUNDAY, FEBRUARY 25, 2035

I've been too cold and too miserable, and too sick to do much writing. We've all had flu. We're made to work anyway. Four people died last week during a long, cold rain. One was pregnant. She gave birth alone in the mud. No one was allowed to help her. She and her baby both died. Two were worked until they dropped. When they dropped, the teachers called them lazy parasites and lashed them. During the night, they died—two men. They were all strangers, highway paupers—"vagrants" who had been forced to come here. They were sick and half-starved when they arrived. Thanks to the cold, wet weather, the lack of heat in our barracks, and the bad diet, we all catch any contagious disease brought to us from the highway or from the towns. Even our "teachers" are suffering with colds and flu. And when they suffer, they take their misery out on us.

All this, and one other thing has made us decide that the time has come to make our own break—or die trying.

We have information—some of us have learned things from our rapists, others just from keeping our eyes and ears open. Also, we have 23 knives—that is, Earthseed, the Sullivans and the Gamas have 23 knives. That's more than one for each guard. Some we've stolen from the trash heap where our "teachers" teach us wastefulness and slovenliness. Other knives are just sharp bits of metal that we've found and wrapped with tape or cloth to protect our hands. They're crude, but they'll cut a human throat. As soon as we've shut our collars off, we'll use the knives. If we're quick and if we move together as we've planned, we should be able to surprise several of our guards before they even think to use their maggots against us.

We know some of us will die in this. Maybe we'll all die. But the way things are going, we'll die anyway. None of us know how long we're to be kept collared. No one who's come here has been released. Even the few people who try to suck up to the "teachers" when they don't have to are still here, still collared. None of us have heard anything about what's happened to our children. And most of us are sick. None of Earthseed has died since Day's rebellion, but we're sick. And Allie . . . Allie might die. Or she might be permanently brain damaged. She's one of the reasons I've decided we've got to risk a breakout soon.

Allie and her lover Mary Sullivan were caught last Sunday.

No, I take that back. They weren't caught. They were betrayed. They were betrayed by Beth and Jessica Faircloth. That's the worst. They were betrayed by people who were part of us, part of Earthseed. They were betrayed by people whom Allie and the rest of us had helped to rescue from starvation and slavery back when they had nothing. We took them in, and when their family decided to join Earthseed, when they had done their probationary year, we Welcomed them.

I watched the betrayal. I couldn't stop it. I couldn't do anything. I'm worthless these days, just worthless.

Last Sunday, we had the usual six hours of preaching, this time on the evils of sexual sinfulness. First we heard from Reverend Locke, who runs this place. Then we heard from Reverend Chandler Benton, a minister from Eureka who sometimes drives out to inflict himself on us. Benton preached a vicious and weirdly salacious sermon on the evil, depraved wickedness of bestiality, incest, pedophilia, homosexuality, lesbianism, pornography, masturbation, prostitution, and adultery. It went on and on—stories from current news, Bible stories, long quotations of Old Testament laws and punishments including death by stoning, the destruction of Sodom and Gomorrah, the life and death of Jezebel, disease, hellfire, on and on.

But there was nothing at all said about rape. The good Reverend Benton himself has, during earlier visits, made use of both Adela Ortiz and Cristina Cho. He goes to the cabin—once the Bailer house—that is reserved now for visiting VIPs and has the woman of his choice brought to him.

We endure these sermons. They give us a chance to come in out of the rain. We are allowed to sit down and not work. We aren't cold because our "teachers" don't want to be cold. They build a big fire in the school's fireplace once a week. And so for a few hours on Sundays, we are warm, dry, and almost comfortable in our rows on the floor. We're hungry, but we know we'll soon be fed. We're in a drowsy, passive state. Without the rest we get on Sundays, several more of us would be dead. I'm sure of that. Nevertheless, we're being preached at while we're in that drowsy, passive state. I doze sometimes, though we're lashed if we're caught sleeping. I sit up, lean against a wall, and I let myself doze.

I didn't realize it, but the two female Faircloths, it seems, had begun to listen. Worse, they had begun to believe, to be frightened, to be converted. Or perhaps not. Perhaps they had other motives.

We're always being called upon to testify, to give public thanks for all the kindness and generosity that God has shown us in spite of our unworthiness. And we must confess that unworthiness and make a public repentance and a public appeal for God's mercy. We have each been required to do this many times. The more you yield, the more you are required to yield. Our teachers know we don't mean it, know we act out of fear of pain. We simply do as we are told. They hate us for this. They look at us with unmistakable hatred, disgust, and contempt, and they insist that it's love that they feel. Their God requires them to love us, after all. And it's only love that makes them try so hard to help us see the light. They say we're blinded by our own sinful stubbornness to the love and the help that they offer. "Spare the rod and spoil the child," they tell us, and we are, at best, still children as far as morality is concerned.

Right.

Anyway, Reverend Benton issued a call to testify. Three people had been ordered to testify. I was one of them. How I was selected, I don't know, but a scrawny "teacher" with bad teeth had put his hand on my shoulder before services began and ordered me to give testimony. The other two who had been ordered to testify were Ed Gama and a redhaired, one-armed woman, fresh from the highway. Her name was Teal, she had been with us for less than a week, and she was afraid of her shadow. Ed and I have done it before, so we went first to show the stranger what to do. This was the usual practice. I gave thanks for my many blessings, then I confessed to sinful thoughts, to anger, and to resistance to my teachers who were only trying to help me. I apologized to God and to all present again and again for my wickedness. I begged for forgiveness, begged for the strength and the wisdom to do God's will.

That's how you do it. That's how I've done it for over a year.

When I finished, Ed did pretty much the same thing. He had his own scripted list of sins and apologies. Teal was bright enough to do as we had done, but she was very frightened. Her voice trembled, and she all but whispered.

In his loud, nasty voice, Reverend Benton said, "Speak up, sister. Let the church hear your testimony."

Tears spilled from the woman's eyes, but she managed to raise her voice and repent and ask forgiveness for "all the things she had done wrong." She must have forgotten the kind of thing that the sermons had "suggested" she confess to. Then she collapsed to her knees and began to sob, out of control, terrified, begging, "Don't hurt me. Please don't hurt me. I'll do anything."

If I had tried to go to her, help her up, and take her back to her space on the floor, I would have been lashed. Human decency is a sin here. Ed and I looked at each other, but neither of us dared to touch her. I suspect that some "teacher" would have helped her back to her place. Lashing her back to her place wouldn't be quite the thing to do under the circumstances.

But there was an interruption. Beth and Jessica Faircloth had gotten up and were picking their way through the congregation, trying not to step on anyone, heading for the altar. When they reached the altar, they fell to their knees. People did this sometimes, gave voluntary testimony in hope of currying favor with the "teachers." It was harmless—or had always been harmless before. And it might buy you a piece of bread or an apple later. In fact, the Faircloths had done it several times. Some of us sneered at them for it, but it had never seemed important to me. Stupid me.

"We've sinned too," Beth cried. "We didn't mean to. We didn't know what to do. We knew it was wrong, but we were afraid."

They were not lashed. I saw Reverend Benton hold up his hand, no doubt telling the "teachers" to let them alone. "Speak, sisters," he said. "Confess your sin. God loves you. God will forgive."

They didn't follow the form this time. Instead they spoke the way they do when they're afraid, when they know they've done something other people might not like, when they're standing together against others. They're not twins. In fact, they're 18- and 19-year-old sisters, but under stress, they act much younger, and they act like twins, finishing one another's sentences, speaking in unison, or repeating one another's words. Their testimony was like that.

"We saw them doing it," Beth said.

"They've been doing it for a long time now," Jessica added. "We saw them."

"At night," Beth continued. "We knew it was wrong."

"It's dirty and filthy and perverted!" Jessica said.

"You can hear them kissing and making noises," Beth said, making a face, to show her disgust. "Perverted!"

"I never knew Allie was like that, but even before you came to teach us, she lived with another woman," Jessica said. "I thought she was okay because she had a little boy, but now I know she wasn't."

"She must have been doing it with women all the time," Beth echoed.

"Now she does it with Mary Sullivan." Jessica had begun to cry. "It's wrong, but we were afraid to tell before."

"She's strong like a man, and she's mean," Beth said. "We're afraid of her."

And I thought, *Oh no, damnit, no!* Our "teachers" have mistreated us every day, humiliated us and harangued us. But the misery has gone on for so long, and the sermons have gone on for so long, and we've stood together against it all. . . .

But I suppose something like this was bound to happen sooner or later. I only wish the traitors had been strangers from outside. That's happened before in lesser ways, but after a night or two, we've always managed to teach outsiders to keep their mouths shut about anything they've seen among their fellow inmates. No member of Earthseed has ever betrayed us in any way—until now.

As Allie was dragged to the front of the room to be punished, she shouted at Beth and Jessica, "They'll still rape you, and they'll still lash you and when they're done with you they'll still kill you!"

And I screamed at them, "She gave you food when you were hungry!"

So the "teachers" lashed me too.

But what they did to Allie and to Mary Sullivan, that went on and on. Mary Sullivan's father Arthur begged them to stop, managed to hit one of them and knock him down. So, of course he was lashed. But he bought no mercy for his daughter. Mary was having terrible convulsions, and they went on lashing her. They lashed both women until neither could scream anymore. They made us watch. I didn't watch. To survive, I kept my head down, my eyes half shut. I've been lashed for this behavior from time to time, but not today. Today, all attention was on the two "sinners."

They lashed Allie and Mary until Mary died.

They lashed them until Allie was lost somewhere within herself. She hasn't spoken a full sentence since the lashing.

Because I spoke for Allie, I was made to dig Mary's grave. Better me than Mary's father. He isn't in his right mind either. He was forced to watch his child tortured to death. He just wanders around, staring. Our teachers lash him, and he screams from the pain, but when they finish, he's no different. They seem to think they can torture him into forgetting his terrible grief and his hate.

I can't stand this. I can't. I don't care if they kill me. I will break free of this or I will be dead.

The Faircloth girls have been given a room in what used to be the King house. They have a whole room to themselves now instead of a room shared with thirty other women. They still wear collars, but they're on permanent cooking duty now. They don't have to chop wood or do fieldwork or construction work or clear brush or dig wells or graves or do any of the other hard, heavy, dirty work that the rest of us must do. And they don't know how to cook. Somehow, they've never learned to put together a decent meal. So they don't cook for our "teachers." They just cook for us.

Of course, they're hated. No one talks to them, but no one does anything to them either. We've been warned to let them alone. And they have been given a certain power over us. They can season our food with spit or dirt or shit, and we know it. Maybe that's what they're doing, and that's why the food is so much worse than it was. I didn't think that was possible—for it to get worse. The Faircloths have managed to ruin garbage. The Sullivan brothers and sisters might kill both Faircloth girls if they get the chance. Old Arthur Sullivan has been sent away. We don't know where. He's out of his mind and our "teachers" weren't able to lash him back to sanity, so they got rid of him.

We've learned that the master unit, the unit that powers or controls all the collars in Camp Christian, is in my old cabin. For months it was kept in one of the maggots—or we heard that's where it was kept. We've had to put together hints, rumors, and overheard comments, any of which might be misinterpreted, or untrue. But at long last, I believe we have it right.

Reverend Locke's two assistants live in my cabin, and from time to time, some of us are taken there for the night. The next time that happens, we'll make our break.

The women who have been taken there most often are Noriko, Cristina Cho, and the Mora girls.

"They say they like small, ladylike women," Noriko says with terrible bitterness. "Those flabby, ugly men. They like us because it's easy for them to hurt us. They like to use their hands, leave bruises, make you beg them to stop."

She, Cristina, and the Moras all say they would rather risk death than go on with things as they are. Whichever of them is taken to my cabin next will cut their rapist's throats during the night. They can do that now. I don't believe they could have a few months ago. Then they will try to find and disable the master unit. Problem is, we don't know what the master unit looks like. None of us has ever seen it.

All we know—or think we know about it—we've learned from those among us who have been collared before. They say once you disable the master unit, the smaller units won't work. The only way I can understand this is to compare it to one of the phones in the Balter house down south in Robledo, so long ago. This was a big, old-fashioned dinosaur of a "cordless" phone. You had to plug the base unit into an electrical outlet and a phone jack. Then you could walk around the house and yard talking into the hand unit. But unplug the two cords of the base, and the hand unit didn't work anymore. I'm told that that's close to what happens with a network of collars.

I don't know anything for sure. I only half believe that we can do what we think we can and survive. Tampering with the master unit might kill the woman who does it. It might kill us all. But the truth is, we couldn't last much longer, no matter what. We're only just human now—most of us. I've said this to the people I trust—people who have helped me gather the fragments of information that we have. I've asked each of them if they're willing to take the risk.

They are. We all are.

WEDNESDAY, FEBRUARY 28, 2035

Day before yesterday, we had a terrible storm—truly terrible. And yet, it was a wonderful thing: wind and rain and cold . . . and a landslide. The hill where our cemetery once was with all its new and old trees, that hill has slumped down into our valley. Our teachers had made us cut down the older trees for firewood and lumber and God. I never found out how they came to believe we prayed to trees, but they went on believing it. We begged them to let the hill alone, told them it was our cemetery, and they lashed us. Because they forced us to do this, the hillside has broken away and come rumbling down to us. It has buried a maggot and three cabins, including the cabin that Bankole and I had built and then lived in for our six brief years together.

Also, it buried the men who slept alone in that cabin. I'm sorry to say that there were two women in each of the other cabins. They were from squatter camps. Natividad had been friendly with one of them, but I didn't know them at all. They are dead, however, buried and dead. Six "teachers," four captive women, *and all of our collars* were dead. Last Sunday, we resolved to free ourselves or die trying. Now, instead, the weather, and our "teachers'" own stupidity has freed us.

Here is what happened.

The storm began as a cold rain whipped by a brisk wind on Monday afternoon, and for a while, we were made to go on working in it. At last, though, our "teachers," who are much more willing to inflict suffering than to endure it, drove us back to our prison rooms to sit in the cold dimness while they went to our cabins, to warm fires, light, and food.

After a while, the lowest-ranking "teacher" brought Beth and Jessica Faircloth out with our disgusting dinner—a lot of half-boiled, half-spoiled cabbage with potatoes.

We had put Allie where the Faircloths could not avoid seeing her, being confronted by her when they came in. She is a little better. I've looked after her as best I could. She walks like a bent old woman, talks in monosyllables, and does not always seem to understand when we speak to her. I don't believe she even remembers what the Faircloths did to her, but she seems to trust me. I told her to watch them—watch them every second.

She did.

The Faircloths trembled and stumbled over one another, putting down pots of awful food and backing out. We all stared at them in silence, but I suspect they saw only saw Allie.

After dinner, we rested as best we could, feeling cold, stiff, miserable, and damp on the bare wood floor wrapped in our filthy blankets. Some of us slept, but the storm grew much worse, shaking the building and making it creak. Rain beat against the window and blew roofing off cabins, limbs off trees, and trash from the dump that the teachers had made us create. We had had no dump before. We had a salvage heap and a compost heap. Neither was trash. We could not afford to be wasteful. Our teachers have made trash of our entire community.

Sometimes there was lightning and thunder, sometimes only heavy rain. It went on all night, tearing the world apart outside. Then sometime this morning before dawn, not long after I had managed to get to sleep, I was awakened by a terrible noise. It wasn't like thunder—wasn't like anything I'd ever heard. It was just this incredible rumbling, breaking, cracking noise.

I reacted without thinking. My place is near the window, and I jumped up and looked out. I leaned against the sill and peered out into the darkness. A moment later there was a flare of lightning, and I saw rock and dirt where my cabin should have been. Rock and dirt.

It took me a moment to understand this. Then I realized that I was leaning against the windowsill, leaning halfway out the window. And I had not convulsed and fallen to the floor. No pain. None of that filthy, twisting agony that made us all slaves.

I touched my collar. It was still there, still capable of delivering the agony. But for some reason, it no longer cared that I leaned against the windowsill. In the dark room, I reached for Natividad. She slept on one side of me and Allie slept on the other. Natividad trusts me, and she knows how to be quiet.

"Freedom!" I whispered. "The collars are dead! They're dead!"

She let me lead her to the door between our quarters and the men's. We managed to get there, each of us waking people as we went, whispering to them, but not stepping on anyone, feeling our way. At the door, Natividad pulled back a little, then she let me lead her through. The door's never been locked. Collars were always enough to keep everyone away from it. But not this time.

No pain.

We woke the men—those who were still asleep. We couldn't see well enough to wake only the men we trusted. We woke them all. We couldn't do this with silent stealth. We were quiet, but they awoke in confusion and chaos. Some were already awake and confused and grabbing me, and realizing that I was a woman. I hit one who wouldn't let me go—a stranger from the road.

OCTAVIA E. BUTLER

"Freedom!" I whispered into his face. "The collars are dead! We can get away!"

He let me go, and scrambled for the door. I went back and gathered the women. When I got them into the men's room, the men were already pouring out of the building. We followed them through the big outside doors. Travis and Natividad, Mike and Noriko, others of Earthseed, the Gamas, and the Sullivans somehow found one another. We all clustered together, male and female members of families greeting one another, crying, hugging. They had not been able even to touch one another through the eternity of our captivity. Seventeen months. Eternity.

I hugged Harry because neither of us had anyone left. Then he and I stood together watching the others, probably feeling the same mixture of relief and pain. Zahra was gone. Bankole was gone. And where were our children?

But there was no time for joy or grief.

"We've got to get into the cabins now," I said, all but herding them before me. "We've got to stop them from fixing the collars. We've got to get their guns before they know what's going on. They'll waste time trying to lash us. Groups of four or more to a cabin. Do it!"

We all know how to work together. We've spent years working together. We separated and went to the houses. Travis, Natividad, and I grabbed the Mora girls and we burst into what had been the Kardos house just as the screaming began outside.

Some of our "teachers" came rushing out of their cabins to see what was wrong, and they were torn to pieces by the people they had so enjoyed tormenting.

Some of the captives, desperate to escape while they could, tried to find their way through the Lazor wire in the dark, and the wire cut their flesh to the bone when they ran into it.

Earthseed made no such lethal mistake. We went into the cabins to arm ourselves, to rid ourselves of our "teachers," and to cut off our damned collars.

My group piled onto the two "teachers" who were there, out of bed, one with his pants and shirt on, and one in long underwear. They could have shot us. But they were so used to depending on their belts to protect them that it was the belts they tried to reach.

One stood and said, "What's going on?" The other lunged at Natividad and me with a wordless shout.

We grappled with them, dragged them down, and strangled them. That simple. Even simple for me. It hurt when they hit me. It hurt when I hit them. And it didn't matter a good goddamn! Once I had my hands on one of them, I just shut my eyes and did it. I never felt their deaths. And I have never been so eager and so glad to kill people.

We couldn't see them very well anyway in the dark cabin, but we made sure they were dead. We didn't let go of them until they were very, very dead. Our makeshift knives were still in the walls and floor of our barracks, but our hands did the job.

And then we had guns. We used a chair, then a night table to smash open a gun cabinet.

More important, then we had wire cutters.

Tori Mora found the cutters in what had once been Noriko Kardos's silverware drawer. Now it was full of small hand tools. We took turns cutting one another's collars off. As long as we wore them, we were in terrible danger. I was afraid every minute, anticipating the convulsing agony that could end our freedom, begin our final torture. Our "teachers" would kill us if they regained control of us. They would kill us very, very slowly. The collars alone would kill us if they somehow switched back on while we were trying to cut through them and twist them off. I had learned over the months that nothing was more tamperproof than a functioning collar.

I cut the Mora girls' collar off, and Tori cut off mine. Travis and Natividad did the same for one another. And then we were free. Then, no matter what, we were truly free. We all hugged one another again. There was still danger, still work to do, but we were free. We allowed ourselves that moment of intense relief.

OCTAVIA E. BUTLER

Then we went out to find that our people and some of the others had finished the job. The teachers were all dead. I saw that some of the inmates still wore their collars, so I went back into the Kardos cabin for the wire cutters. Once people realized what I was doing—cutting off collars—both outsiders and members of the Earthseed community made a ragged line in front of me. I spent the next several minutes cutting off collars. It was cold, the wind was blowing, but at least it had stopped raining. The eastern sky was beginning to brighten with the dawn. We were free people, all of us.

Now what?

We stripped what we could from the cabins. We had to. The outsiders were running around grabbing things, tearing or smashing whatever they didn't want, screaming, cheering, ripping curtains from windows, breaking windows, grabbing food and liquor. Amazing how much liquor our "teachers" had had.

We took guns first. We didn't try to stop the outsiders from their orgy of destruction, but we did guard the things we collected: guns, ammunition, clothing, shoes, food. Outsiders understood that. We were like them, taking what we wanted and guarding it. Some of them had found guns, too, but there was a respectful wariness between us. Even people who got crazy drunk didn't come after us.

Someone shot the locks off the gate, and people began to leave.

Several people tried to shoot their way into the single unburied maggot, but it was locked and impervious to any effort we could make. In fact, if even one of our "teachers" had slept in the maggot, he could have defeated our escape. He could have killed us all.

Our own trucks were long gone. One had been destroyed when Gray Mora said his final "no" to slavery. The other had been taken and driven away. We had no idea where.

When it was light, I counted seven people dead on the Lazor wire. I suspect most had bled to death, although two had opened their own abdomens, even slicing into their intestines propelled by their mindless lunge for freedom. Lazor wire is impossible to see at night in the rain, and even the lowest street pauper should know the dangers of it. When we were ready to leave, I collected Allie, who had stayed inside the school and just stood at a window, staring out at us. I cut off her collar, then I thought about the Faircloths. I had not cut off their collars. They had not come to me. The two Faircloth boys, of course, had been taken away with the rest of our young children. Alan Faircloth, the father of Beth and Jessica, must have taken his daughters and slipped away—or perhaps the Sullivans had found them and taken their revenge.

I sighed. Either the girls were dead or they were with Alan. Best to say nothing. There had been enough killing.

I gathered what was left of the Earthseed community around me. The sun wasn't visible through the clouds, but the wind had died down, and the sky was pale gray. It was cold, but for once, with our fresh clothing, we were warm enough.

"We can't stay here," I told my people. "We'll have to take as much as we can carry and go. The church will send people here sooner or later."

"Our homes," Noriko Kardos said in a kind of moan.

I nodded. "I know. But they're already gone. They've been gone for a long time." And a particular Earthseed verse occurred to me.

In order to rise
From its own ashes
A phoenix
First
Must
Burn.

It was an apt Earthseed verse, but not a comforting one. The problem with Earthseed has always been that it isn't a very comforting belief system.

OCTAVIA E. BUTLER

"Let's take one last look through the houses," I said. "We need to look for evidence of what they've done with our children. That's the most important thing we can do next: find the children."

I left Michael and Travis to guard the goods we had collected, and the rest of us went in groups to search the ruins of the houses.

But we found nothing that related to the children. There was money hidden here and there around the cabins, missed by the marauding inmates. There were piles of religious tracts, Bibles, lists of "inmates" brought from Garberville, Eureka, Arcata, Trinidad, and other nearby towns. There was a plan for spring planting, a few books written by President Jarret, or by some ghostwriter. There were personal papers, but nothing about our children, and no addresses. None. Nothing. This could only be deliberate. They feared being found out. Was it us they feared, or someone else?

We searched until almost midday. Then we knew we had to go, too. The roads were mud and water, and it was unlikely that anyone would try to drive up today, but we needed to get a good start. In particular, I wanted to go to our secret caches where we had not only the necessities but copies of records, journals, and in two places, the hand and foot prints of some of our children. Bankole took hand and foot prints of every child he delivered. He labeled them, gave a copy to the parents, and kept a copy. I had distributed these copies among two of our caches—the two that only a few of us knew about. I don't know whether the prints will help us get our children back. When I let myself think about it, I have to admit that I don't know even whether our children are alive. I only know that now I have to get to those two caches. They are back in the mountains toward the sea, not toward the road. We can disappear in that country. There are places there where we can shelter and decide what to do. It's one thing to say that we must find our children, and another to figure out how to do that, how to begin.

Who to trust?

We burned Acorn. No. No, we burned Camp Christian. We burned Camp Christian so that it couldn't be used as Camp Christian anymore. If Christian America still wants the land it stole from us, it will have some serious rebuilding to do. We spread lamp oil and diesel fuel inside the cabins that we built from the trees we cut and the stone and concrete we hauled. We spread oil in the school Grayson Mora had designed and we had all worked so hard to build and make beautiful. We spread it on the bodies of our "teachers." All that we could not take with us, all that the other inmates had not taken or destroyed, we burned. The buildings might not burn to the ground because the rain had soaked everything, but they would be gutted and unsafe. The furniture that we had built or salvaged would burn. The hated flesh would burn.

So, once more, we watched our homes burn. We went into the hills, separating from the last of the other inmates, who went their own ways back to the highway or wherever else they might want to go. From the hills, for a time, we watched. Most of us had seen our homes burn before, but we had not been the ones to set the fires. This time, though, it's too late for fire to be the destroyer that we remembered. The things that we had created and loved had already been destroyed. This time, the fires only cleansed.

15

○ ○ ○

From EARTHSEED: THE BOOKS OF THE LIVING

We have lived before.
We will live again.
We will be silk,
Stone,
Mind,
Star.
We will be scattered,
Gathered,
Molded,
Probed.
We will live
And we will serve life.
We will shape God
And God will shape us
Again,
Always again,
Forevermore.

The crusaders deliberately divided siblings because if they were together, they might support one another in secret heathen practices or beliefs. But if each child was isolated and dropped into a family of good Christian Americans, then each would be changed. Parent pressure, peer pressure, and time would remake them as good Christian Americans.

Sometimes it did, even among the older children of Acorn. Look at the Faircloth boys. One became a Christian American minister. The other rejected Christian America completely. And sometimes the division was utterly destructive. Some of us died of it. Ramon Figueroa Castro committed suicide because, according to one of his foster brothers, "He was too stubborn to try to fit in and forget about his sinful past." Christian America was, at first, much more a refuge for the ignorant and the intolerant than it should have been. Even people who would never beat or burn another person could treat suddenly orphaned or abducted children with cold, self-righteous cruelty.

"Give in," my mother said to the adults of Acorn. "Do as you're told and keep your own council. Don't give them excuses to hurt you. Bide your time. Watch your captors. Listen to them. Collect information, pool it, and use it against them." But we kids never heard any of this. We were snatched away and given alone into the hands of people who believed that it was their duty to break us and remake us in the Christian American image. And, of course, breaking people is much easier than putting them together again.

So much agony caused, so much evil done in God's name.

And yet, Christian America had begun by trying to help and to heal as well as to convert. Long before Jarret was elected President, his church had begun to rescue children. But in those early days, they only rescued kids who really needed help. Along the Gulf Coast where Jarret began his work, there were several Christian American children's homes that were over a decade old by 2032. These homes collected street orphans, fed them, cared for them, and raised them to be "the bulwark of Christian America." Only later did the fanatics take over and begin stealing the children of "heathens" and doing terrible harm.

In preparation for this book, I spoke with several people who were raised in "CA" children's homes or were adopted from CA homes into CA families. What they told me reminded me of my own life with the Alexanders. The homes and adoptive families were not meant to be cruel. Even in the homes, there were no collars except as punishment for the older children, and then only after warnings and lesser punishments had failed. The homes weren't kept by sadists or perverts but by people who believed deeply in what they were doing—or at least by workers who wanted very much to please their employers and keep their jobs. The believers wanted "their" children to believe absolutely in God, in Jarret and in being good Christian American soldiers ready to do battle with every sort of anti-American heathenism. The mercenaries were easier to please. They wanted no children injured or killed while they were on duty. They wanted the required lessons learned, the required tests passed. They wanted peace.

The Alexanders were like a combination of the believer and the mercenary. The Alexanders wanted me to believe, and if they did not love me, at least they took care of me. By the time I was old enough for school—Christian American school, of course—I had learned to be quiet and keep out of their way. When I succeeded at this, Kayce and Madison would reward me by letting me alone. Kayce took a break from telling me how much inferior I was to Kamaria. Madison took a break from trying to get his sweaty hands under my dress. I would take a book to a quiet corner of the house or yard and read. My earliest books were all either Bible stories or stories of Christian American heroes who, like Asha Vere, did great deeds for the faith. These influenced me. How could they not? I dreamed of doing great deeds myself. I dreamed of making Kayce so proud of me, making her love me the way she loved Kamaria. Both my biological parents were big, strong people. Thanks to them, I was always big for my age, and strong—one more strike against me, since Kamaria had been "small and dainty." I dreamed of doing great, heroic things, but all I really tried to do was hide, vanish, make myself invisible.

It should have been hard for an oversized kid like me to hide that way, but it wasn't. If I did my chores and my homework, I was encouraged to vanish—or rather, I wasn't encouraged to do anything else. In my neighborhood there were only a few kids, and they were all older than I was. To them I was either a nuisance or a pawn. They ignored me or they got me into trouble. Kayce and her friends didn't appreciate any attempts I made to join in their adult conversation. Even when Kayce was alone, she wasn't really interested in anything I had to say. She either told me more than I wanted to know about Kamaria, or she punished me for asking questions about anything else.

Quiet was good. Questioning was bad. Children should be seen and not heard. They should believe what their elders told them, and be content that it was all they needed to know. If there were any brutality in the way I was raised, that was it. Stupid faith was good. Thinking and questioning were bad. I was to be like a sheep in Christ's flock—or Jarret's flock. I was to be quiet and meek. Once I learned that, my childhood was at least physically comfortable.

From *THE JOURNALS OF LAUREN OYA OLAMINA*
SUNDAY, MARCH 4, 2035

So much has happened. . . .

No, that's wrong. Things haven't just happened. I've caused them to happen. I must get back to normal, to knowing and admitting, at least to myself, when I cause things. Slaves are always told that they've caused something bad, done something sinful, made stupid mistakes. Good things were the acts of our "teachers" or of God. Bad things were our fault. Either we had done some specific wrong or God was so generally displeased with us that He was punishing the whole camp.

If you hear nonsense like that often enough for long enough, you begin to believe it. You weight yourself down with blame for all the world's pain. Or you decide that you're an innocent victim. Your masters are at fault or God is or Satan is—or maybe things just happen on their own. Slaves protect themselves in all sorts of ways.

But we're not slaves anymore.

I've done this: I sent my people away. We survived slavery together, but I didn't believe that we could survive freedom together. I broke up the Earthseed community and sent its parts in all directions. I believe it was the right thing to do, but I can hardly bear to think about it. Once I've written this, perhaps I can begin to heal. I don't know. All I know now is that I've torn a huge hole in myself. I've sent away those who mean most to me. They were all I had left, and I know I may not see them ever again.

On Tuesday we escaped from Camp Christian, burning the camp and our keepers as we went. We left behind the bones of our dead and the dream of Acorn as the first Earthseed community. The Sullivans and the Gamas went their own ways. We would not have asked them to leave us, but I was glad they did. We had between us only the money in our caches and the money we had taken from our "teachers." Since we are all now homeless, jobless, and on foot, that money won't go far.

I did ask both families who were going to stay with relatives or friends to get whatever information they could about the children, about the legality of the camp, about the existence of other camps. We all must find out what we can. I've asked them to leave word with the Holly family. The Hollys were neighbors, more distant than the Sullivans and the Gamas, but neighbors. They were good friends of the Sullivans, and there was no rumor of their having been enslaved. We must be careful not to get them into trouble, but if we are careful, and if we check with them now and then, we can all exchange information.

Problem is, we didn't dare take any of the phones from Camp Christian. The outsiders took some of them, but we were afraid we could somehow be traced if we used them. We can't take the chance of being collared again. We might be enslaved for life or executed because we've killed good Christian American citizens. The fact that those citizens had stolen our homes, our land, our freedom, and our children just might be overlooked if the citizens were influential enough. We believe it could happen. Look what had already happened! We're all afraid.

Among ourselves—Earthseed only—we've agreed on a place that we can use as a message drop. It's down near what's left of Humboldt Redwoods State Park. There any of us can leave information to be read, copied, and acted on by the rest of us. It's a good place because we all know where it is and because it's isolated. Getting to it isn't easy. We don't dare leave information or meet in groups in some more convenient place near the highway or near local roads, and we need a way of reaching one another without depending on the Hollys. We'll check with them, but who knows how they'll feel about us now. We'll communicate among ourselves by leaving messages at our secret place, and perhaps by meeting there.

But I'm going too fast. We had some time together after leaving Camp Christian.

We walked deeper into the mountains, away from paved roads, south and west to the largest of our caches where we knew there was the cold shelter of a small cave. At the cave, we rested and shared the food that we had brought from Camp Christian. Then we dug out the supplies that we had stored in heavy, heat-sealed plastic sacks and stored there. That gave us all packets of dried foods—fruit, nuts, beans, eggs, and milk—plus blankets and ammunition. Most important, I passed out the infant foot and hand prints that had been stored at this particular cache to the parents present. I gave the Mora girls their younger brothers' prints and they sat staring at them, each holding one. Both their parents were dead. They have only each other and their little brothers, if they can find them.

"They should be with us!" Doe muttered. "No one has the right to take them from us."

Adela Ortiz folded her son's prints and put them inside her shirt. Then she folded her arms in front of her as though cradling a baby. Larkin's prints and those of Travis and Natividad's kids were at a different location, but I found the prints of Harry's kids, Tabia and Russell, and I gave them to Harry. He just sat looking at them, frowning at them and shaking his head. It was as though he were trying to read an explanation in them for all that had happened to him. Or maybe he was seeing the faces of his children, and Zahra's face, long gone.

We sat warming ourselves around the fire we had finally dared to start. We had collected wood outside during the last hour of daylight, but we waited until it was dark to try to use it. The wood was wet and wouldn't burn at first. When we did get a small fire going, it seemed to make more smoke than heat. We hoped no one would see the smoke sliding up and out of the cave, or that if people did see it, they would think it was from one of the many squatter camps in the mountains. In winter, these mountains are cold, wet, uncomfortable places, difficult places in which to live without modern conveniences, but they're also places where sensible people mind their own business.

I sat with Harry, and he went on staring at the prints and shaking his head. Then he began to rock back and forth. His expression in the firelight seemed to crack, to break down, somehow, unable to hold itself together.

I pulled him to me and held him while he cursed and cried in a harsh, strained, whisper. I realized at some point that I was crying too. I think that within ourselves, we both howled, but somehow, we never got much above a whisper, a rasp. I could feel the howling straining to get out of my throat, the screams that came out as small, ragged cries, his and mine. I don't know how long we sat together, holding one another, going mad inside ourselves, wailing and moaning for the dead and the lost, unable to contain for one more minute 17 months of humiliation and pain.

We wept ourselves to sleep like tired children. The next day Natividad told me she and Travis had done much the same thing. The others, alone or in groups, had found their own comfort in cathartic weeping, deep sleep, or frantic, furtive lovemaking at the back of the cave. We were together at last, comforting one another, and yet I think each of us was alone, straining toward the others, some part of ourselves still trapped back in the uncertainty and fear, the pain and desolation of Camp Christian. We strained toward some kind of release, some human contact, some way into the normal, human grieving that had been denied us for so long. It amazes me that we were able to behave as sanely as we did.

The next morning Lucio Figueroa and Adela Ortiz awoke tangled together at the back of the cave. They stared at one another first in horror and confusion, then in deep embarrassment, then in resignation. He put his arm around her, pulled one of the blankets we had salvaged around her, and she leaned against him.

Jorge Cho and Diamond Scott awoke in a similar tangle, although they seemed both unsurprised and unembarrassed.

Michael and Noriko awoke together and lay still against one another for a long time, saying nothing, doing nothing. It seemed enough for each of them that at last they could wake up in each other's arms.

The Mora girls awoke together, their faces still marked with the tears they had shed the night before.

Somehow Aubrey Dovetree and Nina Noyer had found one another during the night, although they had never paid much attention to one another before. Once they were awake, they moved apart in obvious discomfort.

Only Allie awoke alone, huddled in fetal position in her blanket. I had forgotten her. And hadn't she lost even more than the rest of us?

I put her between Harry and me, and we started a breakfast fire with the wood we had left over from the night. We put together a breakfast of odds and ends, and Harry and I made her eat. I borrowed a comb from Diamond Scott, who had, in her neatness, managed to find one before we left Camp Christian. With it I combed Allie's hair, then my own. Things like that had begun to matter again, somehow. We all began to try to put ourselves together as respectable human beings again. For so long we had been filthy slaves in filthy rags cultivating filthy habits in the hope of avoiding rape or lashing. I found myself longing for a deep tub of hot, clean water. Thanks to our "teachers," filth and degradation had become so ordinary that sometimes we forgot that we were in rags and that we stank. In our exhaustion, fear, and pain, we came to treasure those moments when we could just lie down and forget, when no one was hurting us, when we had something to eat. Such animal comforts were all we could afford. Remembering wasn't safe. You could lose your mind, remembering.

My ancestors in this hemisphere were, by law, chattel slaves. In the

U.S., they were chattel slaves for two and a half centuries—at least 10 generations. I used to think I knew what that meant. Now I realize that I can't begin to imagine the many terrible things that it must have done to them. How did they survive it all and keep their humanity? Certainly, they were never intended to keep it, just as we weren't.

"Today or tomorrow, we must separate," I said. "We must leave here in small groups." Breakfast was over, and we had all made ourselves a little more presentable. I could see that the others had begun to look at one another, begun to wonder what to do next.

I knew what we had to do. I had known almost from the time we were collared that even if we managed to free ourselves, we wouldn't be able to stay together.

"Earthseed continues," I said into the silence, " but Acorn is dead. There are too many of us. We would be too easy to spot, too easy to recapture or kill."

"What can we do?" Aubrey Dovetree demanded.

And Harry Balter said in a dead voice, "We've got to split up. We've got to go our separate ways and find our kids."

"No," Nina Noyer whispered, and then louder, "No! Everybody's gone, and now you want me to go away by myself again? No!" Now it was a shout.

"Yes," I said to her, only to her, my voice as soft as I could make it. "Nina, you come with me. My family is gone too. Come with me. We'll look for your sisters and my daughter and Allie's son."

"I want us all to stay together," she whispered, and she began to cry.

"If we stay together, we'll be collared or dead in no time," Harry said. He looked at me. "I'll go with you too. You'll need help. And . . . I want my kids back. I'm scared to death of what might be happening to them. That's all I can think about now. That's all I care about."

And Allie put her hand on his shoulder, trying to give comfort.

"No one should leave alone," I said. It's too dangerous to be alone. But don't gather into groups of more than five or six."

"What about us?" Doe Mora said, holding her sister's hand. It was hard at that moment to remember that the two were not blood relatives. Two lonely, frightened ex-slaves met and loved one another and married, and their daughters Doe and Tori became sisters. And they're sisters now, orphaned and alone. I envy their closeness, and I fear for them. They're still kids, and they were abused almost past bearing at Camp Christian. They look starved and haunted. In a way that I can't quite describe, they look old. Our "teachers" realized that they were sharers back during Day's rebellion, and abused them all the more for it, but the girls never gave any of the rest of us away. Yet in spite of their courage, it would be so easy for them to wind up with new collars around their necks. Or they could wind up deciding to prostitute themselves—just to eat.

"You come with us," Natividad said. "We intend to find our children. If we can, we'll find your brothers as well."

Doe bit her lips. "I'm pregnant," she said. "Tori isn't, but I am."

"It's a wonder we all aren't," I said. "We were slaves. Now we're free." I looked at her. She's a tall, slender, delicate-looking girl, large-eyed like her namesake. "What do you want to do, Doe?"

Doe swallowed. "I don't know."

"We'll take care of her," Travis said. "Whatever she decides to do, we'll help her. Her father was a good man. He was a friend of mine. We'll take care of her."

I nodded, relieved. Travis and Natividad are two of the most competent, dependable people I know. They'll survive, and if the girls are with them, the girls will survive too.

Others began forming themselves into groups. Adela Ortiz, who first thought that she would join Travis, Natividad, and the Moras, decided in the end to stay with Lucio Figueroa and his sister. I'm not sure how she and Lucio wound up in each other's arms the night before, but I think now that Adela may be looking for a permanent relationship with Lucio. He's much older than she is, and I think she hopes he'll want her and want to take care of her. But Adela is pregnant too. She's not showing yet, but according to what she's told me, she believes she's at least two months pregnant.

Also, Lucio is still carrying Teresa Lin around with him. Her death and the way she died has made him very, very quiet—kind, but distant. He wasn't like that back in Acorn. His own wife and children were killed before he met us. He had invested all his time and energy in helping his sister with her children. He had only begun to reach out again when Teresa joined us. Now . . . now perhaps he's decided that it hurts too much to begin to care for someone, then lose her.

It does hurt. It's terrible. I know that. But I know Adela, too. She needs to be needed. I remember she hated being pregnant the first time, hated the men who had gang-raped her. But she loved taking care of her baby. She was an attentive, loving mother, and she was happy. What's in store for her now, I don't know.

And yet in spite of my fears for my friends, my people, in spite of my longing to hold together a community that must divide, all this was easier than I had thought it would be—easier than I thought it *could* be. We'd all worked so well together for six years, and we'd endured so much as slaves. Now we were dividing ourselves, deciding how to go our separate ways. I don't mean that it was easy—just that it wasn't as hard as I expected. God is Change. I've taught that for six years. It's true, and I suppose it's paved the way for us now. Earthseed prepares you to live in the world that is and try to shape the world that you want. But none of it is really easy.

We spent the rest of the day going around to the other caches and parceling out the supplies we'd left in them and gathering the other sets of children's hand and foot prints. Then we had one more night together. Once we had gone to all the caches—one had been raided, but the rest were intact—we spent the night in another shallow cave. It was raining again, and cold. That was good because it would make tracking us pretty much impossible. On that last night, when we'd eaten, we dropped off quickly to sleep. We'd been tramping through the mountains all day, carrying packs that got heavier with each stop, and we were tired. But the next morning before we parted, we held a final Gathering. We sang Earthseed verses, to the tunes that Gray Mora and Travis had written. We Remembered our dead, including our dead Acorn. Each of us spoke of it, Remembering.

"You are Earthseed," I said to them, at last. "You always will be. I love you. I love you all." I stopped for a moment, struggling to hold on to what was left of my self-control.

Somehow, I went on. "Not everyone in this country stands with Andrew Jarret," I said. "We know that. Jarret will pass, and we will still be here. We know more about survival than most people. The proof is that we have survived. We have tools that other people don't have, and that they need. The time will come again when we can share what we know." I paused, swallowed. "Stay well," I told them. "Take care of one another."

We agreed to visit the newly designated Humboldt Redwoods information drop every month or two for a year—at least that long. We agreed that it was best that each group not know yet where the other groups were going—so that if one group was caught, it couldn't be forced to betray the others. We agreed it was best not to live in the Eureka and Arcata area because that's where most of our jailers lived, both the dead ones and the off-shift ones who were still alive. Each city was home to a big Christian American church and several affiliated organizations. We might have to go to these cities to look for our children, but once we've found them and taken them back, we should go elsewhere to live.

"And change your names," I told them. "As soon as you can, buy yourselves new identities. Then relax. You're honest people. If anyone says otherwise, attack their credibility. Accuse them of being secret cultists, witches, Satanists, thieves. Whatever you think will endanger your accusers the most, say it! Don't just defend yourselves. Attack. And keep attacking until you scare the shit out of your accusers. Watch them. Pay attention to their body language. Their own reactions will tell you how best to damage them or scare them off.

OCTAVIA E. BUTLER

"I don't think you'll have to do much of that kind of thing. The chances of any of us running into someone who knew us at Camp Christian are small. It's just that we need to be mentally prepared for it if it happens. God is Change. Look after yourselves."

And we went our separate ways. Travis said we would be better off not walking on the highway unless we could lose ourselves in a crowd. If there were no crowds, he said, we should walk through the hills. It would be harder, but safer. I agreed.

We hugged one another. It took a lot of hugging. It took the possibility of coming together again someday in another state or another country or a post-Jarret America. It took tears and fear and hope. It was terrible, that final leavetaking. Deciding to do it was easier than I thought. Doing it was much harder. It was the hardest thing I've ever had to do.

Then I was alone with Allie, Harry, and Nina. We four slogged through the mud, heading north. We traveled through the familiar hills, to the outskirts of Eureka, and finally, to Georgetown. I was the one who suggested Georgetown once we had separated from the others.

"Why?" Harry demanded in a cold voice that didn't sound much like Harry.

"Because it's a good place to pick up information," I said. "And because I know Dolores Ramos George. She may not be able to help us, but she won't talk about our being there."

Harry nodded.

"What's Georgetown?" Nina asked.

"A squatter settlement," I told her. "A big, nasty one. We went there when we were looking for you and your sister. You can get lost in there. People aren't nosy, and the Georges are all right."

"They're all right." Allie agreed. "They don't turn people in." These were her first voluntary sentences since her lashing. I looked at her, and she repeated, "They're all right. We can look for Justin from Georgetown."

16

○ ○ ○

From EARTHSEED: THE BOOKS OF THE LIVING

The Destiny of Earthseed
Is to take root among the stars.

It is to live and to thrive
On new earths.

It is to become new beings
And to consider new questions.

It is to leap into the heavens
Again and again.

It is to explore the vastness
Of heaven.

It is to explore the vastness
Of ourselves.

My first clear memory is of a doll. I was about three years old, maybe four. I don't know where the doll came from. I still don't know. I had never seen one before. I had never been told that they were sinful or forbidden or even that they existed. I suspect now that this doll had been thrown over our fence and abandoned. I found it at the foot of the big pine tree that grew in our backyard.

The doll had been made in the image of an adolescent blond-haired, blue-eyed girl. I remember that it was very straight and thin. It was dressed in a scrap of pink cloth. I remember feeling the knot in the back of it where three ends of the scrap were tied over one shoulder and around the waist. The knot was an oddly soft lump against the hard plastic of the doll's body, and as soon as my fingers found it, I began to pick at it. Then I chewed on it. Then I examined the coarse, yellow hair. It looked like hair, but when I touched it, it didn't feel right. And it bothered me that the legs didn't move. They just stuck out stiff, the feet shaped in permanent tiptoes. I didn't know how to play with a doll, but I knew how to look at it, feel it, taste it, file it away in my memory as one of the new, strange things to come into my world.

Then Kayce was there, snatching the doll from me. When I reached for it, wanting it back, she slapped me. She had come up behind me, seen what was in my hands, and in her sudden rage, lost control. She was a stern disciplinarian, but she rarely hit me. To give her her due, this was the only time I remember her just lashing out at me that way in anger. Maybe that's why I remember it so well.

A man who grew up at the Pelican Bay Christian American Children's Home told me about a Matron who went into a similar rage and killed a child.

Her victim was a seven-year-old boy who had Tourette's syndrome. My informant said, "We kids didn't know anything about Tourette's syndrome, but we knew this particular kid couldn't help yelling insults and making noises. He didn't mean it. Some of us didn't like him. Some of us thought he was crazy. But we all knew he didn't mean the things he yelled out. We knew he couldn't help it. But Matron said he had a devil in him, and she was always screaming at him—every day.

"Then one day she hit him, knocked him into the edge of a kitchen cabinet. He hit the cabinet with his head, and he died.

"I don't believe Matron was sentenced and collared, but she was fired. I just hope that she couldn't find another professional job and had to indenture herself. One way or another, a person like her should wind up wearing a collar."

There was a mindless rigidity about some Christian Americans—about the ones who did the most harm. They were so certain that they were right that, like medieval inquisitors, they would kill you, even torture you to death, to save your soul. Kayce wasn't that bad, but she was more rigid and literal-minded than any human being with normal intelligence should have been, and I suffered for it.

Anyway, she snatched the doll from me and began slapping my face. All the while, she was shouting at me. I was so scared, and screaming so loud myself that I didn't know what she was saying. Looking back now, I know it must have been something to do with idolatry, heathenism, or graven images. Christian America had created whole new categories of sin and expanded old ones. We were not permitted pictures of any kind. Movies and television were forbidden, but somehow Dreamasks were not—although only religious topics were permitted. Later, when I was in school, older kids would pass around secular masks that offered stories of adventure, war, and sex. I had my first pleasurable sexual experience, wearing a deliberately mislabeled Dreamask. The label said "The Story of Moses." In fact, it was the story of a girl who had wild sex with her pastor, the deacons, and anyone else she could seduce. I was eleven years old when I discovered that Mask. If Kayce had ever known what it was, she might have done more than just slap my face. I kept the dirty Mask well hidden.

But at three, I hadn't known enough to hide the doll. Only Kayce's reaction told me what a terrible thing it was. She made me watch while she dug a hole in our backyard, put the doll in, covered it with cooking oil and old papers, and burned it. This, she said, was what would happen to me if I went on defying God and working for Satan. I would go down to hell, and what she had done to the doll, the devil would do to me. I remember she made me look at the shapeless blackened plastic lump that the doll had become. She made me hold it, and I cried because it was still hot, and it burned my hand.

"If you think that hurts," she said, "you just wait until you get to hell."

Years Later, when I was a grown woman, the small daughter of a friend showed me her doll. I managed to stand up quickly and get out of the house. I didn't scream or thrust the dolt away. I just ran. I panicked at the sight of a little girl's doll—real panic. I had to think and remember for a long time before I understood why.

The purpose of Christian America was to make America the great, Christian country that it was supposed to be, to prepare it for a future of strength, stability, and world leadership, and to prepare its people for life everlasting in heaven. Yet sometimes now when I think about Christian America and all that it did when it held power over so many lives, I don't think about order and stability or greatness or even places like Camp Christian or Pelican Bay. I think about the other extremes, the many small, sad, silly extremes that made up so much of Christian American life. I think about a little girl's doll and I try to banish the shadows of panic that I still can't help feeling when I see one.

From *THE JOURNALS OF LAUREN OYA OLAMINA*
WEDNESDAY, MARCH 28, 2035

We have found Justin Gilchrist—or rather, he has found us. In the weeks we've been at Georgetown, this is the best thing that's happened to us.

We've been working for the Georges for room and board while we regained our health, tried to find out where our children might be, caught up on the news, and tried to find ways of fitting ourselves into the world as it is now. Because we've worked for our keep, we still have most of the money we arrived with. I've even managed to earn a little more by reading and writing for people. Most people in Georgetown are illiterate. I've begun to teach reading and writing to some of the few who want to learn. That's also bringing in a little hard currency. And I sell pencil sketches of people's children or other loved ones. This last, I must be careful about. It seems that some of the more rabid Christian America types have decided that a picture of your child might be seen as a graven image. That seems too extreme to catch on with most

OCTAVIA E. BUTLER

people even though Jarret is much loved in Georgetown. Many people here have sons, brothers, husbands, or other male relatives who have been injured or killed in the Al-Can War, but still, they love Jarret.

In fact, Jarret is both loved and despised here. The religious poor who are ignorant, frightened, and desperate to improve their situations are glad to see a "man of God" in the White House. And that's what he is to them: a man of God.

Even some of the less religious ones support him. They say the country needs a strong hand to bring back order, good jobs, honest cops, and free schools. They say he has to be given plenty of time and a free hand so he can put things right again.

But those dedicated to other religions, and those who are not religious at all sneer at Jarret and call him a hypocrite. They sneer, they hate him, but they also fear him. They see him for the tyrant that he is. And the thugs see him as one of them. They envy him. He is the bigger, the more successful thief, murderer, and slaver.

The working poor who love Jarret want to be fooled, need to be fooled. They scratch a living, working long, hard hours at dangerous, dirty jobs, and they need a savior. Poor women, in particular, tend to be deeply religious and more than willing to see Jarret as the Second Coming. Religion is all they have. Their employers and their men abuse them. They bear more children than they can feed. They bear everyone's contempt.

And yet, whether or not extreme Jarretites say it is a sin, they want pictures of their little ones. And I charge less than local photographers. I'm kinder than photographers too. I've never drawn a child's dirt or its sores, or its rags. That isn't necessary. I've made older plain boys handsome and plain girls pretty for their lovers or for their parents. I've even managed after many tries to draw the dead, guided by the loving memory of a relative or friend. I don't know how accurate these drawings are, of course, but they please people.

I think I'll be able to earn a living sketching, teaching, reading, and writing for people as long as I stick to squatter settlements and the poor sections of towns. And there is a bonus to my becoming acquainted with the people in these places. Many of the people in the squatter settlements work in the yards and homes of somewhat-better-off people in the towns and cities. The squatters do gardening, housecleaning, painting, carpentry, childcare, even some plumbing and electrical work. They serve people who have houses or apartments to live in but can't afford to support even unsalaried live-in servants. Such people pay small sums of money or provide food or clothing to get their work done. Squatters who do this kind of work get a chance to see and hear any number of useful things. If, for instance new children have appeared at an employer's home or at a home nearby, regular day laborers know of it. And if the price is right, they'll tell what they know. Information is as much for sale here as is anything else.

In spite of my efforts, though, we found Justin not by buying information, but because he escaped from his new family and came looking for us. He's 11 years old now—old enough to decide for himself what's true and what isn't and too old to be told that the woman he's called mother for eight of his 11 years was evil and worshipped the devil.

I had just finished a pen-and-ink sketch of a woman and her two youngest kids, sitting outside their wood-and-plastic shack. I was headed back up to my room at the hotel. The streets in Georgetown are all dirt tracks or trash-filled ditches—open sewers—where you might step in anything. The Georges were sensible enough to build their collection of businesses upslope from the worst of the mess, but I can only do my work by going down to where most of the people are. I haven't bought much since I've been here, but I have invested in a pair of well-made, water-resistant boots.

I was thinking, as I walked, about the woman whom I had just drawn with her three-month-old and her 18-month-old. The mother isn't 30 yet, but she looks fifty. She has nine kids, sparse, graying hair, and almost no teeth. I felt as though I had gone back in time. Farther

OCTAVIA E. BUTLER

back, I mean. We were nineteenth-century in Acorn. What is this, I wondered? Eighteenth? And yet, perversely, I found myself filled with envy.

Sometimes I look at these poor, sad women and I'm almost sick with envy. *At least they have their children.* If they have nothing else, they have their children. I look at the children and I draw them, and I can hardly stand it.

As I tramped up the hill toward my room at George's, I saw a little boy squatting by the side of the path, his head in his hands. He was just another scrawny little kid in rags. I thought he might be having a nosebleed, and that made me want to hurry past him. My sharing makes me a coward sometimes. But it also makes me resist being a coward.

I stopped. "Are you all right, honey?" I asked.

He jumped at the sound of my voice, then stared up at me. He was not bleeding, but his lips were cut and swollen and he had an old slash in his cheek and a big black-and-blue swelling on the left side of his forehead. I froze the way I had learned to freeze when confronted with unexpected pain, and the kid mumbled something that I didn't understand because his mouth was so swollen. Then he just launched himself at me.

I thought at first that it was some kind of attack. I thought he might have a knife or an old-style razor or even a skin patch of some poison or a drug. There's nothing new about thieving or murderous children. In a big squatter settlement like Georgetown, there were quite a few of them, although they tended to go after the small, the weak, or the sick. And they tended to travel in packs. Then somehow, before the boy touched me, I knew him. I recognized his wounded, distorted face in spite of the pain he was giving me.

Justin! Justin beaten and cut, but alive. I held him, ignoring the people around us who stared or muttered. Justin is small and wiry. I suspect he still has quite a bit of growing to do. He's White, red-haired, and freckled. In short, he doesn't look like someone who should be hugging me. But in Georgetown although people might stare, they don't interfere. They mind their own business. They don't need anyone else's trouble.

I held him away from me and looked him over. He was filthy and bloody, and he didn't look as though he had had much to eat recently. The cuts on his face and mouth and his bruised head weren't his only injuries. He moved as though he hurt elsewhere.

"Is Mama here, too?" he asked.

"She's here," I said.

"Where?"

"I'm taking you to her." We had begun to walk together up toward the George complex.

"Is the Doctor there too?"

I stopped, staring up toward the complex, and looked down, waiting until I could keep my voice steady. "No, Jus. He's not here."

The Justin I had known back before Camp Christian would have accepted these words at face value. He might have asked where Bankole was, but he wouldn't have said what this much older, wounded, wiser child said.

"Shaper?"

I hadn't heard that title for a while. In fact, I hadn't heard my name for a while. In Georgetown, I called myself Cory Duran. It was my step-mother's maiden name, and I used it in the hope of attracting my brother's attention if he happened to be around. The false name is accepted here because even though I'd been to Georgetown several times before the destruction of Acorn, among the permanent residents, only Dolores George and her husband knew my name. And the Georges don't gossip.

As for the title, in Acorn, all the children called me "Shaper." It was the title that seemed right for one teaching Earthseed. Travis, too, was called Shaper. So was Natividad.

"Shaper?"

"Yes, Jus."

"Is the Doctor dead?"

"Yes. He's dead."

"Oh." He had begun to cry. He had not been crying over his own injuries, but he cried for my Bankole. I took his hand and we walked up the hill to George's.

Like the rest of us, Allie has been working for Dolores George. I never worried about my own ability to earn my way. I worried about Harry's depression, but not about his resourcefulness. He would have little trouble. Nina Noyer didn't give me time to worry about her. She arrived at Georgetown and almost immediately fell in love with one of the younger George sons. In spite of her two lost sisters, in spite of Dolores George's disapproval, Nina and the boy are so intense, so wrapped up in one another that Dolores knows she could only alienate her son by objecting. She hopes the sudden passion will burn itself out. I'm not so sure.

But I worried about Allie. She is healing. She talks now as much as she ever did—which is to say, not a lot. She can think and reason. But not all of her memory has come back. For that reason, I told Dolores some of her story and hoped aloud that some permanent job could be found for her. Dolores first gave her small jobs to do, cleaning floors, repairing steps, painting railings. . . . When she saw that Allie worked well and made no trouble, she said Allie could stay as long as she wanted to. No salary, just room and board.

I stopped at a tree stump about halfway up the hill and sat down and took both of Justin's hands between mine. His face looked bad, and it was hard to look at him, but I made myself do it. "Jus, they hurt your mother."

He began to look afraid. "Hurt her how?"

"They put a collar on her. They put collars on all of us. They hurt her with the collar. I don't know whether you've ever seen—"

"I have. I saw collar gangs working on the highway and in Eureka, fixing potholes, pulling weeds, stuff like that. I saw how a collar can hurt you and make you fall down and twitch and scream."

I nodded. "Collars can do more than that. Someone got really mad at your mother and used the collar to hurt her badly. She's almost okay now, but she's still having some trouble with her memory."

"Amnesia?"

"Yes. Most of what she's lost is what happened in the weeks and months just before she was hurt. That was a bad time for us all, and it may be a mercy that she's lost it. But don't be surprised if you ask her about something and she doesn't remember. She can't help it."

He thought about that for a while, then asked in almost a whisper, "Will she remember me?"

"Absolutely. We've been in contact with all sorts of people trying to find out where you and the others were." Then I couldn't help myself. I had to ask a few questions for myself. "Justin, were you with any of the other kids? Were you with Larkin?"

He shook his head. "They took us all to Arcata to the church there. Then they made us all separate. They said we were going to have new Christian American families. They said . . . they said you were all dead. I believed them at first, and I didn't know what to do. But then I saw how they would lie whenever they felt like it. They would say things about us and about Acorn that were nothing but lies. Then I didn't know what to believe."

"Do you know where they sent Larkin—or any of the others?"

He shook his head again. "They made me go with some people who had a girl and a boy of their own. I was almost the first one to go. I didn't get to see who got the other kids. I guess they went with other families. The people who got me, the man was a deacon. He said it was his duty to take me. I guess it was his duty to beat me up, too!"

"Did he do this to your face?"

Justin nodded. "He did and his son—Carl. Carl said my mother was a devil worshiper and a witch. He was always saying that. He's 12, and he thinks he knows everything. Then a few days ago, he said she was a . . . a whore. And I hit him. We got into a big fight and his father came out and called me an ungrateful little devil-worshiping bastard.

Then they both beat the hell out of me. They locked up me in my room and I went out the window. Then I didn't know where to go, so I just went south, out of town, down toward Acorn. The deacon had said it wasn't there anymore, but I had to see for myself. Then a woman saw me on the road and she brought me here. She gave me some food and put some medicine on my face. She had a lot of kids, but she let me stay with her for a couple of days. I guess she would have let me live there. But I wanted to go home."

I listened to all this, then sighed. "Acorn really is gone," I said. "When we finally broke free, we burned what was left of it."

"*You* burned it?"

"Yes. We couldn't stay there. We would have been caught and collared again or killed. So we took what we could carry, and we burned the rest. Why should they be able to steal it and use it? We burned it!"

He drew back from me a little, and I was afraid I was scaring him. He's a tough little kid, but he had been through a lot. I felt ashamed of letting my feelings show more than I should have.

Then he came close and whispered, "Did you kill them?" So I hadn't been scaring him. The look on his thin, battered face was intense and angry and far more full of hate than a child's face should have been.

I just nodded.

"The ones who hurt my mother—did you kill them, too?"

"Yes."

"Good!"

We got up, and I took him to Allie. I watched them meet, saw Allie's joyous tears, heard her cries. I could hardly stand it, but I watched.

Then Harry got an idea about where his kids might be. He had gotten a job driving one of the George trucks or riding shotgun— something he had had plenty of experience doing back at Acorn. He was even able to make friends with the clannish George men. He would never be one of them, but they liked him, and once he'd proved himself by spotting and helping to prevent an attempted hijacking, they trusted him. This enabled him to see more of the state than he could have by just wandering on foot. But it also kept him on the job, with the trucks most of the time. He couldn't look for his children himself—couldn't walk through the little towns, looking at the children as they worked or played. Doing that would probably get him into trouble, anyway.

Justin had given us two sad, useful bits of information. First, all the kids' names were changed. Justin had been called Matthew Landis, just another of Deacon Landis's sons. The older kids like Justin would remember their real names and who their parents were, but the younger ones, the babies, my Larkin. . . .

The second bit of information was that sibling groups were always broken up. This seemed an unnecessary bit of sadism, even for the Church of Christian America. Justin didn't know why it was done, hadn't seen it done, but he had heard Deacon Landis mention it to another man. So children who had already lost their homes and their parents or guardians had also had their sisters or brothers and their own names taken from them.

With all that, how will I find Larkin?

How will I ever find my child? I've asked all the day laborers I know to look for a Black girlchild, dark-skinned, not yet two years old, but probably big for her age, who has suddenly appeared in a household where there had been no pregnancy, in a household that might not be Black, or in a foster home. I've pretended to be a day laborer myself and substituted for two of the cleaning women so that I could look at two children who had been reported to me as possible candidates. Neither was anything like Larkin.

But is Larkin anything like the Larkin I remember anymore? How can she be? Babies grow and change so fast. She was only two months old when they took her. I'm afraid I won't know her now. But I still have the hand and foot prints. I've made copies of them so that I can always carry one. I've even gone to the police—the Humboldt County

OCTAVIA E. BUTLER

Sheriff—with my false name and told them a false story of how my daughter had been stolen from me as I walked along the highway. I left them a copy of the hand and foot prints and paid the "fee for police services" that you have to pay for anything other than an immediate emergency. I don't know whether that was wise or useful, but I did it. I'm doing everything I can think of.

That's why I don't blame Harry for what he's done. I wish like hell he hadn't done it, but I don't blame him. When you're desperate, you do desperate things.

Harry came to see me two days ago.

He'd just returned from a three-day trip up into Oregon and then over to Tahoe and back. The usual thing for him to do after a trip like that should have been to eat something and go to bed. Instead, he came to my room to see me. I was working at a small, rickety table I had bought. I had sketched a mother and her three children and made the table the price of the sketch. My tiny, closetlike room itself came with a window, a block of wood to wedge it open or bar it shut, a narrow shelfbed, a lot of dirt, and a few bugs. I had bought a pitcher and basin for quick washing, some soap, a chair and table for working, and a jug with the best available water purifier for drinking water. And bug spray.

"Fancy," Dolores had said when she came to look at it. "Why the hell don't you spring for a decent room? You can afford it."

"When I find my daughter, maybe I'll be able to think about things like that," I said. "I don't know what it will cost me to find her, then maybe buy her. I don't know what I might have to do." And maybe, I did not say, maybe I'll have to kidnap her and run. Maybe I'll have to pay the Georges for a fast trip across one or two state lines. Maybe anything. I couldn't waste money.

"Yeah," she said. "I haven't heard anything more, but my people are listening."

They're still listening. So are the freelancers to whom I had paid a little and promised a lot—people like Cougar, I'm sorry to say—

except that they deal in even younger children. I feel filthy every time I have to talk to one of them. If anyone deserves to be collared and put to work, they do, and yet there hasn't been any particular Christian American crackdown on them.

Apparently we represent the greater danger to Jarret's America. What was done to us was illegal, by the way. We've learned that much. No new laws have been made to okay any of it. But, as Day Turner said long ago, a lot of people are convinced that cracking down on the poor and the different is a good idea. There are now a number of legal cases—Hindus, Jews, Moslems, and others who have managed to avoid being caught when Crusaders came for them. But even among these people, young children who are taken away are not often returned. Charge after charge of neglect and abuse are made against the parents or guardians. In fact, the parents or guardians might wind up collared legally for the horrible things they were supposed to have done to their children. Sometimes brainwashed or terrorized children are produced to give testimony against biological parents they haven't seen for months or years. I wasn't sure what to make of that last. Justin had not turned against Allie, no matter what he had been told about her. What kind of brainwashing would make a child turn against its own parents?

So the legal road seems not to lead to a return of abducted children—or it hasn't so far. It hasn't even led to an end of the camps. Camps are mentioned on the nets and disks as being strictly for the rehabilitation and reeducation of minor criminals—vagrants, thieves, addicts, and prostitutes. That's all. No problem.

We are, as we have always been, on our own.

"I quit my job today," Harry said to me. He sat on my bed and leaned forward on my table, looking across at me with disturbing intensity. "I'm leaving."

I put aside the lessons I had been writing for one of my students—a woman who wanted to learn to read so that she could teach her children. My students can't or won't afford books of any kind. I write lessons for them on sheets of paper that they buy from George's and bring to me. I've taught them to practice first letters, then words on the ground in a smooth patch of dirt. They write with their forefingers to learn to feel the shapes of letters and words. Then I make them write with sharp, slender sticks so they can get used to the feel of using a pencil or pen.

It seems I've always taught. With four younger brothers, I feel as though I were born teaching. I like doing it. I'm just not sure how much good it does. How much good does anything do now?

"What have you heard?" I asked Harry.

He stared off to one side, out my window.

I reached across the table to take his hand. "Tell me, Harry."

He looked at me and tried, I think, to smile a little. "I've heard that there's a big children's home run by Christian America down in Marin County," he said, "and there's another in Ventura County. I don't have addresses, but I'll find them. Truth is, I've heard there are a lot of children's homes run by CA. But those are the only two I know of in California." He paused, looked out the window again. "I don't know whether they would send our kids to one of those places. Justin says he didn't hear anything about children's homes or orphanages. He says all he heard was that he and the other kids were going to new families to be raised the right way as patriotic Christian Americans."

"But you're going down to Ventura and Marin to find out for sure?"

"I have to."

I thought about this, then shook my head. "I don't believe they'd send kids as young as yours and mine down there. They have them adopted or fostered around here somewhere. At worst they'd be here in small group homes. The Ventura home would have kids pouring into it from all of southern California. The Marin home would be full of kids from the Bay Area and Sacramento."

"So you go on looking here," he said. "I want you to. If you find our kids, it will be as good as if I found them. They won't be in the hands of crazy people—of their own mother's murderers."

"*Here* is where it makes sense to look!" I said. "If CA is doing any moving of kids, chances are, it's from south to north. It's still crowded down there—with all the immigration from Latin America plus the people from Arizona and Nevada and those who were already there."

"I've got to go," he said. "I know you're right, but it doesn't matter. I don't know where to look up here. Adoptions, foster homes, even small group homes don't call enough attention to themselves. We've been checking them, one by one, and we could go on doing that for years. But if the kids are down south, I might be able to get a job at first one, then the other of the big homes and get a look at them."

I sat back, thinking. "I believe you're wrong," I said. "But if you insist on going—"

"I'm going."

"You shouldn't go alone. You need someone to watch your back."

"I don't want you with me. I want you here, searching." He took two palm-sized debit phones from his jacket pocket and pushed one toward me. They were a cheap version of the prepaid renewable kind of satellite phone that we used to use at Acorn. "I bought these yesterday," he said. "I paid for five hours of in-country use. They're cheap, simple, and anonymous. All you can do with them is call and receive, voice only. No screen, no net access, no message storage. But at least we'll be able to talk to one another."

"But your chances of surviving alone on the road—"

He got up and walked toward the door.

"Harry!" I said, standing myself.

"I'm tired," he said. "I've got to get some sleep. I'm half dead."

I let him go. His depression was bad enough. Depression and exhaustion together were too much to fight against. He hadn't been himself since Zahra's death. I would let him rest, then try to make him see reason. I wouldn't try to make him stay, but going alone was suicide. He knew it. Once he had rested, he would be able to admit it.

But the next day—today—Harry was gone.

He left George's early this morning, buying a ride in a truck headed for Santa Barbara. I didn't know about it until I saw Dolores this morning. She handed me the note that he had left with her for me.

"I have to go, Lauren," it said. "Keep the phone with you and stay put. I'll come hack. If I don't find the kids down south, I'll help you continue the search up here. Don't worry, and take care of yourself."

All his life, he's been a funny, gentle, bright person with an under-current of seriousness. We've known one another all our lives, and felt comfortable enough together to be brother and sister. He and Zahra were my best friends. I've lost count of the number of times we've saved one another's lives.

And now it's over. Truly over. Zahra is dead. Harry is gone. Everyone is gone. Allie meant to live in Georgetown with Justin. She had the one thing she cared about: her son. And Nina Noyer just wanted to get married and settle down with people who could take care of her and protect her. I don't blame her, but I find I don't like her much. Her little sisters might be wearing collars now or living with people who abused and terrorized them in God's name. Or they might be in some huge warehouse of a children's home, lost in the crowd, but separated from one another if Justin was right—lost to everyone who had ever loved them.

It isn't that Nina doesn't care. She just doesn't think she can do anything to help them. "I'm not Dan," she's told me more than once. "Maybe it means I'm weak, but I can't help it. I can't do what he did. I can't! It's not fair to expect me to. He was a boy—almost a man! I just want to get married and be happy!"

She's 16. Her brother was only 15 when he rescued her and brought her to us. But as she says, she's not him.

17

○ ○ ○

From EARTHSEED: THE BOOKS OF THE LIVING

All prayers are to Self
And, in one way or another,
All prayers are answered.
Pray,
But beware.
Your desires,
Whether or not you achieve them,
Will determine who you become.

I wonder what my life would have been like if my mother had found me. I don't doubt that she would have stolen me from the Alexanders—or died trying. But then what? How long would it have been before she put me aside for Earthseed, her other kid? Earthseed was never long out of her thoughts. If it didn't comfort her during her captivity—and I suspect it did—at least it sustained her. It enabled her to survive without giving up or truly giving in to her captors. I couldn't have helped her. I was her weakness. Earthseed was her strength. No wonder it was her favorite.

From *THE JOURNALS OF LAUREN OYA OLAMINA*
SUNDAY, APRIL 8, 2035

I'm on my own.

I've left Georgetown, left my students old and young, left my room furnished with junk. I left some of my money and one of my guns with Allie so that I'll have something to fall back on if I'm robbed. I've come first to the message cache—two days' walk—to see whether anything has been left. I'm there now. I'll sleep there in the shelter of a living coast redwood tree that time and rot have hollowed out enough to hold a human or three. I've found unsigned messages from Travis and Natividad and from Michael and Noriko. Both identified themselves by referring to incidents that any member of the community would remember and understand but that would mean nothing to strangers. I did the same in the message I left.

Neither couple had found their kids. Both had left numbers. They had bought new phones—the cheap, talk-and-listen, debit phones like Harry's and mine. I left three numbers—mine, Harry's, and one where Allie could be reached. Then I wrote a message to those who might come later.

"Justin is with us again! He's all right. There is hope. God is Change!"

God is Change. I wrote the words, then settled back to think about that. I find that I haven't thought much about Earthseed in the past few months. I believe its teachings helped me, helped all of us to survive Camp Christian. God is Change. I've lost none of my belief. All that I said to Bankole so long ago—two years ago—is still true.

So much has been destroyed, but it is still true. Earthseed is true. The Destiny is as significant a human purpose as it ever was. Only Acorn is gone. Acorn was precious, but it wasn't essential.

I sit here now, trying to think, to plan. I must find my daughter, and I must teach Earthseed, make Earthseed real to as many people as I can reach, and send them out to teach others.

The truth is, when I taught reading, I used a few simple Earthseed verses. This is what I did in Acorn, and I did it automatically in Georgetown. Strange to say, no one objected. People sometimes looked puzzled, sometimes disagreed or agreed with enthusiasm, but no one complained. Some people even seemed to think that what I read was from the Bible. I couldn't bring myself to let them go on thinking that.

"No," I told them. "It's from something else called *Earthseed: The Books of the Living*." And I showed them one of the few surviving copies—retrieved from one of the caches. Since I've been calling myself Cory Duran, no one connected me with the strangely named author, Lauren Oya Olamina.

Lines like the familiar,

> *"All that you touch,*
> *You Change. . . ."*

And

> *"To get along with God*
> *Consider the consequences of your behavior."*

And

> *"Belief*
> *Initiates and guides action*
> *Or it does nothing."*

And

> *"Kindness eases Change."*

People seemed to like brief fragments of verses or complete rhythmic verses because rhythmic verses are easy to memorize. And memorizing verses made it easier to spot individual words and learn to recognize them in their written forms. In that way, I guess I never stopped teaching Earthseed. But without the Destiny, without a more complete understanding of the belief system, what I taught was no more than a few scattered verses and aphorisms. Nothing unifies them.

I must find at least a few people who are willing to learn more, and who will be willing to teach what they've learned. I must build . . . not a physical community this time. I guess I understand at last how easy it is to destroy such a community. I need to create something wide-reaching and harder to kill. That's why I must teach teachers. I must create not only a dedicated little group of followers, not only a collection of communities as I once imagined, but a movement. I must create a new fashion in faith—a fashion that can evolve into a new religion, a new guiding force, that can help humanity to put its great energy, competitiveness, and creativity to work doing the truly vast job of fulfilling the Destiny.

But first, somehow, I must find my child.

I am alone, and I know that's stupid. To travel alone is to make yourself more vulnerable than you need to be. I wish I could have talked Harry into working with me. He's endangering himself and wasting his time down in southern California and around the Bay Area. I don't believe there's any chance at all that our kids have been shipped down there. They're here. And his kids and mine are so young that they've surely been adopted. My Larkin could grow up believing that she is the daughter of one her kidnappers. His kids were four and two when they were taken, so I suspect the same could happen to them—if we let it.

Tomorrow, I'll start walking toward Eureka. I'm armed. I've got the old .45 semiautomatic that made the trip up from Robledo with me. I had tucked it into one of the caches, thinking I wouldn't need it again. Also, I've done all that seemed reasonable to make myself look both poor and male. I'm big and plain. That's good camouflage, at least. It's not real protection, but it's the best I can do. If someone shoots me, I've got no backup, so chances are, I'm dead. But I'm not the only solitary walker out there, and maybe the robbers and the crazies will go for the smaller ones who look like less trouble. And there are fewer robbers and crazies. Or there were. At Georgetown and on my way here, I saw more and more men in military uniforms—or parts of uniforms. They helped fight Jarret's stupid Al-Can war. Now a lot of them are having a hard time earning a living—and they're often very well armed.

There are more slavers now that Jarret's Crusaders have joined Cougar and his friends in the game of collaring people and grabbing their kids. I'm hoping to be invisible to them. I want to keep quiet, do my work, and to look just crazy enough to encourage people to let me alone. As a man, though, I must be very careful how I follow up the few leads I have on small Black children who have appeared all of a sudden in families where no one was pregnant. I don't want to be mistaken for a lurking child molester or a kidnapper.

I hope to work for meals in Eureka and Arcata—a little yard work, some painting, some minor carpentry, wood that needs chopping. . . . If I stay away from the wealthier neighborhoods, I should be all right. Wealthy people wouldn't need to hire me anyway. They would keep a few servants—people working for room and board. I would be working for what was left of the middle class. I would be just one more day laborer working for his next meal.

Down south and in the Bay Area, a laborer's life would be harder. People are too distrustful of one another, too walled off from one another if they can afford walls. But up here, men are hired, and then at least decently fed. They might even be allowed to sleep in a shed, a garage, or a barn. And they might—often do—get a look at the kids of the family. They might—often do—hear talk that later proves useful. For most laborers, useful means they might be steered toward other jobs or away from trouble or let in on where people keep their valuables. For me, useful might mean rumors of adoptions, fosterings, and children's homes.

I'll wander around the Eureka-Arcata complex and the surrounding towns for as long as I can. Allie has promised to go on collecting information for me, and she says I can crash in her rooms at Georgetown when I need a rest in a real bed. Also, if I'm picked up and collared, Dolores will vouch for me—for a fee, of course. She knows what I'm doing. She doesn't think I've got a chance in hell of succeeding, but she's got kids and grandkids, so she knows I have to do this.

"I'd do the same thing myself," she said when I talked to her. "I'd do all I could. Goddamn these so-called religious people. Thieves and murderers—that's all they are. They should wear the collar. They should roast in hell!"

There are times when I wish I believed in hell—other than the hells we make for one another, I mean.

SUNDAY, APRIL 15 , 2035

I've spent my first week doing other people's scutwork. Odd how familiar all the jobs are—helping to plant vegetable or flower gardens, chopping weeds, pruning bushes and small trees, cleaning up a winter's accumulation of trash, repairing fences, and so on. These are all things I did at Acorn where everyone did everything. People seem pleased and a little surprised that I do good work. I've even earned some money by suggesting extra jobs that I was willing to take care of for a fee. People warn their kids away from me most of the time, but I do get to see the kids, from babies in their mothers' arms to toddlers to older kids and neighbor kids. I haven't seen any familiar faces yet, but, of course, I've just begun. I've gone to as many Black or mixed-race families as I could. I don't know what kind of people I should be checking, but it seemed best to begin with these people. If they seem at all friendly, I ask them if they have friends who might hire me. That's gotten me a couple of jobs so far.

My problem has turned out to be having a place to sleep. A guy offered to let me sleep in his garage that first night if I'd give him a blow job.

I wasn't sure whether he thought I was a man or had spotted that I was a woman, and I didn't care. I bedded down that night in a shabby park where a few redwood trees survive. There, among a small flock of other homeless people, I slept safely and awoke early to avoid the police. People in Georgetown have warned me that collaring vagrants is what cops do when they need some arrests to justify their paychecks. It's also what some of the meaner ones do when they've had no amusement for a while.

It was cold, but I've got warm, lightweight clothing and a comfortable, shabby old sleepsack that I'd used on the trip up from Robledo.

OCTAVIA E. BUTLER

I woke up aching a little from the uneven ground, but otherwise all right. I needed a bath, but compared to the amount of crud I used to accumulate back in Camp Christian, I was almost presentable. I had already decided that I'd wash when I could, sleep sheltered when I could. I can't afford to let myself worry about things like that.

On Tuesday, I was allowed to sleep in a toolshed, which was a good thing, because it rained hard.

On Wednesday I was back in the park, although the woman I worked for told me that I should go to the shelter at the Christian America Center on Fourth Street.

Hell of a thought. I've known for weeks that the place existed, and I've kept well clear of it. Laborers at Georgetown say they avoid the place. People have been known to vanish from there. I'm afraid I'll have to go there someday, though. I need to hear more about what the CA people do with orphans. Problem is, I don't know how I'll be able to stand it. I hate those bastards so much. There are moments when I'd kill them all if I could. *I hate them.*

And I'm terrified of them. What if someone recognizes me? That's unlikely, but what if? I can't go to the CA Center yet. I'll make myself do it soon, but not yet. I'd rather blow my own brains out than wear a collar again.

On Thursday, I was in the park, but on Friday and Saturday, I slept in the garage of an old woman who wanted her fence repaired and painted and her windowsills sanded and painted. Her neighbor kept coming over "to chat." I understood that the neighbor was just making sure that I wasn't murdering her friend, and I didn't mind. It turned out well in the end. The neighbor wound up hiring me herself to chop weeds, prepare the soil, and put in her vegetable and flower gardens. That was good because she was my reason for going to her part of town. She was a blond woman with a blond husband, and yet I had heard through my contacts at Georgetown that she had two beautiful dark-haired, dark-skinned toddlers.

The woman turned out to be not well off at all, and yet she paid me a few dollars in addition to a couple of good meals for the work I did. I liked her, and I was glad when I saw that the two children she had adopted were strangers. I write now in her garage, where there is an electric light and a cot. It's cold, of course, but I'm wrapped up and warm enough except for my hands. I need to write now more than ever because I have no one to talk to, but writing is cold work on nights like this.

SUNDAY, MAY 13, 2035

I've been to the Christian America Center. I've finally made myself go there. It was like making myself step into a big nest of rattlesnakes, but I've done it. I couldn't sleep there. Even without Day Turner's experience to guide me, I couldn't have slept in the rattler's nest. But I've eaten there three times now, trying to hear what there might be to hear. I remember Day Turner telling me that he had been offered a bed, meals, and a few dollars if he helped paint and repair a couple of houses that were to be part of a CA home for orphaned children. He had not known the addresses of the houses. Nor had he known Eureka well enough to give me an idea where these houses might be, and that was a shame. Our children might not still be there—if they were ever there. But I might be able to learn something from the place. There might be records that I could steal or rumors, memories, stories that I could hear about. And if several of our children had been sent there, then perhaps I could find one or two of them still there.

That last thought scared me a little. If I did find a couple of our kids, I couldn't leave them in CA hands. One way or another, I would have to free them and try to reunite them with their families. That would draw such attention to me that I would have to leave the area, and, I suspect, leave my Larkin. This is assuming that I would be able to leave, that I didn't wind up wearing another collar.

The food at the CA Center was edible—a couple of slices of bread

OCTAVIA E. BUTLER

and a rich stew of potatoes and vegetables flavored with beef, although I never found meat of any kind in it. People around me complained about the lack of meat, but I didn't mind. Over the past several months, I've learned to eat whatever was put in front of me, and be glad of it. If I could keep it down, and there was enough of it to fill my stomach, I considered myself lucky. But it amazed me that I could keep anything down while sitting so close to my enemies at the CA Center.

My first visit was the worst. My memory of it isn't as clear as it ought to be. I know I went there. I sat and I ate with several dozen other homeless men. I managed not to go crazy when someone began to preach at us. I know I did all that, and I know that afterward, I needed the long, long walk to the park to get my head back into working order. Walking, like writing, helps.

I did it all in blind terror. How I looked to others I don't know. I think I must have seemed too mentally sick even to talk to. No one tried to make conversation with me, although some of the men talked to one another. I got in line and after that I moved automatically, did what others did. Once I sat down with my food, I found myself crouching over it, protecting it, gulping it like a hawk who's caught a pigeon. I used to see people doing that at Camp Christian. You got so damned hungry there sometimes, it made you a little crazy. This time, though, it wasn't the food that I cared about. I wasn't that hungry. And if I'd wanted to, I could have changed my clothing, gone in to a decent restaurant, and bought a real meal. It's just that somehow, if I focused on the food and filled my mind with it as well as my body, I could keep myself still and not get up and run, screaming, out of that place.

I have never, in freedom, been so afraid. People edged away from me. I mean crazies, junkies, whores, and thieves edged away from me. I didn't think about it at the time. I didn't think about anything. I'm surprised that I manage to remember any of it now. I moved through it in a cloud of blank terror and an absolute readiness to kill.

I had wrapped my gun in my spare clothes and put it at the bottom of my pack. I did this on purpose so that there would be no quick way for me to get at it. I didn't want to be tempted to get at it. If I needed it inside the CA Center, I was already dead. I couldn't leave it anywhere, but I could unload it. I took a lot of time earlier that evening, unloading it and wrapping it up, watching myself wrap it up so that even in the deepest panic I would know I couldn't get at it.

It worked. It was necessary, and it worked.

Years ago, when my neighborhood in Robledo burned, when so much of my family burned, I had to go back. I got away in the night, and the next day, I had to go back. I had to retrieve what I could of that part of my life that was over, and I had to say good-bye. I had to. Up to that moment, and long afterward, going back to my Robledo neighborhood was the hardest thing I had ever done. This was worse.

When I went to the CA Center for the second time several days later, it wasn't as bad. I could look and think and listen. I have no memory of any word said during the first visit. I tried to listen, but I couldn't take anything in. But during the second, I heard people talking about the food, about employers who didn't pay, about women—I was in the men's section—about places up north, out east, or down south were there was work, about joints that hurt, about the war. . . . I listened and I looked. After a while, I saw myself. I saw a man crouching over his food, spooning it into his mouth with intense and terrible concentration. His eyes, when he looked up, looked around, were vacant and scary. In line, he shambled more than he walked. If anyone got close to him, he looked insanity and death at them. He was barely human. People kept away from him. Maybe he was on something. He was big. He might be dangerous. I kept away from him myself. But he was me a few days before. I never found out what his particular problems were, but I know they were as terrible to him as mine are to me.

I heard almost nothing about orphaned children or Jarret's Crusaders. A couple of the men mentioned that they had kids. Most don't talk much, but some can't stop talking: their long-lost homes, women, money, brave deeds and suffering during the war. . . . Nothing useful.

Still I went back for the third time last night. Same food. They

OCTAVIA E. BUTLER

throw in different vegetables—whatever they happen to have, I suppose. The only inevitable ingredient in the stew is potatoes, but dinner is always vegetable stew and bread. And after the meal, there's always at least an hour of sermon to bear. The doors are shut. You eat, then you listen. Then you can leave or try to get a bed.

My first sermon I couldn't remember if my life depended on it. The second was about Christ curing the sick and being willing to cure us too if we only asked. The third was about Jesus Christ, the same yesterday, today, and forever.

The lay minister who delivered this third sermon was Marc.

It was him, my brother, a lay minister in the Church of Christian America.

In fear and surprise, I lowered my head, wondering whether he had seen me. There were about two hundred other people in the men's cafeteria that night—men of all races, ethnicities, and degrees of sanity. I sat toward the back of the cafeteria, and off to the left of the podium or pulpit or whatever it was. After a while I looked up without raising my head. Nothing of Marc's body language indicated that he had seen me. As he warmed to his sermon, though, he did mention that he had a sister who was steeped in sin, a sister who had been raised in the way of the Lord, but who had permitted herself to be pulled down by Satan. This sister had, through the influence of Satan, done him a great injury, he said, but he had forgiven her. He loved her. It hurt him that she would not turn from sin. It hurt him that he had had to turn from her. He shed a few tears and shook his head. At last he said, "Jesus Christ was your Savior yesterday. He is your Savior today. He will be your Savior forever. Your sister might desert you. Your brother might betray you. Your friends might try to pull you down into sin. But Jesus will always be there for you. So hold on to the Lord! Hold on! Stand firm in your faith. Be courageous. Be strong. Be a soldier of Christ. He will help you and protect you. He will raise you up and never, never, never let you down!"

When it was over, I started to slip away with the crowd. I needed to think. I had to figure out how to reach Marc outside the CA Center.

At the last minute, I went back and left a note for the lay minister with one of the servers. It said, "Heard you preach tonight. Didn't know you were here. Need to see you. Out front tomorrow evening where dinner line forms up." And I signed it Bennett O.

One of our brothers was named Bennett Olamina. Olamina was an unusual name. Someone in CA might notice it and remember it from records of the inmates at Camp Christian. Also, it occurred to me that signing the name I was using, "Cory Duran," might be cruel. Cory was Marc's mother, after all, not mine. I didn't want to remind him of the pain of losing her or hint that she might be alive. And if I had written Lauren O., I thought Marc might decide not to come. We hadn't parted on the best of terms, after all. Perhaps it's also cruel to hint to him that one of our two youngest brothers might still be alive. Perhaps he'll know or guess that I wrote the note. But I had to use a name that would get his attention. I must see him. If he won't do anything else, surely he'll help me find Larkin. He can't know what happened to us. I don't believe he would have joined CA if he knew it was made up of thieves, kidnappers, slavers, and murderers. He wanted to lead, to be important, to be respected, but he had been a slave prostitute himself. No matter how angry he was at me, he wouldn't wish me captivity and a collar. At least, I don't believe he would.

The truth is, I don't know what to believe.

An old man is letting me sleep in his garage tonight. I chopped weeds and cleared trash for him today. Now I'm content. I've spread some flat boards over the concrete and covered the boards with rags. In my sleepsack on top of these, I'm pretty comfortable. There's even a filthy old flush toilet and a sink with running water out here—a real luxury. I had a wash. Now I want to sleep, but all I can do, all I can think of is Marc in *that place*, Marc with *those people*. Maybe he was even there at the time of my first visit. We might have seen each other and not known. What would he have done, I wonder, if he had recognized me?

18

○ ○ ○

Beware:
All too often,
We say
What we hear others say.
We think
What we're told that we think.
We see
What we're permitted to see.
Worse!
We see what we're told that we see.
Repetition and pride are the keys to this.
To hear and to see
Even an obvious lie
Again
And again and again
May be to say it,
Almost by reflex
Then to defend it
Because we've said it
And at last to embrace it
Because we've defended it
And because we cannot admit
That we've embraced and defended
An obvious lie.
Thus, without thought,
Without intent,
We make

Mere echoes
Of ourselves—
And we say
What we hear others say.

From *WARRIOR* by Marcos Duran

I've always believed in the power of God, distant and profound. But more immediately, I believe in the power of religion itself as a great mover of masses. I wonder if that's odd in the son of a Baptist minister. I think my father honestly believed that faith in God was enough. He lived as though he believed it. But it didn't save him.

I began preaching when I was only a boy. I prayed for the sick and saw some of them healed under my hands. I was given tithings of money and food by people who had not enough to eat themselves. People who were old enough to be my parents came to me for advice, reassurance, and comfort. I was able to help them. I knew the Bible. I had my own version of my father's quiet, caring, confident manner. I was only in my teens, but I found people interesting. I liked them and I understood how to reach them. I've always been a good mimic, and I'd had more education than most of the people I dealt with. Some Sundays in my Robledo slum church, I had as many as 200 people listening as I preached, taught, prayed, and passed the plate.

But when the city authorities decided that we were no more than trash to be swept out of our homes, my prayers had no power to stop them. The city authorities were stronger and richer. They had more and better guns. They had the power, the knowledge, and the discipline to bury us.

The governments, city, county, state, and federal plus the big rich companies were the sources of money, information, weapons—real physical power. But in post-Pox America, successful churches were only sources of influence. They offered people safe emotional catharsis,

OCTAVIA E. BUTLER

a sense of community, and ways to organize their desires, hopes, and fears into systems of ethics. Those things were important and necessary, but they weren't power. If this country was ever to be restored to greatness, it wasn't the little dollar-a-dozen preachers who would do it.

Andrew Steele Jarret understood this. When he created Christian America and then moved from the pulpit into politics, when he pulled religion and government together and cemented the link with money from rich businessmen, he created what should have been an unstoppable drive to restore the country. And he became my teacher.

I love my Uncle Marc. There were times when I was more than half in love with him. He was so good-looking, and a beautiful person, male or female, can get away with saying and doing things that would destroy a plainer one. I never stopped loving him. Even my mother, I think, loved him in spite of herself.

What Uncle Marc had been through as a slave marked him, I'm sure, but I don't know how much. How can you know what a man would be like if he had grown up unmarked by horror? What did my mother's time as a beaten, robbed, raped slave do to her? She was always a woman of obsessive purpose and great physical courage. She had always been willing to sacrifice others to what she believed was right. She recognized that last characteristic in Uncle Marc, but I don't believe she ever saw it clearly in herself.

From *THE JOURNALS OF LAUREN OYA OLAMINA*
MONDAY, MAY 14, 2035

I met with my brother earlier tonight.

I spent the day helping my latest employer—a likable old guy full of stories of his adventures as a young man in the 1970s. He was a singer and guitar player, with a band. They traveled the world, played raucous music, and had wild sex with hundreds, maybe thousands, of eager young girls. Lies, I suppose.

We put in a vegetable garden and pruned some of the dead limbs from his fruit trees. I don't mean "we," of course. He said, "Well, how about we do this?" Or, "Do you think we can do that?" And he tried to help, and that was all right. He needed to feel useful, just as he needed someone to hear his outrageous stories. He told me he was 88 years old. His two sons are dead. His middle-aged granddaughter and his several young great-grandchildren live in Edmonton, Alberta, up in Canada. He was alone except for a neighbor lady who looked in now and then. And she was 74 herself.

He said I could stay as long as I wanted to if I would help him out in the house and outside. The house wasn't in good shape. It had been neglected for years. I couldn't have done all the repairs, of course, even if he could have afforded the needed materials. But I decided to stay for a few days to do what I could. I didn't dare stay long enough for him to begin to depend on me, but a few days.

I thought that would give me a base to work from while I got to know my brother again.

I'm trying to decide how to talk about my meeting with Marc. Tonight's walk back to the old man's house has helped me to relax a little, calm down a little. But not enough.

Marc was waiting near the long dinner line when I arrived. He looked so handsome and at ease in his clean, stylish, casual clothing. He had worn a dark blue suit when he preached the night before, and he had managed, even as he told a couple of hundred thieves and winos how awful I was, to look startlingly beautiful.

"Marc," I said.

He jumped, then turned to stare at me. He had glanced in my direction, but it was obvious that he hadn't recognized me until I spoke to him. He had been encouraging a man in line ahead of me to accept Jesus Christ as his personal Savior and let Jesus help with his drinking problem. It seemed that the CA Center had a rigorous drying-out program, and Marc had been working hard to sell it.

"Let's take a walk around the corner and talk," I said, and before he could recover or answer, I turned and walked away, certain that he would follow. He did. We were well away from the line and well away from any listening ears when he caught up.

"Lauren!" he said. "My God, Lauren, is it you? What in hell are you—?"

I led him around the corner, out of sight of the line, and onto a dirty little side street that led to the bay. I went on several steps down that street, then stopped and turned and looked at him.

He stood frowning, staring at me, looking uncertain, surprised, almost angry. There was no shame or defensiveness about him. That was good. His reaction on seeing me would have been different, I'm sure, if he had known what his Camp Christian friends had been doing to me.

"I need your help," I said. "I need you to help me to find my daughter."

This made nothing at all clear to him, but it did shift him away from anger, which was what I wanted. "What?" he said.

"Your people have her. They took her. I don't. . . . I don't believe that they've killed her. I don't know what they've done with her, but I suspect that one of them has adopted her. I need you to help me find her."

"Lauren, what are you talking about? What are you doing here? Why are you trying to look like a man? How did you find me?"

"I heard you preach last night."

And again he was reduced to saying, "What?" This time he looked a little embarrassed, a little apprehensive.

"I've been coming here in the hope of finding out what CA does with the children it takes."

"But these people don't take children! I mean, they rescue orphans from the streets, but they don't—"

"And they 'rescue' the children of heathens, don't they? Well, they 'rescued' my daughter Larkin and all the rest of the younger children of Acorn! They killed my Bankole! And Zahra! Zahra Moss Balter from Robledo! They killed her! They put a collar around my neck and around the necks of my people. CA did that! And then those holy Christians worked us like slaves every day and used us like whores at night! That's what they did. That's what kind of people they are. Now I need your help to find my daughter!" All that came out in a rush, in a harsh, ugly whisper, my face up close to his, my emotions almost out of control. I hadn't meant to spit it all out at him that way. I needed him. I meant to tell him everything, but not like that.

He stared at me as though I were speaking to him in Chinese. He put his hand on my shoulder. "Lauren, come in. Have some food, a bath, a clean bed. Come on in. We need to talk."

I stood still, not letting him move me. "Listen," I said in a more human voice. "Listen, I know I'm dumping a lot on you, Marc, and I'm sorry." I took a deep breath. "It's just that you're the only person I've felt that I could dump it on. I need your help. I'm desperate."

"Come on in." He wasn't quite humoring me. He seemed to be in denial, but not speaking of it. He was trying to divert me, tempt me with meaningless comforts.

"Marc, if it's possible, I will never set foot in that poisonous place again. Now that I've found you, I shouldn't have to."

"But these people will help you, Lauren. You're making some kind of mistake. I don't understand it, but you are. We would rather take in whole families than separate them. I've worked on the apartments that we're renovating to help get people off the streets. I know—"

Now he was humoring me. "Have you ever heard of a place called Camp Christian?" I asked, letting the harshness come back into my voice. He was silent for a moment, but I knew before he spoke that the answer to my question was *yes*.

"I wouldn't have named it that," he said. "It's a reeducation camp— one of the places where the worst people we handle are sent. These are people who would go to prison if we didn't take them. Minor criminals, most of them—thieves, junkies, prostitutes, that kind of thing. We try to reach them, teach them skills and self-discipline, stop them from graduating to real prisons."

I listened, shaking my head. He was either a great actor or he believed what he was saying. "Camp Christian *was* a prison," I said. "For seventeen months it was a prison. Before that, it was Acorn. My people and I built Acorn with our own hands, then your Christian America took it, stole it from us, and turned it into a prison camp."

He just stood there, staring at me as though he didn't know what to believe or what to do.

"Back in September," I said, keeping my voice low and even. "Back in September of '33, they came with seven maggots, smashing through our thorn fence, picking off our watchers. I knew we couldn't fight a force like that. I signaled everyone to run like hell, scatter. You know we had drills—drills for fighting and drills for fading into the hills. None of it mattered. They gassed us. Three people might have gotten away: the mute woman named May and the two little Noyer girls. I don't know. They were the only ones we never heard anything about. The rest of us were captured, collared, and used for work and for sex. Our younger children were taken away. No one would tell us where. My Bankole, Zahra Balter, Teresa Lin, and some others were killed. If we asked anything, we were punished with the collars. If we were caught talking at all, we were punished. We slept on the floor or on shelves in the school. Your holy men took our houses. And they took us, too, when they felt like it. Listen!"

He had stopped looking at me and begun to look past me, looking over my right shoulder.

"They brought in street people and travelers and minor criminals and other mountain families, and they collared them too," I said. "Marc! Do you hear me?"

"I don't believe you," he said at last. "I don't believe any of this!"

"Go and look at what's left of Acorn. Look for yourself. Go to one of the other so-called reeducation camps. I'll bet they're just as bad. Check them out."

He began to shake his head. "This is not true! I know these people! They wouldn't do what you're accusing them of."

"Maybe some of them wouldn't. But some of them did. All that we built they stole."

"I don't believe you," he said. But he did believe. "You're making some kind of mistake."

"Go and see for yourself," I repeated. "Be careful how you ask questions. I don't want you to get into trouble. These are dangerous, vicious people. Go and see."

He said nothing for a few seconds. It bothered me that he was frowning, and again, not looking at me. "You were collared?" he asked at last.

"For seventeen months. Forever."

"How did you get away? Was your sentence up?"

"What? What sentence?"

"I mean did they let you go?"

"They never let anyone go. They killed quite a few of us, but they never released anyone. I don't know what their long-range plans were for us, if they had any, but I don't see how they could have dared to let us go after what they'd done to us."

"How did you get free? You don't escape once someone's put a collar on you. There's no escape from a collar."

Unless someone deals with the devil and buys your freedom, I thought. But I didn't say it. "There was a landslide," I did say. "It smashed the cabin where the control unit was kept—my cabin. The control unit powered all the individual belt control units somehow. Maybe it even powered the collars themselves. I'm not sure. Anyway, once it was smashed and buried, the collars stopped working, and we went into our homes and killed our surviving guards—those who hadn't been killed by the landslide. Then we burned the cabins with their bodies inside. *We* burned them. They were ours! We built every one with our own hands."

"You killed people . . . ?"

"Their names were Cougar, Marc. Every one of them was named Cougar!"

He turned—wrenched himself around as though he had to uproot himself to move—and started back toward the corner.

"Marc!"

He kept walking.

"Marc!" I grabbed his arm, pulled him back around to face me. "I didn't tell you this to hurt you. I know I have hurt you, and I'm sorry, but these bastards have my child! I need your help to get her back. Please, Marc."

He hit me.

I never expected it, never saw it coming. Even when we were kids, he and I didn't hit each other.

I stumbled backward, more startled than hurt. And he was gone. By the time I got to the corner, he had already vanished into the CA Center.

I was afraid to go in after him. In his present frame of mind, he might turn me in. How will I get to see him again? Even if he decides to help me, how will I contact him? Surely he will decide to help me once he's had time to think. Surely he will.

SUNDAY, JUNE 3 , 2035

I've left the Eureka-Arcata area.

I'm back at the message tree for the night. I brought a flashlight so that I could have light where I wanted it without taking risks with fire. Now, shielding my light, I'm reading what's been left here. Jorge and Di have left a number, and Jorge says he's found his brother Mateo. In fact, as with Justin, his brother found him. On the northern edge of Garberville where there are still big redwoods, Mateo found Jorge's group sleeping on the ground. He had been looking for them for months. Like Justin, he had run away from abuse, although in his case, the abuse was sexual. Now he's wounded and bitter, but he's with his brother again.

There was no news from Harry. Too soon for him to have gotten back, I suppose. I phoned him several times, but there was no answer. I'm worried about him.

I wrote a note, warning the others to avoid the CA Center in Eureka. I wrote that Marc had been there, but that he wasn't to be trusted.

He isn't to be trusted.

I made myself go back to the CA Center on Wednesday of last week—went back as a sane, but shabby woman rather than as a dirty, crazy man. It took me too long to get up the courage to do that—to go. I worried that Marc might have warned his CA friends about me. I couldn't really believe he would do that, but he might, and I'd had nightmares about them grabbing me as soon as I showed up. I could feel them putting on the collar. I'd wake up soaking wet and scared to death.

At last, I went to a used-clothing store and bought an old black skirt and a blue blouse. From a cheap little shop, I bought a some makeup and a scarf for my hair. I dressed, made up, then dirtied up a little, like maybe I'd been rolling around on the ground with someone.

At CA, I got in line with the other women and ate in the small, walled-off women's section. No one seemed to pay any attention to me, although my height was much more noticeable when I was among only women. I slumped a little and kept my head down when I was standing. I tried to look weary and bedraggled rather than furtive, but I discovered that furtive wasn't all that unusual. Most of the women, like most of the men, were stolid, indifferent, enduring. But a few were chattering crazies, whiners, or frightened little rabbits. There was also a fat woman with only one eye who prowled the room and tried to grab bread from your hands even while you were eating it. She was crazy, of course, but her particular craziness made her nasty and possibly dangerous. She let me alone, but harassed several of the smaller women until a tiny, feisty woman pulled a knife on her.

Then the servers called security, and security men came out of a back room and grabbed both women from behind.

It bothered me very much that they took both women away. The fat crazy woman had been permitted to go about her business until someone resisted. Then both victim and victimizer were treated as equally guilty.

It bothered me even more that the women were not thrown out. They were taken away. Where? They didn't come back. No one I spoke to knew what had happened to them.

Most troubling of all, I recognized one of the security men. He had been at Acorn. He had been one of our "teachers" there. I had seen him take Adela Ortiz away to rape her. I could shut my eyes and see him dragging her off to the cabin he used. There had to be many such men still alive and free—men who were not at Camp Christian when we took back our freedom, then took our revenge. But this was the first one that I had seen.

My fear and my hate returned full force and all but choked me. It took all my self-control to sit still, eat my food, and go on being the lump I had to seem to be. Day Turner had been collared after a fight that he said he had had nothing to do with. Christian America officials made themselves judges, juries, and, when they chose to be, executioners. They didn't waste any effort trying to be fair. I had heard on one of my earlier visits that the all-male CA Center Security Force was made up of retired and off-duty cops. That, if it were true, was terrifying. It made me all the more certain that I was right not to go to the police with the true story of what had been done to me and to Acorn. Hell, I hadn't even been able to get my own brother to believe me. What chance would I have to convince the cops if some of them were working for CA?

After dinner, after the sermon, I managed to make myself go up to one of the servers—a blond woman with a long red scar on her forehead. She was one of the few who laughed and talked with us as she scooped stew into bowls and passed out bread. I asked her to give my note to lay minister Marcos Duran. As it happened, she knew him.

"He's not here anymore," she said. "He was transferred to Portland."

"Oregon?" I asked, and then felt stupid. Of course she meant Portland, Oregon.

"Yeah," the server said. "He left a few days ago. He was offered a chance to do more preaching at our new center in Portland, and he's always wanted that. What a nice man. We were sorry to lose him. Did you ever hear him preach?"

"A couple of times," I said. "Are you sure he's gone?"

"Yeah. We had a party for him. He'll be a great minister someday. A great minister. He's so spiritual." She sighed.

Maybe "spiritual" is another word for fantastically good-looking in her circles. Anyway, he was gone. Instead of helping me find Larkin or even seeing me again, he had gone.

I thanked the server and headed out into the evening toward the home of the 88-year-old man where I was still staying. I had left my spare clothing and my sleepsack in his garage. For once, I was traveling light. My backpack was half-empty. I walked automatically, not thinking about where I was going. I was wondering whether I could reach Marc again, wondering whether it would do me any good to reach him. What would he do if I showed up in Portland? Run for Seattle? Why had he run, anyway? I wouldn't have hurt him—wouldn't have said or done anything that could damage his lay-minister reputation. Did he run because I mentioned Cougar? Maybe it had been a mistake for me to tell him what happened to us, to Acorn. Maybe I should have told him the same thing I had told the police. "Well, I was walking north on U.S. 101, heading for Eureka, and these guys. . . ."

Was it so essential for him to be important in CA that he didn't care what vicious things CA was doing, didn't care even what CA did to the only family he had left?

Then there was a man looming in front of me—a huge man, tall and broad and wearing a CA Center Security uniform. I stopped just before I would have slammed into him. I jumped back. My impulse was to run like hell. This guy looked scary enough to make anyone run. But the truth was, I was frozen with fear. I couldn't move. I just stared up at him.

He put a huge hand inside his uniform jacket, and I had a flash of it coming out holding a gun—not that this guy needed a gun to kill me. He was a giant.

But his hand came out of his jacket holding an envelope—a little white paper envelope like the kind mail used to come in. Back when we lived in Robledo my father sometimes brought home paper mail from the college in such envelopes.

"Reverend Duran said to give this to anyone tall and Black and asking for him by name," the giant said. He had a soft, quiet voice that made his appearance less threatening somehow. "Looks like you qualify," he finished.

I had to make myself reach out and take the envelope.

The giant stared at me for a moment, then said, "He told me you were his sister."

I nodded.

"He said you might be dressed as a man."

I didn't answer. I couldn't quite form words yet.

"He said he's sorry. He asked me to tell you that you could get a bed at the Center for as long as you needed one. I'll be around. He's my friend. I'll look out for you."

"No," I said, getting my voice to work at last. "But thank you." I stood straight, never knowing when I had crouched in my fear. I extended a hand, and the giant took it and shook it. "Thank you," I repeated, and he was gone, striding back toward the Center.

I didn't stop to think. I tucked Marcus's envelope into my blouse and walked on. You didn't stand opening things on dark streets in this part of town. I kept my ears open now, and paid attention to my surroundings. The giant had caught up with me, passed me, and gotten in front of me and I hadn't heard a thing. That kind of inattention was beyond stupid. It was suicidal.

And yet I had almost relaxed again by the time I was only three blocks from the old man's little house. I was tired, full of food, looking forward to my warm pallet, and eager to see what my brother had written.

Then, through my preoccupations, I began to hear footsteps. I swung around just in time to startle and confront the two men who were creeping up behind me. My gun was out of reach in my backpack, but my knife was in my pocket. I grabbed it and flipped it open before these guys could recover and clean the street with me. They weren't big, but there were two of them. I put my back against someone's redwood fence, and let them decide how much they wanted what they thought I had. In fact I was carrying not only my gun but enough money to make them happy for days, as well as Marcus's note, and I wasn't eager to give up any of it.

"Just put the pack down, girl," one said. "Put the pack down and back away from it. We'll let you go."

I didn't move. To take my pack off, I would have had to lower my knife and trust these two not to jump me. That I didn't dare do. I didn't answer them. I wasn't interested in talking to them. I hated hearing the one call me "girl." It was what Bankole called me with love. And here was the word in someone else's mouth with contempt.

I don't know whether or not I was being stupid. I know I was scared to death and I was angry. I tried to stoke the anger.

I saw that one of them had a knife too. It was an old steak knife, but it was a knife—made for cutting meat.

The one with the knife lunged at me. An instant later, the other lunged too—one to cut, one to grab.

I dropped to the ground and stabbed upward into the belly of the knife-wielder. As I jerked my knife free, not looking, not wanting to see what I had done. I rammed my body backward against the legs of the other man—or against where his legs should have been. I only hit one of them—enough to trip him, but he seemed to recover without falling. Then he did fall. He toppled like a tree as I scrambled to my feet.

OCTAVIA E. BUTLER

They were both down, one curled around his belly wound, groaning, and the other making no sound at all except his rasping breathing. The steak knife stuck out of him just below the breastbone.

Shit.

I fell to my knees, my body a flaming mass of agony, from other people's knife wounds. I twisted away from them both, crawled away from them on all fours, dripping tears at the terrible, terrible pain. I dragged myself around a corner and sat there on the broken concrete for a long time. I was shaking with the pain, gasping with it until at last, it began to ease. I got up before it was altogether gone. I went to the old man's garage as quickly as I could. The pain was gone by the time I got there, and the anger had long since gone. There was nothing left but the fear. I got my things together as fast as I could, stuffed them into my pack, and headed out of town. Maybe I didn't have to leave. Maybe the tramp who had been living in the old man's garage would never be connected with the two dead or soon-to-be dead men on the street nearby. Maybe.

But I would not risk a collar.

So I ran.

So I run. I had to check the tree before I headed for Portland, and I'm going to stop at Georgetown. Then I'll take an inland route and avoid Eureka. Meanwhile, here are the words my brother left me:

"Lauren, I'm sorry I hit you—really sorry. I hope I didn't hurt you too much. It's just that I couldn't stand to lose everything again. I just couldn't. That keeps happening to me. Mom and Dad, the Durans, and even Acorn, where I thought maybe I could stay. And I couldn't see how anyone connected with Christian America could do what you say has been done. I could barely stand to hear you say it. I knew it was just wrong. It had to be.

"And I was right. The people who do the kind of thing you described are a splinter group. Jarret has disclaimed all connection with them. They call themselves Jarret's Crusaders, but they lie. They're extremists who believe that reeducating heathen adults and placing their young children in Christian American homes is the only way to restore order and greatness. If Acorn was attacked, these are the likely attackers. I've talked to my friends in CA, and they say it isn't safe to probe too deeply into what the Crusaders are doing. The Crusaders are a kind of secret society, absolutely dedicated, and ruthless. They're courageous people. Misguided, but courageous. I've been told they really do find good homes for the children they rescue. That's what they call it—rescuing the children. They take them into their own homes if necessary and raise them as their children or they find others to raise them. Problem is, they're a nationwide group. They send the kids out of their home areas—often out of their home states. They're serious about raising these kids as good Christian Americans. They believe it would be a sin against God and a crime against America to let them be reunited with their heathen parents.

"I've heard all this second- or third-hand from at least half a dozen people. I don't know how much of it is true. I don't know where Larkin is, and don't have any idea how to find out. I'm sorry about that, sorry about Bankole, sorry about everything.

"You probably won't like this, Lauren, but I think that if you really want to find your daughter, you should join us—join Christian America. Your cult has failed. Your god of change couldn't save you. Why not come back to where you belong? If Mom and Dad were alive, they would join. They would want you to be part of a good Christian organization that's trying to put the country back together again. I know you're smart and strong and too stubborn for your own good. If you can also be patient and join us in our work, you'll have the only chance possible of getting information about your daughter.

"I have to warn you, though, the movement won't let you preach. They agree with Saint Paul in that: 'Let the woman learn in silence with all subjection. But I suffer not a woman to teach nor to usurp authority over the man but to be in silence.' But don't worry. There's plenty of other more suitable work for women to do to serve the movement.

OCTAVIA E. BUTLER

"Some of our people have relatives or friends who are Crusaders. Join us, work hard, keep your eyes and ears open, and maybe you'll learn things that will help you find your daughter—and help you into a good, decent life as a Christian American woman.

"I don't know what else to tell you. I'm enclosing a few hundred in hard currency. I wish I could give you more. I wish I could help you more. I do wish you well, whatever you decide to do, and again, I'm sorry. Marc."

And that was that. There wasn't a word about his going to Portland—no explanation, no good-bye. No address. Had he, in fact, gone to Portland? I thought about that and decided he had—or at least the server who told me he had believed what she was saying.

But why did my brother not mention where he was going—or even *that* he was going—in his letter? Did he think I wouldn't find out? Or was he just signaling me in a cold, deliberate way that he wanted no further contact with me. Was he saying, in effect, "You're my sister and I have a duty to help you. So here's some advice and some money. Too bad about your troubles, but I can't do any more. I've got to get on with my life."

Well, the money I could use. As far as the advice was concerned, my first impulse was to curse it, and to curse my brother for giving it. Then, for a moment, I wondered whether I could join the enemy and find my child. Perhaps I could.

Then I remembered the man I had seen at the Center—the one whom I had last seen acting as one of our "teachers" at Acorn, and raping Adela Ortiz. Perhaps he was the father of the child she would soon be having. Marc might be able to convince himself that the Crusaders are outcast extremists, but I know better. Whether CA chooses to admit it or not, they and the Crusaders have members in common. How many? What are the real connections? What does Jarret really think about the Crusaders? Does he control them? If he doesn't like what they're doing, he should make some effort to stop them. He shouldn't want them to make their insanity part of his political image.

On the other hand, one way to make people afraid of you is to have a crazy side—a side of yourself or your organization that's dangerous and unpredictable—willing to do any damned thing.

Is that what's going on? I don't know and my brother doesn't want to know.

19

○ ○ ○

From EARTHSEED: THE BOOKS OF THE LIVING

All religions are ultimately cargo cults.
Adherents perform required rituals, follow specific
rules, and expect to be supernaturally
gifted with desired rewards—long life,
honor, wisdom, children, good health, wealth,
victory over opponents, immortality after
death, any desired rewards.
Earthseed offers its own rewards—room
for small groups of people to begin new lives and
new ways of life with new opportunities, new wealth,
new concepts of wealth, new challenges to
grow and to learn and to decide what to become.
Earthseed is the dawning adulthood
of the human species. It offers the only
true immortality. It enables the seeds of the
Earth to become the seeds of new life, new communities on new earths. The Destiny of Earthseed is to
take root among the stars, and there, again, to grow,
to learn, and to fly.

I began creating secret Dreamask scenarios when I was 12. By then,
I was very much the timid, careful daughter of Kayce and Madison
Alexander. I knew that even though I was allowed to use Dreamasks
with strict Christian American scenarios—like the old "Asha Vere"
stories—no one would be likely to approve my creating new, uncen-
sored scenarios. I knew this because back when I was nine, I began
making up plain, linear installment stories to amuse myself and my

331

few friends at Christian America School. It was fun. My friends liked it until we all got into trouble. Then some teacher eavesdropped, realized what I was doing, and punished me for lying. My friends were punished for not reporting my lies. We had to memorize whole chapters of Exodus, Psalms, Proverbs, Jeremiah, and Ezekiel. Until we had memorized and been tested on every single assigned chapter, we were allowed no free time—no recess or lunch breaks. We were kept an hour late every day. We were monitored even in the bathroom to make sure we weren't indulging in more wickedness—like stealing a minute or two "from God."

It didn't matter that I had said from the beginning that my stories were only made up. I never tried to convince anyone that they were true. And it didn't matter that the Dreamask scenarios we were all allowed to experience were equally imaginary. It was as though my teachers believed that all the possible stories had already been created, and it was a sin to make more—or at least it was a sin for me to make more.

But by the time I reached puberty, except for the pornography I managed to find, most of the scenarios I was permitted were tired, dull, boring things. Characters were always being shown the error of their ways, suffering for their sins, and then returning to God. Boys fought for Christian America. They went to war against heathens, or went out as missionaries in dangerous, wicked, foreign jungles and deserts. Girls, on the other hand, were always cooking, cleaning, sewing, crying, praying, taking care of babies or old people, and going to church. Asha Vere was unusual because she did interesting things. She saved people. She made them return to God. She was one of the few. In fact as a Black and a woman, she was the only one.

A very old woman—she was in her nineties and lived in one of the nursing homes that Christian America had set up for elderly members— once told me that Asha Vere was my generation's Nancy Drew. It was years before I found out who Nancy Drew was.

Anyway, I wrote scenarios—had to write them down with a stylus in my notebook since even outside of Christian America, no one was going to trust a kid to work with a scenario recorder. At least our notebooks had a lot of memory and I could code them to erase the scenarios if someone else tried to get into them. Or I thought I could.

I wrote about having different parents—parents who cared about me and didn't wish always that I were another person, the sainted Kamaria. I didn't know at this time that I was adopted. All I had was the usual child's suspicion that I might be, and that somewhere, somehow, I might have beautiful, powerful "real" parents who would come for me someday.

I wrote about having four brothers and three sisters. The idea of eight children appealed to me. I didn't think you could be lonely in such a big family. My brothers and sisters and I had huge parties on holidays and birthdays and we were always having adventures, and I had a handsome boyfriend who was crazy about me, and the girls at school were all jealous.

Instead of living in shabby, patched-together old Seattle with its missile-strike scars, we lived in a big corporate town. We were important and had plenty of money. We spent our time speeding around in fast cars or making flashy scientific discoveries in laboratories or catching gangs of spies, embezzlers, and saboteurs. Since this was a Mask, I could live the adventures as any of my brothers or sisters or as either of our parents. That meant I could "experience" being a boy or an adult. But since it wasn't like a real Dreamask experience, I had no sensation guidance beyond research and my imagination. I watched other people, tried to make myself feel what it might be like to drive a car or fire a gun or be an older brother who worked in the South Pacific as a deep-sea miner or an older sister who was an architect in Antarctica or a father who was CEO of a major corporation or a mother who was a molecular biologist. The father was a big, godlike man who was rich and smart and . . . not there most of the time. I had the hardest time being him. Research didn't help much. He was more of a shell than the others. What should a father be like inside, in his thoughts and feelings? I wasn't sure. Not like Madison, for sure. Like the fathers of my occasional friends? I saw my friends' fathers now and then, but I didn't know them. Like the minister, maybe—stern and sure of himself and usually surrounded by a lot of deferential men and smiling women, some of whom were rumored to sleep with him even though they had husbands and he had a wife. But how did he feel? What did he believe? What did he want? What scared him?

I read a lot. I watched people and I eavesdropped. I got a lot of the ideas from kids whose parents let them have nonreligious Masks and books—bad books, we called them. In short, I tried to do what my biological mother hated, but couldn't help doing. I tried to feel what other people felt and know them—really know them.

It was all nonsense, of course. Harmless nonsense. But when I was caught at it, it was suddenly all but criminal.

There was a theft in my Christian American History class. Someone stole a small personal phone that the teacher had left on her desk. We were all searched and our belongings collected and thoroughly examined. Someone examined my notebook too thoroughly, in spite of my self-destruct codes, and found my scenario.

I had to attend special religion classes for delinquents and get counseling. I had to confess my sins before our local church. I had to memorize a dozen or so more chapters of the Bible. While I was working off my punishment, I began to hear whispers that I was, indeed adopted, and that I was the daughter not of rich, important, beautiful people but of the worst heathen devils—murderers, thieves, and perverters of God's word. The kids started it. There were plenty of kids around who were known to be adopted, so it was commonplace to ridicule them and make up lies about how evil their real parents were. And if you weren't adopted, and someone got mad at you, they might call you a heathen bastard whether you were or not.

So first the kids started in on me, then the adults, some of whom knew that I was adopted, began to talk. "Well, after all, think about what kind of woman her real mother must be. That's got to leave a mark on her." Or, "You wait. That girl is no good. My grandmother used to say the fruit doesn't fall far from the tree!" Or, "Well, what can you expect?

'Vere' means truth, doesn't it? And the truth is, there's bad blood in her if there ever was bad blood!"

I remember turning around in church to confront the nasty old woman who had stage-whispered this last bit of stupidity to her equally ancient friend. The two were sitting directly behind Kayce, Madison, and me during Sunday evening service. I looked at her, and she just stared back at me as though I were an animal who had somehow invaded the church.

"'God is love,'" I quoted to her in as sweet a voice as I could manage. And then, "'Love is the fulfilling of the law.'" I tried to make sure that my words carried as well as her ugly stage whisper had carried. Bad blood, for heaven's sake. Kayce had told me people said things like that because they were ignorant, but that I had to respect even the ignorant because they were older.

On that particular night, Kayce nudged me with a sharp elbow the moment I spoke, and I saw the ignorant old woman's mouth turn down in a grimace of dislike and disapproval.

I had just turned 13 when that happened. I remember after church, Kayce and I had a huge fight because she said I was rude to an older person, and I said I didn't care. I said I wanted to know whether I really was adopted and if so, who were my real parents.

Kayce said she and Madison were the only parents I had to worry about, and I was an ungrateful little heathen not to appreciate what I had.

That was that.

When I was 15, an enemy at school told me my real mother was not only a heathen but a whore and a murderer. I hit her before I even thought about it—and I discovered that I didn't know my own strength. I broke her jaw. She was screaming and crying and bleeding, and I was horrified—scared to death. I got kicked out of school, and very nearly collared as a juvenile felon. Only Madison and our minister working together managed to keep my neck out of a collar. This was the beginning of the worst part of my adolescence. I was grateful to Madison. I hadn't thought he would fight for me. I hadn't thought he would fight for anything. He had become even more of a shadow as I had grown. He repaired aging computers for poor working people. He had seemed closer to his tools than he did to me, except when he was feeling me up.

Then, on Saturday, after my troubles had been papered over, while Kayce was attending some women's-group thing at Church, Madison explained to me how grateful I should be to him. He had saved me from a collar. He read me an article about collars—how they hurt, how they can "pacify" even the most violent criminal and still leave him able to do useful work, how the holder of a collar control unit is "a virtual puppet master" as far as the convict is concerned. And although the pain that the collar can deliver is intense, it leaves no mark and does no permanent harm no matter how often it must be used.

Madison gave me some other articles to read. As I took them, he reached out with both sweaty little hands and felt my breasts.

"It wouldn't hurt you to show some gratitude," he said to me when I pulled away. "I saved you from something really brutal. I don't know. You're so ungrateful. Maybe I won't be able to save you next time." He paused. "You know, your mama wanted to let you go on and be collared. She thinks you hurt that girl on purpose." Another pause. "You need to be nice to me, Asha. I'm all you've got."

He kept after me. There were times when I thought I should just sleep with him and be done with it. But I was back in school by then and I could stay away from home most of the time. He was such a godawful whiny man. My only good luck was that he was small, and after a while, I realized he was a little bit afraid of me. That was a shock. I had grown up timid and afraid of almost everyone—resentful, but afraid. I had to be provoked suddenly and severely to make me react with anything other than argument. That's why I was so upset when I broke the girl's jaw. Not only did I not know that I could hurt someone that badly, but I wasn't the kind of person who hurt people at all.

But somehow, Madison didn't know that.

He wouldn't let me alone, but at least he didn't use physical force on me. His moist little hands kept wandering and he kept pleading, and he

OCTAVIA E. BUTLER

watched me. His eyes followed me so much, I was afraid Kayce would notice and blame me. He tried to peek at me in the bathroom—I caught him at it twice. He tried to watch me in my bedroom when I was dressing.

At 15, I couldn't wait to get out of the house and away from both of them for good.

From *THE JOURNALS OF LAUREN OYA OLAMINA*
THURSDAY, JUNE 7, 2035

I'm back at Georgetown. I need to rest a little, check in with Allie, clean up, pick up some of the things I left with her, and gather what information I can. Then I'll head for Oregon. I need to get out of the area for a while, and going up where Marc is seems a good choice. He won't want to see me. He needs to be part of Christian America even though he knows that Christian America's hands are far from clean. If he doesn't want me around reminding him what kind of people he's mixed up with, let him help me. Once I've got my child back, he'll never have to see me again—unless he wants to.

It's hard to accept even the comforts of Georgetown now. It seems that I can only stand myself when I'm moving, working, searching for Larkin. I've got to get out of here.

Allie says I should stay until next week. She says I look like hell. I suppose I did when I arrived. After all, I was pretending to be a vagrant. I've cleaned up now and gone back to being an ordinary woman. But even when I was clean, she said I looked older. "Too much older," she said.

"You've got your Justin back," I told her, and she looked away, looked at Justin, who was playing basketball with some other Georgetown kids. They had nailed an honest-to-goodness basket-without-a-bottom high up on someone's cabin wall. Early Georgetown cabins were made of notched logs, stone, and mud. They're heavy, sturdy things—so heavy that a few have fallen in and killed people during earthquakes. But a nailed-on basket and the blows of a newly stolen basketball did them no harm at all. One of the men who had a job cleaning office buildings in Eureka had brought the ball home the day before, saying he had found it in the street.

"How is Justin?" I asked Allie. She had set up a work area behind the hotel. There she made or repaired furniture, repaired or sharpened tools, and did reading and writing for people. She didn't teach reading or writing as I had. She claimed she didn't have the patience for that kind of teaching—although she was willing to show kids how to work with wood, and she fixed their broken toys for free. She continued to do repair work for the various George businesses, but no more cleaning, no more fetching and carrying. Once Dolores George had seen the quality of her work, Allie was allowed to do the things she loved for her living and for Justin's. The repair work she was doing now for other people was for extra cash to buy clothing or books for Justin.

"I wish you'd stay and teach him," she said to me. "I'm afraid he spends too much time with kids who are already breaking into houses and robbing people. If anything makes me leave Georgetown, it will be that."

I nodded, wondering what sort of things my Larkin was learning. And the unwanted question occurred to me as it sometimes did: Was she still alive to learn anything at all? I turned my back on Allie and stared out into the vast, jumbled forest of shacks, cabins, tents, and lean-tos that was Georgetown.

"Lauren?" Allie said in a voice too soft to trust.

I looked around at her, but she was hand-sanding the leg of a chair, and not looking at me. I waited.

"You know . . . I had a son before Justin," she said.

"I know." Her father, who had prostituted her and her sister Jill had also murdered her baby in a drunken rage. That was why she and Jill had left home. They had waited until their father drank himself to sleep. Then they set fire to their shack with him in it and ran away. Fire again. What a cleansing friend. What a terrible enemy.

OCTAVIA E. BUTLER

"I never even knew who my first son's father was," she said, "but I loved him—my little boy. You can't know how I loved him. He came from me, and he knew me, and he was mine." She sighed and looked up from the chair leg. "For eight whole months, he was mine."

I stared at Georgetown again, knowing where she was going with this, not really wanting to hear it. It had a nasty enough sound when I heard it in my own head.

"I wanted to die when Daddy killed my baby. I wished he had killed me too." She paused. "Jill kept me going—kind of like back at Camp Christian, you kept me going." Another pause, longer this time. *"Lauren, you might never find her."*

I didn't say anything, didn't move. "She might be dead."

After a while, I turned to look at her. She was staring at me, looking sad.

"I'm sorry," she said. "But it's true. And even if she's alive, you might never find her."

"You knew about your baby," I said. "You knew he was dead, not suffering somewhere, not being abused by crazy people who think they're Christians. I don't know anything. But Justin is back, and now Jorge's brother Mateo is back."

"I know, and you know that's different. Both boys are old enough to know who they are. And . . . and they're old enough to survive abuse and neglect."

I thought about that, understood it, turned away from it.

"You still have a life," she said.

"I can't give up on her."

"You can't now. But the time might come. . . ."

I didn't say anything. After a while I spotted one of the men I had gotten information from back before I began working in Eureka. I went off to talk to him, see whether he'd heard anything. He hadn't.

It seems I'm to have a companion for my trip north. I don't know how I feel about that. Allie sent her to me. She's a woman who should have been rich and secure with her family down in Mendocino County, but, according to her, her family didn't want her. They wanted her brother, but they'd never wanted her. She was born from the body of a hired surrogate back when that was still unusual, and although she looks much like her mother and nothing like the surrogate, her parents never quite accepted her—especially after her brother was born the old-fashioned way from the body of his own mother. At 18, she was kidnapped for ransom, but no ransom was ever paid. She knew her parents had the money, but they never paid. Her brother was the prince, but somehow, she was never the princess. Her captors had kept her for a while for sex. Then, she got the idea to make herself seem sick. She would put her finger down her throat whenever they weren't looking. Then she'd throw up all over everything. At last, in disgust and fear, her captors abandoned her down near Clear Lake. When she tried to go home, she discovered that just before the Al-Can War began, her family left the area, moved to Alaska. Now, more than a year after her kidnapping, she was on her way to Alaska to find them. The fact that the war was not yet officially over didn't faze her. She had nothing and no one except her family, and she was going north. Allie had told her to go with me, at least as far as Portland. "Watch one another's backs," she said when she brought us together. "Maybe you'll both manage to live for a while longer."

Belen Ross, the girl's name was. She pronounced it Bay-LEN, and wanted to be called Len. She looked at me—at my clean but cheap men's clothing, my short hair, my boots.

"You don't need me," she said. She's tall, thin, pale, sharp-nosed, and black-haired. She doesn't look strong, but she looks impressive, somehow. In spite of all that's happened to her, she hasn't broken. She still has a lot of pride.

"Know how to use a gun?" I asked.

She nodded. "I'm a damned good shot."

"Then let's talk."

The two of us went up to Allie's room and sat down together at the pine table Allie had made for herself. It was simple and handsome. I ran a hand over it. "Allie shouldn't be in a place like this," I said. "She's good at what she does. She should have a shop of her own in some town."

"No one belongs in a place like this," Len said. "If children grow up here, what chance do they have?"

"What chance do you have?" I asked her.

She looked away. "This is only about our traveling together to Portland," she said.

I nodded. "Allie's right. We will have a better chance together. Lone travelers make good targets."

"I've traveled alone before," she said.

"I have too. And I know that alone, you have to fight off attacks that might not even happen at all if you aren't alone, and if you and your companion are armed."

She sighed and nodded. "You're right. I suppose I don't really mind traveling with you. It won't be for long."

I shook my head. "That's right. You won't have to put up with me for long."

She frowned at me. "Well, what more do you want? We'll get to Portland, and that will be that. We'll never see each other again."

"For now, though, I want to know that you're someone I can trust with my life. I need to know who you are, and you need to know who I am."

"Allie told me you were from a walled community down south."

"In Robledo, yes."

"Wherever. Your community got wiped out, and you came up here to start another community. It got wiped out and you wound up here." That sounded like Allie, giving only the bare bones of my life.

"My husband was killed, my child kidnapped, and my community destroyed," I said. "I'm looking for my child—and for any children of my former community. Only two have been found so far—two of the oldest. My daughter was only a baby."

"Yeah." Len looked away. "Allie said you were looking for your daughter. Too bad. Hope you find her."

Just as I was beginning to get angry with this woman, it occurred to me that she was acting. And as soon as the thought came to me, it was followed by others. Much of what she had shown me so far was false. She had not lied with her words. It was her manner that was a lie—filled with threads of wrongness. She was not the bored, indifferent person she wanted to seem to be. She was just trying to keep her distance. Strangers might be dangerous and cruel. Best to keep one's distance.

Problem was, even though this girl had been treated very badly, she wasn't distant. It wasn't natural to her. It made her a little bit uncomfortable all the time—like an itch, and in her body language, she was communicating her discomfort to me. And, I decided, watching her, there was something else wrong.

"Shall we travel together?" I asked. "I usually travel as a man, by the way. I'm big enough and androgynous-looking enough to get away with it."

"Fine with me."

I looked at her, waiting.

She shrugged. "So we travel together. All right." I went on looking at her.

She shifted in her hard chair. "What's the matter? What is it?"

I reached out and took her hand before she could flinch away. "I'm a sharer," I said. "And so are you."

She snatched her hand away and glared at me. "For godsake! We're only traveling together. Maybe not even that. Keep your accusations to yourself!"

"That's the kind of secret that gets companion travelers killed. If you're still alive, it's obvious that you can handle sudden, unexpected pain. But believe me, two sharers traveling together need to know how to help one another."

She got up and ran out of the room.

I looked after her, wondering whether she would come back. I didn't care whether or not she did, but the strength of her reaction surprised me. Back at Acorn, people were always surprised to be recognized as sharers when they came to us. But once they were recognized, and no one hurt them, they were all right. I never identified another sharer without identifying myself. And most of the ones I did identify realized that sharers do need to learn to manage without crippling one another. Male sharers were touchy—resenting their extra vulnerability more than females seemed to, but none of them, male or female, had just turned and run away.

Well, Belen Ross had been rich, if not loved. She had been protected from the world even better than I had been down in Robledo. She had learned that the people within the walls of her father's compound were of one kind, and those outside were of another. She had learned that she had to protect herself from that other kind. One must never let them see weakness. Perhaps that was it. If so, she wouldn't come back. She would get her things and leave the area as soon as she could. She would not stay where someone knew her dangerous secret.

All this happened on Friday. I didn't see Len again until yesterday—Saturday. I met with a few of the men who had provided me with useful information before—in particular with those who had been to Portland. I bought them drinks and listened to what they had to say, then I left them and bought maps of northern California and Oregon. I bought dried fruit, beans, cornmeal, almonds, sunflower seeds, supplies for my first aid kit, and ammunition for my rifle and my handgun. I bought these things from the George's even though their prices are higher than those of most stores in Eureka. I wouldn't be going to Eureka again soon. I would go inland for a while toward Interstate 5. I might even travel along I-5 if it seemed wise once I'd gotten there and had a look at it. In some parts of California, I-5 has become frightening and dangerous—or at least it was back in '27 when I walked it for a few miles. In any case, I-5 would take me right into Portland. If I circled back to the coast and walked up U.S. 101, I'd have a longer walk. And U.S. 101 looked lonelier. There were fewer towns, smaller towns.

"Big towns are good," a man from Salem, Oregon, had told me. "You can be anonymous. Small towns can be mean and suspicious when strangers show up. If they just had a robbery or something, they might pull you in, put a collar on you, or lock you up or even shoot you. Big cities are bad news. They chew you up and spit you out in pieces. You're nobody, and if you die in the gutter, nobody cares but the sanitation department. Maybe not even them."

"You gotta think about there's still a war on," a man from Bakersfield, California, had said. "It could flare back up anytime, no matter how much they talk peace. Nobody knows what more war's going to mean to people walking on the highway. More guns, I guess. More crazy guys, more guys who don't know how to do anything but kill people."

He was probably right. He had, as he put it, "been bummin' around for more than 20 years," and he was still around. That alone made his opinion worth something. He told me he had had no trouble going back and forth to Portland, even last year during the war, and that was good news. There were fewer people on the road than there had been back in the 2020s, but more than just before the war. I remember when I hoped that fewer travelers were a sign that things were getting better. I suppose things are getting better for some people.

Len came to me just as I finished my purchases at George's. Without a word, she helped me carry my stuff back to Allie's room, where, in continuing silence, she watched while I packed it. She couldn't really help with that.

OCTAVIA E. BUTLER

"Your pack ready?" I asked her.

She shook her head.

"Go get it ready."

She caught my arm and waited until she had my full attention. "First tell me how you knew." she said. "I've never had anyone spot me like that."

I drew a long breath. "You're what, 19?"

"Yes."

"And you've never spotted anyone?"

She shook her head again. "I had just about decided that there weren't any others. I thought the ones who let themselves be discovered were collared or killed. I've been terrified that someone would notice. And then you did. I almost left without you."

"I thought you might, but there didn't seem to be anything I could say to you that wouldn't upset you even more."

"And you really are. . . . You really . . . have it too?"

"I'm a sharer, yes." I stared past her for a moment. "One of the best days of my life was when I realized that my daughter probably wasn't. You can't be 100 percent sure with babies, but I don't believe that she was. And I had a friend who had four sharer kids. He said he didn't think she was either." And where were Gray Mora's children now? What was happening to the lost little boys? Could there be anyone more vulnerable than little male sharers at the mercy of both men and other boys?

"Four sharer children?" Len demanded. "Four?"

I nodded.

"I think . . . I think my life would have been so different if my brother had been a sharer, too, instead of his normal, perfect self." Len said. "It was as though I had leprosy and he didn't. You know what I mean? There was an idea once that people who had leprosy were unclean and God didn't much like them."

I nodded. "Who was the Paracetco addict in your family?"

"They both were—both of my parents."

"Oh, my. And you were the evidence of their misbehavior, the constant reminder. I suppose they couldn't forgive you for that."

She thought about that for a while. "You're right. People do blame you for the things they do to you. The men who kidnapped me blamed me because they had gone to so much trouble to get me, then there was no ransom. I don't remember how many times they hit me for that—as though it were all my fault."

"These days, projecting blame is almost an art form."

"You still haven't told me how you knew."

"Your body language. Everything about you. If you have a chance to meet others, you'll begin to recognize them. It just takes practice."

"Some people think sharing is a power—like some kind of extra-sensory perception."

I shrugged. "You and I know it isn't."

She began to look a little happier. "When do we leave?"

"Monday morning just before dawn. Don't say anything about it to anyone."

"Of course not!"

"Are you all right for supplies?"

In a different tone, she repeated, "Of course not. But I'll be all right. I can take care of myself."

"We'll be traveling together for almost a month," I said. "The idea is that we should take care of ourselves and of one another. What do you need?"

We sat together quiet for a while, and she wrestled in silence with her pride and her temper.

"It's sometimes best to avoid towns," I said. "Some towns fear and hate travelers. If they don't arrest them or beat them, they chase them away. Sometimes at the end of the day, there are no towns within reach. And fasting and hiking don't go well together. Now let's go get you some supplies. I assume you stole the things you have now."

"Thank you," she said, "for assuming that."

I laughed and heard bitterness in my own laughter. "We do what we have to do to live. But don't steal while you're with me." I let my voice harden a little. "And don't steal from me."

"You'll take my word that I won't?"

"Will you give me your word?"

She looked down her long, thin nose at me. "You enjoy telling people what to do, don't you?"

I shrugged. "I like living, and I like being free. And you and I need to be able to trust one another." I watched her now, needing to see all that there was to be seen.

"I know," she said. "It's just that . . . I've always had things. I used to give clothing, shoes, food, things like that to the families of our servants at Christmas. About five years ago, my mother stopped seeing anyone except members of the family, and my father got into the habit of leaving the house servants to me. Now I'm poorer than our servants were. *And, yes, everything I have, I've stolen.* I was so idealistic when I was at home. I wouldn't steal anything. Now I feel moral because I'm a thief instead of a prostitute."

"While we're together, you won't be either."

". . . all right."

And I let myself relax a little. She seemed to mean it. "Let's go get what you need, then. Come on."

WEDNESDAY, JUNE 13, 2035

We're on our way and we've had no trouble. Len asked me whether I had anything to read when we stopped last night, and I handed her one of my two remaining copies of *The First Book of the Living.* We're not rushing and the days are long, so we don't have to push on until it's too dark to read.

We've traveled south to a state highway that will take us inland to 1-5. Len gave no trouble about this. She did ask, "Why not walk right up the coast?"

"I want to avoid Eureka," I told her. "I was mugged last time I was there."

She made a grim face, then nodded. "God, I hope we can avoid that kind of thing."

"The best way to avoid it is to be ready for it." I said. "Accept the reality that it might happen, and keep your eyes and ears open."

"I know."

She's a good traveler. She complains, but she's willing to keep her share of the watches. One of the scary things about being alone is having no one to watch while you sleep. You have to sleep on your belongings, using them as a pillow or at least keeping them in your sleepsack with you, or someone will make off with them. The violent thieves are the ones who present the most obvious and immediate danger, but sneak thieves can hurt you. For one thing, they can force you to join them. If they steal your money or if you don't have enough money to replace the essentials they've stolen, then you have to steal to survive. My experience with collars has made me a very reluctant thief—not that I was ever an eager one.

Anyway, Len is a good traveling companion. And she's an avid reader with an active mind. She says one of the things she misses most about home is computer access to the libraries of the world. She's well read. She rushed through *Earthseed: The First Book of the Living* in one evening. Problem is, it wasn't intended to be rushed through.

"I know you wrote this book." she said when she'd finished it—a couple of hours ago. "Allie told me you wrote a book about something called Earthseed. Is this your real name? Lauren Oya Olamina?"

I nodded. It didn't matter that she knew. We've bedded down off the road, between of a pair of hills where we can have some privacy. We're still in country that I know—hills, scattered ranches, small communities, stands of young trees, open ground. Nice country. We walked through it many times from Acorn. It's less populated than it should be because during the worst years of the 2020s, a lot of people were burned out, robbed, abducted, or just killed. The small communities were vulnerable and the gangs swept over them like locusts. Many of the survivors looked for less crime-ridden places to live—places like Canada, Alaska, and Russia. That's why so much was abandoned to the likes of us when we hunted building materials, useful plants, and old tools. Now, though, the land's familiarity doesn't comfort me. Then Len asks me a familiar question, and that is comforting, somehow.

"Why did you write this?"

"Because it's true," I answered, and from then until the time she lay down to sleep, we talked about Earthseed and what it meant, what it could mean and how anyone could ever accept it even if they happened to hear about it. She doesn't sneer, but she doesn't understand yet either. I find that I look forward to teaching her.

SUNDAY, JUNE 17 , 2035

We're taking the day off. We're in Redding—a little west of Redding in a park, really. Redding is a sizable city. We've made camp, for once in a place where people are supposed to camp, and we're eating heavy, tasty food bought in town. We've also had a chance to bathe and do our laundry. It always puts me in a better mood not to stink and not to have to endure the body odor of my companion. Somehow, no matter how awful I smell, I can still smell other people.

We've had a hot stew of potatoes, vegetables, and jerked beef with a topping of lovely Cheddar cheese. It turns out that Len can't cook. She says her mother could but never did. Never had to. Servants did the cooking, the cleaning, repairing things. Teachers were hired for Len and her brother—mostly to guide their use of the computer courses and to be sure they did the work they were supposed to do. Their father, their computer connections, and their older servants provided them with most of what they knew about the world. Ordinary living skills like cooking and sewing were never on the agenda.

"What did your mother do?" I asked.

Len shrugged. "Nothing, really. She lived in her virtual room—her own private fantasy universe. That room could take her anywhere, so why should she ever come out? She was getting fat and losing her physical and mental health, but her v-room was all she cared about."

I frowned. "I've heard of that kind of thing—people being hooked on Dreamasks or on virtual-world fantasies. I don't know anything about it, though."

"What is there to know? Dreamasks are nothing—cheap kid's toys. Really limited. In that room she could go anywhere, be anyone, be with anyone. It was like a womb with an imagination. She could visit fourteenth-century China, present-day Argentina, Greenland in any imagined distant future, or one of the distant worlds circling Alpha Centauri. You name it, she could create some version of it. Or she could visit her friends, real and imaginary. Her real friends were other wealthy, idle people—mostly women and children. They were as addicted to their v- rooms as she was to hers. If her real friends didn't indulge her as much as she wanted them to, she just created more obliging versions of them. By the time I was abducted, I didn't know whether she really had contact with any flesh-and-blood people anymore. She couldn't stand real people with real egos of their own."

I thought about this. It was worse than anything I had heard about this particular addiction. "What about food?" I asked. "What about bathing or just going to the bathroom?"

"She used to come out for meals. She had her own bathroom. All by itself, it was big as my bedroom. Then she began to have all her meals sent in. After that, there were whole months when I didn't see her. Even when I took her meals in myself, I had to just leave them. She was in the v-bubble inside the room, and I couldn't even see her. If I went into the bubble—you could just walk into it—she would scream at me. I wasn't part of her perfect fantasy life. My brother, on the other hand, was. He got to visit her once or twice a week and share in her fantasies. Nice, isn't it."

I sighed. "Didn't your father mind any of this? Didn't he try to help her—or you?"

"He was busy making money and screwing the maids and their

children—some of whom were also his children. He wasn't cut off from the outside, but he had his own fantasy life." She hesitated. "Do I seem normal to you?"

I couldn't help seeing where she was going with that. "We're survivors, Len. You are. I am. Most of Georgetown is. All of Acorn was. We've been slammed around in all kinds of ways. We're all wounded. We're healing as best we can. And, no, we're not normal. Normal people wouldn't have survived what we've survived. If we were normal, we'd be dead."

That made her cry. I just held her. No doubt she had been repressing far too much in recent years. When had anyone last held her and let her cry? I held her. After a while, she lay down, and I thought she was falling asleep. Then she spoke.

"If God is Change, then . . . then who loves us? Who cares about us? Who cares for us?"

"We care for one another." I said. "We care for ourselves and one another." And I quoted,

> *"Kindness eases Change.*
> *Love quiets fear."*

At that, she surprised me. She said, "Yes, I liked that one." And she finished the quote:

> *"And a sweet and powerful*
> *Positive obsession*
> *Blunts pain,*
> *Diverts rage,*
> *And engages each of us*
> *In the greatest,*
> *The most intense*
> *Of our chosen struggles."*

"But I have no obsession, positive or otherwise. I have nothing."

"Alaska?" I said.

"I don't know what else to do, where else to go."

"If you get there, what will you do? Go back to being your parents' housekeeper?"

She glanced at me. "I don't know whether they would let me. I might never make it over the borders anyway, especially with the war. Border guards will probably shoot me." She said this with no fear, no passion, no feeling at all. She was telling me that she was committing a kind of suicide. She wasn't out to kill herself, but she was going to arrange for others to kill her—because she didn't know what else to do. Because no one loved her or needed her for anything at all. From her parents to her abductors, people were willing to use her and discard her, but she mattered to no one. Not even to herself. Yet she had kept herself alive through hell. Did she struggle for life only out of habit, or because some part of her still hoped that there was something worth living for?

She can't be allowed to go off to be shot by thugs, border guards, or soldiers. I can't let her do that. And, I think, she wants to be stopped. She won't ask to be, and she will fight for her own self-destructive way. People are like that. But I must think about what she can do instead of dying—what she should be doing. I must think about what she can do for Earthseed, and what it can do for her.

20

○ ○ ○

From EARTHSEED: THE BOOKS OF THE LIVING

Are you Earthseed?
Do you believe?
Belief will not save you.
Only actions
Guided and shaped
By belief and knowledge
Will save you.
Belief
Initiates and guides action—
Or it does nothing.

When I was 19, I met my Uncle Marc.

He was, by then, the Reverend Marcos Duran, a slight, still-beautiful middle-aged man who had become in English and in Spanish the best-known minister of the Church of Christian America. There was even some talk of his running for president, although he seemed uncomfortable about this. By then, though, the Church, was just one more Protestant denomination. Andrew Steele Jarret had been dead for years, and the Church had gone from being an institution that everyone knew about and either loved or feared to being a smaller, somewhat defensive organization with much to answer for and few answers.

I had left home. Even though a girl who left home unmarried was seen by church members as almost a prostitute, I left as soon as I was 18.

"If you go," Kayce said, "don't come back. This is a decent, God-fearing house. You will not bring your trash and your sin back here!"

I had gotten a job caring for children in a household where the father had died. I had deliberately looked for a job that did not put me at the mercy of another man—a man who might be like Madison, or worse than Madison. The pay was room, board, and a tiny salary. I believed I had clothing and books enough to get me through a few years of working there, helping to raise another woman's children while she worked in public relations for a big agribusiness company. I had met the kids—two girls and a boy—and I liked them. I believed that I could do this work and save my salary so that when I left, I would have enough money to begin a small business—a small café, perhaps—of my own. I had no grand hopes. I only wanted to get away from the Alexanders who had become more and more intolerable.

There was no love in the Alexander house. There was only the habit of being together, and, I suppose, the fear of even greater loneliness. And there was the Church—the habit of Church with its Bible class, men's and women's missionary groups, charity work, and choir practice. I had joined the young people's choir to get away from Madison. As it happened, the choir provided relief in three ways. First, I discovered that I really liked to sing. I was so shy at first that I could hardly open my mouth, but once I got into the songs, lost myself in them, I loved it. Second, choir practice was one more excuse that I could use to get out of the house. Third, singing in the choir was a way to avoid having to sit next to Madison in church. It was a way to avoid his nasty, moist little hands. He used to feel me up in church. He really did that. We would sit down with Kayce between us, then he would get up to go to the men's room and come back and sit next to me with his coat or his jacket on his lap to hide his touching me.

I believe Kayce realized what was happening. In the days before I left, we were enemies, she and I. Neither of us said anything about Madison. We just spent a lot of time hating one another. We didn't talk unless we had to. Any talk that we couldn't avoid might become a screaming fight. Then she'd call me a little whore, an ungrateful little bastard, a heathen witch. . . . During my seventeenth year, I don't think she and I ever had anything like a conversation.

Anyway, I joined the choir. And I discovered that I had a big alto voice that people enjoyed hearing. I even discovered that church wasn't so bad if I didn't have to sit between the devil and the deep blue sea.

OCTAVIA E. BUTLER

Because of my singing, I tried to stay with the church after I moved out of Kayce and Madison's house. I did try. But I couldn't do it.

The rumors began at once: I was having sex with any number of men. I was pregnant. I had had an abortion. I had cursed God and joined my real mother in a heathen cult. I was spreading lies about Madison. . . . People I had grown up with, people I had thought of as friends, stopped speaking to me. Men who had paid no attention to me while I was at home now began to edge up to me with whispered invitations and unwanted little touches, and then angry denunciations when I wouldn't give them what they now seemed to think they had a right to get from me.

I couldn't take it. A few months after I left home, I left the church. That was all right with my employer. She didn't go to church. She had been raised a Unitarian, but now seemed to have no religious interests. She liked to spend Sundays with her kids. Sunday was my day off. What I did with it was up to me.

But to my amazement, I missed my adoptive parents. I missed the church. I missed the life I had grown up with. I missed everything. And I was so lonely. I dragged myself through my days. Sometimes I barely wanted to be alive.

Then I heard that Reverend Marcos Duran was coming to town, that he would be preaching at the First Christian American Church of Seattle. That was the big church, not our little neighborhood thing. The moment I read that Reverend Duran was coming, I knew I would go to see him. I knew what a great preacher he was. I had disks of him preaching to thousands in great CA cathedrals on the Gulf Coast and in Washington, D.C. He had a big church of his own in New York. He was young to be so successful, and I had quite a crush on him. God, he was beautiful. And unlike every other preacher I knew of, he wasn't married. That must have been rough. Every woman would be after him. Other ministers would pressure him to get married, accept adult responsibilities, family responsibilities. Men would look at his handsome face and think he was a homosexual. Was he? I had heard rumors. But then, I knew about rumors.

I camped out all night outside the big church to make sure that I would be able to get in for services. As soon as I was off duty on Saturday night, I took a blanket roll, some sandwiches, and a bottle of water, and went to get a place outside the church. I wasn't the only one. Even though services would be broadcast free, there were dozens of people camped around the church when I got there. More kept coming. We were mostly women and girls sleeping out that night—not that anyone slept much. There were some men either trying to get close to the women or looking as though they hoped to get close to Reverend Duran. But there was nothing blatant. We sang and talked and laughed. I had a great time. These people were all strangers to me, and I had a great time with them. They liked my voice and got me to sing some solos. Doing that was still hard for me, but I had done it in church, so I just put myself back in church mentally. Then I was into the singing, and the faces of the others told me they were into my songs.

And then a woman came out of the big, handsome house near the church and made straight for me. I stopped singing because it occurred to me suddenly that I was disturbing people. It was late. We were having something very like a party in the street and on the steps of the church. None of us had even thought that we might be keeping people awake. I just stopped singing in the middle of a word and everyone stared at me, then at the woman striding toward me. She was a light-skinned Black woman with red hair and freckles—a plump, middle-aged woman, wearing a long green caftan. She came right up to me as though I were the only one there.

"Would your name be Asha Alexander?" she asked.

I nodded. "Yes, ma'am. I'm sorry if we disturbed you."

She put an envelope in my hand and smiled. "You didn't disturb me, dear, you have a lovely voice. Read the note. I think you'll want to answer it."

The note said, "If your name is Asha Vere Alexander, I would like to speak with you. I believe I have information concerning your biological parents. Marcos Duran."

I stared at the red-haired woman's face in shock, and she smiled. "If

OCTAVIA E. BUTLER

you're interested, come with me," she said, and she turned and walked back toward her house.

I wasn't sure I should.

"What is it?" one of my new friends asked. She was sitting, wrapped in her blankets on the church steps, looking from me to the departing red-haired woman. They were all looking from me to the woman.

"I don't know," I said. "Family stuff." And I ran after the woman.

And he was there, Marcos Duran, in that big house. The house was the home of the minister of the First Church. The red-haired woman was the minister's wife. God, Reverend Duran was even more beautiful in person than he was on the disks. He was an amazing-looking man.

"I've been watching you and your friends and listening to your singing," he said. "I thought I recognized you. Your adoptive parents are Kayce and Madison Alexander." It wasn't a question. He was looking at me as though he knew me, as though he were honestly glad to see me.

I nodded.

He smiled—a sad kind of smile. "Well, I think we may be related. We can do a gene check later if you like, but I believe your mother was my half-sister. She and your father are dead now." He paused, gave me an odd, uncertain look. "I'm sorry to have to tell you that. They were good people. I thought you should know about them if you wanted to."

"You're sure they're dead?" I asked.

He nodded and said again, "I'm sorry."

I thought about this, and didn't know what to feel. My parents were dead. Well, I had thought they might be, in spite of my fantasies. But . . . but all of a sudden, I had an uncle. All of a sudden one of the best-known men in the country was my uncle.

"Would you like to hear about your parents?" he asked.

"Yes!" I said. "Yes, please. I want to hear everything."

So he began to tell me. As I recall it now, he talked about my mother as a girl with four younger brothers to ride herd on, about Robledo being wiped out, about Acorn. Not until he began to talk about Acorn did he begin to lie. Acorn, he said, was a small mountain community—a real community, not a squatter settlement. But he said nothing about Earth-seed, Acorn's religion. Acorn was destroyed like Robledo, he continued. My parents met there, married there, and were killed there. I was found crying in the ruins of the community.

He hadn't found out about all this until a couple of years later, and by then, I had a home and new parents—good Christian Americans, he believed. He had kept track of me, always meaning to speak to me when I was older, let me know my history, let me know that I still had a living member of my biological family.

"You look like her," he said to me. "You look so much like her, I can't believe it. And your voice is like hers. When I heard you singing out there, I had to get up and go look."

He looked at me with something like amazement, then turned and wiped away a tear.

I wanted to touch him, comfort him. That was odd, because I didn't like touching people. I had been too much alone in my life. Kayce didn't like to touch people—or at least she didn't like to touch me. She always said it was too hot or she was too busy or something. She acted as though hugging or kissing me would somehow have been *nasty*. And of course, being touched by Madison's moist little hands was nasty. But this man, my uncle . . . *my uncle!* . . . made me want to reach out to him. I believed everything he told me. It never occurred to me not to. I was awed, flattered, confused, almost in tears.

I begged him to tell me more about my parents. I knew nothing, and I was hungry for any information he could give me. He spent a lot of time with me, answering my questions and putting me at my ease. The pastor and his red-haired wife put me up for what was left of the night. And all of a sudden, I had family.

My mother had blundered through the first few years of her life, knowing early what she wanted to do, but not knowing how to do it, improvising as she went along. She recruited the people of Acorn because she came to believe that she could accomplish her purpose by creating

Earthseed communities where children would grow up learning the "truths" of Earthseed and go on to shape the human future according to those "truths." This was her first attempt, as she put it, to plant seeds. But she had the bad luck to begin her work at almost the same time that Andrew Steele Jarret began his, and he was, at least in the short term, much the stronger. Her only good luck was that he was so much stronger than she was that he never noticed her. His fanatical Crusaders, very much one of the fingers of his hand, utterly destroyed her first effort, but there's no record at all of her ever having come to Jarret's attention. She was just an ant that he happened to step on.

If she had been anything more than that, she would not have survived.

It is interesting, however, to see that after Acorn, she seemed to lose her direction until she found Belen Ross. She had written about wanting to find me, then begin her Earthseed work again—but begin it how? By establishing another Acorn? One even more hidden away and low-key?

Surely, a new Acorn would be just as vulnerable as the first one. One gesture of authority could erase it completely. What then? She needed a different idea, and, in fact, she had one. She knew that she had to teach teachers. Gathering families had not worked. She had to gather single people, or at least independent people—people who would learn from her, then scatter to preach and teach as, in effect, her disciples. Instead, she was still, reflexively, looking for me. I'm not sure there was much left of that search but reflex by the time Belen Ross came into the picture. I've wondered whether Allison Gilchrist—Allie—guessed this and brought her together with Len just to shake her up.

From *THE JOURNALS OF LAUREN OYA OLAMINA*
TUESDAY, JUNE 19, 2035

There are three of us now, in a way. We've had an interesting time becoming three, and I'm not altogether comfortable with the way I brought it about. It isn't exactly what I expected to do, but I've found it interesting. We're on the road again, just north of a shiny, new company town called Hobartville. We bought supplies outside of the walls of Hobartville at the inevitable squatter settlement. Then we circled around the town and moved on. It's good to be moving again. We've been three days in one place.

Until three days ago, we had been walking and making no lingering contacts on the road—which is an odd way for me to behave. Back in '27 when I was walking from Los Angeles to Humboldt County, I gathered people, gathered a small community. I thought then that Earthseed would be born through small, cooperating communities. Once Acorn was established, I invited others to join us. This time, I haven't felt that I could invite anyone other than Len to join me.

This time, after all, I was only going to Portland to look for my daughter and to get my brother to help me find her whether he wanted to or not.

And was that any more realistic a goal than Len's intention to walk to Alaska to rejoin her family? It was, perhaps less suicidal, but . . . no more sensible.

It is my uneasiness, my fear that perhaps this is true, that has kept me from reaching out to people. I've fed a few ragged parent-child groups because it's hard for me to see hungry children and do nothing at all. Yet I couldn't do much. What's a meal, after all? With Acorn, I had done more. With Earthseed, I had hoped to do much more. So much more. . . . I still have hopes. Even during the 17 months of Camp Christian, I never forgot Earthseed, although there were times when I thought I might not survive to teach it or use it to shape our future.

But all I've been able to do on this trip is to feed a mother and child here, a father and child there, then send them on their ways. They don't always want to go.

"How do you know they won't lie in wait and rob us later?" Len asked as we tramped along I-5 after leaving a father and his two small, ragged boys eating what I suspected was their first good meal in some time.

"I don't *know*," I said. "It's unlikely, but it could happen."

"Then why take the chance?"

I looked at her. She met my eyes for a second, then looked away. "I know," she said in a voice I could hardly hear. "But what good is a meal? I mean, they'll be hungry again soon."

"Yes," I said. "Jarret would be easier to take if he cared half as much about children's bodies and minds as he pretends to care about their souls."

"My father voted for him," she said.

"I'm not surprised."

"My father said he would bring order and stability, get the country back on its feet again. I remember that. He got my mother to vote for him too, not that she cared. She would have voted for the man in the moon if he had told her to, just so he would let her alone. I was still living at home during the '32 election. I had never been outside our walls. I thought my father must know what he was talking about, so I was for Jarret, too. I was too young to vote, though, so it didn't matter. All the adult servants voted for him. My father stood by the only phone in the house that servants were allowed to use. He watched as their finger and retinal prints were scanned in. Then he watched them vote."

"I wonder whether it was your abduction that made your father give up on Jarret."

"Give up on him?"

"On him and on the United States. He's left the country, after all."

After a moment, she nodded. "Yes. Although I'm still having trouble thinking of Alaska as a foreign country. I guess that should be easy now, since the war. But it doesn't matter. None of this matters. I mean, those people—that man and his kids who you just fed—they matter, but no one cares about them. Those kids are the future if they don't starve to death. But if they manage to grow up, what kind of men will they be?"

"That's what Earthseed was about," I said. "I wanted us to understand what we could be, what we could do. I wanted to give us a focus, a goal, something big enough, complex enough, difficult enough, and in the end, radical enough to make us become more than we ever have been. We keep falling into the same ditches, you know? I mean, we learn more and more about the physical universe, more about our own bodies, more technology, but somehow, down through history, we go on building empires of one kind or another, then destroying them in one way or another. We go on having stupid wars that we justify and get passionate about, but in the end, all they do is kill huge numbers of people, maim others, impoverish still more, spread disease and hunger, and set the stage for the next war. And when we look at all of that in history, we just shrug our shoulders and say, well, that's the way things are. That's the way things always have been."

"It is," Len said.

"It is," I repeated. "There seem to be solid biological reasons why we are the way we are. If there weren't, the cycles wouldn't keep replaying. The human species is a kind of animal, of course. But we can do something no other animal species has ever had the option to do. We can choose: We can go on building and destroying until we either destroy ourselves or destroy the ability of our world to sustain us. Or we can make something more of ourselves. We can grow up. We can leave the nest. We can fulfill the Destiny, make homes for ourselves among the stars, and become some combination of what we want to become and whatever our new environments challenge us to become. Our new worlds will remake us as we remake them. And some of the new people who emerge from all this will develop new ways to cope. They'll have to. That will break the old cycle, even if it's only to begin a new one, a different one.

"Earthseed is about preparing to fulfill the Destiny. It's about learning to live in partnership with one another in small communities, and at the same time, working out a sustainable partnership with our environment. It's about treating education and adaptability as the absolute essentials that they are. It's. . . ." I glanced at Len, caught a little smile on her face, and wound down. "It's about a lot more than that," I said. "But those are the bones."

"Makes a strange sermon."

"I know."

"You need to do what Jarret does."

"What!" I demanded, not wanting to do anything Jarret did.

"Focus on what people want and tell them how your system will help them get it. Tell folksy stories that illustrate your points and promise the moon and stars—literally in your case. Why should people want to go to the stars, anyway? It will cost a lot of money, and time. It will force us to create whole new technologies. And I doubt that anyone who's alive when the effort starts will live to see the end of it. Some scientists might like it. It will give them the chance to work on their pet projects. And some people might think it's a great adventure, but no one's going to want to pay for it."

Now I smiled. "Exactly. I've been saying things like that for years. Some people might want to do it for the sake of their children—to give them the chance to begin again and do things right this time. But that idea alone won't do it. It won't bring in enough people, money, or persistence. Fulfilling the Destiny is a long-term, expensive, uncertain project—or rather it's hundreds of projects. Maybe thousands. And with no guarantees of anything. Politicians, on the other hand, are short-term thinkers, opportunists, sometimes with consciences, but opportunists nevertheless. Business people are hungry for profit, short- and long-term. The truth is, preparing for interstellar travel and then sending out ships filled with colonists is bound to be a job so long, thankless, expensive, and difficult that I suspect that only a religion could do it. A lot of people will find ways to make money from it. That might get things started. But it will take something as essentially human and as essentially irrational as religion to keep them focused and keep it going—for generations if it takes generations. I suspect it will. You see, I have thought about this."

Len thought about it herself for a while, then said, "If that's what you believe, why don't you tell people to go to the stars because that's what God wants them to do—and don't start explaining to me that your God doesn't want anything. I understand that. But most people won't understand it."

"The people of Acorn did."

"And where are they?"

That hurt like a punch in the face. "No one knows better than I do how miserably I failed my people," I said.

Len looked away, embarrassed. "I didn't mean it that way," she said. "I'm sorry. I just mean that what you're saying just isn't something people are going to understand and get enthusiastic about—at least not quickly. Did people join Acorn for Earthseed or in the hope of feeding their kids?"

I sighed and nodded. "They did it to feed their kids and to live in a community that didn't look down on them for being poor or enslave them when they were vulnerable. It took some of the adults years to accept Earthseed. The kids got into it right away, though. I thought the kids would be the missionary teachers."

"Maybe they would have been, if they'd had the chance. But that way didn't work. What are you going to do now?"

"With Jarret's Crusaders still running loose? I don't know." This wasn't entirely true. I did have some ideas, but I wanted to hear what Len had to say. She had been interesting and thoughtful so far.

"You're good at talking to people," she said. "They like you. Hell, they trust you. Why can't you just preach to them like any other minister? Preach the way Jarret does. Have you ever heard any of his speeches? Most of them are sermons. Newspeople have a hard time opposing anything he wants because he's always on God's side. Guess whose side that puts them on?"

"And you think I should do that?"

"Of course you should do that if you believe what you say."

"I'm not a demagogue."

"That's too bad. That leaves the field to people who are demagogues—to the Jarrets of the world. And there have always been Jarrets. Probably there always will be."

We walked in silence for a while, then I said, "What about you?"

"What do you mean? You know where I'm going."

"Stay with me. Go somewhere else."

"You're going to Oregon to see your brother and find your child."

"Yes. And I'm also going to make Earthseed what it should be—the way we humans finally manage to grow up."

"You intend to try again?"

"I don't really have any choice. Earthseed isn't just what I believe. It's who I am. It's why I exist."

"You say in your book that we don't have purpose, but potential."

I smiled. She had a photographic memory or nearly so. But she wasn't above using it unfairly to win an argument.

I quoted,

> *"We are born*
> *Not with purpose,*
> *But with potential."*

"We choose our purpose," I said. "I chose mine before I was old enough to know any better—or it chose me. Purpose is essential.

Without it, we drift."

"Purpose," she said, and with an air of showing off, she quoted:

> *"Purpose Unifies us:*
> *It focuses our dreams,*
> *Guides our plans,*
> *Strengthens our efforts.*
> *Purpose*
> *Defines us,*
> *Shapes us,*
> *And offers us*
> *Greatness."*

She sighed. "Sounds wonderful. But then a lot of things sound wonderful. What are you going to do?"

"I'm no Jarret," I said, "but you're probably right about the need to simplify and focus my message. You can help me do that."

"Why should I?"

"Because it will keep you alive."

She looked away again. After a long silence, she said with great bitterness, "What makes you think I want to be kept alive?"

"I know you do. But if you stick with me, you'll have to prove it."

"What?"

"As a matter of fact, if you stick with me, you'll have all you can do to stay alive. Ideas like those in Earthseed aren't going to be popular for a while. Jarret wouldn't like them if he knew about them."

"If you have any sense, you won't draw attention to yourself. Not now."

"I don't intend to draw huge crowds or get on the nets. Not until Jarret has worn out his welcome, anyway. I do intend to reach out to people again."

"How?"

And I knew. I had been wondering as we spoke, scrambling for ideas. Len's comments had helped focus me. So had my own recent experience. "I'll reach people in their homes," I said. "There's nothing new about door-to-door missionaries in small cities like Eureka, for instance. In L.A. you couldn't do it. We may not be able to do it in Portland either. Portland's gotten so big. But on the way there, and in the larger towns around Portland, it might work. Small cities and big towns. People in very large cities and the very small towns can be—will be—suspicious and vicious."

"Free towns only, I assume," Len said.

"Of course. If I managed to get into a company town, I might be collared for vagrancy. That can be a life sentence. They just keep charging you more to live than they pay you for your labor, and you never get out of debt."

"So I've heard. You want to just knock on people's doors and ask to tell them about Earthseed? I hear the Jehovah's Witnesses do that. Or they did it. I'm not sure they still do."

"It's gotten more dangerous." I said. "But other people did it too. The Mormons and some other lesser-known groups."

"Christian groups."

"I know." I thought for a moment. "Did you know I was 18 when I began collecting people and establishing Acorn? Eighteen. A year younger than you are now."

"I know. Allie told me."

"People followed me, though," I continued. "And they didn't only do it because they were convinced that I could help them get what they wanted. They followed me because I seemed to be going somewhere. They had no purpose beyond survival. Get a job. Eat. Get a room somewhere. Exist. But I wanted more than that for myself and for my people, and I meant to have it. They wanted more too, but they didn't think they could have it. They weren't even sure what 'it' was."

"Weren't you wonderful?" Len murmured.

"Don't be an idiot," I said. "Those people were willing to follow an 18-year-old girl because she seemed to be going somewhere, seemed to know where she was going. People elected Jarret because he seemed to know where he was going too. Even rich people like your dad are desperate for someone who seems to know where they're going."

"Dad wanted someone who would protect his investments and keep the poor people in their places."

"And when he realized that Jarret either couldn't or wouldn't do either, he left the country. Other people will turn their backs on Jarret, too, in different ways. But they'll still want to follow people who seem to know where they're going."

"You?"

I sighed. "Perhaps. More likely, though, it will be people I've taught. I don't really have the skills that will be needed. Also, I don't know how long it will take to make Earthseed a way of life and the Destiny a goal that much of humanity struggles to achieve. I'm afraid that alone might take my lifetime and yours. It won't be quick. But we'll be the ones who plant the first seeds, you and I."

Len pushed her black hair away from her face. "I don't believe in Earthseed. I don't believe in any of this. It's just a lot of simplistic nonsense. You'll get killed knocking on the doors of strangers, and that will be the end of it."

"That could happen."

"I want no part of it."

"Yes, you do. If you live, you'll accomplish more that's good and important than anyone you've ever known. If you die, you'll die trying to accomplish it."

"I said I want no part of it. It's ridiculous. It's impossible."

"And you have more important things to do?"

Silence.

We didn't talk anymore until we came to a road leading off into the hills. I turned to follow it, ignoring Len's questions. Where was I going? I didn't know at all. Perhaps I would just have a look at what lay up the road, then turn back to the highway. Perhaps not.

Hidden away in the hills, there was a large, two-story wooden farmhouse set back off the road. It was much in need of paint. It had once been white. Now it was gray. Alongside it, a woman was weeding her large vegetable garden. Without telling Len what I meant to do, I walked off the road, went to her, and asked if we could do her weeding for a meal.

"We'll do a good job," I said. "We'll satisfy you, or no food."

She stared at us both with fear and suspicion. She seemed to be alone, but might not be. We were clearly armed, but offering no threat. I smiled. "Just a few sandwiches would be awfully welcome," I said. "We'll work hard for them." I was dressed in loose clothing as a man. My hair was cut short. Len tells me I don't make a bad-looking man. We were both reasonably clean.

The woman smiled in spite of herself—a tentative little smile. "Do you think you can tell the weeds from the vegetables?" she asked.

I laughed and said, "Yes, ma'am." In my sleep, I thought. But Len was another matter. She had never done any gardening at all. Her father hired people to work in their gardens and orchards. She had thin, soft, uncallused hands and no knowledge of plants. I told her to watch me for a while. I pointed out the carrots, the various green vegetables, the herbs, then set her weeding the herbs on hands and knees. She'd have more control over what she pulled that way. I depended on her memory and her good sense. If she was angry with me, she would let me know about it later. Raging at people in public wasn't her style. In fact, we had plenty of food in our packs, and we weren't yet low on money. But I wanted to begin at once to reach out to people. Why not stop for a day on our way to Portland and leave a few words behind in this old gray house? It was good practice, if nothing else.

We worked hard and got the garden cleaned up. Len muttered and complained, but I didn't get the impression that she was really suffering. In fact, she seemed interested in what she was doing and content to be doing it, although she complained about bugs and worms, about the way the weeds smelled, about the way the damp earth smelled, about getting dirty. . . .

I realized that while Len had talked about experiences with her family and with the servants and experiences with her kidnappers and with living on her own, scavenging and stealing, she's never talked about working. She must have done some small jobs for food, but working seems still to be a novelty for her. I'll have to see that she gets more experience so that even if she decides to go off on her own, she'll be better able to take care of herself.

Later in the day, when we had finished the weeding, the woman—who told us her name was Nia Cortez—gave us a plate of three kinds of sandwiches. There was egg, toasted cheese, and ham. And there was a bowl of strawberries, a bowl of oranges, and a pitcher of lemonade sweetened with honey. Nia sat with us on her side porch, and I got the impression that she was lonely, shy, and still more than a little afraid of us. What a solitary place the old house was, dropped amid grassy hills.

"This is beautiful country," I said. "I sketch a little. These rolling hills, blond grasses, and green trees make me want to sit drawing all day."

"You can draw?" Nia asked me with a little smile.

And I took my sketchpad from my pack and began to draw not the rolling hills but Nia's own plump, pleasant face. She was in her late forties or early fifties and had dark brown hair streaked with gray. Drawn back into a long, thick horsetail, it hung almost to her waist. Her plumpness had helped her avoid wrinkles, and her smooth skin was tanned a good even brown—a nice, uncomplicated face. Her eyes were as clear as a baby's, and the same dark brown as most of her hair. Drawing someone gives me an excellent excuse to study them and let myself feel what it seems to me that they feel. That's what sharing is, after all, and it comes to me whether I want it or not. I might as well use it. In a rough and not altogether dependable way, drawing a person helps me become that person and, to be honest, it helps me manipulate that person. Everything teaches.

She was lonely, Nia was. And she was taking an uncomfortable interest in me-as-a-man. To curb that interest, I turned to Len, who was watching everything with sharp, intelligent interest. "Wrap up a couple of sandwiches for me, would you?" I asked her. "I'd like to finish this while the light is right."

Len gave me a sidelong glance and used paper napkins to wrap two sandwiches. Nia, on the other hand, looked at Len almost as though she had forgotten her. Then, in a moment of confusion, she looked down at her hands—tools of work, those hands. She seemed more contained, more restrained when she looked at me again.

I didn't hurry with the drawing. I could have finished it much more quickly. But working on it, adding detail, gave me a chance to talk about Earthseed without seeming to proselytize. I quoted verses as though quoting any poetry to her until one verse caught her interest. That she could not conceal from me. To her credit, it was this verse:

OCTAVIA E. BUTLER

"To shape God
With wisdom and forethought,
To benefit your world,
Your people,
Your life.
Consider consequences.
Minimize harm.
Ask questions.
Seek answers.
Learn.
Teach."

She had once been a teacher in a public school in San Francisco. The school had closed 15 years after she began teaching. That was during the early twenties when so many public school systems around the country gave up the ghost and closed their doors. Even the pretense of having an educated populace was ending. Politicians shook their heads and said sadly that universal education was a failed experiment. Some companies began to educate the children of their workers at least well enough to enable them to become their next generation of workers. Company towns began then to come back into fashion. They offered security, employment, and education. That was all very well, but the company that educated you owned you until you paid off the debt you owed them. You were an indentured person, and if they couldn't use you themselves, they could trade you off to another division of the company—or another company. You, like your education, became a commodity to be bought or sold.

There were still a few public school systems in the country, limping along, doing what they could, but these had more in common with city jails than with even the most mediocre private, religious, or company schools. It was the business of responsible parents to see to the education of their children, somehow. Those who did not were bad parents. It was to be hoped that social, legal, and religious pressures would sooner or later force even bad parents to do their duty toward their offspring.

"So," Nia said, "poor, semiliterate, and illiterate people became financially responsible for their children's elementary education. If they were alcoholics or addicts or prostitutes or if they had all they could do just to feed their kids and maybe keep some sort of roof over their heads, that was just too bad! And no one thought about what kind of society we were building with such stupid decisions. People who could afford to educate their children in private schools were glad to see the government finally stop wasting their tax money, educating other people's children. They seemed to think they lived on Mars. They imagined that a country filled with poor, uneducated, unemployable people somehow wouldn't hurt them!"

Len sighed. "That sounds like the way my dad thinks. I'm his punishment, I guess—not that he cares!"

Nia gave her a look of chilly interest. "What? Your father?"

Len explained, and I watched as, almost against her will, Nia thawed. "I see." She sighed. "I suppose I could have wound up homeless myself, but my aunt and uncle owned this house and surrounding farmland outright. This is mother's family home. I came to live here and care for them when my job ended. They were old and not doing well anymore. Even then they were renting the farmland to neighboring farmers. They left the house, the land, and the rest of their possessions to me when they died. I keep a garden, some chickens, goats, rabbits. I rent the land. I survive."

I tried to ignore a sharp stab of envy and nostalgia.

Len said, " I like your garden." She stared out at the long, neat rows of vegetables, fruits, and herbs.

"Do you?" Nia asked. "I heard you complaining out there."

Len blushed, then looked at her hands. "I've never done that kind of thing before. I liked it, but it was hard work."

I smiled. "She's game, if nothing else. I've been doing work like that all my life."

OCTAVIA E. BUTLER

"You were a gardener?" Nia asked.

"No, it was just a matter of eating or not eating. I've done a number of things, including teach—although I'm not academically qualified to teach. But I'm literate, and the idea of leaving children illiterate is criminal."

As she smiled her delight at hearing such agreement with her own thoughts, I handed her the drawing. On the lower right side of it I had written the first verse of Earthseed, "All that you touch, / You Change. . . ." On the other I had written the "To shape God" verse that she liked.

She read the verses and looked at the picture for a long, long time. It was a detailed drawing, not just a sketch, and I felt almost pleased with it. Then she looked at me and said in a voice almost too soft to hear, "Thank you."

She asked us to stay the night, offered to let us sleep in her barn, proving that she hadn't altogether lost her fear of us. We stayed, and the next day I did a few odd repair jobs around the house for her. I could have stolen her blind if I'd wanted to, but what I had decided that I wanted from her, I couldn't steal. She had to give it.

I told her that evening that I was a woman. First, though, I told her about Larkin. We were in her kitchen. She was cooking. She'd told me to sit down and talk to her. I'd worked hard, she said. I'd earned a rest.

I never took my eyes off her as I told her. It was important that she not feel foolish, frightened, or angry when she understood. A little confusion and mild embarrassment was inevitable, but that should be all.

She looked as though she might cry when she heard about my Larkin. That was all right. Len was in the living room, delighting in reading real books made of paper. She would not see any tears Nia shed—in case Nia was sensitive about that kind of thing. You could never be altogether sure what another person might feel as a humiliation or an invasion of privacy.

"What happened to . . . to the child's mother?" Nia asked.

I didn't answer until she turned to look at me. "It's dangerous on the road," I said. "You know that. People vanish out there. I walked from the Los Angeles area to Humboldt County in '27, so I know it. Know it too well."

"She vanished on the road? She was killed?"

"She vanished on the road to avoid being killed." I paused. "She's me, Nia."

Silence. Confusion. "But. . . ."

"You've trusted us. Now I'm trusting you. I'm a man on the road. I have to be. Two women out there would be everyone's target." There. I was not correcting her, not smiling at the joke I'd played on her. I was making myself vulnerable to her, and asking her to understand and keep my secret. Just right, I hoped. It felt right.

She blinked and then stared at me. She left her pots and came over to take a good look. "I can hardly believe you," she whispered.

And I smiled. "You can, though. I wanted you to know." I drew a deep breath. "Not that it's safe for a man out there either. The people who took my child also killed my husband and wiped out my community—all in the name of God, of course."

She sat down at the table with me. "Crusaders. I've heard of them, of course—that they rescue homeless orphans and . . . burn witches, for heaven's sake. But I've never heard that they . . . just killed people and . . . stole their children." But it seemed that what the Crusaders had done could not quite get her mind off what I had done. "But you . . . ," she said. "I can't get over it. I still feel. . . . I still feel as though you were a man. I mean. . . ."

"It's all right."

She sighed, put her head back and looked at me with a sad smile. "No, it isn't."

No, it wasn't. But I went to her and hugged her and held her. Like Len, she needed to be hugged and held, needed to cry in someone's arms. She'd been alone far too long. To my own surprise, I realized that under other circumstances, I might have taken her to bed. I had

OCTAVIA E. BUTLER

gone through 17 months at Camp Christian without wanting to be with anyone. I missed Bankole—missed him so much sometimes that it was an almost physical pain. And I had never been tempted to want to make love with a woman. Now, I found myself almost wanting to. And she almost wanted me to. But that wasn't the relationship that I needed between us.

I mean to see her again, this kind, lonely woman in her large, empty, shabby house. I need people like her. Until I met her, I had not realized how much I needed such people. Len had been right about what I should be doing, although she had known no more than I about how it must be done. I still don't know enough. But there's no manual for this kind of thing. I suppose that I'll be learning what to do and how to do it until the day I die.

The three of us talked about Earthseed again over dinner. Most often we talked of it from the point of view of education. By the time we parted for the night, I could speak of it as Earthseed without worrying that Nia would feel harassed or proselytized. We stayed one more day and I told her more about Acorn, and about the children of Acorn. I held her once more when she cried. I kissed her lonely mouth, then put her away from me.

I did two more sketches, each accompanied by verses, and I let her offer to look after any of the children of Acorn that I could find until their parents could be contacted. I never suggested it, but I did all I could to open ways for her to suggest it. She was afraid of the children of the road, light-fingered and often violent. But she was not, in theory at least, afraid of the children of Acorn. They were connected with me, and after three days, she had no fear at all of me. That was very compelling, somehow, that complete acceptance and trust. It was hard for me to leave her.

By the time we did leave, she was as much with me as Len was. The verses and the sketches and memories will keep her with me for a while. I'll have to visit her again soon—say within the year—to hold on to her, and I intend to do that. I hope I'll soon be bringing her a child or two to protect and teach—one of Acorn's or not. She needs purpose as much as I need to give it to her.

"That was fascinating," Len said to me this morning as we got under way again, "I enjoyed watching you work."

I glanced at her. "Thank you for working with me."

She smiled, then stopped smiling. "You seduce people. My God, you're always at it, aren't you?"

"People fascinate me," I said. "I care about them. If I didn't, Earth-seed wouldn't mean anything at all to me."

"Are you really going to bring that poor woman children to look after?"

"I hope to."

"She can barely look after herself. That house looks as though the next storm will knock it over."

"Yes. I'll have to see what I can do about that, too."

"Do you have that kind of money?"

"No, of course not. But someone does. I don't know how I'm going to do it, Len, but the world is full of needy people. They don't all need the same things, but they all need purpose. Even some of the ones with plenty of money need purpose."

"What about Larkin?"

"I'll find her. If she's alive, I'll find her. I've sworn that."

We walked in silence for a while. There were a few other walkers in clusters, passing us or walking far ahead or behind us. The broad highway was broken and old and stretched long in front of us, but it wasn't threatening, somehow. Not now.

After a while, Len caught my arm and I turned to look at her. It was good to be walking with someone. Good to have another pair of eyes, another pair of hands. Good to hear another voice say my name, another brain questioning, demanding, even sneering.

"What do you want of me?" she asked. "What is it that you want me to do? You have to tell me that."

"Help me reach people," I said. "Go on working with me, and helping me. There's so much to be done."

THURSDAY, JUNE 21 , 2035

As my father used to quote from his old King James Bible, "Pride goeth before destruction and an haughty spirit before a fall." He liked to be accurate about his quotes.

I'm bruised and wounded about the pride, but not destroyed, at least.

I decided yesterday that things had worked out so well with Nia that I could go on recruiting people as we walked toward Portland. Walking through a roadside town that seemed big enough for people not to be alarmed at the sight of a stranger, I stopped to ask a woman who was sweeping her front porch whether we could do some yard work for a meal. With no warning, she opened her front door, called her two big dogs, and told them to get us. We barely got out of her yard in time to avoid being bitten. Interesting that neither of us drew a gun or uttered a sound. It turns out that Len's fear of dogs is as strong as mine. Last night, she showed me some scars given her by a dog that her former owners had allowed to get too close.

Anyway, the woman with the two dogs cursed us, called us "thieves, killers, heathens, and witches." She promised to call the cops on us.

"All that just because you asked for work," Len said. "Thank heavens you didn't try to tell her about Earthseed!" She was cleaning a long, deep scratch on her arm. It came from a nail that stuck out from the woman's wooden gate. I had spotted the dogs in time to shove her back through the gate, dive through myself, then slam the gate by grabbing a bottom slat and yanking. I only just let go in time to avoid a lot of long, sharp teeth, and damned if the dog didn't bite one of the wooden slats of the fence in frustration at not being able to get at me. I had skinned hands and a bruised hip. Len had her long scratch, which hurt and bled enough to scare me. Later, I treated us both to tetanus skin tabs. They cost more than they should, but neither of us are up-to-date on our immunizations anymore. Best not to take unnecessary chances.

"I wonder what happened to that woman to make her willing to do a thing like that," I said as we walked this morning.

"She was out of her mind," Len said. "That's all."

"That's rarely all," I said.

Then early today, a farm woman drove us off with a rifle and I decided to quit trying for a day or two. A storekeeper told us that Jarret's Crusaders have been active in the area. They've been rounding up vagrants, singling out witches and heathens, and generally scaring the hell out of householders by warning them about the dangers and evils of strangers from the road.

It was interesting to see how angry the storekeeper was. The Crusaders, he said, are bad for business. They collar his highway customers or frighten them away, and they intimidate his local customers so that he's lost a lot of his regulars—the ones who live a long way from his store. They've learned to shop as close to home as they can with little regard for quality or price.

"Jarret says he can't control his own Crusaders," the man said. "Next time out, I'll vote for someone who'll put the bastards in jail where they belong!"

OCTAVIA E. BUTLER

21

○ ○ ○

From EARTHSEED: THE BOOKS OF THE LIVING

To survive,
Let the past
Teach you—
Past customs,
Struggles,
Leaders and thinkers.
Let
These
Help you.
Let them inspire you,
Warn you,
Give you strength.
But beware:
God is Change.
Past is past.
What was
Cannot
Come again.

To survive,
Know the past.
Let it touch you.
Then let
The past
Go.

I don't know that Uncle Marc would ever have told me the truth about my mother. I don't believe he intended to. He never wavered from his story that she was dead, and I never suspected that he was lying. I loved him, believed in him, trusted him completely. When he found out how I was living, he invited me to live with him and continue my education. "You're a bright girl," he said, "and you're family—the only family I have. I couldn't help your mother. Let me help you."

I said yes. I didn't even have to think about it. I quit my job and went to live in one of his houses in New York. He hired a housekeeper and tutors and bought computer courses to see to it that I had the college education that Kayce and Madison wouldn't have provided for me if they could have. Kayce used to say, "You're a girl! If you know how to keep a clean, decent house and how to worship God, you know enough!"

I even went back to church because of Uncle Marc. I went back to the Church of Christian America, physically, at least. I lived at his second home in upstate New York, and I attended church on Sundays because he wanted me to, and because I was so used to doing it. I was comfortable doing it. I sang in the choir again and did regular charity work, helping to care for old people in one of the church nursing homes. Doing those things again was like slipping into a comfortable old pair of shoes.

But the truth was, I had lost whatever faith I once had. The church I grew up in had turned its back on me just because I moved out of the home of people who, somehow, never learned even to like me. Forget love. Fine behavior for good Christian Americans, trying to build a strong, united country.

Better, I decided after much thought and much reading of history, to live a decent life and behave well toward other people. Better not to worry about the Christian Americans, the Catholics, the Lutherans, or whatever. Each denomination seemed to think that it had the truth and the only truth and its people were going to bliss in heaven while everyone else went eternal to torment in hell.

But the Church wasn't only a religion. It was a community—my community. I didn't want to be free of it. That would have been—had been—impossibly lonely. Everyone needs to be part of something.

By the time I got my Master's in history, I found that I couldn't muster any belief in a literal heaven or hell, anyway. I thought the best we could all do was to look after one another and clean up the various hells we've made right here on earth. That seemed to me a big enough job for any person or group, and that was one of the good things that Christian America worked hard at.

I went on living in Uncle Marc's upstate New York house. Once I had my Master's, I began work on my Ph.D. Also, I began creating Dreamask scenarios. Dreamask International hired me on the strength of several scenarios I had done for them on speculation.

Now, thanks to Uncle Marc, I had the Dreamask scenario recorder I had longed for when I was little. Now I had the freedom to create pretty much anything I wanted to. I did my work under the name Asha Vere. I wanted no connection with the Alexanders, yet I felt uncomfortable about trading on my connection with Uncle Marc, and calling myself Duran. At the time, I believed Duran was my mother's family name. My father's surname, "Bankole," meant nothing to me since Uncle Mark couldn't tell me much about Taylor Franklin Bankole—only that he was a doctor and very old when I was born. Asha Vere was name enough for me. It dated me as a child born during the popularity of a particular early Mask, but that didn't matter. And the Dreamask people kind of liked it.

I worked at home on my Masks and on my Ph.D., and was so casual about the degree that I was 32 before I completed it. I enjoyed the work, enjoyed Marc's company when he came to me to get away from his public and enjoy some feeling of family. I was happy. I never found anyone I wanted to marry. In fact, I had never seen a marriage that I would have wanted to be part of. There must be good marriages somewhere, but to me, marriage had the feel of people tolerating each other, enduring each other because they were afraid to be alone or because each was a habit that the other couldn't quite break. I knew that not everyone's marriage was as sterile and ugly as Kayce's and Madison's. I knew that intellectually, but emotionally, I couldn't seem to escape Kayce's cold, bitter dissatisfaction and Madison's moist little hands.

Uncle Marc, on the other hand, had said without ever quite saying it that he preferred men sexually, but his church taught that homosexuality was sin, and he chose to live by that doctrine. So he had no one. Or at least, I never knew him to have anyone. That looks bleak on the page, but we each chose our lives. And we had one another. We were a family. That seemed to be enough.

Meanwhile, my mother was giving her attention to her other child, her older and best beloved child, Earthseed.

Somehow we—or at least I—never paid much attention to the growing Earthseed movement. It was out there. In spite of the efforts of Christian America and other denominations, there were always cults out there. Granted, Earthseed was an unusual cult. It financed scientific exploration and inquiry, and technological creativity. It set up grade schools and eventually colleges, and offered full scholarships to poor but gifted students. The students who accepted had to agree to spend seven years teaching, practicing medicine, or otherwise using their skills to improve life in the many Earthseed communities. Ultimately, the intent was to help the communities to launch themselves toward the stars and to live on the distant worlds they found circling those stars.

"Do you know anything about these people?" I asked Uncle Mark after reading and hearing a few news items about them. "Are they serious? Interstellar emigration? My god, why don't they just move to Antarctica if they want to rough it?" And he surprised me by making a straight line of his mouth and looking away. I had expected him to Laugh.

"They're serious," he said. "They're sad, ridiculous, misled people who believe that the answer to all human problems is to fly off to Alpha Centauri."

I did laugh. "Is a flying saucer coming for them or what?"

He shrugged. "They're pathetic. Forget about them."

I didn't, of course. I left my usual haunts on the nets and began to research them. I wasn't serious. I didn't plan to do anything with what I learned, but I was curious—and I might get an idea for a Mask. I found that Earthseed was a wealthy sect that welcomed everyone and was willing to make use of everyone. It owned land, schools, farms, factories, stores, banks, several whole towns. And it seemed to own a lot of well-known people—lawyers, physicians, journalists, scientists, politicians, even members of Congress.

And were they all hoping to fly off to Alpha Centauri?

It wasn't that simple, of course. But to tell the truth, the more I read about Earthseed, the more I despised it. So much needed to be done here on earth—so many diseases, so much hunger, so much poverty, such suffering, and here was a rich organization spending vast sums of money, time, and effort on nonsense. Just nonsense!

Then I found *The Books of the Living* and I accessed images and information concerning Lauren Oya Olamina.

Even after reading about my mother and seeing her I didn't notice anything. I never looked at her image and thought, "Oh, she looks like me." She did look like me, though—or rather, I looked like her. But I didn't notice. All I saw was a tall, middle-aged, dark-skinned woman with arresting eyes and a nice smile. She looked, somehow, like someone I would be inclined to like and trust—which scared me. It made me immediately dislike and distrust her. She was a cult leader, after all. She was supposed to be seductive. But she wasn't going to seduce me.

And all that was only my reaction to her image. No wonder she was so rich, no wonder she could draw followers even into such a ridiculous religion. She was dangerous.

From *THE JOURNALS OF LAUREN OYA OLAMINA*
SUNDAY, JULY 29, 2035

Portland.

I've gathered a few more people. They aren't people who will travel with me or come together in easily targetable villages. They're people in stable homes—or people who need homes.

Isis Duarte Norman, for instance, lives in a park between the river and the burned, collapsed remains of an old hotel. She has a shack there—wood covered with plastic sheeting. Each evening she can be found there. During the day she works, cleaning other women's houses. This enables her to eat and keep herself and her secondhand clothing clean. She has a hard life, but it's as respectable as she can make it. She's 43. The man she married when she was 23 dumped her six years ago for a 14-year-old girl—the daughter of one of his servants.

"She was so beautiful," Isis said. "I knew he wouldn't be able to keep his hands off her. I couldn't protect her from him any more than I could protect myself, but I never thought that he would keep her and throw me out."

He did. And for six years, she's been homeless and all but hopeless. She said she had thought of killing herself. Only fear had stopped her—the fear of not quite dying, of maiming herself and dying a slow, lingering death of pain and starvation. That could happen. Portland is a vast, crowded city. It isn't Los Angeles or the Bay Area, but it is huge. People ignore one another in self-defense. I find this both useful and frightening. When I met Isis, it was because I went to the door of a home where she was working. Otherwise, she would never have dared to talk to me. As it was, she was designated to assemble a meal and bring it to me when I had finished cleaning up the backyard.

She was wary when she brought the food. Then she looked at the backyard and told me I had done a good job. We talked for a while. I walked her to her shack—which made her nervous. I was a man again. I find it inconvenient and dangerous to be on the street as a homeless woman. Other people manage it well. I don't, somehow.

I left Isis without seeing the inside of her shack. Best not to push people. Best, as Len says, to seduce them. I've seen Isis several times since then. I've talked with her, read verses to her, captured her interest. She has two half-grown children who live with their father's mother, so she cares, in spite of herself, about what the future will bring. I intend to find a real home for her by getting her a live-in job looking after children. That might take time, but I intend to do it.

On the other hand, I've met and gathered in Joel and Irma Elford, who hired me when I first came to Portland to paint a garage and a fence and do some yard work. Len and I worked together, first cutting weeds, harvesting row crops, raking, cleaning the yard at the back of the property where a wilderness had begun to grow. Then, when the dust settled, we painted the garage. We would have to get to the fence the next day. We were to get hard currency for this job, and that put us in a good mood. Len is a likable person to work with. She learns fast, complains endlessly, and does an excellent job, however long it takes. Most of the time, she enjoys herself. The complaining was just one of her quirks.

Then Joel and Irma invited us in to eat with them at their table. I had done a quick sketch of Irma to catch her attention, and added a verse that was intended to reach her through environmental interests that I had heard her express:

> *There is nothing alien*
> *About nature.*
> *Nature*
> *Is all that exists.*
> *It's the earth*
> *And all that's on it.*
> *It's the universe*
> *And all that's in it.*
> *It's God,*
> *Never at rest.*
> *It's you,*
> *Me,*
> *Us,*
> *Them,*

Struggling upstream
Or drifting down.

Also, perhaps because her mother had died the year before, Irma also seemed touched by this fragment of funeral oration.

> *We give our dead*
> *To the orchards*
> *And the groves.*
> *We give our dead*
> *To life.*

We were an unexpected novelty, and the Elfords were curious about us. They let us wash up in their back bathroom and change into cleaner clothing from our packs. Then they sat us down, fed us a huge meal, and began to ask us questions. Where were we going? Did we have homes? Families? No? Well, how long had we been homeless? What did we do for shelter in rough weather? Weren't we afraid "out there"?

I answered for both of us at first, since Len did not seem inclined to talk, and I answered as often with Earthseed verses as with ordinary conversation. It didn't take long for Irma to ask, "What is it you're quoting from?" And then, "May I see it? I've never heard of it." And, "Is this Buddhist? No, I see that it isn't. I very nearly became a Buddhist when I was younger." She's 37. "Very simple little verses. Very direct. But some of them are lovely."

"I want to be understood," I said. "I want to make it easy for people to understand. It doesn't always work, but I was serious about the effort."

Irma was all I could have hoped for. "You wrote these? You? Really? Then tell me please, on page 47. . . ."

They're quiet, childless, middle-aged people who choose to live in a modest, middle-class neighborhood even though they could afford their own walled enclave. They're interested in the world around them and worried about the direction the country has taken. I could see their wealth in the beautiful, expensive little things they've scattered around their home—antique silver and crystal, old leather-bound paper books, paintings, and, for a touch of the modern, a cover-the-earth phone net system that includes, according to Len, the latest in Virtual rooms. They can have all the sights and other sensations of visiting anyplace on earth or any programmed-in imaginary place, all without leaving home. And yet they were interested in talking to us.

We had to be careful, though. The Elfords may be bored and hungry for both novelty and purpose, but they're not fools. I had to be more open with them than I have been with people like Isis. I told them much of my own story, and I told them what I'm trying to do. They thought I was brave, nave, ridiculous, and . . . interesting. Out of pity and curiosity they let us sleep in the comfortable little guest house at the back of their property.

The next day, when we had painted the fence, they found more small jobs for us to do, and now and then, they talked to us. And they let us talk to them. They never lost interest.

"What will you ask them to do?" Len said to me that night as we settled in again in the guest house. "You have them, you know, even if they don't realize it yet."

I nodded. "They're hungry for something to do," I said, "starved for some kind of real purpose. I think they'll have some suggestions themselves. They'll feel better if they make the first suggestions. They'll feel in control. Later, I want them to take Allie in. This guest house would be perfect for her and Justin. When they see what she can do with a few sticks of wood and simple tools, they'll be glad to have her. And I think I'll introduce Allie to Isis. I have the feeling they'll hit it off."

"The Elfords have all but seduced themselves for you," Len said.

I nodded. "Think about all the other people we've met who've given us nothing but trouble. I'm glad to meet eager, enthusiastic people now and then."

And of course, I've found my brother again. I find that I've not wanted to talk about that.

Marc has been preaching at one of the big Portland shelters, helping out with shelter maintenance, and attending a Christian American seminary. He wants to be an ordained minister. He was not happy to see me. I kept showing up to hear him and leaving notes that I wanted a meeting. It took him two weeks to give in.

"I suppose if I moved to Michigan, you'd turn up there," he said by way of greeting.

We were meeting in his apartment building—which was more like a big dormitory. Because he wasn't permitted to have guests in his apartment, we met in the large dining room just off the lobby. It was a clean, dim, plain room crowded with mismatched wooden tables and chairs and nothing else. Its walls were a dim gray-green and the floor was gray tile worn through to the wood in spots. We were alone there, drinking what I was told would be hot cinnamon-apple tea. When I bought a cup from the machine, I found that it tasted like tepid, slightly sweet water. The lights in the room were few, weak, and far apart, and the place worked hard at being as dreary and cheerless as could be managed.

"Service to God is what's important," my brother said, and I realized that I had been looking around and making my unspoken criticism obvious.

"I'm sorry," I said. "If you want to be here, then you should be here. I wish, though . . . I wish you could spare a little concern for your niece."

"Don't be so condescending! And I've told you what you should do to find her!"

Join CA. I shuddered. "I can't. I just can't. If Cougar were here, could you enlist with him again—just as a job, you know? Could you become one of his helpers?"

"It's not the same!"

"It's the same to me. What Cougar did to you, CA's Crusaders did to me. The only difference is they did it to me longer. And don't tell me the Crusaders are just renegades. They're not. They're as much part of

OCTAVIA E. BUTLER

CA as the shelters are. I spotted one of the men who raped and lashed us at Acorn. He was working as an armed guard at the Eureka shelter."

Marc stood up. He all but pushed his chair over in his eagerness to get away from me. "I've finally got a chance to have what I want," he said. "You're not going to wreck it for me!"

"This isn't about you," I said, still seated. "I wish you had a child, Marc. If you did, you might be able to understand what it's like not to know where she is, whether she's being well treated, or even . . . even whether she's still alive. *If I could only know!*"

He stood over me for a very long time, looking down at me as though he hated me. "I don't believe you feel anything," he said.

I stared back at him amazed. "Marc, my daughter—"

"You think you're supposed to care, so you pretend to. Maybe you even want to, but you don't."

I think I preferred it when he hit me. I couldn't react except to sit staring at him. Tears spilled from my eyes, but I didn't realize it at the time. I just sat frozen, staring.

After a while, my brother turned and walked away, tears glistening on his own face.

By then, I wanted to hate him. I couldn't quite, but I wanted to.

"Brothers!" Len muttered when I told her what had happened. She had waited for me at the Elford guesthouse. She listened to what I told her and, I suppose, heard it according to her own experience.

"He needs to make everything my fault," I said. "He still can't let himself admit what Christian America did to me. He couldn't stay with them if they did such things, so he's decided that they're innocent, and somehow everything is my fault."

"Why are you making excuses for him?" Len demanded.

"I'm not. I think that's really what he's feeling. He had tears on his face when he walked away from me. He didn't want me to see that, but I saw it. He has to drive me away or he can't have his dreams. Christian America is teaching him to be the only thing I think he's ever wanted to be—a minister. Like our father."

She sighed and shook her head. "So what are you going to do?"

"I . . . don't know. Maybe the Elfords can suggest something."

"Them, yes. . . . Irma asked me while you were gone whether you would be willing to speak to a group of her friends. She wants to have a party and, I suppose, show you off."

"You're kidding!"

"I said I thought you would do it."

I got up and went to look out the window at a pear tree, dark against the night sky. "You know, if I could only find my daughter, I would think my life was going along beautifully."

SUNDAY, SEPTEMBER 16, 2035

I've managed to get Marc to meet with me again at last.

He may be the only relative I have left on earth. I don't want him as an enemy.

"Just tell me you'll help my Larkin if you ever find her," I said. "How could I do less?" he asked, still with a certain coldness.

"I wish you well, Marc. I always have. You're my brother, and I love you. Even with all that's happened, I can't help loving you."

He sighed. We were sitting in his building's vast, drab dining room again. This time there were other people scattered around, eating late lunches or early dinners. Most were men, young and old, individuals and small groups. Some stared at me with what seemed to be disapproval. "You can't know what Christian America has meant to me," he said. His voice had softened. He looked less distant.

"Of course I can," I told him. "I'm here because I do understand. You'll be a Christian American minister, and I'll be your heathen sister. I can stand that. What I find hard to stand is being your enemy. I never meant for that to happen."

After a while, he said, "We aren't enemies. You're my sister, and I love you too."

We shook hands. I don't think I've ever shaken hands with my

OCTAVIA E. BUTLER

brother before, but I got the feeling that it was as much contact as he was willing to endure, at least for now.

Allie and Justin have come to Portland to live. I phoned Allie and told her to use some of the money I left with her to buy a ride up with the Georges. The Elfords have agreed to let the two of them live in their guest house. Len and I have been given rooms above the garage at the home of another supporter—a friend of the Elfords.

That's how I've come to think of these people—as supporters. We speak to groups in their houses. We lead discussions and teach the truths of Earthseed. I say "we" because Len has begun to take a more active part. She will teach on her own someday, and perhaps train someone to help her. As I write those words, I miss her as though she had already gone off on her own, as though I already had some new young skeptic to train.

Through the Elfords and their friends and the friends of their friends, we've received invitations to speak all over town in people's homes and in small halls. I've found that in each group there is one person, perhaps two, who are serious, who hear in Earthseed something that they can accept, something they want, something they need. These are the ones who will make our first schools possible.

In Acorn, it was no accident that the church and the school were the same. They weren't just the same building. They were the same institution. If the Earthseed Destiny is to have any meaning beyond a distant mythical paradise, Earthseed must be not only a belief system but a way of life. Children should be raised in it. Adults should be reminded of it often, refocused on it, and urged toward it. Both should understand how their current behavior is or isn't contributing to fulfillment of the Destiny. By the time we're able to send Earthseed children to college, they should be dedicated not only to a course of study but to the fulfillment of the Destiny. If they are, then any course of study they choose can become a tool for the fulfillment.

SUNDAY, SEPTEMBER 30, 2035

I've found a potential home for Travis and Natividad. I've called them several times, and gotten no answer. I worried about them until last night when I reached them. They've been living in a squatter camp a few miles from Sacramento. They went there on a rumor that some of Acorn's children had been seen there. The rumor was false, but their money had run low. They'd had to stop and take jobs doing agricultural work. This was rough because the work paid little more than room and board in horrible little shacks.

They'll come here with the Mora girls and the new Mora baby. I can't restore their children to them, but I can see to it that they have work that sustains them and a decent place to live. They'll live in the big house that is to be our first school. The house belongs to one of my supporters—one who said those magic words: "What can I do? What do you need?"

What don't we need!

The house is a big empty shell that the Douglas and Mora families will have to work hard on. It needs paint, repairs, landscaping, fencing, everything. But it has living room for a big family upstairs and teaching and working room downstairs. It will be a new beginning in so many ways. And the people who own it have relatives in both city and state government. They're the kind of people Jarret's Crusaders have learned to let alone.

Also, next month, Len and I are invited to teach at several homes in the Seattle area.

TUESDAY, NOVEMBER 13, 2035

I've finally talked Harry into coming north. He's run across the Figueroas and joined with them for the trip. He hasn't found Tabia or Russ, I'm sorry to say, but he has picked up three orphans. He found them on the road just north of San Luis Obispo. Their mother was hit by a truck. He saw it happen and went straight to the kids. There are more and more vehicles on the road during the day now. Walking is becoming more dangerous.

As horrible as the hit and run was, I get the feeling it's given Harry what he needs—children to protect, children who need him, children who run to him and hold his hands when they're scared. He and Zahra always said they wanted a big family. He's such a good daddy. I have a teaching job for him in Seattle. I believe he'll thrive in it if he can let himself.

Jorge Cho and his family are coming. I've found work for Jorge and Di in Portland.

Now I have to look around for places for the Figueroas.

I believe that I've finally done it. I believe that my life has finally educated me enough to enable me to make a real start at planting Earthseed. It may be too soon to say this, but it feels true. I believe it is true.

I've allowed the Elfords to make *The First Book of the Living* available free on the nets. I never expected to make money from the book. My only fear has been that someone would take it and change it, make it an instrument of some other theology or use it for some new brand of demagoguery. Joel Elford says the best way to avoid that is to make it available on every possible net and with my name on it. And, of course, the copyright is my legal fallback if someone does begin to misuse it seriously.

"I don't think you realize what you have," Joel told me.

I looked at him in surprise and realized that he believed what he was saying.

"And you don't realize how many other people will want it," he continued. "I've aimed the book particularly at the nets that are intended to interest American universities and the smaller free cities where so many of those universities are located. It will go out worldwide, but it will draw more attention to itself in those places."

He was smiling, so I asked, "What are you expecting to happen?"

"You're going to start hearing from people," he said. "You'll soon have more attention than you'll know what to do with." He sobered. "And what you actually do with it is important. Be careful." Irma trusted me more than Joel did. Joel was still watching me—watching with a great deal of interest. He says it's like watching a birth.

SUNDAY, DECEMBER 30, 2035

I've been traveling.

That's nothing new for me, but this is different. This time, thanks to the book, I've been invited by university groups and others, and paid to travel, paid to speak—which is a little like paying ice to be cold.

And I've been flying. Flying! I've walked over most of the West Coast, and now I've flown over the interior of the country and over much of the East Coast. I've flown to Newark, Delaware; Clarion, Pennsylvnia; and up to Syracuse, New York. Next, I go to Toledo, Ohio; Ann Arbor, Michigan; Madison, Wisconsin; and Iowa City, Iowa.

"Not a bad first tour," Joel told me before I left. "I thought you'd arouse interest. People are ready for something new and hopeful."

I was scared to death, worried about flying and worried about speaking to so many strangers. What if I attracted the wrong kind of attention? How would Len handle the experience? And I worried about Len, who seemed to be even more afraid than I was, especially about flying. I had spent more money than I should have, buying us both decent clothing.

Then Joel and Irma were taking us to the airport in their huge car. One way in which they do indulge themselves is to keep a late-model armed and armored car—a civilian maggot, really. The thing cost as much as a nice house in a good neighborhood, and it's scary-looking enough to intimidate anyone stupid enough to spend their time hijacking vehicles.

"We've never had to use the guns," Irma told me when she showed them to me. "I don't like them. They frighten me. But being without them would frighten me more."

So now Len and I are lecturing and conducting Earthseed Workshops. We're being paid in hard currency, fed well, and allowed to live in good, safe hotels. And we're being welcomed, listened to, even taken seriously by people who are hungry for something to believe in, some difficult but worthwhile goal to involve themselves in and work toward.

We've also been laughed at, argued with, booed, and threatened with hellfire—or gunfire. But Jarret's kind of religion and Jarret himself are getting less and less popular these days. Both, it seems, are bad for business, bad for the U.S. Constitution, and bad for a large percentage of the population. They always have been, but now more and more people are willing to say so in public. The Crusaders have terrorized some people into silence, but they've just made others very angry.

And I'm finding more and more people who have the leisure now to worry about the nasty, downward slide that the country's been on. In the 2020s, when these people were sick, starving, or trying to keep warm, they had no time or energy to look beyond their own desperate situations. Now, though, as they're more able to meet their own immediate needs, they begin to look around, feel dissatisfied with the slow pace of change, and with Jarret, who with his war and his Crusaders, has slowed it even more. I suppose it would have been different if we'd won the war.

Anyway, some of these dissatisfied people are finding what they want and need in Earthseed. They're the ones who come to me and ask, "What can I do? I believe. Now how can I help?"

So I've begun to reach people. I've reached so many people from Eureka to Seattle to Syracuse that I believe that even if I were killed tomorrow, some of these people would find ways to go on learning and teaching, pursuing the Destiny. Earthseed will go on. It will grow. It will force us to become the strong, purposeful, adaptable people that we must become if we're to grow enough to fulfill the Destiny.

I know things will go wrong now and then. Religions are no more perfect than any other human institutions. But Earthseed will fulfill its essential purpose. *It will force us to become more than we might ever become without it.* And when it's successful, it will offer us a kind of species life insurance. I wish I could live to see that success. I wish I could be one of those who go out to take root among the stars. I can only hope that my Larkin will go—or perhaps some of her children, or even Marc's children.

Whatever happens, as long as I'm alive, I won't stop working, preaching, aiming people toward the Destiny. I've always known that sharing Earthseed was my only true purpose.

OCTAVIA E. BUTLER

EPILOGUE

○ ○ ○

From EARTHSEED: THE BOOKS OF THE LIVING

Earthseed is adulthood.
It's trying our wings,
Leaving our mother,
Becoming men and women.

We've been children,
Fighting for the full breasts,
The protective embrace,
The soft lap.
Children do this.
But Earthseed is adulthood.

Adulthood is both sweet and sad.
It terrifies.
It empowers.
We are men and women now.
We are Earthseed.
And the Destiny of Earthseed
Is to take root among the stars.

Uncle Marc was, in the end, my only family.

I never saw Kayce and Madison again. I sent them money when they were older and in need, and I hired people to look after them, but I never went back to them. They did their duty toward me and I did mine toward them.

My mother, when I finally met her, was still a drifter. She was immensely rich—or, at least, Earthseed was immensely rich. But she had no home of her own—not even a rented apartment. She drifted between the homes of her many friends and supporters, and between the many Earthseed Communities that she established or encouraged in the United States, Canada, Alaska, Mexico, and Brazil. And she went on teaching, preaching, fund-raising, and spreading her political influence. I met her when she visited a New York Earthseed community in the Adirondacks—a place called Red Spruce.

In fact, she went to Red Spruce to rest. She had been traveling and speaking steadily for several months, and she needed a place where she could be quiet and think. I know this because it was what people kept telling me when I tried to reach her. The community protected her privacy so well that for a while, I was afraid I might never get to see her. I'd read that she usually traveled with only an acolyte or two and, sometimes, a bodyguard, but now it seemed that everyone in the community had decided to guard her.

By then, I was 34, and I wanted very much to meet her. My friends and Uncle Marc's housekeeper, had told me how much I looked like this charismatic, dangerous, heathen cult leader. I had paid no attention until, in researching Lauren Olamina's life, I discovered that she had had a child, a daughter, and that that daughter had been abducted from an early Earthseed community called Acorn.

The community, according to Olamina's official biography, had been destroyed by Jarret's Crusaders back in the 30s. Its men and women had been enslaved for over a year by the Crusaders, and all the prepubescent children had been abducted. Most had never been seen again.

The Church of Christian America had denied this and sued Olamina and Earthseed back in the 2040s when Olamina's charge first came to their attention. The church was still powerful, even though Jarret was dead by then. The rumors were that Jarret, after his single term as President, drank himself to death. A coalition of angry business people, protestors against the Al-Can War, and champions of the First Amendment worked hard to defeat him for re-election in 2036. They won by exposing some of the earliest Christian American witch-burnings. It seems that between 2015 and 2019, Jarret himself took part in singling people out and burning them alive. The Pox, then a growing malignancy, had been both the excuse and the cover for this. Jarret and his friends had burned accused prostitutes, drug dealers, and junkies. Also, in their enthusiasm, they burned some innocent people—people who had nothing to do with the sex trade or drugs. When that happened, Jarret's people covered their "mistakes" with denials, threats, more terror, and occasional pay-offs to the bereaved families. Uncle Marc researched this himself several years ago, and he says it's true—true and sad and wrong, and in the end, irrelevant. He says Jarret's teachings were right even if the man himself did wrong.

Anyway, the Church of Christian America sued Olamina for her "false" accusations. She countersued. Then suddenly, without explanation, CA dropped its suit and settled with her, paying her an unreported, but reputedly vast some of money. I was still a kid growing up with the Alexanders when all this happened, and I heard nothing about it. Years later, when I began to research Earthseed and Olamina, I didn't know what to think of it.

I phoned Uncle Marc and asked him, point-blank, whether there was any possibility that this woman could be my mother.

On my phone's tiny monitor, Uncle Marc's face froze, then seemed to sag. He suddenly looked much older than his 54 years. He said, "I'll talk to you about this when I come home." And he broke the connection. He wouldn't take my calls after that. He had never refused my calls before. Never.

Not knowing what else to do, where else to turn, I checked the nets to see where Lauren Olamina might be speaking or organizing. To my surprise, I learned that she was "resting" at Red Spruce, less than a hundred kilometers from where I was.

And all of a sudden, I had to see her.

I didn't try to phone her, didn't try to reach her with Uncle Marc's well-known name or my own name as a creator of several popular Masks. I just showed up at Red Spruce, rented a room at their guest house, and began trying to find her. Earthseed doesn't bother with a lot of formality. Anyone can visit its communities and rent a room at a guest house. Visitors came to see relatives who were members, came to attend Gatherings or other ceremonies, even came to join Earthseed and arrange to begin their probationary first year.

I told the manager of the guest house that I thought I might be a relative of Olamina's and asked him if he could tell me how I might make an appointment to speak with her. I asked him because I had heard people call him "Shaper" and I recognized that from my reading as a title of respect akin to "reverend" or "minister." If he was the community's minister, he might be able to introduce me to Olamina himself.

Perhaps he could have, but he refused. Shaper Olamina was very tired, and not to be bothered, he told me. If I wanted to meet her, I should attend one of her Gatherings or phone her headquarters in Eureka, California, and arrange an appointment.

I had to hang around the community for three days before I could find anyone willing to take my message to her. I didn't see her. No one would even tell me where she was staying within the community. They protected her from me courteously, firmly. Then, all of a sudden, the wall around her gave way. I met one of her acolytes and he took my message to her.

My messenger was a thin, brown-haired young man who said his name was Edison Balter. I met him in the guest-house dining room one morning as we each sat alone, eating bagels and drinking apple cider. I pounced on him as someone I hadn't pestered yet. I had no idea at that time what the Balter name meant to my mother or that this man was an adopted son of one of her best friends. I was only relieved that someone was listening to me, not closing one more door in my face.

"I'm her aide this trip," he told me. "She says I'm just about ready to go out on my own, and the idea scares the hell out of me. What name shall I give her?"

"Asha Vere."

"Oh? Are you the Asha Vere who does Dreamasks?"

I nodded.

"Nice work. I'll tell her. You want to put her in one of your Masks? You know you do look a lot like her. Like a softer version of her." And he was gone. He talked fast and moved very fast, but somehow without seeming to hurry. He didn't look anything like Olamina himself, but there was a similarity. I found that I liked him at once—just as I'd at first found myself liking her. Another likable cultist. I got the feeling that Red Spruce, a clean, pretty mountain community, was nothing but a nest of seductively colorful snakes—a poisonous place.

Then Edison Balter came back and told me he would take me to her. She was somewhere in her fifties—58, I remembered from my reading. She was born way back in 2009, before the Pox. My god. She was old. But she didn't look old, even though her black hair was streaked with gray. She looked big and strong and, in spite of her pleasant, welcoming expression, just a little frightening. She was a little taller than me, and maybe a little more angular. She looked . . . not hard, but as though she could be hard with just the smallest change of expression. She looked like someone I wouldn't want to get on the wrong side of. And, yes, even I could see it. She looked like me.

She and I just stood looking at one another for a long, long time. After a while, she came up to me, took my left hand, and turned it to look at the two little moles I have just below the knuckles. My impulse was to pull away, but I managed not to.

She stared at the moles for a while, then said, "Do you have another mark—a kind of jagged dark patch just here?" She touched a place covered by my blouse on my left shoulder near my neck.

This time, I did step away from her touch. I didn't mean to, but I just don't like to be touched. Not even by a stranger who might be my mother. I said, "I have a birthmark like that, yes."

"Yes," she whispered, and went on looking at me. After a moment, she said, "Sit down. Sit here with me. You are my child, my daughter. I know you are."

I sat in a chair instead of sharing the couch with her. She was open and welcoming, and somehow, that made me want all the more to draw back.

"Have you only just found out?" she asked.

I nodded, tried to speak, and found myself stumbling and stammering. "I came here because I thought . . . maybe . . . because I looked up information about you, and I was curious. I mean, I read about Earthseed, and people said I looked like you, and . . . well, I knew I was adopted, so I wondered."

"So you had adoptive parents. Were they good to you? What's your life been like? What do you. . . ." She stopped, drew a deep breath, covered her face with both hands for a moment, shook her head, then gave a short laugh. "I want to know everything! I can't believe that it's you. I. . . . " Tears began to stream down her broad, dark face. She leaned toward me, and I knew she wanted to hug me. She hugged people. She touched people. She hadn't been raised by Kayce and Madison Alexander.

I looked away from her and shifted around trying to get comfortable in my chair, in my skin, in my newfound identity. "Can we do a gene print?" I asked.

"Yes. Today. Now." She took a phone from her pocket and called someone. No more than a minute later, a woman dressed all in blue came in carrying a small plastic case. She drew a small amount of blood from each of us, and checked it in a portable diagnostic from her case. The unit wasn't much bigger than Olamina's phone. In less than a minute, though, it spit out two gene prints. They were rough and incomplete, but even I could see both their many differences and their many unmistakably identical points.

"You're close relatives," the woman said. "Anyone would guess that just from looking at you, but this confirms it."

"We're mother and daughter," Olamina said.

"Yes," the woman in blue agreed. She was my mother's age or older—a Puerto Rican woman by her accent. She had not a strand of gray in her black hair, but her face was Lined and old. "I had heard, Shaper, that you had a daughter who was lost. And now you've found her."

"She's found me," my mother said.

"God is Change," the woman said, and gathered her equipment. She hugged my mother before she left us. She looked at me, but didn't hug me. "Welcome," she said to me in soft Spanish, and then again, "God is Change." And she was gone.

"Shape God," my mother whispered in a response that sounded both reflexive and religious.

Then we talked.

"I had parents." I said. "Kayce and Madison Alexander. I. . . . We didn't get along. I haven't seen them since I turned 18. They said, 'If you Leave without getting married, don't come back!' So I didn't. Then I found Uncle Marc, and I finally—"

She stood up, staring down at me, staring with such a closed look frozen on her face. It shut me out, that look, and I wondered whether this was what she was really like—cold, distant, unfeeling. Did she only pretend to be warm and open to deceive her public?

"When?" she demanded, and her tone was as cold as her expression. "When did you find Marc? When did you learn that he was your uncle? How did you find out? Tell me!"

I stared at her. She stared back for a moment, then began to pace. She walked to a window, faced it for several seconds, staring out at the mountains. Then she came back to look down at me with what I could only think of as quieter eyes.

"Please tell me about your life," she said. "You probably know some-thing about mine because so much has been written. But I know nothing about yours. Please tell me."

Irrationally, I didn't want to. I wanted to get away from her. She was one of those people who sucked you in, made you like her before you could even get to know her, and only then let you see what she might really be like. She had millions of people convinced that they were going to fly off to the stars. How much money had she taken from them while they waited for the ship to Alpha Centauri? My god, I didn't want to like her. I wanted the ugly persona I had glimpsed to be what she really was. I wanted to despise her.

Instead, I told her the story of my life.

Then we had dinner together, just her and me. A woman who might have been a servant, a bodyguard, or the lady of the house brought in a tray for us.

Then my mother told me the story of my birth, my father, my abduction. Hearing about it from her wasn't like reading an impersonal account. I listened and cried. I couldn't help it.

"What did Marc tell you?" she asked.

I hesitated, not sure what to say. In the end, I told the truth just because I couldn't think of a decent lie. "He said you were dead—that both my mother and my father were dead."

She groaned.

"He . . . he took care of me," I said. "He saw to it that I got to go to college, and that I had a good place to live. He and I . . . well, we're a family. We didn't have anyone before we found one another."

She just looked at me.

"I don't know why he told me you were dead. Maybe he was just . . . lonely. I don't know. We got along, he and I, right from the first. I still live in one of his houses. I can afford a place of my own now, but it's like I said. We're a family." I paused, then said something I had never admitted before. "You know, I never felt that anyone loved me before I met him. And I guess I never loved anyone until he loved me. He made it . . . safe to love him back."

"Your father and I both loved you," she said. "We had tried for two years to have a baby. We worried about his age. We worried about the way the world was—all the chaos. But we wanted you so much. And when you were born, we loved you more than you can imagine. When you were taken, and your father was killed . . . I felt for a while as though I'd died myself. I tried so hard for so long to find you."

I didn't know what to say to that. I shrugged uncomfortably. She hadn't found me. And Uncle Marc had. I wondered just how hard she'd really looked.

"I didn't even know whether you were still alive," she said. "I wanted to believe you were, but I didn't know. I got involved in a lawsuit with Christian America back in the forties, and I tried to force them to tell me what had happened to you. They claimed that any record there may have been of you was lost in a fire an the Pelican Bay Children's Home years before."

Had they said that? I supposed they might have. They would have said almost anything to avoid giving up evidence of their abductions—and giving a Christian American child back to a heathen cult leader. But still, "Uncle Marc says he found me when I was two or three years old," I said. "But he saw that I had good Christian American parents, and he thought it would be best for me to stay with them, undisturbed." I shouldn't have said that. I'm not sure why I did.

She got up and began to walk again—quick, angry pacing, prowling the room. "I never thought he would do that to me," she said. "I never thought he hated me enough to do a thing like that. I never thought he could hate *anyone* that much. I saved him from slavery! I saved his worthless life, goddamnit!"

"He doesn't hate you," I said. "I'm sure he doesn't. I've never known him to hate anyone. He thought he was doing right."

"Don't defend him," she whispered. "I know you love him, but don't defend him to me. I loved him myself, and see what he's done to me—and to you."

"You're a cult leader," I said. "He's Christian American. He believed—"

"I don't care! I've spoken with him hundreds of times since he found you, and he said nothing. Nothing!"

"He doesn't have any children." I said. "I don't think he ever will. But I was like a daughter to him. He was like a father to me."

She stopped her pacing and stood staring down at me with an almost frightening intensity. She stared at me as though she hated me.

I stood up, looked around for my jacket, found it, and put it on.

"No!" she said. "No, don't go." All the stiffness and rage went out of her. "Please don't go. Not yet."

But I needed to go. She is an overwhelming person, and I needed to get away from her.

"All right," she said when I headed for the door. "But you can always come to me. Come back tomorrow. Come back whenever you want to. We have so much time to make up for. My door is open to you, Larkin, always."

I stopped and looked back at her, realizing that she had called me by the name that she had given to her baby daughter so long ago. "Asha," I said, looking back at her. "My name is Asha Vere."

She looked confused. Then her face seemed to sag the way Uncle Marc's had when I phoned him to ask about her. She looked so hurt and sad that I couldn't stop myself from feeling sorry for her. "Asha," she whispered. "My door is open to you, Asha. Always."

The next day Uncle Marc arrived, filled with fear and despair.

"I'm sorry," he said to me as soon as he saw me. "I was so happy when I found you after you left your parents. I was so glad to be able to help you with your education. I guess . . . I had been alone so long that I just couldn't stand to share you with anyone."

My mother would not see him. He came to me almost in tears because he had tried to see her and she had refused. He tried several more times, and over and over again, she sent people out to tell him to go away.

I went back home with him. I was angry with him, but even angrier with her, somehow. I loved him more than I'd ever loved anyone no matter what he had done, and she was hurting him. I didn't know whether I would ever see her again. I didn't know whether I should. I didn't even know whether I wanted to.

My mother lived to be 81.

She kept her word. She never stopped teaching. For Earthseed, she used herself up several times over speaking, training, guiding, writing, establishing schools that boarded orphans as well as students who had parents and homes. She found sources of money and directed them into areas of study that brought the fulfillment of the Earthseed Destiny closer. She sent promising young students to universities that helped them to fulfill their own potential.

All that she did, she did for Earthseed. I did see her again occasionally, but Earthseed was her first "child," and in some ways her only "child."

She was planning a Lecture tour when her heart stopped just after her eighty-first birthday. She saw the first shuttles leave for the first starship assembled partly on the Moon and partly in orbit. I was not on any of the shuttles, of course. Neither was Uncle Marc, and neither of us has children.

But Justin Gilchrist was on that ship. He shouldn't have been at his age, of course, but he was. And the son of Jessica Faircloth has gone, ironically. He's a biologist. The Mora girls, their children, and the whole surviving Douglas family have gone. They, in particular, were her family. All Earthseed was her family. We never really were, Uncle Marc and I. She never really needed us, so we didn't let ourselves need her. Here is the last journal entry of hers that seems to apply to her long, narrow story.

From *THE JOURNALS OF LAUREN OYA OLAMINA*
THURSDAY, JULY 20, 2090

I know what I've done.

I have not given them heaven, but I've helped them to give themselves the heavens. I can't give them individual immortality, but I've helped them to give our species its only chance at immortality. I've helped them to the next stage of growth. They're young adults now, leaving the nest. It will be rough on them out there. It's always rough on the young when they leave the protection of the mother. It will take a toll—perhaps a heavy one. I don't like to think about that, but I know it's true. Out there, though, among the stars on the living worlds we already know about and on other worlds that we haven't yet dreamed of, some will survive and change and thrive and some will suffer and die.

Earthseed was always true. I've made it real, given it substance. Not that I ever had a choice in the matter. If you want a thing—truly want it, want it so badly that you need it as you need air to breathe, then unless you die, you will have it. Why not? It has you. There is no escape. What a cruel and terrible thing escape would be if escape were possible.

The shuttles are fat, squat, ugly, ancient-looking space trucks. They look as though they could be a hundred years old. They're very different from the early ones under the skin, of course. The skin itself is substantially different. But except for being larger, today's space shuttles don't look that different from those a hundred years ago. I've seen pictures of the old ones.

Today's shuttles have been loaded with cargoes of people, already deeply asleep in DiaPause—the suspended-animation process that seems to be the best of the bunch. Traveling with the people are frozen human and animal embryos, plant seeds, tools, equipment, memories, dreams, and hopes. As big and as spaceworthy as they are, the shuttles should sag to the Earth under such a load. The memories alone should overload them. The libraries of the Earth go with them. All this is to be off-loaded on the Earth's first starship, the *Christopher Columbus*.

I object to the name. This ship is not about a shortcut to riches and empire. It's not about snatching up slaves and gold and presenting them to some European monarch. But one can't win every battle. One must know which battles to fight. The name is nothing.

I couldn't have watched this first Departure on a screen or in a virtual room or in some personalized version beneath a Dreamask. I would have traveled across the world on foot to see this Departure if I'd had to. This is my life flying away on these ugly big trucks. This is my immortality. I have a right to see it, hear the thunder of it, smell it.

I will go with the first ship to leave after my death. If I thought I could survive as something other than a burden, I would go on this one, alive. No matter. Let them someday use my ashes to fertilize their crops. Let them do that. It's arranged. I'll go, and they'll give me to their orchards and their groves.

Now, with my friends and the children of my friends, I watch. Lacy Figueroa, Myra Cho, Edison Balter and his daughter, Jan, and Harry Balter, bent, gray, and smiling. It took Harry so long to learn to smile again after the loss of Zahra and the children. He's a man who should smile. He stands with one arm around his granddaughter and the other around me. He's my age. Eighty-one. Impossible. Eighty-one! God is Change.

My Larkin would not come. I begged her, but she refused. She's caring for Marc. He's just getting over another heart transplant. How completely, how thoroughly he has stolen my child. I have never even tried to forgive him.

Now, I watch as, one by one, the ships lift their cargoes from the Earth. I feel alone with my thoughts until I reach out to hug each of my friends and look into their loved faces, this one solemn, that one joyous, all of them wet with tears. Except for Harry, they'll all go soon in these same shuttles. Perhaps Harry's ashes and mine will keep company someday. The Destiny of Earthseed is to take root among the stars, after all, and not to be filled with preservative poisons, boxed up at great expense, as is the revived fashion now, and buried uselessly in some cemetery.

I know what I've done.

For the kingdom of heaven is as a man traveling into a far country, who called his own servants, and delivered unto them his goods. And unto one he gave five talents, to another two, and to another one; to every man according to his several ability; and straightway took his journey.

Then he that had received the five talents went and traded with the same and made them other five talents. And likewise he that had received two, he also gained other two. But he that had received one went and digged in the earth and hid his lord's money.

After a long time the lord of these servants cometh, and reck-

oneth with them. And so he that had received five talents came and brought the other five talents, saying, Lord, thou deliverest unto me five talents: behold, I have gained beside them five talents more.

His lord said unto him, Well done, thou good and faithful servant: thou hast been faithful over a few things, I will make thee ruler over many things: enter thou into the joy of thy lord.

He also that had received two talents came and said, Lord, thou deliverdst unto me two talents: behold, I have gained two other talents beside them.

His lord said unto him, Well done, thou good and faithful servant: thou hast been faithful over a few things, I will make thee ruler over many things: enter thou into the joy of thy lord.

Then he which had received the one talent came and said, Lord, I knew thee that thou art an hard man, reaping where thou hast not sown, and gathering where thou has not strawed: And I was afraid and went and hid thy talent in the earth: lo, there thou hast what is thine.

His lord answered and said unto him, Thou wicked and slothful servant, thou knewest that I reap where I sowed not, and gather where I have not strawed: Thou oughtest therefore to have put my money to the exchangers and then at my coming I should have received mine own with usury.

Take therefore the talent from him and give it unto him which hath ten talents. For unto every one that hath shall be given, and he shall have abundance: but from him that hath not shall be taken away even that which he hath.

THE BIBLE
AUTHORIZED KING JAMES VERSION
ST. MATTHEW 25: 14 - 30

A writer who darkly imagined the future we have destined for ourselves in book after book, and also one who has shown us the way toward improving on that dismal fate, OCTAVIA E. BUTLER (1947–2006) is recognized as among the bravest and smartest of contemporary fiction writers. A 1995 MacArthur Award winner, Butler transcended the science fiction category even as she was awarded that community's top prizes, the Nebula and Hugo Awards. She reaches readers of all ages, all races, and all religious and sexual persuasions. For years the only African-American woman writing science fiction, Butler has encouraged many others to follow in her path.

TOSHI REAGON is a singer, musician, composer, producer, and curator. She has toured nationally and internationally with her band, Toshi Reagon and BIGLovely, and in 2011 she started the community festival Word*Rock & Sword: A Festival Exploration of Women's Lives as an answer to the escalation of legislative violence against and criminalization of women. Her next project is *Octavia E. Butler's Parable of the Sower*, an opera set to debut in the fall of 2017.

ABOUT SEVEN STORIES PRESS

SEVEN STORIES PRESS is an independent book publisher based in New York City. We publish works of the imagination by such writers as Nelson Algren, Russell Banks, Octavia E. Butler, Ani DiFranco, Assia Djebar, Ariel Dorfman, Coco Fusco, Barry Gifford, Martha Long, Luis Negrón, Hwang Sok-yong, Lee Stringer, and Kurt Vonnegut, to name a few, together with political titles by voices of conscience, including Subhankar Banerjee, the Boston Women's Health Collective, Noam Chomsky, Angela Y. Davis, Human Rights Watch, Derrick Jensen, Ralph Nader, Loretta Napoleoni, Gary Null, Greg Palast, Project Censored, Barbara Seaman, Alice Walker, Gary Webb, and Howard Zinn, among many others. Seven Stories Press believes publishers have a special responsibility to defend free speech and human rights, and to celebrate the gifts of the human imagination, wherever we can. In 2012 we launched Triangle Square books for young readers with strong social justice and narrative components, telling personal stories of courage and commitment. For additional information, visit www.sevenstories.com.

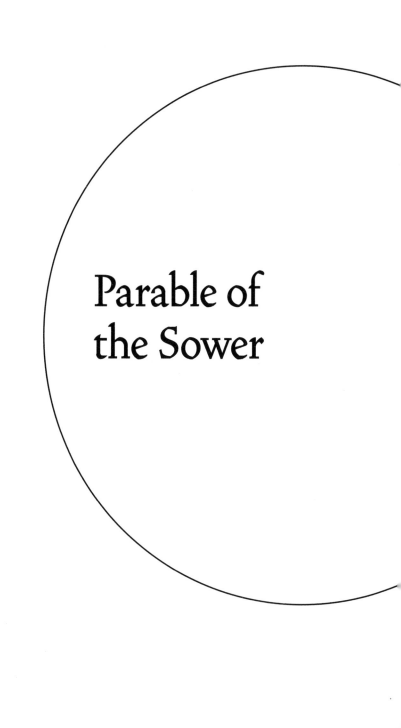

Parable of
the Sower

BOOKS BY OCTAVIA E. BUTLER

Fledgling
Parable of the Talents
Parable of the Sower
Lilith's Brood
Dawn
Adulthood Rites
Imago
Seed to Harvest
Wild Seed
Mind of My Mind
Clay's Ark
Patternmaster
Kindred
Survivor
Bloodchild and Other Stories

OCTAVIA E. BUTLER

Parable of the Sower

GLORIA STEINEM
introduction

Seven Stories Press
NEW YORK • OAKLAND

Copyright © 1993 by Octavia E. Butler
Introduction © 2016 by Gloria Steinem. Reprinted by permission.

Seven Stories Press
140 Watts Street
New York, NY 10013
www.sevenstories.com

Library of Congress Cataloging-in-Publication Data

Names: Butler, Octavia E., author.
Title: Parable of the sower : a novel / Octavia E. Butler.
Description: Seven Stories Press edition. | New Yokr : Seven Stories Press,
   [2016]
Identifiers: LCCN 2016033091 | ISBN 9781609807191 (hardcover)
Subjects: LCSH: African Americans--Fiction. | Twenty-first century--Fiction.
   | California, Southern--Fiction. | BISAC: FICTION / Science Fiction /
   General. | FICTION / Literary. | GSAFD: Science fiction.
Classification: LCC PS3552.U827 P37 2016 | DDC 813/.54--dc23
LC record available at https://lccn.loc.gov/2016033091

Printed in the USA.

19 18 17 16 15 14 13 12

Introduction

by Gloria Steinem

If there is one thing scarier than a dystopian novel about the future, it's one written in the past that has already begun to come true. This is what makes *Parable of the Sower* even more impressive than it was when first published.

Twenty-five years ago, the great Octavia Butler wrote this first volume of what was to be a trilogy. She died at the tragically early age of fifty-eight, but we are lucky to have this novel and its sequel, *Parable of the Talents*. Its title refers to the biblical verse that describes not the seed, but the differing grounds it falls on; a challenge to readers who will be the ground for seeds of warning.

Its story begins in a future California that has become divided into three overlapping worlds: the powerful who own and control water, electricity, and the growth of food; the struggling middle population of those who live in walled communities, protect themselves with guns, and do their best to hang on to an order of the past; and the homeless, illiterate, dying, and prostituted of the city streets and countryside who rob the living and scavenge among unburied corpses that lie wherever they fell.

In all these worlds, water costs more than gasoline, police and firefighters serve only those who can pay, literacy is rare enough to be a marketable skill, designer drugs compel an obsession with fire, and no one is safe from robbery or rape or burning despite arms, walls, locked gates, and layers of protection.

It is in this middle population in walled communities, struggling to preserve a past order, that we meet a teenager named Lauren. She is our narrator. She is smart and subject to hope and fear, friends and betrayals. She is also afflicted with hyperempathy syndrome, something she inherited from her drug-addicted mother. It causes her to feel the pain of any living being around her, including animals, yet the pain may be so great that it immobilizes her and she cannot help the one who is suffering. Hyperempathy can become so painful that she helps the sufferer to die; Butler is no romantic about the cost of empathy. In Lauren's own complicated life, we see her first with her family, then, as she loses them and begins to walk north through lawless territory, with a lover and disparate friends, then, as a leader who not only keeps the group together, but refuses to abandon them in order to be safer herself. She also is a poet who imagines the future. In a book called *Earthseed: The Book of the Living*, she tells us what was to be the theme of Butler's book: "The destiny of the human race is to migrate to other planets and star systems."

This does not mean I'm giving away the story. Events will hook you anyway by their immediacy, intimacy, and odd resonance with what we are already experiencing. In fact, you may find yourself carrying the plot forward in your mind long after you put the book down. For Butler, the future depends not only on a mega-force like global warming—which is depicted here in gradual and frightening reality of long droughts and then floods—but also on human behavior. She makes very clear that human behavior caused global warming, not the other way around; at least, not until it was almost too late. Unlike many in science fiction, but like such feminist science fiction writers as Joanna Russ, Ursula LeGuin, and Marge Piercy, Butler doesn't just create a future based on new science and new technology, she also shows the results of old human behavior that guides them.

In a science fiction world that was, in her lifetime, mostly by and for white male writers and readers, Octavia Butler has always been considered an oddity. She herself felt uniquely well suited. As she explained: "I'm black, I'm solitary, I've always been an outsider." Her characters are young and old, Latina, African American, and more, all in the most natural and uniquely American of ways.

When young Lauren starts walking cross-country to save her future life, for instance, there is an echo of enslaved Africans walking north to save their lives in the past. In defining God, her characters come up with the idea that God is Change, the Truth of Life.

It's not surprising that Octavia Butler became the first science fiction writer ever to receive a MacArthur "Genius" Award; or that she inspired millions of readers who had never seen themselves in science fiction or future fantasy before; or that African American science fiction writers, mostly but not only women, cite her as their almost sole inspiration; or that the science fiction books she read as a child were given to her mother by families who employed her as a maid; or that she now has been translated and read in countries around the world; or that her own life sounds like science fiction.

But as she often pointed out, what she wrote was neither science nor fiction, because "All struggles are essentially power struggles. Who will rule? Who will lead? Who will define, refine, confine, design?"

Octavia Butler was playing out our very real possibilities as humans. I think she can help each of us to do the same.

Parable of
the Sower

2024

❑ ❑ ❑

Prodigy is, at its essence, adaptability and persistent, positive obsession. Without persistence, what remains is an enthusiasm of the moment. Without adaptability, what remains may be channeled into destructive fanaticism. Without positive obsession, there is nothing at all.

EARTHSEED: THE BOOKS OF THE LIVING
by Lauren Oya Olamina

1

☐ ☐ ☐

All that you touch
You Change.

All that you Change
Changes you.

The only lasting truth
Is Change.

God
Is Change.

EARTHSEED: THE BOOKS OF THE LIVING
SATURDAY, JULY 20, 2024

I had my recurring dream last night. I guess I should have expected it. It comes to me when I struggle—when I twist on my own personal hook and try to pretend that nothing unusual is happening. It comes to me when I try to be my father's daughter.

Today is our birthday—my fifteenth and my father's fifty-fifth. Tomorrow, I'll try to please him—him and the community and God. So last night, I dreamed a reminder that it's all a lie. I think I need to write about the dream because this particular lie bothers me so much.

I'm learning to fly, to levitate myself. No one is teaching me. I'm just learning on my own, little by little, dream lesson by dream lesson. Not a very subtle image, but a persistent one. I've had many

13

lessons, and I'm better at flying than I used to be. I trust my ability more now, but I'm still afraid. I can't quite control my directions yet.

I lean forward toward the doorway. It's a doorway like the one between my room and the hall. It seems to be a long way from me, but I lean toward it. Holding my body stiff and tense, I let go of whatever I'm grasping, whatever has kept me from rising or falling so far. And I lean into the air, straining upward, not moving upward, but not quite falling down either. Then I do begin to move, as though to slide on the air drifting a few feet above the floor, caught between terror and joy.

I drift toward the doorway. Cool, pale light glows from it. Then I slide a little to the right; and a little more. I can see that I'm going to miss the door and hit the wall beside it, but I can't stop or turn. I drift away from the door, away from the cool glow into another light.

The wall before me is burning. Fire has sprung from nowhere, has eaten in through the wall, has begun to reach toward me, reach for me. The fire spreads. I drift into it. It blazes up around me. I thrash and scramble and try to swim back out of it, grabbing handfuls of air and fire, kicking, burning! Darkness.

Perhaps I awake a little. I do sometimes when the fire swallows me. That's bad. When I wake up all the way, I can't get back to sleep. I try, but I've never been able to.

This time I don't wake up all the way. I fade into the second part of the dream—the part that's ordinary and real, the part that did happen years ago when I was little, though at the time it didn't seem to matter.

Darkness.

Darkness brightening.

Stars.

Stars casting their cool, pale, glinting light.

"We couldn't see so many stars when I was little," my stepmother says to me. She speaks in Spanish, her own first language. She stands still and small, looking up at the broad sweep of the Milky Way. She

OCTAVIA E. BUTLER

and I have gone out after dark to take the washing down from the clothesline. The day has been hot, as usual, and we both like the cool darkness of early night. There's no moon, but we can see very well. The sky is full of stars.

The neighborhood wall is a massive, looming presence nearby. I see it as a crouching animal, perhaps about to spring, more threatening than protective. But my stepmother is there, and she isn't afraid. I stay close to her. I'm seven years old.

I look up at the stars and the deep, black sky. "Why couldn't you see the stars?" I ask her. "Everyone can see them." I speak in Spanish, too, as she's taught me. It's an intimacy somehow.

"City lights," she says. "Lights, progress, growth, all those things we're too hot and too poor to bother with anymore." She pauses. "When I was your age, my mother told me that the stars—the few stars we could see—were windows into heaven. Windows for God to look through to keep an eye on us. I believed her for almost a year." My stepmother hands me an armload of my youngest brother's diapers. I take them, walk back toward the house where she has left her big wicker laundry basket, and pile the diapers atop the rest of the clothes. The basket is full. I look to see that my stepmother is not watching me, then let myself fall backward onto the soft mound of stiff, clean clothes. For a moment, the fall is like floating.

I lie there, looking up at the stars. I pick out some of the constellations and name the stars that make them up. I've learned them from an astronomy book that belonged to my father's mother.

I see the sudden light streak of a meteor flashing westward across the sky. I stare after it, hoping to see another. Then my stepmother calls me and I go back to her.

"There are city lights now," I say to her. "They don't hide the stars."

She shakes her head. "There aren't anywhere near as many as there were. Kids today have no idea what a blaze of light cities used to be—and not that long ago."

"I'd rather have the stars," I say.

"The stars are free." She shrugs. "I'd rather have the city lights back myself, the sooner the better. But we can afford the stars."

2

□ □ □

A gift of God
May sear unready fingers.

EARTHSEED: THE BOOKS OF THE LIVING
SUNDAY, JULY 21, 2024

At least three years ago, my father's God stopped being my God. His church stopped being my church. And yet, today, because I'm a coward, I let myself be initiated into that church. I let my father baptize me in all three names of that God who isn't mine anymore.

My God has another name.

We got up early this morning because we had to go across town to church. Most Sundays, Dad holds church services in our front rooms. He's a Baptist minister, and even though not all of the people who live within our neighborhood walls are Baptists, those who feel the need to go to church are glad to come to us. That way they don't have to risk going outside where things are so dangerous and crazy. It's bad enough that some people—my father for one—have to go out to work at least once a week. None of us goes out to school anymore. Adults get nervous about kids going outside.

But today was special. For today, my father made arrangements with another minister—a friend of his who still had a real church building with a real baptistery.

Dad once had a church just a few blocks outside our wall. He began it before there were so many walls. But after it had been slept in by the homeless, robbed, and vandalized several times, someone poured gasoline in and around it and burned it down. Seven of the homeless people sleeping inside on that last night burned with it.

17

But somehow, Dad's friend Reverend Robinson has managed to keep his church from being destroyed. We rode our bikes to it this morning—me, two of my brothers, four other neighborhood kids who were ready to be baptized, plus my father and some other neighborhood adults riding shotgun. All the adults were armed. That's the rule. Go out in a bunch, and go armed.

The alternative was to be baptized in the bathtub at home. That would have been cheaper and safer and fine with me. I said so, but no one paid attention to me. To the adults, going outside to a real church was like stepping back into the good old days when there were churches all over the place and too many lights and gasoline was for fueling cars and trucks instead of for torching things. They never miss a chance to relive the good old days or to tell kids how great it's going to be when the country gets back on its feet and good times come back.

Yeah.

To us kids—most of us—the trip was just an adventure, an excuse to go outside the wall. We would be baptized out of duty or as a kind of insurance, but most of us aren't that much concerned with religion. I am, but then I have a different religion.

"Why take chances," Silvia Dunn said to me a few days ago. "Maybe there's something to all this religion stuff." Her parents thought there was, so she was with us.

My brother Keith who was also with us didn't share any of my beliefs. He just didn't care. Dad wanted him to be baptized, so what the hell. There wasn't much that Keith did care about. He liked to hang out with his friends and pretend to be grown up, dodge work and dodge school and dodge church. He's only twelve, the oldest of my three brothers. I don't like him much, but he's my stepmother's favorite. Three smart sons and one dumb one, and it's the dumb one she loves best.

Keith looked around more than anyone as we rode. His ambition, if you could call it that, is to get out of the neighborhood and go to

OCTAVIA E. BUTLER

Los Angeles. He's never too clear about what he'll do there. He just wants to go to the big city and make big money. According to my father, the big city is a carcass covered with too many maggots. I think he's right, though not all the maggots are in L.A. They're here, too.

But maggots tend not to be early-morning types. We rode past people stretched out, sleeping on the sidewalks, and a few just waking up, but they paid no attention to us. I saw at least three people who weren't going to wake up again, ever. One of them was headless. I caught myself looking around for the head. After that, I tried not to look around at all.

A woman, young, naked, and filthy stumbled along past us. I got a look at her slack expression and realized that she was dazed or drunk or something.

Maybe she had been raped so much that she was crazy. I'd heard stories of that happening. Or maybe she was just high on drugs. The boys in our group almost fell off their bikes, staring at her. What wonderful religious thoughts they would be having for a while.

The naked woman never looked at us. I glanced back after we'd passed her and saw that she had settled down in the weeds against someone else's neighborhood wall.

A lot of our ride was along one neighborhood wall after another; some a block long, some two blocks, some five. . . . Up toward the hills there were walled estates—one big house and a lot of shacky little dependencies where the servants lived. We didn't pass anything like that today. In fact we passed a couple of neighborhoods so poor that their walls were made up of unmortared rocks, chunks of concrete, and trash. Then there were the pitiful, unwalled residential areas. A lot of the houses were trashed—burned, vandalized, infested with drunks or druggies or squatted in by homeless families with their filthy, gaunt, half-naked children. Their kids were wide awake and watching us this morning. I feel sorry for the little ones, but the ones my age and older make me nervous. We ride down the middle of the cracked street, and the kids come out and stand along the curb to stare at us. They just stand and stare. I think if there were only one or two of us, or if they couldn't see our guns, they might try to pull us down and steal our bikes, our clothes, our shoes, whatever. Then what? Rape? Murder? We could wind up like that naked woman, stumbling along, dazed, maybe hurt, sure to attract dangerous attention unless she could steal some clothing. I wish we could have given her something.

My stepmother says she and my father stopped to help an injured woman once, and the guys who had injured her jumped out from behind a wall and almost killed them.

And we're in Robledo—20 miles from Los Angeles, and, according to Dad, once a rich, green, unwalled little city that he had been eager to abandon when he was a young man. Like Keith, he had wanted to escape the dullness of Robledo for big city excitement. L.A. was better then—less lethal. He lived there for 21 years. Then in 2010, his parents were murdered and he inherited their house. Whoever killed them had robbed the house and smashed up the furniture, but they didn't torch anything. There was no neighborhood wall back then.

Crazy to live without a wall to protect you. Even in Robledo, most of the street poor—squatters, winos, junkies, homeless people in general—are dangerous. They're desperate or crazy or both. That's enough to make anyone dangerous.

Worse for me, they often have things wrong with them. They cut off each other's ears, arms, legs. . . . They carry untreated diseases and festering wounds. They have no money to spend on water to wash with so even the unwounded have sores. They don't get enough to eat so they're malnourished—or they eat bad food and poison themselves. As I rode, I tried not to look around at them, but I couldn't help seeing—collecting—some of their general misery.

I can take a lot of pain without falling apart. I've had to learn to do that. But it was hard, today, to keep pedaling and keep up with the others when just about everyone I saw made me feel worse and worse.

My father glanced back at me every now and then. He tells me, "You can beat this thing. You don't have to give in to it." He has always pretended, or perhaps believed, that my hyperempathy syndrome was something I could shake off and forget about. The sharing isn't real, after all. It isn't some magic or ESP that allows me to share the pain or the pleasure of other people. It's delusional. Even I admit that. My brother Keith used to pretend to be hurt just to trick me into sharing his supposed pain. Once he used red ink as fake blood to make me bleed. I was eleven then, and I still bled through the skin when I saw someone else bleeding. I couldn't help doing it, and I always worried that it would give me away to people outside the family.

I haven't shared bleeding with anyone since I was twelve and got my first period. What a relief that was. I just wish all the rest of it had gone away, too. Keith only tricked me into bleeding that once, and I beat the hell out of him for it. I didn't fight much when I was little because it hurt me so. I felt every blow that I struck, just as though I'd hit myself. So when I did decide that I had to fight, I set out to hurt the other kid more than kids usually hurt one another. I broke Michael Talcott's arm and Rubin Quintanilla's nose. I knocked out four of Silvia Dunn's teeth. They all earned what I did to them two or three times over. I got punished every time, and I resented it. It was double punishment, after all, and my father and stepmother knew it. But knowing didn't stop them. I think they did it to satisfy the other kids' parents. But when I beat up Keith, I knew that Cory or Dad or both of them would punish me for it—my poor little brother, after all. So I had to see that my poor little brother paid in advance. What I did to him had to be worthwhile in spite of what they would do to me.

It was.

We both got it later from Dad—me for hurting a younger kid and

Keith for risking putting "family business" into the street. Dad is big on privacy and "family business." There's a whole range of things we never even hint about outside the family. First among these is anything about my mother, my hyperempathy, and how the two are connected. To my father, the whole business is shameful. He's a preacher and a professor and a dean. A first wife who was a drug addict and a daughter who is drug damaged is not something he wants to boast about. Lucky for me. Being the most vulnerable person I know is damned sure not something I want to boast about.

I can't do a thing about my hyperempathy, no matter what Dad thinks or wants or wishes. I feel what I see others feeling or what I believe they feel. Hyperempathy is what the doctors call an "organic delusional syndrome." Big shit. It hurts, that's all I know. Thanks to Paracetco, the small pill, the Einstein powder, the particular drug my mother chose to abuse before my birth killed her, I'm crazy. I get a lot of grief that doesn't belong to me, and that isn't real. But it hurts.

I'm supposed to share pleasure *and* pain, but there isn't much pleasure around these days. About the only pleasure I've found that I enjoy sharing is sex. I get the guy's good feeling and my own. I almost wish I didn't. I live in a tiny, walled fish-bowl cul-de-sac community, and I'm the preacher's daughter. There's a real limit to what I can do as far as sex goes.

Anyway, my neurotransmitters are scrambled and they're going to stay scrambled. But I can do okay as long as other people don't know about me. Inside our neighborhood walls I do fine. Our rides today, though, were hell. Going and coming, they were all the worst things I've ever felt—shadows and ghosts, twists and jabs of unexpected pain.

If I don't look too long at old injuries, they don't hurt me too much. There was a naked little boy whose skin was a mass of big red sores; a man with a huge scab over the stump where his right hand used to be; a little girl, naked, maybe seven years old with blood running down her bare thighs. A woman with a swollen, bloody, beaten face. . . .

OCTAVIA E. BUTLER

I must have seemed jumpy. I glanced around like a bird, not letting my gaze rest on anyone longer than it took me to see that they weren't coming in my direction or aiming anything at me.

Dad may have read something of what I was feeling in my expression. I try not to let my face show anything, but he's good at reading me. Sometimes people say I look grim or angry. Better to have them think that than know the truth. Better to have them think anything than let them know just how easy it is to hurt me.

Dad had insisted on fresh, clean, potable water for the baptism. He couldn't afford it, of course. Who could? That was the other reason for the four extra kids:

Silvia Dunn, Hector Quintanilla, Curtis Talcott, and Drew Balter, along with my brothers Keith and Marcus. The other kids' parents had helped with costs. They thought a proper baptism was important enough to spend some money and take some risks. I was the oldest by about two months. Curtis was next. As much as I hated being there, I hated even more that Curtis was there. I care about him more than I want to. I care what he thinks of me. I worry that I'll fall apart in public some day and he'll see. But not today.

By the time we reached the fortress-church, my jaw-muscles hurt from clinching and unclinching my teeth, and overall, I was exhausted.

There were only five or six dozen people at the service—enough to fill up our front rooms at home and look like a big crowd. At the church, though, with its surrounding wall and its security bars and Lazor wire and its huge hollowness inside, and its armed guards, the crowd seemed a tiny scattering of people. That was all right. The last thing I wanted was a big audience to maybe trip me up with pain.

The baptism went just as planned. They sent us kids off to the bathrooms ("men's," "women's," "please do not put paper of any kind into toilets," "water for washing in bucket at left. . . .") to undress and put on white gowns. When we were ready, Curtis's father took us to an anteroom where we could hear the preaching—from the first chapter of Saint John and the second chapter of The Acts—and wait our turns.

My turn came last. I assume that was my father's idea. First the neighbor kids, then my brothers, then me. For reasons that don't make a lot of sense to me, Dad thinks I need more humility. I think my particular biological humility—or humiliation—is more than enough.

What the hell? Someone had to be last. I just wish I could have been courageous enough to skip the thing altogether.

So, "In the name of the Father, the Son, and the Holy Ghost. . . ." Catholics get this stuff over with when they're babies. I wish Baptists did. I almost wish I could believe it was important the way a lot of people seem to, the way my father seems to. Failing that, I wish I didn't care.

But I do. The idea of God is much on my mind these days. I've been paying attention to what other people believe—whether they believe, and if so what kind of God they believe in. Keith says God is just the adults' way of trying to scare you into doing what they want. He doesn't say that around Dad, but he says it. He believes in what he sees, and no matter what's in front of him, he doesn't see much. I suppose Dad would say that about me if he knew what I believe. Maybe he'd be right. But it wouldn't stop me from seeing what I see.

A lot of people seem to believe in a big-daddy-God or a big-cop-God or a big-king-God. They believe in a kind of super-person. A few believe God is another word for nature. And nature turns out to mean just about anything they happen not to understand or feel in control of.

Some say God is a spirit, a force, an ultimate reality. Ask seven people what all of that means and you'll get seven different answers. So what is God? Just another name for whatever makes you feel special and protected?

There's a big, early-season storm blowing itself out in the Gulf of

OCTAVIA E. BUTLER

Mexico. It's bounced around the Gulf, killing people from Florida to Texas and down into Mexico. There are over 700 known dead so far. One hurricane. And how many people has it hurt? How many are going to starve later because of destroyed crops? That's nature. Is it God? Most of the dead are the street poor who have nowhere to go and who don't hear the warnings until it's too late for their feet to take them to safety. Where's safety for them anyway? Is it a sin against God to be poor? We're almost poor ourselves. There are fewer and fewer jobs among us, more of us being born, more kids growing up with nothing to look forward to. One way or another, we'll all be poor some day. The adults say things will get better, but they never have. How will God—my father's God—behave toward us when we're poor?

Is there a God? If there is, does he (she? it?) care about us? Deists like Benjamin Franklin and Thomas Jefferson believed God was something that made us, then left us on our own.

"Misguided," Dad said when I asked him about Deists. "They should have had more faith in what their Bibles told them."

I wonder if the people on the Gulf Coast still have faith. People have had faith through horrible disasters before. I read a lot about that kind of thing. I read a lot period. My favorite book of the Bible is Job. I think it says more about my father's God in particular and gods in general than anything else I've ever read.

In the book of Job, God says he made everything and he knows everything so no one has any right to question what he does with any of it. Okay. That works. That Old Testament God doesn't violate the way things are now. But that God sounds a lot like Zeus—a super-powerful man, playing with his toys the way my youngest brothers play with toy soldiers. Bang, bang! Seven toys fall dead. If they're yours, you make the rules. Who cares what the toys think. Wipe out a toy's family, then give it a brand new family. Toy children, like Job's children, are interchangeable.

Maybe God is a kind of big kid, playing with his toys. If he is,

what difference does it make if 700 people get killed in a hurricane—
or if seven kids go to church and get dipped in a big tank of expensive water?

But what if all that is wrong? What if God is something else altogether?

OCTAVIA E. BUTLER

3

□ □ □

We do not worship God.
We perceive and attend God.
We learn from God.
With forethought and work,
We shape God.
In the end, we yield to God.
We adapt and endure,
For we are Earthseed
And God is Change.

EARTHSEED: THE BOOKS OF THE LIVING
TUESDAY, JULY 30, 2024

One of the astronauts on the latest Mars mission has been killed. Something went wrong with her protective suit and the rest of her team couldn't get her back to the shelter in time to save her. People here in the neighborhood are saying she had no business going to Mars, anyway. All that money wasted on another crazy space trip when so many people here on earth can't afford water, food, or shelter.

The cost of water has gone up again. And I heard on the news today that more water peddlers are being killed. Peddlers sell water to squatters and the street poor—and to people who've managed to hold on to their homes, but not to pay their utility bills. Peddlers are being found with their throats cut and their money and their handtrucks stolen. Dad says water now costs several times as much as gasoline. But, except for arsonists and the rich, most people have given up buying gasoline. No one I know uses a gas-powered car, truck, or cycle. Vehicles like that are rusting in driveways and being cannibalized for metal and plastic.

It's a lot harder to give up water.

Fashion helps. You're supposed to be dirty now. If you're clean, you make a target of yourself. People think you're showing off, trying to be better than they are. Among the younger kids, being clean is a great way to start a fight. Cory won't let us stay dirty here in the neighborhood, but we all have filthy clothes to wear outside the walls. Even inside, my brothers throw dirt on themselves as soon as they get away from the house. It's better than getting beaten up all the time.

Tonight the last big Window Wall television in the neighborhood went dark for good. We saw the dead astronaut with all of red, rocky Mars around her. We saw a dust-dry reservoir and three dead water peddlers with their dirty-blue armbands and their heads cut halfway off. And we saw whole blocks of boarded up buildings burning in Los Angeles. Of course, no one would waste water trying to put such fires out.

Then the Window went dark. The sound had flickered up and down for months, but the picture was always as promised—like looking through a vast, open window.

The Yannis family has made a business of having people in to look through their Window. Dad says that kind of unlicensed business isn't legal, but he let us go to watch sometimes because he didn't see any harm in it, and it helped the Yannises. A lot of small businesses are illegal, even though they don't hurt anyone, and they keep a household or two alive. The Yannis Window is about as old as I am. It covers the long west wall of their living room. They must have had plenty of money back when they bought it. For the past couple of years, though, they've been charging admission—only letting in people from the neighborhood—and selling fruit, fruit juice, acorn bread, or walnuts. Whatever they had too much of in their garden,

OCTAVIA E. BUTLER

they found a way to sell. They showed movies from their library and let us watch news and whatever else was broadcast. They couldn't afford to subscribe to any of the new multisensory stuff, and their old Window couldn't have received most of it, anyway.

They have no reality vests, no touch-rings, and no headsets. Their setup was just a plain, thin-screened Window.

All we have left now are three small, ancient, murky little TV sets scattered around the neighborhood, a couple of computers used for work, and radios. Every household still has at least one working radio. A lot of our everyday news is from radio.

I wonder what Mrs. Yannis will do now. Her two sisters have moved in with her, and they're working so maybe it will be all right. One is a pharmacist and the other is a nurse. They don't earn much, but Mrs. Yannis owns the house free and clear. It was her parents' house.

All three sisters are widows and between them they have twelve kids, all younger than I am. Two years ago, Mr. Yannis, a dentist, was killed while riding his electric cycle home from the walled, guarded clinic where he worked. Mrs. Yannis says he was caught in a crossfire, hit from two directions, then shot once more at close range. His bike was stolen. The police investigated, collected their fee, and couldn't find a thing. People get killed like that all the time. Unless it happens in front of a police station, there are never any witnesses.

SATURDAY, AUGUST 3, 2024

The dead astronaut is going to be brought back to Earth. She wanted to be buried on Mars. She said that when she realized she was dying. She said Mars was the one thing she had wanted all her life, and now she would be part of it forever.

But the Secretary of Astronautics says no. He says her body might be a contaminant. Idiot.

Can he believe that any microorganism living in or on her body would have a prayer of surviving and going native in that cold, thin, lethal ghost of an atmosphere? Maybe he can. Secretaries of Astronautics don't have to know much about science. They have to know about politics. Theirs is the youngest Cabinet department, and already it's fighting for its life. Christopher Morpeth Donner, one of the men running for President this year, has promised to abolish it if he's elected. My father agrees with Donner.

"Bread and circuses," my father says when there's space news on the radio. "Politicians and big corporations get the bread, and we get the circuses."

"Space could be our future," I say. I believe that. As far as I'm concerned, space exploration and colonization are among the few things left over from the last century that can help us more than they hurt us. It's hard to get anyone to see that, though, when there's so much suffering going on just outside our walls.

Dad just looks at me and shakes his head. "You don't understand," he says. "You don't have any idea what a criminal waste of time and money that so-called space program is." He's going to vote for Donner. He's the only person I know who's going to vote at all. Most people have given up on politicians. After all, politicians have been promising to return us to the glory, wealth, and order of the twentieth century ever since I can remember. That's what the space program is about these days, at least for politicians. Hey, we can run a space station, a station on the moon, and soon, a colony on Mars. That proves we're still a great, forward-looking, powerful nation, right?

Yeah.

Well, we're barely a nation at all anymore, but I'm glad we're still in space. We have to be going some place other than down the toilet.

And I'm sorry that astronaut will be brought back from her own chosen heaven. Her name was Alicia Catalina Godinez Leal. She was a chemist. I intend to remember her. I think she can be a kind of model for me. She spent her life heading for Mars—preparing herself, becoming an astronaut, getting on a Mars crew, going to Mars, beginning to figure out how to terraform Mars, beginning to create sheltered places where people can live and work now. . . .

Mars is a rock—cold, empty, almost airless, dead. Yet it's heaven in a way. We can see it in the night sky, a whole other world, but too nearby, too close within the reach of the people who've made such a hell of life here on Earth.

MONDAY, AUGUST 12, 2024

Mrs. Sims shot herself today—or rather, she shot herself a few days ago, and Cory and Dad found her today. Cory went a little crazy for a while afterward.

Poor, sanctimonious, old Mrs. Sims. She used to sit in our front-room church every Sunday, large-print Bible in hand, and shout out her responses: "Yes, Lord!" "Hallelujah!" "Thank you, Jesus!" "Amen!" During the rest of the week she sewed, made baskets, took care of her garden, sold what she could from it, took care of pre-school children, and talked about everyone who wasn't as holy as she thought she was.

She was the only person I've ever known who lived alone. She had a whole big house to herself because she and the wife of her only son hated each other. Her son and his family were poor, but they wouldn't live with her. Too bad.

Different people frightened her in some deep, hard, ugly way. She didn't like the Hsu family because they were Chinese and His-panic, and the older Chinese generation is still Buddhist. She's lived a couple of doors up from them for longer than I've been alive, but they were still from Saturn as far as she was concerned.

"Idolaters," she would call them if none of them were around. At least she cared enough about neighborly relations to do her talking about them behind their backs. They brought her peaches and figs and a length of good cotton cloth last month when she was robbed.

That robbery was Mrs. Sims's first major tragedy. Three men

climbed over the neighborhood wall, cutting through the strands of barbed wire and Lazor wire on top. Lazor wire is terrible stuff. It's so fine and sharp that it slices into the wings or feet of birds who either don't see it or see it and try to settle on it. People, though, can always find a way over, under, or through.

Everyone brought Mrs. Sims things after the robbery, in spite of the way she is. Was. Food, clothing, money. . . . We took up collections for her at church. The thieves had tied her up and left her—after one of them raped her. An old lady like that! They grabbed all her food, her jewelry that had once belonged to her mother, her clothes, and worst of all, her supply of cash. It turns out she kept that—all of it—in a blue plastic mixing bowl high up in her kitchen cabinet. Poor, crazy old lady. She came to my father, crying and carrying on after the robbery because now she couldn't buy the extra food she needed to supplement what she grew. She couldn't pay her utility bills or her upcoming property taxes. She would be thrown out of her house into the street! She would starve!

Dad told her over and over that the church would never let that happen, but she didn't believe him. She talked on and on about having to be a beggar now, while Dad and Cory tried to reassure her. The funny thing is, she didn't like us either because Dad had gone and married "that Mexican woman Cory-ah-zan." It just isn't that hard to say "Corazon" if that's what you choose to call her. Most people just call her Cory or Mrs. Olamina.

Cory never let on that she was offended. She and Mrs. Sims were sugary sweet to one another. A little more hypocrisy to keep the peace.

Last week Mrs. Sims's son, his five kids, his wife, her brother, and her brother's three kids all died in a house fire—an arson fire. The son's house had been in an unwalled area north and east of us, closer to the foothills. It wasn't a bad area, but it was poor. Naked. One night someone torched the house. Maybe it was a vengeance fire set by some enemy of a family member or maybe some crazy just set it

OCTAVIA E. BUTLER

for fun. I've heard there's a new illegal drug that makes people want to set fires.

Anyway, no one knows who did it to the Sims/Boyer families. No one saw anything, of course.

And no one got out of the house. Odd, that. Eleven people, and no one got out.

So about three days ago, Mrs. Sims shot herself. Dad said he'd heard from the cops that it was about three days ago. That would have been just two days after she heard about her son's death. Dad went to see her this morning because she missed church yesterday. Cory forced herself to go along because she thought she should. I wish she hadn't. To me, dead bodies are disgusting. They stink, and if they're old enough, there are maggots. But what the hell? They're dead. They aren't suffering, and if you didn't like them when they were alive, why get so upset about their being dead? Cory gets upset. She jumps on me for sharing pain with the living, but she tries to share it with the dead.

I began writing this about Mrs. Sims because she killed herself. That's what's upset me. She believed, like Dad, that if you kill yourself, you go to hell and burn forever. She believed in a literal acceptance of everything in the Bible. Yet, when things got to be too much for her, she decided to trade pain for eternal pain in the hereafter.

How could she do that?

Did she really believe in anything at all? Was it all hypocrisy?

Or maybe she just went crazy because her God was demanding too much of her. She was no Job. In real life, how many people are?

SATURDAY, AUGUST 17, 2024

I can't get Mrs. Sims out of my mind. Somehow, she and her suicide have gotten tangled up with the astronaut and her death and her expulsion from heaven. I need to write about what I believe. I need to begin to put together the scattered verses that I've been writing about God since I was twelve. Most of them aren't much good. They say what I need to say, but they don't say it very well. A few are the way they should be. They press on me, too, like the two deaths. I try to hide in all the work there is to do here for the household, for my father's church, and for the school Cory keeps to teach the neighborhood kids. The truth is, I don't care about any of those things, but they keep me busy and make me tired, and most of the time, I sleep without dreaming. And Dad beams when people tell him how smart and industrious I am.

I love him. He's the best person l know, and I care what he thinks. I wish I didn't, but I do.

For whatever it's worth, here's what I believe. It took me a lot of time to understand it, then a lot more time with a dictionary and a thesaurus to say it just right—just the way it has to be. In the past year, it's gone through twenty-five or thirty lumpy, incoherent rewrites. This is the right one, the true one. This is the one I keep coming back to:

> *God is Power—*
> *Infinite,*
> *Irresistible,*
> *Inexorable,*
> *Indifferent.*
> *And yet, God is Pliable—*
> *Trickster,*
> *Teacher,*
> *Chaos,*
> *Clay.*
> *God exists to be shaped.*
> *God is Change.*

This is the literal truth.
God can't be resisted or stopped, but can be shaped and focused.

This means God is not to be prayed to. Prayers only help the person doing the praying, and then, only if they strengthen and focus that person's resolve. If they're used that way, they can help us in our only real relationship with God. They help us to shape God and to accept and work with the shapes that God imposes on us. God is power, and in the end, God prevails.

But we can rig the game in our own favor if we understand that God exists to be shaped, and will be shaped, with or without our forethought, with or without our intent.

That's what I know. That's some of it anyway. I'm not like Mrs. Sims. I'm not some kind of potential Job, long suffering, stiff necked, then, at last, either humble before an all-knowing almighty, or destroyed. My God doesn't love me or hate me or watch over me or know me at all, and I feel no love for or loyalty to my God. My God just is.

Maybe I'll be more like Alicia Leal, the astronaut. Like her, I believe in something that I think my dying, denying, backward-looking people need. I don't have all of it yet. I don't even know how to pass on what I do have. I've got to learn to do that. It scares me how many things I've got to learn. How will I learn them?

Is any of this real?

Dangerous question. Sometimes I don't know the answer. I doubt myself. I doubt what I think I know. I try to forget about it. After all, if it's real, why doesn't anyone else know about it? Everyone knows that change is inevitable. From the second law of thermodynamics to Darwinian evolution, from Buddhism's insistence that nothing is permanent and all suffering results from our delusions of permanence to the third chapter of Ecclesiastes ("To everything there is a season . . . ."), change is part of life, of existence, of the common wisdom. But I don't believe we're dealing with all that that means. We haven't even begun to deal with it.

We give lip service to acceptance, as though acceptance were enough. Then we go on to create super-people—super-parents, super-kings and queens, super-cops—to be our gods and to look after us—to stand between us and God. Yet God has been here all along, shaping us and being shaped by us in no particular way or in too many ways at once like an amoeba—or like a cancer. Chaos.

Even so, why can't I do what others have done—ignore the obvious. Live a normal life. It's hard enough just to do that in this world.

But this thing (this idea? Philosophy? New religion?) won't let me alone, won't let me forget it, won't let me go. Maybe. . . . Maybe it's like my sharing: One more weirdness; one more crazy, deep-rooted delusion that I'm stuck with. I am stuck with it. And in time, I'll have to do something about it. In spite of what my father will say or do to me, in spite of the poisonous rottenness outside the wall where I might be exiled, I'll have to do something about it.

That reality scares me to death.

WEDNESDAY, NOVEMBER 6, 2024

President William Turner Smith lost yesterday's election. Christopher Charles Morpeth Donner is our new President—President-elect. So what are we in for? Donner has already said that as soon as possible after his inauguration next year, he'll begin to dismantle the "wasteful, pointless, unnecessary" moon and Mars programs. Near space programs dealing with communications and experimentation will be privatized—sold off.

Also, Donner has a plan for putting people back to work. He hopes to get laws changed, suspend "overly restrictive" minimum wage, environmental, and worker protection laws for those employers willing to take on homeless employees and provide them with training and adequate room and board.

What's adequate, I wonder: A house or apartment? A room? A bed in a shared room? A barracks bed? Space on a floor? Space on the ground? And what about people with big families? Won't they be seen as bad investments? Won't it make much more sense for companies to hire single people, childless couples, or, at most, people with only one or two kids? I wonder.

And what about those suspended laws? Will it be legal to poison, mutilate, or infect people—as long as you provide them with food, water, and space to die?

Dad decided not to vote for Donner after all. He didn't vote for anyone. He said politicians turned his stomach.

2025

□ □ □

Intelligence is ongoing, individual adaptability.
Adaptations that an intelligent species may make in
a single generation, other species make over many
generations of selective breeding and selective dying.
Yet intelligence is demanding. If it is misdirected by
accident or by intent, it can foster its own orgies of
breeding and dying.

EARTHSEED: THE BOOKS OF THE LIVING

4

□ □ □

A victim of God may,
Through learning adaption,
Become a partner of God,
A victim of God may,
Through forethought and planning,
Become a shaper of God.
Or a victim of God may,
Through shortsightedness and fear,
Remain God's victim,
God's plaything,
God's prey.

EARTHSEED: THE BOOKS OF THE LIVING
SATURDAY, FEBRUARY 1, 2025

We had a fire today. People worry so much about fire, but the little kids will play with it if they can. We were lucky with this fire. Amy Dunn, three years old, managed to start it in her family's garage.

Once the fire began to crawl up the wall, Amy got scared and ran into the house. She knew she had done something bad, so she didn't tell anyone. She hid under her grandmother's bed.

Out back, the dry wood of the garage burned fast and hot. Robin Balter saw the smoke and rang the emergency bell on the island in our street. Robin's only ten, but she's a bright little kid— one of my stepmother's star students. She keeps her head. If she hadn't alerted people as soon as she saw the smoke, the fire could have spread.

I heard the bell and ran out like everyone else to see what was wrong. The Dunns live across the street from us, so I couldn't miss the smoke.

The fire plan worked the way it was supposed to. The adult men and women put the fire out with garden hoses, shovels, wet towels and blankets. Those without hoses beat at the edges of the fire and smothered them with dirt. Kids my age helped out where we were needed and put out any new fires started by flying embers. We brought buckets to fill with water, and shovels, blankets, and towels of our own. There were a lot of us, and we kept our eyes open. The very old people watched the little kids and kept them out of the way and out of trouble.

No one missed Amy. No one had seen her in the Dunn backyard, so no one thought about her. Her grandmother found her much later and got the truth out of her.

The garage was a total loss. Edwin Dunn salvaged some of his garden and carpentry equipment, but not much. The grapefruit tree next to the garage and the two peach trees behind it were half-burned, too, but they might survive. The carrot, squash, collard, and potato plants were a trampled mess.

Of course, no one called the fire department. No one would take on fire service fees just to save an unoccupied garage. Most of our households couldn't afford another big bill, anyway. The water wasted on putting out the fire was going to be hard enough to pay for.

What will happen, I wonder, to poor little Amy Dunn. No one cares about her. Her family feeds her and, now and then, cleans her up, but they don't love her or even like her. Her mother Tracy is only a year older than I am. She was 13 when Amy was born. She was 12 when her 27-year-old uncle who had been raping her for years managed to make her pregnant.

Problem: Uncle Derek was a big, blond, handsome guy, funny and bright and well-liked. Tracy was, is, dull and homely, sulky and dirty-looking. Even when she's clean, she looks splotchy, dirty. Some of her problems might have come from being raped by Uncle Derek

OCTAVIA E. BUTLER

for years. Uncle Derek was Tracy's mother's youngest brother, her favorite brother, but when people realized what he had been doing, the neighborhood men got together and suggested he go live somewhere else. People didn't want him around their daughters. Irrational as usual, Tracy's mother blamed Tracy for his exile, and for her own embarrassment. Not many girls in the neighborhood have babies before they drag some boy to my father and have him unite them in holy matrimony. But there was no one to marry Tracy, and no money for prenatal care or an abortion. And poor Amy, as she grew, looked more and more like Tracy: scrawny and splotchy with sparse, stringy hair. I don't think she'll ever be pretty.

Tracy's maternal instincts didn't kick in, and I doubt that her mother Christmas Dunn has any. The Dunn family has a reputation for craziness. There are sixteen of them living in the Dunn house, and at least a third are nuts. Amy isn't crazy, though. Not yet. She's neglected and lonely, and like any little kid left on her own too much, she finds ways to amuse herself.

I've never seen anyone hit Amy or curse her or anything like that. The Dunns do care what people think of them. But no one pays any attention to her, either. She spends most of her time playing alone in the dirt. She also eats the dirt and whatever she finds in it, including bugs. But not long ago, just out of curiosity, I took her to our house, sponged her off, taught her the alphabet, and showed her how to write her name. She loved it. She's got a hungry, able little mind, and she loves attention.

Tonight I asked Cory if Amy could start school early. Cory doesn't take kids until they're five or close to five, but she said she'd let Amy in if I would take charge of her. I expected that, though I don't like it. I help with the five- and six-year-olds, anyway. I've been taking care of little kids since I was one, and I'm tired of it. I think, though, that if someone doesn't help Amy now, someday she'll do something a lot worse than burning down her family's garage.

Some cousins of old Mrs. Sims have inherited her house. They're lucky there's still a house to inherit. If it weren't for our wall, the house would have been gutted, taken over by squatters, or torched as soon as it was empty. As it was, all people did was take back things they had given to Mrs. Sims after she was robbed, and take whatever food she had in the house. No sense letting it rot. We didn't take her furniture or her rugs or her appliances. We could have, but we didn't. We aren't thieves.

Wardell Parrish and Rosalee Payne think otherwise. They're both small, rust-brown, sour-looking people like Mrs. Sims. They're the children of a first cousin that Mrs. Sims had managed to keep contact and good relations with. He's a widower twice over, no kids, and she's been widowed once, seven kids. They're not only brother and sister, but twins. Maybe that helps them get along with each other. They damn sure won't get along with anyone else.

They're moving in today. They've been here a couple of times before to look the place over, and I guess they must have liked it better than their parents' house. They shared that with 18 other people. I was busy in the den with my class of younger school kids, so I didn't meet them until today, though I've heard Dad talking to them—heard them sit in our living room and insinuate that we had cleaned out Mrs. Sims's house before they arrived.

Dad kept his temper. "You know she was robbed during the month before she died," he said. "You can check with the police about that—if you haven't already. Since then the community has protected the house. We haven't used it or stripped it. If you choose to live among us, you should understand that. We help each other, and we don't steal."

"I wouldn't expect you to say you did," Wardell Parrish muttered.

His sister jumped in before he could say more. "We're not accusing anyone of anything," she lied. "We just wondered. . . . We knew

Cousin Marjorie had some nice things—jewelry that she inherited from her mother. . . . Very valuable. . . ."

"Check with the police," my father said.

"Well, yes, I know, but. . . ."

"This is a small community," my father said. "We all know each other here. We depend on each other."

There was a silence. Perhaps the twins were getting the message.

"We're not very social," Wardell Parrish said. "We mind our own business."

Again his sister jumped in before he could go on. "I'm sure everything will be all right," she said. "I'm sure we'll get along fine."

I didn't like them when I heard them. I liked them even less when I met them. They look at us as though we smell and they don't. Of course, it doesn't matter whether I like them or not. There are other people in the neighborhood whom I don't like. But I don't trust the Payne-Parrishes. The kids seem all right, but the adults. . . . I wouldn't want to have to depend on them. Not even for little things.

Payne and Parrish. What perfect names they have.

SATURDAY, FEBRUARY 22, 2025

We ran into a pack of feral dogs today. We went to the hills today for target practice—me, my father, Joanne Garfield, her cousin and boyfriend Harold—Harry—Balter, my boyfriend Curtis Talcott, his brother Michael, Aura Moss and her brother Peter. Our other adult Guardian was Joanne's father Jay. He's a good guy and a good shot. Dad likes to work with him, although sometimes there are problems. The Garfields and the Balters are white, and the rest of us are black. That can be dangerous these days. On the street, people are expected to fear and hate everyone but their own kind, but with all of us armed and watchful, people stared, but they let us alone. Our neighborhood is too small for us to play those kinds of games.

Everything went as usual at first. The Talcotts got into an argument first with each other, then with the Mosses. The Mosses are always blaming other people for whatever they do wrong, so they tend to have disputes outstanding with most of us. Peter Moss is the worst because he's always trying to be like his father, and his father is a total shit. His father has three wives. All at once, Karen, Natalie, and Zahra. They've all got kids by him, though so far, Zahra, the youngest and prettiest, only has one. Karen is the one with the marriage license, but she let him get away with bringing first one, then another new woman into the house and calling them his wives. I guess the way things are, she didn't think she could make it on her own with three kids when he brought in Natalie and five by the time he found Zahra.

The Mosses don't come to church. Richard Moss has put together his own religion—a combination of the Old Testament and historical West African practices. He claims that God wants men to be patriarchs, rulers and protectors of women, and fathers of as many children as possible. He's an engineer for one of the big commercial water companies, so he can afford to pick up beautiful, young homeless women and live with them in polygamous relationships. He could pick up twenty women like that if he could afford to feed them. I hear there's a lot of that kind of thing going on in other neighborhoods. Some middle class men prove they're men by having a lot of wives in temporary or permanent relationships. Some upper class men prove they're men by having one wife and a lot of beautiful, disposable young servant girls. Nasty. When the girls get pregnant, if their rich employers won't protect them, the employers' wives throw them out to starve.

Is that the way it's going to be, I wonder? Is that the future: Large numbers of people stuck in either President-elect Donner's version of slavery or Richard Moss's?

We rode our bikes to the top of River Street past the last neighborhood walls, past the last ragged, unwalled houses, past the last stretch of broken asphalt and rag and stick shacks of squatters and street poor who stare at us in their horrible, empty way, and then higher into the hills along a dirt road. At last we dismounted and walked our bikes down the narrow trail into one of the canyons that we and others use for target practice. It looked all right this time, but we always have to be careful. People use canyons for a lot of things. If we find corpses in one, we stay away from it for a while. Dad tries to shield us from what goes on in the world, but he can't. Knowing that, he also tries to teach us to shield ourselves.

Most of us have practiced at home with BB guns on homemade targets or on squirrel and bird targets. I've done all that. My aim is good, but I don't like it with the birds and squirrels. Dad was the one who insisted on my learning to shoot them. He said moving targets would be good for my aim. I think there was more to it than that. I think he wanted to see whether or not I could do it—whether shooting a bird or a squirrel would trigger my hyperempathy.

It didn't, quite. I didn't like it, but it wasn't painful. It felt like a big, soft, strange ghost blow, like getting hit with a huge ball of air, but with no coolness, no feeling of wind. The blow, though still soft, was a little harder with squirrels and sometimes rats than with birds. All three had to be killed, though. They ate our food or ruined it. Tree-crops were their special victims: Peaches, plums, figs, persimmons, nuts. . . . And crops like strawberries, blackberries, grapes . . . Whatever we planted, if they could get at it, they would. Birds are particular pests because they can fly in, yet I like them. I envy their ability to fly. Sometimes I get up and go out at dawn just so I can watch them without anyone scaring them or shooting them. Now that I'm old enough to go target shooting on Saturdays, I don't intend to shoot anymore birds, no matter what Dad says. Besides, just because I can shoot a bird or a squirrel doesn't mean l could shoot a person—a thief like the ones who robbed Mrs. Sims. I don't know whether I could do that. And if I did it, I don't know what would happen to me. Would I die?

It's my father's fault that we pay so much attention to guns and shooting. He carries a nine millimeter automatic pistol whenever he leaves the neighborhood. He carries it on his hip where people can see it. He says that discourages mistakes. Armed people do get killed—most often in crossfires or by snipers—but unarmed people get killed a lot more often.

Dad also has a silenced nine millimeter submachine gun. It stays at home with Cory in case something happens there while he's away. Both guns are German—Heckler & Koch. Dad has never said where he got the submachine gun. It's illegal, of course, so I don't blame him. It must have cost a hell of a lot. He's only had it away from home a few times so he, Cory, and I could get the feel of it. He'll do the same for the boys when they're older.

Cory has an old Smith & Wesson .38 revolver that she's good with. She's had it since before she married Dad. She loaned that one to me today. Ours aren't the best or the newest guns in the neighborhood, but they all work. Dad and Cory keep them in good condition. I have to help with that now. And they spend the necessary time on practice and money on ammunition.

At neighborhood association meetings, Dad used to push the adults of every household to own weapons, maintain them, and know how to use them. "Know how to use them so well," he's said more than once, "that you're as able to defend yourself at two a.m. as you are at two p.m."

At first there were a few neighbors who didn't like that—older ones who said it was the job of the police to protect them, younger ones who worried that their little children would find their guns, and religious ones who didn't think a minister of the gospel should need guns. This was several years ago.

"The police," my father told them, "may be able to avenge you, but they can't protect you. Things are getting worse. And as for your children. . . . Well, yes, there is risk. But you can put your guns out of their reach while they're very young, and train them as they grow older. That's what I mean to do. I believe they'll have a better chance of growing up if you can protect them." He paused, stared at the people, then went on. "I have a wife and five children," he said. "I will pray for them all. I'll also see to it that they know how to defend themselves. And for as long as I can, I will stand between my family and any intruder." He paused again. "Now that's what I have to do. You all do what you have to do."

By now there are at least two guns in every household. Dad says he suspects that some of them are so well hidden—like Mrs. Sims's gun—that they wouldn't be available in an emergency. He's working on that.

All the kids who attend school at our house get gun handling instruction. Once they've passed that and turned fifteen, two or three of the neighborhood adults begin taking them to the hills for target practice. It's a kind of rite of passage for us. My brother Keith has been whining to go along whenever someone gets a shooting group together, but the age rule is firm.

I worry about the way Keith wants to get his hands on the guns. Dad doesn't seem to worry, but I do.

There are always a few groups of homeless people and packs of feral dogs living out beyond the last hillside shacks. People and dogs hunt rabbits, possums, squirrels, and each other. Both scavenge whatever dies. The dogs used to belong to people—or their ancestors did. But dogs eat meat. These days, no poor or middle class person who had an edible piece of meat would give it to a dog. Rich people still keep dogs, either because they like them or because they use them to guard estates, enclaves, and businesses. The rich have plenty of other security devices, but the dogs are extra insurance. Dogs scare people.

I did some shooting today, and I was leaning against a boulder, watching others shoot, when I realized there was a dog nearby, watching me. Just one dog—male, yellow-brown, sharp-eared, short-haired. He wasn't big enough to make a meal of me, and I still had the Smith & Wesson, so while he was looking me over, I took a good look at him. He was lean, but he didn't look starved. He looked alert and curious. He sniffed the air, and I remembered that dogs were supposed to be oriented more toward scent than sight.

"Look at that," I said to Joanne Garfield who was standing nearby.

She turned, gasped, and jerked her gun up to aim at the dog. The dog vanished into the dry brush and boulders. Turning, Joanne tried to look everywhere as though she expected to see more dogs stalking us, but there was nothing. She was shaking.

"I'm sorry," I said. "I didn't know you were afraid of them."

She drew a deep breath and looked at the place where the dog had been. "I didn't know I was either," she whispered. "I've never been so close to one before. I . . . I wish I had gotten a better look at it."

At that moment, Aura Moss screamed and fired her father's Llama automatic.

I pushed away from the boulder and turned to see Aura pointing her gun toward some rocks and babbling.

"It was over there!" she said, her words tumbling over one another. "It was some kind of animal—dirty yellow with big teeth. It had its mouth open. It was huge!"

"You stupid bitch, you almost shot me!" Michael Talcott shouted. I could see now that he had ducked down behind a boulder. He would have been in Aura's line of fire, but he didn't seem to be hurt.

"Put your gun away, Aura," my father said. He kept his voice low, but he was angry. I could see that, whether Aura could or not.

"It was an animal," she insisted. "A big one. It might still be around."

"Aura!" My father raised his voice and hardened it.

Aura looked at him, then seemed to realize that she had more than a dog to worry about. She looked at the gun in her hand, frowned, fumbled it safe, and put it back into her holster.

"Mike?" my father said.

"I'm okay," Michael Talcott said. "No thanks to her!"

"It wasn't my fault," Aura said, right on cue. "There was an animal. It could have killed you! It was sneaking up on us!"

"I think it was just a dog," I said. "There was one watching us over here. Joanne moved and it ran away."

"You should have killed it," Peter Moss said. "What do you want to do? Wait until it jumps someone."

"What was it doing?" Jay Garfield asked. "Just watching?"

"That's all," I said. "It didn't look sick or starved. It wasn't very big. I don't think it was a danger to anyone here. There are too many of us, and we're all too big."

"The thing I saw was huge," Aura insisted. "It had its mouth open!"

I went over to her because I'd had a sudden thought. "It was panting," I said. "They pant when they're hot. It doesn't mean they're angry or hungry." I hesitated, watching her. "You've never seen one before, have you?"

She shook her head.

"They're bold, but they're not dangerous to a group like this. You don't have to worry."

She didn't look as though she quite believed me, but she seemed to relax a little. The Moss girls were both bullied and sheltered. They were almost never allowed to leave the walls of the neighborhood. They were educated at home by their mothers according to the religion their father had assembled, and they were warned away from the sin and contamination of the rest of the world. I'm surprised that Aura was allowed to come to us for gun handling instruction and target practice. I hope it will be good for her—and I hope the rest of us will survive.

"All of you stay where you are," Dad said. He glanced at Jay Garfield, then went a short way up among the rocks and scrub oaks to see whether Aura had shot anything. He kept his gun in his hand and the safety off. He was out of our sight for no more than a minute.

He came back with a look on his face that I couldn't read. "Put your guns away," he said. "We're going home."

"Did I kill it?" Aura demanded.

"No. Get your bikes." He and Jay Garfield whispered together for a moment, and Jay Garfield sighed. Joanne and I watched them, wondering, knowing we wouldn't hear anything from them until they were ready to tell us.

"This is not about a dead dog," Harold Balter said behind us. Joanne moved back to stand beside him.

"It's about either a dog pack or a human pack," I said, "or maybe it's a corpse."

It was, as I found out later, a family of corpses: A woman, a little boy of about four years, and a just-born infant, all partly eaten. But Dad didn't tell me that until we got home. At the canyon, all we knew was that he was upset.

"If there were a corpse around here, we would have smelled it," Harry said.

"Not if it were fresh," I countered.

Joanne looked at me and sighed the way her father sighs. "If it's that, I wonder where we'll go shooting next time. I wonder when there'll be a next time."

Peter Moss and the Talcott brothers had gotten into an argument over whose fault it was that Aura had almost shot Michael, and Dad had to break it up. Then Dad checked with Aura to see that she was all right. He said a few things to her that I couldn't hear, and I saw a tear slide down her face. She cries easily. She always has.

Dad walked away from her looking harassed. He led us up the path out of the canyon. We walked our bikes, and we all kept looking around. We could see now that there were other dogs nearby. We were being watched by a big pack. Jay Garfield brought up the rear, guarding our backs.

"He said we should stick together," Joanne told me. She had seen me looking back at her father.

"You and I?"

"Yeah, and Harry. He said we should look out for one another."

"I don't think these dogs are stupid enough or hungry enough to attack us in daylight. They'll go after some lone street person tonight."

"Shut up, for godsake."

The road was narrow going up and out of the canyon. It would have been a bad place to have to fight off dogs. Someone could trip and step off the crumbling edge. Someone could be knocked off the edge by a dog or by one of us. That would mean falling several hundred feet.

Down below, I could hear dogs fighting now. We may have been close to their dens or whatever they lived in. I thought maybe we were just close to what they were feeding on.

"If they come," my father said in a quiet, even voice, "freeze, aim, and fire. That will save you. Nothing else will. Freeze, aim, and fire. Keep your eyes open and stay calm."

I replayed the words in my mind as we went up the switchbacks. No doubt Dad wanted us to replay them. I could see that Aura was still leaking tears and smearing and streaking her face with dirt like a little kid. She was too wrapped up in her own misery and fear to be of much use.

We got almost to the top before anything happened. We were beginning to relax, I think. I hadn't seen a dog for a while. Then, from the front of our line, we heard three shots.

We all froze, most of us unable to see what had happened.

"Keep moving," my father called. "It's all right. It was just one dog getting too close."

"Are you okay?" I called.

"Yes," he said. "Just come on and keep your eyes open."

One by one, we came abreast of the dog that had been shot and walked past it. It was a bigger, grayer animal than the one I had seen. There was a beauty to it. It looked like pictures I had seen of wolves. It was wedged against a hanging boulder just a few steps up the steep canyon wall from us.

It moved.

I saw its bloody wounds as it twisted. I bit my tongue as the pain I knew it must feel became my pain. What to do? Keep walking? I couldn't. One more step and I would fall and lie in the dirt, helpless against the pain. Or I might fall into the canyon.

"It's still alive," Joanne said behind me. "It's moving."

Its forefeet were making little running motions, its claws scraping against the rock.

I thought I would throw up. My belly hurt more and more until I felt skewered through the middle. I leaned on my bike with my left arm. With my right hand, I drew the Smith & Wesson, aimed, and shot the beautiful dog through its head.

I felt the impact of the bullet as a hard, solid blow—something beyond pain. Then I felt the dog die. I saw it jerk, shudder, stretch its body long, then freeze. I saw it die. I felt it die. It went out like a match in a sudden vanishing of pain. Its life flared up, then went out. I went a little numb. Without the bike, I would have collapsed.

People had crowded close before and behind me. I heard them before I could see them clearly.

"It's dead," I heard Joanne say. "Poor thing."

"What?" my father demanded. "Another one?"

I managed to focus on him. He must have skirted close to the cliff-edge of the road to have gotten all the way back to us. And he must have run.

"The same one," I said, managing to straighten up. "It wasn't dead. We saw it moving."

"I put three bullets into it," he said.

"It was moving, Reverend Olamina," Joanne insisted. "It was suffering. If Lauren hadn't shot it, someone else would have had to."

Dad sighed. "Well, it isn't suffering now. Let's get out of here." Then he seemed to realize what Joanne had said. He looked at me. "Are you all right?"

I nodded. I don't know how I looked. No one was reacting to me as though I looked odd, so I must not have shown much of what I had gone through. I think only Harry Balter, Curtis Talcott, and Joanne had seen me shoot the dog. I looked at them and Curtis grinned at me. He leaned against his bike and in a slow, lazy motion, he drew an imaginary gun, took careful aim at the dead dog, and fired an imaginary shot.

"Pow," he said. "Just like she does stuff like that every day. Pow!"

"Let's go," my father said.

We began walking up the path again. We left the canyon and made our way down to the street. There were no more dogs.

I walked, then rode in a daze, still not quite free of the dog I had killed. I had felt it die, and yet I had not died. I had felt its pain as though it were a human being. I had felt its life flare and go out, and I was still alive.

Pow.

5

□ □ □

Belief
Initiates and guides action—
Or it does nothing.

EARTHSEED: THE BOOKS OF THE LIVING

SUNDAY, MARCH 2, 2025

It's raining.

We heard last night on the radio that there was a storm sweeping in from the Pacific, but most people didn't believe it. "We'll have wind," Cory said. "Wind and maybe a few drops of rain, or maybe just a little cool weather. That would be welcome. It's all we'll get."

That's all there has been for six years. I can remember the rain six years ago, water swirling around the back porch, not high enough to come into the house, but high enough to attract my brothers who wanted to play in it. Cory, forever worried about infection, wouldn't let them. She said they'd be splashing around in a soup of all the waste-water germs we'd been watering our gardens with for years. Maybe she was right, but kids all over the neighborhood covered themselves with mud and earthworms that day, and nothing terrible happened to them.

But that storm was almost tropical—a quick, hard, warm, September rain, the edge of a hurricane that hit Mexico's Pacific coast. This is a colder, winter storm. It began this morning as people were coming to church.

In the choir we sang rousing old hymns accompanied by Cory's piano playing and lightning and thunder from outside. It was wonderful. Some people missed part of the sermon, though, because they went home to put out all the barrels, buckets, tubs, and pots they could find to catch the free water. Other went home to put pots and buckets inside where there were leaks in the roof.

I can't remember when any of us have had a roof repaired by a professional. We all have Spanish tile roofs, and that's good. A tile roof is, I suspect, more secure and lasting than wood or asphalt shingles. But time, wind, and earthquakes have taken a toll. Tree limbs have done some damage, too. Yet no one has extra money for anything as nonessential as roof repair. At best, some of the neighborhood men go up with whatever materials they can scavenge and create makeshift patches. No one's even done that for a while. If it only rains once every six or seven years, why bother?

Our roof is all right so far, and the barrels and things we put out after services this morning are full or filling. Good, clean, free water from the sky. If only it came more often.

MONDAY, MARCH 3, 2025

Still raining.

No thunder today, though there was some last night. Steady drizzle, and occasional, heavy showers all day. All day. So different and beautiful. I've never felt so overwhelmed by water. I went out and walked in the rain until I was soaked. Cory didn't want me to, but I did it anyway. It was so wonderful. How can she not understand that? It was so incredible and wonderful.

TUESDAY, MARCH 4, 2025

Amy Dunn is dead.

Three years old, unloved, and dead. That doesn't seem reasonable or even possible. She could read simple words and count to thirty. I taught her. She so much loved getting attention that she stuck to me during school hours and drove me crazy. Didn't want me to go to the bathroom without her.

Dead.

I had gotten to like her, even though she was a pest.

Today I walked her home after class. I had gotten into the habit of walking her home because the Dunns wouldn't send anyone for her.

"She knows the way," Christmas said. "Just send her over. She'll get here all right."

I didn't doubt that she could have. She could look across the street, and across the center island, and see her house from ours, but Amy had a tendency to wander. Sent home alone, she might get there or she might wind up in the Montoya garden, grazing, or in the Moss rabbit house, trying to let the rabbits out. So I walked her across, glad for an excuse to get out in the rain again. Amy loved it, too, and we lingered for a moment under the big avocado tree on the island. There was a navel orange tree at the back end of the island, and I picked a pair of ripe oranges—one for Amy and one for me. I peeled both of them, and we ate them while the rain plastered Amy's scant colorless hair against her head and made her look bald.

I took her to her door and left her in the care of her mother.

"You didn't have to get her so wet," Tracy complained.

"Might as well enjoy the rain while it lasts," I said, and I left them.

I saw Tracy take Amy into the house and shut the door. Yet somehow Amy wound up outside again, wound up near the front gate, just opposite the Garfield/Balter/Dory house. Jay Garfield found her there when he came out to investigate what he thought was another bundle that someone had thrown over the gate. People toss us things sometimes—gifts of envy and hate: A maggoty, dead animal, a bag of shit, even an occasional severed human limb or a dead child. Dead adults have been left lying just beyond our wall. But these were all outsiders. Amy was one of us.

Someone shot Amy right through the metal gate. It had to be an accidental hit because you can't see through our gate from the outside. The shooter either fired at someone who was in front of the gate or fired at the gate itself, at the neighborhood, at us and our supposed wealth and privilege. Most bullets wouldn't have gotten through the gate. It's supposed to be bulletproof. But it's been penetrated a couple of times before, high up, near the top. Now we have six new bullet holes in the lower portion—six holes and a seventh dent, a long, smooth gauge where a bullet had glanced off without breaking through.

We hear so much gunfire, day and night, single shots and odd bursts of automatic weapons fire, even occasional blasts from heavy artillery or explosions from grenades or bigger bombs. We worry most about those last things, but they're rare. It's harder to steal big weapons, and not many people around here can afford to buy the illegal ones—or that's what Dad says. The thing is, we hear gunfire so much that we don't hear it. A couple of the Balter kids said they heard shooting, but as usual, they paid no attention to it. It was outside, beyond the wall, after all. Most of us heard nothing except the rain.

Amy was going to turn four in a couple of weeks. I had planned to give her a little party with my kindergartners.

God, I hate this place.

I mean, I love it. It's home. These are my people. But I hate it. It's like an island surrounded by sharks—except that sharks don't bother you unless you go in the water. But our land sharks are on their way in. It's just a matter of how long it takes for them to get hungry enough.

WEDNESDAY, MARCH 5, 2025

I walked in the rain again this morning. It was cold, but good. Amy has already been cremated. I wonder if her mother is relieved. She doesn't look relieved. She never liked Amy, but now she cries. I don't think she's faking. The family has spent money it could not afford to get the police involved to try to find the killer. I suspect that the only good this will do will be to chase away the people who live on the sidewalks and streets nearest to our wall. Is that good? The street poor will be back, and they won't love us for siccing the cops on them. It's illegal to camp out on the street the way they do—the way they must—so the cops knock them around, rob them if they have anything worth stealing, then order them away or jail them. The miserable will be made even more miserable. None of that can help Amy. I suppose, though, that it will make the Dunns feel better about the way they treated her.

On Saturday, Dad will preach Amy's funeral. I wish I didn't have to be there. Funerals have never bothered me before, but this one does.

"You cared about Amy," Joanne Garfield said to me when I complained to her. We had lunch together today. We ate in my bedroom because it's still raining off and on, and the rest of the house was full of all the kids who hadn't gone home to eat lunch. But my room is still mine. It's the one place in the world where I can go and not be followed by anyone I don't invite in. I'm the only person I know who has a bedroom to herself. These days, even Dad and Cory knock before they open my door. That's one of the best things about being the only daughter in the family. I have to kick my brothers out of here all the time, but at least I can kick them out. Joanne is an only child, but she shares a room with three younger girl cousins—whiny Lisa, always demanding and complaining; smart, giggly Robin with her near-genius I.Q.; and invisible Jessica who whispers and stares at her feet and cries if you give her a dirty look. All three are Balters—Harry's sisters and the children of Joanne's mother's sister. The two adult sisters, their husbands, their eight children, and their parents Mr. and Mrs. Dory are all squeezed into one five-bedroom house. It isn't the most crowded house in the neighborhood, but I'm glad I don't have to live like that.

"Almost no one cared about Amy," Joanne said. "But you did."

"After the fire, I did," I said. "I got scared for her then. Before that, I ignored her like everyone else."

"So now you're feeling guilty?"

"No."

"Yes, you are."

I looked at her, surprised. "I mean it. No. I hate that she's dead, and I miss her, but I didn't cause her death. I just can't deny what all this says about us."

"What?"

I felt on the verge of talking to her about things I hadn't talked about before. I'd written about them. Sometimes I write to keep from going crazy. There's a world of things I don't feel free to talk to anyone about.

But Joanne is a friend. She knows me better than most people, and she has a brain. Why not talk to her? Sooner or later, I have to talk to someone.

"What's wrong?" she asked. She had opened a plastic container of bean salad. Now she put it down on my night table.

"Don't you ever wonder if maybe Amy and Mrs. Sims are the lucky ones?" I asked. "I mean, don't you ever wonder what's going to happen to the rest of us?"

There was a clap of dull, muffled thunder, and a sudden heavy shower. Radio weather reports say today's rain will be the last of the four-day series of storms. I hope not.

"Sure I think about it," Joanne said. "With people shooting little kids, how can I not think about it?"

"People have been killing little kids since there've been people," I said.

"Not in here, they haven't. Not until now."

"Yes, that's it, isn't it? We got a wake-up call. Another one."

"What are you talking about?"

"Amy was the first of us to be killed like that. She won't be the last."

OCTAVIA E. BUTLER

Joanne sighed, and there was a little shudder in the sigh. "So you think so, too."

"I do. But I didn't know you thought about it at all."

"Rape, robbery, and now murder. Of course I think about it. Everyone thinks about it. Everyone worries. I wish I could get out of here."

"Where would you go?"

"That's it, isn't it? There's nowhere to go."

"There might be."

"Not if you don't have money. Not if all you know how to do is take care of babies and cook."

I shook my head. "You know much more than that."

"Maybe, but none of it matters. I won't be able to afford college. I won't be able to get a job or move out of my parents' house because no job I could get would support me and there are no safe places to move. Hell, my parents are still living with their parents."

"I know," I said. "And as bad as that is, there's more."

"Who needs more? That's enough!" She began to eat the bean salad. It looked good, but I thought I might be about to ruin it for her.

"There's cholera spreading in southern Mississippi and Louisiana," I said. "I heard about it on the radio yesterday. There are too many poor people—illiterate, jobless, homeless, without decent sanitation or clean water. They have plenty of water down there, but a lot of it is polluted. And you know that drug that makes people want to set fires?"

She nodded, chewing.

"It's spreading again. It was on the east coast. Now it's in Chicago. The reports say that it makes watching a fire better than sex. I don't know whether the reporters are condemning it or advertising it." I drew a deep breath. "Tornadoes are smashing hell out of Alabama, Kentucky, Tennessee, and two or three other states. Three hundred people dead so far. And there's a blizzard freezing the northern midwest, killing even more people. In New York and New Jersey, a measles epidemic is killing people. Measles!"

"I heard about the measles," Joanne said. "Strange. Even if people can't afford immunizations, measles shouldn't kill."

"Those people are half dead already," I told her. "They've come through the winter cold, hungry, already sick with other diseases. And, no, of course they can't afford immunizations. We're lucky our parents found the money to pay for all our immunizations. If we have kids, I don't see how we'll be able to do even that for them."

"I know, I know." She sounded almost bored. "Things are bad. My mother is hoping this new guy, President Donner, will start to get us back to normal."

"Normal," I muttered. "I wonder what that is. Do you agree with your mother?"

"No. Donner hasn't got a chance. I think he would fix things if he could, but Harry says his ideas are scary. Harry says he'll set the country back a hundred years."

"My father says something like that. I'm surprised that Harry agrees."

"He would. His own father thinks Donner is God. Harry wouldn't agree with him on anything."

I laughed, distracted, thinking about Harry's battles with his father. Neighborhood fireworks—plenty of flash, but no real fire.

"Why do you want to talk about this stuff?" Joanne asked, bringing me back to the real fire. "We can't do anything about it."

"We have to."

"Have to what? We're fifteen! What can we do?"

"We can get ready. That's what we've got to do now. Get ready for what's going to happen, get ready to survive it, get ready to make a life afterward. Get focused on arranging to survive so that we can do more than just get batted around by crazy people, desperate people, thugs, and leaders who don't know what they're doing!"

She just stared at me. "I don't know what you're talking about."

I was rolling—too fast, maybe. "I'm talking about this place, Jo, this cul-de-sac with a wall around it. I'm talking about the day a big gang of those hungry, desperate, crazy people outside decide to come in. I'm talking about what we've got to do before that happens so that we can survive and rebuild—or at least survive and escape to be something other than beggars."

"Someone's going to just smash in our wall and come in?"

"More likely blast it down, or blast the gate open. It's going to happen some day. You know that as well as I do."

"Oh, no I don't," she protested. She sat up straight, almost stiff, her lunch forgotten for the moment. I bit into a piece of acorn bread that was full of dried fruit and nuts. It's a favorite of mine, but I managed to chew and swallow without tasting it.

"Jo, we're in for trouble. You've already admitted that."

"Sure," she said. "More shootings, more break-ins. That's what I meant."

"And that's what will happen for a while. I wish I could guess how long. We'll be hit and hit and hit, then the big hit will come. And if we're not ready for it, it will be like Jericho."

She held herself rigid, rejecting. "You don't know that! You can't read the future. No one can."

"You can," I said, "if you want to. It's scary, but once you get past the fear, it's easy. In L.A. some walled communities bigger and stronger than this one just aren't there anymore. Nothing left but ruins, rats, and squatters. What happened to them can happen to us. We'll die in here unless we get busy now and work out ways to survive."

"If you think that, why don't you tell your parents? Warn them and see what they say."

"I intend to as soon as I think of a way to do it that will reach them. Besides . . . I think they already know. I think my father does, anyway. I think most of the adults know. They don't want to know, but they do."

"My mother could be right about Donner. He really could do some good."

"No. No, Donner's just a kind of human banister."

"A what?"

"I mean he's like . . . like a symbol of the past for us to hold on to as we're pushed into the future. He's nothing. No substance. But having him there, the latest in a two-and-a-half-century-long line of American Presidents, makes people feel that the country, the culture that they grew up with is still here—that we'll get through these bad times and back to normal."

"We could," she said. "We might. I think someday we will." No, she didn't. She was too bright to take anything but the most superficial comfort from her denial. But even superficial comfort is better than none, I guess. I tried another tactic.

"Did you ever read about bubonic plague in medieval Europe?" I asked.

She nodded. She reads a lot the way I do, reads all kinds of things. "A lot of the continent was depopulated," she said. "Some survivors thought the world was coming to an end."

"Yes, but once they realized it wasn't, they also realized there was a lot of vacant land available for the taking, and if they had a trade, they realized they could demand better pay for their work. A lot of things changed for the survivors."

"What's your point?"

"The changes." I thought for a moment. They were slow changes compared to anything that might happen here, but it took a plague to make some of the people realize that things *could* change."

"So?"

"Things are changing now, too. Our adults haven't been wiped out by a plague so they're still anchored in the past, waiting for the good old days to come back. But things have changed a lot, and they'll change more. Things are always changing. This is just one of the big jumps instead of the little step-by-step changes that are easier to take. People have changed the climate of the world. Now they're waiting for the old days to come back."

"Your father says he doesn't believe people changed the climate in spite of what scientists say. He says only God could change the world in such an important way."

"Do you believe him?"

She opened her mouth, looked at me, then closed it again. After a while, she said, "I don't know."

"My father has his blind spots," I said. "He's the best person I know, but even he has blind spots."

"It doesn't make any difference," she said. "We can't make the climate change back, no matter why it changed in the first place. You and I can't. The neighborhood can't. We can't do anything."

I lost patience. "Then let's kill ourselves now and be done with it!"

She frowned, her round, too serious face almost angry. She tore bits of peel from a small navel orange. "What then?" she demanded. "What can we do?"

I put the last bite of my acorn bread down and went around her to my night table. I took several books from the deep bottom drawer and showed them to her. "This is what I've been doing—reading and studying these over the past few months. These books are old like all the books in this house. I've also been using Dad's computer when he lets me—to get new stuff."

Frowning, she looked them over. Three books on survival in the wilderness, three on guns and shooting, two each on handling medical emergencies, California native and naturalized plants and their uses, and basic living: log-cabin-building, livestock raising, plant cultivation, soap making—that kind of thing. Joanne caught on at once.

"What are you doing?" she asked. "Trying to learn to live off the land?"

"I'm trying to learn whatever I can that might help me survive out there. I think we should all study books like these. I think we should bury money and other necessities in the ground where thieves won't find them. I think we should make emergency packs—grab and run packs—in case we have to get out of here in a hurry. Money, food, clothing, matches, a blanket. . . . I think we should fix places outside where we can meet in case we get separated. Hell, I think a lot of things. And I know—I know!—that no matter how many things I think of, they won't be enough. Every time I go outside, I try to imagine what it might be like to live out there without walls, and I realize I don't know anything."

"Then why—"

"I intend to survive."

She just stared.

"I mean to learn everything I can while I can," I said. "If I find myself outside, maybe what I've learned will help me live long enough to learn more."

She gave me a nervous smile. "You've been reading too many adventure stories," she said.

I frowned. How could I reach her? "This isn't a joke, Jo."

"What is it then?" She ate the last section of her orange. "What do you want me to say?"

"I want you to be serious. I realize I don't know very much. None of us knows very much. But we can all learn more. Then we can teach one another. We can stop denying reality or hoping it will go away by magic."

"That's not what I'm doing."

I looked out for a moment at the rain, calming myself.

"Okay. Okay, what are you doing?"

She looked uncomfortable. "I'm still not sure we can really do anything."

"Jo!"

"Tell me what I can do that won't get me in trouble or make everyone think I'm crazy. Just tell me something."

At last. "Have you read all your family's books?"

"Some of them. Not all. They aren't all worth reading. Books aren't going to save us."

"Nothing is going to save us. If we don't save ourselves, we're dead.

Now use your imagination. Is there anything on your family book-shelves that might help you if you were stuck outside?"

"No."

"You answer too fast. Go home and look again. And like I said, use your imagination. Any kind of survival information from ency-clopedias, biographies, anything that helps you learn to live off the land and defend ourselves. Even some fiction might be useful."

She gave me a sidelong glance. "I'll bet," she said.

"Jo, if you never need this information, it won't do you any harm. You'll just know a little more than you did before. So what? By the way, do you take notes when you read?"

Guarded look. "Sometimes."

"Read this." I handed her one of the plant books. This one was about California Indians, the plants they used, and how they used them—an interesting, entertaining little book. She would be sur-prised. There was nothing in it to scare her or threaten her or push her. I thought I had already done enough of that.

"Take notes," I told her. "You'll remember better if you do."

"I still don't believe you," she said. "Things don't have to be as bad as you say they are."

I put the book into her hands. "Hang on to your notes," I said. "Pay special attention to the plants that grow between here and the coast and between here and Oregon along the coast. I've marked them."

"I said I don't believe you."

"I don't care."

She looked down at the book, ran her hands over the black cloth-and-cardboard binding. "So we learn to eat grass and live in the bushes," she muttered.

"We learn to survive," I said. "It's a good book. Take care of it. You know how my father is about his books."

THURSDAY, MARCH 6, 2025

The rain stopped. My windows are on the north side of the house, and I can see the clouds breaking up. They're being blown over the mountains toward the desert. Surprising how fast they can move. The wind is strong and cold now. It might cost us a few trees.

I wonder how many years it will be before we see rain again.

6

◻ ◻ ◻

Drowning people
Sometimes die
Fighting their rescuers.

EARTHSEED: THE BOOKS OF THE LIVING
SATURDAY, MARCH 8, 2025

Joanne told.

She told her mother who told her father who told my father who had one of those serious talks with me.

Damn her. *Damn her!*

I saw her today at the service we had for Amy and yesterday at school. She didn't say a word about what she had done. It turns out she told her mother on Thursday. Maybe it was supposed to be a secret between them or something. But, oh, Phillida Garfield was so concerned for me, so worried. And she didn't like my scaring Joanne. Was Joanne scared? Not scared enough to use her brain, it seems. Joanne always seemed so sensible. Did she think getting me into trouble would make the danger go away? No, that's not it. This is just more denial: A dumb little game of "If we don't talk about bad things, maybe they won't happen." Idiot! I'll never be able to tell her anything important again.

What if I'd been more open? What if I'd talked religion with her? I'd wanted to. How will I ever be able to talk to anyone about that?

What I did say worked its way back to me tonight. Mr. Garfield talked to Dad after the funeral. It was like the whispering game that little kids play. The message went all the way from, "We're in danger here and we're going to have to work hard to save ourselves," to "Lauren is talking about running away because she's afraid that outsiders are going to riot and tear down the walls and kill us all."

Well, I had said *some* of that, and Joanne had made it clear that she didn't agree with me. But I hadn't just let the bad predictions stand alone: "We're going to die, boo-hoo." What would be the point of that? Still, only the negative stuff came home to me.

"Lauren, what did you say to Joanne?" my father demanded. He came to my room after dinner when he should have been doing his final work on tomorrow's sermon. He sat down on my one chair and stared at me in a way that meant, "Where is your mind, girl? What's the matter with you?" That look plus Joanne's name told me what had happened, what this was about. My friend Joanne. *Damn her!*

I sat on my bed and looked back at him. "I told her we were in for some bad, dangerous times," I said. "I warned her we ought to learn what we could now so we could survive."

That was when he told me how upset Joanne's mother was, how upset Joanne was, and how they both thought I needed to "talk to someone," because I thought our world was coming to an end.

"Do you think our world is coming to an end?" Dad asked, and with no warning at all, I almost started crying. I had all I could do to hold it back. What I thought was, "No, I think *your* world is coming to an end, and maybe you with it." That was terrible. I hadn't thought about it in such a personal way before. I turned and looked out a window until I felt calmer. When I faced him again, I said, "Yes. Don't you?"

He frowned. I don't think he expected me to say that. "You're fifteen," he said. "You don't really understand what's going on here. The problems we have now have been building since long before you were born."

"I know."

He was still frowning. I wondered what he wanted me to say. "What were you doing, then?" he asked. "Why did you say those things to Joanne?"

I decided to go on telling the truth for as long as I could. I hate to lie to him. "What I said was true," I insisted.

OCTAVIA E. BUTLER

"You don't have to say everything you think you know," he said. "Haven't you figured that out yet?"

"Joanne and I were friends," I said. "I thought I could talk to her."

He shook his head. "These things frighten people. It's best not to talk about them."

"But, Dad, that's like . . . like ignoring a fire in the living room because we're all in the kitchen, and, besides, house fires are too scary to talk about."

"Don't warn Joanne or any of your other friends," he said. "Not now. I know you think you're right, but you're not doing anyone any good. You're just panicking people."

I managed to suppress a surge of anger by shifting the subject a little. Sometimes the way to move Dad is to go at him from several directions.

"Did Mr. Garfield give you back your book?" I asked.

"What book?"

"I loaned Joanne a book about California plants and the ways Indians used them. It was one of your books. I'm sorry I loaned it to her. It's so neutral, I didn't think it could cause trouble. But I guess it has."

He looked startled, then he almost smiled. "Yes, I will have to have that one back, all right. You wouldn't have the acorn bread you like so much without that one—not to mention a few other things we take for granted."

"Acorn bread . . . ?"

He nodded. "Most of the people in this country don't eat acorns, you know. They have no tradition of eating them, they don't know how to prepare them, and for some reason, they find the idea of eating them disgusting. Some of our neighbors wanted to cut down all our big live oak trees and plant something useful. You wouldn't believe the time I had changing their minds."

"What did people eat before?"

"Bread made of wheat and other grains—corn, rye, oats . . . things like that."

"Too expensive!"

"Didn't use to be. You get that book back from Joanne." He drew a deep breath. "Now, let's get off the side track and back onto the main track. What were you planning? Did you try to talk Joanne into running away?"

Then I sighed. "Of course not."

"Her father says you did."

"He's wrong. This was about staying alive, learning to live outside so that we'd be able to if we ever had to."

He watched me as though he could read the truth in my mind. When I was little, I used to think he could. "All right," he said. "You may have meant well, but no more scare talk."

"It wasn't scare talk. We do need to learn what we can while there's time."

"That's not up to you, Lauren. You don't make decisions for this community."

Oh hell. If I could just find a balance between holding back too much and pushing, poaching. " Yes, sir."

He leaned back and looked at me. "Tell me exactly what you told Joanne. All of it."

I told him. I was careful to keep my voice flat and passionless, but I didn't leave anything out. I wanted him to know, to understand what I believed. The nonreligious part of it, anyway. When I finished, I stopped and waited. He seemed to expect me to say more. He just sat there for a while and stared at me. I couldn't tell what he felt. Other people never could if he didn't want them to, but I've been able to most of the time. Now I felt shut out, and there was nothing I could do about it. I waited.

At last he let his breath out as though he had been holding it. "Don't talk about this anymore," he said in a voice that didn't invite argument.

I looked back at him, not wanting to give a promise that would be a lie.

"Lauren."

"Dad."

"I want your promise that you won't talk about this anymore."

What to say? I wouldn't promise. I couldn't. "We could make earthquake packs," I suggested. "Emergency kits that we can grab in case we have to get out of the house fast. If we call them earthquake packs, the idea might not bother people so much. People are used to worrying about earthquakes." All this came out in a rush.

"I want your promise, daughter."

I slumped. "Why? You know I'm right. Even Mrs. Garfield must know it. So why?"

I thought he would yell at me or punish me. His voice had had that warning edge to it that my brothers and I had come to call the rattle—as in a rattlesnake's warning sound. If you pushed him past the rattle, you were in trouble. If he called you "son" or "daughter" you were close to trouble.

"Why?" I insisted.

"Because you don't have any idea what you're doing," he said. He frowned and rubbed his forehead. When he spoke again, the edge went out of his voice. "It's better to teach people than to scare them, Lauren. If you scare them and nothing happens, they lose their fear, and you lose some of your authority with them. It's harder to scare them a second time, harder to teach them, harder to win back their trust. Best to begin by teaching." His mouth crooked into a little smile. "It's interesting that you chose to begin your efforts with the book you lent to Joanne. Did you ever think of teaching from that book?"

"Teaching . . . my kindergartners?"

"Why not. Get them started on the right foot. You could even put together a class for older kids and adults. Something like Mr. Ibarra's wood carving class, Mrs. Balter's needlework classes, and young Robert Hsu's astronomy lectures. People are bored. They wouldn't mind another informal class now that they've lost the Yannis television. If you can think of ways to entertain them and teach them at the same time, you'll get your information out. And all without making anyone look down."

"Look down . . . ?"

"Into the abyss, daughter." But I wasn't in trouble anymore. Not at the moment. "You've just noticed the abyss," he continued. "The adults in this community have been balancing at the edge of it for more years than you've been alive."

I got up, went over to him and took his hand. "It's getting worse, Dad."

"I know."

"Maybe it's time to look down. Time to look for some hand and foot holds before we just get pushed in."

"That's why we have target practice every week and Lazor wire and our emergency bell. Your idea for emergency packs is a good one. Some people already have them. For earthquakes. Some will assemble them if I suggest it. And, of course, some won't do anything at all. There are always people who won't do anything."

"Will you suggest it?"

"Yes. At the next neighborhood association meeting."

"What else can we do? None of this is fast enough."

"It will have to be." He stood up, a tall, broad wall of a man. "Why don't you ask around, see if anyone in the neighborhood knows anything about martial arts. You need more than a book or two to learn good dependable unarmed combat."

I blinked. "Okay."

"Check with old Mr. Hsu and Mr. and Mrs. Montoya."

"Mr. *and* Mrs.?"

"I think so. Talk to them about classes, not about Armageddon."

I looked up at him, and he looked more like a wall than ever, standing and waiting. And he had offered me a lot—all I would get, I suspected. I sighed. "Okay, Dad, I promise. I'll try not to scare anyone else. I just hope things hold together long enough for us to do it your way."

And he echoed my sigh. "At last. Good. Now come out back with me. There are some important things buried in the yard in sealed containers. It's time for you to know where they are—just in case."

SUNDAY, MARCH 9, 2025

Today, Dad preached from Genesis six, Noah and the ark: "And God saw that the wickedness of man was great in the earth, and that every imagination of the thoughts and of his heart was only evil continually. And it repented the Lord that he had made man on the earth, and it grieved him at his heart. And the Lord said, I will destroy man whom I have created from the face of the earth; both man, and beast, and the creeping thing and the fowls of the air; for it repenteth me that I have made them. But Noah found grace in the eyes of the Lord."

And then, of course, later God says to Noah, "Make thee an ark of gopher wood; rooms shalt thou make in the ark, and shalt pitch it within and without with pitch."

Dad focused on the two-part nature of this situation. God decides to destroy everything except Noah, his family, and some animals. But if Noah is going to be saved, he has plenty of hard work to do.

Joanne came to me after church and said she was sorry for all the craziness.

"Okay," I said.

"Still friends?" she asked.

And I hedged: "Not enemies, anyway. Get my father's book back to me. He wants it."

"My mother took it. I didn't know she'd get so upset."

"It isn't hers. Get it back to me. Or have your dad give it to mine. I don't care. But he wants his book."

"All right."

I watched her leave the house. She looks so trustworthy—tall and straight and serious and intelligent—I still feel inclined to trust her.

But I can't. I don't. She has no idea how much she could have hurt me if I had given her just a few more words to use against me. I don't think I'll ever trust her again, and I hate that. She was my best friend. Now she isn't.

WEDNESDAY, MARCH 12, 2025

Garden thieves got in last night. They stripped citrus trees of fruit in the Hsu yard and the Talcott yard. In the process, they trampled what was left of winter gardens and much of the spring planting.

Dad says we have to set up a regular watch. He tried to call a neighborhood association meeting for tonight, but it's a work night for some people, including Gary Hsu who sleeps over at his job whenever he has to report in person. We're supposed to get together for a meeting on Saturday. Meanwhile, Dad got Jay Garfield, Wyatt and Kayla Talcott, Alex Montoya, and Edwin Dunn together to patrol the neighborhood in shifts in armed pairs. That meant that except for the Talcotts who are already a pair (and who are so angry about their garden that I pity any thief who gets in their way), the others have to find partners among the other adults of the neighborhood.

"Find someone you trust to protect your back," I heard Dad tell the little group. Each pair was to patrol for two hours from just before dark to just after dawn. The first patrol, walking through or looking into all the backyards, would get people used to the idea of watchers while they were still awake enough to understand.

"Make sure they see you if you get first watch," Dad said. "The sight of you will remind them that there will be watchers all through the night. We don't want any of them mistaking you for thieves."

Sensible. People go to bed soon after dark to save electricity, but between dinner and darkness they spend time on their porches or in their yards where it isn't so hot. Some listen to their radio on front or back porches. Now and then people get together to play music, sing, play board games, talk, or get out on the paved part of the street for volleyball, touch football, basketball, or tennis. People used to play baseball, but we just can't afford what that costs in windows. A few people just find a corner and read a book while there's still daylight. It's a good, comfortable, recreational time. What a pity to spoil it with reminders of reality. But it can't be helped.

"What will you do if you catch a thief?" Cory asked my father before he went out. He was on the second shift, and he and Cory were having a rare cup of coffee together in the kitchen while he waited. Coffee was for special occasions. I couldn't miss the good smell of it in my room where I lay awake.

I eavesdrop. I don't put drinking glasses to walls or crouch with my ear against doors, but I do often lie awake long after dark when we kids are all supposed to be asleep. The kitchen is across the hall from my room, the dining room is nearby at the end of the hall, and my parents' room is next door. The house is old and well insulated. If there's a shut door between me and the conversation, I can't hear much. But at night with all or most of the lights out, I can leave my door open a crack, and if other doors are also open, I can hear a lot. I learn a lot.

"We'll chase him off, I hope," Dad said. "We've agreed to that. We'll give him a good scare and let him know there are easier ways to get a dollar."

"A dollar . . . ?"

"Yes, indeed. Our thieves didn't steal all that food because they were hungry. They stripped those trees—took everything they could."

"I know," Cory said. "I took some lemons and grapefruits to both the Hsus and the Wyatts today and told them they could pick from our trees when they needed more. I took them some seed, too. They both had a lot of young plants trampled, but this early in the season, they should be able to repair the damage."

"Yes." My father paused. "But you see my point. People steal that way for money. They're not desperate. Just greedy and dangerous. We might be able to scare them into looking for easier pickings."

"But what if you can't?" Cory asked, almost whispering. Her voice fell so low that I was afraid I would miss something.

"If you can't, will you shoot them?"

"Yes," he said.

". . . yes?" she repeated in that same small voice. "Just . . . 'yes?'" She was like Joanne all over again—denial personified. What planet do people like that live on?

"Yes," my father said.

"Why!"

There was a long silence. When my father spoke again, his own voice had gone very soft. "Baby, if these people steal enough, they'll force us to spend more than we can afford on food—or go hungry. We live on the edge as it is. You know how hard things are."

"But . . . couldn't we just call the police?"

"For what? We can't afford their fees, and anyway, they're not interested until after a crime has been committed. Even then, if you call them, they won't show up for hours—maybe not for two or three days."

"I know."

"What are you saying then? You want the kids to go hungry? You want thieves coming into the house once they've stripped the gardens?"

"But they haven't done that."

"Of course they have. Mrs. Sims was only their latest victim."

"She lived alone. We always said she shouldn't do that."

"You want to trust them not to hurt you or the kids just because there are seven of us? Baby, we can't live by pretending this is still twenty or thirty years ago."

"But you could go to jail!" She was crying—not sobbing, but speaking with that voice-full-of-tears that she can manage sometimes.

"No," Dad said. "If we have to shoot someone, we're together in it. After we've shot him we carry him into the nearest house. It's still legal to shoot housebreakers. After that we do a little damage and get our stories straight."

OCTAVIA E. BUTLER

Long, long silence. "You could still get in trouble."

"I'll risk it."

Another long silence. "Thou shalt not kill," Cory whispered.

"Nehemiah four," Dad said. "Verse 14."

There was nothing more. A few minutes later, I heard Dad leave. I waited until I heard Cory go to her room and shut the door. Then I got up, shut my door, moved my lamp so the light wouldn't show under the door, then turned it on and opened my grandmother's Bible. She had had a lot of Bibles and Dad had let me keep this one.

Nehemiah, chapter four, Verse 14: "And I looked and rose up and said unto the nobles, and to the rulers, and to the rest of the people, be not afraid of them: remember the Lord which is great and terrible, and fight for your brethren, your sons, and your daughters, your wives and your houses."

Interesting. Interesting that Dad had that verse ready, and that Cory recognized it. Maybe they've had this conversation before.

SATURDAY, MARCH 15, 2025

It's official.

Now we have a regular neighborhood watch—a roster of people from every household who are over eighteen, good with guns—their own and others'—and considered responsible by my father and by the people who have already been patrolling the neighborhood. Since none of the watchers have ever been cops or security guards, they'll go on working in pairs, watching out for each other as well as for the neighborhood. They'll use whistles to call for help if they need it. Also, they'll meet once a week to read, discuss, and practice martial arts and shoot-out techniques. The Montoyas will give their martial arts classes, all right, but not at my suggestion. Old Mr. Hsu is having back problems, and he won't be teaching anything for a while, but the Montoyas seem to be enough. I plan to sit in on the classes as often as I can stand to share everyone's practice pains.

Dad has collected all his books from me this morning. All I have left are my notes. I don't mind. Thanks to the garden thieves, people are preparing themselves for the worst. I feel almost grateful to the thieves.

They haven't come back, by the way—our thieves. When they do, we should be able to give them something they don't expect.

SATURDAY, MARCH 29, 2025

Our thieves paid us another visit last night.

Maybe they weren't the same ones, but their intentions were the same: To take away what someone else has sweated to grow and very much needs.

This time they were after Richard Moss's rabbits. Those rabbits are the neighborhood's only livestock except for some chickens the Cruz and Montoya families tried to raise a few years ago. Those were stolen as soon as they were old enough to make noise and let outsiders know they were there. The Moss rabbits have been our secret until this year when Richard Moss insisted on selling meat and whatever his wives could make from raw or tanned rabbit hides out beyond the wall. The Mosses had been selling to us all along, of course, meat, hides, fertilizer, everything except live rabbits. Those he hoarded as breeding stock. But now, stubborn, arrogant, and greedy, he had decided he could earn more if he peddled his merchandise outside. So, now the word is out on the street about the damned rabbits, and last night someone came to get them.

The Moss rabbit house is a converted three-car garage added to the property in the 1980s according to Dad. It's hard to believe any household once had three cars, and gas fueled cars at that. But I remember the old garage before Richard Moss converted it. It was huge with three black oil spots on the floor where three cars had once been housed. Richard Moss repaired the walls and roof, put in windows for cross ventilation, and in general, made the place almost fit for people to live in. In fact, it's much better than what a lot of people live in now on the outside. He built rows and tiers of cages—hutches—and put in more electric lights and ceiling fans. The fans can be made to work on kid power. He's hooked them up to an old bicycle frame, and every Moss kid who's old enough to manage the pedals sooner or later gets drafted into powering the fans. The Moss kids hate it, but they know what they'll get if they don't do it.

I don't know how many rabbits the Mosses have now, but it seems they're always killing and skinning and doing disgusting things to pelts. Even a little monopoly is worth a lot of trouble.

The two thieves had managed to stuff 13 rabbits into canvas sacks by the time our watchers spotted them. The watchers were Alejandro Montoya and Julia Lincoln, one of Shani Yannis's sisters. Mrs. Montoya has two kids sick with the flu so she's off the watch roster for a while.

Mrs. Lincoln and Mr. Montoya followed the plan that the group of watchers had put together at their meetings. Without a word of command or warning, they fired their guns into the air two or three times each, at the same time, blowing their whistles full blast. They kept to cover, but inside the Moss house, someone woke up and turned on the rabbit house lights. That could have been a lethal mistake for the watchers, but they were hidden behind pomegranate bushes.

The two thieves ran like rabbits.

Abandoning sacks, rabbits, pry bars, a long coil of rope, wire cutters, and even an excellent long aluminum ladder, they scrambled up that ladder and over the wall in seconds. Our wall is three meters high and topped off with pieces of broken glass as well as the usual barbed wire and the all but invisible Lazor wire. All the wire had been cut in spite of our efforts. What a pity we couldn't afford to electrify it or set other traps. But at least the glass—the oldest, simplest of our tricks—had gotten one of them. We found a broad stream of dried blood down the inside of the wall this morning.

We also found a Glock 19 pistol where one of the thieves had dropped it. Mrs. Lincoln and Mr. Montoya could have been shot. If the thieves hadn't been scared out of their minds, there could have been a gun battle. Someone in the Moss house or a neighboring house could have been hurt or killed.

Cory went after Dad about that once they were alone in the kitchen tonight.

"I know," Dad said. He sounded tired and miserable. "Don't think we haven't thought about those things. That's why we want to scare the thieves away. Even shooting into the air isn't safe. Nothing's safe."

"They ran away this time, but they won't always run."

"I know."

"So what, then? You protect rabbits or oranges, and maybe get a child killed?"

Silence.

"*We can't live this way!*" Cory shouted. I jumped. I've never heard her sound like that before.

"We do live this way," Dad said. There was no anger in his voice, no emotional response at all to her shouting. There was nothing. Weariness. Sadness. I've never heard him sound so tired, so . . . almost beaten. And yet he had won. His idea had beaten off a pair of armed thieves without our having to hurt anyone. If the thieves had hurt themselves, that was their problem.

Of course they would come back, or others would come. That would happen no matter what. And Cory was right. The next thieves might not lose their guns and run away. So what? Should we lie in our beds and let them take all we had and hope they were content with stripping our gardens? How long does a thief stay content? And what's it like to starve?

"We couldn't make it without you," Cory was saying. She wasn't shouting now. "That could have been you out there, facing criminals. Next time it might be you. You could be shot, protecting the neighbors' rabbits."

"Did you notice," Dad said, "that every off-duty watcher answered the whistles last night? They came out to defend their community."

"I don't care about them! It's you I'm worried about!"

"No," he said. "We can't think that way anymore. Cory, there's nobody to help us but God and ourselves. I protect Moss's place in spite of what I think of him, and he protects mine, no matter what he thinks of me. We all look out for one another." He paused. "I've got plenty of insurance. You and the kids should be able to make it all right if—"

"No!" Cory said. "Do you think that's all it is? Money? Do you think—?"

"No, babe. No." Pause. "I know what it is to be left alone. This is no world to be alone in."

There was a long silence, and I didn't think they would say anymore. I lay on my bed, wondering if I should get up and shut my door so I could turn on my lamp and write. But there was a little more.

"What are we supposed to do if you die?" she demanded, and I think she was crying. "What do we do if they shoot you over some damn rabbits?"

"Live!" Dad said. "That's all anybody can do right now. Live. Hold out. Survive. I don't know whether good times are coming back again. But I know that won't matter if we don't survive these times."

That was the end of their talk. I lay in the dark for a long time, thinking about what they had said. Cory was right again. Dad might get hurt. He might get killed. I don't know how to think about that. I can write about it, but I don't feel it. On some deep level, I don't believe it. I guess I'm as good at denial as anyone.

So Cory is right, but it doesn't matter. And Dad is right, but he doesn't go far enough. God is Change, and in the end, God prevails. But God exists to be shaped. It isn't enough for us to just survive, limping along, playing business as usual while things get worse and worse. If that's the shape we give to God, then someday we must

become too weak—too poor, too hungry, too sick—to defend ourselves. Then we'll be wiped out.

There has to be more that we can do, a better destiny that we can
shape. Another place. Another way. Something!

7

□ □ □

We are all Godseed, but no more or less so than any
other aspect of the universe, Godseed is all there
is—all that Changes. Earthseed is all that spreads
Earthlife to new earths. The universe is Godseed. Only
we are Earthseed. And the Destiny of Earthseed is to
take root among the stars.

EARTHSEED: THE BOOKS OF THE LIVING
SATURDAY, APRIL 26, 2025

Sometimes naming a thing—giving it a name or discovering its
name—helps one to begin to understand it. Knowing the name of
a thing *and* knowing what that thing is for gives me even more of a
handle on it.

The particular God-is-Change belief system that seems right to
me will be called Earthseed. I've tried to name it before. Failing that,
I've tried to leave it unnamed. Neither effort has made me comfortable. Name plus purpose equals focus for me.

Well, today, I found the name, found it while I was weeding the
back garden and thinking about the way plants seed themselves,
windborne, animalborne, waterborne, far from their parent plants.
They have no ability at all to travel great distances under their own
power, and yet, they do travel. Even they don't have to just sit in one
place and wait to be wiped out. There are islands thousands of miles
from anywhere—the Hawaiian Islands, for example, and Easter
Island—where plants seeded themselves and grew long before any
humans arrived.

Earthseed.

I am Earthseed. Anyone can be. Someday, I think there will be a lot of us. And I think we'll have to seed ourselves farther and farther from this dying place.

I've never felt that I was making any of this up—not the name, Earthseed, not any of it. I mean, I've never felt that it was anything other than real: discovery rather than invention, exploration rather than creation. I wish I could believe it was all supernatural, and that I'm getting messages from God. But then, I don't believe in that kind of God. All I do is observe and take notes, trying to put things down in ways that are as powerful, as simple, and as direct as I feel them. I can never do that. I keep trying, but I can't. I'm not good enough as a writer or poet or whatever it is I need to be. I don't know what to do about that. It drives me frantic sometimes. I'm getting better, but so slowly.

The thing is, even with my writing problems, every time I understand a little more, I wonder why it's taken me so long—why there was ever a time when I didn't understand a thing so obvious and real and true.

Here's the only puzzle in it all, the only paradox, or bit of illogic or circular reasoning or whatever it should be called:

> *Why is the universe?*
> *To shape God.*
>
> *Why is God?*
> *To shape the universe.*

I can't get rid of it. I've tried to change it or dump it, but I can't. I *cannot*. It feels like the truest thing I've ever written. It's as mysterious and as obvious as any other explanation of God or the universe that I've ever read, except that to me the others feel inadequate, at best.

All the rest of Earthseed is explanation—what God is, what God

OCTAVIA E. BUTLER

does, what we are, what we should do, what we can't help doing. . . . Consider: Whether you're a human being, an insect, a microbe, or a stone, this verse is true.

> *All that you touch,*
> *You Change.*
>
> *All that you Change,*
> *Changes you.*
>
> *The only lasting truth*
> *Is Change.*
>
> *God*
> *Is Change.*

I'm going to go through my old journals and gather the verses I've written into one volume. I'll put them into one of the exercise notebooks that Cory hands out to the older kids now that there are so few computers in the neighborhood. I've written plenty of useless stuff in those books, getting my high school work out of the way. Now I'll put one to better use. Then, someday when people are able to pay more attention to what I say than to how old I am, I'll use these verses to pry them loose from the rotting past, and maybe push them into saving themselves and building a future that makes sense.

That's if everything will just hold together for a few more years.

SATURDAY, JUNE 7, 2025

I've finally assembled a small survival pack for myself—a grab-and-run pack. I've had to dig some things I need out of the garage and the attic so that no one complains about my taking things they need. I've collected a hatchet, for instance, and two small, light, all-metal pots. There's plenty of stuff like that around because no one throws anything away that has any possibility of someday being useful or salable.

I packed my few hundred dollars in savings—almost a thousand. It *might* feed me for two weeks if I'm allowed to keep it, and if I'm very careful what I buy and where I buy it. I've kept up with prices, questioning Dad when he and the other neighborhood men do the essential shopping. Food prices are insane, always going up, never down. Everyone complains about them.

I found an old canteen and a plastic bottle both for water, and I resolved to keep them clean and full. I packed matches, a full change of clothing, including shoes in case I have to get up at night and run, comb, soap, toothbrush and toothpaste, tampons, toilet paper, bandages, pins, needles and thread, alcohol, aspirin, a couple of spoons and forks, a can opener, my pocket knife, packets of acorn flour, dried fruit, roasted nuts and edible seeds, dried milk, a little sugar and salt, my survival notes, several plastic storage bags, large and small, a lot of plantable raw seed, my journal, my Earthseed notebook, and lengths of clothesline. I stowed all this in a pair of old pillowcases, one inside the other for strength. I rolled the pillowcases into a blanket pack and tied it with some of the clothesline so that I could grab it and run without losing things, but I made it easy to open at the top so that I could get my journal in and out, change the water to keep it fresh, and less often, change the food and check on the seed. The last thing I wanted to find out was that instead of carrying plantable seed or edible food, I had a load of bugs and worms.

I wish I could take a gun. I don't own one and Dad won't let me keep one of his in my room. I mean to try to grab one if trouble comes, but I may not be able to. It would be crazy to wind up outside with nothing but a knife and a scared look, but it could happen. Dad and Wyatt Talcott took us out for target practice today, and afterward I tried to talk Dad into letting me keep one of the guns in my room.

"No," he said, sitting down, tired and dusty, behind his desk in his cluttered office. "You don't have anywhere to keep it safe during the day, and the boys are always in and out of your room."

I hesitated, then told him about the emergency pack that I had put together.

He nodded. "I thought it was a good idea back when you first suggested it," he said. "But, think, Lauren. It would be like a gift to a burglar. Money, food, water, a gun. . . . Most burglars don't find what they want all bundled up and waiting for them. I think we'd better make it a little harder for any burglar who comes here to get hold of a gun."

"It will just be a rolled up blanket mixed in with some other rolled or folded bed clothes in my closet," I said. "No one will even notice it."

"No." He shook his head. "No, the guns stay where they are."

And that's that. I think he's more worried about the boys snooping around than about burglars. My brothers have been taught how to behave around guns all their lives, but Greg is only eight and Ben is nine. Dad just isn't ready to put temptation in their paths yet. Marcus at 11 is more trustworthy than a lot of adults, but Keith at almost 13 is a question mark. He wouldn't steal from Dad. He wouldn't dare. But he has stolen from me—only little things so far. He wants a gun, though, the way thirsty people want water. He wants to be all grown up—yesterday. So maybe Dad's right. I hate his decision, but maybe he's right.

"Where would you go?" I asked him, changing the subject. "If we were forced out of here, where would you take us?"

He blew out a breath, puffing up his cheeks for a second. "To the neighbors or to the college," he said. "The college has temporary emergency accommodations for employees who are burned or driven out of their homes."

"And then?"

"Rebuilding, fortifying, doing whatever we can do to live and be safe."

"Would you ever think about leaving here, heading north to where water isn't such a problem and food is cheaper?"

"No." He stared into space. "My job down here is as secure as a job can be. There are no jobs up there. Newcomers work for food if they work at all. Experience doesn't matter. Education doesn't matter. There are just too many desperate people. They work their lives away for a sack of beans and they live on the streets."

"I heard it was easier up there," I said. "Oregon, Washington, Canada."

"Closed," he said. "You've got to sneak into Oregon if you get in at all. Even harder to sneak into Washington. People get shot every day trying to sneak into Canada. Nobody wants California trash."

"But people do leave. People are always moving north."

"They try. They're desperate and they have nothing to lose. But I do. This is my home. Beyond taxes, I don't owe a penny on it. You and your brothers have never known a hungry day here, and God willing, you never will."

In my Earthseed notebook, I've written,

> *A tree*
> *Cannot grow*
> *In its parents' shadows.*

Is it necessary to write things like that? Everyone knows them. What do they mean now, anyway? What does this one mean if you live in a cul-de-sac with a wall around it? What does it mean if you're damned lucky to live in a cul-de-sac with a wall around it?

MONDAY, JUNE 16, 2025

There was a long report on the radio today about the findings of the big Anglo-Japanese cosmological station on the moon. The station, with its vast array of telescopes and some of the most sensitive spectroscopic equipment ever made, has detected more planets orbiting nearby stars. That station has been detecting new worlds for a dozen years now, and there's even evidence that a few of the discovered worlds may be life-bearing. I've listened to and read every scrap of information I could find on this subject, and I've noticed that there's less and less argument against the likelihood that some of these worlds are alive. The idea is gaining scientific acceptance. Of course, no one has any idea whether the extrasolar life is anything more than a few trillion microbes. People speculate about intelligent life, and it's fun to think about, but no one is claiming to have found anyone to talk to out there. I don't care. Life alone is enough. I find it . . . more exciting and encouraging than I can explain, more important than I can explain. There *is* life out there. There are living worlds just a few light years away, and the United States is busy drawing back from even our nearby dead worlds, the moon and Mars. I understand why they are, but I wish they weren't.

I suspect that a living world might be easier for us to adapt to and live on without a long, expensive umbilical to Earth. *Easier* but not easy. Still, that's something, because I don't think there could be a multi-light-year umbilical. I think people who traveled to extrasolar worlds would be on their own—far from politicians and business people, failing economies and tortured ecologies—and far from help. Well out of the shadow of their parent world.

SATURDAY, JULY 19, 2025

Tomorrow, I'll be sixteen. Only sixteen. I feel older. I want to be older. I need to be older. I hate being a kid. Time drags!

Tracy Dunn has disappeared. She's been depressed since Amy was killed. When she talked at all, it was about dying and wanting to die and deserving to die. Everyone kept hoping she would get over her grief—or her guilt—and get on with her life. Maybe she couldn't. Dad talked with her several times, and I know he was worried about her. Her crazy family hasn't been any help. They treat her the way she treated Amy: They ignore her.

The rumor is that she went outside sometime yesterday. A group of Moss and Payne kids say they saw her go out of the gate just after they left school. No one has seen her since.

SUNDAY, JULY 20, 2025

Here's the birthday gift that came into my mind this morning as I woke up—just two lines:

> *The Destiny of Earthseed*
> *Is to take root among the stars.*

This is what I was reaching for a few days ago when the story of the new planets being discovered caught my attention. It's true, of course. It's obvious.

Right now, it's also impossible. The world is in horrible shape. Even rich countries aren't doing as well as history says rich countries used to do. President Donner isn't the only one breaking up and selling off science and space projects. No one is expanding the kind of exploration that doesn't earn an immediate profit, or at least promise big future profits. There's no mood now for doing anything that could be considered unnecessary or wasteful. And yet,

> *The Destiny of Earthseed*
> *Is to take root among the stars.*

I don't know how it will happen or when it will happen. There's so much to do before it can even begin. I guess that's to be expected. There's always a lot to do before you get to go to heaven.

OCTAVIA E. BUTLER

8

□ □ □

To get along with God,
Consider the consequences of your behavior.

EARTHSEED: THE BOOKS OF THE LIVING
SATURDAY, JULY 26, 2025

Tracy Dunn has not come home and has not been found by the police. I don't think she will be. She's only been gone for a week, but a week outside must be like a week in hell. People vanish outside. They go through our gate like Mr. Yannis did, and everyone waits for them, but they never come back—or they come back in an urn. I think Tracy Dunn is dead.

Bianca Montoya is pregnant. It isn't just gossip, it's true, and it matters to me, somehow. Bianca is 17, unmarried, and out of her mind about Jorge Iturbe who lives at the Ibarra house and is Yolanda Ibarra's brother.

Jorge admits to being the father. I don't know why they didn't just get married before everything got so public. Jorge is 23, and he, at least, ought to have some sense. Anyway, they're going to get married now. The Ibarra and Iturbe families have been feuding with the Montoyas for a week over this. So stupid. You'd think they had nothing else to do. At least they're both Latino. No interracial feud this time. Last year when Craig Dunn who's white and one of the saner members of the Dunn family was caught making love to Siti Moss who's black and Richard Moss's oldest daughter to boot, I thought someone was going to get killed. Crazy.

But my point isn't who's sleeping with whom or who's feuding.

My point is—my question is—how in the world can anyone get married and make babies with things the way they are now?

I mean, I know people have always gotten married and had kids, but now. . . . Now there's nowhere to go, nothing to do. A couple gets married, and if they're lucky, they get a room or a garage to live in—with no hope of anything better and every reason to expect things to get worse.

Bianca's chosen life is one of my options. It's not one that I intend to exercise, but it is pretty much what the neighborhood expects of me—of anyone my age. Grow up a little more, get married, have babies. Curtis Talcott says the new Iturbe family will get half-a-garage to live in after they marry. Jorge's sister Celia Iturbe Cruz and her husband and baby have the other half. Two couples, and not one paying job among them. The best they could hope for would be to move into some rich people's compound as domestic servants and work for room and board. There's no way to save any money or ever do any better.

And what if they wanted to go north, try for a better life in Oregon or Washington or Canada? It would be much harder to travel with a baby or two, and much more dangerous to try to sneak past hostile guards and over state lines or international borders with babies.

I don't know whether Bianca is brave or stupid. She and her sister are busy altering their mother's old wedding dress, and everyone's cooking and getting ready for a party as though these were the good old days. *How can they?*

I like Curtis Talcott a lot. Maybe I love him. Sometimes I think I do. He says he loves me. But if all I had to look forward to was marriage to him and babies and poverty that just keeps getting worse, I think I'd kill myself.

SATURDAY, AUGUST 2, 2025

We had a target practice today, and for the first time since I killed the dog, we found another corpse. We all saw it this time—an old woman, naked, maggoty, half-eaten, and beyond disgusting.

That did it for Aura Moss. She says she won't do anymore target shooting. Not ever. I tried talking to her, but she says it's the men's job to protect us anyway. She says women shouldn't have to practice with guns.

"What if you have to protect your younger sisters and brothers?" I asked her. She has to babysit them often enough.

"I already know enough to do that," she said.

"You get rusty without practice," I said.

"I'm not going out again," she insisted. "It's none of your business. I don't have to go!"

I couldn't move her. She was afraid, and that made her defensive. Dad said I should have waited until the memory of the corpse faded, then tried to convince her. He's right, I guess. It's the Moss attitude that gets me. Richard Moss lets his wives and daughters pull things like this. He works them like slaves in his gardens and rabbit raising operation and around the house, but he lets them pretend they're "ladies" when it comes to any community effort. If they don't want to do their part, he always backs them up. This is dangerous and stupid. It's a breeding ground for resentment. No Moss woman has ever stood a watch. I'm not the only one who's noticed.

The two oldest Payne kids went with us for the first time. Bad luck for them. They weren't scared off, though. Doyle and Margaret. There's a toughness to them. They're all right. Their uncle Wardell Parrish hadn't wanted them to go. He had made nasty comments about Dad's ego, about private armies and vigilantes, and about his taxes—how he had paid enough in his life to have a right to depend on the police to protect him. Blah, blah, blah. He's a strange, solitary, whiny man. I've heard that he used to be wealthy. Dad agrees with me that he can't be trusted. But he's not Doyle and Margaret's father, and their mother Rosalee Payne doesn't like anyone telling her how to raise her five kids. The only power she has in the world is her authority over her children and her money. She does have a little money, inherited from her parents. Her brother has somehow lost his. So his trying to tell her what to do or what she shouldn't let her kids do was a dumb move. He should have known better—though for the kids' sake, I'm glad he didn't.

My brother Keith begged to go with us as usual. He'll turn thirteen in a few days—August 14—and the thought of waiting two more years until he's 15 must seem impossible to him. I understand that. Waiting is terrible. Waiting to be older is worse than other kinds of waiting because there's nothing you can do to make it happen faster. Poor Keith. Poor me.

At least Dad lets Keith shoot at birds and squirrels with the family BB gun, but Keith still complains. "It's not fair," he said today for the twentieth or thirtieth time. "Lauren's a girl and you let her go. You always let her do things. I could learn to help you guard and scare off robbers. . . ." He had once made the mistake of offering to help "shoot robbers" instead of scaring them off, and Dad all but preached him a sermon. Dad almost never hits us, but he can be scary without lifting a finger.

Keith didn't go today, of course. And our practice went all right until we found the corpse. We didn't see any dogs this time. Most upsetting to me, though, there were a few more rag, stick, cardboard, and palm frond shacks along the way into the hills along River Street. There always seem to be more. They've never bothered us beyond begging and cursing, but they always stare so. It gets harder to ride past them. They're living skeletons, some of them. Skin and bones and a few teeth. They eat whatever they can find up there.

Sometimes I dream about the way they stare at us.

Back at home, my brother Keith slipped out of the neighborhood—out through the front gates and away. He stole Cory's key and took off on his own. Dad and I didn't know until we got home. Keith was still gone, and by then Cory knew he must be outside. She had checked with others in the neighborhood and two of the Dunn kids, twins

Allison and Marie, age six, said they saw him go out the gate. That was when Cory went home and discovered that her key was gone.

Dad, tired and angry and scared, was going to go right back out to look for him, but Keith got home just as Dad was leaving. Cory, Marcus, and I had gone to the front porch with Dad, all three of us speculating about where Keith had gone, and Marcus and I volunteering to go with Dad to help search. It was almost dark.

"You get back in that house and stay there," Dad said. "It's bad enough to have one of you out there." He checked the submachine gun, made sure it was fully loaded.

"Dad, look," I said. I had spotted something moving three houses down—quick, shadowy movement alongside the Garfield porch. I didn't know it was Keith. I was attracted by its furtiveness. Someone was sneaking around, trying to hide.

Dad was quick enough to see the movement before it was hidden by the Garfield house. He got up at once, took the gun, and went to check. The rest of us watched and waited.

Moments later Cory said she heard an odd noise in the house. I was too focused on Dad and what was going on outside to hear what she heard, or to pay any attention to her. She went in. Marcus and I were still on the porch when she screamed.

Marcus and I glanced at each other, then at the front door. Marcus lunged for the door. I yelled for Dad. Dad was out of sight, but I heard him answer my call.

"Come quick," I shouted, then I ran into the house.

Cory, Marcus, Bennett, and Gregory were in the kitchen, clustered around Keith. Keith was sprawled, panting, on the floor, wearing only his underpants. He was scraped and bruised, bleeding, and filthy. Cory knelt beside him, examining him, questioning him, crying.

"What happened to you? Who did this? Why did you go outside? Where are your clothes? What—?"

"Where's the key you stole?" Dad cut in. "Did they take it from you?"

Everyone jumped, looked up at Dad, then down at Keith.

"I couldn't help it," Keith said, still panting. "I couldn't, Daddy. There were five guys."

"So they got the key."

Keith nodded, careful not to meet Dad's eyes.

Dad turned and strode out of the house, almost at a run. It was too late now to get George or Brian Hsu to change the gate lock. That would have to be done tomorrow, and new keys made and passed out. I thought Dad must be going out to warn people and to put more watchers on duty. I wanted to offer to help alert people, but I didn't. Dad looked too angry to accept help from one of his kids right then. And when he got back, Keith was in for it. Was he ever in for it. A pair of pants gone, and a shirt and *a pair of shoes*. Cory had never been willing to let us run around barefoot the way a lot of kids did, except in the house. Her definitions of being civilized did not involve dirty, heavily callused feet anymore than they involved dirty, diseased skin. Shoes were expensive, and we were always growing out of ours, but Cory insisted. Each of us had at least one pair of wearable shoes, in spite of what they cost, and they cost a lot. Now money would have to be found to get an extra pair for Keith.

Keith curled up on the floor, smudging the tile with blood from his nose and mouth, hugging himself and crying now that Dad was gone. It took Cory two or three minutes to get him up and half carry him to the bathroom. I tried to help her, but she stared at me like I was the one who beat him up, so I let them alone. It wasn't as though I wanted to help. I just thought I should. Keith was in real pain, and it was hard for me to endure sharing it.

I cleaned up the blood so no one would slip in it or track it around. Then I fixed dinner, ate, fed the three younger boys, and put the rest aside for Dad, Cory, and Keith.

Keith had to confess what he had done this morning at church. He had to stand up in front of the whole congregation and tell them everything, including what the five thugs had done to him. Then he had to apologize—to God, to his parents, and to the congregation that he had endangered and inconvenienced. Dad made him do that over Cory's objections.

Dad never hit him, though last night he must have been tempted. "Why would you do such a thing!" he kept demanding. "How could any son of mine be so stupid! Where are your brains, boy? What did you think you were doing? I'm talking to you! Answer me!"

Keith answered and answered and answered, but the answers never seemed to make much sense to Dad. "I ain't no baby no more," he wept. Or, "I wanted to show you. Just wanted to show you! You always let Lauren do stuff!" Or, "I'm a man! I shouldn't be hiding in the house, hiding in the wall; I'm a man!"

It went on and on because Keith refused to admit he had done anything wrong. He wanted to show he was a man, not a scared girl. It wasn't his fault that a gang of guys jumped him, beat him, robbed him. He didn't do anything. It wasn't his fault.

Dad stared at him in utter disgust. "You disobeyed," he said. "You stole. You endangered the lives and the property of everyone here, including your mother, your sister, and your little brothers. If you were the man you think you are, I'd beat the hell out of you!"

Keith stared straight ahead. "Bad guys come in even if they don't have a key," he muttered. "They come in and steal stuff. It's not my fault!"

It took Dad two hours to get Keith to admit that it was his fault, no excuses. He'd done wrong. He wouldn't do it again.

My brother isn't very smart, but he makes up for it in pure stubbornness. My father is smart and stubborn. Keith didn't have a chance, but he made Dad work for his victory. The next morning,

Dad had his revenge. I don't believe he thought of Keith's forced confession that way, but Keith's expression told me that he did.

"How do I get out of this family," Marcus muttered to me as we watched. I sympathized. He had to share a room with Keith, and the two of them, only a year apart in age, fought all the time. Now things would be worse.

Keith is Cory's favorite. If you asked her, she would say she didn't have a favorite, but she does. She babies him and lets him get away with skipping chores, a little lying, a little stealing.. . . Maybe that's why Keith thinks when he screws up, it's okay.

This morning's sermon was on the ten commandments with extra emphasis on "Honor thy father and thy mother," and "Thou shalt not steal." I think Dad got rid of a lot of anger and frustration, preaching that sermon. Keith, tall, stone-faced, looking older than his thirteen years, kept his anger. I could see him keeping it inside, holding it down, choking on it.

OCTAVIA E. BUTLER

9

□ □ □

All struggles
Are essentially
power struggles.
Who will rule,
Who will lead,
Who will define,
refine,
confine,
design,
Who will dominate.
All struggles
Are essentially
power struggles,
And most
are no more intellectual
than two rams
knocking their heads together.

EARTHSEED: THE BOOKS OF THE LIVING
SUNDAY, AUGUST 17, 2025

My parents' usual good judgement failed them this week on my
brother Keith's birthday. They gave him his own BB gun. It wasn't
new, but it worked, and it looked much more dangerous than it
was. And it was his. He didn't have to share it. I suppose it was
intended to make him feel better about the two years he still had to
wait until he got his hands on the Smith & Wesson, or better yet,
the Heckler & Koch. And, of course, it was supposed to help him

get over his stupid desire to sneak out, and the humiliation of his public confession.

Keith shot a few more pigeons and crows, threatened to shoot Marcus—Marcus just told me about that tonight—then yesterday, he took off for parts unknown. He took the BB gun with him, of course. No one has seen him for about eighteen hours, and there's not much doubt that he's gone outside again.

MONDAY, AUGUST 18, 2025

Dad went out looking for Keith today. He even called in the police. He says he doesn't know how we'll afford the fee, but he's scared. The longer Keith is gone, the more likely he is to get hurt or killed. Marcus says he thinks Keith went looking for the guys who beat him up. I don't believe it. Not even Keith would go looking for five guys—or even one guy—with nothing but a BB gun.

Cory's even more upset than Dad. She's scared and jumpy and sick to her stomach, and she keeps crying. I talked her into going back to bed, then taught her classes myself. I've done that four or five times before when she was sick, so it wasn't too weird for the kids. I just used Cory's lesson plans, and during the first part of the day, I partnered the older kids with my kindergartners and let everyone get a taste of teaching or learning from someone different. Some of my students are my age and older, and a couple of these—Aura Moss and Michael Talcott—got up and left. They knew I understood the work. I got the last of my high school work and tests out of the way almost two years ago. Since then I've done uncredited (free) college work with Dad. Michael and Aura know all that, but they're much too grown up to learn anything from the likes of me. The hell with them. It's a pity, though, that my Curtis has to have a brother like Michael—not that any of us gets to choose our brothers.

OCTAVIA E. BUTLER

No sign of Keith. I think Cory has gone into mourning for him. I handled classes again today, and Dad went out searching again. He came home looking exhausted tonight, and Cory wept and shouted at him.

"You didn't try!" she said with me and all three of my brothers looking on. We'd all come to see whether Dad had brought Keith back. "You could have found him if you'd tried!"

Dad tried to go to her, but she backed away, still shouting: "If it were your precious Lauren out there alone, you would have found her by now! You don't care about Keith."

She's never said anything like that before.

I mean, we were always Cory and Lauren. She never asked me to call her "mother," and I never thought to do it. I always knew she was my stepmother. But still . . . I always loved her. It mystified me that Keith was her favorite, but it didn't make me love her any less. I was her kid, but not her kid. Not quite. Not really. But I always thought she loved me.

Dad shooed us all off to bed. He quieted Cory and took her back to their room. A few minutes ago, he came to see me.

"She didn't mean it," he said. "She loves you as though you were her daughter, Lauren."

I just looked at him.

"She wants you to know she's sorry."

I nodded, and after a few more assurances, he went.

Is she sorry? I don't think so.

Did she mean it. She did. Oh, yes, she meant it.

Shit.

THURSDAY, AUGUST 30, 2025

Keith came back last night.

He just walked into the house during dinner, as though he'd been outside playing football instead of gone since Saturday. And this time he looked fine. Not a mark on him. He was wearing a clean new set of clothing—even new shoes. All of it was of much better quality than he had when he left, and much more expensive than we could have afforded.

He still had the BB gun until Dad took it away from him and smashed it.

Keith wouldn't say where he'd been or how he'd gotten the new things, so Dad beat him bloody.

I've only seen Dad like that once before—when I was 12. Cory tried to stop him, tried to pull him off Keith, screamed at him in English, then in Spanish, then without words.

Gregory threw up on the floor, and Bennett started to cry. Marcus backed away from the whole scene, and slipped out of the house.

Then it was over.

Keith was crying like a two-year-old and Cory was holding him. Dad stood over both of them, looking dazed.

I followed Marcus out the back door and stumbled and almost fell down the back steps. I didn't know what I was doing. Marcus wasn't around. I sat on the steps in the warm darkness and let my body shake and hurt and vomit in helpless empathy with Keith. Then I guess I passed out.

I came to sometime later with Marcus shaking me and whispering my name.

I got up with Marcus hanging on to my arm, trying to steady me, and I got to my bedroom.

"Let me sleep in here," he whispered once I was sitting on my bed, dazed and still in pain. "I'll sleep on the floor, I don't care."

"All right," I said, not caring where he slept. I lay down on the bed without taking off even my shoes, and drew my body into a fetal ball on top of the bedclothes. I either fell asleep that way or I passed out again.

SATURDAY, OCTOBER 25, 2025

Keith has gone outside again. He went yesterday afternoon. Cory didn't admit until tonight that he took not only her key this time, but her gun. He took the Smith & Wesson.

Dad refused to go out and look for him. Dad slept in his office last night. He's sleeping there again tonight.

I never liked my brother much. I hate him now for what he's doing to the family—for what he's doing to my father. I hate him. Damn, I hate him.

MONDAY, NOVEMBER 3, 2025

Keith came home tonight while Dad was visiting over at the Talcott house. I suspect that Keith hung around and watched the house and waited until Dad left. He had come to see Cory. He brought her a lot of money done up in a fat roll.

She stared at it, then took it, dazed. "So much, Keith," she whispered. "Where did you get it?"

"It's for you," he said. "All for you, not him."

He took her hand and closed it around the money—and she let him do it, though she had to know it must be stolen money or drug money or worse.

Keith gave Bennett and Gregory big, expensive bars of milk chocolate with peanuts. He just smiled at Marcus and me—an obvious "fuck you" smile. Then, before Dad could come home and find him here, he left again. Cory hadn't realized that he was leaving again, and she all but screamed and clung to him.

"No! You'll be killed out there! What's the matter with you? Stay home!"

"Mama, I won't let him beat me again," he said. "I don't need him hitting me and telling me what to do. Pretty soon, I'll be able to make more money in a day than he can in a week—maybe in a month."

"You'll be killed!"

"No I won't. I know what I'm doing." He kissed her, then, with surprising ease, took her arms from around him. "I'll come back and see you," he said. "I'll bring you presents."

And he vanished out the back door, and was gone.

2026

□ □ □

Civilization is to groups what intelligence is to individuals. It is a means of combining the intelligence of many to achieve ongoing group adaptation.

Civilization, like intelligence, may serve well, serve adequately, or fail to serve its adaptive function. When civilization fails to serve, it must disintegrate unless it is acted upon by unifying internal or external forces.

EARTHSEED: THE BOOKS OF THE LIVING

10

□ □ □

When apparent stability disintegrates,
As it must—
God is Change—
People tend to give in
To fear and depression,
To need and greed.
When no influence is strong enough
To unify people
They divide.
They struggle,
One against one,
Group against group,
For survival, position, power.
They remember old hates and generate new ones,
They create chaos and nurture it.
They kill and kill and kill,
Until they are exhausted and destroyed,
Until they are conquered by outside forces,
Or until one of them becomes
A leader
Most will follow,
Or a tyrant
Most fear.

EARTHSEED: THE BOOKS OF THE LIVING

Keith came home yesterday, bigger than ever, as tall and lean as Dad is tall and broad. He's not quite 14, but he already looks like the man he wants so much to be. We're like that, we Olaminas—tall, sturdy, fast growing people. Except for Gregory who is only nine, we all tower over Cory. I'm still the tallest, but my height seems to annoy her these days. She loves Keith's size, though—her big son. She just hates the fact that he doesn't live with us anymore.

"I got a room," he said to me yesterday. We talked, he and I. Cory was with Dorotea Cruz who is one of her best friends and who had just had another baby. The other boys were playing in the street and on the island. Dad had gone to the college, and would be gone over-night. Now, more than ever, it's safest to go out just at dawn, and not to try coming home until just at dawn the next morning. That's if you have to go outside at all, which Dad does about once a week. The worst parasites still prowl at night and sleep late into the morning. Yet Keith lives outside.

"I got a room in a building with some other people," he said. Translation: He and his friends were squatting in an abandoned building. Who were his friends? A gang? A flock of prostitutes? A bunch of *astronauts*, flying high on drugs? A den of thieves? All of the above? Whenever he came to see us he brought money to Cory and little gifts to Bennett and Gregory.

How could he get money? There's no honest way.

"Do your friends know how old you are?" I asked.

He grinned. "Hell, no. Why should I tell them that?"

I nodded. "It does help to look older sometimes."

"You want something to eat?"

"You going to cook for me?"

"I've cooked for you hundreds of times. Thousands."

"I know. But you always had to before."

"Don't be stupid. You think I couldn't act the way you did: Skip out on my responsibilities if I felt like it? I don't feel like it. You want to eat or not?"

"Sure."

I made rabbit stew and acorn bread—enough for Cory and all the boys when they came in. He hung around and watched me work for a while, then began to talk to me. He's never done that before. We've never, never liked each other, he and I. But he had information I wanted, and he seemed to want to talk. I must have been the safest person he could talk to. He wasn't afraid of shocking me. He didn't much care what I thought. And he wasn't afraid I'd tell Dad or Cory anything he said. Of course, I wouldn't. Why cause them pain? I've never been much for tattling on people, anyway.

"It's just a nasty old building on the outside," he was saying of his new home. "You wouldn't believe how great it looks once you go in, though."

"Whorehouse or spaceship?" I asked.

"It's got stuff like you never saw," he evaded. "TV windows you go through instead of just sitting and looking at. Headsets, belts, and touchrings . . . you see and feel everything, do anything. Anything! There's places and things you can get into with that equipment that are insane! You don't ever have to go into the street except to get food."

"And whoever owns this stuff took you in?" I asked.

"Yeah."

"Why?"

He looked at me for a long time, then started to laugh. "Because I can read and write," he said at last. "And none of them can. They're all older than me, but not one of them can read or write anything. They stole all this great stuff and they couldn't even use it. Before I got there they even broke some of it because they couldn't read the instructions."

Cory and I had had a hell of a struggle, teaching him to read and write. He had been bored, impatient, anything but eager.

"So you read for a living—help your new friends learn to use their stolen equipment," I said.

"Yeah."

"And what else?"

"Nothin' else."

What a piss-poor liar he is. Always was. He's got no conscience. He just isn't smart enough to tell convincing lies. "Drugs, Keith?" I asked. "Prostitution? Robbery?"

"I said nothing else! You always think you know everything."

I sighed. "You're not done causing Dad and Cory pain are you? Not by a long shot."

He looked as though he wanted to shout back at me or hit me. He might have done one or the other if I hadn't mentioned Cory.

"I don't give a shit about him," he said, his voice low and ugly. He had a man's voice already. He had everything but a man's brain. "I do more for her than he does. I bring her money and nice things. And my friends . . . my friends know she lives here, and they let this place alone. He's nothing!"

I turned and looked at him and saw my father's face, lighter-skinned, younger, thinner, but my father's face, unmistakable. "He's you," I whispered. "Every time I look at you, I see him. Every time you look at him, you see yourself."

"Dogshit!"

I shrugged.

It was a long time before he spoke again. At last he said, "Did he ever hit you?"

"Not for about five years."

"Why'd he hit you—back then?"

I thought about that, and decided to tell him. He was old enough. "He caught me and Rubin Quintanilla in the bushes together."

Keith shouted with abrupt laughter. "You and Rubin? Really? You were doing it with him? You're kidding."

"We were twelve. What the hell."

"You're lucky you didn't get pregnant."

"I know. Twelve can be a dumb age."

He looked away. "Bet he didn't beat you as bad as he beat me!"

"He sent you boys over to play with the Talcotts." I gave him a glass of cold orange juice and poured one for myself.

"I don't remember," he said.

"You were nine," I said. "Nobody was going to tell you what was going on. As I remember, I told you I fell down the back steps."

He frowned, perhaps remembering. My face had been memorable. Dad hadn't beaten me as badly as he beat Keith, but I looked worse. He should remember that.

"He ever beat up Mama?"

I shook my head. "No. I've never seen any sign of it. I don't think he would. He loves her, you know. He really does."

"Bastard!"

"He's our father, and he's the best man I know."

"Did you think that when he beat you?"

"No. But later when I figured out how stupid I'd been, I was just glad he was so strict. And back when it happened, I was just glad he didn't quite kill me."

He laughed again—twice in just a few minutes, and both times at things I'd said. Maybe he was ready to open up a little now.

"Tell me about the outside," I said. "How do you live out there?"

He drained the last of his second glass of juice. "I told you. I live real good out there."

"But how did you live when you first went out—when you went to stay."

He looked at me and smiled. He smiled like that years ago when he used red ink to trick me into bleeding in empathy with a wound he didn't have. I remember that particular nasty smile.

"You want to go out yourself, don't you?" he demanded.

"Someday."

"What, instead of marrying Curtis and having a bunch of babies?"

"Yeah. Instead of that."

"I wondered why you were being so nice to me."

The food smelled just about ready, so I got up and took the bread from the oven and bowls from the cupboard. I was tempted to tell him to dish up his own stew, but I knew he would spoon all the meat out of the stew and leave nothing but potatoes and vegetables for the rest of us. So I served him and myself, covered the pot, left it on the lowest possible fire, and put a towel over the bread.

I let him eat in peace for a while, though I thought the boys would be coming in any time now, starving.

Then I was afraid to wait any longer. "Talk to me, Keith," I said. "I really want to know. How did you survive when you first went out there."

His smile this time was less evil. Maybe the food had mellowed him. "Slept in a cardboard box for three days and stole food," he said. "I don't know why I kept going back to that box. Could have slept in any old corner. Some kids carry a piece of cardboard to sleep on—so they won't be right down on the ground, you know.

"Then I got a sleepsack from an old man. It was new, like he never used it. Then I—"

"You stole it?"

He gave me a look of scorn. "What you think I was going to do? I didn't have no money. Just had that gun—Mama's .38."

Yes. He had brought it back to her three visits ago, along with two boxes of ammunition. Of course he never said how he got the ammunition—or how he got his replacement gun—a Heckler & Koch nine millimeter just like Dad's. He just showed up with things and claimed that if you had the money, you could buy anything out-side. He had never admitted how he got the money.

"Okay," I said. "So you stole a sleepsack. And you kept stealing food? It's a wonder you didn't get caught."

"The old guy had some money. I used it to buy food. Then I started walking toward L.A."

That old dream of his. For reasons that make sense to him alone, he's always wanted to go to L.A. Any sane person would be thankful for the twenty miles that separate us from that oozing sore.

"There's people all over the freeway coming away from L.A.," he said. "There's even people walking up from way down in San Diego. They don't know where they're going. I talked to this guy, he said he was going to Alaska. Goddamn. Alaska!"

"Good luck to him," I said. "He's got a lot of guns to face before he gets there."

"He won't get there. Alaska must be a thousand miles from here!"

I nodded. "More than that, and with hostile state lines and borders along the way. But good luck to him anyhow. It's a goal that makes sense."

"He had twenty-three thousand dollars in his pack."

I didn't say anything. I just froze, stared at him in disgust and renewed dislike. But of course. Of course.

"You wanted to know," he said. "That's what it's like outside. If you got a gun, you're somebody. If you don't, you're shit. And a lot of people out there don't have guns."

"I thought most of them did—except the ones too poor to be worth robbing."

"I thought so too. But guns cost a lot. And it's easier to get one if you already got one, you know?"

"What if that Alaska guy had had one. You'd be dead."

"I sneaked up on him while he was sleeping. Just sort of followed him until he went off the road to go to sleep. Then I got him. He led me away from L.A., though."

"You shot him?"

The nasty smile again.

"He talked to you. He was friendly to you. And you shot him."

"What was I supposed to do? Wait for God to come and give me some money? What was I supposed to do?"

"Come home."

"Shit."

"Doesn't it even bother you that you took someone's life—you killed a man?"

He seemed to think about that for a while. Then he shook his head. "It don't bother me," he said. "I was scared at first, but then . . . after I did it, I didn't feel nothing. Nobody saw me do it. I just took his stuff and left him there. Besides, maybe he wasn't dead. People don't always die just because you shoot them."

"You didn't check?"

"I just wanted his stuff. He was crazy anyway. Alaska!"

I didn't say anymore to him, didn't ask anymore questions. He talked a little about meeting some guys and joining up with them, then discovering that even though they were all older than he was, none of them could read or write. He was a help to them. He made their lives pleasanter. Maybe that's why they didn't just wait until he was asleep and kill him and take his loot for themselves.

After a while, he noticed that I wasn't saying anything, and he laughed. "You better marry Curtis and make babies," he said. "Out there, outside, you wouldn't last a day. That hyperempathy shit of yours would bring you down even if nobody touched you."

"You think that," I said.

"Hey, I saw a guy get both of his eyes gouged out. After that, they set him on fire and watched him run around and scream and burn. You think you could stand to see that?"

"Your new friends did that?" I asked.

"Hell no! Crazies did that. Paints. They shave off all their hair—even their eyebrows—and they paint their skin green or blue or red or yellow. They eat fire and kill rich people."

"They do what?"

"They take that drug that makes them like to watch fires. Sometimes a camp fire or a trash fire or a house fire. Or sometimes they grab a rich guy and set him on fire."

"Why?"

"I don't know. They're crazy. I heard some of them used to be rich kids, so I don't know why they hate rich people so much. That drug is bad, though. Sometimes the paints like the fire so much they get too close to it. Then their friends don't even help him. They just watch them burn. It's like . . . I don't know, it's like they were fucking the fire, and like it was the best fuck they ever had."

"You've never tried it?"

"Hell no! I told you. Those guys are crazy. You know, even the girls shave their heads. Damn, they look ugly!"

"They're mostly kids, then?"

"Yeah. Your age up to maybe twenty. There's a few old ones, twenty-five, even thirty. I hear most of them don't live that long though."

Cory and the boys came in at that moment, Gregory and Bennett excited because their side in soccer had won. Cory was happy and wistful, talking to Marcus about Dorotea Cruz's new baby girl. Things changed when they all saw Keith, of course, but the evening wasn't too bad. Keith had presents for the little boys, of course, and money for Cory and nothing for Marcus and me. This time, though, he was a little shamefaced with me.

"Maybe I'll bring you something next time," he said.

"No, don't," I said, thinking of the Alaska-bound traveler. "It's all right. I don't want anything."

He shrugged and turned to talk to Cory.

MONDAY, JULY 20, 2026

Keith came to see me today just before dark. He found me walking home from the Talcott house where Curtis had been wishing me a very happy birthday. We've been very careful, Curtis and I, but from somewhere or other, he's gotten a supply of condoms. They're old fashioned, but they work. And there's an unused darkroom in a corner of the Talcott garage.

Keith scared me out of a very sweet mood. He came from behind two houses without making a sound. He had almost reached me before I realized someone was there and turned to face him.

He raised his hands, smiling, "Brought you a birthday present," he said. He put something into my left hand. Money.

"Keith, no, give it to Cory."

"You give it to her. You want her to have it, you give it to her. I gave it to you."

I walked him to the gate, concerned that one of the watchers might spot him and shoot him. He was that much taller than he had been when he stopped living with us. Dad was home so he wouldn't come in. I thanked him for the money and told him I would give it to Cory. I wanted him to know that because I didn't want him to bring me anything else, ever.

He seemed not to mind. He kissed the side of my face said, "Happy birthday," and went out. He still had Cory's key, and although Dad knew he had it, he hadn't had the lock changed again.

WEDNESDAY, AUGUST 26, 2026

Today, my parents had to go downtown to identify the body of my brother Keith.

SATURDAY, AUGUST 29, 2026

I haven't been able to write a word since Wednesday. I don't know what to write. The body was Keith's. I never saw it, of course. Dad said he tried to keep Cory from seeing it. The things someone had done to Keith before he died. . . . I don't want to write about this, but I need to. Sometimes writing about a thing makes it easier to stand.

Someone had cut and burned away most of my brother's skin. Everywhere except his face. They burned out his eyes, but left the rest of his face intact—like they wanted him to be recognized. They cut and they cauterized and they cut and they cauterized. . . . Some of the wounds were days old. Someone had an endless hatred of my brother.

Dad got us all together and described to us what had been done. He told it in a flat, dead monotone. He wanted to scare us, to scare Marcus, Bennett, and Gregory in particular. He wanted us to understand just how dangerous the outside is.

The police said drug dealers torture people the way Keith was tortured. They torture people who steal from them and people who compete with them. We don't know whether Keith was doing either of these things. We just know he's dead. His body was dumped across town from here in front of a burned-out old building that was once a nursing home. It was dumped on the broken concrete and abandoned several hours after Keith died. It could have been dumped in one of the canyons and only the dogs would have found it. But someone wanted it to be found, wanted it to be recognized. Had one of his victims' relatives or friends managed to get even at last?

The police seemed to think we should know who killed him. I got the feeling from their questions that they would have been happy to arrest Dad or Cory or both of them. But they both lead very public lives, and neither had any unexplained absences or other breaks in routine. Dozens of people could give them alibis. Of course, I said nothing about what Keith had told me he had been doing. What good would that do? He was dead, and in a horrible way. By accident or by intent, all his victims were avenged.

Wardell Parrish felt called upon to tell the police about the big fight Dad and Keith had had last year. He'd heard it, of course. Half the neighborhood had heard it. Family fights are neighborhood theater—and Dad, the minister, after all!

I know Wardell Parrish was the one who told the cops. His youngest niece Tanya let that much slip. "Uncle Ward said he hated to mention it but . . ."

Oh, I'll bet he hated to mention it. Damned bastard! But nobody backed him up. The cops went nosing around the neighborhood, but no one else admitted knowing anything about a fight. After all, they knew Dad didn't kill Keith. And they knew the cops liked to solve cases by "discovering" evidence against whomever they decided must be guilty. Best to give them nothing. They never helped when people called for help. They came later, and more often than not, made a bad situation worse.

We had the service today. Dad asked his friend Reverend Robinson to take care of it. Dad just sat with Cory and the rest of us and looked bent and old. So old.

Cory cried all day, most of the time without making a sound. She's been crying off and on since Wednesday. Marcus and Dad tried to comfort her. Even I tried, though the way she looked at me . . . as though I had had something to do with Keith's death, as though she almost hated me. I keep reaching out to her. I don't know what else to do. Maybe in time, she'll be able to forgive me for not being her daughter, for being alive when her son is dead, for being Dad's daughter by someone else . . . ? I don't know.

Dad never shed a tear. I've never seen him cry in my life. Today, I wish he would. I wish he could.

Curtis Talcott sort of hung around with me today, and we talked and talked. I guess I needed to talk, and Curtis was willing to put up with me.

He said I should cry. He said no matter how bad things had gotten between Keith and me or Keith and the family, I should let myself cry. Odd. Until he brought it up, I hadn't thought about my own absence of tears. I hadn't cried at all. Maybe Cory had noticed. Maybe my dry face was just one more grudge she held against me.

It wasn't that I was holding back, being stoic. It's just that I hated Keith at least as much as I loved him. He was my brother—half-brother—but he was also the most sociopathic person I've ever been close to. He would have been a monster if he had been allowed to grow up. Maybe he was one already. He never cared what he did. If

OCTAVIA E. BUTLER

he wanted to do something and it wouldn't cause him immediate physical pain, he did it, fuck the earth.

He messed up our family, broke it into something less than a family. Still, I would never have wished him dead. I would never wish anyone dead in that horrible way. I think he was killed by monsters much worse than himself. It's beyond me how one human being could do that to another. If hyperempathy syndrome were a more common complaint, people couldn't do such things. They could kill if they had to, and bear the pain of it or be destroyed by it. But if everyone could feel everyone else's pain, who would torture? Who would cause anyone unnecessary pain? I've never thought of my problem as something that might do some good before, but the way things are, I think it would help. I wish I could give it to people. Failing that, I wish I could find other people who have it, and live among them. A biological conscience is better than no conscience at all.

But as for me crying, if I were going to cry, I think I would have done it back when Dad beat Keith—when the beating was over and Dad saw what he had done, and we all saw how both Keith and Cory looked at him. I knew then that neither of them would ever forgive him. Not ever. That was the end of something precious in the family.

I wish Dad could cry for his son, but I don't feel any need at all to cry for my brother. May he rest in peace—in his urn, in heaven, wherever.

11

□ □ □

Any Change may bear seeds of benefit.
Seek them out.
Any Change may bear seeds of harm.
Beware.
God is infinitely malleable.
God is Change.

EARTHSEED: THE BOOKS OF THE LIVING
SATURDAY, OCTOBER 17, 2026

We are coming apart.

The community, the families, individual family members. . . .
We're a rope, breaking, a single strand at a time.

There was another robbery last night—or an attempted robbery.
I wish that was all. No garden theft this time. Three guys came over
the wall and crowbarred their way into the Cruz house. The Cruz
family, of course, has loud burglar alarms, barred windows, and security gates at all the doors just like the rest of us, but that doesn't seem
to matter. When people want to come in, they come in. The thieves
used simple hand tools—crowbars, hydraulic jacks, things anyone
can get. I don't know how they disabled the burglar alarm. I know
they cut the electrical and phone lines to the house. That shouldn't
have mattered since the alarm had back-up batteries. Whatever else
they did, or whatever went wrong, the alarm didn't go off. And
after the thieves used the crowbar on the door, they walked into the
kitchen and used it on Dorotea Cruz's seventy-five-year-old grandmother. The old lady was a light sleeper and had gotten into the
habit of getting up at night and brewing herself a cup of lemon grass

125

tea. Her family says that's what she was coming into the kitchen to do when the thieves broke in.

Then Dorotea's brothers Hector and Rubin Quintanilla, came running, guns in hand. They had the bedroom nearest to the kitchen and they heard all the noise—the break-in itself and Mrs. Quintanilla being knocked against the kitchen table and chairs. They killed two of the thieves. The third got away, perhaps wounded. There was a lot of blood. But old Mrs. Quintanilla was dead.

This is the seventh incident since Keith was killed. More and more people are coming over our wall to take what we have, or what they think we have. Seven intrusions into house or garden in less than two months—in an 11-household community. If this is what's happening to us, what must it be like for people who are really rich—although perhaps with their big guns, private armies of security guards, and up to date security equipment, they're better able to fight back. Maybe that's why we're getting so much attention. We have a few stealables and we're not that well protected. Of the seven intrusions, three were successful. Thieves got in and out with something—a couple of radios, a sack of walnuts, wheat flour, corn meal, pieces of jewelry, an ancient TV, a computer. . . . If they could carry it, they made off with it. If what Keith told me is true, we're getting the poorer class of thieves here. No doubt the tougher, smarter, more courageous thieves hit stores and businesses. But our lower-class thugs are killing us slowly.

Next year, I'll be 18—old enough, according to Dad, to stand a regular night watch. I wish I could do it now. As soon as I can do it, I will. But it won't be enough.

It's funny. Cory and Dad have been using some of the money Keith brought us to help the people who've been robbed. Stolen money to help victims of theft. Half the money is hidden in our back yard in case of disaster. There has always been some money hidden out there. Now there's enough to make a difference. The other half has gone into the church fund to help our neighbors in emergencies. It won't be enough.

Something new is beginning—or perhaps something old and nasty is reviving. A company called Kagimoto, Stamm, Frampton, and Company—KSF—has taken over the running of a small coastal city called Olivar. Olivar, incorporated in the 1980s, is just one more beach/bedroom suburb of Los Angeles, small and well- to-do. It has little industry, much hilly, vacant land and a short, crumbling coastline. Its people, like some here in our Robledo neighborhood, earn salaries that would once have made them prosperous and comfortable. In fact, Olivar is a lot richer than we are, but since it's a coastal city, its taxes are higher, and since some of its land is unstable, it has extra problems. Parts of it sometimes crumble into the ocean, undercut or deeply saturated by salt water. Sea level keeps rising with the warming climate and there is the occasional earthquake. Olivar's flat, sandy beach is already just a memory. So are the houses and businesses that used to sit on that beach. Like coastal cities all over the world, Olivar needs special help. It's an upper middle class, white, literate community of people who once had a lot of weight to throw around. Now, not even the politicians it's helped to elect will stand by it. The whole state, the country, the world needs help, it's been told. What the hell is tiny Olivar whining about?

Somewhat richer and less geologically active communities are getting help—dikes, sea walls, evacuation assistance, whatever's appropriate. Olivar, located between the sea and Los Angeles, is getting an influx of salt water from one direction and desperate poor people from the other. It has a solar powered desalination plant on some of its flatter, more stable land, and that provides its people with a dependable supply of water.

But it can't protect itself from the encroaching sea, the crumbling earth, the crumbling economy, or the desperate refugees. Even getting back and forth to work, for those few who can't work at home, was becoming as dangerous for them as it is for our people—a kind of terrible gauntlet that has to be run over and over again.

Then the people of KSF showed up. After many promises, much haggling, suspicion, fear, hope, and legal wrangling, the voters and the officials of Olivar permitted their town to be taken over, bought out, privatized. KSF will expand the desalination plant to vast size. That plant will be the first of many. The company intends to dominate farming and the selling of water and solar and wind energy over much of the southwest—where for pennies it's already bought vast tracts of fertile, waterless land. So far, Olivar is one of its smaller coastal holdings, but with Olivar, it gets an eager, educated work force, people a few years older than I am whose options are very limited. And there's all that formerly public land that they now control. They mean to own great water, power, and agricultural industries in an area that most people have given up on. They have long-term plans, and the people of Olivar have decided to become part of them—to accept smaller salaries than their socio-economic group is used to in exchange for security, a guaranteed food supply, jobs, and help in their battle with the Pacific.

There are still people in Olivar who are uncomfortable with the change. They know about early American company towns in which the companies cheated and abused people.

But this is to be different. The people of Olivar aren't frightened, impoverished victims. They're able to look after themselves, their rights and their property. They're educated people who don't want to live in the spreading chaos of the rest of Los Angeles County. Some of them said so on the radio documentary we all listened to last night—as they made a public spectacle of selling themselves to KSF.

"Good luck to them," Dad said. "Not that they'll have much luck in the long run."

"What do you mean?" Cory demanded. "I think the whole idea is wonderful. It's what we need. Now if only some big company would want to do the same thing with Robledo."

"No," Dad said. "Thank God, no."

"You don't know! Why shouldn't they?"

"Robledo's too big, too poor, too black, and too Hispanic to be of interest to anyone—and it has no coastline. What it does have is street poor, body dumps, and a memory of once being well-off—of shade trees, big houses, hills, and canyons. Most of those things are still here, but no company will want us."

At the end of the program it was announced that KSF was looking for registered nurses, credentialed teachers, and a few other skilled professionals who would be willing to move to Olivar and work for room and board. The offer wasn't put that way, of course, but that's what it meant. Yet Cory recorded the phone number and called it at once. She and Dad are both teachers, both Ph.D.'s. She was desperate to get in ahead of the crowd. Dad just shrugged and let her call.

Room and board. The offered salaries were so low that if Dad and Cory both worked, they wouldn't earn as much as Dad is earning now with the college. And out of it they'd have to pay rent as well as the usual expenses. In fact, when you add everything up, it's clear that with the six of us, they couldn't earn enough to meet expenses. It might work if I could find a job of some kind, but in Olivar they don't need me. They've got hundreds of me, at least—maybe thousands. Every surviving community is full of unemployed, half-educated kids or unemployed, uneducated kids.

Anyone KSF hired would have a hard time living on the salary offered. In not very much time, I think the new hires would be in debt to the company. That's an old company-town trick—get people into debt, hang on to them, and work them harder. Debt slavery. That might work in Christopher Donner's America. Labor laws, state and federal, are not what they once were.

"We could *try*," Cory insisted to Dad. "We could be safe in Olivar. The kids could go to a real school and later get jobs with the company. After all, where can they go from here except outside?"

Dad shook his head. "Don't hope for it, Cory. There's nothing safe about slavery."

Marcus and I were still up, listening. The two younger boys had been sent to bed, but we four were still clustered around the radio. Now Marcus spoke up.

"Olivar doesn't sound like slavery," he said. "Those rich people would never let themselves be slaves."

Dad gave him a sad smile. "Not now," he said. "Not at first." He shook his head. "Kagimoto, Stamm, Frampton: Japanese, German, Canadian. When I was young, people said it would come to this. Well, why shouldn't other countries buy what's left of us if we put it up for sale. I wonder how many of the people in Olivar have any idea what they're doing."

"I don't think many do," I said. "I don't think they'd dare let themselves know."

He looked at me, and I looked back. I'm still learning how dogged people can be in denial, even when their freedom or their lives are at stake. He's lived with it longer. I wonder how.

Marcus said, "Lauren, you ought to want to go to some place like Olivar more than anyone. You share pain every time you see someone get hurt. There'd be a lot less pain in Olivar."

"And there would be all those guards," I said. "I've noticed that people who have a little bit of power tend to use it. All those guards KSF is bringing in—they won't be allowed to bother the rich people, at least at first. But new, bare-bones, work-for-room-and-board employees. . . . I'll bet they'll be fair game."

"There's no reason to believe the company would allow that kind of thing," Cory said. "Why do you always expect the worst of everyone?"

"When it comes to strangers with guns," I told her, "I think suspicion is more likely to keep you alive than trust."

She made a sharp, wordless sound of disgust. "You know nothing about the world. You think you have all the answers but you know nothing!"

OCTAVIA E. BUTLER

I didn't argue. There wasn't much point in my arguing with her.

"I doubt that Olivar is looking for families of blacks and Hispanics, anyway," Dad said. "The Balters or the Garfields or even some of the Dunns might get in, but I don't think we would. Even if I were trusting enough to put my family into KSF's hands, they wouldn't have us."

"We could try it," Cory insisted. "We should! We wouldn't be any worse off than we are now if they turn us down. And if we got in and we didn't like it, we could come back here. We could rent the house to one of the big families here—charge them just a little, then—"

"Then come back here jobless and penniless," Dad said. "No, I mean it. This business sounds half antebellum revival and half science fiction. I don't trust it. Freedom is dangerous, Cory, but it's precious, too. You can't just throw it away or let it slip away. You can't sell it for bread and pottage."

Cory stared at him—just stared. He refused to look away. Cory got up and went to their bedroom. I saw her there a few minutes later, sitting on the bed, cradling the urn of Keith's ashes, and crying.

SATURDAY, OCTOBER 24, 2026

Marcus tells me the Garfields are trying to get into Olivar. He's been spending a lot of time with Robin Balter and she told him. She hates the idea because she likes her cousin Joanne a lot better than she does her two sisters. She's afraid that if Joanne goes away to Olivar, she'll never see her again. I suspect she's right.

I can't imagine this place without the Garfields. Joanne, Jay, Phillida. . . . We've lost individuals before, of course, but we've never lost a whole family. I mean . . . they'll be alive, but . . . they'll be gone.

I hope they're refused. I know it's selfish, but I don't care. Not that it makes any difference what I hope. Oh hell. I hope they get whatever will be best for their survival. I hope they'll be all right.

At 13, my brother Marcus has become the only person in the family whom I would call beautiful. Girls his age stare at him when they think he's not looking. They giggle a lot around him and chase him like crazy, but he sticks to Robin. She's not pretty at all—all skin and bones and brains—but she's funny and sensible. In a year or two, she'll start to fill out and my brother will get beauty along with all those brains. Then, if the two of them are still together, their lives will get a lot more interesting.

I've changed my mind. I used to wait for the explosion, the big crash, the sudden chaos that would destroy the neighborhood. Instead, things are unraveling, disintegrating bit by bit. Susan Talcott Bruce and her husband have applied to Olivar. Other people are talking about applying, thinking about it. There's a small college in Olivar. There are lethal security devices to keep thugs and the street poor out. There are more jobs opening up. . . .

Maybe Olivar is the future—one face of it. Cities controlled by big companies are old hat in science fiction. My grandmother left a whole bookcase of old science fiction novels. The company-city subgenre always seemed to star a hero who outsmarted, overthrew, or escaped "the company." I've never seen one where the hero fought like hell to get taken in and underpaid by the company. In real life, that's the way it will be. That's the way it is.

And what should I be doing? What can I do? In less than a year, I'll be 18, an adult—an adult with no prospects except life in our disintegrating neighborhood. Or Earthseed.

To begin Earthseed, I'll have to go outside. I've known that for a long time, but the idea scares me just as much as it always has.

Next year when I'm 18, I'll go. That means now I have to begin to plan how I'll handle it.

OCTAVIA E. BUTLER

I'm going to go north. My grandparents once traveled a lot by car. They left us old road maps of just about every county in the state plus several of other parts of the country. The newest of them is 40 years old, but that doesn't matter. The roads will still be there. They'll just be in worse shape than they were back when my grandparents drove a gas-fueled car over them. I've put maps of the California counties north of us and the few I could find of Washington and Oregon counties into my pack.

I wonder if there are people outside who will pay me to teach them reading and writing—basic stuff—or people who will pay me to read or write for them. Keith started me thinking about that. I might even be able to teach some Earthseed verses along with the reading and writing. Given any chance at all, teaching is what I would choose to do. Even if I have to take other kinds of work to get enough to eat, I can teach. If I do it well, it will draw people to me—to Earthseed.

> *All successful life is*
> *Adaptable,*
> *Opportunistic,*
> *Tenacious,*
> *Interconnected, and*
> *Fecund.*
> *Understand this.*
> *Use it.*
> *Shape God.*

I wrote that verse a few months ago. It's true like all the verses. It seems more true than ever now, more useful to me when I'm afraid.

I've finally got a title for my book of Earthseed verses—Earthseed: The Book of the Living. There are the Tibetan and the Egyptian Books of the Dead. Dad has copies of them. I've never heard of anything called a book of the living, but I wouldn't be surprised to discover that there is something. I don't care. I'm trying to speak—to write—the truth. I'm trying to be clear. I'm not interested in being fancy, or even original. Clarity and truth will be plenty, if I can only achieve them. If it happens that there are other people outside somewhere preaching my truth, I'll join them. Otherwise, I'll adapt where I must, take what opportunities I can find or make, hang on, gather students, and teach.

12

□ □ □

We are Earthseed
The life that perceives itself
Changing.

EARTHSEED: THE BOOKS OF THE LIVING
SATURDAY, NOVEMBER 14, 2026

The Garfields have been accepted at Olivar.

They'll be moving next month. That soon. I've known them all my life, and they'll be gone. Joanne and I have had our differences, but we grew up together. I thought somehow that when I left, she would still be here. Everyone would still be here, frozen in time just as I left them. But no, that's fantasy. God is Change.

"Do you want to go?" I asked her this morning. We had gotten together to pick a few early lemons and navel oranges and some persimmons, almost ripe and brilliant orange. We picked at my house, and then at hers, enjoying the work. The weather was cool. It was good to be outside.

"I have to go," she said. "What else is there for me—for anyone. It's all going to hell here. You know it is."

I stared at her. I guess discussing such things is all right now that she has a way out. "So you move into another fortress," I said.

"It's a better fortress. It won't have people coming over the walls, killing old ladies."

"Your mother says all you'll have is an apartment. No yard. No garden. You'll have less money, but you'll have to use more of it to buy food."

"We'll manage!" There was a brittle quality to her voice.

I put down the old rake I was using as a fruit picker. It worked fine on the lemons and oranges. "Scared?" I asked.

She put down her own real fruit picker with its awkward extension handle and small fruit-catching basket. It was best for persimmons. She hugged herself. "I've lived here, lived with trees and gardens all my life. I . . . don't know how it will be to be shut up in an apartment. It does scare me, but we'll manage. We'll have to."

"You can come back here if things aren't what you hope. Your grandparents and your aunt's family will still be here."

"Harry will still be here," she whispered, looking toward her house. I would have to stop thinking of it as the Garfield house. Harry and Joanne were at least as close as Curtis and I. I hadn't thought about her leaving him—what that must be like. I like Harry Balter. I remember being surprised when he and Joanne first started going together. They'd lived in the same house all their lives. I had thought of Harry almost as her brother. But they were only first cousins, and against the odds, they had managed to fall in love. Or I thought they had. They hadn't gone with anyone else for years. Everyone assumed they would get around to marrying when they were a little older.

"Marry him and take him with you," I said.

"He won't go," she said in that same whisper. "We've talked and talked about it. He wants me to stay here with him, get married soon and go north. Just . . . go with no prospects. Nothing. It's crazy."

"Why won't he go to Olivar?"

"He thinks the way your father does. He thinks Olivar's a trap. He's read about nineteenth and early twentieth century company towns, and he says no matter how great Olivar looks, all we'll get from it in the end is debt and loss of freedom."

I knew Harry had sense. "Jo," I said, "you'll be of age next year. You could stay here with the Balters until then and marry. Or you could talk your father into letting you marry now."

"And then what? Go join the street poor? Stay and stuff more babies into that crowded house. Harry doesn't have a job, and there's no real chance of his getting one that pays money. Are we supposed to live on what Harry's parents earn? What kind of future is that? None! None at all!"

Sensible. Conservative and sensible and mature and *wrong*. Very much in character with Joanne.

Or maybe I was the one who was wrong. Maybe the security Joanne will find in Olivar is the only kind of security to be had for anyone who isn't rich. To me, though, security in Olivar isn't much more attractive than the security Keith has finally found in his urn.

I picked a few more lemons and some oranges and wondered what she would do if she knew I was also planning to leave next year. Would she run to her mother again, frightened for me, and eager to have someone protect me from myself? She might. She wants a future she can understand and depend on—a future that looks a lot like her parents' present. I don't think that's possible. Things are changing too much, too fast. Who can fight God?

We put baskets of fruit inside my back door on the porch, then headed for her house.

"What will you do?" she asked me as we walked. "Are you just going to stay here? I mean . . . are you going to stay and marry Curtis?"

I shrugged and lied. "I don't know. If I marry anyone, it will be Curtis. But I don't know about marrying. I don't want to have children here anymore than you do. I know we'll be staying here for a while longer, though. Dad won't let Cory even apply to Olivar. I'm glad of that because I don't want to go there. But there'll be other Olivars. Who knows what I might wind up doing?" That last didn't feel like a lie.

"You think there'll be more privatized cities?" she asked.

"Bound to be if Olivar succeeds. This country is going to be parceled out as a source of cheap labor and cheap land. When people like those in Olivar beg to sell themselves, our surviving cities are bound to wind up the economic colonies of whoever can afford to buy them."

"Oh, God, there you go again. You've always got a disaster up your sleeve."

"I see what's out there. You see it too. You just deny it."

"Remember when you thought starving hordes were going to come crawling over our walls and we would have to run away to the mountains and eat grass?"

Did I remember? I turned to face her, first angry—furious—then to my own surprise, sad. "I'll miss you," I said.

She must have read my feelings. "I'm sorry," she whispered.

We hugged each other. I didn't ask her what she was sorry for, and she didn't say anymore.

TUESDAY, NOVEMBER 17, 2026

Dad didn't come home today. He was due this morning.

I don't know what that means. I don't know what to think. I'm scared to death.

Cory called the college, his friends, fellow ministers, co-workers, the cops, the hospitals. . . .

Nothing. He isn't under arrest or sick or injured or dead—at least not as far as anyone knows. None of his friends or colleagues had seen him since he left work early this morning. His bike was working all right. He was all right.

He had ridden off toward home with three co-workers who lived in other neighborhoods in our area. Each of these said the same thing: That they had left him as usual at River Street where it intersects Durant Road. That's only five blocks from here. We're at the tip-end of Durant Road.

So where is he?

Today a group of us, all armed, rode bicycles from home to River Street and down River Street to the college. Five miles in all. We checked side streets, alleys, vacant buildings, every place we could think of. I went. I took Marcus with me because if I hadn't, he would have gone out alone. I had the Smith & Wesson. Marcus had only his knife. He's quick and agile with it, and strong for his age, but he's never used it on anything alive. If anything had happened to him, I don't think I would have dared to go home. Cory is already out of her mind with worry. All this on top of losing Keith. . . . I don't know. Everyone helped. Jay Garfield will be leaving soon, but that didn't stop him from leading the search. He's a good man. He did everything he could think of to find Dad.

Tomorrow we're going into the hills and canyons. We have to. No one wants to, but what else can we do?

WEDNESDAY, NOVEMBER 18, 2026

I've never seen more squalor, more human remains, more feral dogs than I saw today. I have to write. I have to dump this onto paper. I can't keep it inside of me. Seeing the dead has never bothered me before, but this . . .

We were looking for Dad's body, of course, though no one said so. I couldn't deny that reality or avoid thinking about it. Cory checked with the police again, with the hospitals, with everyone we could think of who knew Dad.

Nothing.

So we had to go to the hills. When we go for target practice, we don't look around, except to ensure safety. We don't look for what we'd rather not find. Today in groups of three or four, we combed through the area nearest to the top of River Street. I kept Marcus with me—which was not easy. What is it in young boys that makes them want to wander off alone and get killed? They get two chin hairs and they're trying to prove they're men.

"You watch my back and I'll watch yours," I said. "I'm not going to let you get hurt. Don't you let me down."

He gave me the kind of near-smile that said he knew exactly what I was trying to do, and that he was going to do as he pleased. I got mad and grabbed him by the shoulders.

"Dammit, Marcus, how many sisters have you got? How many fathers have you got!" I never used even mild profanity with him unless things were very serious. Now, it got his attention.

"Don't worry," he muttered. "I'll help."

Then we found the arm. Marcus was the one who spotted it—something dark lying just off the trail we were following. It was hung up in the low branches of a scrub oak.

The arm was fresh and whole—a hand, a lower, and an upper arm. A black man's arm, just the color of my father's where color could be seen. It was slashed and cut all over, yet still powerful looking—long-boned, long-fingered, yet muscular and massive. . . . Familiar?

Smooth, white bone stuck out at the shoulder end. The arm had been cut off with a sharp knife. The bone wasn't broken. And, yes. It could have been his.

Marcus threw up when he saw it. I made myself examine it, search it for something familiar, for certainty. Jay Garfield tried to stop me, and I shoved him away and told him to go to hell. I'm sorry for that, and I told him so later. But I had to know. And yet, I still don't know. The arm was too slashed and covered in dried blood. I couldn't tell. Jay Garfield took fingerprints in his pocket notebook, but we left the arm itself. How could we take that back to Cory?

And we kept searching. What else could we do? George Hsu found a rattlesnake. It didn't bite anyone and we didn't kill it. I don't think anyone was in a mood to kill things.

We saw dogs, but they kept away from us. I even saw a cat watching us from under a bush. Cats either run like hell or crouch and freeze. They're interesting to watch, somehow. Or, at any other time, they'd be interesting.

Then someone began to scream. I've never heard screams like that before—on and on. A man, screaming, begging, praying: "No! No more! Oh, God, no more, please. Jesus, Jesus, Jesus, *please*!" Then there were wordless, grating cries and high, horrible mewling.

It was a man's voice, not like my father's but not that different from his. We couldn't locate the source. The echoes bounced around the canyon, confusing us, sending us first in one direction, then in another. The canyon was full of loose rock and spiny,

　　　　　　　　　OCTAVIA E. BUTLER

vicious plants that kept us on the pathways where there were pathways.

The screaming stopped, then began again as a kind of horrible, bubbling noise.

I had let myself fall back to the end of the line of us by then. I wasn't in trouble. Sound doesn't trigger my sharing. I have to see another person in pain before I do any sharing. And this was one I'd do *anything* to avoid seeing.

Marcus dropped back beside me and whispered, "You okay?"

"Yeah," I said. "I just don't want to know anything about what's happening to that man."

"Keith," he said.

"I know," I agreed.

We walked our bikes behind the others, watching the back trail. Kayla Talcott dropped back to see if we were all right. She hadn't wanted us to come, but since we had come, she had come, she had kept an eye on us. She's like that.

"It doesn't sound like your daddy," she said. "Doesn't sound like him at all." Kayla is from Texas like my biological mother. Sometimes she sounded as though she'd never left, and sometimes she sounded as though she'd never been near any part of the south. She seemed to be able to turn the accent on and off. She tended to turn it on for comforting people, and for threatening to kill them. Sometimes when I'm with Curtis, I see her in his face and wonder what kind of relative—what kind of mother-in-law—she would make. Today I think both Marcus and I were glad she was there. We needed to be close to someone with her kind of mothering strength.

The horrible noise ended. Maybe the poor man was dead and out of his misery. I hope so.

We never found him. We found human bones and animal bones. We found the rotting corpses of five people scattered among the boulders. We found the cold remains of a fire with a human femur and two human skulls lying among the ashes.

At last, we came home and wrapped our community wall around us and huddled in our illusions of security.

SUNDAY, NOVEMBER 22, 2026

No one has found my father. Almost every adult in the neighborhood has spent some time looking. Richard Moss didn't, but his oldest son and daughter did. Wardell Parrish didn't, but his sister and oldest nephew did. I don't know what else people could have done. If I did know, I would be out doing it.

And yet nothing, nothing, nothing! The police never came up with any sign of him. He never turned up anywhere. He's vanished, gone. Even the severed arm's fingerprints weren't his.

Every night since Wednesday, I've dreamed that horrible screaming. I've gone out twice more with teams hunting through the canyons. We've found nothing but more of the dead and the poorest of the living—people who are all staring eyes and visible bones. My own bones ached in empathy. Sometimes if I sleep for a while without hearing the screaming, I see these—the living dead. I've always seen them. I've never seen them.

A team I wasn't with found a living child being eaten by dogs. The team killed the dogs, then watched, helpless as the boy died.

I spoke at services this morning. Maybe it was my duty. I don't know. People came for church, all uncertain and upset, not knowing what they should do. I think they wanted to draw together, and they had years of habit drawing them together at our house on Sunday morning. They were uncertain and hesitant, but they came.

Both Wyatt Talcott and Jay Garfield offered to speak. Both did say a few words, both informally eulogizing my father, though neither admitted that that was what they were doing. I was afraid everyone would do that and the service would become an impossible impromptu funeral. When I stood up, it wasn't just to say a couple of words. I meant to give them something they could take home—

something that might make them feel that enough had been said for today.

I thanked them all for the ongoing—emphasize ongoing—efforts to find my father. Then . . . well, then I talked about perseverance. I preached a sermon about perseverance if an unordained kid can be said to preach a sermon. No one was going to stop me. Cory was the only one who might have tried, but Cory was in a kind of walking coma. She wasn't doing anything she didn't have to do.

So I preached from Luke, chapter eighteen, verses one through eight: the parable of the importunate widow. It's one I've always liked. A widow is so persistent in her demands for justice that she overcomes the resistance of a judge who fears neither God nor man. She wears him down.

Moral: The weak can overcome the strong if the weak persist. Persisting isn't always safe, but it's often necessary.

My father and the adults present had created and maintained our community in spite of the scarcity and the violence outside. Now, with my father or without him, that community had to go on, hold together, survive. I talked about my nightmares and the source of those nightmares. Some people might not have wanted their kids to hear things like that, but I didn't care. If Keith had known more, maybe he would still be alive. But I didn't mention Keith. People could say what happened to Keith was his own fault. No one could say that about Dad. I didn't want anyone to be able to say it about this community some day.

"Those nightmares of mine are our future if we fail one another," I said, winding up. "Starvation, agony at the hands of people who aren't human anymore. Dismemberment. Death.

"We have God and we have each other. We have our island community, fragile, and yet a fortress. Sometimes it seems too small and too weak to survive. And like the widow in Christ's parable, its enemies fear neither God nor man. But also like the widow, it persists. *We persist.* This is our place, no matter what."

That was my message. I left it there, hanging before them with an unfinished feel to it. I could feel them expecting more, then realizing that I wasn't going to say more, then biting down on what I had said.

At just the right moment, Kayla Talcott began an old song. Others took it up, singing slowly, but with feeling: "We shall not, we shall not be moved. . . ."

I think this might have sounded weak or even pitiful somehow if it had been begun by a lesser voice. I think I might have sang it weakly. I'm only a fair singer. Kayla, on the other hand, has a big voice, beautiful, clear, and able to do everything she asks of it. Also, Kayla has a reputation for not moving unless she wants to.

Later, as she was leaving, I thanked her.

She looked at me. I'd grown past her years ago, and she had to look up. "Good job," she said, and nodded and walked away toward her house. I love her.

I got other compliments today, and I think they were sincere. Most said, in one way or another, "You're right," and "I didn't know you could preach like that," and "Your father would be proud of you."

Yeah, I hope so. I did it for him. He built this bunch of houses into a community. And now, he's probably dead. I wouldn't let them bury him, but I know. I'm no good at denial and self-deception. That was Dad's funeral that I was preaching—his and the community's. Because as much as I want all that I said to be true, it isn't. We'll be moved, all right. It's just a matter of when, by whom, and in how many pieces.

OCTAVIA E. BUTLER

13

□ □ □

There is no end
To what a living world
Will demand of you.

EARTHSEED: THE BOOKS OF THE LIVING
SATURDAY, DECEMBER 19, 2026

Today Reverend Matthew Robinson in whose church I was baptized came to preach my father's funeral. Cory made the arrangements. There was no body, no urn. No one knows what happened to my father. Neither we nor the police have been able to find out. We're sure he's dead. He would find a way to come home if he were alive, so we're certain he's dead.

No, we're not certain. We're not certain at all. Is he sick somewhere? Hurt? Held against his will for who knows what reason by who knows what monsters?

This is worse than when Keith died. So much worse. As horrible as that was, we knew he was dead. Whatever he suffered, we knew he wasn't suffering anymore. Not in this world, anyway. We *knew*. Now, we don't know anything. He is dead. But we don't *know!*

The Dunns must of felt this when Tracy vanished. Crazy as they are, crazy as she was, they must have felt this. What do they feel now? Tracy never came back. If she's not dead, what must be happening to her outside? A girl alone only faced one kind of future outside. I intend to go out posing as a man when I go.

How will they feel when I go? I'll be dead to them—to Cory, the boys, the neighborhood. They'll hope I'm dead, considering the supposed alternative. Thank Dad for my tallness and my strength.

145

I won't have to leave Dad now. He's already left me. He was 57. What reason would strangers have for keeping a 57-year-old man alive? Once they'd robbed him, they would either let him go or kill him. If they let him go, he'd come home, walking, limping, crawling.

So he's dead.

That's that.

It has to be.

TUESDAY, DECEMBER 22, 2026

The Garfields left for Olivar today—Phillida, Jay, and Joanne. An armored KSF truck came from Olivar to collect them and their belongings. The adults of the community had all they could do to keep the little kids from climbing all over the truck and pestering the drivers to death. Most kids my brothers' ages have never been close to a truck that runs. Some of the younger Moss kids have never seen a truck of any kind. The Moss kids weren't even allowed to visit the Yannis house back when the Yannis television still worked.

The two guys from KSF were patient once they realized the kids weren't thieves or vandals. Those two guys with their uniforms, pistols, whips, and clubs, looked more like cops than movers. No doubt they had even more substantial weapons in the truck. My brother Bennett said he saw bigger guns mounted inside the truck when he climbed onto the hood. But when you consider how much a truck that size is worth, and how many people might want to relieve them of it and its contents, I guess the weaponry isn't surprising.

The two movers were a black and a white, and I could see that Cory considered that hopeful. Maybe Olivar wouldn't be the white enclave that Dad had expected.

Cory cornered the black guy and talked to him for as long as he would let her. Will she try now to get us into Olivar? I think she will. After all, without Dad's salary, she'll have to do something. I don't think we have a prayer of being accepted. The insurance company isn't going to pay—or not for a long time. Its people choose not to believe that Dad is dead. Without proof he can't be declared legally dead for seven years. Can they hold on to our money for that long? I don't know, but it wouldn't surprise me. We could starve many times over in seven years. And Cory must know she alone can't earn enough in Olivar to feed and house us. Is she hoping to get work for me, too? I don't know what we're going to do.

Joanne and I cried all over each other, saying good-bye. We promised to phone each other, to stay in touch. I don't think we'll be able to. It costs extra to call Olivar. We won't be able to afford it. I don't think she will either. Chances are, I'll never see her again. The people I've grown up with are falling out of my life, one by one.

After the truck pulled away, I found Curtis and took him back to the old darkroom to make love. We hadn't done it for a long time, and I needed it. I wish I could imagine just marrying Curtis, staying here, and having a decent life with him.

It isn't possible. Even if there were no Earthseed, it wouldn't be possible. I would almost be doing the family a favor if I left now—one less mouth to feed. Unless I could somehow get a job. . . .

"We've got to get out of here, too," Curtis said as we lay together afterward, lingering, tempting fate, not wanting to lose the feel of each other so soon. But that wasn't what he had meant. I turned my head to look at him.

"Don't you want to go?" he asked. "Wouldn't you like to get out of this dead end neighborhood, out of Robledo."

I nodded. "I was just thinking that. But—"

"I want you to marry me, and I want us to get out of here," he said in a near whisper. "This place is dying."

I raised myself to my elbows and looked down at him. The only light in the room came from a single window up near the ceiling. Nothing covered it anymore, and the glass was broken out of it, but still, only a little light came in. Curtis's face was full of shadows.

"Where do you want to go?" I asked him.

"Not Olivar," he said. "That could turn out to be a bigger dead end than living here."

"Where, then?"

"I don't know. Oregon or Washington? Canada? Alaska?"

I don't think I gave any sign of sudden excitement. People tell me my face doesn't show them what I'm feeling. My sharing has been a hard teacher. But he saw something.

"You've already been thinking about leaving, haven't you," he demanded. "That's why you won't talk about getting married."

I rested my hand on his smooth chest.

"You were thinking about going alone!" He grasped my wrist, seemed ready to push it away. Then he held on to it, kept it. "You were just going to walk away from here and leave me."

I turned so that he couldn't see my face because now I had a feeling my emotions were all too obvious: Confusion, fear, hope. . . . Of course I had intended to go alone, and of course I hadn't told anyone that I was leaving. And I had not decided yet how Dad's disappearance would affect my going. That raised frightening questions. What are my responsibilities? What will happen to my brothers if I leave them to Cory? They're her sons, and she'll move the earth to take care of them, keep them fed and clothed and housed. But can she do it alone? How?

"I want to go," I admitted, moving around, trying to be comfortable on the pallet of old sleepsacks that we had put down on the concrete floor. "I planned to go. Don't tell anyone."

"How can I if I go with you?"

I smiled, loving him. But. . . "Cory and my brothers are going to need help," I said. "When my father was here, I planned to go next year when I'm eighteen. Now . . . I don't know."

"Where were you going?"

"North. Maybe as far as Canada. Maybe not."

"Alone?"

"Yeah."

"Why?" Why alone, he meant.

I shrugged. "I could get killed as soon as I leave here. I could starve. The cops could pick me up. Dogs could get me. I could catch a disease. Anything could happen to me; I've thought about it. I haven't named half the bad possibilities."

"That's why you need help!"

"That's why I couldn't ask anyone else to walk away from food and shelter and as much safety as there is in our world. To just start walking north, and hope you wind up some place good. How could I ask that of you?"

"It's not that bad. Farther north, we can get work."

"Maybe. But people have been flooding north for years. Jobs are scarce up there, too. And statelines and borders are closed."

"There's nothing down there!"

"I know."

"So how can you help Cory and your brothers?"

"I don't know. We haven't figured out what to do. So far, nothing I've thought of will work."

"They'd have more of everything if you left."

"Maybe. But, Curtis, how can I leave them? Could you walk away and leave your family, not knowing how they would manage to survive?"

"Sometimes I think so," he said.

I ignored that. He didn't get along very well with his brother Michael, but his family was probably the strongest unit in the neighborhood. Take on one of them and you've got to deal with them all. He would never walk away from them if they were in trouble.

"Marry me now," he said. "We'll stay here and help your family get on its feet. Then we'll leave."

"Not now," I said. "I can't see how anything is going to work out now. Everything's too crazy."

"And what? You think it's going to get sane? It's never been sane. You just have to go ahead and live, no matter what."

I didn't know what to say, so I kissed him. But I couldn't distract him.

"I hate this room," he said. "I hate hiding to be with you and I hate playing games." He paused. "But I do love you. Damn! Sometimes I almost wish I didn't."

"Don't wish that," I said. He knew so little about me, and he thought he knew everything. I'd never told him about my sharing, for instance. I'll have to before I marry him. If I don't, when he finds out, he'll know I didn't trust him enough to be honest with him. And not much is known about sharing. Suppose I pass it on to my kids?

Then there's Earthseed. I'll have to tell him about that. What will he think? That I've gone crazy? I can't tell him. Not yet.

"We could live at your house," he said. "My parents would help out with food. Maybe I could find some kind of job. . . ."

"I want to marry you," I said. I hesitated, and there was absolute silence. I couldn't believe I'd heard myself say such a thing, but it was true. Maybe I was just feeling bereft. Keith, my father, the Garfields, Mrs. Quintanilla. . . . People could disappear so easily. I wanted someone with me who cared about me, and who wouldn't disappear. But my judgment wasn't entirely gone.

"When my family is back on its feet, we'll marry," I said. "Then we can get out of here. I just have to know that my brothers will be all right."

"If we're going to marry anyway, why not do it now?"

Because I have things to tell you, I thought. Because if you reject me or make me reject you with your reactions, I don't want to have to hang around and watch you with someone else.

"Not now," I said. "Wait for me."

He shook his head in obvious disgust. "What the hell do you think I've been doing?"

It's Christmas Eve.

Last night someone set fire to the Payne-Parrish house. While the community tried to put out the fire, and then tried to keep it from spreading, three other houses were robbed. Ours was one of the three:

Thieves took all our store-bought food: wheat flour, sugar, canned goods, packaged goods. . . . They took our radio—our last one. The crazy thing is, before we went to bed we had been listening to a half-hour news feature about increasing arson. People are setting more fires to cover crimes—although why they would bother these days, I don't know. The police are no threat to criminals. People are setting fires to do what our arsonist did last night—to get the neighbors of the arson victim to leave their own homes unguarded. People are setting fires to get rid of whomever they dislike from personal enemies to anyone who looks or sounds foreign or racially different. People are setting fires because they're frustrated, angry, hopeless. They have no power to improve their lives, but they have the power to make others even more miserable. And the only way to prove to yourself that you have power is to use it.

Then there's that fire drug with it's dozen or so names: Blaze, fuego, flash, sunfire. . . . The most popular name is pyro—short for pyromania. It's all the same drug, and it's been around for a while. From what Keith said, it's becoming more popular. It makes watching the leaping, changing patterns of fire a better, more intense, longer-lasting high than sex. Like Paracetco, my biological mother's drug of choice, pyro screws around with people's neurochemistry. But Paracetco began as a legitimate drug intended to help victims of Alzheimer's disease. Pyro was an accident. It was a homebrew—a basement drug invented by someone who was trying to assemble one of the other higher-priced street drugs. The inventor made a very small chemical mistake, and wound up with pyro. That happened on the east coast and caused an immediate increase in the number of senseless arson fires, large and small.

Pyro worked its way west without making nearly as much trouble as it could have. Now its popularity is growing. And in dry-as-straw Southern California, it can cause a real orgy of burning.

"My God," Cory said when the radio report was over. And in a small, whispery voice, she quoted from the Book of Revelation: " 'Babylon the great is fallen, is fallen, and is become the habitation of devils . . .'"

And the devils set fire to the Payne-Parrish house.

At about two a.m. I woke to the jangling of the bell: Emergency! Earthquake? Fire? Intruders?

But there was no shaking, no unfamiliar noise, no smoke. Whatever was happening, it wasn't at our house. I got up, threw clothing on, debated for a second whether to snatch my survival pack, then left it. Our house didn't seem to be in immediate danger. My pack was safe in the closet, mixed in among blankets and bundles of old clothes. If I had to have it, I could come back and snatch it in seconds.

I ran outside to see what was needed, and saw at once. The Payne-Parrish house was fully involved, surrounded by fire. One of the watchers on duty was still sounding the alarm. People spilled from all the houses, and must have seen as I did that the Parrish house was a total loss. Neighbors were already wetting down the houses on either side. A live oak tree—one of our huge, ancient ones—was afire. There was a light wind blowing, swirling bits of burning leaves and twigs into the air and scattering them. I joined the people who were beating and wetting the grounds.

Where were the Paynes? Where was Wardell Parrish? Had anyone called the fire department? A house full of people, after all, it wasn't like a burning garage.

I asked several people. Kayla Talcott said she had called them. I was grateful and ashamed. I wouldn't have asked if Dad were still with us. One of us would have just called. Now we couldn't afford to call.

No one had seen any of the Paynes. Wardell Parrish I found in the Yannis yard where Cory and my brother Bennett were wrapping him in a blanket. He was coughing so much that he couldn't talk, and wearing only pajama pants.

"Is he okay?" I asked.

"He breathed a lot of smoke," Cory said. "Has someone called—"

"Kayla Talcott called the fire department."

"Good. But no one's at the gate to let them in."

"I'll go." I turned away, but she caught my arm.

"The others?" she whispered. She meant the Paynes, of course.

"I don't know."

She nodded and let me go.

I went to the gate, borrowing Alex Montoya's key on the way. He always seemed to have his gate key in his pocket. It was because of him that I didn't go back into our house and maybe interrupt a robbery and be killed for my trouble.

Firefighters arrived in no great hurry. I let them in, locked the gate after them, and watched as they put out the fire.

No one had seen the Paynes. We could only assume they had never gotten out. Cory tried to take Wardell Parrish to our house, but he refused to leave until he found out one way or the other about his twin sister and his nieces and nephews.

When the fire was almost out, the bell began to ring again. We all looked around. Caroline Balter, Harry's mother, was jerking and pushing at the bell and screaming.

"Intruders!" she shouted. "Thieves! They've broken into the houses!"

And we all rushed without thinking back to our houses. Wardell Parrish came along with my family, still coughing, and wheezing, and as useless—as weaponless—as the rest of us. We could have been killed, rushing in that way. Instead, we were lucky. We scared away our thieves.

Along with our store-bought food and the radio, the thieves got some of Dad's tools and supplies—nails, wire, screws, bolts, that kind of thing. They didn't get the phone, the computer, or anything in Dad's office. In fact, they didn't get into Dad's office at all. I suppose we scared them away before they could search the whole house.

They stole clothing and shoes from Cory's room, but didn't touch my room or the boys'. They got some of our money—the kitchen money, Cory calls it. She had hidden it in the kitchen in a box of detergent. She had thought no one would steal such a thing. In fact, the thieves might have stolen it for resale without realizing that it wasn't just detergent. It could have been worse. The kitchen money was only about a thousand dollars for minor emergencies.

The thieves did not find the rest of our money, some of it hidden out by our lemon tree, and some hidden with our two remaining guns under the floor in Cory's closet. Dad had gone to a lot of trouble to make a kind of floor safe, not locked, but completely concealed beneath a rug and a battered chest of drawers filled with sewing things—salvaged bits of cloth, buttons, zippers, hooks, things like that. The chest of drawers could be moved with one hand. It slid from one side of the closet to the other if you pushed it right, and in seconds you could have the money and the guns in your hands. The concealment trick wouldn't have defeated people who had time to make a thorough search, but it had defeated our thieves. They had dumped some of the drawers onto the floor, but they had not thought to look under the chest.

The thieves did take Cory's sewing machine. It was a compact, sturdy old machine with its own carrying case. Both case and machine were gone. That was a real blow. Cory and I both use that machine to make, alter, and repair clothing for the family. I had thought I might even be able to earn some money with the machine, sewing for other people in the neighborhood. Now the machine is gone. Sewing for the family will have to be done by hand. It will take much more time, and may not look like what we're used to. Bad. Hard. But not a fatal blow. Cory cried over the loss of her machine, but we can get along without it. She's just being worn down by one blow after another.

OCTAVIA E. BUTLER

We'll adapt. We'll have to. God is Change.

Strange how much it helps me to remember that.

Curtis Talcott just came to my window to tell me that the firemen have found charred bodies and bones in the ashes of the Payne-Parrish house. The police are here, taking reports of the robberies and the obvious arson. I told Cory. She can tell Wardell Parrish or let the cops tell him. He's lying down on one of our living room couches. I doubt that he's sleeping. Even though I've never liked him, I feel sorry for him. He's lost his house and his family. He's the only survivor. What must that be like?

TUESDAY, DECEMBER 29, 2026

I don't know how long it can last, but in some way that I suspect is not quite legal, Cory has taken over part of the job Dad held for so long. She'll give the classes Dad gave. With the computer hookups we have already in place, she'll issue assignments, receive homework, and be available for phone and compu-conferences. The administrative part of Dad's work will be handled by someone else who can use the extra money, and who is willing to show up at the college more often than once or twice a month. It will be as though Dad were still teaching, but had decided to give up his other responsibilities.

Cory has arranged this by pleading and begging, by crying and cajoling and calling in every favor and every friend she could think of. People at the college know her. She taught there before Bennett's birth, before she saw the need here and began the front-room school that serves all the children of the neighborhood. Dad was all for her quitting the college because he didn't want her going back and forth outside, exposed to all the dangers that involved. The neighbors pay a per-kid fee, but it isn't much. No one could support a household on it.

Now Cory will have to go outside again. She's already drafting men and older boys in the neighborhood to escort her when she has to go out. There are plenty of unemployed men here, and Cory will be paying them a small fee.

So in a few days, the new term will start and Cory will do Dad's work—while I do her work. I'll handle the school with help from her and from Russel Dory, Joanne and Harry's grandfather. He used to be a highschool math teacher. He's been retired for years, but he's still sharp. I don't think I need his help, but Cory does, and he's willing, so that's that.

Alex Montoya and Kayla Talcott will take over Dad's preaching and other church work. Neither is ordained, but both have substituted for Dad in the past. Both have authority in the community and the church. And, of course, both know their Bible.

This is how we will survive and hold together. It will work. I don't know how long it will last, but for now, it will work.

WEDNESDAY, DECEMBER 30, 2026

Wardell Parrish has finally dragged himself back to his people—to the part of his family that he lived with before he and his sister inherited the Sims house. He's stayed with us since his sister and all her children were killed. Cory gave him some of Dad's clothes which were too big for him. Much too big.

He wandered around, not talking, not seeming to see anything, not eating enough. . . . Then yesterday he said, like a little boy, "I want to go home. I can't stay here. I hate it here; everyone's dead! I have to go home."

So today Wyatt Talcott, Michael, and Curtis escorted him home. Poor man. He's years older than he was a week ago. I think he may not live much longer.

2027

□ □ □

We are Earthseed. We are flesh—self aware, quest-
ing, problem-solving flesh. We are that aspect of
Earthlife best able to shape God knowingly. We are
Earthlife maturing, Earthlife preparing to fall away
from the parent world. We are Earthlife preparing
to take root in new ground, Earthlife fulfilling its
purpose, its promise, its Destiny.

14

□ □ □

In order to rise
From its own ashes
A phoenix
First
Must
Burn.

EARTHSEED: THE BOOKS OF THE LIVING
SATURDAY, JULY 31, 2027 — MORNING

Last night, when I escaped from the neighborhood, it was burning. The houses, the trees, the people: Burning.

Smoke awoke me, and I shouted down the hall to Cory and the boys. I grabbed my clothes and emergency pack and followed Cory as she herded the boys out.

The bell never rang. Our watchers must have been killed before they could reach it.

Everything was chaos. People running, screaming, shooting. The gate had been destroyed. Our attackers had driven an ancient truck through it. They must have stolen a truck just to crash it through our gate.

I think they must have been pyro addicts—bald people with painted heads, faces, and hands. Red faces; blue faces; green faces; screaming mouths; avid, crazy eyes, glittering in the firelight.

They shot us and shot us and shot us. I saw Natalie Moss, running, screaming, then pitching backward, her face half gone, her body still impelled forward. She fell flat on her back, and did not move again.

I fell with her, caught up in her death. I lay there, dazed, strug-

159

gling to move, to get up. Cory and the boys, running ahead of me never noticed. They ran on.

I got up, felt for my pack, found it, and ran. I tried not to see what was happening around me. Hearing the gunfire and the screams didn't stop me. A dead body—Edwin Dunn—didn't stop me. I bent, snatched up his gun, and kept running.

Someone screamed near me, then tackled me, pulled me down. I fired the gun in reflexive terror, and took the terrible impact in my own stomach. A green face hung above mine, mouth open, eyes wide, not yet feeling all his pain. I shot him again, terrified that his pain would immobilize me when he did feel it. It seemed that he took a long time to die.

When I could move again, I pushed his body off me. I got up, still holding the gun, and ran for the wrecked gate.

Best to be in the darkness outside. Best to hide.

I ran up Meredith Street away from Durant Road, away from the fires and the shooting. I had lost track of Cory and the boys. I thought they would go toward the hills and not toward the center of town. Every direction was dangerous, but there was more danger where there were more people. In the night, a woman and three kids might look like a gift basket of food, money, and sex.

North toward the hills. North through the dark streets to where the nearby hills and mountains blotted out the stars.

And then what?

I didn't know. I couldn't think. I had never been outside the walls when it was so dark. My only hope of staying alive was to listen, hear any movement before it got too close to me, see what I could by star-light, be as quiet as I could.

I walked down the middle of the street looking and listening and trying to avoid potholes and chunks of broken asphalt. There was little other trash. Anything that would burn, people would use as fuel. Anything that could be reused or sold had been gathered. Cory used to comment on that. Poverty, she said, had made the streets cleaner.

Where was she? Where had she taken my brothers? Were they all right? Had they even gotten out of the neighborhood?

I stopped. Were my brothers back there? Was Curtis? I hadn't seen him at all—though if anyone were going to survive this insanity, it would be the Talcotts. But we had no way of finding each other.

Sound. Footsteps. Two pairs of running footsteps. I stayed where I was, frozen in place. No sudden moves to draw attention to me. Had I already been seen? Could I be seen—a figure of darker darkness in an otherwise empty street?

The sound was behind me. I listened and knew that it was off to one side, approaching, passing. Two people running down a side street, indifferent to the noise they made, indifferent to woman-shaped shadows.

I let out a breath and drew another through my mouth because I could get more air with less sound that way. I couldn't go back to the fires and the pain. If Cory and the boys were there, they were dead or worse, captive. But they had been ahead of me. They must have gotten out. Cory wouldn't let them come back to look for me. There was a bright glow in the air over what had been our neighborhood. If she had gotten the boys away, all she had to do was look back to know that she didn't want to go back.

Did she have her Smith & Wesson? I wished I had it and the two boxes of ammunition that went with it. All I had was the knife in my pack and Edwin Dunn's old .45 automatic. And all the ammunition I had for it was in it. If it wasn't empty. I knew the gun. It held seven rounds. I'd fired it twice. How many times had Edwin Dunn fired it before someone shot him? I didn't expect to find out until morning. I had a flashlight in my pack, but I didn't intend to use it unless I could be certain I wouldn't be making a target of myself.

During the day the sight of the bulge in my pocket would be enough to make people think twice about robbing or raping me. But during the night the blue gun would be all but invisible even in my hand. If it were empty, I could only use it as a club. And the moment

I hit someone with it, I might as well hit myself. If I lost consciousness for any reason during a fight, I would lose all my possessions if not my life. Tonight I had to hide.

Tomorrow I would have to try to bluff as much as possible. Most people wouldn't insist on my shooting them just to test whether or not the gun was loaded. For the street poor, unable to afford medical care, even a minor wound might be fatal.

I am one of the street poor, now. Not as poor as some, but homeless, alone, full of books and ignorant of reality. Unless I meet someone from the neighborhood, there's no one I can afford to trust. No one to back me up.

Three miles to the hills. I kept to the starlit back streets, listening and looking around. The gun was in my hand. I meant to keep it there. I could hear dogs barking and snarling, fighting somewhere not far away.

I was in a cold sweat. I had never been more terrified in my life. Yet nothing attacked me. Nothing found me.

I didn't go all the way to the hills. Instead I found a burned out, unwalled house a few blocks before the end of Meredith Street. Fear of dogs had made me keep an eye open for anything that might provide shelter.

The house was a ruin, a plundered ruin. It wasn't safe to walk into with or without a light. It was a roofless collection of upright black bones. But it had been built up off the ground. Five con crete steps led up to what had been the front porch. There should be a way under the house.

What if other people were under it?

I walked around it, listening, trying to see. Then, instead of daring to crawl under, I settled in what was left of the attached garage. A corner of it was still standing, and there was enough rubble in front of that corner to conceal me if I didn't show a light. Also, if I were surprised, I could get out of the garage faster than I could crawl out from under a house. The concrete floor could not collapse under me

OCTAVIA E. BUTLER

as the wooden floor might in what was left of the house proper. It was as good as I was going to get, and I was exhausted. I didn't know whether I could sleep, but I had to rest.

Morning now. What shall I do? I did sleep a little, but I kept startling awake. Every sound woke me—the wind, rats, insects, then squirrels, and birds. . . . I don't feel rested, but I'm a little less exhausted. So what shall I do?

How is it that we had never established an outside meeting place—somewhere where the family could reunite after disaster. I remember suggesting to Dad that we do that, but he had never done anything about it, and I hadn't pushed the idea as I should have. (Poor Godshaping. Lack of forethought.)

What now!

Now, I have to go home. I don't want to. The idea scares me to death. It's taken me a long time just to write the word: Home. But I have to know about my brothers, and about Cory and Curtis. I don't know how I can help if they're hurt or being held by someone. I don't know what might be waiting for me back at the neighborhood. More painted faces? The police? I'm in trouble either way. If the police are there, I'll have to hide my gun before I go in—my gun, and my small amount of money. Carrying a gun can win you a lot of unwanted attention from the police if you catch them in the wrong mood. Yet everyone who has one carries it. The trick, of course, is not to get caught carrying it.

On the other hand, if the painted faces are still there, I can't go in at all. How long do those people stay high on pyro and fire? Do they hang around after their fun to steal whatever's left and maybe kill a few more people?

No matter. I have to go and see.

I have to go home.

I have to write. I don't know what else to do. The others are asleep now, but it isn't dark. I'm on watch because I couldn't sleep if I tried. I'm jittery and crazed. I can't cry. I want to get up and just run and run. . . . Run away from everything. But there isn't any away.

I have to write. There's nothing familiar left to me but the writing. God is Change. I hate God. I have to write.

There were no unburned houses back in the neighborhood, although some were burned worse than others. I don't know whether police or firefighters ever came. If they had come, they were gone when I got there. The neighborhood was wide open and crawling with scavengers.

I stood at the gate, staring in as strangers picked among the black bones of our homes. The ruins were still smoking, but men, women, and children were all over them, digging through them, picking fruit from the trees, stripping our dead, quarreling or fighting over new acquisitions, stashing things away in clothing or bundles. . . . Who were these people?

I put my hand on the gun in my pocket—it had four rounds left in it—and I went in. I was grimy from lying in dirt and ashes all night. I might not be noticed.

I saw three women from an unwalled part of Durant Road, digging through what was left of the Yannis house. They were laughing and throwing around chunks of wood and plaster.

Where were Shani Yannis and her daughters? Where were her sisters?

I walked through the neighborhood, looking past the human maggots, trying to find some of the people I had grown up with. I found dead ones. Edwin Dunn lay where he had when I took his gun, but now he was shirtless and shoeless. His pockets had been turned out.

The ground was littered with ash-covered corpses, some burned or half blown apart by automatic weapons fire. Dried or nearly dried blood had pooled in the street. Two men were prying loose our emergency bell. The bright, clear, early morning sunlight made the whole scene less real somehow, more nightmarelike. I stopped in front of our house and stared at the five adults and the child who were picking through the ruins of it. Who were these vultures? Did the fire draw them? Is that what the street poor do? Run to fire and hope to find a corpse to strip?

There was a dead green face on our front porch. I went up the steps and stood looking at him—at her. The green face was a woman—tall, lean, bald, but female. And what had she died for? What was the point of all this?

"Leave her alone." A woman who had a pair of Cory's shoes in her hand strode up to me. "She died for all of us. Leave her alone."

I've never in my life wanted more to kill another human being. "Get the hell out of my way," I said. I didn't raise my voice. I don't know how I looked, but the thief backed away.

I stepped over the green face and went into the carcass of our home. The other thieves looked at me, but none of them said anything. One pair, I noticed, was a man with a small boy. The man was dressing the boy in a pair of my brother Gregory's jeans. The jeans were much too big, but the man belted them and rolled them up.

And where was Gregory, my clownish smartass of a baby brother? Where was he? Where was everyone?

The roof of our house had fallen in. Most things had burned—kitchen, living room, dining room, my room. . . . The floor wasn't safe to walk on. I saw one of the scavengers fall through, give a surprised yell, then climb, unhurt, onto a floor joist.

Nothing left in my room could be salvaged. Ashes. A heat-distorted metal bedframe, the broken metal and ceramic remains of my lamp, bunches of ashes that had been clothing or books. Many books were not burned through. They were useless, but they had been packed so tightly together that the fire had burned in deeply from the edges and the spines. Rough circles of un-burned paper remained, surrounded by ash. I didn't find a single whole page.

The back two bedrooms had survived better. That was where the scavengers were, and where I headed.

I found bundled pairs of my father's socks, folded shorts and T-shirts, and an extra holster that I could use for the .45. All this I found in or under the unpromising-looking remains of Dad's chest of drawers. Most things were burned beyond use, but I stuffed the best of what I found into my pack. The man with the child came over to scavenge beside me, and somehow, perhaps because of the child, because this stranger in his filthy rags was someone's father, too, I didn't mind. The little boy watched the two of us, his small brown face expressionless. He did look a little like Gregory.

I dug a dried apricot out of my pack and held it out to him. He couldn't have been more than six, but he wouldn't touch the food until the man told him to. Good discipline. But at the man's nod, he snatched the apricot, bit off a tiny taste, then stuffed the rest into his mouth whole.

So, in company with five strangers, I plundered my family's home. The ammunition under the closet floor in my parents' room had burned, had no doubt exploded. The closet was badly charred. So much for the money hidden there.

I took dental floss, soap, and a jar of petroleum jelly from my parents' bathroom. Everything else was already gone.

I managed to gather one set of outer clothing each for Cory and my brothers. In particular, I found shoes for them. There was a woman scavenging among Marcus's shoes, and she glared at me, but she kept quiet. My brothers had run out of the house in their pajamas. Cory had thrown on a coat. I had been the last to get out of the house because I had risked stopping to grab jeans, a sweatshirt, and shoes as well as my emergency pack. I could have been killed. If I had thought about what I was doing, if I had had to think, no doubt I would have been killed. I reacted the way I had trained myself to react—though my training was far from up to date—more memory than anything else. I hadn't practiced late at night for ages. Yet my self-administered training had worked.

Now, if I could get these clothes to Cory and my brothers, I might be able to make up for their lack of training. Especially if I could get the money under the rocks by the lemon tree.

I put clothes and shoes into a salvaged pillow case, looked around for blankets, and couldn't find one. They must have been grabbed early. All the more reason to get the lemon-tree money.

I went out to the peach tree, and, being tall, managed to reach a couple of nearly-ripe peaches that other scavengers had missed. Then I looked around as though for something more to take, and surprised myself by almost crying at the sight of Cory's big, well-tended back garden, trampled into the ground. Peppers, tomatoes, squashes, carrots, cucumbers, lettuce, melons, sunflowers, beans, corn. . . . Much of it wasn't ripe yet, but what hadn't been stolen had been destroyed.

I scavenged a few carrots, a couple of handfuls of sunflower seeds from flower heads that lay on the ground, and a few bean pods from vines Cory had planted to run up the sunflower stalks and corn plants. I took what was left the way I thought a late-arriving scavenger would. And I worked my way toward the lemon tree. When I reached it, heavy with little green lemons, I hunted for any with even a hint of paling, of yellow. I took a few from the tree, and from the ground. Cory had planted shade-loving flowers at the base of the tree, and they had thrived there. She and my father had scattered small, rounded boulders among these in a way that seemed no more than decorative. A few of these had been turned over, crushing the flowers near them. In fact, the rock with the money under it had been turned over. But the two or three inches of dirt over the money packet, triple wrapped and heat-sealed in plastic, was undisturbed.

I snatched the packet in no more time than it had taken to pick up a couple of lemons a moment before. First I spotted the hiding place, then I snatched up the money packet along with a hand full of dirt.

Then, eager to leave, but terrified of drawing attention to myself, I picked up a few more lemons and hunted around for more food.

The figs were hard and green instead of purple, and the persimmons were yellow-green instead of orange. I found a single ear of corn left on a downed stalk and used it to stuff the money packet deeper into my blanket pack. Then I left.

With my pack on my back and the pillow case in my left arm, resting on my hip like a baby, I walked down the driveway to the street. I kept my right hand free for the gun still in my pocket. I had not taken time to put on the holster.

There were more people within the walls than there had been when I arrived. I had to walk past most of them to get out. Others were leaving with their loads, and I tried to follow them without quite attaching myself to any particular group. This meant that I moved more slowly than I would have chosen to. I had time to look at the corpses and see what I didn't want to see.

Richard Moss, stark naked, lying in a pool of his own blood. His house, closer to the gate than ours, had been burned to the ground. Only the chimney stuck up blackened and naked from the rubble. Where were his two surviving wives Karen and Zahra? Or had they survived? Where were all his many children?

Little Robin Balter, naked, filthy, bloody between her legs, cold, bony, barely pubescent. Yet she might have married my brother Marcus someday. She might have been my sister. She had always been such a bright, sharp, great little kid, all serious and knowing. Twelve going on thirty-five, Cory used to say. She always smiled when she said it.

Russell Dory, Robin's grandfather. Only his shoes had been taken. His body had been almost torn apart by automatic weapons fire. An old man and a child. What had the painted faces gotten for all their killing?

"She died for us," the scavenger woman had said of the green face. Some kind of insane burn-the-rich movement, Keith had said. We've never been rich, but to the desperate, we looked rich. We were surviving and we had our wall. Did our community die so that addicts could make a help-the-poor political statement?

There were other corpses. I didn't get a close look at most of them. They littered the front yards, the street, and the island. There was no sign of our emergency bell now. The men who had wanted it had carried it away—perhaps to be sold for its metal.

I saw Layla Yannis, Shani's oldest daughter. Like Robin, she had been raped. I saw Michael Talcott, one side of his head smashed in. I didn't look around for Curtis. I was terrified that I might see him lying nearby. I was almost out of control as it was, and I couldn't draw attention to myself. I couldn't be anything more than another scavenger hauling away treasure.

Bodies passed under my eyes: Jeremy Balter, one of Robin's brothers, Philip Moss, George Hsu, his wife and his oldest son, Juana Montoya, Rubin Quintanilla, Lidia Cruz. . . . Lidia was only eight years old. She had been raped, too.

I made it back through the gate. I didn't break down. I hadn't seen Cory or my brothers in the carnage. That didn't mean they weren't there, but I hadn't seen them. They might be alive. Curtis might be alive. Where could I look for them?

The Talcotts had relatives living in Robledo, but I didn't know where. Somewhere on the other side of River Street. I couldn't look for them, though Curtis might have gone to them. Why hadn't anyone else stayed to salvage what they could?

I circled the neighborhood, keeping the wall in sight, then made a greater circle. I saw no one—or at least no one I knew. I saw other street poor who stared at me.

Then because I didn't know what else to do, I headed back toward my burned out garage on Meredith Street. I couldn't call the police. All the phones I knew of were slag. No strangers would let me use their phone if they had phones, and I didn't know anyone whom I could pay to call and trust to make the call. Most people would avoid me or be tempted to keep my money and never call. And anyway, if the police have ignored what's been done to my neighborhood so far, if such a fire and so many corpses can be ignored, why should I go to them? What would they do? Arrest me? Take my cash as their fee? I wouldn't be surprised. Best to stay clear of them.

But *where* was my family!

Someone called my name.

I turned around, my hand in my pocket, and saw Zahra Moss and Harry Balter—Richard Moss's youngest wife and Robin Balter's oldest brother. They were an unlikely pair, but they were definitely together. They managed, without touching each other, to give the appearance of all but clinging together. Both were blood-spattered and ragged. I looked at Harry's battered swollen face and remembered that Joanne had loved him—or thought she had—and that he wouldn't marry her and go with her to Olivar because he believed what Dad believed about Olivar.

"Are you all right?" he asked me.

I nodded, remembering Robin. Did he know? Russell Dory, Robin, and Jeremy. . . . "They beat you up?" I asked, feeling stupid and awkward. I didn't want to tell him his grandfather, brother, and sister were dead.

"I had to fight my way out last night. I was lucky they didn't shoot me." He swayed, looked around. "Let's sit on the curb."

Both Zahra and I looked around, made sure no one else was near by. We sat with Harry between us. I sat on my pillowcase of clothing. Zahra and Harry were fully dressed, in spite of their coating of blood and dirt, but they carried nothing. Did they have nothing, or had they left their things somewhere—perhaps with whatever was left of their families. And where was Zahra's little girl Bibi? Did she know that Richard Moss was dead?

"Everyone's dead," Zahra whispered as though speaking into my thoughts. "Everyone. Those painted bastards killed them all!"

"No!" Harry shook his head. "We got out. There'll be some others."

He sat with his face in his hands, and I wondered whether he was more hurt than I had thought. I wasn't sharing any serious pain with him.

"Have either of you seen my brothers or Cory?" I asked. "Dead," Zahra whispered. "Like my Bibi. All dead."

I jumped. "No! Not all of them. No! Did you see them?"

"I saw most of the Montoya family," Harry said. He wasn't talking to me as much as musing aloud. "We saw them last night. They said Juana was dead. The rest of them were going to walk to Glendale where their relatives live."

"But—" I began.

"And I saw Laticia Hsu. She had been stabbed forty or fifty times."

"But did you see my brothers?" I had to ask.

"They're all dead, I told you," Zahra said. "They got out, but the paints caught them and dragged them back and killed them. I saw. One of them had me down, and he . . . I saw."

She was being raped when she saw my family dragged back and killed? Was that what she meant? Was it true?

"I went back this morning," I said. "I didn't see their bodies. Didn't see any of them." Oh, no. Oh, no. Oh, no. . . .

"I saw. Your mother. All of them. I saw." Zahra hugged herself. "I didn't want to see, but I saw."

We all sat without talking. I don't know how long we sat there. Now and then someone walked past us and looked at us, some dirty, ragged person with bundles. Cleaner people in little bunches rode past us on bikes. A group of three rode past on motorcycles, their electric hum and whine strange in the quiet street.

When I got up, the other two looked at me. For no reason except habit, I picked up my pillowcase. I don't know what I meant to do with the things in it. It had occurred to me, though, that I should get back to my garage before someone else settled there. I wasn't thinking very well. It was as though that garage was home now, and all I wanted in the world was to be there.

Harry got up and almost fell down again. He bent and threw up into the gutter. The sight of his throwing up grabbed at me, and I only just managed to look away in time to avoid joining him. He finished, spat, turned to face Zahra and me, and coughed.

"I feel like hell," he said.

"They hit him in the head last night," Zahra explained. "He got me away from the guy who was . . . Well, you know. He got me away, but they hurt him."

"There's a burned out garage where I slept last night," I said. "It's a long walk, but he can rest there. We can all rest there."

Zahra took my pillowcase and carried it. Maybe something in it could do her some good. We walked on either side of Harry and kept him from stopping or wandering off or staggering too much. Somehow, we got him to the garage.

15

□ □ □

Kindness eases Change

EARTHSEED: THE BOOKS OF THE LIVING
SUNDAY, AUGUST 1, 2027

Harry slept most of the day today. Zahra and I took turns staying with him. He has a concussion, at least, and he needs time to heal. We haven't talked about what we'll do if he gets sicker instead of healing. Zahra doesn't want to abandon him because he fought to save her. I don't want to abandon him because I've known him all my life. He's a good guy. I wonder if there's some way to get in touch with the Garfields. They would give him a home, or at least see that he has medical care.

But he doesn't seem to be getting worse. He totters out to the fenced back yard to urinate. He eats the food and drinks the water that I give him. With no need for discussion, we're eating and drinking sparingly from my supplies. They're all we have. Soon we'll have to risk going out to buy more. But today, Sunday, is a day of rest and healing for us.

The pain of Harry's headache and his bruised, beaten body are almost welcome to me. They're distractions. Along with Zahra's talking and crying for her dead daughter, they fill my mind.

Their misery eases my own, somehow. It gives me moments when I don't think about my family. Everyone is dead. But how can they be? Everyone?

Zahra has a soft, little-girl voice that I used to think was phony. It's real, but it takes on a sandpaper roughness when she's upset. It sounds painful, as though it's abrading her throat as she speaks.

She had seen her daughter killed, seen the blue face who shot Bibi as Zahra ran, carrying her. She believed the blue face was enjoying himself, shooting at all the moving targets. She said his expression reminded her of a man having sex.

"I fell down," she whispered. "I thought I was dead. I thought he had killed me. There was blood. Then I saw Bibi's head drop to one side. A red face grabbed her from me. I didn't see where he came from. He grabbed her and threw her into the Hsu house. The house was burning everywhere. He threw her into the fire.

"I went crazy then. I don't know what I did. Somebody grabbed me, then I was free, then somebody shoved me down and fell on me. I couldn't get my breath, and he tore my clothes. Then he was on me, and I couldn't do anything. That's when I saw your mother, your brothers. . . .

"Then Harry was there, and he pulled the bastard off me. He told me later that I was screaming. I don't know what I was doing. He was beating up the guy he'd pulled off me when a new guy jumped him. I hit the new guy with a rock and Harry knocked the other one out. Then we got away. We just ran. We didn't sleep. We hid between two unwalled houses down the street away from the fire until a guy came out with an ax and chased us away. Then we just wandered until we found you. We didn't even really know each other before. You know, Richard never wanted us to have much to do with the neighbors— especially the white ones."

I nodded, remembering Richard Moss. "He's dead, you know," I said. "I saw him." I wanted to take the words back as soon as I'd said them. I didn't know how to tell someone her husband was dead, but there must be a better, gentler way than that.

She stared at me, stricken. I wanted to apologize for my bluntness, but I didn't think it would help. "I'm sorry," I said in a kind of generic apology for everything. She began to cry, and I repeated, "I'm sorry."

I held her and let her cry. Harry woke up, drank a little water, and listened while Zahra told how Richard Moss had bought her from her homeless mother when she was only fifteen—younger than I had thought—and brought her to live in the first house she had ever known. He gave her enough to eat and didn't beat her, and even when her co-wives were hateful to her, it was a thousand times better than living outside with her mother and starving. Now she was outside again. In six years, she had gone from nothing to nothing.

"Do you have someplace to go?" she asked us at last. "Do you know anybody who still has a house?"

I looked at Harry. "You might be able to get into Olivar if you can walk there from here. The Garfields would take you in."

He thought about that for a while. "I don't want to," he said. "I don't think there's anymore future in Olivar than there was in our neighborhood. But at least in our neighborhood, we had the guns."

"For all the good it did us," Zahra muttered.

"I know. But they were our guns, not hired gunmen. No one could turn them against us. In Olivar, from what Joanne said, no one's allowed to have a gun except the security force. And who the hell are they?"

"Company people," I said. "People from outside Olivar."

He nodded. "That's what I heard, too. Maybe it will be all right, but it doesn't sound all right."

"It sounds better than starving," Zahra said. "You guys have never missed a meal, have you?"

"I'm going north," I said. "I planned to go anyway once my family was back on its feet. Now I have no family, and I'm going."

"North where?" Zahra demanded.

"Up toward Canada. The way things are now, I may not be able to get that far. But I'll get to a place where water doesn't cost more than food, and where work brings a salary. Even a small one. I'm not going to spend my life as some kind of twenty-first century slave."

"North is where I'm headed, too," Harry said. "There's nothing here. I've tried for over a year to get a job here—any job that pays money. There's nothing. I want to work for money, and get some college. The only jobs that pay serious money are the kind our parents had, the kind that require college degrees."

I looked at him, wanting to ask something, hesitating, plunging. "Harry, what about your parents?"

"I don't know," he said. "I didn't see them killed. Zahra says she didn't. I don't know where anyone is. We got separated."

I swallowed. "I didn't see your parents," I said, "but I did see some of your other relatives—dead."

"Who?" he demanded.

I guess there really isn't any way to tell people that their close relatives are dead except to say it—no matter how much you don't want to. "Your grandfather," I said, "and Jeremy and Robin."

"Robin and Jeremy? Kids? Little kids?"

Zahra took his hand. "They kill little kids," she said. "Out here in the world, they kill kids every day."

He didn't cry. Or maybe he cried when we were asleep. First, though, he closed himself up, stopped talking, stopped responding, stopped doing anything until it was nearly dark. By then, Zahra had gone out and come back with my brother Bennett's shirt full of ripe peaches.

"Don't ask me where I got them," she said.

"I assume you stole them," I said. "Not from anyone around here, I hope. No sense making the neighbors mad."

She lifted an eyebrow. "I don't need you to tell me how to live out here. I was born out here. Eat your peaches."

I ate four of them. They were delicious, and too ripe to travel well anyway.

"Why don't you try on some of those clothes," I said. "Take what fits you."

She fit not only into Marcus's shirt and jeans—though she had to roll the jeans legs up—but into his shoes. Shoes are expensive. Now she has two pair.

"You let me do it, I'll trade these little shoes for some food," she said.

I nodded. "Tomorrow. Whatever you get, we'll split it. Then I'm leaving."

"Going north?"

"Yes."

"Just north. Do you know anything about the roads and towns and where to buy stuff or steal it? Have you got money?"

"I have maps," I said. "They're old, but I think they're still good. No one's been building new roads lately."

"Hell no. Money?"

"A little. Not enough, I suspect."

"No such thing as enough money. What about him?" She gestured toward Harry's unmoving back. He was lying down. I couldn't tell whether he was asleep or not.

"He has to decide for himself," I said. "Maybe he wants to hang around to look for his family before he goes."

He turned over slowly. He looked sick, but fully aware. Zahra put the peaches she had saved for him next to him.

"I don't want to wait for anything," he said. "I wish we could start now. I hate this place."

"You going with her?" Zahra asked, jabbing a thumb at me.

He looked at me. "We might be able to help each other," he said. "At least we know each other, and . . . I managed to grab a few hundred dollars as I ran out of the house." He was offering trust. He meant we could trust each other. That was no small thing.

"I was thinking of traveling as a man," I said to him.

He seemed to be repressing a smile. "That will be safer for you. You're at least tall enough to fool people. You'll have to cut your hair, though."

Zahra grunted. "Mixed couples catch hell whether people think they're gay or straight. Harry'll piss off all the blacks and you'll piss off all the whites. Good luck."

I watched her as she said it, and realized what she wasn't saying. "You want to come?" I asked.

She sniffed. "Why should I? I won't cut my hair!"

"No need," I said. "We can be a black couple and their white friend. If Harry can get a reasonable tan, maybe we can claim him as a cousin."

She hesitated, then whispered, "Yeah, I want to go." And she started to cry. Harry stared at her in surprise.

"Did you think we were going to just dump you?" I asked. "All you had to do was let us know."

"I don't have any money," she said. "Not a dollar."

I sighed. "Where did you get those peaches?"

"You were right. I stole them."

"You have a useful skill, then, and information about living out here." I faced Harry. "What do you think?"

"Her stealing doesn't bother you?" he asked.

"I mean to survive," I said.

"'Thou shalt not steal,'" he quoted. "Years and years—a lifetime of Thou shalt not steal.'"

I had to smother a flash of anger before I could answer. He wasn't my father. He had no business quoting scripture at me. He was nobody. I didn't look at him. I didn't speak until I knew my voice would sound normal. Then, "I said I mean to survive," I told him. "Don't you?"

He nodded. "It wasn't a criticism. I'm just surprised."

"I hope it won't ever mean getting caught or leaving someone else to starve," I said. And to my own surprise, I smiled. "I've thought about it. That's the way I feel, but I've never stolen anything."

"You're kidding!" Zahra said.

I shrugged. "It's true. I grew up trying to set a good example for my brothers and trying to live up to my father's expectations. That seemed like what I should be doing."

"Oldest kid," Harry said. "I know." He was the oldest in his family.

"Oldest, hell," Zahra said, laughing. "You're both babies out here."

And that wasn't offensive, somehow. Perhaps because it was true.

OCTAVIA E. BUTLER

"I'm inexperienced," I admitted. "But I can learn. You're going to be one of my teachers."

"One?" she said. "Who have you got but me?"

"Everyone."

She looked scornful. "No one."

"Everyone who's surviving out here knows things that I need to know," I said. "I'll watch them, I'll listen to them, I'll learn from them. If I don't, I'll be killed. And like I said, I intend to survive."

"They'll sell you a bowl of shit," she said.

I nodded. "I know. But I'll buy as few of those as possible."

She looked at me for a long time, then sighed. "I wish I'd known you better before all this happened," she said. "You're a weird preacher's kid. If you still want to play man, I'll cut your hair for you."

MONDAY, AUGUST 2, 2027
(FROM NOTES EXPANDED SUNDAY, AUGUST 8)

We're on our way.

This morning Zahra took us to Hanning Joss, the biggest secure store complex in Robledo. We could get all we needed there. Hanning vendors sell everything from gourmet food to delousing cream, prostheses to homebirthing kits, guns to the latest in touchrings, headsets, and recordings. I could have spent days just wandering through the aisles, staring at the stuff I couldn't afford. I had never been to Hanning before, had never seen anything like it in person.

But we had to go into the complex one at a time, leaving two outside to guard our bundles—including my gun. Hanning, as I had heard many times on the radio, was one of the safest places in the city. If you didn't like their sniffers, metal detectors, package restrictions, armed guards, and willingness to strip-search anyone they thought was suspicious on the way in or out, you could shop somewhere else. The store was full of people eager to put up with the inconvenience and invasion of privacy if only they could buy the things they needed in peace.

No one strip-searched me, though I was required to prove that I wasn't a deadbeat.

"Show your Hanning disc or money," an armed guard demanded at the massive gates. I was terrified that he would steal my money, but I showed the bills that I intended to spend, and he nodded. He never touched them. No doubt we were both being watched, and our behaviors recorded. Such a security conscious store wouldn't want its guards stealing the customers' money.

"Shop in peace," the guard said with no hint of a smile.

I bought salt, a small tube of honey, and the cheapest of dried foods—oats, fruit, nuts, bean flour, lentils, plus a little dried beef—all that I thought Zahra and I could carry. And I bought more water and a few odd items: water purification tablets—just in case—and sun blocker, which even Zahra and I would need, some stuff for insect bites, and an ointment Dad used for muscle aches. We would have plenty of those. I bought more toilet paper, tampons, and lip balm. I bought myself a new notebook, two more pens, and an expensive supply of ammunition for the .45. I felt better once I had that.

I bought three of the cheap, multipurpose sleepsacks—big, tough storage bags, and the preferred bedding of all the more affluent homeless. The country was full of people who could earn or steal food and water, but could not rent even a cot. These might sleep on the street or in makeshift shacks, but if they could, they put a sleepsack between their bodies and the ground. The sacks, with their own strapping, fold to serve as packs during the day. They're light, tough, and able to survive most abuse. They're warm even if you have to sleep on the concrete, but they're thin—more useful than comfortable. Curtis and I used to make love on a pallet of them.

And I bought three oversized jackets of the same thin, breathing synthetic as the sleepsacks. They'll finish the job of keeping us warm at night as we moved north. They look cheap and ugly, and that's good. They might not be stolen.

That was the end of my money—the money I had packed in my emergency pack. I haven't touched the money I took from the foot of the lemon tree. That I had split in half and put in two of my father's socks. I kept it pinned inside my jeans, invisible and unavailable to pickpockets.

It isn't a lot of money, but it's more than I've ever had before— more than anyone could expect me to have. I pinned it where it is, rewrapped in plastic and secure in the socks on Saturday night when I had finished writing and still couldn't stop thinking and remembering and knowing there was nothing I could do about the past.

Then I had a kind of tactile memory of grabbing the money packet and a handful of dirt and stuffing both into my pack. I had an incredible amount of nervous energy that was spending itself in jitteriness. My hands shook so that I could hardly find the money— by feel, in darkness. I made it an exercise in concentration to find the money, socks, and pins, divide the money in half, or as close to in half as I could without seeing, put it into the socks, and pin it in place. I checked it when I went out to urinate the next morning. I'd done a good job. The pins didn't show at all on the outside. I'd put them through the seams down near my ankles. Nothing dangling, no problems.

I took my many purchases out to what was once the ground floor of a parking structure, and was now a kind of semienclosed flea market. Many of the things dug out of ash heaps and landfills wind up for sale here. The rule is that if you buy something in the store, you can sell something of similar value in the structure. Your receipt, coded and dated, is your peddler's license.

The structure was patrolled, though more to check these licenses than to keep anyone safe. Still, the structure was safer than the street.

I found Harry and Zahra sitting on our bundles, Harry waiting to go into the store, and Zahra waiting for her license. They had put their backs against a wall of the store at a spot away from the street and away from the biggest crowd of buyers and sellers. I gave Zahra the receipt and began to separate and pack our new supplies. We would leave as soon as Zahra and Harry finished their buying and selling.

We walked down to the freeway—the 118—and turned west. We would take the 118 to the 23 and the 23 to U.S. 101. The 101 would take us up the coast toward Oregon. We became part of a broad river of people walking west on the freeway. Only a few straggled east against the current—east toward the mountains and the desert. Where were the westward walkers going? To something, or just away from here?

We saw a few trucks—most of them run at night—swarms of bikes or electric cycles, and two cars. All these had plenty of room to speed along the outer lanes past us. We're safer if we keep to the left lanes away from the on and off ramps. It's against the law in California to walk on the freeways, but the law is archaic. Everyone who walks walks on the freeways sooner or later. Freeways provide the most direct routes between cities and parts of cities. Dad walked or bicycled on them often. Some prostitutes and peddlers of food, water, and other necessities live along the freeways in sheds or shacks or in the open air. Beggars, thieves, and murderers live here, too.

But I've never walked a freeway before today. I found the experience both fascinating and frightening. In some ways, the scene reminded me of an old film I saw once of a street in mid-twentieth-century China—walkers, bicyclers, people carrying, pulling, pushing loads of all kinds. But the freeway crowd is a heterogenous mass—black and white, Asian and Latin, whole families are on the move with babies on backs or perched atop loads in carts, wagons or bicycle baskets, sometimes along with an old or handicapped person. Other old, ill, or handicapped people hobbled along as best they could with the help of sticks or fitter companions. Many were armed with sheathed knives, rifles, and, of course, visible, holstered hand-guns. The occasional passing cop paid no attention.

Children cried, played, squatted, did everything except eat. Almost no one ate while walking. I saw a couple of people drink

OCTAVIA E. BUTLER

from canteens. They took quick, furtive gulps, as though they were doing something shameful—or something dangerous.

A woman alongside us collapsed. I got no impression of pain from her, except at the sudden impact of her body weight on her knees. That made me stumble, but not fall. The woman sat where she had fallen for a few seconds, then lurched to her feet and began walking again, leaning forward under her huge pack.

Almost everyone was filthy. Their bags and bundles and packs were filthy. They stank. And we, who have slept on concrete in ashes and dirt, and who have not bathed for three days—we fitted in pretty well. Only our new sleepsack packs gave us away as either new to the road or at least in possession of new stealables. We should have dirtied the packs a little before we got started. We will dirty them tonight. I'll see to it.

There were a few young guys around, lean and quick, some filthy, some not dirty at all. Keiths. Today's Keiths. The ones who bothered me most weren't carrying much. Some weren't carrying anything except weapons.

Predators. They looked around a lot, stared at people, and the people looked away. I looked away. I was glad to see that Harry and Zahra did the same. We didn't need trouble. If trouble came, I hoped we could kill it and keep walking.

The gun was fully loaded now, and I wore it holstered, but half covered by my shirt. Harry bought himself a knife. The money he had snatched up as he ran from his burning house had not been enough to buy a gun. I could have bought a second gun, but it would have taken too much of my money, and we have a long way to go.

Zahra used the shoe money to buy herself a knife and a few personal things. I had refused my share of that money. She needed a few dollars in her pocket.

The day she and Harry use their knives, I hope they kill. If they don't, I might have to, to escape the pain. And what will they think of that?

They deserve to know that I'm a sharer. For their own safety, they should know. But I've never told anyone. Sharing is a weakness, a shameful secret. A person who knows what I am can hurt me, betray me, disable me with little effort.

I can't tell. Not yet. I'll have to tell soon, I know, but not yet. We're together, the three of us, but we're not a unit yet. Harry and I don't know Zahra very well, nor she us. And none of us know what will happen when we're challenged. A racist challenge might force us apart. I want to trust these people. I like them, and . . . they're all I have left. But I need more time to decide. It's no small thing to commit yourself to other people.

"You okay?" Zahra asked.

I nodded.

"You look like hell. And you're so damned poker-faced most of the time. . . ."

"Just thinking," I said. "There's so much to think about now."

She sighed her breath out in a near whistle. "Yeah. I know. But keep your eyes open. You get too wrapped up in your thinking, and you'll miss things. People get killed on freeways all the time."

16

□ □ □

Earthseed
Cast on new ground
Must first perceive
That it knows nothing.

EARTHSEED: THE BOOKS OF THE LIVING
MONDAY, AUGUST 2, 2027
(CONT. FROM NOTES EXPANDED AUGUST 8)

Here are some of the things I've learned today:

Walking hurts. I've never done enough walking to learn that before, but I know it now. It isn't only the blisters and sore feet, although we've got those. After a while, everything hurts. I think my back and shoulders would like to desert to another body. Nothing eases the pain except rest. Even though we got a late start, we stopped twice today to rest. We went off the freeway, into the hills or bushes to sit down, drink water, eat dried fruit and nuts. Then we went on. The days are long this time of year.

Sucking on a plum or apricot pit all day makes you feel less thirsty. Zahra told us that.

"When I was a kid," she said, "there were times when I would put a little rock in my mouth. Anything to feel better. It's a cheat, though. If you don't drink enough water, you'll die no matter how you feel."

All three of us walked along with seeds in our mouths after our first stop, and we felt better. We drank only during our stops in the hills. It's safer that way.

Also, cold camps are safer than cheery campfires. Yet tonight we cleared some ground, dug into a hillside, and made a small fire in the hollow. There we cooked some of my acorn meal with nuts and fruit. It was wonderful. Soon we'll run out of it and we'll have to survive on beans, cornmeal, oats—expensive stuff from stores. Acorns are home-food, and home is gone.

Fires are illegal. You can see them flickering all over the hills, but they are illegal. Everything is so dry that there's always a danger of campfires getting away from people and taking out a community or two. It does happen. But people who have no homes will build fires. Even people like us who know what fire can do will build them. They give comfort, hot food, and a false sense of security.

While we were eating, and even after we'd finished, people drifted over and tried to join us. Most were harmless and easily gotten rid of. Three claimed they just wanted to get warm. The sun was still up, red on the horizon, and it was far from cold.

Three women wanted to know whether two studs like Harry and me didn't need more than one woman. The women who asked this may have been cold, considering how few clothes they had on. It's going to be strange for me, pretending to be a man.

"Couldn't I just roast this potato in your coals?" an old man asked, showing us a withered potato.

We gave him some fire and sent him away—and watched to see where he went, since a burning brand could be either a weapon or a major distraction if he had friends hiding. It's crazy to live this way, suspecting helpless old people. Insane. But we need our paranoia to keep us alive. Hell, Harry wanted to let the old guy sit with us. It took Zahra and me together to let him know that wasn't going to happen. Harry and I have been well-fed and protected all our lives. We're strong and healthy and better educated than most people our age. But we're stupid out here. We want to trust people. I fight against the impulse. Harry hasn't learned to do that yet. We argued about it afterward, low voiced, almost whispering.

"Nobody's safe," Zahra told him. "No matter how pitiful they look, they can steal you naked. Little kids, skinny and big-eyed will make off with all your money, water, and food! I know. I used to do it to people. Maybe they died, I don't know. But I didn't die."

Harry and I both stared at her. We knew so little about her life. But to me, at that moment, Harry was our most dangerous question mark.

"You're strong and confident," I said to him. "You think you can take care of yourself out here, and maybe you can. But think what a stab wound or a broken bone would mean out here: Disablement, slow death from infection or starvation, no medical care, nothing."

He looked at me as though he wasn't sure he wanted to know me anymore. "What, then?" he asked. "Everyone's guilty until proven innocent? Guilty of what? And how do they prove themselves to you?"

"I don't give a piss whether they're innocent or not," Zahra said. "Let them tend to their own business."

"Harry, your mind is still back in the neighborhood," I said. "You still think a mistake is when your father yells at you or you break a finger or chip a tooth or something. Out here a mistake—one mistake—and you may be dead. Remember that guy today? What if that happened to us?"

We had seen a man robbed—a chubby guy of 35 or 40 who was walking along eating nuts out of a paper bag. Not smart. A little kid of 12 or 13 snatched the nuts and ran off with them. While the victim was distracted by the little kid, two bigger kids tripped him, cut his pack straps, dragged the pack off his back, and ran off with it. The whole thing happened so fast that no one could have interfered if they'd wanted to. No one tried. The victim was unhurt except for bruises and abrasions—the sort of thing I had to put up with every day back in the neighborhood. But the victim's supplies were gone. If he had a home nearby and other supplies, he would be all right. Otherwise, his only way of surviving might be to rob someone else—if he could.

"Remember?" I asked Harry. "We don't have to hurt anyone unless they push us into it, but we don't dare let our guard down. We can't trust people."

Harry shook his head. "What if I thought that way when I pulled that guy off Zahra?"

I held on to my temper. "Harry, you know I don't mean we shouldn't trust or help each other. We know each other. We've made a commitment to travel together."

"I'm not sure we do know each other."

"I am. And we can't afford your denial. You can't afford it."

He just stared at me.

"Out here, you adapt to your surroundings or you get killed," I said. "That's obvious!"

Now he did look at me as though I were a stranger. I looked back, hoping I knew him as well as I thought I did. He had a brain and he had courage. He just didn't want to change.

"Do you want to break off with us," Zahra asked, "go your own way without us?"

His gaze softened as he looked at her. "No," he said. "Of course not. But we don't have to turn into animals, for godsake."

"In a way, we do," I said. "We're a pack, the three of us, and all those other people out there aren't in it. If we're a good pack, and we work together, we have a chance. You can be sure we aren't the only pack out here."

He leaned back against a rock, and said with amazement, "You damn sure talk macho enough to be a guy."

I almost hit him. Maybe Zahra and I would be better off without him. But no, that wasn't true. Numbers mattered. Friendship mattered. One real male presence mattered.

"Don't repeat that," I whispered, leaning close to him. "Never say that again. There are other people all over these hills; you don't know who's listening. You give me away and you weaken yourself!"

That reached him. "Sorry," he said.

"It's bad out here," Zahra said. "But most people make it if they're careful. People weaker than us make it—if they're careful."

Harry gave a wan smile. "I hate this world already," he said.

"It's not so bad if people stick together."

He looked from her to me and back to her again. He smiled at her and nodded. It occurred to me then that he liked her, was attracted to her. That could be a problem for her later. She was a beautiful woman, and I would never be beautiful—which didn't bother me. Boys had always seemed to like me. But Zahra's looks grabbed male attention. If she and Harry get together, she could wind up carrying two heavy loads northward.

I was lost in thought about the two of them when Zahra nudged me with her foot.

Two big, dirty-looking guys were standing nearby, watching us, watching Zahra in particular.

I stood up, feeling the others stand with me, flanking me. These guys were too close to us. They meant to be too close. As I stood up, I put my hand on the gun.

"Yeah?" I said. "What do you want?"

"Not a thing," one of them said, smiling at Zahra. Both wore big holstered knives which they fingered.

I drew the gun. "Good deal," I said.

Their smiles vanished. "What, you going to shoot us for standing here?" the talkative one said.

I thumbed the safety. I would shoot the talker, the leader. The other one would run away. He already wanted to run away. He was staring, open-mouthed, at the gun. By the time I collapsed, he would be gone.

"Hey, no trouble!" the talker raised his hands, backing away. "Take it easy, man."

I let them go. I think it would have been better to shoot them. I'm afraid of guys like that—guys looking for trouble, looking for victims. But it seems I can't quite shoot someone just because I'm afraid of him. I killed a man on the night of the fire, and I haven't thought much about it. But this was different. It was like what Harry said about stealing. I've heard, "Thou shalt not kill," all my life, but when you have to, you kill. I wonder what Dad would say about that. But then, he was the one who taught me to shoot.

"We'd better keep a damn good watch tonight," I said. I looked at Harry, and was glad to see that he looked the way I probably had a moment before: mad and worried. "Let's pass your watch and my gun around," I told him. "Three hours per watcher."

"You would have done it, wouldn't you?" he asked. It sounded like a real question.

I nodded. "Wouldn't you?"

"Yes. I wouldn't have wanted to, but those guys were out for fun. Their idea of fun, anyway." He glanced at Zahra. He had pulled one man off her, and taken a beating for it. Maybe the obvious threat to her would keep him alert. Anything that would keep him alert couldn't be all bad.

I looked at Zahra, kept my voice very low. "You never went shooting with us, so I have to ask. Do you know how to use this?"

"Yeah," she said. "Richard let his older kids go out, but he wouldn't let me. Before he bought me, though, I was a good shot."

Her alien past again. It distracted me for a moment. I had been waiting to ask her how much a person costs these days. And she had been sold by her mother to a man who couldn't have been much more than a stranger. He could have been a maniac, a monster. And my father used to worry about future slavery or debt slavery. Had he known? He couldn't have.

"Have you used a gun like this before?" I asked. I reengaged the safety and handed it to her.

"Hell, yeah," she said, examining it. "I like this. It's heavy, but if you shoot somebody with it, they go down." She released the clip, checked it, reinserted it, rammed it home, and handed it back. "I wish I could have practiced with you all," she said. "I always wanted to."

Without warning, I felt a pang of loneliness for the burned neighborhood. It was almost a physical pain. I had been desperate to leave

190   OCTAVIA E. BUTLER

it, but I had expected it still to be there—changed, but surviving. Now that it was gone, there were moments when I couldn't imagine how I was going to survive without it.

"You guys get some sleep," I said. "I'm too wound up to sleep now. I'll take the first watch."

"We should gather more wood for the fire first," Harry said. "It's burning low."

"Let it go out," I said. "It's a spotlight on us, and it messes up our night vision. Other people can see us long before we see them."

"And sit here in the dark," he said. It wasn't a protest. At worst, it was grudging agreement. "I'll take the watch after you," he said, lying back and pulling up his sleepsack and positioning the rest of his gear to serve as a pillow. As an afterthought, he took off his wrist watch and gave it to me. "It was a gift from my mother," he said.

"You know I'll take care of it," I told him.

He nodded. "You be careful," he said, and closed his eyes.

I put the watch on, pulled the elastic of my sleeve down over it so that the glow of the dial wouldn't be visible by accident, and sat back against the hill to make a few quick notes. While there was still some natural light, I could write and watch.

Zahra watched me for a while, then laid her hand on my arm. "Teach me to do that," she whispered.

I looked at her, not understanding.

"Teach me to read and write."

I was surprised, but I shouldn't have been. Where, in a life like hers, had there been time or money for school. And once Richard Moss bought her, her jealous co-wives wouldn't have taught her.

"You should have come to us back in the neighborhood," I said. "We would have set up lessons for you."

"Richard wouldn't let me. He said I already knew enough to suit him."

I groaned. "I'll teach you. We can start tomorrow morning if you want."

"Okay." She gave me an odd smile and began ordering her bag and her few possessions, bundled in my scavenged pillowcase. She lay down in her bag and turned on her side to look at me. "I didn't think I'd like you," she said. "Preacher's kid, all over the place, teaching, telling everybody what to do, sticking your damn nose in everything. But you ain't bad."

I went from surprise into amusement of my own. "Neither are you," I said.

"You didn't like me either?" Her turn to be surprised.

"You were the best looking woman in the neighborhood. No, I wasn't crazy about you. And remember a couple of years ago when you tried your hardest to make me throw up while I was learning to clean and skin rabbits?"

"Why'd you want to learn that, anyway?" she asked. "Blood, guts, worms. . . . I just figured, 'There she goes again, sticking her nose where it don't belong. Well, let her have it!' "

"I wanted to know that I could do that—handle a dead animal, skin it, butcher it, treat its hide to make leather. I wanted to know how to do it, and that I could do it without getting sick."

"Why?"

"Because I thought someday I might have to. And we might out here. Same reason I put together an emergency pack and kept it where I could grab it."

"I wondered about that—about you having all that stuff from home, I mean. At first I thought maybe you got it all when you went back. But no, you were ready for all the trouble. You saw it coming."

"No." I shook my head, remembering. "No one could have been ready for that. But . . . I thought something would happen someday. I didn't know how bad it would be or when it would come. But everything was getting worse: the climate, the economy, crime, drugs, you know. I didn't believe we would be allowed to sit behind our walls, looking clean and fat and rich to the hungry, thirsty, homeless, jobless, filthy people outside."

OCTAVIA E. BUTLER

She turned again and lay on her back, staring upward at the stars. "I should have seen some of that stuff," she said. "But I didn't. Those big walls. And everybody had a gun. There were guards every night. I thought . . . I thought we were so strong."

I put my notebook and pen down, sat on my sleepsack, and put my own pillowcased bundle behind me. Mine was lumpy and uncomfortable to lean on. I wanted it uncomfortable. I was tired. Everything ached. Given a little comfort, I would fall asleep.

The sun was down now, and our fire had gone out except for a few glowing coals. I drew the gun and held it in my lap. If I needed it at all, I would need it fast. We weren't strong enough to survive slowness or stupid mistakes.

I sat where I was for three weary, terrifying hours. Nothing happened to me, but I could see and hear things happening. There were people moving around the hills, sometimes silhouetting themselves against the sky as they ran or walked over the tops of hills. I saw groups and individuals. Twice I saw dogs, distant, but alarming. I heard a lot of gunfire—individual shots and short bursts of automatic weapons fire. That last and the dogs worried me, scared me. A pistol would be no protection against a machine gun or automatic rifle. And dogs might not know enough to be afraid of guns. Would a pack keep coming if I shot two or three of its members? I sat in a cold sweat, longing for walls—or at least for another magazine or two for the gun.

It was nearly midnight when I woke Harry, gave him the gun and the watch, and made him as uncomfortable as I could by warning him about the dogs, the gunfire, and the many people who wandered around at night. He did look awake and alert enough when I lay down.

I fell asleep at once. Aching and exhausted, I found the hard ground as welcoming as my bed at home.

A shout awoke me. Then I heard gunfire—several single shots, thunderous and nearby. Harry?

Something fell across me before I could get out of my sleep-sack—something big and heavy. It knocked the breath out of me. I struggled to get it off me, knowing that it was a human body, dead or unconscious. As I pushed at it and felt its heavy beard stubble and long hair, I realized it was a man, and not Harry. Some stranger.

I heard scrambling and thrashing near me. There were grunts and sounds of blows. A fight. I could see them in the darkness—two figures struggling on the ground. The one on the bottom was Harry.

He was fighting someone over the gun, and he was losing. The muzzle was being forced toward him.

That couldn't happen. We couldn't lose the gun or Harry. I took a small granite boulder from our fire pit, set my teeth, and brought it down with all my strength on the back of the intruder's head. And I brought myself down.

It wasn't the worst pain I had ever shared, but it came close. I was worthless after delivering that one blow. I think I was unconscious for a while.

Then Zahra appeared from somewhere, feeling me, trying to see me. She wouldn't find a wound, of course.

I sat up, fending her off, and saw that Harry was there, too.

"Are they dead?" I asked.

"Never mind them," he said. "Are you all right?"

I got up, swaying from the residual shock of the blow. I felt sick and dizzy, and my head hurt. A few days before, Harry had made me feel that way and we'd both recovered. Did that mean the man I'd hit would recover?

I checked him. He was still alive, unconscious, not feeling any pain now. What I was feeling was my own reaction to the blow I'd struck.

"The other one's dead," Harry said. "This one. . . Well, you caved in the back of his head. I don't know why he's still alive."

"Oh, no," I whispered. "Oh hell." And then to Harry, "Give me the gun."

OCTAVIA E. BUTLER

"Why?" he asked.

My fingers had found the blood and broken skull, soft and pulpy at the back of the stranger's head. Harry was right. He should have been dead.

"Give me the gun," I repeated, and held out a bloody hand for it. "Unless you want to do this yourself."

"You can't shoot him. You can't just . . ."

"I hope you'd find the courage to shoot me if I were like that, and out here with no medical care to be had. We shoot him, or leave him here alive. How long do you think it will take him to die?"

"Maybe he won't die."

I went to my pack, struggling to navigate without throwing up. I pulled it away from the dead man, groped within it, and found my knife. It was a good knife, sharp and strong. I flicked it open and cut the unconscious man's throat with it.

Not until the flow of blood stopped did I feel safe. The man's heart had pumped his life away into the ground. He could not regain consciousness and involve me in his agony.

But, of course, I was far from safe. Perhaps the last two people from my old life were about to leave me. I had shocked and horrified them. I wouldn't blame them for leaving.

"Strip the bodies," I said. "Take what they have, then we'll put them into the scrub oaks down the hill where we gathered wood."

I searched the man I had killed, found a small amount of money in his pants pocket and a larger amount in his right sock. Matches, a packet of almonds, a packet of dried meat, and a packet of small, round, purple pills. I found no knife, no weapon of any kind. So this was not one of the pair that sized us up earlier in the night. I hadn't thought so. Neither of them had been long-haired. Both of these were.

I put the pills back in the pocket I had taken them from. Everything else, I kept. The money would help sustain us. The food might or might not be edible. I would decide that when I could see it clearly.

I looked to see what the others were doing, and was relieved to find them stripping the other body. Harry turned it over, then kept watch as Zahra went through the clothing, shoes, socks, and hair. She was even more thorough than I had been. With no hint of squeamishness, she hauled off the man's clothing and examined its greasy pockets, seams, and hems. I got the feeling she had done this before.

"Money, food, and a knife," she whispered at last.

"The other one didn't have a knife," I said, crouching beside them. "Harry, what—?"

"He had one," Harry whispered. "He pulled it when I yelled for them to stop. It's probably on the ground somewhere. Let's put these two down in the oaks."

"You and I can do it," I said. "Give Zahra the gun. She can guard us."

I was glad to see him hand her the gun without protest. He had not made a move to hand it to me when I asked, but that had been different.

We took the bodies down to the scrub oaks and rolled them into cover. Then we kicked dirt over all the blood that we could see and the urine that one of the men had released.

That wasn't enough. By mutual consent, we moved camp. This meant nothing more than gathering our bundles and sleepsacks and carrying them over the next low ridge and out of sight of where we had been.

If you camped on a hill between any two of the many low, rib-like ridges, you could have, almost, the privacy of a big, open-topped, three-walled room. You were vulnerable from hill or ridge tops, but if you camped on the ridges, you would be noticed by far more people. We chose a spot between two ridges, settled and sat silent for some time. I felt set-apart. I knew I had to speak, and I was afraid that nothing I could say would help. They might leave me. In disgust, in distrust, in fear, they might decide that they couldn't travel with me any longer. Best to try to get ahead of them.

"I'm going to tell you about myself," I said. "I don't know whether it will help you to understand me, but I have to tell you. You have a right to know."

OCTAVIA E. BUTLER

And in low whispers, I told them about my mother—my biological mother—and about my sharing.

When I finished, there was another long silence. Then Zahra spoke, and I was so startled by the sound of her soft voice that I jumped.

"So when you hit that guy," she said, "it was like you hitting yourself."

"No," I said. "I don't get the damage. Just the pain."

"But, I mean it felt like you hit yourself?"

I nodded. "Close enough. When I was little, I used to bleed along with people if I hurt them or even if I saw them hurt. I haven't done that for a few years."

"But if they're unconscious or dead, you don't feel anything."

"That's right."

"So that's why you killed that guy?"

"I killed him because he was a threat to us. To me in a special way, but to you, too. What could we have done about him? Abandon him to the flies, the ants, and the dogs? You might have been willing to do that, but would Harry? Could we stay with him? For how long? To what purpose? Or would we dare to hunt up a cop and try to report seeing a guy hurt without involving ourselves. Cops are not trusting people. I think they would want to check us out, hang on to us for a while, maybe charge us with attacking the guy and killing his friend." I turned to look at Harry who had not said a word. "What would you have done?" I asked.

"I don't know," he said, his voice hard with disapproval. "I only know I wouldn't have done what you did."

"I wouldn't have asked you to do it," I said. "I didn't ask you. But, Harry, I would do it again. I might have to do it again. That's why I'm telling you this." I glanced at Zahra. "I'm sorry I didn't tell you before. I knew I should, but talking about it is . . . hard. Very hard. I've never told anyone before. Now . . ." I took a deep breath. "Now everything's up to you."

"What do you mean?" Harry demanded.

I looked at him, wishing I could see his expression well enough to know whether this was a real question. I didn't think it was. I decided to ignore him.

"So what do you think?" I asked, looking at Zahra.

Neither of them said anything for a minute. Then Zahra began to speak, began to say such terrible things in that soft voice of hers. After a moment, I wasn't sure she was talking to us.

"My mama took drugs, too," she said. "Shit, where I was born, everybody's mama took drugs—and whored to pay for them. And had babies all the time, and threw them away like trash when they died. Most of the babies did die from the drugs or accidents or not having enough to eat or being left alone so much . . . or from being sick. They were always getting sick. Some of them were born sick. They had sores all over or big things on their eyes—tumors, you know—or no legs or fits or can't breathe right. . . . All kinds of things. And some of the ones who lived were dumb as dirt. Can't think, can't learn, just sit around nine, ten years old, peeing in their pants, rocking back and forth, and dripping spit down their chins. There's a lot of them."

She took my hand and held it. "You ain't got nothing wrong with you, Lauren—nothing worth worrying about. That Paracetco shit was baby milk."

How was it that I had not gotten to know this woman back in the neighborhood? I hugged her. She seemed surprised, then hugged back.

We both looked at Harry.

He sat still, near us, but far from us—from me. "What would you do," he asked, "if that guy only had a broken arm or leg?"

I groaned, thinking about pain. I already knew more than I wanted to about how broken bones feel. "I think I'd let him go," I said, "and I'm sure I would be sorry for it. It would be a long time before I stopped looking over my shoulder."

"You wouldn't kill him to escape the pain?"

"I never killed anyone back in the neighborhood to escape pain."

OCTAVIA E. BUTLER

"But a stranger . . ."

"I've said what I would do."

"What if I broke my arm?"

"Then I might not be much good to you. I would be having trouble with my arm, too, after all. But we'd have two good arms between us." I sighed. "We grew up together, Harry. You know me. You know what kind of person I am. I might fail you, but if I could help myself, I wouldn't betray you."

"I thought I knew you."

I took his hands, looked at their big, pale, blunt fingers. They had a lot of strength in them, I knew, but I had never seen him use it to bully anyone. He was worth some trouble, Harry was.

"No one is who we think they are," I said. "That's what we get for not being telepathic. But you've trusted me so far—and I've trusted you. I've just put my life in your hands. What are you going to do?"

Was he going to abandon me now to my "infirmity"—instead of me maybe abandoning him at some future time due to a theoretical broken arm. And I thought: One oldest kid to another, Harry; would that be responsible behavior?

He took his hands back. "Well, I did know you were a manipulative bitch," he said.

Zahra smothered a laugh. I was surprised. I'd never heard him use the word before. I heard it now as a sound of frustration. He wasn't going to leave. He was a last bit of home that I didn't have to give up yet. How did he feel about that? Was he angry with me for almost breaking up the group? He had reason to be, I suppose.

"I don't understand how you could have been like this all the time," he said. "How could you hide your sharing from everyone?"

"My father taught me to hide it," I told him. "He was right. In this world, there isn't any room for housebound, frightened, squeamish people, and that's what I might have become if everyone had known about me—all the other kids, for instance. Little kids are vicious. Haven't you noticed?"

"But your brothers must have known."

"My father put the fear of God into them about it. He could do that. As far as I know, they never told anyone. Keith used to play 'funny' tricks on me, though."

"So . . . you faked everyone out. You must be a hell of an actor."

"I *had* to learn to pretend to be normal. My father kept trying to convince me that I was normal. He was wrong about that, but I'm glad he taught me the way he did."

"Maybe you are normal. I mean if the pain isn't real, then maybe—"

"Maybe this sharing thing is all in my head? Of course it is! And I can't get it out. Believe me, I'd love to."

There was a long silence. Then he asked, "What do you write in your book every night?" Interesting shift.

"My thoughts," I said. "The day's events. My feelings."

"Things you can't say?" he asked. "Things that are important to you?"

"Yes."

"Then let me read something. Let me know something about the you that hides. I feel as though . . . as though you're a lie. I don't know you. Show me something of you that's real."

What a request! Or was it a demand? I would have given him money to read and digest some of the Earthseed portions of my journal. But he had to be eased into them. If he read the wrong thing, it would just increase the distance between us.

"The risks you ask me to take, Harry. . . . But, yes, I'll show you some of what I've written. I want to. It'll be another first for me. All I ask is that you read what I show you aloud so Zahra can hear it. As soon as it's light, I'll show you."

When it was light, I showed him this:

> *"All that you touch*
> *You Change.*

OCTAVIA E. BUTLER

All that you Change
Changes you.

The only lasting truth
Is Change.

God
Is Change."

Last year, I chose these lines to the first page of the first book of *Earthseed: The Books of the Living*. These lines say everything. Everything!

Imagine him asking me for it.

I must be careful.

17

□ □ □

Embrace diversity.
Unite —
Or be divided,
robbed,
ruled,
killed
By those who see you as prey.
Embrace diversity
Or be destroyed.

EARTHSEED: THE BOOKS OF THE LIVING
TUESDAY, AUGUST 3, 2027
(FROM NOTES EXPANDED AUGUST 8)

There's a big fire in the hills to the east of us. We saw it begin as a thin, dark column of smoke, rising into an otherwise clear sky. Now it's massive—a hillside or two? Several buildings? Many houses? Our neighborhood again?

We kept looking at it, then looking away. Other people dying, losing their families, their homes. . . . Even when we had walked past it, we looked back.

Had the people with painted faces done this, too? Zahra was crying as she walked along, cursing in a voice so soft that I could hear only a few of the bitter words.

Earlier today we left the 118 freeway to look for and finally connect with the 23. Now we're on the 23 with charred overgrown wilderness on one side and neighborhoods on the other. We can't see the fire itself now. We've passed it, come a long way from it, put hills between it and us as we head southward toward the coast. But we can still see the smoke. We didn't stop for the night until it was almost dark and we were all tired and hungry.

We've camped away from the freeway on the wilderness side of it, out of sight, but not out of hearing of the shuffling hoards of people on the move. I think that's a sound we'll hear for the whole of our journey whether we stop in Northern California or go through to Canada. So many people hoping for so much up where it still rains every year, and an uneducated person might still get a job that pays in money instead of beans, water, potatoes, and maybe a floor to sleep on.

But it's the fire that holds our attention. Maybe it was started by accident. Maybe not. But still, people are losing what they may not be able to replace. Even if they survive, insurance isn't worth much these days.

People on the highway, shadowy in the darkness, had begun to reverse the flow, to drift northward to find a way to the fire. Best to be early for the scavenging.

"Should we go?" Zahra asked, her mouth full of dried meat. We built no fire tonight. Best for us to vanish into the darkness and avoid guests. We had put a tangle of trees and bushes at our backs and hoped for the best.

"You mean go back and rob those people?" Harry demanded.

"Scavenge," she said. "Take what people don't need no more. If you're dead, you don't need much."

"We should stay here and rest," I said. "We're tired, and it will be a long time before things are cool enough over there to allow scavenging. It's a long way off, anyway."

Zahra sighed. "Yeah."

"We don't have to do things like that, anyway," Harry said.

Zahra shrugged. "Every little bit helps."

"You were crying about that fire a while ago."

"Uh-uh," Zahra drew her knees up against her body. "I wasn't

204   OCTAVIA E. BUTLER

crying about that fire. I was crying about our fire and my Bibi and thinking about how much I hate people who set fires like that. I wish they would burn. I wish I could burn them. I wish I could just take them and throw them in the fire . . . like they did my Bibi." And she began to cry again, and he held her, apologizing and, I think, shedding a few tears himself.

Grief hit like that. Something would remind us of the past, of home, of a person, and then we would remember that it was all gone. The person was dead or probably dead. Everything we'd known and treasured was gone. Everything except the three of us. And how well were we doing?

"I think we should move," Harry said sometime later. He was still sitting with Zahra, one arm around her, and she seemed to welcome the contact.

"Why?" she asked.

"I want to be higher, closer to the level of the freeway or above it. I want to be able to see the fire if it jumps the freeway and spreads toward us. I want to see it before it gets too close. Fire moves fast."

I groaned. 'You're right," I said, "but moving now that it's dark is risky. We could lose this place and find nothing better."

"Wait here," he said, and got up and walked away into the darkness. I had the gun, so I hoped he kept his knife handy—and I hoped he wouldn't need it. He was still raw about what had happened the night before. He had killed a man. That bothered him. I had killed a man in a much more cold-blooded way, according to him, and it didn't bother me. But my "cold-bloodedness" bothered him. He wasn't a sharer. He didn't understand that to me pain was the evil. Death was an end to pain. No Bible verses were going to change that as far as I was concerned. He didn't understand sharing. Why should he? Most people knew little or nothing about it.

On the other hand, my Earthseed verses had surprised him, and, I think, pleased him a little. I wasn't sure whether he liked the writing or the reasoning, but he liked having something to read and talk about.

"Poetry?" he said this morning as he looked through the pages I showed him—pages of my Earthseed notebook, as it happened. "I never knew you cared about poetry."

"A lot of it isn't very poetical," I said. "But it's what I believe, and I've written it as well as I could." I showed him four verses in all—gentle, brief verses that might take hold of him without his realizing it and live in his memory without his intending that they should. Bits of the Bible had done that to me, staying with me even after I stopped believing.

I gave to Harry, and through him to Zahra, thoughts I wanted them to keep. But I couldn't prevent Harry from keeping other things as well: His new distrust of me, for instance, almost his new dislike. I was not quite Lauren Olamina to him any longer. I had seen that in his expression off and on all day. Odd. Joanne hadn't liked her glimpse of the real me either. On the other hand, Zahra didn't seem to mind. But then, she hadn't known me very well at home. What she learned now, she could accept without feeling lied to. Harry did feel lied to, and perhaps he wondered what lies I was still telling or living. Only time could heal that—if he let it.

We moved when he came back. He had found us a new campsite, near the freeway and yet private. One of the huge freeway signs had fallen or been knocked down, and now lay on the ground, propped up by a pair of dead sycamore trees. With the trees, it formed a massive lean-to. The rock and ash leavings of a campfire showed us that the place had been used before. Perhaps there had been people here tonight, but they had gone away to see what they could scavenge from the fire. Now we're here, happy to get a little privacy, a view of the hills back where the fire is, and the security, for what it was worth, of at least one wall.

"Good deal!" Zahra said, unrolling her sleepsack and settling down on top of it. "I'll take the first watch tonight, okay?"

It was okay with me. I gave her the gun and lay down, eager for sleep. Again I was amazed to find so much comfort in sleeping on the ground in my clothes. There's no narcotic like exhaustion.

OCTAVIA E. BUTLER

Sometime in the night I woke up to soft, small sounds of voices and breathing. Zahra and Harry were making love. I turned my head and saw them at it, though they were too much involved with each other to notice me.

And, of course, no one was on watch.

I got caught up in their lovemaking, and had all I could do to lie still and keep quiet. I couldn't escape their sensation. I couldn't keep an efficient watch. I could either writhe with them or hold myself rigid. I held rigid until they finished—until Harry kissed Zahra, then got up to put his pants on and began his watch.

And I lay awake afterward, angry and worried. How in hell could I talk to either of them about this? It would be none of my business except for the time they chose for doing it. But look when that was! We could all have been killed.

Still sitting up, Harry began to snore.

I listened for a couple of minutes, then sat up, reached over Zahra, and shook him.

He jumped awake, stared around, then turned toward me. I couldn't see more than a moving silhouette.

"Give me the gun and go back to sleep," I said.

He just sat there.

"Harry, you'll get us killed. Give me the gun and the watch and lie down. I'll wake you later."

He looked at the watch.

"Sorry," he said. "Guess I was more tired than I thought." His voice grew less sleep-fogged. "I'm all right. I'm awake. Go back to sleep."

His pride had kicked in. It would be almost impossible to get the gun and the watch from him now.

I lay down. "Remember last night," I said. "If you care about her at all, if you want her to live, remember last night."

He didn't answer. I hoped I had surprised him. I supposed I had also embarrassed him. And maybe I had made him feel angry and defensive. Whatever I'd done, I didn't hear him doing anymore snoring.

WEDNESDAY, AUGUST 4, 2027

Today we stopped at a commercial water station and filled ourselves and all our containers with clean, safe water. Commercial stations are best for that. Anything you buy from a water peddler on the freeway ought to be boiled, and still might not be safe. Boiling kills disease organisms, but may do nothing to get rid of chemical residue—fuel, pesticide, herbicide, whatever else has been in the bottles that peddlers use. The fact that most peddlers can't read makes the situation worse. They sometimes poison themselves.

Commercial stations let you draw whatever you pay for—and not a drop more—right out of one of their taps. You drink whatever the local householders are drinking. It might taste, smell, or look bad, but you can depend on it not to kill you.

There aren't enough water stations. That's why water peddlers exist. Also, water stations are dangerous places. People going in have money. People coming out have water, which is as good as money. Beggars and thieves hang around such places—keeping the whores and drug dealers company. Dad warned us all about water stations, trying to prepare us in case we ever went out and got caught far enough from home to be tempted to stop for water. His advice: "Don't do it. Suffer. Get your rear end home."

Yeah.

Three is the smallest comfortable number at a water station. Two to watch and one to fill up. And it's good to have three ready for trouble on the way to and from the station. Three would not stop determined thugs, but it would stop opportunists—and most predators are opportunists. They prey on old people, lone women or women with young kids, handicapped people. . . . They don't want to get hurt. My father used to call them coyotes. When he was being polite, he called them coyotes.

OCTAVIA E. BUTLER

We were coming away with our water when we saw a pair of two-legged coyotes grab a bottle of water from a woman who was carrying a sizable pack and a baby. The man with her grabbed the coyote who had taken the water, the coyote passed the water to his partner, and his partner ran straight into us.

I tripped him. I think it was the baby who attracted my attention, my sympathy. The tough plastic bubble that held the water didn't break. The coyote didn't break either. I set my teeth, sharing the jolt as he fell and the pain of his scraped forearms. Back home, the younger kids hit me with that kind of thing every day.

I stepped back from the coyote and put my hand on the gun. Harry stepped up beside me. I was glad to have him there. We looked more intimidating together.

The husband of the woman had thrown off his attacker, and the two coyotes, finding themselves outnumbered, scampered away. Skinny, scared little bastards out to do their daily stealing.

I picked up the plastic bubble of water and handed it to the man. He took it and said, "Thanks man. Thanks a lot."

I nodded and we went on our way. It still felt strange to be called "man." I didn't like it, but that didn't matter.

"All of a sudden you're a Good Samaritan," Harry said. But he didn't mind. There was no disapproval in his voice.

"It was the baby, wasn't it?" Zahra asked.

"Yes," I admitted. "The family, really. All of them together." All of them together. They had been a black man, a Hispanic-looking woman, and a baby who managed to look a little like both of them. In a few more years, a lot of the families back in the neighborhood would have looked like that. Hell, Harry and Zahra were working on starting a family like that. And as Zahra had once observed, mixed couples catch hell out here.

Yet there were Harry and Zahra, walking so close together that they couldn't help now and then brushing against each other. But they kept alert, looked around. We were on U.S.101 now, and there were even more walkers. Even clumsy thieves would have no trouble losing themselves in this crowd.

But Zahra and I had had a talk this morning during her reading lesson. We were supposed to be working on the sounds of letters and the spelling of simple words. But when Harry went off to the bushes of our designated toilet area, I stopped the lesson.

"Remember what you said to me a couple of days ago?" I asked her. "My mind was wandering and you warned me. 'People get killed on freeways all the time,' you said."

To my surprise, she saw where I was headed at once. "Damn you," she said, looking up from the paper I had given her. "You don't sleep sound enough, that's all." She smiled as she said it.

"You want privacy, I'll give it to you," I said. "Just let me know, and I'll guard the camp from someplace a short distance away. You two can do what you want. But no more of this shit when you're on watch!"

She looked surprised. "Didn't think you said words like that."

"And I didn't think you did things like last night. Dumb!"

"I know. Fun, though. He's a big strong boy." She paused. "You jealous?"

"Zahra!"

"Don't worry," she said. "Things took me by surprise last night. I . . . I needed something, someone. It won't be like that no more."

"Okay."

"You jealous?" she repeated.

I made myself smile. "I'm as human as you are," I said. "But I don't think I would have yielded to temptation out here with no prospects, no idea what's going to happen. The thought of getting pregnant would have stopped me cold."

"People have babies out here all the time." She grinned at me. "What about you and that boyfriend of yours."

"We were careful. We used condoms."

Zahra shrugged. "Well Harry and me didn't. If it happens, it happens."

OCTAVIA E. BUTLER

It had apparently happened to the couple whose water we had saved. Now they had a baby to lug north.

They stayed near us today, that couple. I saw them every now and then. Tall, stocky, velvet-skinned, deep-black man carrying a huge pack; short, pretty, stocky, light-brown woman with baby and pack; medium brown baby a few months old—huge-eyed baby with curly black hair.

They rested when we rested. They're camped now not far behind us. They look more like potential allies than potential dangers, but I'll keep an eye on them.

THURSDAY, AUGUST 5, 2027

Late today we came within sight of the ocean. None of us have ever seen it before, and we had to go closer, look at it, camp within sight and sound and smell of it. Once we had decided to do that, we walked shoeless in the waves, pants legs rolled up. Sometimes we just stood and stared at it: the Pacific Ocean—the largest, deepest body of water on earth, almost half-a-world of water. Yet, as it was, we couldn't drink any of it.

Harry stripped down to his underwear and waded out until the cool water reached his chest. He can't swim, of course. None of us can swim. We've never before seen water enough to swim in. Zahra and I watched Harry with a lot of concern. Neither of us felt free to follow him. I'm supposed to be a man and Zahra attracts enough of the wrong kind of attention with all her clothes on. We decided to wait until after sundown and go in fully clothed, just to wash away some of the grime and stink. Then we could change clothes. We both had soap and we were eager to make use of it.

There were other people on the beach. In fact, the narrow strip of sand was crowded with people, though they managed to stay out of each other's way. They had spread themselves out and seemed far more tolerant of one another than they had during our night in the hills. I didn't hear any shooting or fighting. There were no dogs, no obvious thefts, no rape. Perhaps the sea and the cool breeze lulled them. Harry wasn't the only one to strip down and go into the water. Quite a few women had gone out, wearing almost nothing. Maybe this was a safer place than any we'd seen so far.

Some people had tents, and several had built fires. We settled in against the remnants of a small building. We were always, it seemed, looking for walls to shield us. Was it better to have them and perhaps get trapped against them or to camp in the open and be vulnerable on every side? We didn't know. It just felt better to have at least one wall.

I salvaged a flat piece of wood from the building, went a few yards closer to the ocean, and began to dig into the sand. I dug until I found dampness. Then I waited.

"What's supposed to happen?" Zahra asked. Until now she had watched me without saying anything.

"Drinkable water," I told her. "According to a couple of books I read, water is supposed to seep up through the sand with most of the salt filtered out of it."

She looked into the damp hole. "When?" she asked.

I dug a little more. "Give it time," I said. "If the trick works, we ought to know about it. It might save our lives someday."

"Or poison us or give us a disease," she said. She looked up to see Harry coming toward us, dripping wet. Even his hair was wet.

"He don't look bad naked," she said.

He was still wearing his underwear, of course, but I could see what she meant. He had a nice, strong-looking body, and I don't think he minded our looking at it. And he looked clean and he didn't stink.

I couldn't wait to get into the water.

"Go ahead," he said. "It's sundown. I'll watch our stuff. Go."

We got our soap out, gave him the gun, took off shoes and socks, and went. It was wonderful. The water was cold and it was hard to stand up in the waves and the sand kept being drawn away from our feet, even drawn from under our feet. But we threw water on each other and washed everything—clothing, bodies, and hair—let the waves knock us around, and laughed like crazy people. Best time I've had since we left home.

Quite a lot of water had seeped into the hole I dug by the time we got back to Harry. I tasted it—took a little up in my hand while Harry criticized me.

"Look at all the people in this damned place!" he said. "Do you see any bathrooms? What do you think they do out here. You ought to at least have the sense to use a water purification tablet!"

That thought was enough to make me spit out the mouthful of water that I had taken. He was right, of course. But that one mouthful had told me what I wanted to know. The water had been a little brackish, but not bad—drinkable. It should be boiled or a water purification tablet should be added to it, as Harry had said, and before that, according to my book, it could be strained through sand to get rid of more of the salt. That meant if we stayed near the coast, we could survive even if we ran short of water. That was good to know.

We still had our shadows. The couple with the baby had camped near us, and the woman was now sitting on the sand nursing her baby while the man knelt beside his pack, rummaging through it.

"Do you think they want to wash?" I asked Harry and Zahra.

"What are you going to do?" Zahra responded. "Offer to babysit?"

I shook my head. "No, I think that would be too much. Do either of you mind if I invite them over?"

"Aren't you afraid they'll rob us?" Harry demanded. "You're afraid of everyone else."

"They have better gear than we do," I said. "And they have no natural allies around here except us. Mixed couples or groups are rare out here. No doubt that's why they've kept close to us."

"And you helped them," Zahra said. "People don't help strangers too much out here. And you gave them back their water. That means you have enough so you don't have to rob them."

"So do you mind?" I asked again.

They looked at each other.

"I don't mind," Zahra said. "Long as we keep an eye on them."

"Why do you want them?" Harry asked, watching me.

"They need us more than we need them," I said.

"That's not a reason."

"They're potential allies."

"We don't need allies."

"Not now. But we'd be damned fools to wait and try to get them when we do need them. By then, they might not be around."

He shrugged and sighed. "All right. Like Zahra says, as long as we watch them."

I got up and went over to the couple. I could see them straighten and go tense as I approached. I was careful not to go too close or move too fast.

"Hello," I said. "If you two would like to take turns bathing, you can come over and join us. That might be safer for the baby."

"Join you?" the man said. "You're asking us to join you?"

"Inviting you."

"Why?"

"Why not. We're natural allies—the mixed couple and the mixed group."

"Allies?" the man said, and he laughed.

I looked at him, wondering why he laughed.

"What the hell do you really want?" he demanded.

I sighed. "Come join us if you want to. You're welcome, and in a pinch, five is better than two." I turned and left them. Let them talk it over and decide.

"They coming?" Zahra asked when I got back.

"I think so," I said. "Although maybe not tonight."

We built a fire and had a hot meal last night, but the mixed family did not join us. I didn't blame them. People stay alive out here by being suspicious. But they didn't go away either. And it was no accident that they had chosen to stay near us. It was a good thing for them that they were near us. The peaceful beach scene changed late last night. Dogs came onto the sand.

They came during my watch. I saw movement far down the beach and I focused on it. Then there was shouting, screams. I thought it was a fight or a robbery. I didn't see the dogs until they broke away from a group of humans and ran inland. One of them was carrying something, but I couldn't tell what it was. I watched them until they vanished inland. People chased them for a short distance, but the dogs were too fast. Someone's property was lost—someone's food, no doubt.

I was on edge after that. I got up, moved to the inland end of our wall, sat there where I could see more of the beach. I was there, sitting still with the gun in my lap when I spotted movement perhaps a long city block up the beach. Dark forms against pale sand. More dogs. Three of them. They nosed around the sand for a moment, then headed our way. I sat as still as I could, watching. So many people slept without posting watches. The three dogs wandered among the camps, investigating what they pleased, and no one tried to drive them away. On the other hand, people's oranges, potatoes, and grain meal couldn't be very tempting to a dog. Our small supply of dried meat might be another matter. But no dog would get it.

But the dogs stopped at the camp of the mixed couple. I remembered the baby and jumped up. At the same moment, the baby began to cry. I shoved Zahra with my foot and she came awake all at once. She could do that.

"Dogs," I said. "Wake Harry." Then I headed for the mixed couple. The woman was screaming and beating at a dog with her hands. A second dog was dodging the man's kicks and going for the baby. Only the third dog was clear of the family.

I stopped, slipped the safety, and as the third dog went in toward the baby, I shot it.

The dog dropped without a sound. I dropped, too, gasping, feeling kicked in the chest. It surprised me how hard the loose sand was to fall on.

At the crack of the shot, the other two dogs took off inland. From my prone position, I sighted on them as they ran. I might have been able to pick off one more of them, but I let them go. I hurt enough already. I couldn't catch my breath, it seemed. As I gasped, though, it occurred to me that prone was a good shooting position for me. Sharing would be less able to incapacitate me at once if I shot two-handed and prone. I filed the knowledge away for future use. Also, it was interesting that the dogs had been frightened by my shot. Was it the sound that scared them or the fact that one of them had been hit? I wish I knew more about them. I've read books about them being intelligent, loyal pets, but that's all in the past. Dogs now are wild animals who will eat a baby if they can.

I felt that the dog I had shot was dead. It wasn't moving. But by now a lot of people were awake and moving around. A living dog, even wounded, would be frantic to get away.

The pain in my chest began to ebb. When I could breathe without gasping, I stood up and walked back to our camp. There was so much confusion by then that no one noticed me except Harry and Zahra.

Harry came out to meet me. He took the gun from my hand, then took my arm and steered me back to my sleepsack.

"So you hit something," he said as I sat gasping again from the small exertion.

I nodded. "Killed a dog. I'll be okay soon."

"You need a keeper," he said.

"Dogs were after the baby!"

"You've adopted those damned people."

I smiled in spite of myself, liking him, thinking that I'd pretty much adopted him and Zahra, too. "What's wrong with that?" I asked.

He sighed. "Get in your bag and go to sleep, will you. I'll take the next watch,"

"Some people just came and carried off the dog you killed," Zahra said. "We should have got it."

"I'm not ready to eat a dog yet," Harry told her. "Go to sleep."

The names of the members of the mixed family are Travis Charles Douglas, Gloria Natividad Douglas, and six-month-old Dominic Douglas, also called Domingo. They gave in and joined us tonight after we made camp. We've detoured away from the highway to make camp on another beach, and they've followed. Once we were settled, they came over to us, uncertain and suspicious, offering us small pieces of their treasure: milk chocolate full of almonds. Real milk chocolate, not carob candy. It was the best thing I'd tasted since long before leaving Robledo.

"It was you last night?" Natividad asked Harry. The first thing she had told us was to call her Natividad.

"It was Lauren," Harry said, gesturing toward me.

She looked at me. "Thank you."

"Is your baby all right?" I asked.

"He had scratches and sand in his eyes and mouth from being dragged." She stroked the sleeping baby's black hair. "I put salve on the scratches and washed his eyes. He's all right now. He's so good. He only cried a little bit."

"Hardly ever cries," Travis said with quiet pride. Travis has an unusual deep-black complexion—skin so smooth that I can't believe he has ever in his life had a pimple. Looking at him makes me want to touch him and see how all that perfect skin feels. He's young, good looking, and intense—a stocky, muscular man, tall, but a little shorter and a little heavier than Harry. Natividad is stocky, too—a pale brown woman with a round, pretty face, long black hair bound up in a coil atop her head. She's short, but it isn't surprising somehow that she can carry a pack and a baby and keep up a steady pace all day. I like her, feel inclined to trust her. I'll have to be careful about that. But I don't believe she would steal from us. Travis has not accepted us yet, but she has. We've helped her baby. We're her friends.

"We're going to Seattle," she told us. "Travis has an aunt there. She says we can stay with her until we find work. We want to find work that pays money."

"Don't we all," Zahra agreed. She sat on Harry's sleepsack with him, his arm around her. Tonight could be tiresome for me.

Travis and Natividad sat on their three sacks, spread out to give their baby room to crawl when he woke up. Natividad had harnessed him to her wrist with a length of clothesline.

I felt alone between the two couples. I let them talk about their hopes and rumors of northern edens. I took out my notebook and began to write up the day's events, still savoring the last of the chocolate.

The baby awoke hungry and crying. Natividad opened her loose shirt, gave him a breast, and moved over near me to see what I was doing.

"You can read and write," she said with surprise. "I thought you might be drawing. What are you writing?"

"She's always writing," Harry said. "Ask to read her poetry. Some of it isn't bad."

I winced. My name is androgynous, in pronunciation at least— Lauren sounds like the more masculine Loren. But pronouns are more specific, and still a problem for Harry.

"She?" Travis asked right on cue. "Her?"

"Damn it, Harry," I said. "We forgot to buy that tape for your mouth."

He shook his head, then gave me an embarrassed smile. "I've known you all my life. It isn't easy to remember to switch all your pronouns. I think it's all right this time, though."

"I told you so!" Natividad said to her husband. Then she looked embarrassed. "I told him you didn't look like a man," she said to me. "You're tall and strong, but . . . I don't know. You don't have a man's face."

I had, almost, a man's chest and hips, so maybe I should be glad to hear that I didn't have a man's face—though it wasn't going to help me on the road. "We believed two men and a woman would be more likely to survive than two women and a man," I said. "Out here, the trick is to avoid confrontation by looking strong."

"The three of us aren't going to help you look strong," Travis said. He sounded bitter. Did he resent the baby and Natividad?

"You are our natural allies," I said. "You sneered at that last time I said it, but it's true. The baby won't weaken us much, I hope, and he'll have a better chance of surviving with five adults around him."

"I can take care of my wife and my son," Travis said with more pride than sense. I decided not to hear him.

"I think you and Natividad will strengthen us," I said. "Two more pairs of eyes, two more pairs of hands. Do you have knives?"

"Yes." He patted his pants pocket. "I wish we had guns like you."

I wished we had guns—plural—too. But I didn't say so. "You and Natividad look strong and healthy," I said. "Predators will look at a group like the five of us and move on to easier prey."

Travis grunted, still noncommittal. Well, I had helped him twice, and now I was a woman. It might take him a while to forgive me for that, no matter how grateful he was.

"I want to hear some of your poetry," Natividad said. "The man we worked for, his wife used to write poetry. She would read it to me sometimes when she was feeling lonely. I liked it. Read me something of yours before it gets too dark."

Odd to think of a rich woman reading to her maid—which was who Natividad had been. Maybe I had the wrong idea of rich women. But then, everyone gets lonely. I put my journal down and picked up my book of Earthseed verses. I chose soft, non-preachy verses, good for road-weary minds and bodies.

18

□ □ □

Once or twice
each week
A Gathering of Earthseed
is a good and necessary thing.
It vents emotion, then
quiets the mind.
It focuses attention,
strengthens purpose, and
unifies people.

EARTHSEED: THE BOOKS OF THE LIVING

SUNDAY, AUGUST 8, 2027

"You believe in all this Earthseed stuff, don't you?" Travis asked me.

It was our day off, our day of rest. We had left the highway to find a beach where we could camp for the day and night and be comfortable. The Santa Barbara beach we had found included a partly burned park where there were trees and tables. It wasn't crowded, and we could have a little daytime privacy. The water was only a short walk away. The two couples took turns disappearing while I watched their packs and the baby. Interesting that the Douglases were already comfortable trusting me with all that was precious to them. We didn't trust them to watch alone last night or the night before, though we did make them watch. We had no walls to put our backs against last night so it was useful to have two watchers at a time. Natividad watched with me and Travis watched with Harry. Finally, Zahra watched alone.

I organized that, feeling that it was the schedule that would be most comfortable to both couples. Neither would be required to trust the other too much.

Now, amid the outdoor tables, firepits, pines, palms, and sycamores, trust seems not to be a problem. If you turn your back to the burned portion which is barren and ugly, this is a beautiful place, and it's far enough from the highway not to be found by the ever-flowing river of people moving north. I found it because I had maps—in particular, a street map of much of Santa Barbara County. My grandparents' maps helped us explore away from the highway even though many street signs were fallen or gone. There were enough left for us to find beaches when we were near them.

There were locals at this beach—people who had left real homes to spend an August day at the beach. I eavesdropped on a few fragments of conversation and found out that much.

Then I tried talking to some of them. To my surprise, most were willing to talk. Yes, the park was beautiful except where some painted fools had set fires. The rumors were that they did it to fight for the poor, to expose or destroy the goods hoarded by the rich. But a park by the sea wasn't goods. It was open to everyone. Why burn it? No one knew why.

No one knew where the fad of painting yourself and getting high on drugs and fire had come from, either. Most people suspected it had begun in Los Angeles where, according to them, most stupid or wicked things began. Local prejudice. I didn't tell any of them I was from the L.A. area. I just smiled and asked about the local job situation. Some people said they knew where I could work to earn a meal or a "safe" place to sleep, but no one knew where I could earn money. That didn't mean there weren't any such jobs, but if there were, they would be hard to find and harder to qualify for. That's going to be a problem wherever we go. And yet we know a lot, the three of us, the five of us. We know how to do a great many things. There must be a way to put it all together and make us something other than domestic servants working for room and board. We make an interesting unit.

Water is very expensive here—worse than in Los Angeles or Ventura Counties. We all went to a water station this morning. Still no freeway watersellers for us.

On the road yesterday, we saw three dead men—a group together, young, unmarked, but covered with the blood they had vomited, their bodies bloated and beginning to stink. We passed them, looked at them, took nothing from their bodies. Their packs—if they'd had any—were already gone. Their clothes, we did not want. And their canteens—all three still had canteens—their canteens, no one wanted.

We all resupplied yesterday at a local Hanning Joss. We were relieved and surprised to see it—a good dependable place where we could buy all we needed from solid food for the baby to soap to salves for skin chafed by salt water, sun, and walking. Natividad bought new liners for her baby carrier and washed and dried a plastic bag of filthy old ones. Zahra went with her into the separate laundry area of the store to wash and dry some of our filthy clothing. We wore our sea-washed clothing, salty, but not quite stinking. Paying to wash clothes was a luxury we could not often afford, yet none of us found it easy to be filthy. We weren't used to it. We were all hoping for cheaper water in the north. I even bought a second clip for the gun—plus solvent, oil, and brushes to clean the gun. It had bothered me, not being able to clean it before. If the gun failed us when we needed it, we could be killed. The new clip was a comfort, too. It gave us a chance to reload fast and keep shooting.

Now we lounged in the shade of pines and sycamores, enjoyed the sea breeze, rested, and talked. I wrote, fleshing out my journal notes for the week. I was just finishing that when Travis sat down next to me and asked his question:

"You believe in all this Earthseed stuff, don't you?"

"Every word," I answered.

"But . . . you made it up."

I reached down, picked up a small stone, and put it on the table between us. "If I could analyze this and tell you all that it was made of, would that mean I'd made up its contents?"

He didn't do more than glance at the rock. He kept his eyes on me. "So what did you analyze to get Earthseed?"

"Other people," I said, "myself, everything I could read, hear, see, all the history I could learn. My father is—was—a minister and a teacher. My stepmother ran a neighborhood school. I had a chance to see a lot."

"What did your father think of your idea of God?"

"He never knew."

"You never had the guts to tell him."

I shrugged. "He's the one person in the world I worked hard not to hurt."

"Dead?"

"Yes."

"Yeah. My parents, too." He shook his head. "People don't live long these days."

There was a period of silence. After a while, he said, "How did you get your ideas about God?"

"I was looking for God," I said. "I wasn't looking for mythology or mysticism or magic. I didn't know whether there was a god to find, but I wanted to know. God would have to be a power that could not be defied by anyone or anything."

"Change."

"Change, yes."

"But it's not a god. It's not a person or an intelligence or even a thing. It's just . . . I don't know. An idea."

I smiled. Was that such a terrible criticism? "It's a truth," I said.

"Change is ongoing. Everything changes in some way—size, position, composition, frequency, velocity, thinking, whatever. Every living thing, every bit of matter, all the energy in the universe changes in some way. I don't claim that everything changes in every way, but everything changes in some way."

Harry, coming in dripping from the sea, heard this last. "Sort of like saying God is the second law of thermodynamics," he said, grinning. He and I had already had this conversation.

"That's an aspect of God," I said to Travis. "Do you know about the second law?"

He nodded. "Entropy, the idea that the natural flow of heat is from something hot to something cold—not the other way—so that the universe itself is cooling down, running down, dissipating its energy."

I let my surprise show.

"My mother wrote for newspapers and magazines at first," he said. "She taught me at home. Then my father died and she couldn't earn enough for us to keep the house. And she couldn't find any other work that paid money. She had to take a job as a live-in cook, but she went on teaching me."

"She taught you about entropy?" Harry asked.

"She taught me to read and write," Travis said. "Then she taught me to teach myself. The man she worked for had a library—a whole big room full of books."

"He let you read them?" I asked.

"He didn't let me near them." Travis gave me a humorless smile. "I read them anyway. My mother would sneak them to me."

Of course. Slaves did that two hundred years ago. They sneaked around and educated themselves as best they could, sometimes suffering whipping, sale, or mutilation for their efforts.

"Did he ever catch you or her at it?" I asked.

"No." Travis turned to look toward the sea. "We were careful. It was important. She never borrowed more than one book at a time. I think his wife knew, but she was a decent woman. She never said anything. She was the one who talked him into letting me marry Natividad."

The son of the cook marrying one of the maids. That was like something out of another era, too.

"Then my mother died and all Natividad and I had was each other, and then the baby. I was staying on as gardener-handyman, but then the old bastard we worked for decided he wanted Natividad. He would try to watch when she fed the baby. Couldn't let her alone. That's why we left. That's why his wife helped us leave. She gave us money. She knew it wasn't Natividad's fault. And I knew I didn't want to have to kill the guy. So we left."

In slavery when that happened, there was nothing the slaves could do about it—or nothing that wouldn't get them killed, sold, or beaten.

I looked at Natividad who sat a short distance away, on spread out sleepsacks, playing with her baby and talking to Zahra. She had been lucky. Did she know? How many other people were less lucky—unable to escape the master's attentions or gain the mistress's sympathies. How far did masters and mistresses go these days toward putting less than submissive servants in their places?

"I still can't see change or entropy as God," Travis said, bringing the conversation back to Earthseed.

"Then show me a more pervasive power than change," I said. "It isn't just entropy. God is more complex than that. Human behavior alone should teach you that much. And there's still more complexity when you're dealing with several things at once—as you always are. There are all kinds of changes in the universe."

He shook his head. "Maybe, but nobody's going to worship them."

"I hope not," I said. "Earthseed deals with ongoing reality, not with supernatural authority figures. Worship is no good without action. With action, it's only useful if it steadies you, focuses your efforts, eases your mind."

He gave me an unhappy smile. "Praying makes people feel better even when there's no action they can take," he said. "I used to think that was all God was good for—to help people like my mother stand what they had to stand."

"That isn't what God is for, but there are times when that's what prayer is for. And there are times when that's what these verses are for. God is Change, and in the end, God prevails. But there's hope in understanding the nature of God—not punishing or jealous, but infinitely malleable. There's comfort in realizing that everyone and everything yields to God. There's power in knowing that God can be focused, diverted, shaped by anyone at all. But there's no power in having strength and brains, and yet waiting for God to fix things for you or take revenge for you. You know that. You knew it when you took your family and got the hell out of your boss's house. God will shape us all every day of our lives. Best to understand that and return the effort: Shape God."

"Amen!" Harry said, smiling.

I looked at him, wavered between annoyance and amusement, and let amusement win. "Put something on before you burn, Harry."

"You sounded like you could use an 'amen,' " he said as he put on a loose blue shirt. "Do you want to go on preaching or do you want to eat?"

We had beans cooked with bits of dried meat, tomatoes, peppers, and onions. It was Sunday. There were public firepits in the park, and we had plenty of time. We even had a little wheat-flour bread and the baby had real baby food with his milk instead of mashed or mother-chewed bits of whatever we were eating.

It's been a good day. Every now and then, Travis would ask me another question or toss me another challenge to Earthseed, and I would try to answer without preaching him a sermon—which was hard. I think I managed it most of the time. Zahra and Natividad got into an argument about whether I was talking about a male god or a female god. When I pointed out that Change had no sex at all and wasn't a person, they were confused, but not dismissive. Only Harry refused to take the discussion seriously. He liked the idea of keeping a journal, though. Yesterday he bought a small notebook, and now he's writing, too—and helping Zahra with her reading and writing lessons.

I'd like to draw him into Earthseed. I'd like to draw them all in. They could be the beginning of an Earthseed community. I would love to teach Dominic Earthseed as he grows up. I would teach him and he would teach me. The questions little children ask drive you insane because they never stop. But they also make you think. For now, though, I had to deal with Travis's questions.

I took a chance. I told Travis about the Destiny.

He had asked and asked me what the point of Earthseed is. Why personify change by calling it God? Since change is just an idea, why not call it that? Just say change is important.

"Because after a while, it won't be important!" I told him. "People forget ideas. They're more likely to remember God—especially when they're scared or desperate."

"Then they're supposed to do what?" he demanded. "Read a poem?"

"Or remember a truth or a comfort or a reminder to action," I said. "People do that all the time. They reach back to the Bible, the Talmud, the Koran, or some other religious book that helps them deal with the frightening changes that happen in life."

"Change does scare most people."

"I know. God is frightening. Best to learn to cope."

"Your stuff isn't very comforting."

"It is after a while. I'm still growing into it myself. God isn't good or evil, doesn't favor you or hate you, and yet God is better partnered than fought."

"Your God doesn't care about you at all," Travis said.

"All the more reason to care about myself and others. All the more reason to create Earthseed communities and shape God together. 'God is Trickster, Teacher, Chaos, Clay.' We decide which aspect we embrace—and how to deal with the others."

"Is that what you want to do? Set up Earthseed communities?"

"Yes."

"And then what?"

There it was. The opening. I swallowed and turned a little so that I could see the burned over area. It was so damn ugly. Hard to think anyone had done that on purpose.

"And then what?" Travis insisted. "A God like yours wouldn't have a heaven for people to hope for, so what is there?"

"Heaven," I said, facing him again. "Oh, yes. Heaven."

He didn't say anything. He gave me one of his suspicious looks and waited.

"'The Destiny of Earthseed is to take root among the stars,'" I said. "That's the ultimate Earthseed aim, and the ultimate human change short of death. It's a destiny we'd better pursue if we hope to be anything other than smooth-skinned dinosaurs—here today, gone tomorrow, our bones mixed with the bones and ashes of our cities, and so what?"

"Space?" he said. "Mars?"

"Beyond Mars," I said. "Other star systems. Living worlds."

"You're crazy as hell," he said, but I like the soft, quiet way he said it—with amazement rather than ridicule.

I grinned. "I know it won't be possible for a long time. Now is a time for building foundations—Earthseed communities—focused on the Destiny. After all, my heaven really exists, and you don't have to die to reach it. 'The Destiny of Earthseed is to take root among the stars,' or among the ashes." I nodded toward the burned area.

Travis listened. He didn't point out that a person walking north from L.A. to who-knows-where with all her possessions on her back was hardly in a position to point the way to Alpha Centauri. He listened. He laughed a little—as though he were afraid to get caught being too serious about my ideas. But he didn't back away from me. He leaned forward. He argued. He shouted. He asked more questions. Natividad told him to stop bothering me, but he kept it up. I didn't mind. I understand persistence. I admire it.

SUNDAY, AUGUST 15, 2027

I think Travis Charles Douglas is my first convert. Zahra Moss is my second. Zahra has listened as the days passed, and as Travis and I went on arguing off and on. Sometimes she asked questions or pointed out what she saw as inconsistencies. After a while, she said. "I don't care about no outer space. You can keep that part of it. But if you want to put together some kind of community where people look out for each other and don't have to take being pushed around, I'm with you. I've been talking to Natividad. I don't want to live the way she had to. I don't want to live the way my mama had to either."

I wondered how much difference there was between Natividad's former employer who treated her as though he owned her and Richard Moss who purchased young girls to be part of his harem. It was all a matter of personal feeling, no doubt. Natividad had resented her employer. Zahra had accepted and perhaps loved Richard Moss.

Earthseed is being born right here on Highway 101—on that portion of 101 that was once El Camino Real, the royal highway of California's Spanish past. Now it's a highway, a river of the poor. A river flooding north.

I've come to think that I should be fishing that river even as I follow its current. I should watch people not only to spot those who might be dangerous to us, but to find those few like Travis and Natividad who would join us and be welcome.

And then what? Find a place to squat and take over? Act as a kind of gang? No. Not quite a gang. We aren't gang types. I don't want gang types with their need to dominate, rob and terrorize. And yet we might have to dominate. We might have to rob to survive, and even terrorize to scare off or kill enemies. We'll have to be very careful how we allow our needs to shape us. But we must have arable land, a dependable water supply, and enough freedom from attack to let us establish ourselves and grow.

It might be possible to find such an isolated place along the coast, and make a deal with the inhabitants. If there were a few more of us, and if we were better armed, we might provide security in exchange for living room. We might also provide education plus reading and writing services to adult illiterates. There might be a market for that kind of thing. So many people, children and adults, are illiterate these days. . . . We might be able to do it—grow our own food, grow ourselves and our neighbors into something brand new. Into Earthseed.

19

□ □ □

Changes.
The galaxies move through space.
The stars ignite,
burn,
age,
cool,
Evolving.
God is Change.
God prevails.

EARTHSEED: THE BOOKS OF THE LIVING
FRIDAY, AUGUST 27, 2027
(FROM NOTES EXPANDED SUNDAY, AUGUST 29)

Earthquake today.

It hit early this morning just as we were beginning the day's walk, and it was a strong one. The ground itself gave a low, grating rumble like buried thunder. It jerked and shuddered, then seemed to drop. I'm sure it did drop, though I don't know how far. Once the shaking stopped, everything looked the same—except for sudden patches of dust thrown up here and there in the brown hills around us.

Several people screamed or shouted during the quake. Some, burdened by heavy packs, lost their footing and fell into the dirt or onto the broken asphalt. Travis, with Dominic on his chest and a heavy pack on his back was almost one of these. He stumbled, staggered, and managed somehow to catch himself. The baby, unhurt, but jolted by the sudden shaking, began to cry, adding to the noise of two older children walking nearby, the sudden talking of almost everyone, and the gasps of an old man who had fallen during the quake.

I put aside my usual suspicions and went to see whether the old man was all right—not that I could have done much to help him if he hadn't been. I retrieved his cane for him—it had landed beyond his reach—and helped him up. He was as light as a child, thin, toothless, and frightened of me.

I gave him a pat on the shoulder and sent him on his way, checking when his back was turned to see that he hadn't lifted anything. The world was full of thieves. Old people and young kids were often pickpockets.

Nothing missing.

Another man nearby smiled at me—an older, but not yet old black man who still had his teeth, and who pushed his belongings in twin saddlebags hanging from a small, sturdy metal-framed cart. He didn't say anything, but I liked his smile. I smiled back. Then I remembered that I was supposed to be a man, and wondered whether he had seen through my disguise. Not that it mattered.

I went back to my group where Zahra and Natividad were comforting Dominic and Harry was picking up something from the roadside. I went to Harry, and saw that he had found a filthy rag knotted into a small, tight ball around something. Harry tore the rotten cloth and a roll of money fell out into his hands. Hundred-dollar bills. Two or three dozen of them.

"Put it away!" I whispered.

He pushed the money into a deep pants pocket. "New shoes," he whispered. "Good ones, and other things. Do you need anything?"

I had promised to buy him a new pair of shoes as soon as we reached a dependable store. His were worn out. Now another idea occurred to me. "If you have enough," I whispered, "buy yourself a gun. I'll still get your shoes. You get a gun!" Then I spoke to the others, ignoring his surprise. "Is everyone all right?"

Everyone was. Dominic was happy again, riding now on his mother's back, and playing with her hair. Zahra was readjusting her pack, and Travis had gone on and was taking a look at the small community ahead. This was farm country. We'd passed through nothing for days except small, dying towns, withering roadside communities and farms, some working, some abandoned and growing weeds.

We walked forward toward Travis.

"Fire," he said as we approached.

One house down the hill from the road smoked from several of its windows. Already people from the highway had begun to drift down toward it. Trouble. The people who owned the house might manage to put out their fire and still be overwhelmed by scavengers.

"Let's get away from here," I said. "The people down there are still strong, and they're going to feel besieged soon. They'll fight back."

"We might find something we can use," Zahra argued.

"There's nothing down there worth our getting shot over," I said. "Let's go!" I led the way past the small community and we were almost clear of it when the gunfire began.

There were people still on the road with us, but many had flooded down into the small community to steal. The crowd would not confine its attention to the one burning house, and all the households would have to resist.

There were more shots behind us—first single shots, then an uneven crackling of exchanged fire, then the unmistakable chatter of automatic weapons fire. We walked faster, hoping that we were beyond the range of anything aimed in our direction.

"Shit!" Zahra whispered, keeping up with me. "I should have known that was going to happen. People out here in the middle of nowhere gotta be tough."

"I don't think their toughness will get them through this day, though," I said, looking back. There was much more smoke rising now, and it was rising from more than one place. Distant shouts and screams mixed with the gunfire. Stupid place to put a naked little community. They should have hidden their homes away in the mountains where few strangers would ever see them. That was something for me to keep in mind. All the people of this community could do now was take a few of their tormentors with them. Tomorrow the survivors of this place would be on the road with scraps of their belongings on their backs.

It's odd, but I don't think anyone on the road would have thought of attacking that community en masse like that if the earthquake—or something—had not started a fire. One small fire was the weakness that gave scavengers permission to devastate the community—which they were no doubt doing now. The shooting could scare away some, kill or wound others, and make the remainder very angry. If the people of the community chose to live in such a dangerous place, they should have set up overwhelming defenses—a line of explosive charges and incendiaries, that kind of thing. Only power that strong, that destructive, that sudden would scare attackers off, would drive them away in a panic more overwhelming than the greed and the need that had drawn them in the first place. If the people of the community were without explosives, they should have grabbed their money and their kids and run like crazy the moment they saw the horde coming. They knew the hills better than migrating scavengers could. They should have had hiding places already prepared or at least been able to lose themselves among the hills while scavengers were ransacking their homes. But they had done none of this. And now vast thick clouds of smoke rose behind us, drawing even more scavengers.

"Whole world's gone crazy," a voice near me said, and I knew before I looked that it was the man with the saddlebagged cart. We'd slowed down a little, looking back, and he had caught up. He too had had the sense not to try to go scavenging in the little community. He didn't look like a man who scavenged. His clothes were dirty and ordinary, but they fit him well and they looked almost new. His jeans were still dark blue, and still creased down the legs. His

OCTAVIA E. BUTLER

red, short-sleeved shirt still had all its buttons. He wore expensive walking shoes and had had, not too long ago, an expensive professional haircut. What was he doing out here on the road, pushing a cart? A rich pauper—or at least, a once-rich pauper. He had a short, full, salt and pepper beard. I decided that I liked his looks as much as I had before. What a handsome old man.

Had the world gone crazy?

"From what I've read," I said to him, "the world goes crazy every three or four decades. The trick is to survive until it goes sane again." I was showing off my education and background; I admit it. But the old man seemed unimpressed.

"The nineteen nineties were crazy," he said, "but they were rich. Nothing like this bad. I don't think it's ever been this bad. Those people, those animals back there . . ."

"I don't see how they can act that way," Natividad said. "I wish we could call the police—whoever the police are around here. The householders back there should call."

"It wouldn't do any good," I said. "Even if the cops came today instead of tomorrow, they'd just add to the death toll."

We walked on, the stranger walking with us. He seemed content to walk with us. He could have dropped back or walked on ahead since he didn't have to carry his load. As long as he stayed on the road, he could speed along. But he stuck with us. I talked to him, introduced myself and learned that his name was Bankole—Taylor Franklin Bankole. Our last names were an instant bond between us. We're both descended from men who assumed African surnames back during the 1960s. His father and my grandfather had had their names legally changed, and both had chosen Yoruba replacement names.

"Most people chose Swahili names in the '60s," Bankole told me. He wanted to be called Bankole. "My father had to do something different. All his life he had to be different."

"I don't know my grandfather's reasons," I said. "His last name was Broome before he changed it, and that was no loss. But why he chose Olamina . . . ? Even my father didn't know. He made the change before my father was born, so my father was always Olamina, and so were we."

Bankole was one year older than my father. He had been born in 1970, and he was, according to him, too damn old to be tramping along a highway with everything he owned in a couple of saddlebags. He was 57. I caught myself wishing he were younger so he would live longer.

Old or not, he heard the two girls calling for help sooner than we did.

There was a road, more dirt than asphalt, running below and alongside the highway, then veering away from the highway into the hills. Up that road was a half-collapsed house, the dust of its collapse still hanging over it. It couldn't have been much of a house before it fell in. Now it was rubble. And once Bankole alerted us, we could hear faint shouts from it.

"Sounds like women," Harry said.

I sighed. "Let's go see. It might just be a matter of pushing some wood off them or something."

Harry caught me by the shoulder. "You sure?"

"Yeah." I took the gun out and gave it to him in case someone else's pain made me useless. "Watch our backs," I said.

We went in wary and tentative, knowing that a call for help could be false, could lure people to their attackers. A few other people followed us off the road, and Harry hung back, staying between them and us. Bankole shoved his cart along, keeping up with me.

There were two voices calling from the rubble. Both sounded like women. One was pleading, the other cursing. We located them by the sound of their voices, then Zahra, Travis and I began throwing off rubble—dry, broken wood, plaster, plastic, and brick from an ancient chimney. Bankole stood with Harry, watching, and looking formidable. Did he have a gun? I hoped he did. We were drawing a small audience of hungry-eyed scavengers. Most people looked to see what we were doing, and went on. A few stayed and stared. If the women had been trapped since the earthquake, it was surprising that no one had come already to steal their belongings and set fire to the rubble, leaving them in it. I hoped we would be able to get the women out and get back on the highway before someone decided to rush us. No doubt they already would have if there had been anything of value in sight.

Natividad spoke to Bankole, then put Dominic in one of his saddlebags and felt to see that her knife was still in her pocket. I didn't like that much. Better she should keep wearing the baby so we could leave at a run if she had to.

We found a pale leg, bruised and bleeding but unbroken, pinned under a beam. A whole section of wall and ceiling plus some of the chimney had fallen on these women. We moved the loose stuff then worked together to lift heavier pieces. At last we dragged the women out by their exposed limbs—an arm and a leg for one, both legs for the other. I didn't enjoy it anymore than they did.

On the other hand, it wasn't that bad. The women had lost some skin here and there, and one was bleeding from the nose and mouth. She spat out blood and a couple of teeth and cursed and tried to get up. I let Zahra help her up. All I wanted to do now was get away from here.

The other one, face wet with tears, just sat and stared at us. She was quiet now in a blank, unnatural way. Too quiet. When Travis tried to help her up, she cringed and cried out. Travis let her alone. She didn't seem to be hurt beyond a few scratches, but she might have hit her head. She might be in shock.

"Where's your stuff?" Zahra was asking the bloody one. "We're going to have to get away from here fast."

I rubbed my mouth, trying to get past an irrational certainty that two of my own teeth were gone. I felt horrible—scraped and bruised and throbbing, yet whole and unbroken, undamaged in any major way. I just wanted to huddle somewhere until I felt less miserable. I took a deep breath and went to the frightened, cringing woman.

"Can you understand me?" I asked.

She looked at me, then looked around, saw her companion wiping away blood with a grimy hand, and tried to get up and run to her. She tripped, started to fall, and I caught her, grateful that she wasn't very big.

"Your legs are all right," I said, "but take it easy. We have to get out of here soon, and you've got to be able to walk."

"Who are you?" she asked.

"A total stranger," I said. "Try to walk."

"There was an earthquake."

"Yeah. Walk!"

She took a shaky step away from me, then another. She staggered over to her friend. "Allie?" she said.

Her friend saw her, stumbled to her, hugged her, smeared her with blood. "Jill! Thank God!"

"Here's their stuff," Travis said. "Let's get them out of here while we still can."

We made them walk a little more, tried to make them see and understand the danger of staying where we were. We couldn't drag them with us, and what would have been the point of digging them out, then leaving them at the mercy of scavengers. They had to walk along with us until they were stronger and able to take care of themselves.

"Okay," the bloody one said. She was the smaller and tougher of the two, not that there was that much physical difference between them. Two medium-size, brown-haired white women in their twenties. They might be sisters.

"Okay," the bloody one repeated. "Let's get out of here." She was walking without limping or staggering now, though her companion was less steady.

"Give me my stuff," she said.

Travis waved her toward two dusty sleepsack packs. She put one on her back, then looked at the other and at her companion.

"I can carry it," the other woman said. "I'm all right."

She wasn't, but she had to carry her own things. No one could carry a double pack for long. No one could fight while carrying a double pack.

There were a dozen people standing around staring as we brought the two women out. Harry walked ahead of us, gun in hand. Something about him said with great clarity that he would kill. If he were pushed even a little, he would kill. I hadn't seen him that way before. It was impressive and frightening and wrong. Right for the situation and the moment, but wrong for Harry. He wasn't the kind of man who ought ever to look that way.

When had I begun thinking of him as a man rather than a boy? What the hell. We're all men and women now, not kids anymore. Shit.

Bankole walked behind, looking even more formidable than Harry in spite of his graying hair and beard. He had a gun in his hand. I had gotten a look at it as I walked past him. Another automatic—perhaps a nine millimeter. I hoped he was good with it.

Natividad pushed his cart along just ahead of him with Dominic still in one of the bags. Travis walked beside her, guarding her and the baby.

I walked with the two women, fearful that one of them might fall or that some fool might grab one. The one called Allie was still bleeding, spitting blood and wiping her bloody nose with a bloody arm. And the one called Jill still looked dull and shaky. Allie and I kept Jill between us.

Before the attack began, I knew it would happen. Helping the two trapped women had made us targets. We might already have been attacked if the community down the road had not drawn off so many of the most violent, desperate people. The weak would be attacked today. The quake had set the mood. And one attack could trigger others.

We could only try to be ready.

Out of the blue, a man grabbed Zahra. She's small, and must have looked weak as well as beautiful.

An instant later, someone grabbed me. I was spun around, and I tripped and started to fall. It was that stupid. Before anyone could hit me, I tripped and fell. But because my attacker had pulled me toward him, I fell against him. I dragged him down with me. Somehow, I managed to get my knife out. I flicked it open. I jabbed it upward into my attacker's body.

The six inch blade went in to the hilt. Then, in empathic agony, I jerked it out again.

I can't describe the pain.

The others told me later that I screamed as they'd never heard anyone scream. I'm not surprised. Nothing has ever hurt me that much before.

After a while, the agony in my chest ebbed and died. That is, the man on top of me bled and died. Not until then could I begin to be aware of something other than pain.

The first thing I heard was Dominic, crying.

I understood then that I had also heard shots fired—several shots. Where was everyone? Were they wounded?

Dead? Being held prisoner?

I kept my body still beneath the dead man. He was painfully heavy as deadweight, and his body odor was nauseating. He had bled all over my chest, and, if my nose was any judge, in death, he had urinated on me. Yet I didn't dare move until I understood the situation.

I opened my eyes just a little.

Before I could understand what I was seeing, someone hauled the stinking dead man off me. I found myself looking into two worried faces: Harry and Bankole.

I coughed and tried to get up, but Bankole held me down.

"Are you hurt anywhere?" he demanded.

"No, I'm all right," I said. I saw Harry staring at all the blood, and I added, "Don't worry. The other guy did all the bleeding."

They helped me up, and I discovered I was right. The dead man had urinated on me. I was almost frantic with the need to strip off my filthy clothes and wash. But that had to wait. No matter how disgusting I was, I wouldn't undress in daylight where I could be seen. I'd had enough trouble for one day.

I looked around, saw Travis and Natividad comforting Dominic who was still screaming. Zahra was with the two new girls, standing guard beside them as they sat on the ground.

"Are those two okay?" I asked.

Harry nodded. "They're scared and shaken up, but they're all right. Everyone's all right—except him and his friends." He gestured toward the dead man. There were three more dead lying nearby.

"There were some wounded," Harry said. "We let them go."

I nodded. "We'd better strip these bodies and go, too. We're too obvious here from the highway."

We did a quick, thorough job, searching everything except body cavities. We weren't needy enough to do that yet. Then, at Zahra's insistence, I did go behind the ruined house for a quick change of clothing. She took the gun from Harry and stood watch for me.

"You're bloody," she said. "If people think you're wounded, they might jump you. This ain't a good day to look like you got something wrong with you."

I suspected that she was right. Anyway, it was a pleasure to have her talk me into something I already wanted so much to do.

I put my filthy, wet clothes into a plastic bag, sealed it, and stuffed it into my pack. If any of the dead had owned clothing that would fit me, and that was still in wearable condition, I would have thrown mine away. As it was, I would keep them and wash them the next time we came to a water station or a store that permitted washing. We had collected money from the corpses, but it would be best to use that for necessities.

We had taken about twenty-five hundred dollars in all from the four corpses—along with two knives that we could sell or pass on to the two girls, and one gun pulled by a man Harry had shot. The gun turned out to be an empty, dirty Beretta nine millimeter. Its owner had had no ammunition, but we can buy that—maybe from Bankole. For that we will spend money. I had found a few pieces of jewelry in the pocket of the man who attacked me—two gold rings, a necklace of polished blue stones that I thought were lapis lazuli, and a single earring which turned out to be a radio. The radio we would keep. It could give us information about the world beyond the highway. It would be good not to be cut off any longer. I wondered who my attacker had robbed to get it.

All four of the corpses had little plastic pill boxes hidden somewhere on them. Two boxes contained a couple of pills each. The other two were empty. So these people who carried neither food nor water nor adequate weapons did carry pills when they could steal them or steal enough to buy them. Junkies. What was their drug of choice, I wondered. Pyro? For the first time in days, I found myself thinking of my brother Keith. Had he dealt in the round purple pills we kept finding on people who attacked us? Was that why he died?

A few miles later along the highway, we saw some cops in cars, heading south toward what must now be a burned out hulk of a community with a lot of corpses. Perhaps the cops would arrest a few late-arriving scavengers. Perhaps they would scavenge a little themselves. Or perhaps they would just have a look and drive away. What had cops done for my community when it was burning? Nothing.

The two women we'd dug out of the rubble want to stay with us. Allison and Jillian Gilchrist are their names. They are sisters, 24 and 25 years old, poor, running away from a life of prostitution. Their pimp was their father. The house that had fallen on them was empty when they took shelter in it the night before. It looked long abandoned.

"Abandoned buildings are traps," Zahra told them as we walked. "Out here in the middle of nowhere, they're targets for all kinds of people."

OCTAVIA E. BUTLER

"Nobody bothered us," Jill said. "But then the house fell on us, and nobody helped us either, until you guys came along."

"You're very fortunate," Bankole told her. He was still with us, and walking next to me. "People don't help each other much out here."

"We know," Jill admitted. "We're grateful. Who are you guys, anyway?"

Harry gave her an odd little smile. "Earthseed," he said, and glanced at me. You have to watch out for Harry when he smiles that way.

"What's Earthseed?" Jill asked, right on cue. She had let Harry direct her gaze to me.

"We share some ideas," I said. "We intend to settle up north, and found a community."

"Where up north?" Allie demanded. Her mouth was still hurting, and I felt it more when I paid attention to her. At least her bleeding had almost stopped.

"We're looking for jobs that pay salaries and we're watching water prices," I said. "We want to settle where water isn't such a big problem."

"Water's a problem everywhere," she proclaimed. Then, "What are you? Some kind of cult or something?"

"We believe in some of the same things," I said.

She turned to stare at me with what looked like hostility. "I think religion is dog shit," she announced. "It's either phony or crazy."

I shrugged. "You can travel with us or you can walk away."

"But what the hell do you stand for?" she demanded. "What do you pray to?"

"Ourselves," I said. "What else is there?"

She turned away in disgust, then turned back. "Do we have to join your cult if we travel with you?"

"No."

"All right then!" She turned her back and walked ahead of me as though she'd won something.

I raised my voice just enough to startle and projected it at the back of her head. I said, "We risked ourselves for you today."

She jumped, but refused to look back.

I continued. "You don't owe us anything for that. It isn't something you could buy from us. But if you travel with us, and there's trouble, you stand by us, stand with us. Now will you do that or not?"

Allie swung around, stiff with anger. She stopped right in front of me and stood there.

I didn't stop or turn. It wasn't a time for giving way. I needed to know what her pride and anger might drive her to. How much of that apparent hostility of hers was real, and how much might be due to her pain? Was she going to be more trouble than she was worth?

When she realized that I meant to walk over her if I had to, that I would do it, she slid around me to walk beside me as though she had intended to do that all along.

"If you hadn't been the ones to dig us out," she said, "we wouldn't bother with you at all." She drew a deep, ragged breath.

"We know how to pull our own weight. We can help our friends and fight our enemies. We've been doing that since we were kids."

I looked at her, thinking of the little that she and her sister had told us about their lives: prostitution, pimp father. . . . Hell of a story if it were true. No doubt the details would be even more interesting. How had they gotten away from their father, anyway? They would bear watching, but they might turn out to be worth something.

"Welcome," I said.

She stared at me, nodded, then walked ahead of me in long quick strides. Her sister, who had dropped to walk near us while we were talking, now walked faster to join her. And Zahra, who had dropped back to keep an eye on the sister, grinned at me and shook her head. She went up to join Harry who was leading the group.

Bankole came up beside me again, and I realized he had gotten out of the way as soon as he saw trouble between Allie and me.

"One fight a day is enough for me," he said when he saw me looking at him.

I smiled. "Thank you for standing by us back there."

He shrugged. "I was surprised to see that anyone else cared what happened to a couple of strangers."

"You cared."

"Yes. That kind of thing will get me killed someday. If you don't mind, I'd like to travel with your group, too."

"You have been. You're welcome."

"Thank you," he said, and smiled back at me. He had clear eyes with deep brown irises—attractive eyes. I like him too much already. I'll have to be careful.

Late today we reached Salinas, a small city that seemed little touched by the quake and its aftershocks. The ground has been shuddering off and on all day. Also, Salinas seemed untouched by the hordes of overeager scavengers that we had been seeing since that first burning community this morning. That was a surprise. Almost all of the smaller communities we'd passed had been burning and swarming with scavengers. It was as though the quake had given yesterday's quiet, plodding paupers permission to go animal and prey on anyone who still lives in a house.

I suspected that the bulk of the predatory scavengers were still behind us, still killing and dying and fighting over the spoils. I've never worked as hard at not seeing what was going on around me as I did today. The smoke and the noise helped veil things from me. I had enough to do dealing with Allie's throbbing face and mouth and the ambient misery of the highway.

We were tired when we reached Salinas, but we had decided to walk on after resupplying and washing. We didn't want to be in town when the worst of the scavengers arrived. They might be calm, tired after their day of burning and stealing, but I doubted it. I thought they would be drunk with power and hungry for more. As Bankole said, "Once people get the idea that it's all right to take what you want and destroy the rest, who knows when they'll stop."

But Salinas looked well-armed. Cops had parked all along the shoulders of the highway, staring at us, some holding their shot-guns or automatic rifles as though they'd love an excuse to use them. Maybe they knew what was coming.

We needed to resupply, but we didn't know whether we would be allowed to. Salinas had the look of a "stay on the road" type town—the kind that wanted you gone by sundown unless you lived there. This week and last, we had run across a few little towns like that.

But no one stopped us when we headed off the road to a store. There were only a few people on the road now, and the cops were able to watch all of us. I saw them watching us in particular, but they didn't stop us. We were quiet. We were women and a baby as well as men, and three of us were white. I don't think any of that harmed us in their eyes.

The security guards in the stores were as well-armed as the cops—shot-guns and automatic rifles, a couple of machine guns on tripods in cubicles above us. Bankole said he could remember a time when security guards had revolvers or nothing but clubs. My father used to talk like that.

Some of the guards either weren't very well trained—or they were almost as power-drunk as the scavengers. They pointed their guns at us. It was crazy. Two or three of us walked into a store and two or three guns were trained on us. We didn't know what was going on at first. We froze, staring, waiting to see what was going to happen.

The guys behind the guns laughed. One of them said, "Buy some-thing or get the fuck out!"

We got out. These were little stores. There were plenty of them to choose from. Some of them turned out to have sane guards. I couldn't help wondering how many accidents the crazy guards have with those guns. I suppose that after the fact, every accident was an armed robber with obvious homicidal inclinations.

The guards at the water station seemed calm and professional. They kept their guns down and confined themselves to cursing people to speed them along. We felt safe enough not only to buy water and give our clothes a quick wash and dry, but to rent a couple of cubicles—men's and women's—and sponge ourselves off from a basin of water each. That settled the question of my sex for any of the new people who hadn't already figured it out.

At last, somewhat cleaner, resupplied with food, water, ammunition for all three guns, and, by the way, condoms for my own future, we headed out of town. On our way, we passed through a small street market at the edge of town. It was just a few people with their merchandise—mostly junk—scattered on tables or on filthy rags spread on the bare asphalt. Bankole spotted the rifle on one of the tables.

It was an antique—a bolt action Winchester, empty, of course, with a five-round capacity. It would be, as Bankole admitted, slow. But he liked it. He inspected it with eyes and fingers and bargained with the well-armed old man and woman who were offering it for sale. They had one of the cleaner tables with merchandise laid out in a neat pattern—a small, manual typewriter; a stack of books; a few hand tools, worn, but clean; two knives in worn leather sheaths; a couple of pots, and the rifle with sling and scope.

While Bankole haggled with the man over the rifle, I bought the pots from the woman. I would get Bankole to carry them in his cart. They were large enough to contain soup or stew or hot cereal for all of us at once. We were nine now, and bigger pots made sense. Then I joined Harry at the stack of books.

There was no nonfiction. I bought a fat anthology of poetry and Harry bought a western novel. The others, either from lack of money or from lack of interest ignored the books. I would have bought more if I could have carried them. My pack was already about as heavy as I thought I could stand, and still walk all day.

Our bargaining finished, we stood away from the table to wait for Bankole. And Bankole surprised us.

He got the old man down to a price he seemed to think was fair, then he called us over. "Any of you know how to handle a relic like this?" he asked.

Well, Harry and I did, and he had us look the rifle over. In the end, everyone had a look at it, some with obvious awkwardness and some with familiarity. Back in the neighborhood, Harry and I had practiced with the guns of other households—rifles and shotguns as well as handguns. Whatever was legal back home was shared, at least in practice sessions. My father had wanted us to be familiar with whatever weapons might be available. Harry and I were both good, competent shots, but we'd never bought a used gun. I liked the rifle, I liked the look and feel of it, but that didn't mean much. Harry seemed to like it, too. Same problem.

"Come over here," Bankole said. He herded us out of earshot of the old couple. "You should buy that gun," he told us. "You took enough money off those four junkies to pay the price I got that guy to agree to. You need at least one accurate, long-range weapon, and this is a good one."

"That money would buy a lot of food," Travis said.

Bankole nodded. "Yes, but only living people need food. You buy this, and it will pay for itself the first time you need it. Anyone who doesn't know how to use it, I'll teach. My father and I used to hunt deer with guns just like this."

"It's an antique," Harry said. "If it were automatic . . ."

"If it were automatic, you couldn't afford it." Bankole shrugged. "This thing is cheap because it's old and it's legal."

"And it's slow," Zahra said. "And if you think that old guy's price is cheap, you're crazy."

"I know I'm new here," Allie said, "but I agree with Bankole. You guys are good with your handguns, but sooner or later, you're going to meet someone who sits out of handgun range and picks you off. Picks us off."

"And this rifle is going to save us?" Zahra demanded.

"I doubt that it would save us," I said. "But with a decent shot behind it, it might give us a chance." I looked at Bankole. "You hit any of those deer?"

He smiled. "One or two."

I did not return the smile. "Why don't you buy the rifle for yourself?"

"I can't afford it," he said. "I've got enough money to keep me going and take care of necessities for a while. Everything else that I had was stolen from me or burned."

I didn't quite believe him. But then, no one knew how much money I had either. In a way, I suppose he was asking about our solvency. Did we have enough money to spend an unexpected windfall on an old rifle? And what did he intend to do if we did? I hoped, not for the first time, that he wasn't just a handsome thief. Yet I did like the gun, and we do need it.

"Harry and I are decent shots, too," I said to the group. "I like the feel of this gun, and it's the best we can afford right now. Has anyone seen any real trouble with it?"

They looked at one another. No one answered.

"It just needs a cleaning and some 30-06 ammunition," Bankole said. "It's been stored for a while, but it appears to have been well maintained. If you buy it, I think I can manage to buy a cleaning kit and some ammunition."

At that, I spoke up before anyone else could. "If we buy, that's a deal. Who else can handle the rifle?"

"I can," Natividad said. And when that won her a few surprised looks, she smiled. "I had no brothers. My father needed to teach someone."

"We never had a chance to do any shooting," Allie said. "But we can learn."

Jill nodded. "I always wanted to learn," she said.

"I'll have to learn, too," Travis admitted. "Where I grew up, guns were either locked away or carried by hired guards."

"Let's go buy it, then," I said. "And let's get out of here. The sun will be down soon."

Bankole kept his word, bought cleaning things and plenty of ammunition—insisted on buying them before we left town, because, as he said, "Who knows when we'll need it, or when we'll find other people willing to sell it to us."

Once that was settled, we left town.

As we left, Harry carried the new rifle and Zahra carried the Beretta, both empty and in need of attention before we loaded them. Only Bankole and I carried fully loaded guns. I led the group and he brought up the rear. It was getting dark. Behind us in the distance, we could hear gunfire and the dull thunder of small explosions.

20

□ □ □

God is neither good nor evil,
neither loving
nor hating.
God is Power.
God is Change.
We must find the rest of what we need within ourselves,
in one another,
in our Destiny.

EARTHSEED: THE BOOKS OF THE LIVING
SATURDAY, AUGUST 28, 2027
(FROM NOTES EXPANDED TUESDAY, AUGUST 31)

Today or tomorrow should be a rest day, but we've agreed not to rest.
Last night was full of distant shooting, explosions and fire. We could
see fire behind us, though not in front. Moving on seems sensible, in
spite of our weariness.

Then, this morning, I cleaned the little black earring radio with
alcohol from my pack, turned the thing on, and put it in my ear. I
had to relay what it said since its sound could not reach the others.

What it said told us we should not only forget about resting, but
change our plans.

We had intended to follow U.S. 101 up through San Francisco
and across the Golden Gate Bridge. But the radio warned us to stay
away from the Bay Area. From San Jose up through San Francisco,
Oakland, and Berkeley, there is chaos. The quake hit hard up there,
and the scavengers, predators, cops, and private armies of security

guards seem bent on destroying what's left. Also, of course, pyro is doing its part. This far north, the radio reporters shorten the name to "pro" or "ro" and they say there are plenty of addicts.

Addicts are running wild, setting fires in areas that the earthquake didn't damage. Bands of the street poor precede or follow them, grabbing whatever they can from stores and from the walled enclaves of the rich and what's left of the middle class. Yeah.

In some places, the rich are escaping by flying out in helicopters. The bridges that are still intact—and most of them are—are guarded either by the police or by gangs. Both groups are there to rob desperate, fleeing people of their weapons, money, food, and water—at the least. The penalty for being too poor to be worth robbing is a beating, a rape, and/or death. The National Guard has been activated to restore order, and I suppose it might. But I suspect that in the short term, it will only add to the chaos. What else could another group of well-armed people do in such an insane situation. The thoughtful ones might take their guns and other equipment and vanish to help their families. Others might find themselves at war with their own people. They'll be confused and scared and dangerous. Of course, some will discover that they enjoy their new power—the power to make others submit, the power to take what they want—property, sex, life . . .

Bad situation. The Bay Area will be a good place to avoid for a long time.

We spread maps on the ground, studied them as we ate breakfast, and decided to turn off U.S. 101 this morning. We'll follow a smaller, no doubt emptier road inland to the little town of San Juan Bautista, then east along State Route 156. From 156 to 152 to Interstate 5. We'll use I-5 to circle around the Bay Area. For a time we'll walk up the center of the state instead of along the coast. We might have to bypass I-5 and go farther east to State 33 or 99. I like the emptiness around much of I-5. Cities are dangerous. Even small towns can be deadly. Yet we have to be able to resupply. In particular, we have to be

OCTAVIA E. BUTLER

able to get water. If that means going into the more populated areas around one of the other highways, we'll do it. Meanwhile we'll be careful, resupply every time we get a chance, never pass up a chance to top off our water and food, waste nothing. But, hell, the maps are old. Maybe the area around I-5 is more settled now.

To reach I-5, we'll pass a big freshwater lake—San Luis Reservoir. It might be dry now. Over the past few years a lot of things had gone dry. But there will be trees, cool shade, a place to rest and be comfortable. Perhaps there will at least be a water station. If so, we'll camp there and rest for a day or even two days. After hiking up and over a lot of hills, we'll need the extra rest.

For now, I suspect that we'll soon have scavengers being driven north toward us from Salinas, and refugees being driven south toward us from the Bay Area. The best thing we can do is get out of the way.

We got an early start, fortified by the good food we had bought at Salinas—some extra stuff that Bankole had wheeled in his cart, though we all chipped in to buy it. We made sandwiches—dried beef, cheese, sliced tomatoes—all on bread made from wheat flour. And we ate grapes. It was a shame we had to hurry. We hadn't had anything that good tasting for a long time.

The highway north was emptier today than I've ever seen it. We were the biggest crowd around—eight adults and a baby—and other people kept away from us. Several of the other walkers were individuals and couples with children. They all seemed in a hurry—as though they, too, knew what might be coming behind them. Did they also know what might be ahead—what was ahead if they stayed on 101. Before we left 101 I tried to warn a couple of women traveling alone with kids to avoid the Bay Area. I told them I'd heard there was a lot of trouble up there—fires, riots, bad quake damage. They just held on to their kids and edged away from me.

Then we left 101 and took our small, hilly road, our short cut to San Juan Bautista. The road was paved and not too badly broken up. It was lonely. For long stretches we saw no one at all. No one had followed us from 101. We passed farms, small communities, and shanties, and the people living in these came out with their guns to stare at us. But they let us alone. The shortcut worked. We managed to reach and pass through San Juan Bautista before dark. We've camped just east of the town. We're all exhausted, footsore, full of aches and pains and blisters. I long for a rest day, but not yet. Not yet.

I put my sleepsack next to Bankole's and lay down, already half asleep. We had drawn straws for the watch schedule, and my watch wasn't until the early morning. I ate nuts and raisins, bread and cheese, and I slept like a corpse.

SUNDAY, AUGUST 29, 2027
(FROM NOTES EXPANDED TUESDAY, AUGUST 31)

Early this morning I awoke to the sound of gunfire, nearby and loud. Short bursts of automatic weapons fire. And there was light from somewhere.

"Be still," someone said. "Stay down and keep quiet." Zahra's voice. She had the watch just before mine.

"What is it?" one of the Gilchrists demanded. And then, "We've got to get away!"

"Stay!" I whispered. "Be still, and it will pass."

I could see now that two groups were running from the highway—the 156—one group chasing the other, both firing their guns as though they and their enemies were the only people in the world. We could only stay down and hope they didn't shoot us by accident. If nobody moved, accidents were less likely.

The light came from a fire burning some distance from us. Not buildings. We hadn't camped near buildings. Yet something was burning. It was, I decided, a big truck of some kind. Perhaps that was the reason for the shooting. Someone, some group had tried to hijack a truck on the highway and things had gone wrong. Now, whatever the truck was carrying—food, I suspected—the fire would get it. Neither the hijackers nor the defenders would win.

We would win if we could just keep out of the fighting.

I reached over to feel for Bankole, wanting assurance that he was all right.

He wasn't there.

His sleepsack and his things were still there, but he was gone.

Moving as little as I could, I looked toward our designated toilet area. He must be there. I couldn't see him, but where else could he be? Bad timing. I squinted, trying to pick him out, not knowing whether to be glad or afraid because I couldn't. After all, if I could see him, so could other people.

The shooting went on and on while we lay still and quiet and scared. One of the trees we'd camped under was hit twice, but well above our heads.

Then the truck exploded. I don't know what exploded in it. It hadn't looked like an old truck—one of those that used diesel fuel, but it might have been. Would diesel fuel explode? I didn't know.

The explosion seemed to end the gunfight. A few more shots were exchanged, then nothing. I saw people, visible in the firelight, walking back toward the truck. Sometime later, I saw others—several together in a bunch—moving away toward the town. Both groups were moving away from us, and that was good.

Now. Where was Bankole? In as low a voice as I could manage, I spoke to the others. "Can anyone see Bankole?"

No answer.

"Zahra, did you see him go?"

"Yeah, a couple of minutes before the shooting started," she answered.

All right. If he didn't come out soon, we would have to go looking for him. I swallowed, tried not to think about finding him hurt or dead. "Is everyone else all right?" I asked. "Zahra?"

"I'm fine."

"Harry?"

"Yeah," he said. "I'm okay."

"Travis? Natividad?"

"We're all right," Travis said.

"What about Dominic?"

"Didn't even wake up."

That was good. If he had, his crying could have gotten us killed. "Allie? Jill?"

"We're okay," Allie said.

I sat up, keeping my movements slow and cautious. I couldn't see anyone or hear anything beyond insects and the distant fire. When no one shot me, others sat up, too. Where noise and light had not awakened Dominic, his mother's movement did the trick. He awoke and began to whimper, but Natividad held him and he quieted.

But still no Bankole. I wanted to get up and go looking for him. I had two mental images of him: One of him lying wounded or dead, and one of him crouching behind a tree holding his own Beretta nine millimeter. If the latter was true, I could scare him into shooting me. There might also be other people out there with ready guns and frayed nerves.

"What time is it?" I asked Zahra who had Harry's watch.

"Three-forty," she said.

"Let me have the gun," I said. "Your watch is almost over anyway."

"What about Bankole?" She passed both the watch and the gun over.

"If he isn't back in five minutes I'm going to go look for him."

"Wait a minute," Harry said. "You aren't going to do that by yourself. I'll go with you."

I almost said no. I don't think he would have paid any attention if I had, but I never spoke the word. If Bankole were injured and conscious, I would be useless the moment I saw him. I would be lucky to drag myself back to camp. Someone else would have to drag him back.

"Thank you," I said to Harry.

Five minutes later, he and I went first to the toilet area, then around it, searching. There was no one, or rather, we could see no one. Still, there might be other people around—others camping overnight, others involved in the shooting, others prowling. . . . Still, I called Bankole's name once, aloud. I touched Harry as a kind of warning and he jumped, settled, then jumped again as I said the name. We both listened in absolute silence.

There was a rustling off to our right where there were several trees blotting out the stars, creating a space of impenetrable darkness. Anything could be there.

The rustling came again, and with it a whimper—a child's whimper. Then Bankole's voice:

"Olamina!"

"Yes," I answered, almost limp with relief. "Here!"

He came out of the pool of darkness, a tall, broad shadow that seemed bulkier than it should have been. He was carrying something.

"I have an orphaned child," he said. "The mother was hit by a stray bullet. She just died."

I sighed. "Is the child hurt?"

"No, just scared. I'll carry him back to our camp. Will one of you get his things?"

"Take us to his camp," I said.

Harry collected the child's things, and I collected the mother's and searched her body. Between us, we gathered everything. By the time we finished, the little boy, perhaps three years old, was crying. That scared me. I left Harry to push the dead woman's pack along in her baby carriage and Bankole to carry the whimpering child. All I carried was the gun, drawn and ready. Even when we got back to our own camp, I couldn't relax. The little boy wouldn't be quiet and Dominic joined him with even louder cries. Zahra and Jill worked to comfort the new child, but he was surrounded by strangers in the middle of the night, and he wanted his mother!

I saw movement over near the burned out carcass of the truck.

The fire was still burning, but it was smaller now, burning itself out. There were still people near it. They had lost their truck. Would they care about a crying child? And if they did care, would they want to help the kid or just shut its mouth?

A lone, dark figure came away from the truck and took several steps toward us. At that moment, Natividad took the new child, and in spite of his age, gave him one breast and Dominic the other.

It worked. Both children were comforted almost at once. They made a few more small sounds, then settled down to nursing.

The shadow figure from the truck stood still, perhaps confused now that it was no longer guided by noise. After a moment, it turned and went back past the truck and out of sight. Gone. It couldn't have seen us. We could look out of the darkness under the trees that sheltered our campsite and see by firelight, by starlight. But others could only follow the baby noise to us.

"We ought to move," Allie whispered. "Even if they can't see us, they know we're here."

"Watch with me," I said.

"What?"

"Stay awake and watch with me. Let the others get a little more rest. Trying to move in the dark is more dangerous than staying put."

".. . all right. But I don't have a gun."

"Do you have a knife?"

"Yeah."

"That will have to be enough until we get the other guns clean and ready." We've been too tired and in too much of a hurry to do that so far. Also, I don't want Allie or Jill to have guns yet. Not yet. "Just keep your eyes open." The only real defense against automatic rifles is concealment and silence.

"A knife is better than a gun now," Zahra said. "If you have to use it, it will be quiet."

I nodded. "The rest of you, try to get a little more rest. I'll wake you at dawn."

Most of them lay down to sleep, or at least to rest. Natividad kept both children with her. Tomorrow, though, one of us would have to take charge of the little boy. We didn't need the burden of such a big child—one who had reached the "run around and grab everything" stage. But we had the little boy, and there was no one to hand him off to. No woman camping alongside a highway with her child would have other relatives handy.

"Olamina," Bankole said into my ear. His voice was low and soft and only I reacted to it. I turned, and he was so close that I felt his beard brush my face. Soft, thick beard. This morning he combed it more carefully than he combed the hair on his head. He has the only mirror among us. Vain, vain old man. I moved almost by reflex toward him.

I kissed him, wondering what it would feel like to kiss so much beard. I did kiss the beard at first, missing his mouth by a little in the dark. Then I found it and he moved a little and slipped his arms around me and we settled to it for a little while.

It was hard for me to make myself push him away. I didn't want to. He didn't want to let me.

"I was going to say thank you for coming after me," he said. "That woman was conscious almost until she died. The only thing I could do for her was stay with her."

"I was afraid you might have been shot out there."

"I was flat on the ground until I heard the woman groaning."

I sighed. "Yeah." And then, "Rest."

He lay down next to me and rubbed my arm—which tingled wherever he touched it. "We should talk soon," he said.

"At least," I agreed.

He grinned—I could see the flash of teeth—and turned over and tried to sleep.

The boy's name was Justin Rohr. His dead mother had been Sandra Rohr. Justin had been born in Riverside, California just three years ago. His mother had gotten him this far north from Riverside. She had saved his birth certificate, some baby pictures, and a picture of a stocky, freckled, red-haired man who was, according to a notation on the back of the photo, Richard Walter Rohr, born January 9, 2002, and died May 20, 2026. The boy's father—only twenty-four when he died. I wondered what had killed him. Sandra Rohr had saved her marriage certificate and other papers important to her. All were wrapped in a plastic packet that I had taken from her body. Elsewhere on her, I had found several thousand dollars and a gold ring.

There was nothing about relatives or a specific destination. It seemed that Sandra had simply been heading north with her son in search of a better life.

The little boy tolerated us all well enough today, although he got frustrated when we didn't understand him at once. When he cried, he demanded that we produce his mother.

Allie, of all people, was his choice for substitute mother. She resisted him at first. She ignored him or pushed him away. But when he was not being wheeled along, he chose to walk with her or demand to be carried by her. By the end of the day, she had given in. The two of them had chosen each other.

"She used to have a little boy," her sister Jill told me as we walked along State 156 with the few other walkers who had chosen this route. It was empty. There were times when we could see no one at all, or when, as we headed east and north, the only people we could see were heading west and south toward us, toward the coast.

"She called her little boy Adam," Jill continued. "He was only a few months old when . . . he died."

I looked at her. She had a big swollen purple bruise in the middle of her forehead, like a misshapen third eye. I don't think it hurt her much, though. It didn't hurt me much.

"When he died," I repeated. "Who killed him?"

She looked away and rubbed her bruise. "Our father. That's why we left. He killed the baby. It cried. He hit it with his fists until it stopped."

I shook my head and sighed. It was no news to me that other people's fathers could be monsters. I'd heard about such things all my life, but I'd never before met people who were so clearly their father's victims.

"We burned the house," Jill whispered. I heard her say it, and I knew without asking what she wasn't saying. But she looked like a person talking to herself, forgetting that anyone was listening. "He was passed out drunk on the floor. The baby was dead. We got our stuff and our money—we earned it!—and we set fire to the trash on the floor and the couch. We didn't stay to see. I don't know what happened. We ran away. Maybe the fire went out. Maybe he didn't die." She focused on me. "He might still be alive."

She sounded more scared than anything else. Not hopeful or sorry. Scared. The devil might still be alive.

"Where did you run from?" I asked. "What city?"

"Glendale."

"Way down in L.A. County?"

"Yeah."

"Then he's more than three hundred miles behind you."

". . . yeah."

"He drank a lot, didn't he."

"All the time."

"Then he'd be in no shape to follow you even if the fire never touched him. What do you think would happen to a drunk on the highway? He'd never even make it out of L.A."

She nodded. "You sound like Allie. You're both right. I know. But . . . I dream about him sometimes—that he's coming, that he's found us. . . . I know it's crazy. But I wake up covered in sweat."

"Yeah," I said, remembering my own nightmares during the search for my father. "Yeah."

Jill and I walked together for a while without talking. We were moving slowly because Justin demanded to be allowed to walk now and then. He had too much energy to spend hours sitting and riding. And, of course, when he was allowed to walk, he wanted to run all around, investigate everything. I had time to stop, swing my pack around, and dig out a length of clothesline. I handed it to Jill.

"Tell your sister to try harnessing him with this," I said. "It might save his life. One end around his waist, the other around her arm."

She took the rope.

"I've taken care of a few three-year-olds," I said, "and I'll tell you, she's going to need a lot of help with that little kid. If she doesn't know that now, she will."

"Are you guys just going to leave all the work to her?" Jill demanded.

"Of course not." I watched Allie and Justin walking along—lean, angular woman and pudgy, bumblebee of a child. The boy ran to investigate a bush near the roadside, then, startled by the approach of strangers, ran back to Allie and hung on to the cloth of her jeans until she took his hand. "They do seem to be adopting each other, though," I said. "And taking care of other people can be a good cure for nightmares like yours and maybe hers."

"You sound as though you know."

I nodded. "I live in this world, too."

We passed through Hollister before noon. We resupplied there, not knowing when we would see well-equipped stores again. We had already discovered that several of the small communities shown on the maps no longer existed—had not existed for years. The earthquake had done a lot of damage in Hollister, but the people hadn't gone animal. They seemed to be helping one another with repairs and looking after their own destitute. Imagine that.

21

☐ ☐ ☐

The Self must create
Its own reasons for being.
To shape God,
Shape Self.

EARTHSEED: THE BOOKS OF THE LIVING
MONDAY, AUGUST 30, 2027

There is still a little water in the San Luis Reservoir. It's more fresh water than I've ever seen in one place, but by the vast size of the reservoir, I can see that it's only a little compared to what should be there—what used to be there.

The highway runs through the recreational area for several miles. That gave us a chance to travel through on the road until we spotted an area that would make a good rest-day camp and that wasn't occupied.

There are a lot of people in the area—people who have set up permanent camps in everything from rag-and-plastic tents to wooden shacks that look almost fit for human habitation. Where are so many people going to the bathroom? How clean is the water in the reservoir? No doubt cities that use it purify the water when it reaches them. Whether they do or not, I think it's time for us to break out the water purification tablets.

Around several of the tents and shacks, there are small, ragged gardens—new plantings and remnants of summer vegetable gardens. There are a few things left to harvest: big squashes, pumpkins, and gourds still growing along with carrots, peppers, greens, and a little corn. Good, cheap, filling foods. Not enough protein, but perhaps the people hunt. There must be game around here, and I saw plenty of guns. People wear holstered handguns or carry rifles or shotguns. The men in particular go armed.

They all stared at us.

As we went past, people stopped their gardening, outdoor cooking, or whatever to stare at us. We had pushed ourselves, had been eager to arrive ahead of the crowd I believe will soon come in from the Bay Area. So we didn't arrive with the usual human river. Yet by ourselves we are enough of a crowd to make the local squatters nervous. They let us alone, though. Except during disaster-induced feeding frenzies like the ones after the earthquake, most people let one another alone. I think Dominic and Justin are making it easier for us to fit in. Justin, now tethered to Allie's wrist, runs around staring at the squatters until they make him nervous. Then he runs back to Allie and demands to be carried. He's a cute little kid. Lean, grim-faced people tend to smile at him.

No one shot at us or challenged us as we walked along the highway. No one bothered us later when we left the highway and headed into the trees toward what we thought might be a good area. We found old campsites and toilet places and avoided them. We didn't want to be within sight of the highway or of anyone else's tent or shack. We wanted privacy, not too many rocks to sleep on, and a way of reaching the water that didn't put us too much on display. We looked for over an hour until we found an isolated old campsite, long abandoned and a little higher upslope than others we'd seen. It suited all of us. Then, with hours of daylight left, we rested in enormous comfort and laziness, knowing we had the rest of today and all of tomorrow to do almost nothing. Natividad fed Dominic and the two of them drifted off to sleep. Allie followed her example with Justin, although preparing him a meal was a little more complicated. Both women had more reason to be tired and to need sleep than the rest of us, so we left them out when we drew lots for a watch schedule—one for day and night. We shouldn't get *too* comfortable. Also, we agreed that no one should go off exploring or getting water alone. I thought the couples would soon start going off together—And I thought it was just about time for Bankole and me to have that talk.

I sat with him and cleaned our new handgun while he cleaned the rifle. Harry was on watch and needed my gun. When I went over to give it to him, he let me know he understood exactly what was going on between Bankole and me.

"Be careful," he whispered. "Don't give the poor old guy a heart attack."

"I'll tell him you were worried," I said.

Harry laughed, then sobered. "Be careful, Lauren. Bankole is probably all right. He seems to be. But, well. . . . Yell if anything goes wrong."

I rested my hand on his shoulder for a moment and said, "Thank you."

The nice thing about sitting and working alongside someone you don't know very well, someone you'd like to know much better, is that you can talk with him or be quiet with him. You can get comfortable with him and with the awareness that you'll soon be making love to him.

Bankole and I were quiet for a while, a little shy. I sneaked glances at him and caught him sneaking glances at me. Then, to my own surprise, I began to talk to him about Earthseed—not preaching, just talking, testing I guess. I needed to see his reaction. Earthseed is the most important thing in my life. If Bankole were going to laugh at it, I needed to know now. I didn't expect him to agree with it or even to be much interested in it. He's an old man. I thought he was probably content with whatever religion he had. It occurred to me as I spoke that I had no idea what his religion was. I asked him.

"None at all," he said. "When my wife was alive, we went to a Methodist church. Her religion was important to her, so I went along. I saw how it comforted her, and I wanted to believe, but I never could."

"We were Baptists," I said. "I couldn't make myself believe either, and I couldn't tell anyone. My father was the minister. I kept quiet and began to understand Earthseed."

"Began to invent Earthseed," he said.

"Began to discover it and understand it," I said. "Stumbling across the truth isn't the same as making things up." I wondered how many times and ways I would have to say this to new people.

"It sounds like some combination of Buddhism, existentialism, Sufism, and I don't know what else," he said. "Buddhism doesn't make a god of the concept of change, but the impermanence of everything is a basic Buddhist principle."

"I know," I said. "I've done a lot of reading. Some other religions and philosophies do contain ideas that would fit into Earthseed, but none of them *are* Earthseed. They go off in their own directions."

He nodded. "All right. But tell me, what do people have to do to be good members of an Earthseed Community?"

A nice, door-opening question. "The essentials," I answered, "are to learn to shape God with forethought, care, and work; to educate and benefit their community, their families, and themselves; and to contribute to the fulfillment of the Destiny."

"And why should people bother about the Destiny, farfetched as it is? What's in it for them?"

"A unifying, purposeful life here on Earth, and the hope of heaven for themselves and their children. A real heaven, not mythology or philosophy. A heaven that will be theirs to shape."

"Or a hell," he said. His mouth twitched. "Human beings are good at creating hells for themselves even out of richness." He thought for a moment. "It sounds too simple, you know."

"You think it's simple?" I asked in surprise.

"I said it *sounds* too simple."

"It sounds overwhelming to some people."

"I mean it's too . . . straightforward. If you get people to accept it, they'll make it more complicated, more open to interpretation, more mystical, and more comforting."

"Not around me they won't!" I said.

"With you or without you, they will. All religions change. Think about the big ones. What do you think Christ would be these days?

A Baptist? A Methodist? A Catholic? And the Buddha—do you think he'd be a Buddhist now? What kind of Buddhism would he practice?" He smiled. "After all, if 'God is Change,' surely Earthseed can change, and if it lasts, it will."

I looked away from him because he was smiling. This was all nothing to him. "I know," I said. "No one can stop Change, but we all shape Change whether we mean to or not. I mean to guide and shape Earthseed into what it should be."

"Perhaps." He went on smiling. "How serious are you about this?"

The question drove me deep into myself. I spoke, almost not knowing what I would say. "When my father . . . disappeared," I began, "it was Earthseed that kept me going. When most of my community and the rest of my family were wiped out, and I was alone, I still had Earthseed. What I am now, all that I am now is Earthseed."

"What you are now," he said after a long silence, "is a very unusual young woman."

We didn't talk for a while after that. I wondered what he thought. He hadn't seemed to be bottling up *too* much hilarity. No more than I'd expected. He had been willing to go along with his wife's religious needs. Now, he would at least permit me mine.

I wondered about his wife. He hadn't mentioned her before. What had she been like? How had she died?

"Did you leave home because your wife died?" I asked.

He put down a long slender cleaning rod and rested his back against the tree behind him. "My wife died five years ago," he said. "Three men broke in—-junkies, dealers, I don't know. They beat her, tried to make her tell where the drugs were."

"Drugs?"

"They had decided that we must have something they could use or sell. They didn't like the things she was able to give them so they kept beating her. She had a heart problem." He drew in a long breath, then sighed. "She was still alive when I got home. She was able to tell me what had happened. I tried to help her, but the bastards had taken her medicine, taken everything. I phoned for an ambulance. It arrived an hour after she died. I tried to save her, then to revive her. I tried so damned hard. . . ."

I stared down the hill from our camp where just a glint of water was visible in the distance through the trees and bushes. The world is full of painful stories. Sometimes it seems as though there aren't any other kind and yet I found myself thinking how beautiful that glint of water was through the trees.

"I should have headed north when Sharon died," Bankole said. "I thought about it."

"But you stayed." I turned away from the water and looked at him. "Why?"

He shook his head. "I didn't know what to do, so for some time I didn't do anything. Friends took care of me, cooked for me, cleaned the house. It surprised me that they would do that. Church people most of them. Neighbors. More her friends than mine."

I thought of Wardell Parrish, devastated after the loss of his sister and her children—and his house. Had Bankole been some community's Wardell Parrish? "Did you live in a walled community?" I asked.

"Yes. Not rich, though. Nowhere near rich. People managed to hold on to their property and feed their families. Not much else. No servants. No hired guards."

"Sounds like my old neighborhood."

"I suppose it sounds like a lot of old neighborhoods that aren't there anymore. I stayed to help the people who had helped me. I couldn't walk away from them."

"But you did. You left. Why?"

"Fire—and scavengers."

"You, too? Your whole community?"

"Yes. The houses burned, most of the people were killed. . . . The rest scattered, went to family or friends elsewhere. Scavengers and squatters moved in. I didn't decide to leave. I escaped."

Much too familiar. "Where did you live? What city?"

"San Diego."

"That far south?"

"Yes. As I said, I should have left years ago. If I had, I could have managed plane fare and resettlement money."

Plane fare *and* resettlement money? He might not call that rich, but we would have.

"Where are you going now?" I asked.

"North." He shrugged.

"Just anywhere north or somewhere in particular?"

"Anywhere where I can be paid for my services and allowed to live among people who aren't out to kill me for my food or water."

Or for drugs, I thought. I looked into his bearded face and added up the hints I'd picked up today and over the past few days. "You're a doctor, aren't you?"

He looked a little surprised. "I was, yes. Family practice. It seems a long time ago."

"People will always need doctors," I said. "You'll do all right."

"My mother used to say that." He gave me a wry smile. "But here I am."

I smiled back because, looking at him now, I couldn't help myself, but as he spoke, I decided he had told me at least one lie. He might be as displaced and in distress as he appeared to be, but he wasn't just wandering north. He wasn't looking for just anywhere he could be paid for his services and not robbed or murdered. He wasn't the kind of man who wandered. He knew where he was going. He had a haven somewhere—a relative's home, another home of his own, a friend's home, *something*—some definite destination.

Or perhaps he just had enough money to buy a place for himself in Washington or Canada or Alaska. He had had to choose between fast, safe, expensive air travel and having settling-in money when he got where he was going. He had chosen settling-in money. If so, I agreed with him. He was taking the kind of risk that would enable him to make a new beginning as soon as possible—if he survived.

On the other hand, if I were right about any of this, he might disappear on me some night. Or perhaps he would be more open about it—just walk away from me some day, turn down a side road and wave good-bye. I didn't want that. After I'd slept with him I would want it even less.

Even now, I wanted to keep him with me. I hated that he was lying to me already—or I believed he was. But why should he tell me everything? He didn't know me very well yet, and like me, he meant to survive. Perhaps I could convince him that he and I could survive well together. Meanwhile, best to enjoy him without quite trusting him. I may be wrong about all this, but I don't believe I am. Pity.

We finished the guns, loaded them, and went down to the water to wash. You could go right down to the water, scoop some up in a pot, and take it away. It was free. I kept looking around, thinking someone would come to stop us or charge us or something. I suppose we could have been robbed, but no one paid any attention to us. We saw other people getting water in bottles, canteens, pots, and bags, but the place seemed peaceful. No one bothered anyone. No one paid any attention to us.

"A place like this can't last," I told Bankole. "It's a shame. Life could be good here."

"I suspect that it's against the law to live here," he said. "This is a State Recreation Area. There should be some kind of limit on how long you can stay. I'm certain that there should be—used to be— some group policing the place. I wonder if officials of some kind come around to collect bribes now and then."

"Not while we're here, I hope." I dried my hands and arms and waited for him to dry his. "Are you hungry?" I asked.

"Oh, yes," he said. He looked at me for a while, then reached for me. He took me by both arms, drew me to him, kissed me, and spoke into my ear. "Aren't you?"

I didn't say anything. After a while I took his hand and we went back to camp to pick up one of his blankets. Then we went to an isolated little spot that we'd both noticed earlier.

It felt natural and easy to lie down with him, and explore the

OCTAVIA E. BUTLER

smooth, hard, broad feel of his body. He'd kept himself fit. No doubt walking hundreds of miles in the past few weeks had burned off whatever fat he'd been carrying. He was still big—barrel-chested and tall. Best of all, he took a lot of uncomplicated pleasure in my body, and I got to share it with him. It isn't often that I can enjoy the good side of my hyperempathy. I let the sensation take over, intense and wild. I might be more in danger of having a heart attack than he is. How had I done without this for so long?

There was an odd, unromantic moment when we both reached into crumpled clothing and produced condoms. It was funny because of the way it hit us both at once, and we laughed, then went on to the serious business of loving and pleasuring one another. That combed and trimmed beard that he's so vain about tickles like mad.

"I knew I should have let you alone," he said to me when we had made love twice and were still not willing to get up and go back to the others. "You're going to kill me. I'm too old for this stuff."

I laughed and made a pillow of his shoulder.

After a while, he said, "I need to be serious for a minute, girl."

"Okay."

He drew a long breath, sighed, swallowed, hesitated. "I don't want to give you up," he said.

I smiled.

"You're a kid," he said. "I ought to know better. How old are you, anyway?"

I told him.

He jumped, then pushed me off his shoulder. "Eighteen?" He flinched away from me as though my skin burned him. "My god," he said. "You're a baby! I'm a child molester!"

I didn't laugh, though I wanted to. I just looked at him.

After a while he frowned and shook his head. In a little more time, he moved back against me, touching my face, my shoulders, my breasts.

"You're not just eighteen," he said.

I shrugged.

"When were you born? What year?"

"Twenty oh nine."

"No." He drew the word out: "Nooo."

I kissed him and said in the same tone, "Yesss. Now stop your nonsense. You want to be with me and I want to be with you. We're not going to split up because of my age, are we?"

After a while he shook his head. "You should have a nice youngster like Travis," he said. "I should have the sense and the strength to send you off to find one."

That made me think of Curtis, and I cringed away from thinking of him. I've thought as little as possible about Curtis Talcott. He isn't like my brothers. He may be dead, but none of us ever saw his body. I saw his brother Michael. I was terrified of seeing Curtis himself, but I never did. He may not be dead. He's lost to me, but I hope he's not dead. He should be here with me on the road. I hope he's alive and all right.

"Who have I reminded you of?" Bankole asked me, his voice soft and deep.

I shook my head. "A boy I knew at home. We were going to get married this year. I don't even know whether he's still alive."

"You loved him?"

"Yes! We were going to marry and leave home, walk north. We had decided to go this fall."

"That's crazy! You intended to walk this road even though you didn't have to?"

"Yes. And if we had left earlier, he'd be with me. I wish I knew he was all right."

He lay down on his back and drew me down beside him. "We've all lost someone," he said. "You and I seem to have lost everyone. That's a bond, I suppose."

"A terrible one," I said. "But not our only one."

He shook his head. "You're really eighteen?"

OCTAVIA E. BUTLER

"Yes. As of last month."

"You look and act years older."

"This is who I am," I said.

"You were the oldest kid in your family, weren't you?"

I nodded. "I had four brothers. They're all dead."

"Yes," he sighed. "Yes."

TUESDAY, AUGUST 31, 2027

I've spent all of today talking, writing, reading, and making love to Bankole. It seems such a luxury not to have to get up, pack, and walk all day. We all lay sprawled around the campsite resting aching muscles, eating, and doing nothing. More people flowed into the area from the highway and made their camps, but none of them bothered us.

I began Zahra's reading lesson and Jill and Allie looked interested. I included them as though I had intended to from the first. It turned out that they could read a little, but hadn't learned to write. Toward the end of the lesson, I read a few Earthseed verses to them in spite of Harry's groans. Yet when Allie proclaimed that she would never pray to any god of change, Harry was the one who corrected her. Zahra and Travis both smiled at that, and Bankole watched us all with apparent interest.

After that, Allie began to ask questions instead of making scornful proclamations, and for the most part, the others answered her— Travis and Natividad, Harry and Zahra. Once Bankole answered, expanding on something I told him yesterday. Then he caught himself and looked a little embarrassed.

"I still think it's too simple," he said to me. "A lot of it is logical, but it will never work without a sprinkling of mystical confusion."

"I'll leave that to my descendants," I said, and he busied himself, digging a bag of almonds out of his pack, pouring some into his hand, and passing the rest around.

Just before nightfall a gun battle began over toward the highway.

We couldn't see any of it from where we were, but we stopped talking and lay down. With bullets flying, it seemed best to keep low.

The shooting started and stopped, moved away, then came back. I was on watch, so I had to stay alert, but in this storm of noise, nothing moved near us except the trees in the evening breeze. It looked so peaceful, and yet people out there were trying to kill each other, and no doubt succeeding. Strange how normal it's become for us to lie on the ground and listen while nearby, people try to kill each other.

22

□ □ □

As wind,
As water,
As fire,
As life,
God
Is both creative and destructive,
Demanding and yielding,
Sculptor and clay.
God is Infinite Potential:
God is Change.

EARTHSEED: THE BOOKS OF THE LIVING
THURSDAY, SEPTEMBER 9, 2027

We've had over a week of weary, frightening, nerve-wracking walking. We've reached and passed through the city of Sacramento without real trouble. We've been able to buy enough food and water, been able to find plenty of empty places in the hills where we could make camp. Yet none of us have had any feelings of comfort or well-being along the stretch of Interstate-5 that we've just traveled.

I-5 is much less traveled than U.S. 101, in spite of the earthquake chaos. There were times when the only people we could see were each other. Those times never lasted long, but they did happen.

On the other hand, there were more trucks on I-5. We had to be careful because trucks traveled during the day as well as at night. Also, there were more human bones on I-5. It was nothing to run across skulls, lower jaws, or bones of the pelvis and torso. Arm and leg bones were rarer, but now and then, we spotted them, too.

"I think it's the trucks," Bankole told us. "If they hit someone along here, they wouldn't stop. They wouldn't dare. And the junkies and alcoholics wouldn't be that careful where they walked."

I suppose he's right, although along that whole empty stretch of road, we saw only four people whom I believed were either not sober or not sane.

But we saw other things. On Tuesday we camped in a little hollow back in the hills to the west of the road, and a big black and white dog came wandering down toward our camp with the fresh- looking, bloody hand and forearm of a child in its mouth.

The dog spotted us, froze, turned, and ran back the way it had come. But we all got a good look before it went, and we all saw the same thing. That night, we posted a double watch. Two watchers, two guns, no unnecessary conversation, no sex.

The next day we decided not to take another rest day until we had passed through Sacramento. There was no guarantee that anything would be better on the other side of Sacramento, but we wanted to get away from this grim land.

That night, looking for a place to camp, we stumbled across four ragged, filthy kids huddled around a campfire. The picture of them is still clear in my mind. Kids the age of my brothers—twelve, thirteen, maybe fourteen years old, three boys and a girl. The girl was pregnant, and so huge it was obvious she would be giving birth any day. We rounded a bend in a dry stream bed, and there these kids were, roasting a severed human leg, maneuvering it where it lay in the middle of their fire atop the burning wood by twisting its foot. As we watched, the girl pulled a sliver of charred flesh from the thigh and stuffed it into her mouth.

They never saw us. I was in the lead, and I stopped the others before they all rounded the bend. Harry and Zahra, who were just behind me, saw all that I saw. We turned the others back and away, not telling them why until we were far from those kids and their cannibal feast.

OCTAVIA E. BUTLER

No one attacked us. No one bothered us at all. The country we walked through was even beautiful in some places—green trees and rolling hills; golden dried grasses and tiny communities; farms, many overgrown and abandoned, and abandoned houses. Nice country, and compared to Southern California, rich country. More water, more food, more room. . . .

So why were the people eating one another?

There were several burned out buildings. It was obvious that there had been trouble here, too, but much less than on the coast. Yet we couldn't wait to get back to the coast.

Sacramento was all right to resupply in and hurry through. Water and food were cheap there compared to what you could buy along the roadside, of course. Cities were always a relief as far as prices went. But cities were also dangerous. More gangs, more cops, more suspicious, nervous people with guns. You tiptoe through cities. You keep up a steady pace, keep your eyes open, and try to look both too intimidating to bother and invisible. Neat trick. Bankole says cities have been like that for a long time.

Speaking of Bankole, I haven't let him get much rest on this rest day. He doesn't seem to mind. He did say something that I should make note of, though. He said he wanted me to leave the group with him. He has, as I suspected, a safe haven—or as safe as any haven can be that isn't surrounded by high-tech security devices and armed guards. It's in the hills on the coast near Cape Mendocino maybe two weeks from here.

"My sister and her family have been living there," he said. "But the property belongs to me. There's room on it for you."

I could imagine how delighted his sister would be to see me. Would she try to be polite, or would she stare at me, then at him, then demand to know whether he was in his right mind?

"Did you hear what I said?" he demanded.

I looked at him, interested in the anger I heard in his voice. Why anger?

"What am I doing? Boring you?" he demanded.

I took his hand and kissed it. "You introduce me to your sister and she'll measure you for a straitjacket."

After a while, he laughed. "Yes." And then, "I don't care."

"You might, sooner or later."

"You'll come with me, then."

"No. I'd like to, but no."

He smiled. "Yes. You'll come."

I watched him. I tried to read the smile, but it's hard to read a bearded face. It's easier to say what I didn't see—or didn't recognize. I didn't see condescension or that particular kind of disregard that some men reserve for women. He wasn't deciding that my "no" was a secret "yes." Something else was going on.

"I own three hundred acres," he said. "I bought the property years ago as an investment. There was going to be a big housing development up there, and speculators like me were going to make tons of money, selling our land to the developers. The project fell through for some reason, and I was stuck with land that I could either sell at a loss or keep. I kept it. Most of it is good for farming. It's got some trees on it, and some big tree stumps. My sister and her husband have built a house and a few outbuildings."

"You might have dozens or hundreds of squatters on that land now," I said.

"I don't think so. Access is a problem. It's not convenient to any real road, and it's well away from the big highways. It's a great place to hide."

"Water?"

"There are wells. My sister says the area is getting dryer, warmer. That's no surprise. But the ground water seems dependable so far."

I thought I could see where he was headed now, but he was going to have to get there all by himself. His land; his choice.

"There aren't many black people up that way, are there?" I asked.

"Not many," he agreed. "My sister hasn't had much trouble, though."

"What does she do for a living? Farm the land?"

"Yes, and her husband does odd jobs for cash—which is dangerous because it leaves her and the children alone for days, weeks, even months at a time. If we can manage to support ourselves without becoming a drain on her few resources, we might be useful to her. We might give her more security."

"How many kids?"

"Three. Let's see. . . eleven, thirteen, and fifteen years old by now. She's only forty herself." His mouth twitched. Only. Yeah. Even his little sister was old enough to be my mother. "Her name's Alex. Alexandra. Married to Don Casey. They both hate cities. They thought my land was a godsend. They could raise children who might live to grow up." He nodded. "And their children have done all right."

"How have you kept in touch?" I asked. "Phone?"

"That was part of our agreement," he said. "They don't have a phone, but when Don goes to one of the towns to get work, he phones me and lets me know how everyone is. He won't know what's happened to me. He won't be expecting me. If he's tried to phone, both he and Alex will be worried."

"You should have flown up," I said. "But I'm glad you didn't."

"Are you? So am I. Listen, you are coming with me. I can't think of anything I want as much as I want you. I haven't wanted anything at all for a long time. Too long."

I leaned back against a tree. Our campsite wasn't as completely private as the one at San Luis had been, but there were trees, and the couples could get away from each other. Each couple had one gun, and the Gilchrist sisters were babysitting Dominic as well as Justin. We had put them in the middle of a rough triangle and given them my gun. On I-5 they and Travis had had a chance to do a little target practice. It was all of our duty to look around now and then and make sure no strangers wandered into the area. I looked around.

Sitting up I could see Justin running around, chasing pigeons. Jill was keeping an eye on him, but not trying to keep up with him.

Bankole took me by the shoulder and turned me to face him. "I'm not boring you, am I?" he asked for the second time.

I had been trying not to look at him. I looked now, but he had not yet said what he had to say if he wanted to keep me with him. Did he know? I thought he did.

"I want to go with you," I said. "But I'm serious about Earthseed. I couldn't be more serious. You have to understand that." Why did this sound strange to me? It was the absolute truth, but I felt odd telling it.

"I know my rival," he said.

Maybe that's why it sounded strange. I was telling him there was someone else—something else. Maybe it would have sounded less strange if the something were another man.

"You could help me," I said.

"Help you what? Do you have any real idea what you want to do?"

"Begin the first Earthseed Community."

He sighed.

"You could help me," I repeated. "This world is falling apart. You could help me begin something purposeful and constructive."

"Going to fix the world, are you?" he said with quiet amusement.

I looked at him. For a moment I was too angry to let myself speak. When I could control my voice, I said, "It's all right if you don't believe, but don't laugh. Do you know what it means to have something to believe in? Don't laugh."

After a while he said, "All right."

After a longer while, I said, "Fixing the world is not what Earthseed is about."

"The stars. I know." He lay flat on his back, but turned his head to look at me instead of looking up.

"This world would be a better place if people lived according to Earthseed," I said. "But then, this world would be better if people lived according to the teachings of almost any religion."

"That's true. Why do you think they'll live according to the teaching of yours?"

OCTAVIA E. BUTLER

"A few will. Several thousand? Several hundred thousand? Millions? I don't know. But when I have a home base, I'll begin the first community. In fact, I've already begun it."

"Is that what you need me for?" He didn't bother to smile or pretend it was a joke. It wasn't. I moved over closer to him and sat next to him so that I could look down into his face.

"I need you to understand me," I said. "I need you to take me the way I am or go off to your land by yourself."

"You need me to take you and all your friends off the street so you can start a church." Again, he was altogether serious.

"That or nothing," I said with equal seriousness. He gave me a humorless smile. "So now we know where we stand."

I smoothed his beard, and saw that he wanted to move away from my hand, but that he did not move. "Are you all that sure you want God as your rival?" I asked.

"I don't seem to have much choice, do I?" He covered my caressing hand with one of his own. "Tell me, do you ever lose your temper and scream and cry?"

"Sure."

"I can't picture it. In all honesty, I can't."

And that reminded me of something that I hadn't told him, had better tell him before he found out and felt cheated or decided that I didn't trust him—which I still didn't, quite. But I didn't want to lose him to stupidity or cowardice. I didn't want to lose him at all.

"Still want me with you?" I asked.

"Oh, yes," he said. "I intend to marry you once we've settled."

He had managed to surprise me. I stared at him with my mouth open.

"A genuine spur-of-the-moment reaction," he said. "I'll have to remember it. Will you marry me, by the way?"

"Listen to me first."

"No more. Bring your church. Bring your congregation. I doubt they care anymore about the stars than I do, but bring them. I like them, and there's room for them."

If they would come. My next effort would be to convince them. But this effort wasn't over yet.

"That isn't all," I said. "Let me tell you one more thing. Then, if you still want me, I'll marry you anytime you say. I want to. You must know I want to."

He waited.

"My mother was taking—abusing—a prescription drug when she got pregnant with me. The drug was Paracetco. As a result, I have hyperempathy syndrome."

He took that in with no sign of how he felt about it. He sat up and looked at me—looked at me with great curiosity, as though he hoped to see some sign of my hyperempathy on my face or body. "You feel other people's pain?" he asked.

"I share other people's pain and pleasure," I said. "There hasn't been much pleasure to share lately, except with you."

"Do you share bleeding?"

"No more. I did when I was little."

"But you . . . I saw you kill a man."

"Yes." I shook my head, remembering what he had seen. "I had to, or he would have killed me."

"I know that. It's just that. . . I'm surprised you were able to do it."

"I told you, I had to."

He shook his head. "I've read about the syndrome, of course, although I've never seen a case. I remember thinking that it might not be so bad a thing if most people had to endure all the pain they caused. Not doctors or other medical people, of course, but most people."

"Bad idea," I said.

"I'm not sure."

"Take my word for it. Bad, bad idea. Self-defense shouldn't have to be an agony or a killing or both. I can be crippled by the pain of a wounded person. I'm a very good shot because I've never felt that I could afford just to wound someone. Also . . ." I stopped, looked past him for a moment and drew a deep breath, then focused on him again. "The worst of it is, if you got hurt, I might not be able to help you. I might be as crippled by your injury—by your pain, I mean—as you are."

"I suspect you'd find a way." He smiled a little.

"Don't suspect that, Bankole." I stopped and hunted for words that would make him understand. "I'm not looking for compliments or even reassurance. I want you to understand: If you broke your leg badly, if you were shot, if anything serious and disabling happened to you, I might be disabled, too. You must know how disabling real pain can be."

"Yes. I know a little about you, too. No, don't tell me again that you aren't fishing for compliments. I know. Let's go back to camp. I've got some pain medications in my bag. I'll teach you how and when to use them on me or whoever needs them. If you can just hold on and be yourself long enough to use them, you can do whatever else may be necessary."

". . . okay. So . . . do you still want to marry me?" It surprised me how much I didn't want to ask the question. I knew he still wanted me. Yet there I was, asking him, almost begging him to say it. I needed to hear it.

He laughed. Big, full laughter that sounded so real, I couldn't take offense. "I'll have to remember this," he said. "Do you imagine for one minute, girl, that I would let you get away?"

23

□ □ □

Your teachers
Are all around you.
All that you perceive,
All that you experience,
All that is given to you
or taken from you,
All that you love or hate,
need or fear
Will teach you—
If you will learn.
God is your first
and your last teacher.
God is your harshest teacher:
subtle,
demanding.
Learn or die.

EARTHSEED: THE BOOKS OF THE LIVING
FRIDAY, SEPTEMBER 10, 2027

We had another battle to try to sleep through before dawn this morning. It began to the south of us out on or near the highway, and worked its way first toward, then away from us.

We could hear people shooting, screaming, cursing, running. . . . Same old stuff—tiresome, dangerous, and stupid. The shooting went on for over an hour, waxing and waning. There was a final barrage that seemed to involve more guns than ever. Then the noise stopped.

I managed to sleep through some of it. I got over being afraid, even got over being angry. In the end, I was only tired. I thought, *if the bastards are going to kill me, I can't stop them by staying awake.* If that wasn't altogether true, I didn't care. I slept.

And somehow, during or after the battle, in spite of the watch, two people slipped into our camp and bedded down among us. They slept, too.

We awoke early as usual so that we could start walking while the heat wasn't too terrible. We've learned to wake up without prompting at the first light of dawn. Today, four of us sat up in our bags at almost the same time. I was crawling out of my bag to go off and urinate when I spotted the extra people—two gray lumps in the dawn light, one large and one small, lying against each other, asleep on the bare ground. Thin arms and legs extended like sticks from rags and mounds of clothing.

I glanced around at the others and saw that they were staring where I was staring—all of them except Jill, who was supposed to be on watch. We began trusting her to stand night watch last week with a partner. This was only her second solitary watch. And where was she looking? Away into the trees. She and I would have to talk.

Harry and Travis were already reacting to the figures on the ground. In silence, each man was peeling out of his bag in his underwear, and standing up. More fully clothed, I matched them, move for move, and the three of us closed in around the two intruders.

The larger of the two awoke all at once, jumped up, darted two or three steps toward Harry, then stopped. It was a woman. We could see her better now. She was brown-skinned with a lot of long, straight, unkempt black hair. Her coloring was as dark as mine, but she was all planes and angles—a wiry, hawk-faced woman who could have used a few decent meals and a good scrubbing. She looked like a lot of people we've seen on the road.

The second intruder awoke, saw Travis standing nearby in his underwear, and screamed. That got everyone's attention. It was the high, piercing shriek of a child—a little girl who looked about seven.

She was a tiny, pinched image of the woman—her mother, or her sister perhaps.

The woman ran back to the child and tried to scoop her up. But the child had folded herself into a tight fetal knot and the woman, trying to lift her, could not get a grip. She stumbled, fell over, and in an instant she too had rolled herself into a tight ball. By then everyone had come to see.

"Harry," I said, and waited until he looked at me. "Would you and Zahra keep watch—make sure nothing else surprises us."

He nodded. He and Zahra detached from the cluster, separated, and took up positions on opposite sides of the camp, Harry nearest to the approach from the highway and Zahra on the approach from the nearest lesser road. We had buried ourselves as well as we could in a deserted area that Bankole said must once have been a park, but we didn't kid ourselves that we were alone. We'd followed I-5 to a small city outside Sacramento, away from the worst of the sprawl, but there were still plenty of poor people around—local paupers and refugees like us.

Where had this pair of ragged, terrified, filthy people come from?

"We won't hurt you," I said to them as they lay, still rolled up on the ground. "Get up. Come on, get up. You've come into our camp unasked. You can at least talk to us."

We didn't touch them. Bankole seemed to want to, but he stopped when I grasped his arm. They were already scared to death. A strange man, reaching out to them, might make them hysterical.

Trembling, the woman unrolled herself and gazed up at us. Now I realized she looked Asian except for her coloring. She put her head down and whispered something to the child. After a moment, the two of them stood up.

"We didn't know this was your place," she whispered. "We'll go away. Let us go away."

I sighed and looked at the terrified face of the little girl. "You can go," I said. "Or if you like, you can eat with us."

They both wanted to run away. They were like deer, frozen in terror, about to bolt. But I'd said the magic word. Two weeks ago, I wouldn't have said it, but I said today to these two starved- looking people: "eat."

"Food?" the woman whispered.

"Yes. We'll share a little food with you."

The woman looked at the little girl. I was certain now that they were mother and daughter. "We can't pay," she said. "We don't have anything."

I could see that. "Just take what we give you and nothing more than we give you," I said. "That will be pay enough."

"We won't steal. We aren't thieves."

Of course they were thieves. How else could they live. Some stealing and scavenging, maybe some whoring. . . . They weren't very good at it or they'd look better. But for the little kid's sake, I wanted to help them at least with a meal.

"Wait, then," I said. "We'll put a meal together."

They sat where they were and watched us with hungry, hungry eyes. There was more hunger in those eyes than we could fill with all our food. I thought I had probably made a mistake. These people were so desperate, they were dangerous. It didn't matter at all that they looked harmless. They were still alive and strong enough to run. They were not harmless.

It was Justin who eased some of the tension in those bottomless, hungry eyes. Stark naked, he toddled over to the woman and the girl and looked them over. The little girl only stared back, but after a moment, the woman began to smile. She said something to Justin, and he smiled. Then he ran back to Allie who held on to him long enough to dress him. But he had done his work. The woman was seeing us with different eyes. She watched Natividad nursing Dominic, then watched Bankole combing his beard. This seemed funny to her and to the child, and they both giggled.

"You're a hit," I told Bankole.

"I don't see what's so funny about a man combing his beard," he muttered, and put away his comb.

I dug sweet pears out of my pack, and took one each to the woman and the girl. I had just bought them two days before, and I had only three left. Other people got the idea and began sharing what they could spare. Shelled walnuts, apples, a pomegranate, Valencia oranges, figs. . . . little things.

"Save what you can," Natividad told the woman as she gave her almonds wrapped in a piece of red cloth. "Wrap things in here and tie the ends together."

We all shared corn bread made with a little honey and the hard-boiled eggs we bought and cooked yesterday. We baked the corn bread in the coals of last night's fire so that we could get away early this morning. The woman and the girl ate as though the plain, cold food were the best they had ever tasted, as though they couldn't believe someone had given it to them. They crouched over it as though they were afraid we might snatch it back.

"We've got to go," I said at last. "The sun's getting hotter."

The woman looked at me, her strange, sharp face hungry again, but now not hungry for food.

"Let us go with you," she said, her words tumbling over one another. "We'll work. We'll get wood, make fire, clean dishes, anything. Take us with you."

Bankole looked at me. "I assume you saw that coming."

I nodded. The woman was looking from one of us to the other.

"Anything," she whispered—or whimpered. Her eyes were dry and starved, but tears streamed from the little girl's eyes.

"Give us a moment to decide," I said. I meant, *Go away so my friends can yell at me in private,* but the woman didn't seem to understand. She didn't move.

"Wait over there," I said, pointing toward the trees nearest to the road. "Let us talk. Then we'll tell you."

She didn't want to do it. She hesitated, then stood up, pulled her even more reluctant daughter up, and trudged off to the trees I had indicated.

"Oh God," Zahra muttered. "We're going to take them, aren't we?"

"That's what we have to decide," I said.

"What, we feed her, and then we get to tell her to go away and finish starving?" Zahra made a noise of disgust.

"If she isn't a thief," Bankole said. "And if she doesn't have any other dangerous habits, we may be able to carry them. That little kid. . . ."

"Yes," I said. "Bankole, is there room for them at your place?"

"His place?" three others asked. I hadn't had a chance to tell them about it. And I hadn't had the nerve.

"He has a lot of land up north and over by the coast," I said. "There's a family house that we can't live in because his sister and her family are there. But there's room and trees and water. He says . . ." I swallowed, looked at Bankole who was smiling a little. "He says we can start Earthseed there—build what we can."

"Are there jobs?" Harry asked Bankole.

"My brother-in-law manages with year-round gardens and temporary jobs. He's raising three kids that way."

"But the jobs do pay money?"

"Yes, they pay. Not well, but they pay. We'd better hold off talking about this for a while. We're torturing that young woman over there."

"She'll steal," Natividad said. "She says she won't, but she will. You can look at her and tell."

"She's been beaten," Jill said. "The way they rolled up when we first spotted them. They're used to being beaten, kicked, knocked around."

"Yeah." Allie looked haunted. "You try to keep from getting hit in the head, try to protect your eyes and . . . your front. She thought we would beat her. She and the kid both."

Interesting that Allie and Jill should understand so well. What a terrible father they had. And what had happened to their mother? They had never talked about her. It was amazing that they had escaped alive and sane enough to function.

"Should we let her stay?" I asked them.

Both girls nodded. "I think she'll be a pain in the ass for a while, though," Allie said. "Like Natividad says, she'll steal. She won't be able to stop herself. We'll have to watch her real good. That little kid will steal, too. Steal and run like hell."

Zahra grinned. "Reminds me of me at that age. They'll both be pains in the ass. I vote we try them. If they have manners or if they can learn manners, we keep them. If they're too stupid to learn, we throw them out."

I looked at Travis and Harry, standing together. "What do you guys say?"

"I say you're going soft," Harry said. "You would have raised hell if we'd tried to take in a beggar woman and her child a few weeks ago."

I nodded. "You're right. I would have. And maybe that's the attitude we should keep. But these two . . . I think they might be worth something—and I don't think they're dangerous. If I'm wrong, we can always dump them."

"They might not take to being dumped," Travis said. Then he shrugged. "I don't want to be the one to send that little kid out to be one more thief-beggar-whore. But think, Lauren. If we let them stay, and it doesn't work out, it might be damned hard to get rid of them. And if they turn out to have friends around here—friends that they're scouting for, we might have to kill them."

Both Harry and Natividad began to protest. Kill a woman and a child? No! Not possible! Never!

The rest of us let them talk. When they ran down, I said, "It could get that bad, I suppose, but I don't think it will. That woman wants to live. Even more, she wants the kid to live. I think she'd put up with a lot for the kid's sake, and I don't think she'd put the kid in danger by scouting for a gang. Gangs are more direct out here, anyway. They don't need scouts."

Silence.

"Shall we try them?" I asked. "Or shall we turn them away now?"

"I'm not against them," Travis said. "Let them stay, for the kid's sake. But let's go back to having two watchers at once during the night. How the hell did those two get in here like that, anyway?"

Jill shrank a little. "They could have gotten in anytime last night," she said. "Anytime."

"What we don't see can kill us," I said. "Jill, you didn't see them?"

"They could have been there when I took over the watch!"

"You still didn't see them. They could have cut your throat—or your sister's."

"Well. They didn't."

"The next one might." I leaned toward her. "The world is full of crazy, dangerous people. We see signs of that every day. If we don't watch out for ourselves, they will rob us, kill us, and maybe eat us. It's a world gone to hell, Jill, and we've only got each other to keep it off us."

Sullen silence.

I reached out and took her hand. "Jill."

"It wasn't my fault!" she said. "You can't prove I—"

"Jill!"

She shut up and stared at me.

"Listen, no one is going to beat you up, for heaven sake, but you did something wrong, something dangerous. You know you did."

"So what do you want her to do?" Allie demanded. "Get on her knees and say she's sorry?"

"I want her to love her own life and yours enough not to be careless. That's what I want. That's what you should want, now more than ever. Jill?"

Jill closed her eyes. "Oh shit!" she said. And then, "All right, all right! I didn't see them. I really didn't. I'll watch better. No one else will get by me."

I clasped her hand for a moment longer, then let it go. "Okay. Let's get out of here. Let's collect that scared woman and her scared little kid and get out of here."

The two scared people turned out to be the most racially mixed that I had ever met. Here's their story, put together from the fragments they told us during the day and tonight. The woman had a Japanese father, a black mother, and a Mexican husband, all dead. Only she and her daughter are left. Her name is Emery Tanaka Solis. Her daughter is Tori Solis. Tori is nine years old, not seven as I had guessed. I suspect she has rarely had enough to eat in her life. She's tiny, quick, quiet, and hungry-eyed. She hid bits of food in her filthy rags until we made her a new dress from one of Bankole's shirts. Then she hid food in that. Although Tori is nine, her mother is only twenty-three. At thirteen, Emery married a much older man who promised to take care of her. Her father was already dead, killed in someone else's gunfight. Her mother was sick, and dying of tuberculosis. The mother pushed Emery into marriage to save her from victimization and starvation in the streets.

Up to that point, the situation was dreary, but normal. Emery had three children over the next three years—a daughter and two sons. She and her husband did farm work in trade for food, shelter, and hand-me-downs. Then the farm was sold to a big agribusiness conglomerate, and the workers fell into new hands. Wages were paid, but in company scrip, not in cash. Rent was charged for the workers' shacks. Workers had to pay for food, for clothing—new or used—for everything they needed, and, of course they could only spend their company notes at the company store. Wages—surprise!—were never quite enough to pay the bills. According to new laws that might or might not exist, people were not permitted to leave an employer to whom they owed money. They were obligated to work off the debt either as quasi-indentured people or as convicts. That is, if they refused to work, they could be arrested, jailed, and in the end, handed over to their employers.

Either way, such debt slaves could be forced to work longer hours for less pay, could be "disciplined" if they failed to meet their quotas, could be traded and sold with or without their consent, with or without their families, to distant employers who had temporary or permanent need of them. Worse, children could be forced to work off the debt of their parents if the parents died, became disabled, or escaped.

Emery's husband sickened and died. There was no doctor, no medicine beyond a few expensive over-the-counter preparations and the herbs that the workers grew in their tiny gardens. Jorge Francisco Solis died in fever and pain on the earthen floor of his shack without ever seeing a doctor. Bankole said it sounded as though he died of peritonitis brought on by untreated appendicitis. Such a simple thing. But then, there's nothing more replaceable than unskilled labor.

Emery and her children became responsible for the Solis debt. Accepting this, Emery worked and endured until one day, without warning, her sons were taken away. They were one and two years younger than her daughter, and too young to be without both their parents. Yet they were taken. Emery was not asked to part with them, nor was she told what would be done with them. She had terrible suspicions when she recovered from the drug she had been given to "quiet her down." She cried and demanded the return of her sons and would not work again until her masters threatened to take her daughter as well.

She decided then to run away, to take her daughter and brave the roads with their thieves, rapists, and cannibals. They had nothing for anyone to steal, and rape wasn't something they could escape by remaining slaves. As for the cannibals . . . well, perhaps they were only fantasies—lies intended to frighten slaves into accepting their lot.

"There are cannibals," I told her as we ate that night. "We've seen them. I think, though, that they're scavengers, not killers. They take advantage of road kills, that kind of thing."

"Scavengers kill," Emery said. "If you get hurt or if you look sick, they come after you."

I nodded, and she went on with her story. Late one night, she and Tori slipped out past the armed guards and electrified fences, the sound and motion detectors and the dogs. Both knew how to be quiet, how to fade from cover to cover, how to lie still for hours. Both were very fast. Slaves learned things like that—the ones who lived did. Emery and Tori must have been very lucky.

Emery had some notion of finding her sons and getting them back, but she had no idea where they had been taken. They had been driven away in a truck; she knew that much. But she didn't know even which way the truck turned when it reached the highway. Her parents had taught her to read and write, but she had seen no writing about her sons. She had to admit after a while that all she could do was save her daughter.

Living on wild plants and whatever they could "find" or beg, they drifted north. That was the way Emery said it: they found things. Well, if I were in her place, I would have found a few things, too.

A gang fight drove her to us. Gangs are always a special danger in cities. If you keep to the road while you're in individual gang territories, you might escape their attentions. We have so far. But the overgrown park land where we camped last night was, according to Emery, in dispute. Two gangs shot at each other and called insults and accusations back and forth. Now and then they stopped to shoot at passing trucks. During one of these intervals, Emery and Tori who had camped close to the roadside had slipped away.

"One group was coming closer to us," Emery said. "They would shoot and run. When they ran, they got closer. We had to get away. We couldn't let them hear us or see us. We found your clearing, but we didn't see you. You know how to hide."

That, I suppose was a compliment. We try to disappear into the scenery when that's possible. Most of the time it isn't. Tonight it isn't. And tonight we watch two at a time.

SUNDAY, SEPTEMBER 12, 2027

Tori Solis has found us two more companions today: Grayson Mora and his daughter Doe. Doe was only a year younger than Tori, and the two little girls, walking along, going the same way, became friends. Today we turned west on State Highway 20 and were heading back toward U.S. 101. We spent a lot of time talking about settling on Bankole's land, about jobs and crops and what we might build there.

Meanwhile, the two little girls, Tori and Doe were making friends and pulling their parents together. The parents were alike enough to attract my attention. They were about the same age—which meant that the man had become a father almost as young as the woman had become a mother. That wasn't unusual, but it was unusual that he had taken charge of his child.

He was a tall, thin, black Latino, quiet, protective of his child, yet tentative, somehow. He liked Emery. I could see that. Yet on some level he wanted to get away from her—and away from us. When we left the road to make camp, he would have gone on if his daughter had not begged, then cried to stay with us. He had his own food so I told him he could camp near us if he wanted to. Two things hit me as I talked to him.

First, he didn't like us. That was obvious. He didn't like us at all. I thought he might resent us because we were united and armed. You tend to resent the people you're afraid of. I told him we kept a watch, and that if he could put up with that, he was welcome. He shrugged and said in his soft, cold voice, "Oh, yeah."

He'll stay. His kid wants it and some part of him wants it, but something's wrong. Something beyond ordinary traveler caution.

The second thing is only my suspicion. I believe Grayson and Doe Mora were also slaves. Yet Grayson is now a rich pauper. He has a pair of sleepsacks, food, water, and money. If I'm right, he took them off someone—or off someone's corpse.

Why do I think he was a slave? That odd tentativeness of his is just too much like Emery's. And Doe and Tori, though they don't look alike at all, seem to understand each other like sisters. Little kids can do that sometimes, without it meaning anything. Just being little kids together is enough. But I've never seen any kids but these two both show the tendency to drop to the ground and roll into a fetal knot when frightened.

OCTAVIA E. BUTLER

Doe did just that when she tripped and fell, and Zahra stepped over to see whether she was hurt. Doe's body snapped into a trembling ball. Was that, as Jill and Allie supposed, what people did when they expected to be beaten or kicked—a posture of protection and submission both at once?

"Something wrong about that fellow," Bankole said, glancing at Grayson as we bedded down next to each other. We had eaten and heard more of Emery's story, and talked a little, but we were tired. I had my writing to do, and Travis and Jill were on watch. Bankole, who had an early morning watch with Zahra just wanted to talk. He sat beside me and spoke into my ear in a voice so low that if I leaned away from him, I lost words. "Mora's too jumpy," he said. "He flinches if someone walks close to him."

"I think he's another ex-slave," I said in a voice just as low. "That might not be his only problem, but it's his most obvious one".

"So you picked up on that, too." He put his arm around me and sighed. "I agree. Both he and the child."

"And he doesn't love us."

"He doesn't trust us. Why should he? We'll have to watch all four of them for a while. They're . . . odd. They might be stupid enough to try to grab some of our packs and leave some night. Or it might just be a matter of little things starting to disappear. The children are more likely to get caught at it. Yet if the adults stay, it will be for the children's sake. If we take it easy on the children and protect them, I think the adults will be loyal to us."

"So we become the crew of a modern underground railroad," I said. Slavery again—even worse than my father thought, or at least sooner. He thought it would take a while.

"None of this is new." Bankole made himself comfortable against me. "In the early 1990s while I was in college, I heard about cases of growers doing some of this—holding people against their wills and forcing them to work without pay. Latins in California, blacks and Latins in the south. . . . Now and then, someone would go to jail for it."

"But Emery says there's a new law—that forcing people or their children to work off debt that they can't help running up is legal."

"Maybe. It's hard to know what to believe. I suppose the politicians may have passed a law that could be used to support debt slavery. But I've heard nothing about it. Anyone dirty enough to be a slaver is dirty enough to tell a pack of lies. You realize that that woman's children were sold like cattle—and no doubt sold into prostitution."

I nodded. "She knows, too."

"Yes. My God."

"Things are breaking down more and more." I paused. "I'll tell you, though, if we can convince ex-slaves that they can have freedom with us, no one will fight harder to keep it. We need better guns, though. And we need to be so careful. . . . It keeps getting more dangerous out here. It will be especially dangerous with those little girls around."

"Those two know how to be quiet," Bankole said. "They're little rabbits, fast and silent. That's why they're still alive."

24

□ □ □

Respect God:
Pray working.
Pray learning,
planning,
doing.
Pray creating,
teaching,
reaching.
Pray working.
Pray to focus your thoughts,
still your fears,
strengthen your purpose.
Respect God.
Shape God.
Pray working.

EARTHSEED: THE BOOKS OF THE LIVING
FRIDAY, SEPTEMBER 17, 2027

We read some verses and talked about Earthseed for a while this morning. It was a calming thing to do—almost like church. We needed something calming and reassuring. Even the new people joined in, asking questions, thinking aloud, applying the verses to their experiences.

God is Change, and in the end, God *does* prevail. But we have something to say about the whens and the whys of that end.

Yeah.

It's been a horrible week.

We've taken both today and yesterday as rest days. We might take tomorrow as well. I need it whether the others do or not. We're all sore and sick, in mourning and exhausted—yet triumphant. Odd to be triumphant. I think it's because most of us are still alive. We are a harvest of survivors. But then, that's what we've always been.

This is what happened.

At our noon stop on Tuesday, Tori and Doe, the two little girls, went away from the group to urinate. Emery went with them. She had kind of taken charge of Doe as well as her own daughter. The night before, she and Grayson Mora had slipped away from the group and stayed away for over an hour. Harry and I were on watch, and we saw them go. Now they were a couple—all over each other, but at arm's length from everyone else. Strange people.

So Emery took the girls off to pee—not far away. Just across the hill face and out of sight behind a patch of dead bushes and tall, dry grass. The rest of us sat eating, drinking, and sweating in what shade we could get from a copse of oak trees that looked only half dead. The trees had been robbed of a great number of branches, no doubt by people needing firewood. I was looking at their many jagged wounds when the screaming began.

First there were the high, needle thin, needle sharp shrieks of the little girls, then we heard Emery shouting for help. Then we heard a man's voice, cursing.

Most of us jumped up without thinking and ran toward the noise. In midstride, I grabbed Harry and Zahra by the arms to get their attention. Then I gestured them back to guard our packs and Natividad and Allie who had stayed with the babies. Harry had the rifle and Zahra had one of the Berettas, and in that moment, they both resented the hell out of me. No matter. For the moment, I was just glad to see them go back. They could cover us if necessary, and keep us from being overwhelmed.

We found Emery fighting with a big bald man who had grabbed Tori. Doe was already running back to us, screaming. She ran straight into her father's arms. He swept her up and ran off toward the highway, then he veered back toward the oaks and our people. There were other bald people coming up from the highway. Like us, they ran toward the screams. I saw metal gleaming among them— perhaps only knives. Perhaps guns. Travis spotted the group, too, and yelled a warning before I could.

I fell back, dropped to one knee, aimed my .45 two-handed, and waited for a clear shot at Emery's attacker. The man was much taller than Emery, and his head and shoulders were exposed except where he held Tori against him. The little girl looked like a doll that he was clutching in one arm. Emery was the problem. She, small and quick, was darting at the man, tearing at his face, trying to reach his eyes. He was trying to protect his eyes and to knock or throw her away from him. With both hands free, he might have been quick enough to bat her aside, but he wouldn't let go of the struggling Tori, and Emery wouldn't be beaten off.

For an instant, he did knock Emery back from him. In that brief window of time, my own ears ringing from his blow, I shot him.

I knew at once that I'd hit him. He didn't fall, but I felt his pain, and I wasn't good for anything else for a while. Then he toppled, and I collapsed with him. But I could still see and hear, and I still had the gun.

I heard shouting. The bald gang from the highway was almost on us—six, seven, eight people. I couldn't do anything while I was dealing with the pain, but I saw them. Instants later when the man I had shot lost consciousness or died, I was free—and needed.

Bankole had our only other gun away from camp.

I got up before I should have, almost fell down again, then shot a second attacker off Travis who was carrying Emery.

I went down again, but didn't lose consciousness. I saw Bankole grab Tori and all but throw her to Jill. Jill caught her, turned, and ran back toward camp with her.

Bankole reached me, and I was able to get up and help him cover our retreat.

We had only the scarred trees to retreat to, but they had thick, solid-looking trunks. An attacker fired several bullets into them as we reached them.

It took me several seconds to understand that someone was shooting at us. Once I did, I dropped behind the trees with the others and looked for the opposing gun.

Our rifle thundered behind me before I could spot anything. Harry, on the job. He fired twice more. I fired twice myself, barely aiming, barely in control. I believe Bankole fired. Then I was lost, no more good for anything. I died with someone. The shooting stopped.

I died with someone else. Someone laid hands on me and I came within a finger's twitch of squeezing the trigger once more.

Bankole.

"You stupid asshole!" I whimpered. "I almost killed you."

"You're bleeding," he said.

I was surprised. I tried to remember whether I'd been shot. Maybe I had just come down on a sharp piece of wood. I had no sense of my own body. I hurt, but I couldn't have said where—or even whether the pain was mine or someone else's. The pain was intense, yet defuse somehow. I felt . . . disembodied.

"Is everyone else all right?" I asked.

"Be still," he said.

"Is it over, Bankole?"

"Yes. The survivors have run away."

"Take my gun, then, and give it to Natividad—in case they decide to come back."

I think I felt him take the gun from my hand. I heard muffled talk that I didn't quite understand. That was when I realized I was losing consciousness. All right then. At least I had held on long enough to do some good.

Jill Gilchrist is dead.

She was shot in the back as she ran toward the trees carrying

Tori. Bankole didn't tell me, didn't want me to know before I had to because, as it turned out, I was wounded myself. I was lucky. My wound was minor. It hurt, but other than that, it didn't matter much. Jill was unlucky. I found out about her death when I came to and heard Allie's hoarse screaming grief.

Jill had gotten Tori back to the trees, put her down, then, without a sound, folded to the ground as though taking cover. Emery had grabbed Tori and huddled, crying with her in terror and relief. Everyone else had been busy, first taking cover, then firing or directing fire. Travis was the first to see the blood pooling around Jill. He shouted for Bankole, then turned Jill onto her back and saw blood welling from what turned out to be an exit wound in her chest. Bankole says she died before he reached her. No last words, no last sight of her sister, not even the assurance that she had saved the little girl. She had. Tori was bruised, but fine. Everyone was fine except Jill.

My own wound, to be honest, was a big scratch. A bullet had plowed a furrow straight through the flesh of my left side, leaving little damage, a lot of blood, a couple of holes in my shirt, and a lot of pain. The wound throbbed worse than a burn, but it wasn't disabling.

"Cowboy wound," Harry said when he and Zahra came to look me over. They looked dirty and miserable, but Harry tried to be upbeat for me. They had just helped to bury Jill. The group had, with hands, sticks, and our hatchet, dug a shallow grave for her while I was unconscious. They put her among the trees' roots, covered her, and rolled big rocks atop her grave. The trees were to have her, but the dogs and the cannibals were not.

The group had decided to bed down for the night where we were, even though our oak copse should have been rejected as an overnight camp because it was too close to the highway.

"You're a goddamn fool and too big to carry," Zahra told me. "So just rest there and let Bankole take care of you. Not that anyone could stop him."

"You've just got a cowboy wound," Harry repeated. "In that book I bought, people are always getting shot in the side or the arm or the shoulder, and it's nothing—although Bankole says a good percentage of them would have died of tetanus or some other infection."

"Thanks for the encouragement," I said.

Zahra gave him a look, then patted my arm. "Don't worry," she said. "No germ will get past that old man. He's mad as hell at you for getting yourself shot. Says if you had any sense, you would have stayed back here with the babies."

"What?"

"Hey, he's old," Harry said. "What do you expect."

I sighed. "How's Allie?"

"Crying." He shook his head. "She won't let anyone near her except Justin. Even he keeps trying to comfort her. It upsets him that she's crying."

"Emery and Tori are kind of beaten up, too," Zahra said. "They're the other reason we're not moving." She paused. "Hey, Lauren, you ever notice anything funny about those two—Emery and Tori, I mean? And about that guy Mora, too."

Something clicked into place for me, and I sighed again. "They're sharers, aren't they?"

"Yes, all of them—both adults and both kids. You knew?"

"Not until now. I did notice something odd: that tentativeness and touchiness—not wanting to be touched, I mean. And they were all slaves. My brother Marcus once said what good slaves sharers would make."

"That Mora guy wants to leave," Harry said.

"So let him go," I answered. "He tried to run out on us just before the shooting."

"He came back. He even helped dig Jill's grave. I mean he wants us all to leave. He says that gang we beat will come back when it's dark."

"He's sure?"

"Yeah. He's going crazy, wanting to get his kid out of here."

"Can Emery and Tori make it?"

"I'll carry Tori," a new voice said. "Emery can make it." Grayson Mora, of course. Last seen abandoning ship.

I got up slowly. My side hurt. Bankole had cleaned and bandaged the wound while I was unconscious, and that was a piece of luck. Now, though, I felt half-conscious, half-detached from my body. I felt everything except pain as though through a thick layer of cotton. Only the pain was sharp and real. I was almost grateful for it.

"I can walk," I said after trying a few steps. "But I feel like I'm walking on stilts. I don't know if I can keep the usual pace."

Grayson Mora stepped close to me. He glanced at Harry as though he wished Harry would go away. Harry just stared back at him.

"How many times did you die?" Mora asked me.

"Three at least," I answered, as though this were a sane conversation. "Maybe four. I never did it like that before—over and over. Insane. But you look well enough."

His expression hardened as though I'd slapped him. Of course, I had insulted him. I'd said, *Where were you, man and fellow sharer, while your woman and your group were in danger.* Funny. There I was, speaking a language I hadn't realized I knew.

"I had to get Doe out of danger," he said. "I had no gun, anyway."

"Can you shoot?"

He hesitated. "Never shot before," he admitted, dropping his voice to a mumble. Again I'd shamed him—this time without meaning to.

"When we teach you to shoot, will you, to protect the group?"

"Yeah!" Though at that moment, I think he would have preferred to shoot me.

"It hurts like hell," I warned.

He shrugged. "Most things do."

I looked into his thin, angry face. Were all slaves so thin— underfed, overworked, and taught that most things hurt? "Are you from this area?"

"Born in Sacramento."

"Then we need all the information you can give us. Even without a gun, we need you to help us survive here."

"My information is to get out of here before those things up the hill throw paint on themselves and start shooting people and setting fires."

"Oh, shit," I said. "So that's what they are."

"What'd you think they were?"

"I didn't have a chance to think about them. It wouldn't have mattered anyway. Harry, did you guys strip the dead?"

"Yeah." He gave me a thin smile. "We got another gun—a .38. I put some stuff in your pack from the ones you killed."

"Thank you. I don't know that I can carry my pack yet. Maybe Bankole—"

"He's already got it on his cart. Let's go."

We headed out toward the road.

"Is that how you do it?" Grayson Mora asked, walking next to me. "Whoever kills takes?"

"Yes, but we don't kill unless someone threatens us," I said. "We don't hunt people. We don't eat human flesh. We fight together against enemies. If one of us is in need, the rest help out. And we don't steal from one another, *ever*."

"Emery said that. I didn't believe her at first."

"Will you live as we do?"

" . . . yeah. I guess so."

I hesitated. "So what else is wrong? I can see that you don't trust us, even now."

He walked closer to me, but did not touch me. "Where'd that white man come from?" he demanded.

"I've known him all my life," I said. "He and I and the others have kept one another alive for a long time, now."

"But. . . him and those others, they don't feel anything. You're the only one who feels."

"We call it sharing. I'm the only one."

"But they . . . You . . ."

"We help each other. A group is strong. One or two people are easier to rob and kill."

"Yeah." He looked around at the others. There was no great trust or liking in his expression, but he looked more relaxed, more satisfied. He looked as though he had solved a troubling puzzle.

Testing him, I let myself stumble. It was easy. I still had little feeling in my feet and legs.

Mora stepped aside. He didn't touch me or offer help. Sweet guy.

I left Mora, went over to Allie, and walked with her for a while. Her grief and resentment were like a wall against me—against everyone, I suppose, but I was the one bothering her at the moment. And I was alive and her sister was dead, and her sister was the only family she had left, and why didn't I just get the hell out of her face?

She never said anything. She just pretended I wasn't there. She pushed Justin along in his carriage and wiped tears from her stony face now and then with a swift, whiplike motion. She was hurting herself, doing that. She was rubbing her face too hard, too fast, rubbing it raw. She was hurting me, too, and I didn't need anymore pain. I stayed with her, though, until her defenses began to crumble under a new wave of crippling grief. She stopped hurting herself and just let the tears run down her face, let them fall to her chest or to the broken blacktop. She seemed to sag under a sudden weight.

I hugged her then. I put my hands on her shoulders and stopped her half-blind plodding. When she swung around to face me, hostile and hurting, I hugged her. She could have broken free. I was feeling far from strong just then, but after a first angry pulling away, she hung on to me and moaned. I've never heard anyone moan like that. She cried and moaned there at the roadside, and the others stopped and waited for us. No one spoke. Justin began to whimper and Natividad came back to comfort him. The wordless message was the same for both child and woman: *In spite of your loss and pain, you aren't alone. You still have people who care about you and want you to be all right. You still have family.*

After a while, Allie and I let each other go. She isn't a chatty woman, especially not in her pain. She took Justin from Natividad, smoothed his hair, and held him. When we began walking again, she carried him for a while, and I pushed the carriage. We walked together, and there didn't seem to be any need to say anything.

On the road, there was a fair amount of foot traffic in both directions. Still, I worried that a big group like ours would be noticeable and locatable, no matter what. I worried because I didn't understand the ways of our attackers.

Sometime later when Allie put Justin back into the carriage and took the carriage from me, I moved to walk with Bankole and Emery. Emery was the one who explained things to me, and she was the one who spotted the smoke from the first fire—no doubt because she was looking for it. We couldn't tell for sure, but the fire looked as though it might have begun back as far as where we had stopped at the oak copse.

"They'll burn everything," Emery whispered to Bankole and me. "They won't stop until they've used up all the 'ro they have. All night, they'll be burning things. Things and people."

'Ro, pyro, pyromania. That damned fire drug again.

"Will they follow us?" I asked.

She shrugged. "There are a lot of us, and you killed some of them. I think they'll take their revenge on other, weaker travelers." Another shrug. "To them we're all the same. A traveler is a traveler."

"So unless we get caught in one of their fires . . ."

"We'll be okay, yeah. They hate everybody who isn't them. They would have sold my Tori to get some more 'ro."

I looked at her bruised, swollen face. Bankole had given her something for her pain. I was grateful for that, and half-angry at him for refusing to give me anything. He didn't understand my numbness and grogginess back at the copse, and it disturbed him. Well at least that had faded away. Let him die three or four times and see how he feels. No, I'm glad he'll never know how it feels. It makes no sense. That brief, endless agony, over and over. It makes no sense at all. I keep catching myself wondering how it is that I'm still alive.

"Emery?" I said, keeping my voice low.

She looked at me.

"You know I'm a sharer."

She nodded, then glanced sidelong at Bankole.

"He knows," I assured her. "But. . . look, you and Grayson are the first sharers I've known who had children." There was no reason to tell her she and Grayson and their children were the first sharers I'd known period. "I hope to have kids myself someday, so I need to know . . . do they always inherit the sharing?"

"One of my boys didn't have it," she said. "Some feelers— sharers—can't have any kids. I don't know why. And I knew some who had two or three kids who didn't have it at all. Bosses, though, they like you to have it."

"I'll bet they do."

"Sometimes," she continued, "sometimes they pay more for people who have it. Especially kids."

Her kids. Yet they had taken a boy who wasn't a sharer and left a girl who was. How long would it have been before they came back for the girl? Perhaps they had a lucrative offer for the boys as a pair, so they sold them first.

"My god," Bankole said. "This country has slipped back two hundred years."

"Things were better when I was little," Emery said. "My mother always said they would get better again. Good times would come back. She said they always did. My father would shake his head and not say anything." She looked around to see where Tori was and spotted her on Grayson Mora's shoulders. Then she caught sight of something else, and she gasped.

We followed her gaze and saw fire creeping over the hills behind us—far behind us, but not far enough. This was some new fire, whipping along in the dry evening breeze. Either the people who attacked us had followed us, setting fires, or someone was imitating them, echoing them.

We went on, moving faster, trying to see where we could go to be safe. On either side of the highway, there was dry grass, there were trees, living and dead. So far, the fire was only on the north side.

We kept to the south side, hoping it would be safe. There was a lake ahead, according to my map of the area—Clear Lake, it was called. The map showed it to be large, and the highway followed its northern shore for a few miles. We would reach it soon. How soon?

I calculated as we walked. Tomorrow. We should be able to camp near it tomorrow evening. Not soon enough.

I could smell the smoke now. Did that mean the wind was blowing the fire toward us?

Other people began hurrying and keeping to the south side of the road and heading west. No one went east now. There were no trucks yet, but it was getting late. They would be barreling through soon. And we should be camping for the night soon. Did we dare?

The south side still seemed free of fire behind us, but on the north side the fire crawled after us, coming no closer, but refusing to be left behind.

We went on for a while, all of us looking back often, all of us tired, some of us hurting. I called a halt and gestured us off the road to the south at a place where there was room to sit and rest.

"We can't stay here," Mora said. "The fire could jump the road any time."

"We can rest here for a few moments," I said. "We can see the fire, and it will tell us when we'd better start walking again."

"We'd better start now!" Mora said. "If that fire gets going good, it will move faster than we can run! Best to keep well ahead of it!"

"Best to have the strength to keep ahead of it," I said, and I took a water bottle from my pack and drank. We were within sight of the road and we had made it a rule not to eat or drink in such exposed places, but today that rule had to be suspended. To go into the hills away from the road might mean being cut off from the road by fire. We couldn't know when or where a windblown piece of burning debris might land.

Others followed my example and drank and ate a little dried fruit, meat, and bread. Bankole and I shared with Emery and Tori. Mora seemed to want to leave in spite of us, but his daughter Doe was sitting half asleep on the ground against Zahra. He stooped next to her and made her drink a little water and eat some fruit.

"We might have to keep moving all night," Allie said, her voice almost too soft to hear. "This might be the only rest we get." And to Travis, "You'd better put Dominic into the carriage with Justin when he's finished eating."

Travis nodded. He'd carried Dominic this far. Now he tucked him in with Justin. "I'll push the carriage for a while," he said.

Bankole looked at my wound, rebandaged it, and this time gave me something for the pain. He buried the bloody bandages he had removed, digging a shallow hole with a flat rock.

Emery, with Tori gone to sleep against her, looked to see what Bankole was doing with me, then jumped and looked away, her hand going to her own side.

"I didn't know you were hurt so much," she whispered.

"I'm not," I said, and made myself smile. "It looks nastier than it is with all the blood, but it isn't bad. I'm damned lucky compared to Jill. And it doesn't stop me from walking."

"You didn't give me any pain when we were walking," she said.

I nodded, glad to know I could fake her out. "It's ugly," I said, "but not too painful."

She settled down as though she felt better. No doubt she did. If I moaned and groaned, I'd have all four of them moaning and groaning. The kids might even bleed along with me. I would have to be careful and keep lying at least as long as the fire was a threat—or as long as I could.

The truth was, those blood-saturated bandages scared the hell out of me, and the wound hurt worse than ever. But I knew I had to keep going or burn. After a few minutes, Bankole's pills began to take the edge off my pain, and that made the whole world easier to endure.

We had about an hour's rest before the fire made us too nervous to stay where we were. Then we got up and walked. By then, at some point behind us, the fire had already jumped the road. Now, neither the north nor the south side looked safe. Until it was dark, all we could see in the hills behind us was smoke. It was a terrifying, looming, moving wall.

Later, after dark, we could see the fire eating its way toward us. There were dogs running along the road with us, but they paid no attention to us. Cats and deer ran past us, and a skunk scuttled by. It was live and let live. Neither humans nor animals were foolish enough to waste time attacking one another. Behind us and to the north, the fire began to roar.

We put Tori in the carriage and Justin and Dominic between her legs. The babies never even woke up while we were moving them. Tori herself was more than half asleep. I worried that the carriage might break down with the extra weight, but it held. Travis, Harry, and Allie traded off pushing it.

Doe, we put atop the load on Bankole's cart. She couldn't have been comfortable there, but she didn't complain. She was more awake than Tori, and she had been walking on her own most of the time since our encounter with the would-be kidnappers. She was a strong little kid—her father's daughter.

Grayson Mora helped push Bankole's cart. In fact, once Doe was loaded aboard, Mora pushed the cart most of the time. The man wasn't likeable, but in his love for his daughter, he was admirable.

At some point in the endless night, more smoke and ash than ever began to swirl around us, and I caught myself thinking that we might not make it. Without stopping, we wet shirts, scarves, whatever we had, and tied them around our noses and mouths.

The fire roared and thundered its way past us on the north, singeing our hair and clothing, making breathing a terrible effort. The babies woke up and screamed in fear and pain, then choked and almost brought me down. Tori, crying herself with their pain and her own, held on to them and would not let them struggle out of the carriage.

I thought we would die. I believed there was no way for us to survive this sea of fire, hot wind, smoke, and ash. I saw people— strangers—fall, and we left them lying on the highway, waiting to burn. I stopped looking back. In the roar of the fire, I could not hear whether they screamed. I could see the babies before Natividad threw wet rags over them. I knew they were screaming. Then I couldn't see them, and it was a blessing.

We began to run out of water.

There was nothing to do except keep going or burn. The terrible, deafening noise of the fire increased, then lessened, and again, increased, then lessened. It seemed that the fire went north away from the road, then whipped back down toward us.

It teased like a living, malevolent thing, intent on causing pain and terror. It drove us before it like dogs chasing a rabbit. Yet it didn't eat us. It could have, but it didn't.

In the end, the worst of it roared off to the northwest. Firestorm, Bankole called it later. Yes. Like a tornado of fire, roaring around, just missing us, playing with us, then letting us live.

We could not rest. There was still fire. Little fires that could grow into big ones, smoke, blinding and choking smoke. . . . No rest.

But we could slow down. We could emerge from the worst of the smoke and ash, and escape the lash of hot winds. We could pause by the side of the road for a moment, and gag in peace. There was a lot of gagging. Coughing and gagging and crying muddy tracks onto our faces. It was incredible. We were going to survive. We were still alive and together—scorched and miserable, in great need of water, but alive. We were going to make it.

Later, when we dared, we went off the road, unloaded my pack from Bankole's cart, and dug out his extra water bottle. He dug it out. He'd told us he had it when he could have kept it for himself.

"We'll reach Clear Lake sometime tomorrow," I said. "Early tomorrow, I think. I don't know how far we've come or where we are now, so I can only guess that we'll get there early. But it is there waiting for us tomorrow."

People grunted or coughed and downed swallows from Bankole's extra bottle. The kids had to be prevented from guzzling too much water. As it was, Dominic choked and began to cry again.

We camped where we were, within sight of the road. Two of us had to stay awake on watch. I volunteered for first watch because I was in too much pain to sleep. I got my gun back from Natividad, checked to see that she had reloaded it—she had—and looked around for a partner.

"I'll watch with you," Grayson Mora said.

That surprised me. I would have preferred someone who knew how to use a gun—someone I would trust with a gun.

"I'm not going to be able to sleep until you do," he said. "It's that simple. So let's both put our pain to good use."

I looked at Emery and the two girls to see whether they'd heard, but they seemed to be already asleep. "All right," I said. "We've got to watch for strangers and fire. Give me a yell if you see anything unusual."

"Give me a gun," he said. "If anybody comes close, I can at least use it to scare them."

In the dark, sure. "No gun," I said. "Not yet. You don't know enough yet."

He stared at me for several seconds, then went over to Bankole. He turned his back to me as he spoke to Bankole. "Look, you know I need a gun to do any guarding in a place like this. She doesn't know how it is. She thinks she does, but she doesn't."

Bankole shrugged. "If you can't do it, man, go to sleep. One of us will take the watch with her."

"Shit." Mora made the word long and nasty. "Shiiit. First time I saw her, I knew she was a man. Just didn't know she was the only man here."

Absolute silence.

Doe Mora saved the situation to the degree that it could be saved. At that moment she stepped up behind her father and tapped him on the back. He spun around, more than ready to fight, spun with such speed and fury that the little girl squealed and jumped back.

"What the hell are you doing up!" he shouted. "What do you want!"

Frightened, the little girl just stared at him. After a moment, she extended her hand, offering a pomegranate. "Zahra said we could have this," she whispered. "Would you cut it?"

Good thinking, Zahra! I didn't turn to look at her, but I was aware of her watching. By now, everyone still awake was watching.

"Everyone's tired and everyone's hurting," I told him. "Everyone, not just you. But we've managed to keep ourselves alive by working together and by not doing or saying stupid things."

"And if that's not good enough for you," Bankole added, in a voice low and ugly with anger, "tomorrow you can go out and find yourself a different kind of group to travel with—a group too goddamn macho to waste its time saving your child's life twice in one day."

There must be something worthwhile in Mora. He didn't say anything. He took out his knife and cut the pomegranate into quarters for Doe, then kept half of it because she insisted that he was supposed to have half. They sat together and ate the juicy, seedy, red fruit, then Mora tucked Doe in again and found himself a perch where, gunless, he began his first watch.

He said nothing more about guns, and he never apologized. Of course he didn't leave us. Where would he go? He was a runaway slave. We were the best thing he'd found so far—the best he was going to find as long as he had Doe with him.

We didn't reach Clear Lake the next morning. To tell the truth it was already the next morning when we went to sleep. We were too tired and sore to get up at dawn—which came early in the second watch. Only the need for water made us move out when we did—at a hot, smoky 11 a.m.

We found the corpse of a young woman when we got back to the road. There wasn't a mark on her, but she was dead.

"I want her clothes," Emery whispered. She was near me or I wouldn't have heard her. The dead woman was about her size, and dressed in a cotton shirt and pants that looked almost new. They were dirty, but far less so than Emery's clothes.

"Strip her, then," I said. "I'd help you, but I'm not bending too well this morning."

"I'll give her a hand," Allie whispered. Justin was asleep in his carriage with Dominic, so she was free to help with the ordinary, unspeakable things that we did now to live.

The dead woman had not even soiled herself in her dying. That made the job less disgusting than it could have been. Rigor mortis had set in, however, and stripping her was a job for two.

There was no one but us on this stretch of road, so Emery and Allie had all the time they needed. We had seen no other walkers yet this morning.

Emery and Allie took every scrap of clothing, including under-wear, socks, and boots, though Emery thought the boots would be too big for her. No matter. If no one could wear them, she could sell them.

In fact, it was the boots that yielded Emery the first cash she had ever owned. On the farm where she had been a slave, she had been paid only in company scrip, worthless except on the farm, and almost worthless there.

Stitched into the tongue of each of the dead woman's boots were five, folded one hundred-dollar bills—a thousand dollars in all. We had to tell her how little that was. If she were careful, and shopped only at the cheapest stores, and ate no meat, wheat, or dairy products, it might feed her for two weeks. It might feed both her and Tori for a week and a half. Still, it seemed riches to Emery.

Late that day, when we reached Clear Lake—much smaller than I had expected—we came across a tiny, expensive store, being run from the back of an old truck near a cluster of half-burned, collapsed cabins. It sold fruit, vegetables, nuts, and smoked fish. We all had to buy a few things, but Emery squandered too much money on pears and walnuts for everyone. She delighted in passing these around, in being able to give us something for a change. She's all right. We'll have to teach her about shopping and the value of money, but she's worth something, Emery is. And she's decided she's one of us.

SUNDAY, SEPTEMBER 26, 2027

Somehow, we've reached our new home—Bankole's land in the coastal hills of Humboldt County. The highway—U.S. 101—is to the east and north of us, and Cape Mendocino and the sea are to the west. A few miles south are state parks filled with huge redwood trees and hoards of squatters. The land surrounding us, however, is as empty and wild as any I've seen. It's covered with dry brush, trees, and tree stumps, all far removed from any city, and a long, hilly walk from the little towns that line the highway. There's farming around here, and logging, and just plain isolated living. According to Bankole, it's best to mind your own business and not pay too much attention to how people on neighboring plots of land earn a living. If they hijack trucks on 101, grow marijuana, distill whisky, or brew up more complicated illegal substances. . . . Well, live and let live.

Bankole guided us along a narrow blacktopped road that soon became a narrow dirt road. We saw a few cultivated fields, some scars left by past fires or logging, and a lot of land that seemed unused. The road all but vanished before we came to the end of it. Good for isolation. Bad for getting things in or out. Bad for traveling back and forth to get work. Bankole had said his brother-in- law had to spend a lot of time in various towns, away from his family. That was easier to understand now. There's no possibility here of coming home every day or two. So what did you have to do to save cash? Sleep in door- ways or parks in town? Maybe it was worth the inconvenience to do just that if you could keep your family together and safe—far from the desperate, the crazy, and the vicious.

Or that's what I thought until we reached the hillside where Ban- kole's sister's house and outbuildings were supposed to be.

There was no house. There were no buildings. There was almost nothing: A broad black smear on the hillside; a few charred planks sticking up from the rubble, some leaning against others; and a tall brick chimney, standing black and solitary like a tombstone in a picture of an old-style graveyard. A tombstone amid the bones and ashes.

25

□ □ □

Create no images of God.
Accept the images
that God has provided.
They are everywhere,
in everything.
God is Change—
Seed to tree,
tree to forest;
Rain to river,
river to sea;
Grubs to bees,
bees to swarm.
From one, many;
from many, one;
Forever uniting, growing, dissolving—
forever Changing.
The universe
is God's self-portrait.

EARTHSEED: THE BOOKS OF THE LIVING
FRIDAY, OCTOBER 1, 2027

We've been arguing all week about whether or not we should stay
here with the bones and ashes.

We've found five skulls—three in what was left of the house and
two outside. There were other scattered bones, but not one complete skeleton. Dogs have been at the bones—dogs and cannibals,
perhaps. The fire happened long enough ago for weeds to begin to

grow in the rubble. Two months ago? Three? Some of the far-flung neighbors might know. Some of the far-flung neighbors might have set the fire.

There was no way to be certain, but I assumed that the bones belonged to Bankole's sister and her family. I think Bankole assumed that, too, but he couldn't bring himself to just bury the bones and write off his sister. The day after we got here, he and Harry hiked back to Glory, the nearest small town that we had passed through, to talk to the local cops. They were, or they professed to be, sheriff's deputies. I wonder what you have to do to become a cop. I wonder what a badge is, other than a license to steal. What did it used to be to make people Bankole's age want to trust it. I know what the old books say, but still, I wonder.

The deputies all but ignored Bankole's story and his questions. They wrote nothing down, claimed to know nothing. They treated Bankole as though they doubted that he even had a sister, or that he was who he said he was. So many stolen IDs these days. They searched him and took the cash he was carrying. Fees for police services, they said. He had been careful to carry only what he thought would be enough to keep them sweet-tempered, but not enough to make them suspicious or more greedy than they already were. The rest—a sizeable packet—he left with me. He trusted me enough to do that. His gun he left with Harry who had gone shopping.

Jail for Bankole could have meant being sold into a period of hard, unpaid labor—slavery. Perhaps if he had been younger, the deputies might have taken his money and arrested him anyway on some trumped-up charge. I had begged him not to go, not to trust *any* police or government official. It seemed to me such people were no better than gangs with their robbing and slaving.

Bankole agreed with me, yet he insisted on going.

"She was my little sister," he said. "I have to try, at least, to find out what happened to her. I need to know who did this. Most of all, I need to know whether any of her children could have survived. One or more of those five skulls could have belonged to the arsonists." He stared at the collection of bones. "I have to risk going to the sheriff's office," he continued. "But you don't. I don't want you with me. I don't want them getting any ideas about you, maybe finding out by accident that you're a sharer. I don't want my sister's death to cost you your life or your freedom."

We fought about it. I was afraid for him; he was afraid for me, and we were both angrier than we had ever been at each other. I was terrified that he would be killed or arrested, and we'd never find out what happened to him. No one should travel alone in this world.

"Look," he said at last, "you can do some good here with the group. You'll have one of the four guns left here, and you know how to survive. You're needed here. If the cops decide they want me, you won't be able to do a thing. Worse, if they decide they want you, there'll be nothing I can do except take revenge, and be killed for it."

That slowed me down—the thought that I might cause his death instead of backing him up. I didn't quite believe it, but it slowed me down. Harry stepped in then and said he would go. He wanted to anyway. He could buy some things for the group, and he wanted to look for a job. He wanted to earn some money.

"I'll do what I can," he told me just before they left. "He's not a bad old guy. I'll bring him back to you."

They brought each other back, Bankole a few thousand dollars poorer, and Harry still jobless—though they did bring back supplies and a few hand tools. Bankole knew no more than he had when he left about his sister and her family, but the cops had said they would come out to investigate the fire and the bones.

We worried that sooner or later, they might show up. We're still keeping a lookout for them, and we've hidden—buried—most of our valuables. We want to bury the bones, but we don't dare. It's bothering Bankole. Bothering him a lot. I've suggested we hold a funeral and go ahead and bury the bones. The hell with the cops. But he says no. Best to give them as little provocation as possible. If they came, they would do enough harm with their stealing. Best not to give them reason to do more.

There's a well with an old-fashioned hand pump under the rubble of an outbuilding. It still works. The solar-powered electric pump near the house does not. We couldn't stay here long without a dependable water source. With the well, though, it's hard to leave— hard to walk away from possible sanctuary—in spite of arsonists and cops.

Bankole owns this land, free and clear. There's a huge, half ruined garden plus citrus trees full of unripe fruit. We've already been pulling carrots and digging potatoes here. There are plenty of other fruit and nut trees plus wild pines, redwoods, and Douglas firs. None of these last were very big. This area was logged sometime before Bankole bought it. Bankole says it was clear-cut back in the 1980s or 1990s, but we can make use of the trees that have grown since then, and we can plant more. We can build a shelter, put in a winter garden from the seed I've been carrying and collecting since we left home. Granted, a lot of it is old seed. I hadn't renewed it as often as I should have while I was at home. Strange that I hadn't. Things kept getting worse and worse at home, yet I had paid less and less attention to the pack that was supposed to save my life when the mob came. There was so much else to worry about—and I think I was into my own brand of denial, as bad in its way as Cory's or Joanne's mother's. But all that feels like ancient history. Now was what we had to worry about. What were we going to do now?

"I don't think we can make it here," Harry said earlier this evening as we sat around the campfire. There should be something cheerful about sitting around a campfire with friends and a full stomach. We even had meat tonight, fresh meat. Bankole took the rifle and went off by himself for a while. When he came back, he brought three rabbits which Zahra and I skinned, cleaned, and roasted. We also roasted sweet potatoes that we had dug out of the garden. We should have been content. Yet all we were doing was rehashing what had become an old argument over the past few days. Perhaps it was the bones and ashes just over the rise that were bothering us. We had camped out of sight of the burned area in the hope of recovering a little peace of mind, but it hadn't helped. I was thinking that we should figure out a way to capture a few wild rabbits alive and breed them for a sure meat supply. Was that possible? Why not, if we stay here? And we should stay.

"Nothing we find farther north will be any better or any safer than this," I said. "It will be hard to live here, but if we work together, and if we're careful, it should be possible. We can build a community here."

"Oh, god, there she goes with her Earthseed shit again," Allie said. But she smiled a little as she said it. That was good. She hadn't smiled much lately.

"We can build a community here," I repeated. "It's dangerous, sure, but, hell, it's dangerous everywhere, and the more people there are packed together in cities, the more danger there is. This is a ridiculous place to build a community. It's isolated, miles from everywhere with no decent road leading here, but for us, for now, it's perfect."

"Except that someone burned this place down last time," Grayson Mora said. "Anything we build out here by itself is a target."

"Anything we build *anywhere* is a target," Zahra argued. "But the people out here before . . . I'm sorry, Bankole, I gotta say this: They couldn't have kept a good watch—a man and a woman and three kids. They would have worked hard all day, then slept all night. It would have been too hard on just two grown people to try to sit up and watch for half the night each."

"They didn't keep a night watch," Bankole said. "We'll have to keep one, though. And we could use a couple of dogs. If we could get them as puppies and train them to guard—"

"Give meat to dogs?" Mora demanded, outraged.

"Not soon." Bankole shrugged. "Not until we have enough for

ourselves. But if we can get dogs, they'll help us keep the rest of our goods."

"I wouldn't give a dog nothing but a bullet or a rock," Mora said. "I saw dogs eat a woman once."

"There are no jobs in that town Bankole and I went to," Harry said. "There was nothing. Not even work for room and board. I asked all over town. No one even knew of anything."

I frowned. "The towns around here are all close to the highway," I said. "They must get a lot of people passing through, looking for a place to settle—or maybe a place to rob, rape, kill. The locals wouldn't welcome new people. They wouldn't trust anyone they didn't know."

Harry looked from me to Bankole.

"She's right," Bankole said. "My brother-in-law had a hard time before people began to get used to him, and he moved up here before things got so bad. He knew plumbing, carpentry, electrical work, and motor vehicle mechanics. Of course, it didn't help that he was black. Being white might help you win people over faster than he did. I think, though, that any serious money we make here will come from the land. Food is gold these days, and we can grow food here. We have guns to protect ourselves, so we can sell our crops in nearby towns or on the highway."

"If we survive long enough to grow anything to sell," Mora muttered. "If there's enough water, if the bugs don't eat our crops, if no one burns us out the way they did those people over the hill, if, if, if!"

Allie sighed. "Shit, it's if, if, if anywhere you go. This place isn't so bad." She was sitting on her sleepsack, holding the sleeping Justin's head in her lap. As she spoke, she stroked the boy's hair. It occurred to me, not for the first time, that no matter how tough Allie tried to seem, that little boy was the key to her. Children were the keys to most of the adults present.

"There are no guarantees anywhere," I agreed. "But if we're willing to work, our chances are good here. I've got some seed in my pack. We can buy more. What we have to do at this point is more like gardening than farming. Everything will have to be done by hand—composting, watering, weeding, picking worms or slugs or whatever off the crops and killing them one by one if that's what it takes. As for water, if our well still has water in it now, in October, I don't think we have to worry about it going dry on us. Not this year, anyway.

"And if people threaten us or our crop, we kill them. That's all. We kill them, or they kill us. If we work together, we can defend ourselves, and we can protect the kids. A community's first responsibility is to protect its children—the ones we have now and the ones we will have."

There was silence for a while, people digesting, perhaps measuring it against what they had to look forward to if they left this place and continued north.

"We should decide," I said. "We have building and planting to do here. We have to buy more food, more seed and tools." It was time for directness: "Allie, will you stay?"

She looked across the dead fire at me, stared hard at me as though she hoped to see something on my face that would give her an answer.

"What seed do you have?" she asked.

I drew a deep breath. "Most of it is summer stuff—corn, peppers, sunflowers, eggplant, melons, tomatoes, beans, squash. But I have some winter things; peas, carrots, cabbage, broccoli, winter squash, onions, asparagus, herbs, several kinds of greens. . . . We can buy more, and we've got the stuff left in this garden plus what we can harvest from the local oak, pine, and citrus trees. I brought tree seeds too: more oak, citrus, peach, pear, nectarine, almond, walnut, a few others. They won't do us any good for a few years, but they're a hell of an investment in the future."

"So is a kid," Allie said. "I didn't think I would be dumb enough to say this, but yeah, I'll stay. I want to build something, too. I never had a chance to build anything before."

Allie and Justin were a yes, then.

"Harry? Zahra?"

"Of course we're staying," Zahra said.

Harry frowned. "Wait a minute. We don't have to."

"I know. But we are. If we can make a community like Lauren says and not have to hire out to strangers and trust them when they shouldn't be trusted, then we should do it. If you grew up where I did, you'd know we should."

"Harry," I said, "I've known you all my life. You're the closest thing to a brother that I have left. You aren't really thinking about leaving, are you?" It wasn't the world's best argument. He had been both cousin and lover to Joanne, and he'd let her go when he could have gone with her.

"I want something of my own," he said. "Land, a home, maybe a store or a small farm. Something that's mine. This land is Bankole's."

"Yes," Bankole said. "And you'll be getting the use of it rent free— and all the water you need. What are those things going to cost you farther north—if you can get them at all farther north—if you can get yourself out of California."

"But there's no work here!"

"There's nothing but work here, boy. Work, and a lot of cheap land. How cheap do you think land will be up where you and all the rest of the world are heading?"

Harry thought about that, then spread his hands. "What I'm worried about is spending all our money here, then discovering we can't make it here."

I nodded. "I've thought about that, too, and it bothers me. But it's a possibility anywhere, you know. You could settle in Oregon or Washington, not be able to get a job, and run out of money. Or you could be forced to work under the conditions that Emery and Grayson found. After all, with rivers of people flowing north, looking for work, employers can take their pick, and pay what they feel like paying."

Emery put her arm around Tori, who sat drowsing next to her. "You might be able to get a job as a driver," she said. "They like white men to be drivers. If you can read and write, and if you'd do the work, you might get hired."

"I don't know how to drive, but I could learn," Harry said. "You mean driving those big armored trucks, don't you?"

Emery looked confused. "Trucks? No, I mean driving people. Making them work. Pushing them to work faster. Making them do . . . whatever the owners says."

Harry's expression had dissolved from hopeful to horrified to outraged. "Jesus God, do you think I'd do that! How could you think I'd do anything like that?"

Emery shrugged. It startled me that she could be indifferent about such a thing, but she seemed to be. "Some people think it's a good job," she said. "Last driver we had, he used to do something with computers. I don't know what. His company went out of business and he got a job driving us. I think he liked it."

"Em," Harry said. He pitched his voice low and waited until she looked at him. "Are you telling me you believe I'd like a job pushing slaves around and taking away their children?"

She stared back, searching his face. "I hope not," she said. And then, "Sometimes jobs like that are the only jobs—slave or slave driver. I heard that just on this side of the Canada border there are a lot of factories with jobs like that."

I frowned. "Factories that use slave labor?"

"Yeah. Workers make things for companies in Canada or Asia. They don't get paid much, so they get into debt. They get hurt or sick, too. Their drinking water's not clean and the factories are dangerous—full of poisons and machines that crush or cut you. But people think they can make some cash and then quit. I worked with some women who had gone up there, taken a look, and come back."

"And you were going up there?" Harry demanded.

"Not to work in those places. The women warned me."

"I've heard of places like that," Bankole said. "They were supposed to provide jobs for that northward-flowing river of people. President Donner's all for them. The workers are more throwaways than slaves. They breathe toxic fumes or drink contaminated water or get caught in unshielded machinery. . . . It doesn't matter. They're easy to replace—thousands of jobless for every job."

"Borderworks," Mora said. "Not all of them are that bad. I heard some pay cash wages, not company scrip."

"Is that where you want to go?" I asked. "Or do you want to stay here?"

He looked down at Doe who was still nibbling at a piece of sweet potato. "I want to stay here," he said, surprising me. "I'm not sure you have a hope in hell of building anything here, but you're just crazy enough to make it work." And if it didn't work, he'd be no worse off than he was when he escaped slavery. He could rob someone and continue his journey north. Or maybe not. I'd been thinking about Mora. He did a lot to keep people away from him—keep them from knowing too much about him, keep them from seeing what he was feeling, or that he was feeling anything—a male sharer, desperate to hide his terrible vulnerability? Sharing would be harder on a man. What would my brothers have been like as sharers? Odd that I hadn't thought of that before.

"I'm glad you're staying," I said. "We need you." I looked at Travis and Natividad. "We need you guys, too. You're staying, aren't you?"

"You know we are," Travis said. "Although I think I agree more than I want to with Mora. I'm not sure we have a prayer of succeeding here."

"We'll have whatever we can shape," I said. And I turned to face Harry. He and Zahra had been whispering together. Now he looked at me.

"Mora's right," he said. "You're nuts."

I sighed.

"But this is a crazy time," he continued. "Maybe you're what the time needs—or what we need. I'll stay. I may be sorry for it, but I'll stay."

Now the decision is acknowledged, and we can stop arguing about it. Tomorrow we'll begin to prepare a winter garden. Next week, several of us will go into town to buy tools, more seed, supplies. Also, it's time we began to build a shelter. There are trees enough in the area, and we can dig into the ground and into the hills. Mora says he's built slave cabins before. Says he's eager to build something better, something fit for human beings. Besides, this far north and this near the coast, we might get some rain.

SUNDAY, OCTOBER 10, 2027

Today we had a funeral for Bankole's dead—the five people who died in the fire. The cops never came. At last Bankole has decided that they aren't going to come, and that it's time his sister and her family had a decent burial. We collected all the bones that we could find, and yesterday, Natividad wrapped them in a shawl that she had knitted years ago. It was the most beautiful thing she owned.

"A thing like that should serve the living," Bankole said when she offered it.

"You are living," Natividad said. "I like you. I wish I could have met your sister."

He looked at her for a while. Then he took the shawl and hugged her. Then, beginning to cry, he went off by himself into the trees, out of our sight. I let him alone for an hour or so, then went after him.

I found him, sitting on a fallen log, wiping his face. I sat with him for some time, saying nothing. After a while, he got up, waited for me to stand, then headed back toward our camp.

"I would like to give them a grove of oak trees," I said. "Trees are better than stone—life commemorating life."

He glanced back at me. "All right."

"Bankole?"

He stopped, looked at me with an expression I could not read.

"None of us knew her," I said. "I wish we had. I wish I had, no matter how much I would have surprised her."

He managed a smile. "She would have looked at you, then looked at me, then, right in front of you, I think she would have said, 'Well, there's no fool like an old fool.' Once she got that out of her system, I think she would have gotten to like you."

"Do you think she could stand. . . or forgive company now?"

"What?"

I drew a deep breath and wondered about what I meant to say. It could go wrong. He could misunderstand. It still needed to be said.

"We'll bury your dead tomorrow. I think you're right to want to do it. And I think we should bury our dead as well. Most of us have had to walk away—or run—away from our unburned, unburied dead. Tomorrow, we should remember them all, and lay them to rest if we can."

"Your family?"

I nodded. "Mine, Zahra's, Harry's, Allie's—both her son and her sister—maybe Emery's sons, maybe others that I don't know about. Mora doesn't talk about himself much, but he must have losses. Doe's mother, perhaps."

"How do you want to do it?" he asked.

"Each of us will have to bury our own dead. We knew them. We can find the words."

Words from the Bible, perhaps?

"Any words, memories, quotations, thoughts, songs. . . . My father had a funeral, even though we never found his body. But my three youngest brothers and my stepmother had nothing. Zahra saw them die, or I wouldn't have any idea what happened to them." I thought for a moment. "I have acorns enough for each of us to plant live oak trees to our dead—enough to plant one for Justin's mother, too. I'm thinking about a very simple ceremony. But everyone should have a chance to speak. Even the two little girls."

He nodded. "I don't have any objection. It isn't a bad idea." And a few steps later: "There's been so much dying. There's so much more to come."

"Not for us, I hope."

He said nothing for a while. Then he stopped and put his hand on my shoulder to stop me. At first he only stood looking at me, almost studying my face. "You're so young," he said. "It seems almost criminal that you should be so young in these terrible times. I wish you could have known this country when it was still salvageable."

"It might survive," I said, "changed, but still itself."

"No." He drew me to his side and put one arm around me. "Human beings will survive of course. Some other countries will survive. Maybe they'll absorb what's left of us. Or maybe we'll just break up into a lot of little states quarreling and fighting with each other over whatever crumbs are left. That's almost happened now with states shutting themselves off from one another, treating state lines as national borders. As bright as you are, I don't think you understand—I don't think you can understand what we've lost. Perhaps that's a blessing."

"God is Change," I said.

"Olamina, that doesn't mean anything."

"It means everything. Everything!"

He sighed. "You know, as bad as things are, we haven't even hit bottom yet. Starvation, disease, drug damage, and mob rule have only begun. Federal, state, and local governments still exist—in name at least—and sometimes they manage to do something more than collect taxes and send in the military. And the money is still good. That amazes me. However much more you need of it to buy anything these days, it is still accepted. That may be a hopeful sign—or perhaps it's only more evidence of what I said: We haven't hit bottom yet."

"Well, the group of us here doesn't have to sink any lower," I said.

He shook his shaggy head, his hair, beard, and serious expression making him look more than a little like an old picture I used to have of Frederick Douglass.

"I wish I believed that," he said. Perhaps it was his grief talking. "I don't think we have a hope in hell of succeeding here."

I slipped my arm around him. "Let's go back," I said. "We've got work to do."

So today we remembered the friends and the family members we've lost. We spoke our individual memories and quoted Bible passages, Earthseed verses, and bits of songs and poems that were favorites of the living or the dead.

Then we buried our dead and we planted oak trees.

Afterward, we sat together and talked and ate a meal and decided to call this place Acorn.

A sower went out to sow his seed: and as he sowed, some fell by the way side; and it was trodden down, and the fowls of the air devoured it. And some fell upon a rock; and as soon as it was sprung up, it withered away because it lacked moisture. And some fell among thorns; and the thorns sprang up with it, and choked it. And others fell on good ground, and sprang up, and bore fruit an hundredfold.

THE BIBLE
Authorized King James Version
St. Luke 8: 5-8

OCTAVIA E. BUTLER

A writer who darkly imagined the future we have destined for ourselves in book after book, and also one who has shown us the way toward improving on that dismal fate, OCTAVIA E. BUTLER (1947–2006) is recognized as among the bravest and smartest of contemporary fiction writers. A 1995 MacArthur Award winner, Butler transcended the science fiction category even as she was awarded that community's top prizes, the Nebula and Hugo Awards. She reaches readers of all ages, all races, and all religious and sexual persuasions. For years the only African-American woman writing science fiction, Butler has encouraged many others to follow in her path.

GLORIA STEINEM is a feminist, journalist, activist, and author. She is well known for her contributions to the women's rights movement, and for her tireless advocacy for equality ever since. Her most recent book is *My Life on the Road*, published in 2015 to wide acclaim.

ABOUT SEVEN STORIES PRESS

Seven Stories Press is an independent book publisher based in New York City. We publish works of the imagination by such writers as Nelson Algren, Russell Banks, Octavia E. Butler, Ani DiFranco, Assia Djebar, Ariel Dorfman, Coco Fusco, Barry Gifford, Martha Long, Luis Negrón, Hwang Sok-yong, Lee Stringer, and Kurt Vonnegut, to name a few, together with political titles by voices of conscience, including Subhankar Banerjee, the Boston Women's Health Collective, Noam Chomsky, Angela Y. Davis, Human Rights Watch, Derrick Jensen, Ralph Nader, Loretta Napoleoni, Gary Null, Greg Palast, Project Censored, Barbara Seaman, Alice Walker, Gary Webb, and Howard Zinn, among many others. Seven Stories Press believes publishers have a special responsibility to defend free speech and human rights, and to celebrate the gifts of the human imagination, wherever we can. In 2012 we launched Triangle Square books for young readers with strong social justice and narrative components, telling personal stories of courage and commitment. For additional information, visit www.sevenstories.com.